# BY DARK DEEDS

## BLADE AND ROSE SERIES BOOK 2

## MIRANDA HONFLEUR

*To my friends at Enclave,*
*this book wouldn't exist without you,*
*and Wednesdays wouldn't be nearly as awesome.*

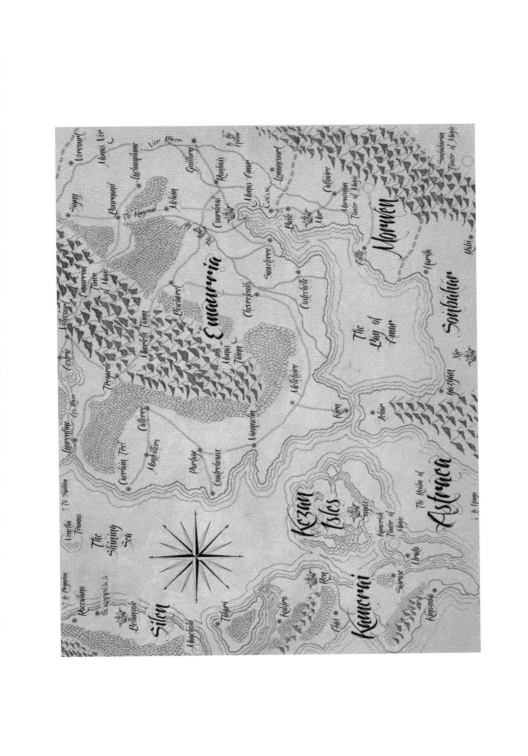

# CHAPTER 1

*a* s Rielle sat chained to a twelve-pound cannon, a shadow covered her almost entirely. She rattled her arcanir shackles at the towering figure, the captain of the *Siren*, who outsized even the large chair behind him. Throne, more like.

He peered down at her from that throne, surrounded by the riches adorning his cabin, extolling his brutal triumphs—antiques, no doubt pillaged from once-hallowed places desecrated by these most brutally pragmatic of men; exotic rugs and expensive cloth; and heavy, ornate precious metals. All stolen or paid for by the trade in human lives.

Crumpled in a ragged pile against the cannon, she looked him over through her tangled hair. Dressed like a king—in a stunning black brocade overcoat, silk breeches, polished black leather boots, a crisp white shirt, and the most garish captain's tricorne she'd ever seen—he ought to be holding court in some nightmare realm, not captaining a pirate ship. But in the pirate world, captains dressed as richly as their reputations allowed.

She shivered. He was a powerful man.

As he rubbed the ebony-and-gray stubble on his jaw, his calculating eyes raked over her frame. On any other day, she would have met such a gaze with unflinching disdain. Today, however, her dry throat betrayed her as she swallowed.

Water... Divine, just a drop—

And they'd taunted her with it. Bound in arcanir, she couldn't use her magic. For three days, she'd been neglected. And she'd spent the last half-hour being unceremoniously washed and scrubbed by a pirate —water all around her but not a drop to drink—and stuffed into a threadbare scratchy cotton dress before being brought here.

And *here* was a place of dread.

The excess, the silence, the posturing, the shackles—all of it made their disparate bargaining positions clear. But her former captor—that vengeful harpy, Shadow—planned to assassinate Jon. And she had a head start.

*I need to stop her. Yesterday.*

She suppressed a grimace. Calm, collected reason first. She needed to negotiate her release.

Licking her cracked lower lip, she raised her eyes to the captain. A full bottle of wine sat upon his desk, making her salivate.

*Not now.* She focused on the captain; it was time to open the door to negotiating her ransom. *I can do this.* "Captain, if I may—"

He dragged in a breath, and she paused. For a man of near silence, even a breath was deafening.

Leaning back in his throne, he regarded her coldly, with a small glimmer in his dark eyes. "Do you know what they call me, girl?"

His voice was weathered, always low. Not in a way that would ever go unheard. When he spoke, people quieted. *She* quieted.

"Captain Sincuore."

A measured smile cloaked his mouth. In his youth, he might have been handsome, until the years and the cruelty of the life he'd led etched in the lines and shaded in the furrows. "And do you know what *sincuore* means?"

"Heartless."

He grinned. But it wasn't happiness behind the grin. It was victory.

Her heart raced, and she clenched her teeth to stop her lips from trembling.

"Do you think that's my real name?"

*Of course not.* "I—I don't know, Captain."

Coolly, he rose from the chair and looked out at the Bay of Amar through the square windows astern.

Everything about his erect posture—stony, towering, still—directed her to remain quiet, but she couldn't. Shadow had sworn to assassinate Jon.

Her heart twisted.

She needed to get off this ship.

It was time to appeal to greed. "There is a massive sum of gold coronas awaiting you, should you ransom me to the March of Laurentine. You would be paid quickly and permitted to depart unhindered."

Captain Sincuore let out an amused breath through his nose.

She stilled her trembling body by pressing it against the twelve-pounder. "The Duchy of Melain, the March of Tregarde, and"—she paused—"the Kingdom of Emaurria itself would pay you handsomely for my release." Jon would do anything for her, including pay a ransom... Of that, she was certain.

*He will forget about you between the thighs of many women.* Shadow's words echoed in her mind anew.

But they were lies.

Jon loved her, and she loved him; they could overcome anything. Including this.

The captain didn't move, didn't flinch, didn't give any indication he'd even heard her.

Did he care about coin? It wasn't as though he were—

Her gaze darted around the room. All the riches... All the gold he likely possessed...

The stupidity, the foolishness of attempting to sway this man with more riches...

But she'd needed to try.

"Do you know on whose order I bear you to your fate?" His voice was even, business like.

Her chin quivered, and she clicked her teeth together, clenched her jaw, willing it to stop. The answer was obvious. "On the order of Shadow, Mage Captain of the Crag Company."

He laughed. "It's a wonder you've survived this long, girl." He turned to her at last, arms behind his back. "The one I work for, I would not cross for all the gold in your country."

Whose power outstripped even that of a whole kingdom?

And why was she—one of hundreds of master mages, a disgraced marquise, removed from court and all its schemes—their target? To have crossed someone of significance, she would have had to move in the same circles. And she most certainly didn't. "Who, then?"

Silence.

A shiver snaked down her spine and slithered through her limbs. She crumpled her fingers into fists. There would be no negotiating her way off the ship. No magic. No fighting. She'd tried them all to no effect.

She had a powerful unknown enemy, one even these pirates wouldn't dare cross. A serpent.

But that wasn't the problem before her now. *Focus.*

Her options were few—finding some way to jump ship... and, being shackled, drown... or holding out for a better chance of freedom at her destination. And although death could be preferable to the things she might endure, she was the only one who knew about Shadow's treachery, the only one who could now protect Jon, and the only one who could atone for the massacre at Laurentine nine years ago.

And she was no coward.

Raising her head, she met Captain Sincuore's gaze without fear or hesitation. Whatever lay ahead, she would persevere. She had to. For Jon's sake. She needed to live to escape. She needed to live to save herself, and him.

And someday, she would see this captain reduced to no more than a red stain on all his expensive possessions.

A red stain. Someday, he would be no more. So would Shadow. And the serpent who'd ordered this. She narrowed her eyes and lifted her chin.

"Such fury." His grin turned predatory. He uncorked the bottle of wine, poured a goblet, and rose.

He strolled toward her and stopped two feet away, a giant.

She looked away. Obvious posturing. Unnecessary, too, as she was already well aware of who had all the power here. At least while *she* was shackled in arcanir. *Remove these shackles, and then we'll see how strong you think you are.*

When he crouched and grabbed her face, angling it upward, she heaved deep breaths. Whatever happened, she would endure. She would endure, see him dead, herself freed, Jon saved, Shadow defeated.

"You have no hope of escape, girl." His grip on her chin tightened. "But I am not entirely without heart." He smiled with cold eyes, a chilling mixture of malice and joy. "The Rose of Laurentine. A lady such as yourself shouldn't have to countenance the horrors of piracy. It's cruel, even for me."

So close, the wine's sweetly bitter scent was intoxicating. She turned her head farther from the goblet.

The captain exhaled sharply. "Truly, girl? The wine? Now?"

Stiffly, she shrugged. Let him live three days without a drop of water, and then he could question thirst.

Sighing, he brought the goblet to her nose, then pressed it to her lips and tipped it.

Holy blood of the Divine, the bittersweet red danced in her mouth, invigorated, its oaky body embracing her tongue, fruity notes dancing on her palate, and it cooled its way down her throat. It wasn't the water she needed, but she'd never tasted anything so soothing.

He pulled it away long before she had her fill, and stood. "Now, as I was saying"—he strolled back to the desk, set down the goblet, and recorked the bottle—"I may be heartless, but you're no use to me dead. This ship, my crew and cargo, can have an... effect on sheltered girls such as yourself. As my very special guest, I was going to offer you a choice." A smile playing on his mouth, he leaned against the massive desk. "Stay fully aware and conscious throughout the rest of your time aboard this ship—"

She blinked, and he blurred before her. Two captains... Three captains. Blurry eyes—she just needed to rub them—

But her hands were chained to the twelve-pounder. Her head spun.

"—or drink this wine, specially prepared for you, and choose to be fully unaware and unconscious throughout the rest of your time aboard this ship. Everybody wins. You avoid injury, I avoid your feeble attempts at rebellion, the job goes as planned, and my generous patron is satisfied."

She tried to raise her head, but it wouldn't cooperate.

"The... wine..." She blinked sluggishly, weakness vining through her limbs.

"Drugged."

The door to the cabin opened, and the captain nodded to the—she turned her head, so slowly she wondered when she'd ever see—

Shades blotted out the light, tall and dark, a circle of large forms closing in. She willed her limbs close to protect her body, but they wouldn't move. Couldn't. She struggled in the chains.

*Break... free...*

Metal clinked and thudded to the floor. Large callused hands grabbed her. The shades. Her gaze traveled their faces, but they were just—shadows. No faces. Shades. Their arms bore her to the door, and she craned her neck to look at the captain—

A shade amid streaks of crimson and gold. Laughter rumbled like thunder, amusement and malice, distant and massive.

The fading light poured in from the windows behind him, and she was through the doorway. The sky turned to shadow, to black, a storm rolling in over the sea, clouds stealing what little light remained. She rolled her head along her shoulders.

As the ship bobbed, darkness shrouded her completely.

Feet thumped, again and again—stairs?—and into blackness they went, the shades and she, but somewhere across the vast waters freedom waited, and at the opportune moment, she would seize it, no matter what a red stain thought.

If she could survive the storm.

HER HAND CLAMPED over his mouth, Drina Heidrun slit the man's throat in the night's cloak. He raised his hands, and she pinned one to the tree with her blade and twisted the other behind his back. Blood gushing, muffled whimpers, gurgles. Old notes, as beautiful now as the first time.

Bent, she held the man as he bled out onto the forest floor. A strong, cool, northeasterly wind swayed the tall pines bearing quiet witness, watching the last of his life abandon his body. Without a sound, she lowered him to the ground, listened for any signs of presence, then stripped him of his gear.

After the siege, she'd buried a weapons supply cache outside Courdeval, and for days, she'd bided her time, watching the coast southwest of the capital, waiting for the right target. A lone traveler, someone whose identity she could easily assume. Finally, one had come.

This traveling apothecary, a hedge witch healer who also sold remedies for illness, traveled alone. Her father, Lyuben, had been a medicine man, and she'd studied herbalism extensively at the Kezani Tower. Perfect.

She'd hidden in the tree cover, planning to cut his throat as he slept, but the fool had gone among the trees and stopped just shy of her spot to relieve himself.

Easy prey.

She donned his tunic and loose breeches, his many-pocketed belt, and his faded black cloak. She pulled up the hood and headed into his camp to sort through his possessions—a donkey, ample provisions, and plenty of stock to sell. The animal bucked at her touch, but she patiently waited for its ears to rise once more, its breath to slow, the whites of its eyes to disappear.

She stroked the donkey's neck and whispered in soft Kezani.

*Everything surrenders with time.*

She settled at the campfire and stirred the stew bubbling there, then removed her gloves. The brand had faded, but it yet remained. Pine bark, corroded bronze, gall, and vitriol. Such a simple thing, but when she and Marko had wed, they hadn't wanted rings in gold or silver, or anything that could ever be removed. They'd wanted a symbol of their union that represented what they truly were: forever.

*I don't want you tonight,* volyena. *I want you forever.* Marko... It had been nine years since she'd seen his face, black curls about his shoulders, gamesome smile. She rubbed the brand.

At the Kezani Tower, she'd been content to do no more than needed for her daily meals and lodging—it had been more than her farming family had provided on the lifeship. In birth, she'd killed her mother, and her family had always cared for her begrudgingly, a runt whose insignificant life had taken the place of a hard worker, a beautiful woman, a breeder, someone worth ten runts among the Kezani Dragos.

And as soon as her shadowmancy had manifested, her father had been eager to be rid of her and sent her from the Dragomir lifeship *Spas* to the Tower. She'd hated farming anyway.

There, she'd met a handsome young apprentice named Marko, whose far-seeing eyes had drawn her in, stolen her heart. Marko, who'd loved her as no one else had ever done, brightening every day at the Tower with his dreams of the future.

The Tower... Daily meals, clothes, a warm bed—she could live out her days content with such luxuries. But Marko, virtuoso augur, had always had his eye on the North.

*Silen, volyena,* he'd said. *Magehold. If we become hensarin, the Grand Divinus's most trusted agents, we'll want for nothing. A few years. A few years, and we'll take our coin and start a proper life, volyena.*

Laurentine was supposed to have been Marko's last job. Disguised as a pirate with his squad, sent to awaken a girl the hensarin augur had predicted would become a quaternary elementalist, a great asset. To liberate her from her noble parents, who had kept their eldest son from the Divinity, who would keep the girl from the Divinity as well. Dominique Amadour Lothaire, the eldest girl they presumed, who had not yet had her éveil.

Only it hadn't been Dominique who'd awakened.

It had been her younger sister Favrielle who'd burned Marko alive, along with her own family. Favrielle, who the Divinity had chosen to retain, to protect, denying Drina her rightful vengeance.

She rubbed the brand until it hurt.

The day two hensarin had found her on mission and delivered word of Marko's death, she'd descended into fureur—stopped only by the arcanir they'd come with. Her inner barriers and her life had shattered that day. Forever with Marko had been reduced to a lone brand for a two-hearted promise.

The two hensarin had stopped her descent into madness, had

brought her back from the brink, called her wandering mind back from the Lone, restored her inner barriers. *The Grand Divinus needs you, shadowmancer*, they'd said.

A shadowmancer. A master of subterfuge and stealth. The Divinity didn't release what it could well use.

She'd stayed. Stayed long enough to steal anything she'd needed from Magehold—records, artifacts, weapons. A recondite skeleton key. Enchanted daggers. Anything that she could use to finally achieve her justice. She'd taken it all back to her home, the ruined tower on the Isle of Khar'shil.

And she'd planned, for years. Someday the girl would become a woman and fall in love with a man—a man with whom she'd make a two-hearted promise. A man who could be torn away from her.

Nine years later, Drina had given up and decided to simply torture and kill the girl herself.

She laughed under her breath. Fate spun her threads in such strange ways. When she'd tired of waiting, the girl had finally found the man, and the Crag Company's reconnaissance had incidentally passed on the intelligence in time.

And now Favrielle Amadour Lothaire was on her way to a life of well-earned punishment and waiting.

Waiting for the day she, too, would know that keen pain of losing forever.

A bitter taste in her mouth, she rose and laid the camp wards. Tonight, she would rest well, and then... Then she would plant herself in Courdeval, deep, invisible, and prepared for desire to meet opportunity.

For her chance to kill Jonathan Dominic Armel Faralle.

*You will finally have justice, Marko. And so will I.*

# CHAPTER 2

From beneath a dark hood in the corner of the dimly lit pub, Flagon & Flotsam, Brennan Karandis Marcel had a clear view of Radovan Vilín, an otherwise unremarkable sailor but for his rumored time aboard the pirate ship *Siren*.

Vilín sat with a table of drunken sailors, downing his ninth ale. The sling around his arm explained why, despite being on the *Siren's* crew list at the office of the Registrar General, he remained in the port of Suguz.

Days of careful investigation had led to this hole in the wall in the densely populated Shoal district, which he had learned Vilín frequented nightly. After several hours of waiting, Brennan's patience wore dangerously thin.

Nursing his second flagon, he tried to ignore the mounting annoyance within, fed by the loud guffaws in the pub. His hands brushed against the sticky surface of the worn wooden table, and he cringed while trying to focus on the conversation at Vilín's table. A night of bawdy anecdotes had paved the way for trading estimations of some cheap brothel's wenches and no useful information. The stretch of boredom made it seem like Vilín would never leave, and Flagon & Flotsam's poor-quality ale did not mitigate the annoyance.

But tonight, one way or another, he'd learn the whereabouts of the *Siren*. And Rielle.

A shiver wove down his spine. It had been too long. Too long. And the more time these fools cost him here, the worse Rielle's odds of survival became.

It had taken about three weeks to travel from Courdeval to Suguz, and his time in the Kezan Isles, with Rielle missing, was a far cry from the never-ending party that he'd remembered from his late teens. The bars every fifty steps, the free-flowing ale, the enthusiastic gambling, and the abundant beautiful women had served a young scoundrel well, but they wouldn't quench the needs of a man on the verge of losing his humanity. And certainly not the Wolf ripping it away inch by inch.

The peace, the solitude, the level of control he longed for didn't exist in this densely populated place. And neither did she.

The night of his last Change, it had been sheer luck that he'd found a small island and the Wolf hadn't been keen on swimming toward the Shoal. Without her blood, it was only a matter of time before he fully lost control.

Finally, with a drunken swagger, Vilín rose from his chair and slammed down his empty stein.

"'Night, boys," he slurred. "Time to pay ol' Milena a visit!" He patted his groin for effect.

Common boor.

Brennan's upper lip curled as he placed several coins upon the table, and when Vilín stumbled out, Brennan slipped away, drawing as little attention to himself as possible. He seemed to escape notice but for the barmaid, whose eyes snapped to the coins left behind before suspending care.

Outside, he drew in the air deeply, separating away the smells of the humid night—seawater, trash, and a tannery, among others—to single out Vilín's faint, malodorous scent. Brennan fell into step behind him down the littered thoroughfare.

The Wolf in him raged for a hunt, mouth watering, catching scents of stray dogs and humans, but he fought the urge, breathing slow, deep breaths in an attempt to pacify it. Since his bond with Rielle had gone silent, the Wolf had been winning more battles than it lost, but he couldn't kill Vilín—not until he extracted the information he needed.

*Once I have what I need, you can kill him.*

The Wolf calmed, receding a measure.

The streets of Suguz were busy even after the midnight hour, but he needed to get Vilín alone. Of course, the red-light district had an active nightlife, but the last thing he needed was the Wolf taking over in full view of witnesses; he could do without a mob bearing torches and pitchforks calling for the slaying of an abomination.

Vilín tottered toward a small alley—the chance Brennan had been waiting for. Vilín braced himself against a building before the alleyway, and Brennan dashed in the shadows, a fluid breeze of darkness that wrapped around Vilín and stole him into the alley.

With a hand clamped tight over the man's mouth, he dragged him to a dead end, muscles bulging, barely containing the Change. *Not yet. Patience.* His body stabilized, just enough.

The pressure and rumbling against his palm was Vilín's screaming.

"Be silent," he hissed into the man's ear.

Vilín persisted, his one uninjured hand clamping down on Brennan's gauntlet and pulling to no avail.

He had to chuckle—what hope did this fool have of getting away?

Vilín continued to scream against his palm and kicked his legs in protest. Annoying. Brennan executed a quick strike to the fourth lumbar vertebra. Vilín's legs went predictably limp. A deft strike to the seventh cervical vertebra, the vertebra prominens, and Vilín's shoulders and arm also went limp, falling away from Brennan's gauntlet. His years of study with his own hand-to-hand Faris master had lasting benefits.

He leaned in close to Vilín's ear. "Be silent, or the next one kills you."

The vibrations against his hand stopped, and Vilín nodded.

"I'm going to take my hand off your mouth," Brennan said, "but if you make any sound other than to answer my questions, I will kill you. Nod if you understand."

Vilín nodded again, wheezing.

Slowly, his fingers curled away from Vilín's mouth. The man's breath came harsh and ragged. The sharp stink of alcohol stung Brennan's nose.

"Where's the *Siren?*"

Vilín's breath came faster. He quivered. "I-I don't know." Irregular heartbeat. Terror and—something else. The man knew something.

*And he will tell us.* Brennan knocked a knuckle against Vilín's seventh thoracic vertebra. "You know if I hit you here just right, you will die a horrible death."

The unmistakable smell of urine inundated the air. Brennan stepped back, getting his boots clear.

"I-I really don't know!" Vilín sobbed.

Brennan pulled his hand away to strike.

"Please," Vilín begged, "you—you can check with the Registrar General!"

Narrowing his eyes, Brennan sighed. "I already checked his office. Try again."

"N-not his office," Vilín stammered, "or his home... but he does keep a second set of records for bribes. If Cap was sailing somewhere off the books, the Registrar recorded it in his second set. Please, will you let me go?"

*Off the books.* He hadn't considered that anything was worth going off the books for in Suguz. His mouth watered, and his hands tingled with violent intention. The Wolf wanted its way.

"Where?" He grabbed Vilín's chin.

"An apartment above the Bonded Jacky!" he immediately answered. "W-will you let me... let me go?"

The Wolf in him lingered just on the edge.

"Yes," Brennan replied. He grabbed Vilín's temple with his other hand.

The man gasped just before Brennan wrenched his head to the side with a gruesome crunch of bone—and let him go.

The sound riled the Wolf within. As Vilín's body thudded to the filthy ground, the Wolf brushed up against Brennan's precarious control, sending a shiver through his unwilling body.

The Change rode the shiver closely, pulling up tufts of fur, claws, and teeth in a beastly ripple, emerging and—when he forced them to recede—fading.

*Soon. Soon we'll hunt. I promise.*

Nostrils flaring, he focused on breathing until the Wolf was calm once more. The full moon was weeks away, but the Wolf had been pushing its advantage at every opportunity—every frustration, every rage, every kill. Its manifestations had been getting stronger, and desperate deals wouldn't work forever. If he tasted blood, tasted flesh—

It wouldn't be long before his control failed completely.

He needed to find Rielle. Soon. For her sake and for his own.

But first, that fucking logbook.

The mouth of the alley was empty; he grabbed the collar of Vilín's shirt and dragged him to a shadowy corner behind some sacks of refuse.

He headed to the Reef, a district on the outskirts of Suguz known for its tobacco, a favorite lodging area of sailors.

A fog had settled over the docks, obfuscating all but the immediate surroundings, but the smells and sounds of the city declared its continuing pulse well into the early morning hours. Laughter, coughing, clatter, and revelry played a chaotic serenade in accompaniment to the scattered human scents drenched in smoke, alcohol, sex, and sweat.

The fumes intensified; the Reef was close. There, among the other smoking dens, was the Bonded Jacky. Through the steamy panes of glass, he could see a gray fog hanging over the merrymaking patrons hunched over tables, gambling with worn cards and smoking pipes or cigars.

Higher, on the second level, neither light nor sound emerged. By all appearances, it was vacant. Shrugging into his hood, he stalked to the gangway between the Bonded Jacky and the brick wall of a small tobacco shop, wading into the shadows. Near the end, he deftly leaped up, kicked off from the brick wall of the shop, and jumped toward a second-story window sill.

He clamped the sill with his fingers and pulled himself up, then planted an elbow and palm flat upon it. He applied pressure to the double panes of the window until the latch broke with a small crunch.

The panes creaked open. It was all he needed: he nudged them farther apart and slipped inside.

He rolled out of the dim light coming through the window and through its billowing white curtains, stopping in a crouch just short of a dresser. His vision quickly adjusted to the darkness. A bedchamber.

He could neither hear nor smell any occupants—the smoke from downstairs didn't help. Nevertheless, he proceeded carefully, his leather boots silent upon the wood beneath, until he reached the doorway to a dark parlor.

The books would be here somewhere.

He crept along the wall until he found a study. Casting a cursory glance toward the apartment's entrance, he stayed close to the wall and skulked toward the room. Carefully, he crossed the threshold toward the large desk dominating the space, bathed in the silvery light of a nearby window.

Atop its large surface, disorder ruled: papers strewn about, an open ink bottle, a quill, a half-burned candle, and a bottle of rum. Below, a lock secured the first wide, shallow drawer in the center.

He swept a hand beneath until his fingers smoothed over a groove. With one good yank, the wood splintered around the lock. The drawer pulled free, and therein lay an assortment of items: a pouch of coins, some scattered keys, two signet rings, and a book. He carefully removed the book and approached the dim light of the window.

Human eyes would be unable to discern any text in such darkness, but he was no mere human. He caught a whiff of a man's scent from the item; it had been used recently and only by one individual. Running a finger along the cover, he hesitated only a second before opening the book. Its information could be devastating.

But he needed to know.

Lists of names and numbers and short, scrawled descriptions littered its pages. He thumbed through it until he found a blank page, then worked backward until he at last came upon a writing about the *Siren*:

*KPV* Siren, *set sail from Suguz, K.I. on Primidi, the second day of Vende-mair, in the year 1342 G.A., with thirty-eight head in cargo, bound for Harifa, Sonbahar.*

A crew list, its numbers skeletal for a caravel, followed. None of that mattered. All he cared about was the destination. Harifa in Sonbahar. Great Wolf, the place was a hotbed of whores, drugs, and slavery, but Rielle had survived worse. She just needed to wait long enough for him to arrive.

The Wolf's snarl rumbled deep within.

He paused, staring at the page until the letters and numbers blurred, memorizing the words while trying not to think of their implications. Stave off the Wolf. He had to stave off the Wolf. *Not now. Not now.*

He closed the book and replaced it within the drawer. With the lock broken, he needed to mask his true purpose; he snatched the pouch of coins and quickly headed for the window through which he had entered. The broken lock would be discovered, but it would seem like nothing more than a burglary, with no indication that the book had been disturbed. With silent finesse, he exited the apartment and jumped down to the gangway below before heading for the docks.

*Thirty-eight head in cargo.*

The *Siren* was a slave ship.

Rielle had been captured and carted away to Harifa on a slave ship.

His precarious control broke. As the Wolf clawed its way out, Brennan ran, hoping to get far enough away from the thick of the city to avoid killing humans this night, even as his mouth watered at the mere thought of blood and flesh.

A massacre would reveal him as a werewolf, a dreaded beast of legend, and mobs to kill him. And he couldn't die, especially not here and not now.

He wouldn't.

Rielle needed help. And he was it.

# CHAPTER 3

$\mathcal{T}$he door opened. "Dinner is ready, Your Majesty."

Jon looked up from his desk. The small-statured woman's chestnut gaze shifted away from his own. "My thanks."

"And a dove for you." She approached with quiet, hesitant steps and held out the sealed paper.

He accepted it. The Principal Secretary's wax seal was unbroken. Brennan. "My thanks."

"I live to serve, Your Majesty." The servant bowed, then walked backward three steps, rearranged her fawn-colored braid over her shoulder, and departed.

*Live to serve. So do I.* He stared at the door, running his thumb over the wax seal. Good news or bad?

If Rielle weren't alive, he wouldn't be getting a *message* from Brennan, but news of a massacre... by werewolf.

She was alive.

He tore open the message.

*The ship was bound for Harifa. Setting sail today.*

He sat up. Harifa, Sonbahar.

Rielle was just across the Bay of Amar. Taken—by Shadow of the Crag Company, if Olivia's theory was correct—but what had happened to her? A prisoner? A hostage? A slave?

With no description of Shadow, information was painfully scarce.

He reached for the Laurentine signet ring she'd given him on the eve of battle. Nobles were ransomed, and Rielle would alert any captor to her value.

He'd give anything to see her safe.

But there'd been no ransom note. There'd been ample time to contact—well, anyone. Post from Sonbahar for most of Emaurria went through Courdeval, and there'd been nothing. He'd sent countless knights in search of her, and the Order had sent paladins, and they'd reported back nothing about her, nor rumors of anyone like her. She wasn't being held for ransom.

Pain radiated from his clenched jaw.

He rose, scraping the chair against the heavy-pile rug. He grasped the note and shoved it into his pocket. If anyone had hurt Rielle, there would be—

Blood. Fingernails bit into his palms and drew blood. He rubbed his hands against his black wool trousers.

He would go to the docks and make inquiries. He couldn't just trust Rielle to Brennan's care; he had to find out what had happened to her himself.

He stormed out of his study toward the hall. At his door, he uncurled rigid fingers and breathed deep.

Two paladin guards stood at attention outside, brought their right hands to their hearts in salute, and bowed. "Your Majesty," they acknowledged in unison.

He turned to one of his guards, Sir Raoul, immediately recognizable by the scar stretching from his forehead across his nose to his cheek, a paladin ten or so years his senior. He'd always lived the job, with little interest in anything else. "Send for the dockmaster's list of departures for Sonbahar today. Immediately."

"Yes, Your Majesty," Raoul replied as Jon strode back into his quarters.

He traversed the vast quarters to enter the privy wardrobe, where his clothes, armor, and treasure—such as it was—were stored. His armor, clean and maintained since the Battle for Courdeval, shone dimly in the afternoon sunlight.

Although made of arcanir, it no longer bore arcanir's signature sage tint but the dark gray Helene Forgeron had achieved in Bournand. The coat of arms, once the Order's Terran moon, had been changed to the Emaurrian coat of arms—a winged serpent clutching a laurel leaf and a rose curled around a four-paneled shield of white and black flanking an ivy leaf.

Once standard issue for a paladin swordsman, this armor would never blend in now when he went into the city.

But who would dare to stop him? Could a man be king and yet unable to walk his own kingdom?

He threw on his arming jacket and hose, fingers stiff with nerves, and hastily donned his armor. Blessed Terra, it felt like coming home, wearing it again. As he put on his knuckle-dusters, light footsteps neared.

Eloi Charbonnau, his young shaggy-haired clerk, bowed and held out a roll of paper. "A list of today's departures, Your Majesty."

"My thanks." He grabbed the offered list and scanned it for ships departing for Harifa. One—and within the hour. The *Mirage*. He needed to get to the docks. Now. No time to think—or he would think himself out of it. "That will be all."

Another bow, and he was alone again. He made quick work of the rest of his armor, fastened his sword belt with Faithkeeper and his dagger. No time for supplies—he'd have to buy some at the docks. He grabbed his belt pouch, donned his helm and cloak, and headed for the door.

On his way out, he paused. As much as he wanted to, he couldn't leave without telling anyone. A missing king could cause a state of emergency, instability—

"Wait an hour," he said to Raoul and his fellow paladin, Florian, "and then tell the Lord Chancellor he's regent until I return." Did it sound as ridiculous to them as it did to him?

Face set to a permanently blank expression, Raoul looked to Florian with tight eyes.

Florian grimaced. "Your Majesty——" A well-timed objection.

"With all due respect," Raoul said grimly, his blue eyes icy, "our orders are to guard you at all times."

And their orders came from Paladin Grand Cordon Raphaël Guérin. Bureaucratic inefficiency indeed. Jon didn't have command of his own guards.

He exhaled slowly, letting his temper cool. "Then guard me as I make my way to the docks." He would worry about losing them in the crowds nearer the docks. "You will not be disobeying your orders."

A compromise.

Both guards raised their right hands to their hearts and bowed. "Majesty."

Flanked by the two paladins, he lowered the visor on his helm and headed for the stables. At least so covered, he didn't have to make eye contact with anyone, only nods of acknowledgment to bows and salutes.

Being king...

The whole experience still lacked tactile fabric; it was a phantom of reality in which he couldn't recall how he'd arrived.

And while he spent days in paperwork, learning from his collection of tutors on every subject from force magic to dancing to *seduction*—Terra have mercy—casting his eye over every corner of Emaurria's map and beyond, acknowledging bows and salutes, exchanging niceties—

While he did all that, Rielle *suffered* somewhere, abandoned by the very last person who should ever abandon her, the man who loved her, who wanted to spend his life eliciting that sweep of heartening brightness across her face.

He'd failed her, failed her when she'd most needed him.

No more.

In the stable, he went to his white destrier's stall, but when he began to saddle the stallion, stable boys rushed in to take over. And within moments, he headed not for Trèstellan's Royal Gate but for the Noble Gate. Noblemen came and went with their guards regularly, and he, eschewing the fanfare of royalty, might pass for one of them, if fortune were fair.

Bows and salutations fluttered with increasing frequency the nearer he rode to the gate, and even in the dense commotion at its center, he was recognized.

No matter. As he swept down into the city through the Azalée District toward the innumerable cascades of red roofs, fewer heads bobbed, fewer backs bent, until he mingled among the masses of travelers, vendors, foreigners, courtiers, nobles, warriors—a mere drop in a churning sea.

The open air at the crown of the capital had condensed to narrow streets, corridors walled by edifices in cruelly cheery coastal hues of sand, sunshine, and sunset with high arched doorways, guarded by unlit lanterns. Stilted elegance in script adorned signboards at Courdeval's higher elevations but gave way past the Triumphal Arch to comfortable straightforwardness and practicality deeper and lower into the city.

At the end of the lane, nothing but sky and greenery awaited, shouldered between endless buildings in parallel that disappeared over the horizon downhill.

From beneath the relative anonymity of his closed helm, Jon assessed the faces of those who turned to him. Thieves, pickpockets, scoundrels, and the like. The narrowing roads offered less and less room to maneuver, with only rare alleyways for relief—dark alleyways. His mind calculated threat and evaluated the terrain unbidden. When he glanced toward his guards, they appeared to be doing the same, hands in uneasy vigil near hilts.

He'd overburdened his two guards. But they'd only have to waste time on him for another half hour, and then he'd be gone.

They made their way lower into the city until the docks came into view, tall ships dotting the Bay of Amar and lining the pier. Beyond the infinite stretch of blue, somewhere, Rielle needed help. She needed *him*.

It was time to lose his guards.

"Majesty." Raoul tipped his head toward the way they had come.

Jon followed the path with his eyes. A banner and palace colors of deep blue and white. So much for a king being able to walk his kingdom.

The crown was an illusion of power.

"It's just a more elegant chain," he muttered under his breath. And someone from the palace was here to give it a yank. There was no time to lose his guards.

He turned to Raoul and raised the visor on his helm. "You know what business has brought me here."

Raoul's face shadowed beneath his scar. "I..."

The palace host drew nearer, a squad of paladins and the Constable of Emaurria himself at the head, Torrance Auvray Marcel, former paladin and Jon's former master.

*Tor.* As Constable of Emaurria, he was the highest officer of the military, second only to Jon himself.

No time. He urged his horse toward the ships, scanning their names as far as he could read. He just needed to find the *Mirage* and embark—

"Come," Raoul beckoned to Florian. "We serve."

Florian gave an emphatic nod of his curly-haired head, his brow creased.

Jon could have smiled at their support, but it'd be premature; he hadn't found the *Mirage* yet. Courdevallans cleared the way, space enough for their horses to get through.

"Make way!" Raoul bellowed, pulling his horse up to Jon.

Jon gave him an appreciative look.

"Close crowds are a potential threat." Raoul surveyed the area.

The *Mirage.* It was just off the coast, a carrack, brilliant and bright, its two square-rigged masts, lateen-rigged mizzenmast, and spars in stark relief, its sails full.

It had departed already.

He shuddered. *No.*

"The Constable of Emaurria!" someone called, a distant voice, clearing a path for Tor and the other riders.

*Faster.* Jon pushed his horse as fast as he dared in the crowd along the docks, past one berth after another, flanked by voices breaking the crowd. *I need to make it to Sonbahar.*

*Unneeded. Outclassed. Abandoning duty.* He shook off his doubts with every set of hoof beats, unwilling to entertain their reason. A decision of the heart couldn't be measured on an abacus.

He closed on the *Mirage's* berth. He rode to the end of the pier, staring out into the bay.

The carrack bobbed off the coast.

He glared at the faraway ship while his horse hoofed the pier. The distant voices of Tor and his host drew nearer and nearer.

*Damn it!*

He squeezed his eyes shut and pinched the bridge of his nose. He could leave the palace, ride to the docks, win over his guards, and lead his former master and a squad of paladins on a chase, but he couldn't force a ship back into port.

A quiet settled. Raoul and Florian closed ranks between him and Tor.

"Move aside," Tor's booming voice commanded.

"Orders, Your Majesty?" Raoul asked.

A bold move to defy Torrance Auvray Marcel. But Jon wouldn't leave Raoul to fight a battle not his own.

"Do as he says." Jon turned his horse to face Tor as Raoul and Florian stood down. The paladins behind his Constable of Emaurria sat poised for—

Jon drew in a bitter breath. "Here to stop me?"

Tor's fists tightened around the reins, his hazel eyes hard. Despite no longer being a paladin, Tor had continued to keep his dark-brown hair short and his face clean-shaven, although he now wore the trappings of nobility.

Any elegance lent by his attire was tempered by the dark circles under his eyes, deeper than they'd ever been when he'd commanded paladins. But he now guided an entire kingdom's military.

"I'm here to protect you," Tor said, meeting his eyes squarely, sincerely, with that same fatherly concern as always. "As I always have. What are you doing?"

Jon kept his voice low. "Rielle's in Sonbahar. Alive. No ransom."

Tor glanced away, lips pressed tight, and closed his eyes as he let out a long sigh. "I know you feel—"

"Don't tell me how I feel."

"Yes, Favrielle needs you. But she is one person, one person my nephew is already tracking." Tor met his eyes.

Jon looked away. It had been fifty-one days since Spiritseve. Fifty-one days since Rielle had disappeared from the shores of Emaurria. The kingdom didn't care that the love of his life was in peril; it needed and needed and needed—and it took and took and took. And he'd allowed the Grands to convince him to place the country's needs above his own need to rescue Rielle.

And they were right.

He had no hope of tracking her, not like Brennan did, with his superior senses. The paladin in him knew that, knew his own strengths and weaknesses, and that worrying here would do nothing. Out in the field, worry crippled a man, endangered the mission, made him a liability instead of an asset. Like he was being now.

Concrete intelligence—knowing Rielle was in Sonbahar—deceived him into feeling capable of finding her. Deceived. He closed his eyes and sighed.

Brennan would find Rielle; she would return; and he had to trust that and perform his duty here.

"What about the rest of your people?"

He didn't need Tor to remind him.

"Look at them." Tor urged his horse forward, close enough to limit who was in earshot, too close—Raoul and Florian moved in defensively.

*I can't.*

"Look at them!" Tor urged, his voice low but firm.

Jon raised his eyes to Tor's and then looked around. A whispering crowd had gathered, ringing their group. A shoeless boy of no more than six stood nearby. Emaciated. So poor, he didn't even see the king.

*I've blinded myself.* Jon bit the inside of his mouth. *It is I who haven't been seeing them.*

"Who will lead them while you're off endangering yourself and self-ishly trying to do what's already being done?" Tor asked quietly. "Do you consider Brennan incapable?"

Brennan was many things. But not incapable. Jon looked away.

"Emaurrian arms will save her, but *you* need them to be yours. And for that selfishness, you are willing to abandon an entire kingdom that needs you."

A shudder cut down Jon's back. *Selfish*.

He'd known it, deep down, and ignored it.

He took in the sight of those around him—the emaciated boy, the many others like him, the dock workers who had so few ships to tend, the thieves who had less and less to steal.

He glared out at the *Mirage*, still at sea. Too late. He'd been too late. Worrying was crippling inaction, and he had his duty. It was time to devote himself to it entirely, to the exclusion of all else. Focus on the mission before him now. Protecting the kingdom.

"Majesty?" Raoul asked, but the word rippled through the crowd, spreading far and wide, and rolled back louder, more urgently, until the whole crowd chanted the word.

The Order of Terra would find the person responsible for the regicide, and Brennan would find Rielle, Jon knew that, and his own presence was... unnecessary, no matter how badly he wanted to be there to find Rielle.

But Brennan couldn't take his place as king—nor could anyone. The Emaurrian people needed the stability of the Faralle dynasty, and he, a bastard and former paladin, was all there was.

He couldn't just leave. He would never be able to just leave. Ever again.

"Terra's blessings upon you, Your Majesty!" a voice rang out.

"Divine keep you, Your Majesty!" The crowd closed in, arms outstretched in need, open and begging.

His hand immediately went to his belt, and he took off his coin purse and handed it to one of Tor's paladins, maintaining eye contact. "See that its contents are distributed to these people fairly."

The paladin hesitated, but at last nodded. "As you command, Your Majesty."

The cacophony of cheers and shouts grew louder, but Jon raised a hand and waited until it quieted. "Good people of Courdeval, I see you."

All eyes fixed upon him.

"I am of you, raised in a monastery, nothing to my name but hunger for something more"—he scanned the crowd, a few faces downturned —"and Emaurrian vigor in my blood."

Cheers erupted from the crowd, all faces to him once more.

"I am your king, and I see you." He let his gaze rest on the young boy for a moment. "Tonight, the palace will see you well fed and clothed, on my word."

A roar rose up from the crowd, booming, humming through his chest, spooking a few of the horses.

"Long live King Jonathan!"

"The Generous!"

"The Vigorous!"

He suppressed a smile.

The state of affairs in Courdeval had improved since the siege, and while the epithets brought a smile to his face, he had no right to any of them until the city and the kingdom could breathe again.

He raised a hand for the crowd to quiet, and it did, just barely. "A night's meal and clothes on your back are a blessing, but too few ships make berth at these docks—"

Shouts of agreement.

"—and I will see many more here with enough paying work to keep your families fed and warm not just for one night, but every night. We *will* have safe lands again, if I have to fight every last new beast or creature myself."

The crowd grew wild, and paladins swooped in to close ranks.

Tor glared at him, his brow creased. "We need to return to the palace, Your Majesty."

"Lead the way." Jon allowed the paladins to lead him back up to Trèstellan, acknowledging his people as word spread of his declarations. And he meant them.

Bright faces greeted him and cheered his name, but none of it warmed. He lowered his gaze for a moment to his gauntleted hand.

Grotesque scales, a gleaming black snakeskin covered his hand, his wrist, his arm.

Gasping, he squeezed his eyes shut, and when he looked again, it was only his armor.

He managed a veil of a smile; he didn't have the freedom to chase ghosts.

The cost to fulfill today's promises would be staggering—he could almost picture Derric's grimace—but he didn't care. With so few ships coming into port to trade, these people had nothing, and if the capital was to survive, to *thrive*, that needed to be addressed.

As much as it hurt, he would stay and see the kingdom safe from threats within and without. And trust Brennan to find Rielle.

*But maybe it's time to delegate the investigation of the regicide to someone with a more... personal stake.* He would see to that later.

And the promise of ships meant ensuring secure passage—keeping the Immortals at bay. He would need allies.

# CHAPTER 4

Olivia's footsteps echoed through the Abbey of Amaranth, soft clicks on the shining marble. Vaulted ceilings soared majestically overhead, and the fading light poured in through the stained-glass clearstory windows, painting winding patterns of blue, purple, gold, green, and red, joined by the blooming cast of the rose windows from the towers. Majesty and beauty in a place where life took its leave.

She continued her pilgrimage to the apsidal eastern end, her gaze drawn to the hemispherical semidome depicting a great full moon over a densely wooded forest, and the Terran goddess descending from it in a sweep, arm outstretched, palm offered.

*James.*

She couldn't wait to see him. Every day for over a month she'd come to see him.

Her feet trod the familiar path to the Farallan chapel and into the colonnaded rotunda, a round building crowned with a dome. Dying sunlight illuminated the statuary at the center, a tomb for the first Farallan king, Tristan Armand Marcel Faralle, and his queen, Rosalie Aimée Vignon Lothaire. The Blade and his Rose. Cast in bronze, the king and queen stood in worship, arms held up to the sky. Off to the side, the newest tombs awaited.

There he was, her James: tall, well-muscled, in his best finery... Shoulder-length hair, prominent jaw, straight regal nose, a neatly trimmed beard, his hands lying palm up at his sides, waiting in eternal repose. The gisant had captured him well. She knelt and slipped her hand in his.

*I've missed you.*

He lay here, ever to slumber, never to change, and she with the lover's curse, heart entombed as tightly as he, but left to live. She squeezed his hand. *The palace has been so cold without you.*

She'd buried herself in work day after day, loudening the turning of her mind, muffling the solitary beating of her heart. But here, once a day, she let in the quiet whispers of love, of longing, and of justice.

King Jonathan had slain Evrard Gilles, and for a time, it had given her comfort, but ultimately not peace. Evrard Gilles had tortured and killed James—she shuddered—but for all his brutality, Gilles had been no more than a sword. And the man who'd commanded that sword remained at large.

Unpunished.

Who had looked upon James and seen a resource, one whose exhaustion was desirable, even at the cost of his life? Who had seen him as deserving death, when he'd been an honorable man, a good man, *her* man?

Her fingertips pressed into the grain of the gisant's stone, and her skin heated, moistened by hot tears. She dragged a sleeve across her face. The Order of Terra had been investigating the regicide for nearly two months and remained empty-handed. But someone had to bring James's killer to justice. Someone had to find the person responsible, who would answer for the murders, the siege, the atrocities. Who would know where Rielle had been taken.

The Swordsman who'd hired Gilles.

Boots clicked behind her, and she glanced over her shoulder. A man liveried in Trèstellan's royal blue and white. He bowed deeply.

"Pardon me, Lady Archmage. His Majesty requests your presence." He remained bent in obeisance.

She rose. "Thank you. I shall leave forthwith."

He straightened, inclined his head, and left.

With a final glance at James' gisant, she took a deep breath and left the abbey to meet with his son.

After a short ride in a coach-and-four, the white-stoned majesty of Trèstellan Palace came into view. She exited the coach, pulled off her gloves, and strode to the king's quarters, exchanging greetings with passers-by as doors opened before her and closed behind her in perfect service.

Lydia, her young lady's maid, rushed to her side, brown curls bouncing. "Rumor says His Majesty took the Constable of Emaurria and several paladins on a merry chase today," she whispered.

Did that have anything to do with his summons? Every evening at their force-magic lessons, he'd been growing more and more restless as he awaited correspondence from Brennan Karandis Marcel.

"The king has reached his breaking point." She swallowed. *And so have I.*

"Small wonder. None of the paladin investigators have returned with good news." Lydia leaned in conspiratorially.

"Rielle came here to save my life, and succeeded. And for that success, she's still missing." With a sigh, Olivia bowed her head. "And it seems even the Order can't find her."

"The Tower has been a *great* help, too," Lydia added.

"Divine forbid they pull a muscle waving us off dismissively." She had sent to the Emaurrian Tower for a spiritualist, but the interim Proctor had replied that none could be spared, and good luck with finding Lothaire.

She smoothed an imaginary wrinkle from her black velvet gown. How Kieran Atterley had managed to secure a position as interim Proctor was anyone's guess.

"We're on our own," she whispered. Spirit magic performed by any mage other than a spiritualist required massive amounts of anima and, for all its costs, rarely succeeded. She would have to inquire about hedge-witch spiritualists with her mage contacts...

...or go to Bournand and twist Feliciano's arm. She shuddered. That dirty peddler of poison could rot in the Lone, even if he was one of the rare few spiritualists. But if her contacts proved worthless, she'd have no other choice.

*I'll do no less than Rielle did for me.*

Lydia gave her a warm smile. "You'll see her again, Your Ladyship. You aren't one to give up easily."

Definitely not. She'd find her best friend no matter what it took. Even if she had to run a company of paladins into Feliciano's filthy resonance den.

"Well, I'm off to see His Majesty." She handed Lydia her cloak and gloves.

Lydia inclined her head. "I'll have your tea brought to your study later."

It was where evenings always found her. And with that, Lydia left.

At the heart of the palace, Olivia took a deep breath, reaching for her braided bun to make sure every hair was in place. A couple of new console tables bearing vast floral arrangements lined the halls, and it didn't feel as empty as it had yesterday. The Crown slowly replaced tapestries, paintings, and furnishings stolen or ruined during the siege, but not fast enough to restore Trèstellan Palace to even a fraction of its former glory.

But restoration was at hand. Soon, it would be as if the siege had never happened, as if Gilles had never invaded, as if James had never died. The court could pretend nothing had gone awry at all, even if she couldn't. The Swordsman needed to be found well before then, before Courdeval, Emaurria, and the world lost interest in him and in justice.

The Order would find him soon. They had to.

Finally, she arrived at the king's quarters, and upon sight, the two paladin guards admitted her. The entrance opened into the antechamber, the first of an enfilade of rooms with massive south-facing windows—a dining room, a study, a bedchamber, a wardrobe, and a garderobe.

The antechamber's golden upholstered walls shimmered in the luminance of the lit sconces, its tufted sofas and armchairs inviting, its portraits regal, softened by massive arrangements of flowers grown magically by the aged Grand Master of Botany, an appointed geomancer who kept the royal greenhouses in bloom year round.

On a nearby winged armchair, she could almost see James again, gazing intently at his brother, King Marcus, while he discussed plans to ban sen'a and trux, and create assistance programs for recovery.

But those days were long past.

"Your Majesty?" she called.

"Join me in the study, Olivia," His Majesty called back to her.

She traversed the dining room, which sat twenty, and entered the study. Nearly every available inch of its twenty-foot-high walls overflowed with books. Magnificent chandeliers, lit with candles and fitted with mirrors to reflect the sunlight in the daytime, hung from the frescoed ceiling, upon which the Great Hunt unfolded. It was said that the Faralles had come to power in the ancient days as a clan of dragon hunters, a myth they had taken to heart, incorporating a winged serpent in the royal coat of arms.

At the massive purple-heartwood desk, His Majesty sat, leaning deep in his high-backed chair, his chin resting on a fist as his sea-blue Bay of Amar gaze pierced a document he held. He wore a black brocade doublet with the first closure unfastened. He still kept his hair close cropped, his face shaven, so like the other paladins of the Order. A show of solidarity, perhaps.

Like his father, he was uncommonly handsome, with a chiseled jaw, dark angled eyebrows—one sporting a slash of a scar—and an irresistible smile. And at twenty-six years of age, royal, and the richest man in the realm, he could certainly have his pick of fine ladies, but only had eyes for one. Her best friend. She smiled.

He still sported the poorly healed scar on his neck—when she'd offered to fade it for him, he'd revealed that it had been Rielle's work.

He was an honorable, strong, and capable man. And he loved Rielle. *Together, we'll find her.*

His Majesty looked up from the document he was reading and inclined his head toward one of the armchairs before his enormous desk.

"What is it you have there, Your Majesty?" She sat.

He lowered the paper to his desk and sighed. "Word from the Order." He closed his eyes and rested his head against the high back of his chair. "Or rather, *no word* from the Order."

She frowned. "About Rielle or the regicide? Both? Or should I say 'neither'?"

He cracked his eyes open and nodded tightly, then crossed his arms, tapping his bicep with a finger. His piercing eyes pinned her to the chair. Evaluative.

She squirmed.

"You've been working a lot lately."

As the Archmage of Emaurria, she was head of all magic affairs, managing and financing the Grand Library; teaching the royal family magic; investigating any magic-related offenses in the kingdom; serving as ambassador to the Divinity of Magic; and commanding the Guardians of Emaurria, the specially appointed mages working as warders in the palace. She oversaw the Grand Healer, the Mage-Commander of the Guardians, the Grand Alchemist, and the Grand Master of Botany, the only immediately subordinate posts to hers that had been filled since the siege.

On top of that, she'd been named Liaison to the King's Council on Immortals, which had her buried in research on every new beast threatening the land since the Rift and advising relevant offices on how to defeat them. Although she delegated what was impossible to fit into her schedule, she thrived on long, busy days.

Keeping the turning of her mind loud.

She shrugged. "No more than I can handle."

His Majesty chuckled darkly.

"Truly," she added, stroking the Ring of the Archmage. The more she worked, the better. "If there's anything else you need of me, you have only to ask."

His Majesty peered at the document on his desk, his finger tapping restlessly. At last, he exhaled deeply. "I want you to investigate the regicide."

A frisson along her spine made her jump in her seat. *Yes,* she wanted to scream. *I'll do it. Let it be me. I'll find out who's responsible for James's murder. I'll work tirelessly until it's solved.*

But... The Order of Terra, headed by Paladin Grand Cordon Raphaël Guérin himself, investigated the regicide. His Majesty had been a paladin himself. Why would he distrust the Order?

Paladins filled every available military office.

Did His Majesty wonder if the Order had schemed to put one of its own on the throne?

If he did, if he withheld his trust from the Order of Terra, then he wouldn't delegate to his adoptive father, Derric Lazare—or even to his former paladin-master, Torrance Auvray Marcel, who, aside from formerly serving the Order, was brother to the most influential noble in the realm.

And if His Majesty didn't trust the Order, he certainly didn't trust the Divinity. So that removed the former Proctor, Pons Olivier, from the list.

But why her? She'd been of the Divinity herself.

He fixed his gaze on her. "Olivia, you loved him. No one will look harder."

James—and Anton—would not find peace in the Lone until there was justice for their deaths.

Justice she could secure.

Justice she *would* secure.

She leaned forward. "I'll do it."

A tentative smile spread across His Majesty's face, his eyes lit with an inner glow. "Good."

He looked to his desk and riffled through the documents, raising his eyebrows at last.

With a quick dip of his quill in the inkwell, he signed the paper and then handed it to her. "This will give you unfettered access to every-thing I have access to. I'll send word to Paladin Grand Cordon Guérin that I've appointed you as Special Investigator on Magic to assist with the regicide. To impede you would be as if to impede me."

Faced with his hardened expression, she shivered at the thought of anyone doing so. She accepted the document.

After handling a few investigations of crimes involving magic, she knew where to begin. She'd see whom the Order had in custody. The paladins had made several arrests of Crag Company mercenaries, offi-cers, and Evrard Gilles's associates.

"I'll begin tonight," she said. "But first, your force-magic lesson."

His Majesty rolled his eyes. "I'm not improving much, and it's not for your lack of effort. Magic... is not my area."

She waved him off. "Small steps, Your Majesty. You can't expect to complete training in a month that normally takes five years or more."

He quirked an eyebrow. "How about training that takes a novice five minutes?"

"Not all novices are created equal." She grinned. "Some require more attention than others."

"Vastly more, clearly."

"Repulsion shields again tonight?"

He grimaced and rose. "Very well. I suppose even the Archmage needs a laugh now and then."

It was his modesty that made her laugh. And for now, she would allow herself that much. His skill with magic—or lack thereof—was indeed remarkable, considering how quickly he learned all else. What little free time he would have had disappeared in lessons—lessons from a dueling master, linguists, historians, etiquette tutors, even a Companion of the Camarilla. What the Companion—infamous flirts, seducers, and lovers—taught, she didn't even want to imagine.

As for the magic... Her work would be entertaining, at least.

But later tonight, the investigation, would be far darker. Somewhere in the Lone, James sharpened his rapier, waiting to greet the man responsible for his death, with Anton close by.

# CHAPTER 5

*A*s soon as the flatbread landed in her open palms, Rielle snatched it away and began stuffing it into her mouth as she crouched, curled, swallowed.

Countless hands reached over her, yanking back her hair, her clothes, pinching, scratching. Fingers closed around her chin as someone grabbed at the remaining flatbread in her hands.

It was gone.

The hands still clawed at her, reaching for her mouth. She shot out blindly with her elbows, colliding with groaning bodies, but they moved on.

She trudged to the side until she hit a wall, and then slumped to the ground.

No more than a mouthful or two each day, and some days, nothing at all. At this rate, she would starve to death.

A sad tease of light stroked her face. Even blindfolded, she discerned the soft morning sun from the scorching, dead heat of the afternoon and its bright, blinding light. The light would stay another few minutes, until the overseers would lock the doors once more, leaving them all in total darkness.

Thick in the air, the smell of filth never relented, but she'd given up hope for any basic human necessities; their importance had crumpled in favor of survival. Even the thought of what covered the ground beneath no longer figured.

Somewhere behind her, cries arose with the crack of a whip and ended with a few erratic sobs. Someone had been too slow. Too loud. Too scared. Or maybe just unlucky. The whip didn't care.

Before long, nearby movement breezed against her skin. Then forceful hands grabbed her, yanked her up, and linked her chains to those of another, already moving.

*Where?* The question flickered in her mind, a mere glimmer, and disappeared.

Chains rattled ahead of her and behind until she was thrown to the ground, colliding with a warm body and bumped by another brought down on her other side. One after another behind her, bodies thudded to the ground. All breathing. All alive.

"Where are we?" a voice dared ask in timid Kamerish amid the whimpers ahead.

A few fearful voices hushed the speaker.

The southern continent. It had to be. The heat, the low Nad'i spoken by the overseers—Sonbahar, or somewhere on the border. Somewhere near water—the salt air sometimes taunted relief it never delivered.

A cry, and more rattling. The body next to her trembled, chains clinking.

A pull on her restrained hands. Sounds of movement from up ahead.

The scrape of sand against her arms made her scramble to her feet. Must keep up. Several large shadows blotted out the light above, a circle of them closing in. Cries erupted from innumerable mouths. Chains clattered. No magic. No sight. No energy. She kept her arms tightly wrapped around herself.

Large, callused hands seized her, prying her arms away from her chest, pulling at her filthy clothes with a savage roughness.

Every inch of her quivered, and she couldn't stop. She resisted, clutching the rags to herself, tears bursting from her eyes to soak the blindfold. Her head bobbed with vertigo. One of her captors shook her

—a violent, unyielding tremor—until the unmistakable chill of nakedness.

She hadn't spoken out of turn—

The inevitable crack of the whip never came. The shadows moved down the line. To someone else.

Sometimes the overseers came into the stable and left with a crying, screaming woman or two, then returned them later, sobbing, weeping. Every creak of the door had been the sign of her turn, but it never came, never came, never came.

She cradled herself, the tiniest amount of disgusting joy springing in her heart even as she stood in utter nudity. The trembling wouldn't stop, racking her bones. She curled her head toward her shoulder, rubbed her cheek against it.

The line was in motion again. Splashing sounded ahead. Her feet moved of their own volition, and when they finally stopped, she was plunged into warm water, the tender skin of her days-old whipped back burning, her blindfold torn away.

Light. Blinding light.

Her sensitive eyes adjusted poorly. Hurried hands soaped and scrubbed her body with all the care of a merciless farmhand washing a tool. She gasped as her head was pushed under the water, then pulled back up. Soap stung as some coarse brush scoured her head. Then it was back under the water, a rough shake beneath it to rinse out most of the lather.

Released, she surfaced, gulping deep breaths, assessing her blurry surroundings. Hundreds of people bound by chains were linked to hers —all unclothed and half-submerged in the massive body of water. Numerous workers darted from person to person with ruthless efficiency, all the while supervised by grim-faced overseers with sharp eyes and whips.

She glanced down at her hands and the arcanir cuffs binding her. The constant, penetrating sting of arcanir had become familiar, almost a comfort, a reminder that she had not gone numb, had not died in the long stretch of darkness and loneliness since Courdeval. Even the thought of that battle her last night there, of being with Jon, Brennan, Olivia, and Leigh, was too much to bear.

*Jon.*

*It's very simple,* he'd said, his breath warm against her lips. *Do you love me, Rielle?* She reached for him, but chains weighed down her hands. He wasn't here.

Her eyes ached, squeezed, watered. Her chest caved inward.

*Return to me,* he'd said, eyes never leaving hers. Never leaving. Never left.

The last words he'd spoken to her. *Return to me.*

Return... She wanted to return. To Jon, a reflection in his Shining Sea eyes. Home.

She wanted to be home.

*Jon...* Her heart cracked and crumbled, her eyes aching with pressure. She had to get to him.

After fighting the Black Mountain Brigands at the Mor Bluffs, she'd defeated fureur. Let love, fear, rage—all of it—back into her heart. Allowed herself to feel.

And here, cuffed in arcanir and far from home, all she did was feel. Fear the overseers, love Jon, rage at Shadow, Sincuore, all of them. Feeling it all, she'd never felt so whole, and yet—

The people around her moved. As she looked ahead, one by one, they stepped out of the bath. Her feet soon followed, bringing her up broad steps and dripping onto the flagstones. They were led outside once more, where guards approached them and unlinked the chains binding the line. They formed new groups, separating people based on age and sex.

The groups were taken in divergent directions. Although she, grouped with the young women, had been taken away from the other groups, they all approached the same place from different sides. A sea of tall wooden posts.

Time after time after time, it unfolded before her eyes, and then it was her turn. Her arms were pulled away from her body, and she had a fleeting taste of freedom as her chains were unfastened, but not the arcanir cuffs. Her arms were yanked back around the rough post and secured tightly along with her feet, forcing her in an upright position— chained to the numbered post, on display, a ware at the souk, along with everyone else.

It had been shocking once, but over the past several weeks, privacy had become a faded memory.

As soon as their work concluded, the overseers moved on to the next post, securing another woman, and another, then another until all were displayed. Left to thirst, to hunger, to bake in the hot sun, and to wonder what misfortune would arrive.

The binding done, her mind wandered. Blindfolded into darkness, bound into stillness, she'd achieved a morbid and peculiar clarity of vision in this Divine-forsaken place. Aboard the ship, the drug-induced haze had left her numbly fantasizing about destroying the crew and its malevolent captain, her only respite the sight of the stars through the porthole every night. The sight of the same stars Jon saw, her only remaining link to him. Drenched in heartache and delirium, she'd been a mess aboard the ship.

But here, ignored like so much cargo, she'd had time to refocus.

Someday, whether tomorrow or years from now, she would be free, no matter the blood and the bodies required. On that day, that fateful day, there would be one name, above all others, demanding her attention. Her gruesome attention.

*Shadow.*

Even the name sent fury coiling around every part of her body. Shadow's suffering would be limited only by her imagination, and for weeks, she'd had nothing but time to do just that.

Fire. It would end in fire. Always fire.

Jon would be safe.

And then there was the matter of the serpent... Who had the captain so feared to cross?

Her shoulders ached. Everything ached.

No one came for nearly an hour, and her arms, back, and shoulders were ready to give out. Soon well-dressed people trickled in, meandering through the rows of posts, pausing to scrutinize the offerings.

The boot of the ship's captain pressed against her face anew; she lowered her chin, avoiding too direct a look. She, like the rest, might have been no more than a rug or a goat or a shovel, on display, powerless, and for sale. Shoppers searched for bargains, for defects, for novelty—and murmured comparisons to one another.

They disgusted her. They outraged her. They terrified her.

She'd almost managed to avoid looking at them altogether until the sun had nearly set.

A rough hand grabbed her jaw, forcing her to look upon the face of a man. Tall and dark-skinned, his severe features were pronounced under his black cotton scarf-like headdress, a *kaffa,* worn to protect against sunburn, dust, and sand in this desert, secured by a rope circlet. Beneath a matching warrior-caste black ankle-length thiyawb, his trained body was obvious, even if by contrast he had a merchant's face.

His discerning brown eyes searched hers for a long moment, and then he spared a brief glance over her before nodding to the woman accompanying him, the one with unequivocal intelligence in her dark gaze.

Although she too wore an ankle-length thiyawb, its heavily embroidered front panel, billowy back, and fine cloth dyed with an expensive violet spoke to her noble caste. Wrapped around her head and face was a *halla,* a cotton headdress similar to the kaffa but worn without a rope circlet; she wore hers tied below her neck, covering but not hiding the shape of her delicate nose and angular chin.

The smooth summer of youth still glowed around her dark, kohl-rimmed eyes—she could be little older than three decades. With a keen gaze, the woman approached, reaching out to examine her.

It was clear that the woman's evaluation was the one that mattered.

If she were bought by a woman... Perhaps she wouldn't be treated so harshly. And beyond the stable, traveling and maybe in a different compound, she might be under lighter guard. Perhaps this auction was the change of fortune she needed.

A flowing probe into her anima from the woman—the unmistakable reach of resonance.

An unnatural wall within her ached. Arcanir's doing. The inability to use magic throbbed as intensely now as it had face to face on the Kezani ship with Shadow. Arcanir's consequences, like its sting, didn't fade while in contact.

*"Tala'anti hadir a Nad'i?"* The woman asked whether she knew the language widely spoken in Sonbahar.

High Nad'i? Here? The languages she'd been hearing for weeks likely included some dialects, but High Nad'i was only spoken by Sonbahar's upper class and scholars.

The woman maintained eye contact, waiting for an answer. Did this woman offer a better fate than the stable? Precious seconds were quickly slipping away.

Life would not improve here; it had been nothing but grim waiting, suffering, and starving, but what did these two strangers offer?

Of all the fates before her, here was the only one she could have some control over, if only by a mere answer.

The woman turned to leave.

*"Tehazara'anti,"* Rielle said, her heart pounding as she commanded the woman to wait. Had she remembered the words properly? Had she said it correctly? She'd learned it initially as part of the subjects the future duchess of Maerleth Tainn would need to know and then at the Tower to read and translate texts on magic.

The woman turned around, her eyes wide—whether it was surprise at Rielle's knowledge of Nad'i, usage of the High Nad'i dialect, or her brazen command to wait, who knew? But it was a reaction.

*"Ani hadir wa sihar kellah a Nad'i,"* Rielle continued, communicating that she both spoke and wrote in Nad'i.

The woman's eyes grew wider still before she finally narrowed them.

Had she smiled beneath the cloth of her halla?

She left with her companion.

*No.*

*Please!* She watched the two walk away before hanging her head once more.

At least she'd tried.

Around her, the other slaves remained fixed to posts. Surely some had been bought? Were they all to be removed at the same time?

Overseers arrived and unchained the others from posts, dragging them off all in the same direction. Away.

Could it—

She breathed one tremulous breath after another, searched the horizon for answers. *Am I actually hoping to be bought?* She shook her head weakly. In a mere few weeks, the world had changed beyond recognition.

It was not long before she met the same fate as the others. Since her legs had long since gone numb, being dragged was her only option. Sand scraped against her bare skin.

One of her captors hoisted her up over his shoulder like a pack; he must have grown tired of dragging her. A whimper of protest formed in her throat and died as blood rushed to her head, building in pounding pressure.

Before the ship, before Shadow, the last person to carry her had been Jon. After dueling Brennan in Melain, despite his own injuries, he'd swept her up into his loving arms, carried her upstairs, let her rest her cheek against his chest. He'd been upset with her, but she'd never felt safer.

She smiled dumbly, weary tears escaping her eyes. *Jon... Please find me. Please. I need you. Please...*

No safety, warmth, or gentleness here. No love. Only pain and no pain.

The numbness in her feet and legs slowly receded. Too much— here, there was too much to bear, too much to feel. The wetness streaming from her eyes down her forehead and into her hairline—

They entered a building where dour-faced men waited with needles and ink; a steady hand pressed the back of her neck, keeping her cheek flat against a cold table, while another set of hands secured her legs. *No, no, no—*

A sharp point pricked against the small of her back. She clenched her teeth against the pain, but then the unmistakable tingle of magic came.

*A rune.*

She squeezed her eyes shut. A runic token of Sonbahar... linked to another rune that, when activated, would function like a tracking spell.

Then she had, indeed, been purchased.

Divine, had she done the right thing? What awaited?

At least she was leaving the stable. An opportunity to escape could present itself and, with it, the chance to kill Shadow and return to Jon.

Night had long fallen by the time she was brought to a caravan, acutely aware of the chill that nakedness magnified. Nearly a dozen others linked to her shivered and shook, just as she did. Soon, they were ushered into a covered wagon, a small mercy. Several cloaked guards awaited them inside, with distinctly curious eyes compared to the auction's men, but a woman seemed to have authority.

A violet thiyawb.

The woman from before. She had removed her halla, revealing a thick bun of shining black hair secured at the nape of her neck, a pointed chin, and thin lips. She moved from one captive to another, conducting what looked like a thorough medical examination before offering a garment. A guard served bread, cheese, and water. Once she finished with the man next to Rielle, it was her turn.

Gentle hands, almost sympathetic. When she opened Rielle's mouth to examine her teeth, some glimmer of hope flickered to life— the suffering would let up. It had to. She met the woman's eyes and did not look away.

"My name is Ihsan," the woman finally said in High Nad'i, her methodical hands roving quickly over Rielle with a sheen of magic. She finished at the belly, and then pulled out a book in which she jotted down a note. "You will henceforth be known as 'Thahab,' " Ihsan said softly, continuing her inspection.

"I already have a name," she blurted. When Ihsan looked up at her, she flinched, but no slap came.

"*Zahibi,*" a guard scolded.

*Master.* She would have to use the word, lull those who meant to lord over her, placate them into thinking she would never rebel.

She swallowed her reluctance. "Zahibi."

Ihsan regarded her with eyes like still waters, wise beyond her twenty-odd years. "It is useful for masters that slaves let go of their former lives, and it is useful for slaves that their masters do not look into them. We do not bargain. We do not ransom. Your former life is over."

She opened her mouth to argue—*Better not.* If they underestimated her, killing them would be all the easier.

Ihsan offered her a loose-fitting *garment*—a loose term, too, as it was more like a bolt of gossamer with an opening for her head. A silken sash cinched in the waist. But it was relief from the chill, warmer than nothing, clean and soft. And no one was hurting anyone. Perhaps the whippings and beatings of the stable were over, too.

When the guard gave her a handful of bread and cheese and offered her a waterskin, she ripped it from his hands, drank, devoured.

The water's cool, clean wetness seeped into her lips, tongue, and cheeks like life, blooming its essence as she gulped it down. Divine, it was as though she'd never tasted water before.

After nearly drinking herself sick, she dragged an arm across her mouth and handed the waterskin back. The dark bread and salty cheese she stuffed into her mouth, filling her belly as swiftly as possible. No hands pried the food from her, for once.

Away from the misery of the stable, with food and water in her belly, her few words of High Nad'i had earned her a better position from which to wrest her freedom, or survive until Jon could. So far, the price was a new name—a worthy trade.

"Thahab," she repeated, the name foreign and unusual on her tongue.

# CHAPTER 6

*O*livia shivered as a paladin guard escorted her through the darkness of Trèstellan's dungeon, not from the biting winter chill but from bygone days spent frozen here. Too many. A left turn, two flights of stairs, a right turn, twenty-eight steps, a left turn...

She rubbed the Ring of the Archmage.

*I'm free. I'm free. I'm free.*

Whenever she visited Leigh, she had to convince herself she wasn't going to her old cell. That she wasn't a prisoner, but the Archmage.

And tonight, she wasn't going to her old cell, or to Leigh's. In this dungeon was a member of Gilles's household, and with him, the chance to unmask the Swordsman.

The stench of filth and mold hung heavier the deeper they went. Disgusting. Familiar. The paladin guard took her to a crowded cell block, where nearly every cell contained a prisoner—or two—who, as she passed by, gasped, clung to the bars, begged.

The Order had made numerous arrests of Crag Company mercenaries after the Battle for Courdeval, as well as Gilles's known associates. Hundreds of prisoners inhabited this dungeon.

"You're not supposed lock more than one prisoner in each cell." She looked up from the list she held.

The paladin eyed her, his green gaze soft, sympathetic, beneath his raised visor, then looked straight ahead again. "The dungeon's full, Lady Archmage. And unless we pack two to a cell, we'll have to start sentencing."

Sentencing... He meant executions. Deaths.

She forced in the stagnant air, held it prisoner, then glanced at the list as she exhaled. "And no one's questioned this... Benoit Donnet?" she read from the document. Donnet had been Gilles's chamberlain, head of his household in Kirn.

"No, Lady Archmage, not since his arrest." The young paladin sighed. "I know it seems as though we've neglected our duty, but there are 231 prisoners here, and we questioned them all when they were arrested, developed agreements with some in exchange for further testimony, cross-referenced that testimony, verified its authenticity, collected corroborating evidence—"

She nodded casually. If he tried to prove his competence, his efforts were wasted. The Order had held 231 prisoners here for nearly two months, and seemed to have no more answers than it had on Spiritseve.

"—and I say this not to inflate my own importance, but to offer you my assistance. I've been posted as a guard to the palace dungeon since Hallowday, and I know every prisoner here by name." He stopped, placing his torch in a holder. "If I can help bring the villain who hired the Crag to justice, then it will be my honor."

Honor. Yes, of course, but there was more to this paladin's offer of assistance than he was saying. She rested a hand on her hip. "What's your name, Sodalis?"

The paladin removed his helm and bent in a practiced bow. "Sir Edgar Armurier, Sodalis of the Order of Terra, second rank, Monas Amar Third Company, at your service, Lady Archmage."

His maple-brown hair shone reddish in the torchlight, a stark contrast to his ivory skin. Clean shaven like all paladins, he nevertheless sported a shadow of facial hair. But in the light, the freshness of youth still in his face, he could be no more than a year or two over twenty.

"Armurier?" she asked.

Straightening, he nodded. "My father is an armorer in Sauveterre. I'm his third son."

Even tradesmen groomed only an heir and a spare, but unlike the Houses, they could rarely countenance the cost of caring for many more children.

Papa and Mama had been less obvious, but they made no secret of scrambling for a betrothal for her sister, Aerin. And when Killian had taken a job at twelve, they hadn't forbidden it. Such were the ways of poorer families. And Sir Edgar seemed as well versed in them as she.

Yet, as badly as she wanted justice for James and Anton and to find Rielle, she would play unwitting tool to no one. "And what is it you really want, Sir Edgar?" She circled him slowly, and when he opened his mouth, she cut him off. "And don't say 'honor.' You've already said that one."

He closed his mouth and hesitated. "Knighthood."

So that was it. His Majesty and the Paladin Grand Cordon had agreed to offer a limited number of knighthoods to distinguished paladins in order to replenish ranks, and Sir Edgar, of the mere second rank and no more than twenty years of age, couldn't hope to find himself among that number.

But with a grand feather in his cap like apprehending the Crag Company's elusive client, he'd distinguish himself all right.

He could prove useful.

She nodded. "Very well, Sir Edgar. Assist me with this investigation, and when we find the person responsible, I'll put in a good word for you with His Majesty." She extended her hand. "On my word."

He shook it. "To the start of a beautiful partnership." His face brightened with a lopsided smile.

"So, Benoit Donnet?"

Sir Edgar grabbed the torch he'd placed and walked her farther down the cell block. "He's a funny little man, Donnet. We haven't questioned him since intake—we focused on the major players in the Crag Company itself—so other than his daily essentials, he probably hasn't had much contact."

Long days and nights spent in the endless dark, accompanied by the skittering of vermin and the ceaseless sounds of flowing water.

Endless hours of boredom, madness. Yes, she knew it. She knew it well.

*Free.*

When Sir Edgar stopped and placed the torch in a holder, she studied the nearby cells separated by thick stone walls, squinting to discern the figures huddled in dark corners.

"This one." Sir Edgar nodded toward a farther cell. "For your safety, you may not enter it."

"I am the Archmage," she shot back, enunciating each word with the requisite gravity. "But I do not need to enter."

Within, a small, lean man sat primly against the wall, his back ramrod straight, his chin high, dignified. His slicked-back gray hair, secured with a tie at the nape, looked almost neat from afar, until the shine of grease caught the light. What looked like a formerly fashionable mustache had grown into an unruly beard, gray and white whiskers tufting over his jaw and neck.

Despite his rigid dignity, his dark eyes fixed on her, through her, and his silent desperation mirrored what she had once felt. She'd looked at Anton the same way once.

He rose, dusted off his grimy clothes, neatened them, and then took a proper bow.

"Monsieur Donnet?" She presented herself before the bars. "I am Archmage Olivia Sabeyon."

"The pleasure is all mine, Your Ladyship," he replied, his voice a hoarse but refined tenor. He inclined his head toward the bars. "May I approach?"

"Please."

He strode nearer but halted an arm's length away. Non-threatening. Courteous. "To what do I owe the honor?"

The records she'd requested from the Order had said he'd been Gilles's household chamberlain in Kirn, his right hand, and when word of the siege's breaking had reached Kirn, he'd seen the Gilles family safely to a ship, but had remained behind to resolve financial matters. Paladins had taken him into custody before he could complete his task.

"You worked as a chamberlain for Evrard Gilles, did you not?" she asked.

"Yes, that is correct, as I told the fine paladins of the Order nearly two months ago."

She ignored his complaint. "And what did you do for him during the course of your employment?"

He pulled his shoulders back. "I managed the household staff, personally took care of my lord and lady's chamber, and managed the household budget—paying expenses, collecting taxes, payments, and so on."

"You personally collected payments?"

"Yes," he said, recognition flickering in his eyes. "But only for my lord's personal accounts. Regrettably, I have no knowledge of any payments he may have received on behalf of the Crag Company."

She narrowed her eyes. "Regrettably?"

He raised his arms and held them out to his sides. "I am an old man, Your Ladyship, and my lord is dead. If there were anything I could tell you about him to secure my release, I would."

He was still loyal to Gilles, knew nothing relevant, or didn't realize he knew something relevant. She would find out which.

"Did you accept any large sums on Gilles' behalf?"

"Nothing out of the ordinary."

"Did Gilles meet with wealthy individuals?"

He shook his head. "My lord's wealth far exceeded that of his circle's. But he wished to ascend in society, among the Houses. His wish never came to fruition."

Naturally. While nobles who ran Free Companies were held in high esteem and often retained for small border disputes—at criminal fees—a commoner running a Free Company was often retained as a last resort, taking jobs few Free Companies would.

Like killing the entire Emaurrian royal line.

"What about the Gilles family?"

He pressed his lips into a thin line. "Lady Gilles and the children never supported my lord's ambitions. I will not endanger them."

So he did have limits. But would they hold, if pressed? "Even if their testimony could secure your release?"

He lowered his gaze, but then raised it to hers once more. "Even if.

Her Ladyship always treated me respectfully, and I love those children as if they were my own."

"But you have no qualms about destroying the memory of their father?"

He frowned. "My lord did that himself."

"Well said." She ran through the possibilities. A chamberlain managed the lord's household—his activities, coordination, his correspondence—

"His correspondence," she said. "In the past year, what kind of correspondence did Gilles receive?"

He drew in a slow breath. "Typical items. News, letters from his friends—all commoners, to a one—although—"

"Although?" She leaned in, and Sir Edgar lightly took her arm to hold her back.

Donnet frowned. "Well, he had one friend whose identity I did not know. They'd corresponded for years, but in code."

That was it. Sir Edgar stiffened next to her.

"And you didn't think coded letters were worth mentioning to the Order?" She narrowed her eyes.

Donnet held up his hands. "They're gone. My lord burned them. I-I didn't even know who sent them, or from where. I do not know what there is to mention."

Coded letters made for illusive evidence when they no longer existed... and when the witness didn't know the writer, the place of origin, or the content. She frowned.

Since her apprenticeship to Leigh, she'd written countless letters. Read countless more. And living away from her family had added to that sum. And as had earning Archmage.

"Did you have any suspicions about whom it might be?" Sir Edgar interrupted.

Donnet shook his head.

If the man had nurtured suspicions, if he truly wanted his freedom, he would have offered.

No, their answers would come only from what Donnet would have perceived. Sights, sounds, smells... of a letter.

"What about the materials?" she asked. "The paper, the ink, the seal?"

His brow furrowed. "Vellum. Iron gall ink. Dry red wax seal. Plain impression."

All fairly common. "But if the correspondence was sealed, how did you know the contents?"

Donnet's cheeks reddened. "On rare occasions, my lord would... leave open correspondence in his chamber."

Snooping. She stifled a smile. "Do you know the bird he used for this correspondence?"

He shook his head. "No, he didn't use a bird." His mouth fell open. "A courier. Always the same man. He'd wait in a local pub for two days for a reply."

She grabbed the bars. "Do you know the man?"

Sir Edgar pulled her back, but she refused to release them. "Lady Archmage—"

"Yes," Donnet answered, raising his eyebrows.

"If I sent an artist, could you—"

"Yes," Donnet said, his face alight, "in exchange for my release."

She smiled. "If your information leads us to the criminal, you have my word that you will be released. Your sentence will be stayed until our investigation is concluded. Sir Edgar Armurier here, a paladin, a man of impeccable honor, is witness."

Donnet bowed. "Then send me this artist, Your Ladyship, and gods' speed in apprehending the man."

If this courier could be found, perhaps he'd lead them straight to the man responsible for James's death. For Anton's death. For the king, the entire royal family, and so much of Courdeval. For Rielle's disappearance.

She inclined her head. "Thank you for your cooperation, Monsieur Donnet."

He mirrored the gesture.

Sir Edgar took the torch and escorted her back toward the stairs, shaking his head. "A courier..."

She grinned. "A courier."

With a little uncommon thinking, there was finally a solid lead in the search for the Crag Company's client. All thanks to reexamining Donnet. A man whose vocation had been taking care of Gilles was worth questioning thoroughly, no matter that he had nothing to do with the Crag Company itself.

"So what's next?" Sir Edgar asked.

She drew in a deep breath, rubbing her Ring of the Archmage. "After we have a sketch of the courier and the location of the pub in Kirn, that's where I'm going, disguised. Perhaps he'll return there, or maybe someone will know more about him."

Sir Edgar stopped. "I'm coming with you."

She turned and crossed her arms. "Don't be ridiculous. It's a week's ride from here by carriage and—"

He shook his head. "We had a deal. And I'm making sure you deliver. For both our sakes." He shrugged. "Besides, I've been known to be handy in a fight. Just in case." He shot her a smile. To no effect. Smug bastard. "Write a letter to my commander and say you need me for your special investigation."

She grimaced. They *did* have an agreement.

Perhaps she could use the help. No mage partner on this. And she couldn't risk telling her subordinates. Like it or not, her circle of trust for this investigation extended only to His Majesty and Sir Edgar—for his self-interest. Self-interest, after all, was a trustworthy motivator.

A letter. She could do that much. "Fine. As agreed, Sir Edgar."

He smiled that bright, lopsided grin of his. "I don't think our disguise will hold up in Kirn if you keeping throwing around 'Sir.' Please, call me Edgar."

She raised an eyebrow. "Fine, *Edgar.* But it's still 'Lady Archmage' to you until then, and certainly after." *Young upstart.*

He executed an elaborate bow. "I wouldn't dare suggest anything less, Lady Archmage."

She strode toward the stairs, and when his steps fell into line behind her, she grinned.

James, Anton, and countless victims would find justice. Rielle would be found.

Olivia straightened. With her spearheading the effort, they'd find this courier and do what the entire Order couldn't.

~

MOST DAYS, the working-class people who called Coquelicot District their home made up the bulk of Drina's clientele, purchasing potions, preventives, salves, and poultices for common diseases that resisted healing. Healing magic, so useful for injuries, hadn't yet solved the mysteries behind diseases like the Wasting, the Sleeping Sickness, Water-Elf Disease, influenza, hereditary defects, and even the common cold. For these, people flocked to apothecaries for remedies, and her products quickly found a market.

Some days, nobles thinking themselves stealthy arrived, cloaked and hooded, quietly requesting the unmaking herbs or poultices for the Inamorata. Business brought in good money, more than enough to live on and replenish stock, and a steady trickle of information.

Today, a woman would come as she did every week to purchase boar's tooth and fox lungs for her young daughter, who suffered from the Wasting. The remedies were old, and unlikely, but the woman was poor, and it was all she could afford. Or so she believed.

Her name was Sauvanne Gouin, forty-two years old, a serving woman since her maiden years, born and raised in Courdeval's Coquelicot District. Widow for six years. Mother to Claire, nineteen years old, a chambermaid in Trèstellan Palace hired when the Order had established Jonathan Dominic Armel Faralle as king on Hallowday, and Sophie, age nine, suffering from the Wasting in her bones for two years.

The woman's elder daughter had access to anyone and everyone of importance in the palace, and the ability to procure paperwork for a visitor, since courtiers occasionally required apothecaries and surgeons and were often not as outgoing as those nobles who thought themselves so stealthy and visited her stall on some days.

The woman's elder daughter was the key to the palace, and to the king.

Drina spent the day selling and advising, doing her typical business, waiting for the woman to arrive. Sauvanne would be wearing her usual open-weave shawl over her lager-brown frock and white apron.

The day had almost ended when the gray open-weave shawl

appeared in the crowd, wrapped around Sauvanne's strong shoulders. Her long mahogany locks, tamed in a large bun, must have been beautiful unbound, something many a man must have noticed while leaving coins on The Greasy Spoon's tables, but few would find worth taking on the expenses of a sick child.

"How is your young daughter faring?"

Sauvanne drew in a deep breath. "She can barely move, poor thing, but I pray she'll improve."

Drina brightened and nodded hopefully. "She will. There are some very effective remedies." *You'll ask me about them.*

Sauvanne smiled, but her eyes remained cold as glass. "I've tried so many... Well, what I could afford." She looked over the wares, corked bottles, satchets, and boxed powders, amid the many others. "Is there anything new?"

*Never fails.* She kept her satisfaction suppressed and tilted her head thoughtfully. "Have you heard of *oporavak* tea? Sheep sorrel, burdock root, and other purifying herbs used to cure the Wasting. It's ten coronas a pound."

Even among the Houses, few had such funds lying around, but when struck with the Wasting, they usually found the money. And occasionally survived. Oporavak tea was no scheme.

Sauvanne nodded solemnly. "I have, yes, but... Ten coronas a pound, I... Unfortunately, it's just me and my daughter, and I don't make nearly enough serving at The Greasy Spoon. My other daughter, Claire, brings us money every week—she works at the palace, you know—but I don't think we could afford it."

Drina widened her eyes. "At the palace, you say?" When Sauvanne nodded, Drina lowered her gaze and pressed her lips together, furrowing her brow to appear deep in thought. "Although I am most thankful for my business in this district, I have hoped to reach some wealthy clients. Only... It's difficult from Coquelicot."

Sauvanne's head bobbed as she listened, then frowned, but her frown slowly softened. "Wait... Perhaps you and I might help each other?"

Drina leaned in, feigning curiosity. All was unfolding as planned. "How so?"

"My daughter is a chambermaid. Maybe some of the courtiers she serves might be in need of you? Perhaps she could summon you when they need remedies?"

Drina crossed her arms. "Yes... Yes, and nobles pay well for discretion." She gave Sauvanne an encouraging smile. "If you could have her arrange such visits, I could procure you some oporavak tea... a dose per visit?"

Sauvanne's face lit up as she beamed, tears in her eyes. She took Drina's hand. "Terra bless you for your kindness!"

Once Drina had proper documents to enter the palace *and* access, it would be a small matter to make use of her maps of Trèstellan from the siege and slip into one of the many passageways. She hadn't explored the palace much beyond the Hall of Mirrors, the dungeon, and the barracks, but she'd remedy that error. From the passageways, every room of worth would be open to her.

Including the king's own bedchamber.

The woman had just given her the king of Emaurria for a dose of oporavak tea. It was pricey, of course, but she never liked to see a child suffer. Two victories in one transaction. She grinned. "My pleasure."

With profuse words and bows of gratitude, Sauvanne purchased her usual remedy of boar's tooth and fox lungs, and left. A little kindness could buy justice.

Drina packed up her stall and headed home, to her room at Peletier's Inn, beaming a smile of her own.

# CHAPTER 7

*J*on paused. Behind the ornate doors, the palace's courtiers and esteemed guests had assembled for dinner in the great hall. His heart sank.

But at least Derric and the High Council had, reluctantly, done his bidding and distributed food and clothing at the docks. Tonight, the people of Courdeval were warm and well fed.

Now it was his turn to work, to ensure Emaurria's security. And to do that, he needed to keep the suitresses at Trèstellan convinced of his good faith and, thus, keep their countries amicable to assisting Emaurria until more permanent solutions could be found.

If they suspected he was merely acting, it would mean his kingdom's ruin.

*No pressure at all.* He scrubbed a hand through his hair, tugged the hem of his fitted black doublet, and took a deep breath. He gathered his composure—a loosening of the muscles, a faint pleasant smile, a carefree air.

His herald announced him. "His Majesty, King Jonathan Dominic Armel Faralle, Prince of Pryndon, Zahibshada of Zehar, Duke of Guillory, Verneuil, and Ornan, Count of Guigemar, Langue, Buis, Lomiere, and Sauvin, Baron of Milun, Laustic..."

The entire host of guests stood upon his entry. The carved head
table, but for his own seat at the center, was filled end to end with suitresses and faced a sea of courtiers. A few stood out—his political dissi-
dents, Viscount Costechelle, a dapper but graying man; and Marquis
Forel, with his dark tousled hair and hazel eyes... another Marcel—

The herald continued, but Jon kept a smile in place. The mouthful
of titles he'd inherited as the last of his line always felt as lengthy as the
first time he'd heard it. And their length spoke to the kingdom's
desperation, not any sense of prestige. At its conclusion, he took his
seat, initiating a ripple as guests seated themselves. "Good evening."

He received a harmony of greetings and honorifics in reply while
the dinner service began, and in the corner, a single harpist strummed
a light dinner tune. It was a far cry from nights spent alone before the
fire pit as a paladin, eating double-baked bread, cured meat, and whatever he could find nearby.

A seat before the head table remained empty. A young bronze-
skinned woman, her voluminous dark hair arranged in an intricate
style, approached to take it with effortless elegance, fixing him with
her unflinching, hazel-eyed gaze.

Someone he'd met? He hadn't faced such rapt attention for nearly a
decade, since—

"How was your day, Your Majesty?" someone asked from next to
him. Princess Melora Nualláin of Morwen, Emaurria's southeastern
landlocked neighbor, angled her shoulders toward him, flaunting an
ample décolletage framed by a low-cut gown, as she had taken to
wearing in recent days. Her lustrous, chestnut-colored curls fell over
her shoulders and contrasted against the bright green shade of her
dress.

*Just stick to your lessons.* Derric had hired—among his many tutors—a
Companion, Alexandre Sartre, to teach him the finer points of the
game. Flirtation, seduction, things no honorable man discussed.

He forced another smile. "It was entirely unexciting... until now,
Your Highness." He took a sip of his aperitif—not that it made his
dishonor and deception palatable. His advisers, however, would be
proud.

Melora placed her elbow on the table and rested her chin on her hand, grinning broadly in some sort of reverie, but her lady-in-waiting, Aislinn, corrected her with a dispositive throat-clearing.

To his left, Princess Alessandra Ermacora of Silen rolled her eyes and fluttered her dark lashes before turning to him, tossing her cascades of dark hair. When she leaned closer, spiced perfume inundated his nostrils.

"I'd rather know," she began in a low rasp, "how will your *night* be?" She raised a derisive brow.

Terra have mercy—

The dry white wine went down his throat all wrong. He coughed into the glass, his eyes watering. A servant quickly dashed from the corner, but he waved the man away.

Alessandra flashed an amused smile and looked him over, then lost herself in a large glass of wine. His guests gasped about his coughing fit and asked questions of concern; he allayed their worries with niceties. There was no easy way to admit to being intimidated by a twenty-year-old princess. A smirking, gleaming-eyed princess.

But she—and the other suitresses—were no doubt just playing their parts, too. Their countries had demanded this from them as his had from him. None of them actually wanted him; none of them *could*. To them, he was a bastard raised as a commoner, elevated to royalty by circumstance, and a stranger. Perhaps each of them had their own love, too, but their station demanded sacrifice.

The staff served the appetizer course, a savory cheese soufflé in individual ramekins. The suitresses chatted at his table while he said as little as he could get away with.

This was nothing more than a farce, as much as the Grands argued otherwise. The longer he could manage to hold the interest of the other countries in the region, the more time he could buy for Emaurria to stabilize. What happened when that time ran out—he and his officers had vastly differing opinions about.

The servants set the main course, a rosemary-roasted quail in a fig demiglace over root vegetables and rice. How many loaves of bread would that have bought his people? All this for appearances.

Course after elaborate course went by, one light topic of conversation to another, all his guests appearing to enjoy themselves but for

Alessandra, whose dark eyes smoldered as she assessed him for far longer than propriety allowed, finishing her second glass of wine before pouring a third.

The suitresses chatted, and the dark-haired courtier viewed him over the rim of her goblet.

"His Lordship, Magister Pons Olivier, Lord Chancellor of Emaurria!" the herald announced.

The seventy-two-year-old former Proctor of the Emaurrian Tower of Magic, and Jon's current Lord Chancellor, Magister Pons Olivier, approached, adorned with his chain of office. He leaned in. "Your Majesty, how would you like a reprieve?"

*Praise Terra.* He rose. "Pardon me, ladies, but I must take my leave. Please, enjoy your dessert and tea." He added pleasantly, "I will see you all tomorrow." He inclined his head, and the ladies stood to curtsy or bow as was their custom.

The dark-haired courtier's eyes met his, and she gave him a mysterious nod. Who in Blessed Terra's name was that person?

Alessandra lost her balance as she curtsied. He reached out to catch her, and she tumbled into his arms.

"Are you all right?" He looked her over.

She brightened. "Yes, thank you." Rising on her toes, she leaned in to kiss his cheek. "You don't fool me," she whispered, and he froze. Beaming, she pulled away and reached for the arms of her chair. "Too much wine."

Melora rose from her chair. "I've also had too—"

With a shake of her head, Aislinn caught her hand and urged her back to her chair.

He took his leave and followed Pons out into the hall. "My thanks." He heaved a sigh. "I am in your debt."

Pons chuckled as they walked toward Jon's quarters. "Not many men would complain in your position, at least not those of your persuasion."

Jon shook his head. "It's not that I don't enjoy their company. It is that I am doing so disingenuously." He loosened the collar of his fitted black leather doublet. "That, and the Sileni princess is beyond bold."

Laughing, Pons clapped him on the back. "Yes, they do things differently there. She will expect to bed you soon."

"She will... *what?*" He stopped in his tracks, gawking at Pons, and thumbed his Sodalis ring, which had last graced Rielle's finger.

"I know." Pons paused. "You will, however, have to continue with gestures of good faith."

He drew his eyebrows together. Gestures of good faith... There had to be some way to placate them, especially Alessandra. He already dined with them, and what else was there but romancing?

When he'd fallen in love with Rielle... The days and nights they'd spent talking, reading, dancing—

*Dancing.*

This time of year, the Houses usually fussed over the Midwinter Ball, but he'd heard nothing of it. "The Midwinter Ball was canceled due to the siege, wasn't it?"

"Perhaps too hastily."

He nodded. The next occasion was the Terran spring festival of Veris in three months. "Let us have a ball for Veris." It would maintain the appearance of courting a bride; he didn't need Derric, the new Grand Master of Emaurria, to take him to task. And the suitresses would be diverted.

"New, but not unusual. I'll talk to the Master of Ceremonies and see that it is done."

His dance tutor would be pleased, at least.

When they finally arrived at his quarters, he paused. "There was a courtier who arrived late to dinner, a dark-haired woman possessed of unusual intensity. Do you know her?"

Pons pursed his lips, then his face brightened. "Ah, the recently widowed Countess Vauquelin, Nora Marcel Vignon."

Terra have mercy, she'd been familiar with good reason. He stiffened. While he'd been Tor's squire, whenever Tor had brought him to visit Maerleth Tainn, she'd pursued him mercilessly.

But it had been a decade since he'd last seen her, and the years had changed her. He'd invited Vignon's widow to court without knowing her true identity. Faolan Auvray Marcel's daughter and Brennan's sister. "Nora?"

"Do you know her, Your Majesty?"

"We've met. What do you know of her?"

"Her husband died in the siege. She has two sons, ages nine and six. The elder had his éveil early upon learning that his father had died. A master from the Tower tutors him now, Your Majesty." When Jon didn't reply right away, Pons hesitated. "Will you... make overtures?"

Overtures. The kind that would—? "No."

Unthinkable.

Pons inclined his head, perhaps just the slightest show of approval, and took his leave. Jon lifelessly greeted Raoul and Florian.

"That good of an evening, Your Majesty?" Florian asked with a sympathetic shake of his head.

"Makes me long for the monastery," he murmured in reply, earning smiles from them both as he entered his quarters. Removing the restricting doublet, he crossed the antechamber, still feeling Nora's unwavering gaze upon him.

*Nora Karandis Marcel.*

No, Nora Marcel Vignon. A formidable woman. No other woman had pursued him so aggressively. The sinful things she'd whispered in his ear to watch him squirm nearly a decade ago still lingered in his memory. *Aren't you even curious?* A devilish little grin. *I won't tell a soul, promise.*

He shivered.

All these years, a marriage, two children, and a widowing later, and she still looked at him the same way she had then. In a strange way, she wasn't unlike her brother—unsettling in her intensity.

He shook off his thoughts and entered his study.

A woman stood with her back to him, gazing out the window. A simple black velvet gown trimmed with white fur clad her figure. Firelight shone in her bright red hair, secured in a large, braided bun at the nape of her neck with a golden comb.

"Olivia."

She turned, eyes wide, and squeezed a roll of parchment. She bowed. "Your Majesty."

"How did you—"

"I apologize for intruding on your privacy"—she glanced away

—"but I wanted to speak with you... away from other ears." She tipped her head toward the bedchamber, and he accompanied her in, toward his drinks cabinet.

"There are passages in the palace, all throughout. When the Crag struck, James—" Her voice broke.

James. Prince James. His father.

"There are some sensitive matters... At least one that should know no other ear but yours."

"Tell me." He poured two goblets of wine and handed one to her.

After taking a sip, she looked at the goblet pensively, took a deep breath, and handed him the parchment.

He unrolled it. It was a sketch of a man with long hair that brushed his deep-set eyes, a gaunt and stubbled face, an aquiline nose, thin lips, a birthmark on his jaw. He looked to be in his forties. "This is...?"

"A courier." She took a place next to him and peered at the drawing with him. "I questioned Gilles's chamberlain, a man called Benoit Donnet, who said that Gilles received coded messages by courier. Always this man. I believe the other party to be the suspect we are looking for."

He glanced at her, a smile spreading across his lips. "Olivia, you..." Terra have mercy, she'd done it. She'd found a lead. She'd done in a week what the Order hadn't in months. He wrapped an arm around her and drew her in. "Terra bless you and your brilliance."

When he pulled back, she beamed back at him and gave him a confident nod. "We have a sketch, yes, but don't go blessing me yet. We haven't apprehended the man."

"But I know you will." He handed the parchment to her. "What do you need to accomplish this? Name it, and it's yours."

"A believable cover. A coach and guards for a few days in Kirn. Lodging. And permission for one of the Order's dungeon guards to accompany me, as he's familiar with much of the testimony in the investigation. And a lady's maid." She hesitated. "And the guard, the paladin guard... He's a junior member of the Order, and I promised I'd put in a good word with you about knighthood."

"Done." He grinned. "Send me the paperwork, and I'll push it through."

She reflected his pleased expression, but the grin soon faded. "I also have less... promising news."

"What is it?" He leaned against the window and drank his wine.

"Word came from Bisclavret."

He knew Bisclavret as a march near the Marcellan Peaks.

"The strange creatures that have been spotted there—massive giants radiating cold. They've been attacking flocks of livestock and scaring the surrounding villages. Some of the villages' militias are mobilizing, but..."

Bile rose in his throat. He drank deeply. Tragedy. Death. Loss. It spread across the land like a sickness. And the account wasn't unique. His kingdom had been slowly succumbing to the newly awakened Immortals, and if the tide wasn't soon stemmed, there'd be no kingdom to speak of. "Death toll?"

"One hundred and forty-eight."

He slammed down the goblet. Terra have mercy.

"And what's worse, we have little information about them, only what the fleeing villagers can tell us. The marquis is sending forces, but faced with the—I call them *mangeurs*—I doubt his soldiers will be effective." She shook her head.

He grabbed a nearby quill, dipped it in ink, and hastily scrawled a note on some paper. He handed it to her. "See what information you can uncover about them by tomorrow afternoon," he said, "then take this to Paladin Captain Perrault and tell him what you know. He should send paladins."

She nodded. "Pons has also suggested a more... unconventional solution."

Considering the number of problems ever multiplying, if solutions were on offer, he was all ears. She turned back to the window. He joined her and followed her line of sight to the Bay of Amar. Somewhere beyond it, if Brennan's note bore truth, was Rielle.

"The Earthbinding," she whispered.

He raised an eyebrow. The Earthbinding... It was the stuff of legend.

"It is an ancient ritual, but it is real. Performed at a Vein, it binds a king to his land to influence its health, prosperity, and strength." She rolled her shoulders. "Pons wants you to do it, but…"

Anyone who knew Emaurrian legend knew the Earthbinding linked a king and his land. He had read the old tales. A king's will and the state of his realm, forever in contest… An Earthbound king had to fight off the vulnerabilities of his land, strengthen it with his own will, and live as one with it for his whole life.

If he succeeded, the harvest would be abundant, his enemies disadvantaged in Emaurria, the Immortals thwarted by the earth itself.

If.

"Will it work?" he asked.

"Although I have deciphered—"

He exhaled sharply. No half-measures. "Will it work?"

"We believe so, yes."

"What does it require?"

She grimaced but quickly recovered. "Invoking the dead gods…"

His stomach rolled. A former paladin and devout Terran invoking the dead gods? "So, blasphemy."

She bit her lip. "There's some ritual—animal sacrifice—"

More blasphemy.

She bit her lip. "And, um, coupling with a virgin—"

Infidelity. Absolutely not.

"She would represent—"

He brought a weary hand to his face and sighed. Did anyone in this palace care a whit about who he was, or only what he could do? He crossed his arms. "So, what would he be called afterward?"

She eyed him warily. "Who?"

"The stranger who inhabits my body."

She pressed her lips together and looked away.

If only he could abdicate—

He hissed. That was unconscionable. He was the last Faralle; trying to hand off a crown would incite another war altogether, a civil war, and he wasn't about to jeopardize the lives of hundreds of thousands of people for the sake of his own selfish desires.

But he didn't have to perform the Earthbinding. And Olivia didn't deserve his wrath. She was only trying to help.

"I'm sorry." He looked out at the city. Lights shone as far as the bay, although fewer than he would have liked. "I just... don't want to become someone unrecognizable." Too late for that. "Any *more* unrecognizable."

She rested a hand on his arm. "You're doing your best, Your Majesty. You need to stay true to yourself as much as you can. Everyone will tell you that to protect a kingdom, sacrifices must be made. But this ritual, if you do it, you wouldn't be *you* anymore."

At least she agreed. "But we do have to do something," he said. "You heard at the High Council meeting. Princess Sandrine is gathering an army."

Princess Sandrine Elise Faralle El-Amin. His cousin once removed. If the High Council's intelligence was legitimate, then Sandrine was hiring hisaad raiders in Sonbahar and preparing to stake a claim for Emaurria. The Faralles were patrilineal; as the son of the late king's brother, his was the stronger claim. But the longer Parliament stalled on his legitimization and a coronation, the more room Sandrine and her husband would have to maneuver. And even if they invaded, the Order of Terra wouldn't welcome them and remove one of their own. The ensuing civil war would only plunge Emaurria into deeper chaos.

He offered her a thin smile. "Was there another matter?"

She drew in a slow breath. "It's about Leigh."

This had been a long time coming.

He let out an exasperated sigh and headed to his bedchamber, where he sat in an armchair by the fireplace. She followed. Of all the things they could have discussed, she had chosen his most loathed subject. The traitor.

He leaned forward and rested his elbows on his knees, staring into the fire. "You shouldn't waste your efforts on his account."

"It's been two months," she said. "We have no proof that he was involved in Rielle's disappearance in any way, and while he may have subverted the Moonlit Rite, he didn't actually hurt anyone and has been charged with no crime."

"And the one hundred and forty-eight dead in Bisclavret?" His shoulders hardened, but he didn't care about keeping his guard up around her. "He betrayed her, Olivia—and you, me, everyone in this realm."

"Without knowing the consequences."

"He knew them. He just unreasonably disregarded them. That doesn't make him innocent—it makes him reckless." He brought the goblet to his lips and drank deeply.

Had the Moonlit Rite not been thwarted, the kingdom would not be facing the Immortals now. It would have been completed in time.

And when it had first happened, he had been convinced that, had Leigh not betrayed them, the vial of king's blood would not have shattered. His own true identity would never have been revealed then and in that way. The group would never have been separated from Rielle. And she would not have disappeared.

Over the past few weeks, however, reason had slowly crept in and dismantled the wall of illogical pretexts he'd built around that night. Olivia forcing him to confront that was no pleasantry.

"Then charge him," she said.

He turned away.

"The Divinity won't ignore the imprisonment of a master, a successful agent, and one of the world's few wild mages, not without cause."

It was true—Pons had advised him on the matter as well.

"The Divinity's devotion to him is inspiring." He didn't bother to hide his bitterness. "Does it know the feeling isn't mutual?"

He expected word from the interim Proctor of the Emaurrian Tower of Magic any day now—from Kieran Atterley, who was supposed to be dead, if he was the same Kieran Rielle had accused Leigh of killing. Although if Magehold had allowed this Kieran as interim Proctor, perhaps that devotion to Leigh wasn't a given.

She seated herself in the armchair beside him and sighed. "Leigh may suspect the Divinity of a great many things, but he knows better than to leave its protection unless he has grounds—tangible, actionable grounds." She stared into the fire with him. "I know that you worry about Rielle and miss her. So do I." She met his eyes for a long moment. "So does Leigh."

"It doesn't change the fact that he is responsible for... the Rift." He finished the rest of the wine and set the goblet on the floor before leaning back into the armchair. The flames slowly consumed the firewood.

"He wants to atone."

Jon scoffed. How exactly did one atone for setting in motion the destruction of not just one nation but the world?

As he stared into the fire, memories of Leigh fighting alongside him and Rielle invaded his mind. Whatever his faults, Leigh Galvan was a highly capable and powerful mage. Although the paladins had been handling the Immortals since the beginning of the Rift, they were spread thin defending the Terran faith, the capital, the nation, and its citizens. One mage wouldn't be a huge relief, but relief nonetheless. The more he considered the idea, the more reasonable it seemed.

And Leigh's reluctance to leave the Divinity's protection was something he could bargain with. "Very well. I will offer him the opportunity for both freedom and atonement. Soon. We'll discuss it further when you return from Kirn."

"Thank you." She smiled and rose. "I will leave instructions for my clerks to redouble their efforts on researching the Immortals. Oh, and be sure to practice your repulsion shields while I'm gone."

He grimaced. He had yet to successfully cast one. "I will. Be safe out there. Terra's blessings upon you."

She lingered in the doorway. "Divine keep you."

As she left, he settled deeper into his armchair. Perhaps Olivia could finally bring justice to the regicide.

And in the meantime, he'd have to accept the idea of freeing the man whose recklessness had led to the Rift. Perhaps two months in the dungeon had given him the opportunity to feel some remorse.

# CHAPTER 8

Through the coach window, Olivia watched the wintry landscape go by, a vast canvas of white stretching as far as the eye could see, framed by snow-tipped pines. The sun hid behind the clouds, leaving the sky gray, a few shades from the snowy starkness it overlooked. She and James had always planned to travel the kingdom... the forests of the heartland in winter, the coast in the summer, vineyards in early autumn. They'd planned so much that had been taken from them.

Soon she'd be in Kirn—and the courier would be in her custody.

A chill wind swept through the coach; she closed the drapes and shrugged into her miniver-trimmed cloak, grateful for the warm stones at her feet. Divine bless Lydia. The sixteen-year-old maid had a good head on her shoulders.

Across from her, Sir Edgar sat dressed like no paladin she'd ever seen. He wore an inexpensive but well-tailored gray wool overcoat, white cotton shirt, black wool trousers, and well-worn but shined leather boots. An unremarkable brown leather belt bore his arcanir longsword—well camouflaged—along with a dagger, belt pouch, and coin purse. Despite the cold, he appeared unperturbed, his evergreen eyes upon her, a faint smile playing around his mouth.

Lydia gave her a rabbit-fur muff. "To stave off the cold, my lady." She blinked her large, doe-like eyes and smiled.

Olivia dug her hands into the fur's warmth. "Thank you, Lydia. I'm glad we packed it, considering this weather."

Sir Edgar raised an eyebrow. "What, none for me?"

She shot him a scowl.

"I could pull off that look."

Lydia stiffened.

"No, you couldn't. And if it's warmth you're looking for, I know a wonderful pyromancy incantation," Olivia replied loftily. "It'll light you right up, like a torch."

He snorted. "Afraid not." He pulled open his shirt and overcoat near the neck, revealing some of his sigil tattoos—the pyromancy sigil, in particular.

"Keep your clothes on," she scolded, although her voice betrayed her and made it sound like a tease.

He neatened his shirt and overcoat once more, grinning broadly. "You're a healer, aren't you? You've seen it all by now, I'm sure."

Of course she had. She'd probably seen more injuries than a seasoned soldier and more bare flesh than a courtesan. But that was in the context of healing, not the ill-conceived exhibitionism of an unmannered paladin. "What I have and haven't seen is no business of yours."

He leaned back in the coach seat and folded his muscular arms. "So, tell me, how is a charming woman like you unmarried?"

She laughed under her breath. "As though marriage should be my primary goal in life?"

Marriage was something to consider once the grief over James wasn't still so fresh, when the right suitor presented himself, someone who could raise her station and that of her family, and their lot. But what man could possibly measure up to James? To take his place in her heart?

So what if she was alone and unloved? There was plenty in her life to keep her warm. She puffed and gestured to the coach. "I'm a fishmonger's daughter, and look at what I've accomplished."

He half-laughed. "Riding in a coach with an armorer's son and a maid?"

Lydia stifled a giggle, and Olivia glared at her. The girl sobered.

"I'm a master mage, one of the Grands, and completely self-reliant, all at age twenty-six, on my own, without a husband." She grinned confidently. "And having been born a commoner, I've had to work many times as hard as any noble for it."

The carriage jostled over a bump. Sir Edgar sighed. "You say 'having been born a commoner' as though you no longer are one."

She was rich, accomplished, titled.

"Having some money and being the Archmage doesn't change your blood. But you shouldn't be ashamed of who you are, Olivia." He held her gaze.

"Your Ladyship," she corrected.

"I appreciate the gesture, but I prefer 'Edgar.' "

She sighed. "Why must you be so annoying?"

He laughed, his eyes gleaming. "Why must you be so amusing?"

Her mouth dropped open. "I'm not here for your amusement."

He smiled that boyish lop-sided grin. Lydia beamed next to her. Traitor.

Olivia sank back into the coach seat, fidgeting in the rabbit-fur muff. "Don't you have a code to adhere to? Sacred Vows?"

"They don't forbid talking," he replied.

"If you're only going to poke me for effect, then I'd vastly prefer silence."

He snorted.

The rest of the trip to Kirn, however, did pass in silence. At least his ears did what they were supposed to, even if *he* didn't.

The dense cluster of buildings came into view in the evening, two- to three-story peaks clustered around the castle within stone walls. The coachman let them out at a well-to-do inn, The Seabird, where they'd rented a block of rooms. Her cover, a buyer for a wealthy household, would involve arranging delivery of some delicacies to Courdeval, for which she had the paperwork in hand. Sir Edgar would pretend to be her personal bodyguard, along with her squad of guards in escort.

Benoit Donnet had provided a sketch, but additionally, he'd

named the establishment frequented by the courier they tracked. Pierre's. She and Sir Edgar would visit there personally and search out the man.

Lydia unpacked her bags and set down a hand mirror, moonlight reflecting off its silver surface. Beyond the window, it was dark, but the waning gibbous moon shone in the sky.

It was well before midnight; the taverns would still be full of patrons. Olivia removed the sketch from her coat. Perhaps even the courier was about?

She rubbed the leather-wrapped parchment. Why waste a single night more than necessary? His Majesty needed her in Courdeval—while she was in Kirn, her clerks and assistants attempted to complete her duties. But no one would be as thorough.

The longer she stayed in Kirn...

She moved to the adjoining room's door and knocked.

No response.

"Oh, Sir Edgar went downstairs for supper," Lydia chimed in as she stashed clothes.

Olivia rifled through her bags for the map of Kirn she'd studied earlier; to get to Pierre's, she'd need it. She grabbed her cloak off the rack, and her coin purse. "Thank you. I'll meet with him, and we may go for a walk."

"Shall I join you, my lady?"

If they went to Pierre's and the situation deteriorated, the last thing she wanted was for Lydia to get caught in the crossfire. There was no telling who this courier worked for, or how prepared he'd be for them. "That won't be necessary. Order anything you want from the kitchen, and have a comfortable night in."

Lydia beamed at her, twirling a lock of brown hair, and thanked her.

Downstairs, it didn't take long to find Sir Edgar sitting alone, shoveling stew into his mouth, with three empty bowls stacked next to him.

"Divine... have you never seen food before tonight?" She sat at his table.

Sir Edgar looked over the rim of his bowl with those moss-green eyes but kept eating. When he finished, he set down the bowl and downed a cup of tea.

"How uncharacteristically quiet of you," she said.

He gestured to the serving man, who brought him another cup of tea and asked her if she wanted anything. She politely declined.

Sir Edgar speared her with a spirited look. "I thought you said you preferred silence."

She shook her head. "So my only choices are annoyance and quiet?"

Grinning, he shrugged. "When everything I say annoys you, then yes, I suppose so."

She sighed. Perhaps she was being too harsh. It wasn't so long ago that she had been in a similar position—a commoner on the rise. His route differed greatly from hers, and his... manner, but a person of her origin and status should be more sympathetic.

She was just so close to finding the person responsible for James's death—the Swordsman—and the merest hint of flirtation, intentional or unintentional, poked a sore spot in her heart that hadn't yet healed. That perhaps would never heal.

"I'm sorry," she mumbled. "I've been out of sorts lately."

He raised an eyebrow, then exhaled a long breath. Finally, he nodded to the empty bowls. "Eat every meal as if it were your last."

"What?"

"I eat a lot because I eat every meal as if it were my last. I've been hungry too much of my life already."

She'd grown up hungry. Papa had tried to make enough money for Mama, her, Aerin, Ronan, and Killian, but sometimes the fishing had been poor, and his business had suffered. It wasn't until Killian had turned twelve and started taking on odd jobs, and when Olivia had gone to the Tower, that they'd had more to eat. She'd been sending them money since.

"The Order doesn't sufficiently provide?"

"It does," he replied, "but it's difficult to break habit."

She grinned. "I'm surprised you aren't as wide as you are tall."

"Just wait 'til I'm old."

She laughed. He was so young; his waistline still had many years to grow.

"So what brings you down here, to the likes of me?"

Her smile faded.

"It must be something."

"We're going to Pierre's tonight."

Edgar leaned back in his chair. "Tonight? Why?"

"Why wait?"

He rubbed his stubbled jaw. "You're not tired?"

"Not when there's work to do. Are you with me or not?" When he reached for his tea, she took it and drank it herself. His eyes widened. Before he could ask, she said, "I'm drinking like it's my last drink."

He grinned. "Let's go."

She pulled out the map and traced their way to Pierre's. It wasn't far—perhaps fifteen minutes.

Outside, sparse lanterns provided soft yellow light among overhanging snow-mantled oaks arching over the gray cobblestone streets. Narrow avenues winded between stone buildings, light casting a fiery glow on walls, and only a few passersby wandered the city at this hour.

She ducked under awnings with him, caught peeks of the night sky above them. The moon watched, and stars dotted the sky, winking from time to time, silent comrades on their mission.

"You have a gleam in your eye," Edgar whispered. "Like you're going to take over the world."

She smiled. "I am."

According to the map, they should have happened upon Pierre's by now. A few dark alleys branched off from the street, but—

Two forms emerged from the darkness. Swords drawn. Men in leathers. "Greetings—"

She extended her arm and twisted her hand. A sleeping spell. One man collapsed.

As Sir Edgar drew his longsword, the other charged.

She threw a sleeping spell at him, too. He thudded to the cobblestone. Sir Edgar rushed over to him, sword pointed at the man's neck, frowning.

Where was Pierre's? She studied the map. It was right here according to the damned thing. She searched the narrow street for signboards—no Pierre's.

"Olivia..." Sir Edgar backed away from the sleeping men. "That fast?"

There was a butcher shop, a restaurant called The Hungry Shepherd, and an inn, and a door with faded lettering over it—err.

*Pierre's.*

Sir Edgar approached her. "You took down those two men before they could even reach us."

She grabbed his arm. "We're here. I think." She nodded toward the inadequate signage. "Quite a bit of wear and tear. How do they expect anyone to find this place?"

"They don't." He stiffened, eyeing her peripherally.

She smiled. People assumed healers could not properly defend themselves, that they could only help others. A needle could stitch a wound, but it could also open a vein.

He furrowed his brow, then shook his head. "Paladins are susceptible to healing magic, but knowing it and seeing it are very different things."

She grinned. "If I wanted to, I could make your nose run right now." She chuckled under her breath. "Or make you wet your pants."

He rolled his eyes, but a slow laugh escaped him. "Well, I'm glad you're a friend."

She reached for the door and glanced over her shoulder. "For now."

With a shake of his head, he followed.

Soft yellow light escaped the inside, and a wall of odor hit—the reek of unwashed flesh, mud, feces, urine, and over it all, ale and pottage, the ever-bubbling stew over the fire. A tapestry hung precariously above the hearth, a top corner peeling away from the wall. Coats lay thrown over chairs and tables. Groups of men with the rare woman here and there nearly filled the tavern; their voices, laughing and shouting, competed for attention.

A woman climbed the stairs with a man tugging at her skirt. A dog stole a bone off the man's plate.

Tankards, plates, food, and a mixture of mud and things she would not consider mingled on the coarse plank floor.

She pursed her lips and headed for the counter. A portly, balding oldster tended bar, his massive form dwarfing the small area. She flattened an invisible wrinkle in her skirt, took a deep breath, pasted on a smile, and approached.

The man pulling the ascending woman's skirt succeeded, and she plopped into his arms to riotous cheering.

Olivia rested her hands on the sticky bar, Sir Edgar beside her.

"What can I get you?" The barkeep didn't even bother to look at them.

"Two pints of braggot, please." Although she preferred posset ale, braggot was more expensive and would be consistent with their cover.

The barkeep summoned a serving man, who left and returned with two pints. She drank hers while Sir Edgar fiddled with his tankard nervously, his ivory skin even paler than normal.

Although he'd said he wanted out of the Order, it seemed he wasn't willing to play fast and loose with the Sacred Vows after all.

The barkeep eyed them. "Anything else?"

She set down her tankard. "Actually, yes, if you would be so kind. I worked with a courier before the siege, and I can't seem to get a hold of him now. But I know he frequented your fine establishment, and I owe him money and wish to retain him once again."

The barkeep raised a bushy gray eyebrow. "Name?"

She smiled. "You know, he never offered one." She chuckled. "He came so highly recommended that I didn't think to ask."

"You want me to recall a man with no name?" He snorted, then sobered. "You say you have money to give him?"

He caught on at last. She nodded.

"Why don't we step into my office?" He tipped his head to a door off to the side.

A look at Sir Edgar, who nodded, and they followed the barkeep. The so-called office was tiny, no more than a desk and chair surrounded by overstacked boxes. No doubt a man like him didn't want to be seen taking bribes from strangers.

The barkeep shut the door behind them. "What's he look like?" he asked quietly.

She removed the portrait from her cloak and unrolled the leather. The barkeep studied the face drawn there.

"I might've seen him." The barkeep crossed his fleshy arms.

She pulled a small coin purse from her pocket, filled with a dozen argents. "If you could tell me where to find him, perhaps my bodyguard and I can check there, and leave the money with you in case he returns here?"

His eyes gleamed. "I know he boarded over the carriage house."

"Over the carriage house?"

"Aye." He grabbed the small purse and opened it. "The coachman's not supposed to rent it out, but he does."

"Anything else you can tell us about him?"

He counted the argents. "Mostly kept to himself—stayed here from dawn till well after dusk. Always paid well. An old fellow would come in from time to time and drop off a message, and he'd be gone. Never more than a day or two."

Donnet. But if that were so, then he hadn't seen the courier since the siege. She narrowed her eyes at the coin purse. It hadn't been well earned.

"When did you last see him?" she asked.

He shrugged. "Month and a half? Coachman might know his comings and goings better."

A dozen argents to be redirected to a coachman who might not even have information for them. She nudged Sir Edgar. "Come on."

They turned toward the door.

"You didn't pay for your drinks," the barkeep said.

She nodded toward the purse. "I'm sure that more than covers it."

Sir Edgar led the way to the door and out. Perhaps the coachman would still be about.

Her heels crunched on the snow. The rare torches and lanterns provided sparse light, but with her map, it was enough to find their way to the carriage house. If the coachman had answers, if he knew where the courier was, James and Anton would be avenged. Courdeval would be avenged.

And perhaps Gilles' mysterious client even knew Rielle's whereabouts.

The answers were within reach. Perhaps within reach tonight. She lengthened her strides.

Sir Edgar grabbed her arm. "Olivia, it's well past midnight, and you want to burst into the carriage house and rouse a sleeping man?"

She yanked her arm out of his grip and continued walking. "You're here to assist me, not to stop me."

He half-laughed. "Do you hear yourself?" He shook his head. "Even if you get an answer tonight, what will you be able to do with your knowledge in the middle of the night?"

He had a point. She looked away.

"Exactly. Nothing." His footsteps crunched next to hers. "Don't pull innocent folk out of their beds in the middle of the night. You want to terrorize this man for offering someone shelter? You want to scare him? What if he screams? What if he runs? What if he doesn't answer the door when strangers knock at midnight?"

If the coachman raised a ruckus, their cover could be blown. If the courier were near, he might flee, go into deep hiding. It could compromise the mission. It could compromise vengeance and finding Rielle.

She sighed. "Fine." She threw up her hands. "Whatever. If you're so concerned, let's go back to the inn. But we leave for the carriage house before dawn."

A slow smile spread across his face. "I knew you'd see reason."

The audacity. She narrowed her eyes. "Did you?"

"I know this is important to you." He shrugged. "And you're willing to fight... but not to hurt innocent people. You're fair. I admire that."

She laughed, looking away as she shook her head.

"What?"

"I'm not doing this for your admiration."

He chuckled. "And? I'm not asking for your hand in marriage."

"Good," she replied. "Then you're not wasting your breath." When he straightened, she grabbed his arm and yanked him down a dimly lit alley back to The Seabird.

*James, if you're listening, give me the strength to see this through. Guide my steps, my eyes, my ears. Let me ease your rest.*

# CHAPTER 9

he dawn was no more than shades of pink and orange in the sky when Olivia emerged from the inn, Sir Edgar hot on her heels. Their breath fogged in the wintry air, and the cold bit even through layers of fur and wool. She pulled up her hood. All night, she'd hardly been able to sleep, waiting until first light so they could head back out.

The carriage house wasn't far from the inn, and if they walked quickly, there'd be enough people about not to scare the coachman, but few enough not to arouse much notice. A perfect combination to elicit some answers. Finally.

The city slowly woke to life. Merchants set up stalls and shops in the predawn hours, and carts drove by with last-minute inventory.

Before long, the carriage house came into view, a long building made of rough, unhewn stone set in mortar, but not laid in regular courses. Two horses waited outside, harnessed to a small coach. She paused, letting a bay stallion smell her hand before she rubbed its nose. She scanned the area, searching for anyone who'd fit the description of a coachman.

"Let's go inside." Sir Edgar strode past her, brown cloak billowing after him. He was perhaps the friendlier face of this investigation. "Hello?" he called.

She followed, the musky smell of horse intensifying. Inside, a number of coaches and stalls lined the lengthy building, and Sir Edgar searched them.

At the end of the aisle was a staircase. It had to lead to the upstairs lodging. She approached it, looking around for anyone. Movement came from near the staircase. No horse.

A boy, about five feet tall, mucking stalls. He could be no more than thirteen. She didn't want to scare him, so she backed away.

"Good morning," she called.

The boy's blond head popped up. When his eyes found hers, he looked her over and inclined his head. "Good morning to you, lady. Next coach leaves for Melletoire tomorrow at dawn."

Loud voice. She smiled. "I'm looking for the coachman. I owe a friend of his some money." She raised her coin purse.

"How much?" Canting his head, the boy ventured out of the stall and wiped his hands on his breeches.

"Is he here?"

The boy shook his head. "He makes the run to Melletoire and back. Should be back by supper."

They'd missed him, then. She raised a brow at Sir Edgar.

Sighing, he approached to stand at her side. "Who runs the carriage house while he's away?"

The boy turned to at the staircase. "Mama."

Sir Edgar shot her a smug smile and raised his eyebrows. Gloating ass.

She ignored him. "Might we speak with her?"

He nodded and darted toward the staircase. "Mama!" he shouted. "A lady and her man here to see you!"

She winced; the boy had a pair of lungs that belied his size. And her man? In his dreams, and maybe not even then.

A door creaked open, and a woman descended the stairs, her long golden hair wrapped in a bun, a wool dress hugging her buxom frame. Her laugh lines deepened as she smiled. "Good morning, lady, sir. What can I do for you?"

"I owe some money to a man who used to board here, a courier?"

The woman frowned. "What's he look like?"

"In his late forties, long hair, a birthmark right here," she said, pointing to a spot on her jaw.

The woman's eyes widened. "Aye, him! Gerard?"

"Right," Olivia said, exhaling a relieved breath. "Gerard."

The woman nodded. "Quiet one, he. Kept to his business and no more. I was repairing a wheel last time he left us."

Olivia grinned. "When was that?"

"Months ago. Maybe two?"

Two months? The trail had gone cold, then.

"Do you know where he was headed?" Sir Edgar stepped forward.

The woman's brow furrowed. "He always used to rush my husband to Melletoire. Didn't want to miss the coach there. Only the route to Chevrefeuils has a departure from there early in the day. Courdeval's leaves at dusk."

Chevrefeuils... He might live there; his master might live there; or it was simply a stop on his way.

"But last time he left, he wasn't in a rush," the woman added. "Maybe he was going elsewhere."

Excellent. So there was no certainty why he went to Chevrefeuils, and now there was no certainty he had even gone there last time. She sighed.

"Thank you for your time," Sir Edgar offered, extending his hand.

The woman blushed and shook it. "It's no trouble."

Olivia opened her coin purse and removed two argents. "For your help."

The woman accepted the sum. "Thank you, lady."

Olivia inclined her head. "Good day to you."

With goodbyes exchanged, she and Sir Edgar strode back out into the street. Snow fell, shrouding the city in stark white.

"So, Chevrefeuils," Sir Edgar said. "We have more answers."

To useless questions, yes. They certainly did. "He's in the wind. And we're no closer to finding him."

"We're closer than we were."

She stopped in the street. "We have nothing." James's death,

Anton's, the king's, the royal family's—Rielle's disappearance—all for nothing, with no answers.

He took her hands before she could turn, and did not let go. "Look, we know he used to take the road to Chevrefeuils all the time, and last time, probably after the siege, he went elsewhere. There are only three roads out of Melletoire—to Kirn, toward Chevrefeuils, and toward Partage." He squeezed her hands. "He had to be going toward Partage. The question is why."

There could be a thousand reasons why. "To buy a bottle of wine? To avoid the fleeing Crag? To catch some sun on the west coast?"

He sighed. "Or perhaps his master traveled elsewhere, a place he could access by way of Partage. Or perhaps, after the siege, it was a longer but safer route to his usual destination."

She shook her head. They had no certainty of that. The best they could do would be to, on the way back to Courdeval, check with Chevrefeuils' carriage house to see if he usually went farther, and where.

He sighed. "Olivia, we have more than we did. What more do you want?"

"To find this courier."

"I thought that's what we were doing."

She pulled her hands out of his grasp. "That's what *I'm* doing."

Maybe he was content with a snail's pace, but she wasn't. Her James had paid the price; Anton had paid the price; and Rielle might... if she hadn't already. There was no time to waste. The courier had to be found yesterday... *weeks* ago... *months* ago.

"I'd ask you if you're always this abrasive, but I know the answer."

She turned away from him and stormed off to The Seabird. He fell into step behind her. Argument or not, it was time to check with Chevrefeuils' carriage house, and if no answers emerged, return to Courdeval and deliver the disappointing news to the king.

RIELLE SHRANK into her scant garment, hiding under her unkempt curls. The caravan had come to a stop, and the guards and Ihsan stepped away. Nearby, there was only a tent with large pens of camels and elephants behind it.

Camels and elephants? The rough, crowded, and jostling covered wagon had only been a temporary luxury, then. The well-traveled paths of Harifa fed into nothing but sand, as far as the eye could see—and wagon wheels were of no use there.

They were to go into the desert, farther from the coast, farther inland.

Farther inland... To where? She strained to hear Ihsan's voice but couldn't make out the words. For all she knew, Ihsan could be taking them to a mine, to live out their days in the dark, breaking their backs mining gold, gems, arcanir, recondite. A nightmare.

Twelve guards stood watch, their eyes keen but not indifferent like the guards' at the auction. Lingering. Unsettling. Beyond them, Ihsan spoke to a man and gesticulated effusively. Effusively for an Emaurrian. Bargaining.

They persisted, bargaining for what felt like an hour. At last, several men arrived with thirteen camels. Stony faced, Ihsan mounted her camel and barked orders to the guards.

Rielle scratched her head—it had gotten itchier and itchier over the past few weeks—and her chains rattled down the line of others like her. With Ihsan and twelve guards, there was no mystery regarding who would ride. No one, after all, would worry about the discomfort of chattels. Five men, a young girl, four women, and behind her, a small boy no older than seven. Linked together, they were fastened to the harness of a camel. To walk.

They trudged across the desert at the camels' pace, a long and slow crawl in the heat of the scorching sun, their skin sizzling beneath the chains and reddened from the exposure. Her feet burned against the hot sand, the brief rise between every shallow footfall her only respite. Sand dunes reached for the horizon, only tufts of weeping lovegrass interrupting its endless stretch of pale desert.

Wherever they were going, Jon would find her. Someone would have seen the *Siren* leave Courdeval, seen a woman matching her description in Harifa, on this route... Someone. He would look for her, never give up, tirelessly searching until he found her. And then... well, as king, he had the coin to buy her freedom, even.

*King.* Kings didn't dare enter foreign lands unauthorized—an act of war—but Jon was different; he'd been raised a paladin, not a prince. He'd be guided not by royal protocol, but by good, by right, by his love for her. She'd just have to survive long enough for him to find her.

And she would. She'd live to see him again. Warn him about Shadow. They'd take her down together. Jon would find her, and she would help him.

After a long day walking, a woman ahead faltered. A guard paused long enough to crack a whip. Night had already fallen by the time they reached a small oasis, lined with date palms and spiky speargrasses. Ihsan drank, the guards drank, and the camels drank. And then Rielle and the rest of them were allowed to. She pulled three hairs from her head, and while Ihsan and the guards were eating, she knotted them into the bark of a date palm. Jon might never see them, but... he might. And that was better than no hope at all.

After Ihsan, the guards, and the camels finished eating, Rielle and the others each got a handful of plain flatbread and cheese. Meager, but even a meager offering was food, and she snatched it.

The dark-haired woman shackled next to her grabbed at her hands.

Rielle pulled back, kicking her legs out at the woman while stuffing the flatbread and cheese into her mouth with sandy fingers, sating her lamenting belly.

The woman screamed at her in Sileni until the whip cracked again, and then she was silent.

The meal was over far too soon. When would the next one be? But those thoughts led to dark places. Dangerous places. At least in arcanir shackles, she'd never go into fureur—or perhaps, even without them, she'd have full control since the battle with the Brigands.

But all this fear, this frustration, this rage was too much.

Breathing slowly, she listened to the desert wind whistling ghostly elegies of sun-bleached bones and weathered dreams. A fate she hoped to avoid.

Somehow, when she was finally off her feet, the pain that had built over the entire day came all at once. Her feet throbbed and stung enough to force tears from her eyes. The others with her weren't faring much better, some groaning while the rest suffered in silence.

Next to her, the boy lay unmoving. Passed out? His chest rose and fell steadily. He was all right... or as much as he could be here.

Soft footfalls shuffled through the sand. Ihsan approached them where they had been left to bed down in the sand, and crouched next to the man at the head of the line.

Healing magic. The last time she'd used it had been the day she'd healed Jon in the Lunar Chamber. All the things they'd promised each other before then... Their plans to spend the summer in the country, reading books by the fire, taking walks, enjoying each other. He'd teach her the sword, and she'd teach him magic. *And of course, I plan to make love to you until we forget our names,* he'd said. Making love on the bank of the Propré River. She suppressed the inkling of an emerging smile.

She rubbed her fingers together, recalling the feel of his skin beneath her touch.

Her chest tightened. The vivid, happy memory was too stark a contrast to reality; if she lost herself in it now, she'd lose her nerve and die in this sand pit.

No, there'd be no sweet surrender to the depths of memory; she had to focus on now, on these oppressive circumstances, these innumerable reasons why the only option was to never give up. Shaking her head, she studied her surroundings, the people beside her, the guards—anything to supplant the precious, unbearable memory.

Ihsan healed the next person's feet. A small mercy compared to the immense cruelty. Of course forcing the slaves to suffer through the walk was more cost-effective than procuring additional camels. However, if they lost the ability to continue, the entire purpose of Ihsan's sojourn to the auction would be frustrated. So, healing magic.

Finally Ihsan paused before her—a numbing spell, then a probe, then healing. Strange. At home, they began with the probe spell.

"Speak, Thahab," Ihsan said in High Nad'i, continuing her work.

After a moment's hesitation, Rielle replied, "I noticed that you did not begin with a probe, Zahibi."

A small smile curled Ihsan's lips. "Pain is often used in the North as a diagnostic criterion to reduce the scope of a probing and, thus, its anima cost to the healer. Barbaric. Here, it is customary for healers to relieve pain first and then do a thorough, if costlier, probing to detect the abnormalities that would cause pain. It is a courtesy for the patients."

Barbaric? Courtesy? To say that about healing and yet drag slaves across a desert—it didn't—couldn't be reconciled. She bowed her head. "How wise, Zahibi, though it is not my place to say so."

Ihsan's small smile faded. "You know a bit about magic."

*How much will remain a mystery to you. For now.* She kept her face expressionless. Had she just tipped her hand? The less her *masters* knew about the extent of her magical abilities, the better. "As much as any person who has been healed, Zahibi."

Ihsan moved on to the boy. She examined him, frowning. "How long has he been like this?"

"A couple hours, Zahibi. I thought it was due to exhaustion."

Ihsan numbed him and began the magical probe at his feet. "It is," she said with a sigh, then muttered a string of curse words under her breath in High Nad'i. Something about "...should have sold me the elephants."

When all the guards and Ihsan had camels, what use would she have had for elephants? "You didn't intend for us to walk, Zahibi?"

Ihsan glared at her. "Of course not," she snapped, giving her a stern look before returning her attention to the boy. "The merchant was being ridiculous. I mentioned that I'd need elephants with gear capable of holding eleven people, but when he realized it was for the slaves, he refused. He said he needed to save his *beasts of burden* for carrying people of worth—as though hundreds of *shafi* or *nawi* will show up in Harifa, requiring camels and elephants." She grunted. "Had he been of honor, he would have admitted it was because *I* was representing House Hazael here in my brother's stead."

House Hazael. That was the destination, then. One of the Houses of Sonbahar... It likely meant housework or farming. At least it wasn't a mine. Sonbahar's mines—of arcanir and many other precious materials —were infamous.

And the day's events made a lot more sense: why the negotiation at the tent had taken so long, why Ihsan had appeared so angry. But how to reconcile merciful intentions with the purchase of people? It was impossible.

"Why did you choose me, Zahibi?" The question had been hiding in the dark corners of her mind, where hope didn't dare stray. Yet, after all that she had been through, the penalty for impudence here could be no worse than what she'd already survived.

Done healing the boy, Ihsan sighed and folded her hands together. "I needed a scribe. It was obvious you were a Northerner, and when you also understood and spoke High Nad'i, I knew you were learned enough to do the work I needed done." At that, Ihsan departed.

She'd been chosen merely for her knowledge of the language? So simple?

Ihsan stopped to talk to a guard, one of the younger, handsomer men of the group, and disappeared with him into her tent.

Still chained, Rielle lay on her back and took what rest she could. A scribe. At least as a scribe, she wouldn't be under heavy guard like a miner or laborer. With a little luck, she could have access to outgoing correspondence... to Jon. A better chance than what had awaited her at the stable. Arrival at House Hazael would mean no more desert, too.

Just like every night aboard the ship, she looked up at the myriad stars, where the sages of old had looked for their fates. Perhaps House Hazael would be her way home. Was that part of the fate the stars held for her? Her arcanir cuffs clinked together behind her head. She would have to look beyond her magic to make it there, use what strengths she could muster.

*When the enemy takes your sword, you must draw your dagger.* Jon's voice, deep and firm, swept around her like warmth from a fire.

Somewhere out there, Jon was looking at the same night sky, and across deserts, cities, the bay, and all that stood between them, they were in some small way together. It was a comfort now to think of sharing anything with him, no matter how remote.

He was coming for her. He wouldn't abandon her. Not Jon. Never Jon. She would see him again.

Her eyelids grew heavy, the image of him cast against their darkness.

# CHAPTER 10

*J*on paced his study. Olivia had returned from Kirn and sent a message promising to discuss the result of her investigation tonight.

The *investigation*. If she'd found the criminal, she would have come running, wouldn't she? The news had to be disappointing, but it had been too much to hope that a courier would be the bloodied sword they'd needed to find.

He'd worked on those repulsion shields for the nearly two weeks she'd been gone... to no effect. After spending the past decade of his life trying to suppress his magic, perhaps now it demanded some price for his rebuff.

He stood at the window, hands resting on the cold sill, looking out beyond the snow-capped villas and homes to the endless dark of the Bay of Amar.

A knock. "The Archmage, Your Majesty," Raoul called.

"Send her in."

Footsteps clicked from afar, and then the door creaked open behind him. He looked over his shoulder to see Olivia walking in, a book tucked under her gray-velvet-clad arm.

She offered him a soft smile that faded. "I'm afraid I have some... unfortunate news."

"I assumed." He rounded the desk, sat in an armchair by the fire, and gestured for her to do the same.

"We tracked the courier to his usual tavern, Pierre's, and to his usual boarding house, an apartment above Kirn's carriage house. The coachman's wife said he usually took the route toward Chevrefeuils, but last time, probably after the siege, he took the route toward Partage." She sat in the other armchair.

No one had wanted to travel near Courdeval after the siege. The courier's master must have lived somewhere he could travel to by way of Chevrefeuils... which was much of the kingdom. Too much.

"And on the way back to Courdeval, we checked with the coachman at Chevrefeuils, who said the man traveled by a nondescript private coach from there to an unknown destination." She sighed.

"It wouldn't be too far, unless they were willing to change horses."

She shook her head. "He wouldn't want to leave a paper trail."

"Both Sauveterre and Monas Tainn are nearby." A march and a monastery. Marquis Sébastien Duclos Auvray of Sauveterre, Duchess Madeleine Duclos Auvray's son, ruled Sauveterre. His mother certainly had the funds to pay for a regicide, but why would she? What would she have to gain? She hadn't even been considered to rule the kingdom.

The regicide—but for Jon himself—might have led to Duke Faolan Auvray Marcel, the duchess's sister's son, becoming king, and Brennan a prince. Duke Faolan would have broken the betrothal, something the duchess wouldn't have wanted.

It was unlikely Marquis Sauveterre was the courier's master.

And Tor had sworn it wasn't Duke Faolan. He knew his own brother, had investigated, and found no evidence. And Tor's word was iron. If not by reputation or devotion, then by relationship. After all the years they'd spent together, so much like brothers, maybe even father and son, Tor wouldn't lie to help someone trying to kill him.

Which left the monastery, Monas Tainn, managed by High Priest Maxime Vignon Aldair. He'd been to Monas Tainn, and it wasn't much different than Monas Ver. A private coach would have been a strange sight. And how would the High Priest have funded the regicide, unless with the Order of Terra's coin?

But if the Order of Terra was responsible, the bloodied sword would drip first in Monas Tainn. He'd have to send a trusted friend to make inquiries. A trusted friend like Valen Boucher, his former brother in arms since they'd been pages at the monastery with Bastien.

"Your Majesty?" Olivia blinked.

He sighed. "Sorry. Thinking." He leaned back in the armchair. "I'll take it from here. I'll let you know what I find."

She nodded, her gaze falling to his hands. The Sodalis ring. "Any word of Rielle?"

"No." And without further word from Brennan, there was nothing to do but perform his duties as king.

"She'll return to us soon. Rielle's strong. A survivor. We'll see her again."

He took a deep breath. "I know we will."

Her gaze descended to the Laurentine signet ring hanging from the chain around his neck, usually hidden in his shirt.

Although she sat nearby, she looked distant—a world away—biting her lip contemplatively. Firelight reflected in her eyes. "When did you know," she began to ask, her eyes fixed upon the signet ring, "that you loved Rielle? Was it when you first met?"

These days, he tried not to think about that, about her—it opened the door to a useless part of him, who could be neither king nor man, but mere worry personified. A liability.

But he allowed himself to open that door for a moment, just a crack. He closed his eyes. A halo of fire, wild wisps of golden hair, narrowed eyes. A captor. A conqueror. A savior. Determined and powerful, a woman who could challenge a man to be stronger. To be better.

"There was something about her from the moment I saw her, no matter how much I wanted to deny it." He vividly remembered looking up at her from the abyss she'd created on the Tower grounds. Her expressionless face had given nothing away, but the ice in her eyes had said she wouldn't hesitate to kill him. In his life, he'd never seen anything like it.

But when was it he'd fallen for her?

"There was this moment when we escaped some crumbling ruins—she healed me before herself. I'd misjudged her, and that had created distance. But right then, I knew she was good. That she cared. And then that distance disappeared." He shook his head. "I think I knew it then." He smiled. "But I am certain of one thing—whether we had met one another at the Tower, here in the palace, or even passing each other by chance in the street, my heart would have always, always known hers and responded."

Olivia looked up from the signet ring. "She is a blessed woman indeed to inspire such devotion." She glanced at him. "I'm finding the world a darker place. Colder alone."

Unsure of what to say, he bowed his head and twirled his Sodalis ring.

"Your father meant a lot to me," she said softly, "and I lost him. I'm not going to lose my best friend, too."

On that they agreed. "I wish I had some indication—any—that she's all right."

"Indication..." She leaned back, a contemplative frown on her face. "Indication..." She sighed. "The new Proctor all but laughed in my face when I requested a spiritualist, saying 'none could be spared.' "

"I know." A spiritualist was capable of doing just what he needed, but he'd gotten the same message. Although what it really said was that the Tower—and perhaps the Divinity—was uninterested in helping him.

And outside the Tower, there were hedge witches who didn't want to come forward for fear of persecution, and a sen'a baron he'd thrashed. "When we were on our way to Monas Amar and Courdeval, Rielle went to a spiritualist in Bournand to confirm whether you were alive."

Olivia tilted her head. "Not Feliciano?"

He clenched a fist. "The very same."

With a grimace, Olivia looked away. No doubt she shared a similar opinion of Feliciano Donati. "In any case," she said, "I think he could be compelled to help, if it's for her. He wouldn't turn down a quaternary elementalist owing him a favor."

After that altercation in Bournand, not a chance. And he couldn't promise himself he wouldn't finish the flogging he'd begun there. "Are there no other spiritualists in Emaurria?"

With a shrug, Olivia leaned back in the armchair and stared into the fire with lifeless eyes. "Spiritualists are rare. Aside from Feliciano, I only know of suitable ones at the Tower."

"Suitable?" They didn't need *suitable*—anyone who could even attempt the spell was worth a try.

She blinked, frowning, then shot up. "Wait. Unsuitable, yes, but there *is* one. A child, a novice, fresh off his éveil. In Courdeval."

A child? "Could he perform the necessary spell?"

"I think so, yes," she said. "I know his tutor. I'll talk to her, see if the boy's parents will agree. If so, we could have our answer very soon."

"Do it."

"This could be what we've been hoping for."

He wanted to jump from his skin, but it would do no good. Nothing would be negotiated with the boy's parents tonight.

A knock on the door.

"Enter," Jon called.

Raoul entered and saluted. "Your clerk, Your Majesty."

"Send him in." Jon rose.

Eloi mustered a brisk walk, came to an abrupt stop, and bowed deeply, his blond curls flopping over his face. "Your Majesty," he greeted, out of breath.

"What is it?"

Eloi rose from his bow, sparing a brief glimpse at Olivia before nodding to Jon. "An ambassador, Your Majesty."

Every country in the region had already sent diplomats. "From?"

Eloi breathed unevenly. "Forgive me, but I don't know, Your Majesty. The most learned among the party spoke Old Emaurrian. One of the paladins—a scholar's son—recognized it but could understand no more than that they desired to meet with our king. None of the Trèstellan translators speak it, as it is a dead language."

Dead language? An Immortal race, perhaps?

An ambassador... That meant potential allies. But what use was that when no one spoke Old Emaurrian?

Olivia stood. "Both Leigh and I are fluent... but I've never heard it spoken before. The accents, dialects—"

Jon turned to her. "Come. Let us meet this ambassador." He strode past Olivia and Eloi, and they followed. Friend or foe, he couldn't decide, but he resisted the urge to believe that what the kingdom needed most had just arrived.

AT THE HEART of Trèstellan Palace, Jon sat high on the throne upon the dais, twelve steps above the rest of the room. Around him, a squad of sixteen paladins stood in perfect formation, and off to his side, Olivia posed in her impeccable emerald-green Archmage's robes, leaning in to whisper her suspicions about the visitors from time to time. A ruse. A trap. An illusion. And then genuine belief.

Another squad of paladins escorted in a group of twenty strangers, all wearing brown cloaks and light armor of what looked like wood. Beneath their helmets, only small portions of their fair skin, blond hair, and golden eyes were visible. At their sides, they wore rapiers similar to the dueling swords that nobles favored.

The paladins stopped just short of the steps, and the foreigners smoothly took the cue and halted. One of them, an individual at the front of the procession with a sunburst pin, descended to a knee and bowed his head. His entire group followed suit.

"Terra's blessings upon you," Jon greeted, Olivia translating his words into the foreign tongue. Did these strangers believe in the Goddess as he did?

"And upon you, Your Majesty."

"Please rise." As Olivia conveyed his words, they rose. "I am King Jonathan Dominic Armel Faralle of Emaurria," he said with a confidence he didn't feel. "I welcome you here."

The leader removed his helmet and so did his group. The stern-faced strangers' skin was unblemished to the last, with no facial hair but for their eyebrows and eyelashes. Some wore their fair hair braided, others knotted, and a few left their subtly pointed ears visible.

None looked older than three decades. The leader was the only man among them.

Light-elves. Some believed them myth, some legend, but here they stood. Derric had told him stories of the light-elves who worshipped the light and the dark-elves who worshipped the dark, wars that had raged for millennia, and a fantastical feud with the first witches. Tales. Tales that now stood before him.

He exchanged a look with Olivia before the leader spoke again.

"My name is Ambriel Sunheart, envoy of our queen, Narenian Sunheart of Vervewood. I have come seeking the ruler of this land, so that we might nurture an alliance that may benefit both of our nations. Our situation is dire. We have awoken to a world different than what we remembered." He hesitated and dulled his tone. "We can provide a number of soldiers and crafters, but we are in need of food, supplies, and knowledge, and we have no allies to turn to. Without supplies, we will be as leaves to the frost.

"We have come to request a diplomatic envoy empowered to treat with our queen for a formal alliance as soon as possible."

The group behind Ambriel stood to perfect attention; if the soldiers this light-elven queen offered were of like discipline, then perhaps this proposed alliance could provide some of the forces Emaurria needed to address the Rift. He could part with some grain and siege supplies in exchange for capable men and women.

"My household will see that you and your people are fed and sheltered for the night. My council and I will meet tonight and come to a decision. I will summon you here tomorrow for my answer."

Ambriel bowed at the waist.

"The paladins will escort you to our guest quarters," he said, and Olivia translated. He signaled one of his servants along the wall. "See that they receive the highest standard of hospitality tonight." He turned to Sir Florian. "Florian." The paladin approached him. "Please see these guests to quarters for the night," he said before adding covertly, "and I want a patrol outside their rooms to escort them wherever they wish to go. Report any movement directly to me."

The light-elves were to go nowhere without a guard. Florian placed his right hand over his heart and bowed; he would execute his orders flawlessly—he'd always been tenacious.

Ambriel and the rest of the light-elves departed behind him, a squad of paladins, and an assortment of household staff.

These were strange times, indeed, to see tales walking among men.

And now for the bureaucracy.

He turned to Olivia. "Would you please assemble the High Council in my private dining room and meet me there in an hour?"

She nodded.

"And, if you would be so kind, would you find me some materials on Old Emaurrian and Elvish language, if there are any available, and bring them to me at your leisure tomorrow?"

"Need more work, do you?" The corner of her mouth lifted.

"Ever and always." At least it felt that way these days. He rose. One more stop to make.

There was a certain prisoner of considerable power and unparalleled conceit that he would try to persuade for the good of the kingdom. He had both a carrot—atonement—and a stick—report of Leigh's actions to the Divinity. Would the mage be swayed by either?

He gestured to Raoul and a paladin he knew well from Monas Ver, Sir Gregoire Bonfils. "Let's go."

Olivia cocked her head inquisitively. "Is there anything else I can help with?"

"I'm not certain I want another witness present." He cracked his knuckles, and with a parting glance, he led his two guards toward the dungeon.

He sighed heavily. The ever-abrasive Leigh Galvan... After two and a half months in the dungeon...

The night would be a long one.

# CHAPTER 11

*L*eigh sat in the filth and listened to the fanciful tale, paying Jon no more heed than a casual glance. Perhaps the entire country was already happy to bend the knee, but the *king* had done nothing to earn his respect, much less his reverence.

Although Jon's visit was atrociously late, he allowed the man to speak his piece. Freedom was long overdue.

After two months in the austere comforts of the arcanir dungeon, he had begun to wonder if Jon had forgotten him—along with the rats, the snakes, and the mice. It was, however, as his lovers always said: Leigh Galvan was not easily forgotten. He grinned to himself, and from the corner of his eye, devoured Jon's puzzled expression.

The barely believable story of light-elves, Old Emaurrian, and treaties Jon had just recounted was ridiculous, to say the least. He wouldn't have believed it at all had Olivia not visited regularly with reports of strange and legendary creatures appearing all over the kingdom, after the Moonlit Rite had... failed.

"What I am hearing is that you *need* me," Leigh said, with no small amount of conceit.

Jon crossed his arms. To a learned man, it appeared that the former paladin was displeased with his inferior bargaining position. Good.

"You can *hear* whatever you like," Jon said—typical paladin clod —"but what I am actually *saying* is that you have the opportunity to leave these conditions and atone, if that is your wish."

Atone. It appeared that his former-apprentice-turned-Archmage had been running her mouth; no matter—he wouldn't give Jon the satisfaction of an explanation. Leigh puffed an aloof breath. Besides, if he was doing anything upon release, it would be finding Rielle. "You and I both know that you won't be able to hold me here much longer." He rattled his chains for dramatic effect. "Magehold will want me freed. I am much more valuable to it in the field than I am in chains. In fact, I am much more valuable to the Divinity than your favor."

Jon narrowed his eyes, but a smile played about his mouth. What was he thinking?

Regardless, his intellectual tools were blunt; Leigh had deceived him before and could handle him now. He grinned inwardly.

Jon tapped one of the metal bars with a booted foot. "So valuable that no request for your release has arrived."

"It's adorable that you believe yourself so above deception."

An amused grunt.

So Jon had been a paladin, unlikely to deceive, but who knew how many hands had handled such a request? Any of them could have quietly made it disappear, and it was too soon for the Divinity to send an emissary from Magehold. He could wait. The cold, the damp, and the constant sting of arcanir rattling his bones was... unpleasant, but not unbearable.

"It is my understanding that to date, due to Rielle's disappearance, no report on her mission has been turned over to Magehold," Jon said. "Imagine how its valuation of your usefulness will be affected if it discovers your direct defiance of its orders."

Leigh's grin threatened to disappear, but he forced its persistence. The paladin-turned-king had shed the heavy ethics that had once impaired him, it seemed, and... Perhaps his intellectual tools weren't entirely blunt.

"You wouldn't," he challenged. "I'd be of no use to you if the Divinity took me into custody."

Jon leaned in close to the bars. "You're of no use to me *now*." A victorious pause. "I could be persuaded to keep my peace, however, if you were to choose to serve the people of the kingdom you've blighted."

*Choose.*

Somewhere deep, deep, *deep* down, he could find a few specks of respect to scrape together for Jon, but a compromise would be hard won.

He shrugged. "Aside from the warm feelings, what's in it for me?"

"Besides the very tangible benefit of freedom from this place, Olivia and I will agree to keep your interference in the Moonlit Rite a secret, you will be named an Emaurrian Ambassador, and after the alliance has been formed, you are free to do as you like," Jon said, lowering his voice, "so long as you don't cross me again." A sharp edge rode his threat.

"Aren't you the least bit concerned that I may try to seek revenge for this imprisonment?"

Jon rested a hand on his sword's pommel. A look not unlike malice flickered in his expression. "If you do, I will destroy you," he said flatly. A promise, not a threat.

The urge to scoff briefly sparked and died. Jon was serious. Perhaps paladins could handle most mages, but Leigh was not most mages.

Still, he didn't relish the idea of testing probability. Especially considering where his last test of probability had gotten him.

"You will recall that because of your idiotic conspiracy theory," Jon said, "our party was split up that night. Rielle is still missing. I have no mercy to spare for you, Galvan."

"Do not lay the entirety of that blame at my feet, *Your Majesty.* Your little revelation shocked her." That little secret being aired was as much to blame for her disappearance as her abductor. Who would die a very, very, *very* painful death. "It is not my fault you *chose* to divulge it then and there, pushing Rielle away and ultimately leading to her abduction. If you have blame to spare, keep it."

A fire raged to life in Jon's eyes, and his hands clamped tightly around the cell's bars. For a moment, Leigh expected him to pull the cell door off its hinges and summarily execute him, but instead, the fire in his gaze slowly died. Jon exhaled coarsely and bowed his head. He loved her. Through and through. He loved her. This man wanted her found just as much as he did.

"Is there any news of her?" Leigh dared to ask, softly. He would have been the first to find Rielle, but the arcanir chains and prison bars had proved a stalwart obstacle.

"Brennan is following a lead on the Kezani vessel seen departing the bay later that night," Jon informed him in a crestfallen murmur.

"Ah, yes, the beast." Leigh's gaze wandered over the various healing bruises and lacerations on his body. Two months ago, Brennan Karandis Marcel had certainly left an *impression*. "You trust him?"

"He is loyal to Rielle," Jon quickly objected, "and I trust in that loyalty."

"Is it really loyalty, or something else?" Leigh raised an eyebrow. Perhaps the state of those intellectual tools required reevaluation.

"Whatever it is, it's enough for me to trust we share this one, common goal."

Leigh scoffed. "Aside from his unsavory history with Rielle, he turns into a monster with an insatiable thirst for blood and death. How can you trust anything about him?" Even before the torture, he had seen it in his eyes in the Lunar Chamber, when the beast had set upon him like death upon the dying.

"And how are you different?" Jon asked. "How much blood and death have you left in your wake?"

Leigh wrinkled his nose. So he'd killed some. And caused an apocalypse.

But the beast did have an obsession where Rielle was concerned. No man orchestrated so elaborate a revenge scheme for a straying fiancée—and then remained both in contact and betrothed—without being obsessed.

The beast could be trusted to find her, perhaps, if with nothing else. Especially not his intentions.

Jon pinched the bridge of his nose and sighed. "I have no more time to trade barbs with you. Will you be the ambassador to the light-elven kingdom or not?"

Between rotting in an arcanir cell until Jon decided to expose his betrayal to the Divinity and being freed to go to a legendary land accompanied by legendary beings, the winner was always clear.

"Fine," Leigh replied, "but I'll need to visit a bathhouse first. And a brothel."

An irritated growl. "Both of your needs will be met. Do we have a deal?"

"We do."

Jon nodded to a guard—another paladin. "I want this man freed, bathed, clothed, and sent to my private dining room within the hour. After the council meeting, procure a selection of... specialists... from the... local brothel," he said, curling his lip.

Leigh could have guffawed—but he did not want to delay that *procurement* in the least.

"It shall be done, Your Majesty," the paladin replied robustly. He placed a hand over his heart and bowed low before swiftly leaving to execute his orders. Another guard took his post.

Delicious. A paladin would see to the procurement of whores. Leigh smirked to himself.

And he would finally be free of this place.

Jon turned toward the stairs.

"Ordering baths, clothes, and whores... It is good to be king, isn't it?"

Jon stopped and looked over his shoulder, shadows playing across his face. "I'd always imagined it would be more honorable," he said, his voice low, deflated, "but I've learned that sometimes, in order to secure the kingdom's honor, my own must be sacrificed." At that, he strode toward the stairwell, flanked by his guards, and disappeared.

Jon would have to choose whether as king, he would be himself or something more.

Sometimes an individual's honor had to be tarnished for the greater good. Perhaps he and Jon finally understood each other.

Two hours into the meeting, Jon's High Council was still debating how to proceed regarding their Immortal guests, and he needed an agreement to present to the light-elves tomorrow morning. He rubbed the oaken table, its grooves over his fingertips keeping him attentive.

"If these 'elves' coexisted with the other Immortals before, then they have valuable knowledge. Their help is not something we should dismiss." Tor thumped the table, earning some nods and murmurs from the other Grands.

Tor was right. But better to let them keep talking, keep options and ideas flowing. Since his briefing on the situation with Vervewood —its strengths, weaknesses, opportunities, and threats—and explaining Leigh's involvement, the High Council had been disputing negotiation parameters. He would finish hearing their differing views before throwing his weight behind any individual stance.

"But what help is there, Torrance, when no one understands them but two mages?" Derric straightened his long and lean frame in the chair and shook his head; although clean shaven, a white sheen of his hair was still just visible. But if he was feeling his age, he certainly hadn't let it slow down his quest to save the world. "This kingdom needs to focus its energies on consolidation of power and development of a unified identity, not diluting itself through alliances with non-humans."

Tor held his head high, his shoulders back, his spine straight. He didn't waver at all. Jon had expected some problems sorting out the former Order hierarchy from his current officers, but Tor, at least, didn't let Derric's former higher position command his obedience. He may have been a paladin for most of his life, but he'd been a Marcel first.

"There won't *be* a kingdom if we can't stand against the Immortals," Valen argued, sweeping his arm out—he'd always had a presence to match his large size. He'd adapted to the duties of Grand Chamberlain and to palace life well, and at thirty-one years old, handsome, and with perpetual good humor, the court had welcomed him with open arms. "The attacks are constant, and how will we protect the kingdom with such small numbers?"

"Olivia and I aren't the only ones who speak Old Emaurrian," Leigh said, his voice a slow drawl from his relaxed position. Clean, coiffed, and well-dressed, he almost resembled a man who hadn't spent two months in prison after thorough torture. Almost. "Bookworms abound at the Tower. Send to the new Proctor for aid or, if you have the stones, petition the Grand Divinus herself."

Olivia swatted him, not unlike a mother scolding a disobedient child, and whispered in his ear; Leigh frowned as if he'd sucked a lemon. "Although Leigh is correct, we have many practiced linguists here. Learning Old Emaurrian won't present but a modest challenge, simpler than Kamerish or Nad'i, for certain."

After the attempt to thwart the Moonlit Rite, a rejection from the Divinity would be just what Leigh wanted. He'd revealed his bias—the mage looked for any opportunity to sow discord with the Divinity.

"Dead languages are not songs and dances, Archmage Sabeyon," Marquis Auguste Vignon Armel, Secretary of State for Foreign Affairs —and Jon's newfound cousin—argued. "It will take far too long, and we need solutions now." Auguste stroked his pointed, graying beard and scowled at Olivia.

A spark illuminated her eyes. "I appreciate the education, Secretary. Truly enlightening." She and Leigh exchanged amused looks.

Auguste opened his mouth, but Jon held up a hand, before this meeting turned into pages hitting each other with practice swords. "Enough. I've heard your concerns and suggestions, and I thank you all." He motioned for Eloi to approach, and the clerk hurried to his side, quill and paper in hand. "First, I'm issuing a mandate that all palace scribes begin learning Old Emaurrian immediately, under Archmage Sabeyon's guidance. Accelerated achievement shall be rewarded with both coin and position."

Eloi busily transcribed the mandate while general acceptance rippled through the council.

"Our ambassador will depart for Vervewood tomorrow, and he will negotiate with Queen Narenian thus: in return for livestock, horses, grain, other foods, clothing, and supplies, Emaurria seeks independent Immortal hunting squads, which would report to our newly appointed Ambassador to Vervewood, who would, in turn, report to the Constable of Emaurria. The numbers are to be negotiated, but I expect parameters delivered to Eloi by the Grand Master, the Grand

Squire, and the Secretaries of the Treasury, Commerce and Labor, Foreign Affairs, and Agriculture well before dawn."

His respective officers motioned for their clerks in varying degrees of haste.

"The Ambassador to Vervewood will attempt to negotiate the most favorable agreement based on these figures, so make no mistakes." Jon waited for Eloi to finish writing. "As part of that agreement, an assembly of Vervewood's linguists is to meet here with our own under the Archmage's oversight, so that language learning materials may be developed jointly and distributed to any who seek to learn. I also grant broad discretion to our ambassador to negotiate for anything of significant value to our kingdom, within the limits prescribed."

Jon glanced at Olivia, who would become even more indispensable. "In the meantime, Archmage Sabeyon will learn more about their culture and that of any other intelligent races awoken by the Rift, information about the Immortals, and anything else to help us make sense of this new world."

He looked for any sign of objection, but the room remained silent except for Eloi's scribbling. "Very well. That concludes the matter of Vervewood."

"Your Majesty," Tor cut in. "There is the matter of the attacks surrounding Bisclavret."

The march near the Marcellan Peaks. The mangeurs—as Olivia had dubbed them—had begun raiding the villages a few days after the Moonlit Rite, capturing people and livestock. The death toll had, last he knew, been one hundred and forty-eight. Perrault was to have sent paladins to help.

With a long exhale, Jon motioned for him to continue.

"Paladin Captain Perrault dispatched two squads of paladins, along with our three squads of soldiers. With the marquis's men, they mounted a defense at one of the villages." Tor lowered his gaze and hesitated. "The village was lost. Radiating an aura of cold, the mangeurs had frozen every person, animal, and building left behind, affecting all but the paladins. Survivors fled farther and farther to at last flock in the village of Espoire. A scarce few remain in the

Bisclavret infirmary. Enough to inform the Marquis of Bisclavret, Claude Amadour Tremblay, of this intelligence."

Murmurs rippled among the High Council.

*Mangeurs.* No mystery veiled the fates of the captured livestock and villagers. Attacked by a horde of enemies offering no terms of surrender, making no demands, standing twenty feet tall and hungry, the villages had faced only slaughter.

Tor exhaled slowly. "Considering the losses, even if we do send more men, their morale will be very low, and there's no certainty of victory. But if Espoire is lost, the march might not survive the winter. And there's no telling if the mangeurs will stop with Bisclavret."

*And it's my responsibility.*

"We need more allies to combat this menace," Derric interrupted, his honey-brown eyes intent. He swept out a hand. "A marriage tie to a country willing to provide soldiers would benefit us most."

Jon placed both of his hands on the table, staring at them, clean and smooth. It had been too long since he'd been out in the wilds, dispensing Terra's justice where it was needed. Here, he'd grown useless, his roughness dulled, his greatest skills unneeded. His attention moved to his Sodalis ring. As a king, his uses were few, despite his power. Soon, duty could require the last thing he wanted to bargain away.

"That is our boldest démarche," Pons intervened, "but we can only take it once. It is best saved for the direst of situations. We are not yet at that crossroads, Derric. There is another way, something unconventional, but..."

Derric lowered his voice, and the pair whispered in hushed tones. More than one Grand leaned closer.

The words sank in while Jon stared at his hands. *Another way...* "You mean the Earthbinding."

Leigh scoffed. "With all due respect, Your Majesty, that is nothing but a legend," he said, with a small, contemptuous smile.

"And you prove yet again, Master Galvan, that you do not, indeed, know everything," Pons replied with a sigh. He looked back to Jon. "Your Majesty, nearly a millennium ago, it was one of Your Majesty's ancestors who last performed it."

Jon nodded. It had been King Tristan Armand Marcel Faralle, who'd married the Lothaire pirate queen.

But a devout Terran and former paladin performing a pagan ritual...

*Dancing under the moon, naked. You know, black arts stuff.* Rielle's playful voice caressed his thoughts. The firelight in her sky-blue eyes, she had smiled that captivating smile of hers in camp, just a couple days from the Tower.

A hollow formed in his throat. It widened to his chest. When would he see her again? Was she safe?

No. He couldn't think about that now.

"Your Majesty?" Tor's voice cut in.

Jon blinked, sucking in a deep breath. Letting his mind wander that road would only render him useless here. "I won't rule it out, but we are not yet so desperate." And he glanced at Derric. "Marriage would bring an alliance, true, but not in time to save Espoire."

He nodded to Leigh. "You will work on securing an alliance with Vervewood, so that we may have some support in the future to face these threats." He turned to Olivia. "In the meantime, send to the Emaurrian Tower for an elementalist. Pay whatever the interim Proctor wants. It's time the Divinity helped. I want a mage working with our forces to stop these attacks. Arrange for their agent to meet us as soon as possible at Castle Brugière in Bisclavret."

"Us?" Auguste questioned. "You mean to go to the castle for the battle, Your Majesty? After over a hundred have been killed by these—"

"One hundred and forty-eight." He and Auguste often disagreed, and despite being the Secretary of State for Foreign Affairs, the man was a blatant isolationist, but Jon required a High Council capable of more than saying yes. And although Auguste often challenged decisions in closed sessions, he supported them when they were final.

Alliances with Immortals, blasphemous rituals, political marriage... Before he could agree to any of these things, he needed to assess the Immortal threat with his own eyes. "And I don't mean to stay in the castle. I mean to fight."

A few stunned faces contrasted with unsurprised glares from those who knew him well.

"Your Majesty, this is an ill—" Derric began.

"It's brilliant," Tor cut in. He leaned back in his chair. "With their king leading them into battle, our forces' morale will be high." He motioned to Derric. "And regarding Parliament stalling on the legitimization, perhaps His Majesty should remind them that he isn't a soft diplomat whose greatest prowess is warming chairs. He is a warrior king. A paladin king. Exactly what a land in turmoil needs to lead them."

Speechless, Jon raised his eyebrows at Tor, who nodded in reply. "Thank you, Lord Constable." Indeed, while Parliament didn't act on the legitimization, Princess Sandrine Elise Faralle El-Amin's claim to the throne remained. Instead, they wasted time on objecting to the funeral costs for the recently deceased Faralles. Disrespect. And a not-so-subtle clue as to their estimation of his own worth, too.

"Coordinate with Paladin Grand Cordon Guérin. Let's not take chances with numbers—a full company," Jon commanded.

Tor nodded and gestured to his clerk.

"I'm coming, too, Your Majesty." Pons raised his head.

At seventy-two years of age, even the few days' travel to Bisclavret through the snow would be difficult for him. "Lord Chancellor—"

"Your Majesty, I am an old man," Pons declared, his words sucking all the air out of the room, "but I am a magister. I will be of greater use to you there for a few days than here."

A sober-faced Leigh nodded his respect.

"Very well. Thank you, Lord Chancellor. It'll be an honor." Jon inclined his head. "We'll leave as soon as the Paladin Grand Cordon can muster the forces."

After the topic of the raids, the officers of the High Council raised a few more subjects. It was well past midnight by the time the meeting ended. Eloi and the other clerks would have a long night ahead of them, overloaded with work, assembling experts on agriculture, history, culture, and other key areas of interest; amassing lists of items, their inventory, and their value from the Grands for negotiation with Vervewood; and drafting documents for the diplomats departing for the elven nation in the morning.

And Leigh, as promised, would get his... *specialists*.

As Valen, yawning and asleep on his feet, was leaving the dining room, Jon caught him.

"A moment, brother?" Jon tilted his head toward the study.

Shaking off the drowsiness, Valen accompanied him there, blinking his jade-green eyes sluggishly. "What's wrong, Jon?"

Jon grabbed the leather-wrapped portrait of the courier off his desk. "I need you to look into something for me," he said, unrolling the portrait. They'd grown up together, fought together, bled together; Valen was family and utterly trustworthy. "Personally. At the carriage house in Chevrefeuils, at Monas Tainn, and at Partage, discreetly ask whether this man was seen, where he was going, what his habits were. Anything you can learn about him."

Valen accepted the portrait and studied the face there. "Who is he?"

"His name might be Gerard, based on our current intelligence. A courier." Jon crossed his arms. "For the one who hired Gilles."

Valen's thick eyebrows shot up. "Does the Order—"

"No." Jon straightened. "I want this kept to as few people as possible. That's you, me, the man who described this courier, a junior paladin, and Olivia."

Valen's head bobbed slowly. "I take it she was the one who found him?" When Jon nodded, Valen pressed his lips together and sighed. "Good head on her shoulders."

"Talk to her before you go. Tell no one the purpose of your travel, and take whatever you need."

Valen rolled up the portrait. "Maybe we'll finally bring the monster responsible for all this to justice." He lowered his gaze. "Maybe even find your lady love."

Jon swallowed, his throat parched. "Terra willing."

Once Valen left, Jon entered his bedchamber, where a large painting graced the wall over the hearth. Rielle.

He stopped.

It had arrived at last. He'd asked the Duchess of Melain to send it to the palace on loan, and she had acquiesced.

Rielle coyly smiled down at him, and he fell into bed, his body aching with fatigue that did not even approximate the exhaustion of his mind. Thinking about her was a dangerous proposition, but at least with her portrait here, there was some hint of her presence. Enough to soothe the berserker inside that wanted to cast off everything and go after her.

At least he'd be out in the field again. It was a sad state of affairs when what he most looked forward to was staring death in the face. But he could be useful there, keep busy, do something about the mangeurs. Or at least try.

He'd fight them and pray it was enough. If the Immortals could be routed through conventional warfare, then there was hope yet for a normal life as king. If not, the Earthbinding, marriage to some princess, and any manner of solutions became not options but necessities. Necessities he needed to avoid.

Tomorrow he'd make for Bisclavret with Pons, a company of paladins, and Emaurrian soldiers, and he'd finally see the Immortal threat for himself.

# CHAPTER 12

*R*ielle squinted against the bright sun. A large blur loomed in the distance.

A city? Which? Was House Hazael here? Her heart raced. This could be it. Would it truly be better than the stable?

It had to be. She trudged closer with the rest of the chained line.

A massive fortified wall enclosed an intimidating metropolis, the sandy shades of its peaks matching the desert it was situated upon. At its heart was the largest building, a huge cylinder with a domed roof, at its apex the universally known symbol for infinity—representing the union between anima in humans and anima in everything, the infinite, and the Divine.

The Divine's most splendid temple.

It had to be Xir. Rumored to be a city of excess, where every desire could be bought, it was an architectural marvel, larger than every city she'd seen but Courdeval, with defenses that had been maintained for a thousand years.

From the guard towers, watchful eyes searched the horizon beneath kaffa and halla in white coats—mages. Sonbahar readily employed mages everywhere in their society, forsaking the useless

suspicion still present in some countries, like Emaurria, for pure practicality.

She squinted. Two mages per guard tower. Likely enforcers—the
most useful for military applications. Accompanying the mages were
teams of archers, with pikemen guarding the gates and likely the guard
towers' ground level.

The entrances and exits were heavily guarded. Even if she could
overcome insurmountable odds by killing her masters and escaping,
there would be no getting by the mages alive without paperwork.

Could Jon arrange such a thing? She breathed deeply, slowly.
Perhaps it wasn't too much to hope that kingship would come with
some connections through the High Council.

Ihsan led their caravan closer to the gate and pulled out some
documents.

The woman defied categorization. She bought slaves but spoke to
them like people; she forced them to traverse a desert on foot but
healed them; and she commanded the authority of armed guards but
did not punish the impudence of slaves. Why?

Did Ihsan Pleasure-Born of House Hazael struggle with her divergent parentage? Despite being a free woman and a child of a noble,
perhaps Ihsan still carried the burden of her father's slave status and
so, expressed leniency where none was expected.

Or maybe it was something more sinister? The puzzle's solution
could prove useful, whatever awaited at House Hazael.

They passed through the gate without incident, and within the
city's walls, the market's atmosphere was decidedly relaxed. Stores,
stalls, and tents stood amply spaced from one another. A dense crowd
perused wares while strolling lazily between them. Small oases with
wells, trees, and flowers punctuated the buildings, a pacifying whisper
of nature among the man-made surroundings. The smell of spiced food
and incense filled the warm air, and somewhere beyond it all, slow and
rhythmic drumming.

Throughout the narrow city corridors and beneath its peaked
arches, Sonbahar's caste system was clearly represented among Xir's
populace. The nobles were, despite the heat, clad in colorful thiyawb
from head to toe and adorned in jewelry. The warrior caste wore black.

Free men and women wore long robes in neutral tones. And casteless or slaves wore next to nothing, exposing their backs or brands, respectively.

Laborers wore little more than modesty demanded while house servants wore upper and lower robes with bare midriffs. Pleasure slaves wore the least of all, their garments small swaths of silk, transparent gossamer exhibiting every inch of the human body or, most shockingly, fine golden chains alone, sometimes linked to piercings in various uncomfortable places.

It was difficult not to look.

And the city didn't seem perturbed in the least.

The caravan slowed. Ahead, gold gleamed in the sun's radiance. An arch ornamented in an intricate kaleidoscope of river blue, burnt orange, sand yellow, and blood red framed a massive set of gates.

They drew open.

Lush green plants and trees and bright flowers bloomed in a stunning array.

A gasp escaped her lips. Paradise. Someone before her gasped, too —a dark-haired woman, one of the people she'd arrived with: the woman who'd tried to steal her food. Tall, shapely, and olive skinned, she was the picture of Sileni beauty, but her slender frame suggested she'd been at the stable some time, if not as long as Rielle had. She turned her head and widened her dark eyes.

This place was awe inspiring to see, even enslaved, even in chains.

The Sileni woman faced forward again as their entire line entered on a mosaic tile path. It ended in a courtyard surrounded by flora, bright tiles arranged in an enormous, thorned blue rose design. Around and above her, the lilting sounds of songbirds carried on the breeze. A pair of colorful parrots soared from a pomegranate tree to a flowering tree.

Beyond the courtyard, a grand villa graced the property, several stories high, with peaked doors and windows, its balconies and walkways sheltered by latticed screens carved with beautiful patterns. The sun shone through them, casting shadows, flowers that danced on the walls.

Somewhere inside, the ever-present sound of flowing water relaxed the atmosphere to bliss, complemented by the slow strumming of a lute and meandering music of a southern oboe.

Ihsan took them around the side of the villa in a long walk that led out to a smaller courtyard with a pool at its center, its mosaic bottom visible through the clear water. All around, tall palm trees cast some shade over the water, their lush green fronds swaying in the light breeze, lending a distinctly pleasant sweetness that mingled with the fresh scent of water.

Beneath it all, the faint, resonant clash of metal rang in quick succession.

Blades.

Two men dueled on the white flagstones, their rapiers colliding. One wore a reddish-purple thiyawb—Zeharan red—a most expensive dye. Twelve thousand rock snails off the coast of western Sonbahar produced enough dye for a single garment. She had seen its like only once before.

The other wore the black thiyawb of the warrior caste. They moved so fast she struggled to follow their movements. A quick strike, and the Zeharan-red duelist drew blood from his opponent's shoulder.

That was it, then. Won.

But the duel continued.

A group of men reclined on large cushions off to the side, well-muscled like the guards of the warrior caste but wearing the bright colors of the nobility. Blood spattered onto the white flagstones at their feet.

A rapier clattered to the ground. The warrior-caste duelist grabbed his arm. Blood seeped through. The Zeharan-red duelist leveled his blade at his opponent's heart.

She peeked at the reclining men for their reactions, but a strained cry came from one of the duelists.

The Zeharan-red duelist had impaled his opponent. Shocked eyes widened as they faded. He fell to the ground, the blood a slow bloom around his body. The victor pulled his rapier free, wiped it clean on the deceased's body, and sheathed it.

He faced them, unperturbed. A dangerous man. A deadly man.

Fit for his medium build, he had a princely face and shining shoulder-length waves of black hair. As he drew closer, his dark, cool eyes sent a chill up her spine. Blood spatter blotted his otherwise unblemished golden-dark skin. He sauntered toward Ihsan with a wry smile.

"At last you return, half-sister," he said in High Nad'i.

The reclining men rose.

"Farrad," Ihsan greeted, her voice firm, deeper than before. She stood a little taller. Her eyes shifted to the dead man. "What was it this time?"

Farrad's eyes danced, rich like mahogany obsidian. "He offered to purchase Samara."

"And you killed him?"

He smiled. "I asked him to choose between flogging and dueling. He chose poorly."

Ihsan looked away. "Is Grandfather around? I have brought the ten slaves he requested. They are ready for training."

"No." Farrad clasped his hands behind his back, standing with his feet shoulder-width apart. "He's away on business." His gaze wandered to the slaves, moving from one to the next until he reached the last, the boy. "I count not ten but *eleven*, half-sister."

Ihsan approached her.

No. Why? Rigid, she hid under her mess of hair, shrugged her shoulders inward. As small as possible. A guard unlinked her chains from the rest of the group and handed them to Ihsan.

Singled out. No, no, no. What would happen to an eleventh, unrequested slave?

"This one is coming with me—my new scribe."

Through her hair, Farrad's unwavering gaze scorched her. She couldn't help but crumple.

"From where do you hail, golden one?"

Ihsan stepped between her and Farrad, stiffening, curling her upper lip. "She is mine."

Farrad stared her down. His dark eyes narrowed. "You claim much, but you forget, half-sister, soon everything in this house will be mine and mine alone."

Ihsan balled a hand into a fist. "Not yet."

"I know my destiny. It was foretold by an augur, and it will come to pass."

Whatever was happening between Ihsan and Farrad appeared to be a longstanding feud. *And I'm now caught up in it. Divine help me.* She swallowed. So far, absolutely nothing had gone right.

Farrad slowly approached, pushing past Ihsan like day through night. He grabbed Rielle's lowered chin and raised it to meet his face.

Scorching. It was as if the desert sun itself had focused all of its rays upon her. Faced with that gaze and the slight smile on his lips, she quickly averted her eyes, burned.

His hold on her chin persisted. Tremors rippled through her, and she tensed every muscle she could. Without her magic, there was little else she could do.

He released her. She swallowed audibly.

For today, the merciless sun had set: Farrad's gaze turned to a guard.

"Take them all away." He sighed. "And someone clean up that mess." He cocked his head toward the dead body.

Away where?

The guard linked her chain to the end of the line, and it soon moved. Ihsan stared down Farrad. "Stay away from my scribe, or Grandfather will hear of it."

No audible answer. She craned her neck around. Ihsan stood with her gaze lowered while Farrad sauntered back to the cushions and his entourage.

But a small spark of hope flickered to life within her as she and the others were led to the slave quarters. The lines of power here were faulty. She would find the weakest point, sever it, and take back her freedom. She would make it out of House Hazael, and then find some way out of the city. Perhaps she could destroy her brand and lay low until Jon found her.

Survival here depended on remaining beneath notice. Being free to move about the shadows, to learn, to plan.

Barely through the gates, and she had already become a point of contention. So much for keeping a low profile.

*Hurry, Jon. Hurry.*

STANDING at His Majesty's right, Olivia translated the agreement to Ambriel Sunheart as His Majesty dictated, while the morning sunlight streamed into the throne room. Everyone had assembled—his Majesty and his squad of Royal Guard, Tor, Leigh, Ambriel and his squad of light-elves. His Majesty sat upon the throne, an elbow rested on an armrest and his chin upon his fist. Today, he wore finely tailored black trousers, riding boots, and a fitted overcoat of scarlet, the finest woolen fabric available, dyed kermes crimson. A crisp dyaspin shirt collar and samite cravat peeked out from beneath.

He looked alive for the first time in months. The battle. He was eager to get to Bisclavret. To risk his life.

She introduced Leigh to Ambriel, and the two exchanged greetings in Old Emaurrian, looking each other over carefully.

In the sunshine, light reflecting off inlaid gold, the massive Trèstellan throne room was at the height of its grandeur. The largest chamber but for the great hall, its marble floor sprawled a hundred feet in a pattern of massive golden stars down the middle, white and bronze marble playing in geometric patterns rippling outward. Frieze-adorned white pillars depicting the kings and queens of old buttressed the second level, a gallery absent of courtiers today. Its columns supported a high domed ceiling, where a dragon sank its teeth into the shoulder of a legendary armor-clad king who poised his sword at the beast's eye. Knights fought all manner of beasts in the background, victorious, struggling, dying. Fighting to the last breath. Ever Emaurrian.

Like James, who had fought to his last breath against insurrectionists, who'd been murdered in service of political goals.

And his only remaining son now wished to leave the centuries-old royal duties of the Faralles and fight?

She drew in a breath and raised her chin, kept her spine straight.

Leigh, perfectly coiffed and attired in a tailored black brocade overcoat, white shirt, and black wool trousers, looked toward the king and back to her, widened his eyes briefly.

"Olivia." His Majesty touched her arm.

She started, turning from his raised eyebrows to Ambriel Sunheart, who frowned.

"What did he say?" His Majesty asked.

Gathering her composure, she turned back to Ambriel. "I'm sorry," she said in Old Emaurrian. "Could you repeat that?"

Ambriel's golden eyes looked from her to the king and back again. He licked his lips. "Vervewood accepts His Majesty's terms. We will send linguists as soon as we can to develop language-learning materials, and as Queen Narenian's brother, I can authorize the creation and dispatch of independent Immortal hunting squads to handle any predators to your people or ours."

With a nod, she relayed his words to His Majesty.

"Then we have an agreement," His Majesty said, rising, and she translated. He reached out to clasp Ambriel's arm. "We'll await word once our ambassador arrives in Vervewood."

A few words in closing, and His Majesty called for two squads of knights to escort the light-elves, Leigh, the humanitarian-aid group, and the paladins and soldiers that would accompany them from the city.

She descended from the twelve-step dais and stood in the emptying throne room, her gaze caught on a mote of dust falling in a ray of sunshine.

James had loved her, and she'd loved him, and... he was gone. Forever.

She'd lost him, but his son didn't have to face the same fate. Yet, he seemed determined to seek it out, pursue it, fight it. His son, *Jon*, who resembled him so closely, had walked into her life, and it had been as if James's memory had chosen to linger, with his easy grace, charming smile, and warmth.

And here, now, today, it was almost like letting James go all over again. She couldn't face that pain again—she *wouldn't*.

A new crowd gathered in the throne room—Pons, Paladin Captain Perrault, Royal Guard. The beginnings of the forces leaving for Bisclavret. With Jon. Would they be enough? Could anyone protect him, keep him from the harm surrounding him and closing in?

A palm gently rested on her arm. Jon's.

"Please allow me to thank you." He smiled warmly and inclined his head. "None of this could have happened without you."

James was really gone and would never return. And Jon was leaving, no matter the danger, and taking James's living memory with him.

"Don't go," she replied, covering his hand with hers, and when he raised an eyebrow, she added, "into battle."

He hesitated. "Olivia—"

She shook her head. "You shouldn't be risking your life."

"I have to."

It was the right course of action. The only thing *to* do. But—

She squeezed his hand. "Someone else can—"

"I'm the king," he said softly. "There is no one else."

Sucking her lower lip, she looked away. He'd seemed very devoted to being a paladin, to service; and now, as king, he was slowly being consumed by the same trait that had once served as his strength—his need to serve. He would do anything to save lives, to do right by his kingdom. Even at great cost to himself.

But someone had to watch out for him, keep him safe, and she was more useful there than fearing for his life here. She looked back at him. "Then at least let me come with you."

Jon shook his head. "You can't. You know you can't."

"Would you say the same if I were—"

"Don't mistake me for Auguste," he shot back. "I know you're formidable. You're also the only one left who speaks Old Emaurrian. You're needed here."

He was right. She deflated.

"And as for me, swinging a blade happens to be my greatest skill, so it's only fair, isn't it?" He gave her arm a squeeze and winked at her.

James's last surviving child. Her king. Her friend. She couldn't lose him. Couldn't lose him, *too*.

She wrapped her arms around him. "Divine and your Goddess keep you," she whispered, holding back tears.

He didn't move for a moment, and then hesitant arms settled around her. He smelled like a forest, serene at dawn. "Olivia, I plan on living."

"I know," she said as he rested a palm on her back. "And I expect you back here for magic lessons in no more than two weeks."

He chuckled softly, a low rumble in his chest, and gave her a squeeze. "I will be. Promise."

He'd better. She pulled away and drew in a lengthy, deep breath, collecting her decorum. A smile played on his lips, his eyes shining in the sunlight, flanked by glittering gold inlaid in the throne-room walls.

He'd promised.

"Gods' speed, Your Majesty. When you return, we'll find Rielle together." She'd already sent word to the boy spiritualist's tutor, former Tower doyen Erelyn Leonne.

"Terra's blessings upon you, Olivia," he said, gesturing the blessed circle with his palm open to her.

"And upon you." Forcing a smile, she bowed, waiting until his footsteps echoed farther and farther away.

He would be fine. He could handle himself. And with the Divine and Terra both watching over him, he'd be safe. Or at least it was what she had to tell herself.

When had she become so fearful? It was as if the fear Gilles had instilled in her those months in the dungeon had never truly left. Every day was another day a box could arrive, an eye, a hand, James's death. She lived in that fear, and in grief, when she should believe in Jon. Have faith in her friend.

It was untenable. Something had to change. Something new had to come into her life that wasn't a box of fear, grief, and death.

She straightened, eyeing the empty throne room for a moment. She hadn't gone to the abbey yet today to see James.

To her quarters, then, and to the abbey.

In the hallway, servants, guards, and courtiers passed to and fro, but amidst it all, a broad-shouldered man stood with his back to her, conversing with two clerks. Tor. The clerks nodded, bowed, and departed.

He turned, and his eyes met hers, hazel flecked with sunlit gold. Torrance Auvray Marcel. He offered a measured smile, and it always made her want to smile right back. "Archmage Sabeyon," he said, "where are you headed?"

"The abbey," she replied and turned in its direction.

A slight, warm smile lit his lips. "It brings you peace."

She nodded. "It does."

"We could all use a bit," he replied, drawing in a deep breath. His sunlit hazel eyes gleamed.

Was he asking for an invitation? Outside of Jon, she hadn't made the effort to forge friendships, to get to know others, not since the siege. And Tor... with his kind smile, his bronze skin like sun-warmed stones, always trying to keep the peace, pleasant, could be someone she should get to know. A new friend, maybe. "You're welcome to join me."

He opened his mouth, but no words emerged.

Perhaps not. Did he think it more than it was? She looked away.

After a moment's hesitation, he offered his arm. "It would be my honor, Archmage Sabeyon."

Even if he thought it more than it was... Would that be so terrible? Torrance Auvray Marcel, a good man, a handsome man, honorable and pious... Would it be—

She laced her arm through his. "Please, call me Olivia."

# CHAPTER 13

hen the sun set on Sixtidi, Drina left her room at Peletier's and headed downstairs to the tavern. Although she worked her stall from dawn until dusk from Primidi to Quintidi, she took Sixtidi and Septidi for herself, only occasionally accepting clients arriving with dire need at Peletier's counter to ask for her wares.

Downstairs, the usual mixture of kitchen maids, tradesmen, mercenaries, and guards ended the day with a pint or two of pale ale. It was a bland nowhere, exactly where a no one like her wanted to be.

Maxime Deloffre waved at her from his table in the back corner. "Lyuba!"

For the past two months, she'd been Lyuba Vaganay, the Kezani widow of an Emaurrian hedge-witch healer and apothecary, Marc Vaganay, from Aestrie.

Max was a well-meaning man with a mop of black curls, strapping broad shoulders, and rum-gold eyes, in his early thirties and a hedge-witch conjurer working for one of the Free Companies—Broadsteel— guarding the cargo of one of Courdeval's shipping companies.

With a wave to the serving girl for her usual, she sauntered to his table. "Max. Early reprieve from the docks?"

He nodded. "You missed it—the king left the capital today."

While she'd been lounging the day away, the king had left the capital? Her stomach turned to stone. *Fortune shits on this day.*

There were things she missed about working with a Free Company. Intricate spy networks among them.

She raised her eyebrows slightly. "Oh?"

"With a company of paladins, two squads of soldiers, and the Lord Chancellor himself. He left through the North Gate, so you probably wouldn't have heard the commotion."

With such an entourage, it had to be for battle. "What do you suppose he'll be doing?"

"Word has spread that he's going to battle the Immortal giants preying on the march of Bisclavret." Max leaned back in his chair and took a swig of ale. "The situation must be dire if the king's leading the men into battle personally."

Frost giants. She'd heard the news of the twenty-foot-tall Immortals that had come from the mountains, devouring everything they could catch and freezing what they couldn't. After she'd left the Divinity, the ruined tower in Khar'shil where she made her home had housed remnants of an ancient library, and she'd read everything she could in Old Erudi. About dragons, krakens, mermaids, werewolves, and even frost giants. The tower itself had a bell that, according to legend, summoned a dragon to destroy any enemy—requiring only a sangremancy ritual.

Legend no more.

The frost giants had been wreaking havoc. And the marquis had raised an army of his vassals only to see them obliterated in battle.

If the king was going into battle himself, then he'd already sent men previously—to their deaths. And a second force, without him, would only go into battle full of fear, or desert to save their own lives. His presence would give them hope of victory. Illusory hope.

She dropped her mouth open. "But that's so dangerous!"

Max laughed and reached across the table to stroke her hand. "My sweet Lyuba." He shook his head. "That's why he's going. My captain says a dangerous threat such as that makes men either corpses or cowards. If their own king will lead them into battle, then surely the danger isn't as great as they supposed, or he wouldn't risk his own life."

"Is that wise?"

Max shrugged. "It's reckless, especially without an heir. A young king like that, surrounded by eligible women, should produce a few princes to keep the realm secure—safe from utter chaos. But if he wins, his spoils aren't merely the safety and gratitude of Bisclavret's people and marquis, but also the respect and faith of the kingdom."

A warrior-king playing to his strengths. "I suppose there'll be a parade when he returns?"

"Naturally. A Joyeuse Entrée." Max drained his ale while the serving girl placed a pint before her, along with a bowl of goat stew and fine potato bread.

Only half-listening to Max, she ate, catching snippets of chatter from the room—concern for the king, worry about the realm's future, rumors about the Lord Constable, fears about the Immortals, and personal anecdotes. She focused on the anecdotes, learning bits about her ever-growing board of pawns.

"Lyuba. Message for you." Lionel Peletier himself lumbered to the table, laying the leather-wrapped message next to the stew, with his sausage-like fingers. An inn's food had to be good when the innkeeper was as portly as Peletier. And she'd been right to think so.

She sopped up the last bit of stew with the crust of bread and popped it into her mouth. She dragged an arm across her lips and nodded to Peletier. "My thanks."

He winked and waddled back to the counter.

Max tipped his head to the rolled-up message. "What is it?"

"Probably a customer placing an order." She opened the message, her eyebrows rising.

*Madame Vaganay, my mother told me you could provide remedies and discretion. Come to the palace forthwith. I've included the relevant documentation. C.*

Claire, Sauvanne's elder daughter. Documents of entry included. She rubbed the leather wrap.

"Well?" Max asked.

She stood and drained her ale. She kissed Max full on the mouth, earning hoots and whoops from the tavern clientele. "Business is good, Max. Eat up, drink up, and find yourself in my room tonight. You're going to need the energy."

The clientele's teasing escalated, and he flushed. "'Til then."

With a broad grin, she bounded up the stairs and to her room, clutching the message close to her chest. The pieces were falling into place at last. The only thing better than gaining access to the palace would have been if the king were in residence, but even this was a huge victory.

She'd memorized the maps of Trèstellan, and tonight, she would set in motion a perfect trap for His Majesty. She packed her apothecary bag and her recondite skeleton key.

A parade. Naturally. And the Master of Ceremonies would plan it all. Naturally. Musicians, dancers, and trumpeters needed coordination. Flowers had to be ordered. Food. This parade, like all others, would be a well-choreographed event.

Whose choreography she could steal.

And once she knew the king's route, she'd know where she'd need to be to kill him.

The news of a royal assassination would travel far and wide... even to Sonbahar.

DRINA KEPT her gaze on the salon's intricate wool rug, a dizzying pattern of red, gold, black, and violet. She had her way into the palace, but now she needed to ascertain it would remain open.

Lady Vauquelin, Nora Marcel Vignon, paced in her red silk dressing gown, its luxurious length flowing behind her.

"You're an apothecary?" Lady Vauquelin placed an elegant hand on her hip.

"Yes, Your Ladyship," she answered, as she had for the fifth time already.

"But... your clothes are so poor."

She tried not to grimace. "My usual clientele is of a... less fortunate quality."

Lady Vauquelin pursed her plump red-stained lips. Contrary to her facial expression, poverty did not, in and of itself, have an odor. But this fine lady would have rarely left her plush bower to learn the difference.

"But my understanding is that my lack of connections with wealthy clients such as yourself could be an asset, Your Ladyship." She ventured a brief glance at Lady Vauquelin.

Her dark tresses flowed to her hip, shining like polished obsidian, light as silk. Her diamond-shaped face, inlaid with dazzling hazel eyes, could inspire many a bard to song. No doubt the lady had half a dozen maids constantly polishing her to perfection—maintaining that shining hair, smooth face, and high fashion, and calling the fruits of that copious labor *good breeding*. Perhaps there was a beauty beneath it all regardless, but there was a lot of *it* to get beneath in order to find out.

"Discretion," Lady Vauquelin said softly. "Yes..."

The lady closed the distance to her and grabbed her arms.

Lady Vauquelin was lucky she was so clearly harmless. And central to the plan.

"You must understand, he can *never* know. If he finds out, I'll be..." The lady shook her head, her shining locks quivering.

*Divine forbid!* She suppressed the urge to laugh, and swallowed. "I understand. I would never betray a client." She paused. "And I'm so beneath the notice of the Houses, no one would even think to question me." True enough, and just what a fine lady expected to hear.

A slow smile spread across Lady Vauquelin's face. "Yes..." She beamed. "Quite right."

"What may I help with, Your Ladyship?"

Lady Vauquelin released her and straightened, pulling her shoulders back, raising her chin. She sniffed. "Fertility herbs."

So Lady Vauquelin intended to hook a man with a child. Recently widowed, she already wanted another husband? And how could she be so certain an Emaurrian man would be so honorable as to marry her rather than let her bear a bastard? She was clever, naive, or mistaken.

Drina nodded. "Are there any in particular you wish to order, or would you like some suggestions, Your Ladyship?"

Lady Vauquelin took a message rolled in leather off the table, closing her fingers around it. She slid the leather through her grip. "First, my mother tells me that there's a substitute for queen's lace that lacks its contraceptive potency. Should he look to verify that I was careful, then I wish to maintain the appearance."

Cunning. "Yes, Your Ladyship. It's nearly identical, substituting wild carrot for—"

Lady Vauquelin clenched the leather in her fist. "I don't care what's in it, as long as it doesn't prevent me from conceiving a child."

*Haughty bitch.* She smiled. "Yes, Your Ladyship."

Toying with the leather roll, Lady Vauquelin paced the salon, red silk catching air, revealing small, delicate feet in fine slippers. "As for the fertility herbs, what do you recommend?"

"Red raspberry leaf tea, daily, to lengthen the most fertile time of your cycle. Evening primrose extract, during your moonbleed, to render you more accommodating to the seed." When Lady Vauquelin narrowed her eyes, she added, "And during the first half of your cycle, chasteberry."

Lady Vauquelin raised a finely arched eyebrow. "Chaste? It's not quite what I'm looking for."

"Despite its name, it's had much success."

Lady Vauquelin regarded her, playing with the leather roll, then finally smacked it against her palm. Women like her didn't live such comfortable lives by denying themselves luxuries. She would want it. Have to have it. Demand it.

"All right. I want all of it. Deliver it here, to my chambers, personally and discreetly, and I will pay double your prices."

Double? The palace had been worth the effort, in more ways than one.

"How soon will it work?" Lady Vauquelin paced. "Will it work after one time?"

One time? What did she plan to do to the father, that she'd only bed him one time? Or perhaps she planned to catch him in a moment of vulnerability? "It depends whether the difficulty lies with the man or the woman—"

Lady Vauquelin threw her hands up. "How am I supposed to know?"

"There are herbs a man might take to—"

Lady Vauquelin shook her head. "No. I don't have access to his food or drink. And I won't."

No access to...

*The king. She plans to conceive the king's child.*

She bowed her head, hoping she'd successfully suppressed the grin. *When Favrielle discovers the duplicity of the man she loves...* Oh, the joy of that day. Almost as good as the day she would discover his death. After that, making the trip to Sonbahar would be priceless, just to see the look on her face, the understanding of what Marko had meant.

She cleared her throat. "If, after one cycle of lying with the intended father, you are not yet with child, I'll be quite surprised, but we'll work on him then."

Lady Vauquelin bobbed her head and laid the leather roll back on the table. "Very well. I look forward to the delivery."

Another opportunity to move about Trèstellan. "As do I, Your Ladyship. It is my pleasure to serve your needs." *My own.*

Lady Vauquelin dismissed her, and when the hall emptied, Drina cast a shadow cloak over herself, keeping to dark corners, and to the untrained eye, she would look like no more than a shadow herself. She would find the chambers of the Master of Ceremonies and copy his parade plans.

But first, it was time to acquaint herself with a possible field of battle.

The map of Trèstellan had indicated rooms on this floor that led into a passageway—probably intended as a mistress's quarters. Finally, she found them and, when no one was about, unlocked the door with the recondite skeleton key and slipped in.

Unoccupied. Gratefully. Although she was no stranger to killing out of necessity, when courtiers went missing, people noticed.

The map had indicated a passage on the other side of the bedchamber, and therein, a massive tapestry covered an entire wall

—*The Claiming of Solis*, wherein Terra, as the Maiden, conceived the next sun god with the current.

She raised an eyebrow. Subtle.

She moved aside the tapestry, ducked between it and the wall. A panel, smaller than a door. Such a small door for such a big step closer to her ends. Taking a deep breath, she pushed it.

With a soft brush, it opened into darkness.

She listened, and when no sound came, she spelled her eyes to see in the dark and entered. Tonight, she would take all the resonance she wanted from her conjurer-lover.

Obscurity had claimed this passage. She entered and closed the panel behind her. Dust and cobwebs filled the narrow space, only a couple unlit sconces upon the wall. She followed the corridor to a narrow stair, and another passage. Generations of kings and mistresses had traveled these well-worn paths to each other, keeping scandalous trysts secret from the rumormongering court and jealous queens.

If not for the undisturbed layer of dust, Jonathan Dominic Armel Faralle could have made use of these paths yet himself. Would Lady Vauquelin, beautiful as she was, have to work much at all to claim him for herself?

Before another panel, she stopped. If memory served—and it always did—this was the entrance to the king's bedchamber. She should have come here while the Crag were in control, but who could have predicted that a penniless paladin bastard would become king?

She shook her head.

He'd left for Bisclavret, as Max had related, but would a servant or valet be skulking around, taking routine care of the quarters?

She rested her ear to the wall, listening for any disturbance. When none came, she pulled the panel's knob slowly. Quietly.

A dense wall of clothes blocked the entry. The king's wardrobe. After laying her apothecary satchel in the passage, she brushed the clothes aside, paused to ensure no one had stirred, and then entered. Vast, it already brimmed with clothes, more than one man should rightfully own, but that was being king. An armor stand stood bare, mountings for weapons on the wall empty.

Light of foot, she crept to the doorway and peeked into the king's opulent bath. It was practically empty but for a plain olive-oil bar and that woodsy shaving soap from Monas Tainn.

Beyond lay the bedchamber, massive floor-to-ceiling windows allowing in the evening ambient glow. It illuminated a sprawling purple-heartwood four-poster canopied bed, two matching night-stands, and a vanity and washbasin. The Code of the Paladin, massive tome that it was, sat atop a bedside table with a jar of dry yellow flowers. Farther in were tables, armchairs, a fireplace. Above it—

Favrielle Amadour Lothaire looked down at her smugly from a portrait.

Drina's vision clouded. Even across the Bay of Amar, on another continent, the bitch laughed in her face, Marko's killer, a dim-witted girl who would have cowered beneath the broom of her ungrateful family, the Lothaires who spat in the face of the Divinity that had taught them true power.

If not for Corbin's mulish wife, Sylviane, the Lothaire children would have been alive, learning their craft in the Tower, serving magic and all mages and the Divine. And Marko—if not for Sylviane and her ignorant daughter, Marko would have never been sent to correct the imbalance, and would yet walk this earth—

*Love of my heart.*

But the bitch peered at her with that smug grin.

Happy.

Marko's murderer had no right. Ever. Drina smiled tightly, slowing her breathing.

Silent as death, she walked the king's chambers, absorbing their dimensions and orientation. They were clearly laid out in the maps, but standing here, taking it all in, she could close her eyes at any moment hereafter and see these rooms. *Always have a backup plan.* When she returned, she'd know her way around.

She exited through the panel in the wardrobe into the darkness of the passage. She shut it, retrieved her satchel, and followed the passage to another stair, far and lower, near the quarters of the Master of Ceremonies.

Outside the room, she listened.

The shuffle of footsteps.

Unmoving, she waited. The footsteps continued—purposeful, quick. A chambermaid, perhaps. A door closed, then quiet filled the time, undisturbed. After a few minutes, she pulled the knob, paused to ascertain the dark room's emptiness, then entered.

Another bedchamber, modest compared to that of the king. She crept along the wall to the study and on to the antechamber. No sound came from the hall.

Cloaked in shadow, she emerged and locked the door behind her with the skeleton key.

While the hall was empty, she hurried a few doors down, to the Master of Ceremonies' rooms, no more than a shadow to any passerby.

Beneath the door, firelight glowed from within into the hall. He was in. Or someone was.

Night had fallen. And so, too, its darkness would fall in her favor. If she remembered the layout correctly, the door led into the antechamber, then a study, and finally the bedchamber, with a small garderobe off the room.

No voices. No steps. Unlikely that anyone would sit alone in the antechamber. The Master of Ceremonies, if it was he, had to be at his desk, in his bedchamber, or in the garderobe.

Under the veil of silence, she could steal into the antechamber and navigate through the shadows until she found what she needed. And if she drew suspicion—

No killing tonight. If the Master of Ceremonies was found dead, the parade plans might be changed. The whole scheme could fall apart.

No, the Master of Ceremonies had to live.

She removed a carefully sealed sachet from her belt pouch. It contained a soporific sponge, soaked in the juice of flax, unripe mulberry, lettuce seeds, ithara, mandragora leaves, ivy, lapathum, sen'a, and hemlock with hyoscyamus.

Pressed to a man's nose, it would weaken him, render him free of pain, and throw him into a dreamlike state. He would wake within some hours, drowsy and uncertain whether the scattered images in his mind were reality or fantasy.

And all would proceed well.

While the hall was empty and no sound came from within the

rooms, she removed the skeleton key again. Exhaling, she inserted it into the lock and, painstakingly slow, turned it.

A click. Unlocked.

She swept off to the side, away from the hall's sconces, and waited. Would that there were some way to cast sound magic without an incantation. A cantor could have rendered an area soundless with a gesture, but the non-innate casting by incantation usually frustrated the very purpose of the spell.

Time ticked by. Guards walked past. Maids. Couriers.

No one emerged from the quarters. She crept to the door and listened. Footsteps striding nearer.

She leaped away to a dark corner. The knob turned. The door opened.

A man exited. Old, balding, fat. Dressed in peacock-like turquoise-and-violet velvet.

He stood, turning the knob, a frown etched into his plump face. *Curious about the lock.* She held her breath, straining to hear what he murmured.

"...incompetent..." A few more unintelligible grumblings, and he locked the door.

Scowling, he walked right past her.

When he rounded the corner, she dashed to the door, picked the lock, entered, then shut it without a sound and locked it once more.

A fire blazed in the hearth in the bedchamber. He'd return soon.

She rushed to the study, to the desk, and riffled through the papers there. Gatherings, a ball—a ball for Veris? She paused, examining the dance suite.

A lengthy night of dancing, all while the king's so-called beloved was missing? The world, it seemed, went on. Either the king was very devoted to maintaining a charade of seeking a bride, or he didn't love the bitch after all.

She set it aside and searched the other papers.

A map. She pushed the rest of the documents aside. Courdeval.

At last, the parade route. The Joyeuse Entrée would begin in the Chardon District, then meander through the bazaar of Dandelion, traverse Violette's middling residences, Alcea and Orchidée's rich merchant districts, then finally proceed through Azalée. She traced the route through her mind again and again until it rooted firmly.

Lists of guards, a requisition of two hundred barded horses, dancers, and so on... Such pageantry. A waste. The people—children—starved in the streets, while the royals and nobles spent coin like breaths on frivolity. And people expressed shock at the assassination of kings?

She studied the parade route twice more, rearranged the papers as they were, then headed for the antechamber.

A rasp of metal. A key inserted.

She dashed to the bedchamber, to the windows. Three stories. She opened it, climbed out, and lowered herself to hang from the ledge, gently shutting the window behind her.

Although hidden from view, she couldn't afford to wait. Her gloved fingers strained to hold her against the stone.

*"Wings of wind, heed my call, / Bear me down, catch my fall."* She released the ledge.

A sheet of wind caught her, slowing her fall, bringing her to the ground like a feather.

She rolled toward the palace wall, taking cover in its shadows. Her satchel remained secure. Her shadow cloak had held. Her anima had dimmed, but she'd have resonance with Max tonight.

Checking for her entry documents—they were in her shirt—she headed for the service gate. Once outside the walls, she'd find a place to put her mind to paper and plan a regicide.

# CHAPTER 14

Barefoot, Rielle followed the crowd of slaves from the bath house around the outside of the villa. The high-noon sun's blinding light caught the silken threads of a cobweb in a latticed window. Where were they going? The bath house was situated at the back of the property, behind the villa, not far from the barracks. She had a rough, if incomplete, layout, and a hazy schedule of some patrols.

They proceeded around the side into the courtyard with the white-bottomed pool, where Farrad had killed a man. The red stain was gone.

The immaculate flagstones burned her soles. Far in the corner, a cluster of pomegranate trees shaded a woman clad in a balaustine-red thiyawb, long hair shining in the light. She blinked.

Two guards walked by, clad in black thiyawb, eyes narrow with watchfulness.

The woman was gone.

The crowd shuffled into the shade, and Rielle with it. Next to her was the Sileni woman she'd arrived with, wearing little more than modesty demanded—a red silken bra and a belt of skirts. A pleasure slave.

Rielle rearranged her own robes—the upper and lower sandy-colored roughspun of a house slave. Praise the Divine she'd been spared the fate of this poor woman.

Their path took them beneath the palms and their soothing shade, then under a colonnade. At the change of direction, she bumped into someone on her other side.

"Pardon me," she said quickly in High Nad'i as the walk continued past another set of guards at a door. Relief cooled her feet. The shaded walk under the colonnade.

A girl of no more than fourteen smiled up at her, tossing a thick black braid over her shoulder. "Are you new?"

Rielle nodded, mirroring the smile. "I just arrived today."

The girl inclined her head. "I am called Samara. I serve in the apothecary."

Rielle was about to give her name, then cleared her throat. "Thahab. I'm a... scribe, I'm told."

Samara's eyes followed the path of two shackled young men being escorted through the gate, led on a line held by a guard. "You're fortunate to end up here, Thahab."

*Fortunate* wasn't the first word that came to mind.

Samara's dark eyes dulled. "Some, like those men, go to far worse places. The gladiator pits. Fighting to the death every day, sold to the highest bidder every night. It is a sad fate." Her voice died to a whimper.

A sad fate... one those men were being sold to?

"Did you know them well?"

Samara nodded. "Zayn and Azusa. Zayn worked with me in the apothecary last year."

A gleam flashed nearby. The gold of the gates and their ornamental arch, open. Unattended.

The crowd broke—the Sileni woman darting through. Her dark waves and belt of scarves flew behind her as she raced for the gates. Gasps rippled through the crowd.

Her bare feet pounded the flagstones, her figure framed by the gates' arch.

She froze. Levitated to midair.

A black-clad guard shouldered by, his hand raised in a clawed pose. An enforcer.

"No," Samara breathed tremulously next to her.

The Sileni woman cried, writhed, a red butterfly caught in an invisible spider's web. A squad of guards rushed past the crowd; Rielle gestured a geomancy spell, an abyss to drop them into, but nothing came.

No magic. Arcanir bonds.

She gulped down a breath as the guards closed in. One of them tangled a hand in the Sileni woman's hair, and the enforcer released her from his spell. She dropped to the flagstones, hard, her head yanked back in the guard's hold.

Dragged, she thrashed and screamed, one hand grasping her hair and the other clawing at the guard's arm.

Rielle stepped toward her, but a hand closed around her wrist. Samara's.

"You can't," Samara whispered. "There's nothing you can..."

One of the guards kicked the Sileni woman, and kicked her, and kicked her until she folded in on herself and stopped struggling.

Curled, helpless, in the open. Beaten. And no one moved to help. No one dared.

They dragged her past the crowd and toward the back end of the property.

A shudder shook Rielle's body, its ghost lingering. "Where are they taking her?" she asked quietly, her voice breaking. She couldn't look away from the woman. Wouldn't.

Samara sucked in a slow breath. "To the barracks. They're going to..." Her rasping voice died. "She'll be given lashes. At least one hundred."

Impossible. "One hundred?"

Samara nodded grimly.

"No one can survive one hundred lashes." At the stable, fifty lashes had killed people.

"Even if she'd made it past the gates, no one in Xir would help, and there's the Divine Guard and the brand..." Samara swallowed, then rubbed her lips together. "Very rarely, someone survives. But this is the price of attempting escape."

In front of them, cautious heads turned to look over shoulders. Samara lowered her gaze. *Escape.* Even the word instilled fear.

*That poor woman...* Her fists tightened.

But there was nothing she could do. Her fingernails bit into her palms.

An attempted escape meant abuse at the barracks and one hundred lashes... And a successful escape meant activation of the brand and being hunted down in the city.

The golden gates shone in the sunlight. In the distance, a woman screamed.

DRINA SHUT the door to a room at the Verninac Inn in Alcea District, glancing about in the starlight for candles. *"Oh fire bright, in dark of night, / Candles burn, wicks ignite."*

A flame sparked to life on the nightstand, a large candle, and one on the desk. She glanced at the fireplace and spoke another incantation, watching the hearth roar to life. Her anima deteriorated at all the non-innate magic, but if Max awaited at Peletier's, she would take all the resonance she needed later. For now, she still had more than half.

She strode to the desk, retrieved some paper, the quill, and an inkwell from the drawer, and sat. The memory of the parade route still fresh in her mind, she drew its entirety. She worked, filling in every detail she could remember, until no more remained, then grabbed a second sheet and made lists. Lists of everything she could recall from the Master of Ceremonies' papers. It was all coming together. Finally.

Her recollection of the Joyeuse Entrée began in the Chardon District, moved through Dandelion, Violette, Alcea, Orchidée, and finally through Azalée. Her list included names—guards, dancers, a company of players, weavers, tailors, writers, musicians, artists, singers, sculptors...

The Veris Ball. A dance suite of a prelude, quessanade, courante, gavotte, bourrée, furlana, volta, gigue...

She went over it all, again and again, filling in any details that came to mind until three hours had passed and she could remember no more. All the information put to paper. She leaned back in the chair and stared at the route, envisioning its path through the city.

The Joyeuse Entrée would begin through the northern gate, which —as an entry point into Courdeval—would be well guarded. She drew her soulblade and cleaned her nails.

The route would proceed through Chardon, full of low thatched houses and tight streets, where a cutthroat might ambush the king's entourage and risk it all for a well-placed blow. But it was risky. Too risky.

Then would come the massive bazaar of Dandelion. Flat, open, it offered no viable ambush points and no vantage points for a marksman. No opportunities there. She tapped the blade against her fingers.

Violette District? Middling homes... She sucked a tooth. Perhaps some residences, since the siege, were still unoccupied along the route...

But the Master of Ceremonies had ordered tapestries and carpets. They'd be hung all along the way. Choosing a site only to have it draped with a tapestry or a carpet would be playing the odds. And who knew when another chance like this would come again?

Alcea and Orchidée ascended into Azalée, a gradual incline through rich mercantile districts, home to social climbers and nobles who couldn't afford a villa in Azalée, and then a hill. She closed her eyes, picturing the main thoroughfare... Up the cobblestones among homes and shops, toward the citadel enshrining Azalée and Trèstellan Palace... Under the Triumphal Arch.

She sat upright in her chair and tapped the blade against her palm.

The Triumphal Arch.

It marked the boundary between Alcea and Orchidée, one hundred and fifty feet tall, one hundred and twenty feet wide... and as a monument, it wasn't guarded.

No one in his right mind would climb the Triumphal Arch, but a mage... A mage might use a forbidden illusion spell for invisibility, then an aeromancy spell to ascend to the top. And from there, a perfect line of sight extended to the hill in Alcea.

Her eyes closed, she smiled. The sun high in the sky, the Joyeuse Entrée would proceed up the hill, and when the king crested—

A perfect line of sight.

A shot.

There'd be one chance and one chance only, but with the right equipment and adequate preparation, the odds of success were good. And she had the right equipment buried just outside Courdeval.

She grinned.

The king would never see it coming.

LEIGH KEPT HIS ATTENTION AHEAD. The Kingsroad had been unusually clear, even for this time of year. At least it wasn't as boring as the arcanir prison. Ambassador though he was, he needed to ensure as much of the party as possible—and their cargo—made it to Vervewood. Promise of aid wouldn't mean much if the necessary resources didn't make it there.

The Emaurrian humanitarian aid carts slowed the caravan to a crawl. His gray courser gave a bored sniff, his ears uneven, one pointing to the front and one to the back as he plodded along. The light-elven host had traveled to Courdeval on foot, but the king had seen fit to provide them with mounts to hasten their return. Altogether, they numbered about fifty, as paladins, clerks, and linguists also accompanied him and the group of twenty light-elves.

He shuddered to think how much longer a larger group would have taken to travel. The Frimair frost made the conditions just a touch more bearable than the Trèstellan dungeon. A harsh wind blew by, and he puffed the fur of his hood from his lips.

Ambriel Sunheart glanced in his direction from atop his horse, golden eyes inquisitive. Tight-lipped, Ambriel had hardly spoken a word since they'd left Courdeval, but with his flawless skin, chiseled features, fair hair, and hardened expression, speaking was entirely optional. Perhaps even unnecessary.

He could scarcely keep the smile to himself.

When they reached the Western Road, the Old One that had

always stood watch, the figure of a legendary wyvern, was remarkably gone. If the world was to be believed, it had come to life and simply stalked away. The statue had always marked two days' ride to the capital. He took a deep breath, his lungs tingling at the cold air.

"Are you all right, Ambassador?" Ambriel Sunheart asked in Old Emaurrian.

The tight-lipped captain had spoken. Leigh glanced up, but the heavens hadn't parted. He followed his curiosity and turned to the elf. Ambriel watched him, unwavering.

"This is not my first winter, Captain." Explaining the missing statue would have been too lengthy anyway. When the elf nodded and looked him over, Leigh asked, "I'm not the first of my kind you've seen, am I?"

The day they'd met, the captain's gaze hadn't flickered at his whitened hair or eyebrows, the product of his encounter with wild magic.

"Islanders, Ambassador?" The captain dropped his gaze and looked out at the barren, frozen landscape. The wind whistled its presence.

Leigh snorted a breath. The Kamerish half of his ancestry had given him the almond-shaped eyes that distinguished him from Emaurrians, but that hadn't been his implication. The captain continued to watch him, not with the spark of curiosity, but with serenity of knowledge.

Leigh smiled. "You know what I mean."

"Prophet," Ambriel said. His gaze roved over Leigh's brow and up to his hairline. "In my time, your kind were most of the mages. Before your kind, humans weren't born with magic but some with the capacity to attain it."

Perhaps one in a hundred people who tried to obtain wild magic came away successful. How many had died in the captain's day?

And... "How did they become born into it?"

Ambriel exhaled a lengthy breath. "Dragons."

Stunned, Leigh kept his reaction from his face. Dragons?

"Dragons were the first shifters of shape among the Immortals. It is said they were born of the Mother's veins, anima made flesh. They could work magic of all kinds. They *were* magic. Some took human form. Some never changed back. Some forgot. And over time, their power weakened until their children became human, and only a touch more."

All mages descended from dragons?

Ludicrous.

Impossible... wasn't it?

Leigh eyed him. If the captain felt talkative, then Leigh would not miss the opportunity to glean useful information, ridiculous tales notwithstanding. "There are no mages among your kind?"

"No."

*No.* Just plain, simple, *no.* He hesitated, then asked the question on his eager tongue. "And you feel confident in sharing this information?"

Ambriel laughed, something Leigh had not yet seen. The captain's smile dazzled with its earnest amusement. "We are allies, are we not?" the captain asked. "You are coming to our land, Ambassador, where you will see much. Why hide anything from you now?"

Of course, if later they didn't like what he knew, they could always try to kill him.

He sighed and mustered his most pleasant smile. "A wonderful attitude, Captain." He glanced down at the rapier and dagger sheathed at the captain's side.

Ambriel faced forward once more, his self-assured profile against the immaculate countryside.

Just how many humans had the Vervewood light-elves taken to the blade? And how many of them had been *prophets?* Without knowing the light-elves' capabilities, he couldn't evaluate his own considerable power against theirs.

Well, now he'd have an even better reason to learn all he could about them. Fending off a shiver, he caught the beat of clopping hooves behind him. He'd never been so relieved to have a squad of paladins around. Even if all they could do was delay the inevitable.

The rest of the day dragged until they made camp near the forest's edge at dusk, in the shadow of some old ruins Ambriel called *Flumentur*, which roughly translated to "Riverwatch." Who had once held Riverwatch, he didn't say. Leigh had passed by the ruins many times and given them no thought, much less considered them a part of a watchtower. The foundation was large, perhaps two hundred feet in diameter, its tallest section no more than twenty feet high, with many parts absent or no more than three feet tall. A ruined stair, its steps thrice as wide and long as any in an Emaurrian watchtower, went nowhere, four feet high.

Riverwatch's stone had graced the fences of nearby farms. How many generations of Emaurrian farmers had scavenged it? How tall had it been? It hadn't mattered... Not until myth and legend had skipped right into reality. The notion of some massive creatures stomping about somewhere was worth the passing thought.

He took notes in his journal at the fire while some of the Emaurrian host tried to pantomime to the light-elves how to prepare the food sent from Courdeval, to replicate their work.

It would be simpler for him to translate. But he shrugged and retired to his tent.

Sir Marin—one of his paladin guards, a massive man even *more* massive in arcanir plate—came in to check on him, then left.

In his bedroll, Leigh lay awake as the night matured. What about the wards?

Right. There were none. He sighed.

Not that he needed wards, but they'd become routine. How he missed having an apprentice to do the menial things.

He rolled to his side. Rielle was still missing. That's where he should be—on her trail, if there was one. But he'd always been more of a catapult than a hound; once he had a direction, victory was assured. Chasing leads, well, perhaps Jon was right... That rabid hound of a Marcel might be worth something.

Regardless, Olivia had assured him she was on top of it, and he didn't doubt it. Olivia, no matter how she looked at the new king—just what was it about the man that his apprentices so fancied?—didn't have a malicious bone in her body.

Although—he wiggled his aching toes—when she'd healed him, she'd assured him his toes would feel like they used to, before the torture. *A bit of an oversell, Olivia.*

And the werewolf... The fervor with which he'd tortured proved his determination to find Rielle. But just what did a monster like that truly want with her?

A commotion sounded from outside the tent. Branches breaking. Stone crumbling. Voices calling.

He sprang to his feet. He tore out of the tent, ignoring the stabbing chill of the night wind. Small fires littered the camp, burning with no kindling.

Arrows loosed. A roar. Screams.

He followed the sounds, whispering an incantation. His candlelight spell flew toward the noise.

He stepped over a tower shield, abandoned on the ground, and looked ahead.

The slit pupil of a large, marbled yellow eye fixed on the candlelight spell and constricted. The juniper-green scales of its triangular reptilian head flashed against the silvery glow.

The winged creature opened its maw and spat.

A twitch of his finger, and the tower shield flew before him, catching the liquid. It ignited.

Containment. He needed to contain the creature—the wyvern.

With his fingertips, he rooted his magic in the trees at the fringe of the camp and at the wyvern's center.

He threw aside the shield and, as he made a fist, pulled the trees to the center.

The wyvern flapped its membranous wings, sending tents, men, and all else flying, but the trees converged on its location. Thunderous cracking muffled an ear-piercing screech and shook the ground.

Splinters and shards shot clear. He animated the stones littering the ground of the Riverwatch, pulling them free to orbit the crushing wood.

A dark liquid seeped from the wooden mass as it compacted. Blood.

Taking no chances, he pulled the stones in, pulverizing the mass and the wyvern inside, the crunch shaking through his body.

When it would compact no more, he let it drop with a booming thud.

Silence blanketed the camp, only the hum of the river Mel breaking its cover. Archers and swordsmen, human and elf alike, stood still, in varying states of dress, some gasping and murmuring about destroyed trees.

He looked over the shocked faces, pausing only when he alighted upon Ambriel Sunheart. Barefoot in the snow, he wore only pants, the wyvern's violet blood spattered on his sculpted, alabaster-white body and coating his rapier. The wind stirred his long, fair hair, but he didn't move. He just stared, appearing like one of the ancient heroes carved of white stone, perfect, chiseled, sculpted by the hand of some god of war or beauty.

In his golden eyes, the look was unmistakable. Leigh had seen it countless times.

"As you were." Leigh pursed his lips, turned, and headed back to his tent. He let himself think of the intensity in the elven captain's gaze.

Ambriel Sunheart wasn't the first to be seduced by his power, and he certainly wouldn't be the last.

# CHAPTER 15

*J*on looked out across the twilit horizon.

They came from the mountains. Rippling from the Marcellan Peaks, they descended in quakes, swaying the snow-capped flame-yellow larches high up and then the white fir spires, an eerie mist of fleeing birds and hushed air rising. The crepuscular rays of the dying sun illumed the disturbed canopy.

Deafening voices, deep like the giant blowing horns of the monasteries and primal like collapsing earth, called from afar. It wouldn't be long now.

"Your Majesty, I must advise you against this course." Pons peeked over the rammed-earth wall with him, across the river Brise-Lames. More like a trickle, at least in the winter. Since they'd blown out the bridge, the thirty-foot-wide, fifteen-foot-deep river channel offered the only barrier, albeit inadequate.

Brazen crows circled the clearing beyond the far bank.

"Duly noted." Jon ducked behind the wall once more and shivered. The wind presaged the quickly approaching winter cold with increasing boldness.

All along the wall, paladins said their prayers and made their offerings, a few priests giving blessings among them.

"The last of the Faralles volunteering for a suicide mission." Pons grumbled a few curses under his breath and rolled his eyes.

The last... Among the catastrophes bursting at all corners of the kingdom, the Grands—Derric especially—had been most relentless with this one cause.

Jon reached for his belt pouch, the familiar crumple of paper setting his mind at ease. It was still there, the last note he had received from Brennan. *The ship was bound for Harifa. Setting sail today.* "I won't be the last."

Pons eyed him narrowly, and he didn't need to say anything. A few choice words from Derric came to mind: something about twenty-six-year-old unmarried and childless kings being liabilities for a kingdom.

But the kingdom had other—greater—liabilities, the resolution of which afforded the tangential benefit of sparing a man from wasting away in uselessness and frustration.

"You're not the only one to call it a 'suicide mission,' " he whispered to Pons. One hundred and forty-eight had died before he'd sent forces to handle the mangeurs. And both squads of paladins and three squads of Emaurrian soldiers had died on the field—eighty men and women—along with sixty-four more civilians and Bisclavret's seventy-one men. All told, the death toll had risen to three hundred and sixty-three people.

And he couldn't justify sending even one more person into battle unless he himself assumed the risk as well. "But for our strategy to work, our forces must have faith in it and see that their king does, too. And the best way to show my faith is by fighting alongside them."

"Wise, Your Majesty," Perrault said. He'd sat still and contemplative on the other side of Pons and the Divinity geomancer Olivia had contracted. Forty-eight-year-old Paladin Captain Sir Albain Perrault had been known for his settled stomach before battle; Jon hadn't seen his composure abandon him yet.

Perrault continued. "But defending the innocent is a paladin's duty whether a king commands it or not. Our place is here. Yet you are of the Order no longer. A king's duty lies with the entire realm."

A man who hadn't served under Perrault for several campaigns might have misunderstood his statement for a barb, but it was an extenuation. The captain gave him the opportunity to quit the field with the semblance of honor.

"I am a paladin no longer, captain. You have the right of it." He met Perrault's gaze squarely. "Yet discharge from the Order doesn't discharge a lifetime of its training. The Emaurrian throne will never crumble for want of a king, yet for want of a single sword, this village might."

Here, just beyond Espoire, he, a company of paladins, two mages, and a squad of Emaurrian soldiers with four ballistae were all that stood between the mangeurs and their prey.

Perrault inclined his head, a gleam—of pride?—in his brown eyes, and said no more.

Sitting between him and Pons, the young geomancer the Tower had sent quivered with pre-battle jitters. She was a master at no more than twenty years of age, her brassy waves of hair pulled back into a tight knot, a brush stroke of freckles across her nose. Her partner, a healer, had remained behind at the castle infirmary when they'd left. She, along with Pons, comprised the entirety of their mage component here. The measure of her confidence would determine the shape of day's end.

Under his evaluation, she brought her trembling hands together. Familiar. His own skin had hardly contained him before his first major battle.

He nodded at her joined hands. "Have faith."

She glanced up at him and mustered a watery smile. "Thank you, Your Majesty. It's mostly the cold."

He tried to offer her what he hoped was an encouraging smile. "What is your name?"

"Ella Vannier." An ephemeral grin flashed on her face. " 'Ella Basket-Weaver.' Not fit for a mage, is it?"

He'd carried the name *Jonathan Ver,* fit for a common-born bastard, for his entire life until a couple months ago. And yet, with those he'd helped, it had carried disparate weight. "It is not your name that makes you. It is you who make your name. This land will know you for your deeds."

A spark lit her eyes. "I'll give them something to talk about."

The ground shook, debris crumbling into the river channel below. The line of soldiers stiffened. Murmurs wound from end to end.

The tremors intensified. Their enemy neared.

He gave a grim nod to Perrault, who signaled to his officers. Ripples rumbled through the hardness of the winter ground, and a chill crept from across the Brise-Lames. Puffs of white fog misted the air before him. His breath. He squeezed Faithkeeper's hilt.

Primal voices thundered nearby, the sound rattling his bones, reverberating in his chest. He eyed the line along the wall, lingering on an Emaurrian soldier raising a hand mirror. He didn't have an angle on the intended target, but the mirror reflected a corner of her stark-white horror.

Cold slithered in, colder than the winter air had any right to be, misting the crisp air with a macabre opacity.

He squeezed his eyes shut. *Holy Mother, guide my hand... for the faithful, the faith, and the land.* He looked past Pons to Ella, who prayed to her own god and then fixed her eyes upon him.

A quake ripped up from the river, water thrashing with it. The mangeurs.

She stiffened, spine rigid, hands out.

"Not yet," he whispered to her.

Another, the aftershock shaking the wall and everyone behind it. Murmurs rose from the line. Beside him, Ella shuddered and bit her lip.

Heavy thuds came from the Brise-Lames riverbed. And the scraping and scrambling of rocks from the river channel cliff wall. The east bank. Their side.

He closed the visor on his helm and gripped Faithkeeper, every muscle aligned to readiness.

Flinty eyes bored into his, awaiting sanction.

The bank crumbled, near enough to smell the fresh earth.

"Now!" he called to his forces.

Ella sprang into action, covered by paladin heavy crossbowmen.

He stole a look over the wall.

Shaggy white hair—almost a glacial blue—topped snow-white faces, eerily human but for crazed crystalline eyes. An air of cold radiated from their frosty skin, the only covering of the twenty-foot mangeurs.

Two dozen occupied the field of battle—half in the river channel, heads and shoulders peaking over as they attempted to climb, and half still on the farther west bank.

Her hands aglow in ghostly green despite her lined face, Ella gestured along the west bank and pulled in.

The cliff wall crumbled at her motion. Rock and soil tumbled into the river channel, engulfing the mangeurs, burying them deeper and deeper.

Pons pressed his glowing hands together, packed the loose earth tight with force magic. Walkable, but it eliminated their buffer zone.

Yet it left the buried mangeurs' heads and necks vulnerable to attack.

How long would it—

Emaurrian soldiers fired ballistae high at the upright mangeurs approaching from the other side of Brise-Lames. Three hits, one down. A shoulder.

The mangeurs closed in.

"Attack!" He jumped the wall, leading the paladins, drawing Faith-keeper with an eager flourish as they charged the trapped mangeurs in the channel. They swarmed the Immortals, plunging long swords into eyes, ears, and skulls.

He ran a giant eye through, translucent fluid bursting forth to coat him. Ichor. It chilled like the coldest night of the year, an inescapable grasp. *Lend me your fire, Rielle.*

Shuddering, he yanked Faithkeeper free, hard, and rolled away as a ballista bolt flew up and over him and his brothers-in-arms to hit a mangeur square in the chest.

Another frost giant swept its arms across the ground, knocking away men like playthings. She seized a paladin and curled a fist. A scream. A crunch. Crimson spray.

She held the crushed body above her mouth and lapped at the oozing blood.

Pons still held the river channel. Jon scanned its length—the heads still *moved*. The mangeurs in it weren't dead. Ella spelled stone and earth into their eager, chomping mouths.

Paladins with great-axes moved in, hacking at giant necks.

Perrault called the advance, barking orders. Picking his route with care, Jon moved, cutting the air with Faithkeeper, shaking off the ichor.

Booming voices, arcanir squelching into flesh, and agonized screams fed the chaos of battle. Massive hands grabbed for paladins.

He buried his blade in a gigantic heel cord and then jerked it free. Icy blood spurted.

A swipe from the target—the female mangeur—

All instinct, he dodged. A bearded frost giant grabbed for him, and he juked. He found his footing amid his fallen brothers. A squad assaulted the bearded mangeur in a storm of flashing blades and armor, commands and shrieks competing for air.

Two ballista bolts flew past the female mangeur. But she dropped, lop-sided, quickly descending into a pit swallowing one large leg.

Ella's geomancy.

As the female attempted to pull free, great-axes hacked at her arm. He closed the distance, drawing his dagger, and then vaulted over two fallen brothers and onto the mangeur. He buried a dagger for a hold in her hip, then Faithkeeper, and tore her gut open. Liquid frost covered his armor and shot through his helm's visor to spatter and freeze upon his face.

He yanked Faithkeeper and his dagger free and cleared the mangeur as a large steel net descended over her and closed, constricted by Pons' magic.

She grasped at her gut, held in what spilled out as the shrinking net pressed her to pieces. Eerie eyes pierced him.

His gaze caught on the crystal iris of the massive eye beneath the net, shimmering like ice in the dying light. It faded to darkness, and the night-black pupil tethered him, dragging him into its inky depths, a nightmare world of shrieking wind and spikes of thorny grass, phantoms in uncanny shapes haunting a witching circle. A shadow realm. He stepped into a pool of darkness and quickly receded, an unstoppable ripple the ephemeral harbinger before his own image, a shrouded reflection with skin that turned to grotesque scales, grinning with too many teeth, too pointed, and it opened its maw to a forked tongue. The depths of its stygian eyes lengthened to an eternal void, summoned him in a chilling voice that echoed. His own.

Moans and cries broke through the shouts and clash of fighting, and he blinked, gasping, struggling for air, and looked about the field—no monster, no pool of darkness, no shadow realm. His gaze snapped back to the mangeur's eye. Dead. Clouded. The netted mangeur lay dead.

A fragile quiet settled, joined by the stench of blood, viscera, and frost. With a shudder, he removed his helm, blinking through the cold burn of ichor. Perhaps only a few seconds had passed. He shook off the malaise and studied the field.

The mangeurs lay broken, disemboweled, dead. But of the company of paladins, less than half remained standing. Maybe a hundred. Most had fallen. A few clung to life and would, Terra willing, survive.

Priests rushed the field with Pons and Ella on their heels to tend the wounded. An arcanir-clad arm reached out from under a dead mangeur's shaggy head. Trapped. Jon sprang forward and braced the massive skull. The trapped man didn't have long.

"Sodalis!" Jon bellowed to a passing paladin, who stopped and rushed to help. Soon, a squad had gathered to extricate their brother, and slowly, painstakingly, they freed him.

Perrault approached with a grim stride. "Your Majesty, would you come with me?"

The gravity etched into Perrault's face gave him pause. He nodded, and with a reassuring clap on the shoulder of his nearest brother, he left to accompany Perrault toward the wall.

The chaos of the battlefield gave way to purposeful calls and sparse bursts of activity. Great-axemen cut great throats, a macabre thing. His people ministered to their dead with tender ritual. Too many had fallen. Too many had died to his ignorance.

They had known little about their enemies. Had planned too little. But faced with the decimation of all the villages east of the Brise-Lames —the loss of civilians, territory, supplies for the coming winter, and esteem, both at home and abroad—the decision had already been made. And endorsed with his knowing seal. The limb cut to save the life.

Soldiers and paladins arranged a makeshift infirmary, and Perrault led him through the hive of activity directly to a soldier held down by two paladins with a priest nearby. Her frantic eyes darted toward her arm, a belt gnashed between her teeth. A steel short sword glowed a molten red in the nearby fire.

One of the paladins held a bonesaw to her arm, flesh that darkened from gray to black and spread like a pestilence from her elbow both up and down her arm. She fixed her fevered gaze on him, horror humming in dilated pupils.

"Terra have mercy," he breathed, taking a knee and offering his hand to her. "Goddess save you."

She gripped it tight, shrieking through the leather as metal sundered flesh.

"Ichor." Perrault knelt next to him, lines chiseling his face as the teeth of the saw gritted against bone. "Magic was of no use to her."

Her grip tightened along with her squeezed-shut eyes—then as one of the paladins brought the molten-red blade to where her arm had been, she faded. A lanky paladin archer rushed in to take the bonesaw and hurried away.

This soldier would not be the only one losing a limb today.

He tensed his fingers around the soldier's and, receiving no response, leaned in close to her nose, stone-still until her warm breath confirmed her life on his ear. A priest knelt nearby to inspect the work.

"She will live, Your Majesty," the priest offered, with an inclination of his head.

"Terra have mercy." He stared at her face, coated in damp torment. It was his knowing seal that had brought her here. That had cost her an arm. And so many others.

And how cavalierly he'd disregarded the Earthbinding and a political marriage, which might have spared some of the lives lost today. His armies would not be enough. Paladins would not be enough. Immortal hunting squads would not be enough.

"Your Majesty," Perrault began softly, "the ichor..."

The ichor. The ichor that grayed flesh. The ichor that had spattered him.

He raised wary fingers to his face. Nothing. If it had spared him...

"It hasn't affected the paladins."

Perrault sighed and looked out at the field.

So many lay dead—most of them paladins—but the wounded facing amputation were soldiers.

"The sigils," Jon whispered under his breath. Their sigils against magic—against elemental magic—had protected them.

Perrault nodded.

Paladins would be needed now more than ever; there wasn't nearly enough recondite to sigil the entire army. But against an invasion of monsters, demons, creatures of myth and legend, paladins alone, in their current number, could not hold the line.

Emaurria—and its people—needed every possible advantage.

*Composure.* He rose, mind whirling. But now was not the time for theory and conjecture. He needed to get the men and women who had fought so bravely here to safety and medical care, to the castle at Bisclavret. He needed to reassure them, the people of this march, and everyone else, that this victory was the first of many to beat back the Immortals threat.

And then he would think on how to stop the unstoppable.

Across the field, brassy silken waves fought free of a tight knot. Ella Vannier rose from her ministrations to a soldier, her worried gaze catching his. Jon grasped at the Laurentine signet ring hanging from a cord around his neck.

A shadow darkened the battlefield.

Overhead in the distant sky, a massive winged creature soared toward the Marcellan Peaks with a deafening roar. A dragon. From maw to tail, it was the size of a village. A town. Against the evening sky, it was a massive shadow, dark as death and unfathomable. Not a single person moved until it had disappeared far from sight.

Perrault scrutinized him. "Your Majesty?"

Jon collected himself quickly. "A squad to carefully collect samples for the Archmage, draw sketches, write accounts, take trophies for our return, then burn the rest of the remains. To the castle, Captain. And then home to plan our next steps."

Composure. Perhaps if he repeated it to himself enough, it would appear.

No. It wouldn't. Not until the kingdom had a fighting chance. He'd fought battles for the past decade, seen enemies capable of destroying a land, but never anything like this. Never giants, dragons, arcane powers... If this was even a fraction of what the kingdom would face, conventional means of warfare were hopeless without... something more.

His spirits fell. But in the face of frost giants, huge losses, and drag-ons, conventional warfare wouldn't hold the line. As much as he hated the thought, it was time to acknowledge the necessities. As a paladin, it would have been unthinkable, but he was a king now.

The Earthbinding.

# CHAPTER 16

*R*ielle's first week at House Hazael taught her some lessons about her new reality. She had not forgotten the Sileni woman's attempted escape. Vittoria, Samara had called her. After a night in the barracks, Vittoria had died, before a single lash could even mar her skin. Rielle swallowed. *Divine keep you, sister.*

Since her arrival, Rielle had watched, listened, and learned. All the new slaves were trained in entertainment and hospitality, observing and learning from the pleasure slaves and the support staff dealing with guests. She'd never use the skills—being a scribe—but it was the perfect time to gather information. As always, success depended on the possession of information in greater amount and usefulness than that of the enemy. Courdeval had reinforced that lesson.

The Hazael family itself numbered just under sixty here. Just over two hundred slaves farmed its land, staffed its household, and provided entertainment, relaxation, and pleasure to its affluent clientele. A full-service hospitality business for the rich upper class, House Hazael offered gourmet meals and diversion. A company of guards protected the Hazaels and their guests and kept order.

Escape from House Hazael—at least without a solid plan—was

suicide. She would have to earn trust, collect information, bide her time for the right opportunity. And it began with quietly completing her duties.

A day's work as a scribe proved to be long and tedious, but not as dull as she had imagined. After she finished her work every day, Ihsan left her in the solar, which offered private time with the many tomes on magic. Unlike Emaurria and most countries, Sonbahar had no forbidden magic, and House Hazael's books detailed innumerable mind-magic, necromancy, and sangremancy spells. The hours after she finished her work became quiet study, for as long as she could keep her eyes open.

Working the long hours Ihsan demanded and studying the magical tomes meant staying awake long enough that when she finished, nearly everyone else in House Hazael slept. Including the guards.

Her work involved translating news stories and some treatises— familiar work since her days at the Tower. But as her hand ached for the tenth consecutive hour today, she felt a lot like a delinquent novice forced to copy the introduction to *The Way of the Learned Mage* one hundred times for misbehaving. Leigh had happily and frequently doled out that punishment.

What was he doing now? How did he spend his days? Did he still believe in the conspiracy theory that had cost Emaurria so much?

Her vision focused on the black inkwell before her, and blurred. In the news she'd translated in the early morning hours, there had been encounters with strange and monstrous creatures, with death tolls ranging up to hundreds. Times at home were dark, and the darkness was spreading—reports came from the shores of Kamerai and the Kezan Isles, too.

She'd longed for something more, anything, to alleviate the weight of her heavy heart by even hinting at the safety of Jon, Olivia, Leigh, Gran, Brennan, and all those she loved. The news message, however, had ended abruptly, without a shred of mercy for her longing.

Was Jon coming for her? There was no news about whether he remained in Emaurria or had traveled.

The pain in her hand was bad, but the suffering of wondering was worse. Too much. She returned to her work, to lose herself to its tedium. When her mind wandered, she let it wander to the new spells she'd learned. A way of destabilizing the flame cloak to explode... A sangremancy ward that functioned as a trap... Gestures, incantations, ritual...

After moving her finished stack of materials, she found an untended workstation with piles of papers and several books scattered across its surface. Seeing the stool pulled out in invitation, she sat and began the process of deciphering the unfinished project. She was Ihsan's only scribe, so it fell to her.

Documents in several languages were gathered and grouped together. Had the previous scribe been compiling them into separate volumes in High Nad'i? Several were nearly complete, all in the same consistent hand—a masterwork of healing and medicine.

Peering down at the page of an unfinished book, she examined the thin, sloping script. Not rounded like Ihsan's penmanship. Someone else. What had happened to this person?

"Aina always wrote in a beautiful hand," Ihsan said.

Rielle started. Ihsan had stepped away from the alchemy recipe she had been working on to look over her shoulder at the incomplete healing grimoire. *Should I not have*— The hairs on the back of her neck stood. "I'm sorry, Zahibi. I should have—"

"It's all right, Thahab." Ihsan's voice was quiet, soft. Unperturbed. "Aina was my former scribe. She originally came from Kamerai and became a fast favorite of mine."

Aina... She grazed her fingertips across the dried ink. Aina had sat in this chair before, slaved in this solar before, lived this life.

A life *she* now lived. Simple as that; they were interchangeable, like cogs in a contraption.

"Farrad strangled her."

Rielle's hand froze. "Strangled...?"

Ihsan nodded.

Dead. Aina was dead?

A cog was a cog was a cog. Aina had been replaced. *I could be replaced.* They were just lists of qualifications and sums of araqs given form.

But could Ihsan be believed? Had Farrad killed her?

The day she'd arrived at House Hazael, out there in the courtyard, two truths had been clear: Farrad Hazael killed with ease, and the siblings were feuding.

If he wanted to injure Ihsan indirectly, her favorites would be a means for him to exploit. A way to strike at her without touching her at all.

*And I'm next in line.*

Ihsan had already singled her out, so even if she tried to distance herself or curry favor with Farrad, it was hopeless. She could either try to please Ihsan and earn what minor favor was possible for her to earn, or be utterly defenseless against Farrad.

Perhaps in Ihsan's favor, she would gain access to useful knowledge —knowledge that could save her from Aina's fate and enable her survival. Now more than ever, without her magic, survival depended on knowledge.

Softly closing the book, she looked at its title, which translated to *Healing Spells for the Elderly.* Indeed, its spells had all addressed symptoms that disparately affected older people.

"It's inspired by Grandfather," Ihsan said. "He's been ailing for several years now, and although I have been tending him and have managed to prolong his life, it is all too quickly approaching its end." Ihsan swallowed, her face sagging. "The 'business trip' that Farrad referred to when you arrived was Grandfather getting his affairs in order before…"

The silence prevailed between them.

Ihsan's grandfather was none other than Imtiyaz abd Hassan abd Sayid Hazael, the head of the House. If his death was quickly approaching, Farrad's ascension to head of the household was imminent as well.

Ihsan returned to her alchemy.

Unusual, however, that Ihsan had taken her into confidence. She'd only been here a few days. Had they developed a rapport so quickly?

A slave walked in with tea for Ihsan, and Rielle turned to her work. It wouldn't be finished in one day, but the stack of healing-potion recipes was the smallest. With a little determination, she would be finished translating and copying it in a few hours. So, she opened the potions recipe volume to a fresh page and began her task.

By the time she finished, the sun had long since set, but the stack of potion recipes was gone and its corresponding volume a good deal thicker. She breathed a relieved sigh.

"Take it to Samara, and see yourself to the slave quarters." Ihsan didn't lift her head from her work but slid a key to the edge of her table.

"Yes, Zahibi."

The apothecary would be stocked with the ingredients that the latest recipes called for, and she wouldn't complain about any errand that delayed returning to the slave quarters. Cracking the knuckles of her aching hands, she rose from her seat. She tottered a moment on numb legs, then took the volume and the key.

She found the hallway alight with a halo from the nearby radiant sconce on the wall. Farther down the hallway was another, and another, and another—the entire place lit with soft light. Over the railing in the open indoor courtyard, the fountain babbled the continuous and relaxing sound of water tumbling into a pool.

A passing guard with a star tattooed on his neck gave her a once-over. Eyed her from beneath a burst of black hair. A moment too long.

Averting her gaze, she hurried toward the staircase, but he blocked her path.

She moved to avoid him, but he moved again.

"Why the hurry?" He grinned, flashing a gold tooth.

She backed up. "I apologize, *sayyid*," she said, inclining her head as she retreated and headed toward the other staircase.

But as she approached, another guard walked up to her.

"That's rude, *ahabadah*," he crooned through a smile, and tsked.

Frozen, she gaped at him, towering over her, a blade strapped to his side.

He lightly rested a palm on her arm, making her shudder. "No need to be afraid."

His smile didn't set her at ease. At all.

She shifted the book and key in her hands. "Zahibi Ihsan commanded me to deliver this to the apothecary."

A laugh burbled in his throat. "Plenty of time for that."

"Immediately," she said, a little louder.

His muddy-brown gaze fixed on something over her shoulder, and he stood to attention.

"Stand aside," Ihsan's firm voice echoed from behind her.

Ihsan stood in the doorway, straight and tall as a queen.

Rielle bowed. *Save me, save me, save—*

"My slave is carrying out my business," she declared. "Let her pass, and do not detain her while she's working."

"Yes, Zahibi," the guard replied, saluting before returning to his post.

*While she's working.* What did that mean? That he could "detain" her after work?

"Thahab!" Ihsan barked. "Move!"

She started, then inclined her head. "Yes, Zahibi."

Giving the guard a wide berth, she made her way to the staircase and the apothecary.

She couldn't stop shaking. The guards had eyed her before, sometimes made sounds or comments to one another, but they'd never blocked her path before like that.

Like the overseers at the stable, sometimes they'd come into the slave quarter, often in the middle of the night, and drag away a woman or two. After Vittoria, there was no doubt as to the reason.

But never her. She was Ihsan's scribe—didn't that afford her some protection?

*While she's working.*

She shuddered again.

They'd left her alone her first week, so perhaps she'd remain safe. Maybe they'd lose interest.

Tonight, she'd bed down far in the back, close to a corner, well among the other women. They wouldn't find her among the hundreds.

She reached the door. The key fit right into the lock, and inside, only a single candle in the back of the room offered light. There, behind a table littered with several small jars, a stack of papers, and an open envelope of anise, Samara sat, mixing a potion.

Samara looked up from her work, tossing her thick black braid over her shoulder. She smiled. Her round eyes fixed upon the volume. "The potions book is finally complete?"

She walked it over to Samara. "You know of it?"

"Yes." Samara ran her palm over the cover. "Aina was nearly done with it before... before..."

"Before she was murdered?" She cleared her throat.

Samara crinkled her nose. "Murdered?"

"By Farrad."

Samara shook her head. "*Zahib* Farrad," she corrected. "He said he had no choice but to kill her. She was such a peaceful woman, and Zahib took her as his lover. One night, he said she drew a poisoned blade on him. He had no choice."

Rielle stared at a shelf of herb-filled jars. When Ihsan said *murder* and Samara said *self-defense,* who was she to believe? "Ihsan said..."

"*Zahibi* Ihsan." Samara frowned. "Divine! You must learn, Thahab." She shook her head. "Who were you? In your life before this place?"

Who had she been, really? Once upon a time, she'd been a master mage with the magister's mantle in reach. Then an incompetent fool. Her own perceptions had failed under the crushing weight of betrayal in Courdeval.

"Before I was brought to this land, I was... happy." At the memory of Jon giving her his Sodalis ring, the corners of her mouth turned up. She rubbed her thumb, where the precious gift should have remained.

Samara smiled sadly.

"I was in love," Rielle confessed, closing the lid of a slightly open jar of mugwort. "He was strong, loyal, a man of conviction. Honorable. Good. He daydreamed with me about a home, a family, a life together, and he teased me like it was his job." She half-laughed under her breath. A few jars away, next to the crushed pomegranate seeds, she recognized another herb: queen's lace. It had been nearly three months since she had used it herself, and in a place like this, it had to be in high demand. "But I was also reckless. Reckless enough to end up here."

Her work abandoned, Samara looked at her with wistful, watery eyes, and they made her own eyes water, too. Better to change the subject.

"What about you?"

Samara pulled in a deep breath. "My mother was once the apothecary assistant." She arranged the jars before her absentmindedly. "Zahib Farrad was about fifteen when he came here seeking sen'a, and she was a year younger than I am now when she caught his eye. And then I was born."

Samara was Farrad's daughter?

"Zahib Farrad kept her as a concubine, but she kept me close, teaching me about plants and potions whenever she could steal us away to this place. Last year, Zahib's first wife, Nazira, ordered my mother to accompany her to the marketplace," she said with a sad smile. "When Nazira returned, my mother was not with her. Nazira said she ran away."

"Samara," Rielle breathed, taking a step closer with her hand outstretched, but Samara shook her head and shrugged it off.

"I know my mother didn't run away." She looked up, her wide eyes shedding not a single tear. "I was happy once, too..."

"Farrad's first wife," Rielle whispered. "Is she after you?"

"Zahibi Nazira?" Samara shook her head. "When she returned without my mother, she received thirty lashes for losing Zahib Imtiyaz's property. She may be jealous of me, but she is either unwilling or unable to act against me."

That first day, the warrior-caste duelist dying on the flagstones... Farrad had said the man had asked to purchase Samara. "It is natural for a father to protect his daughter."

"Zahib may have sired me, but I am not his daughter. I am property Zahib will inherit, and nothing more, but he does protect his property." Samara lowered her gaze and drew in a slow breath. "Come. If you are dismissed, let's retire."

Head reeling, Rielle agreed. Samara tidied her workspace, put out the candle, and locked up the apothecary room. Together, they ascended the steps to the third floor and returned the second key to Ihsan's solar.

House Hazael's quiet in the midnight hours never achieved utter stillness; the fountain babbled in a hushed whisper, nocturnal birds called in the trees outside, and the faded workings of the city breezed in past the golden gates. The candle sconces provided soft if sparse light, and indoors, only the rare guard stood or patrolled with purpose. Perhaps they'd already taken someone tonight.

The ambient moonlight filtered in through the tall lattices in the slave quarters, where the house slaves slept, and but for the dim illumination, darkness clad its corners. She made her way to the washbasins with Samara and washed as hastily as she could while making nary a sound.

Past the soft snores, all the sleeping mats in the back corners were full, and they tried their luck around the outer walls, whispering apologies to move past. She settled in for the night with Samara close by and gazed through the lattice at the night sky that lay beyond. Without fail, every evening found her with thoughts of Jon and her loved ones, how they spent their days, whether they were in good health, whether they—

Lived.

It had been months since Shadow had declared her intention to kill Jon. Since there had been no news of his death, he still lived, at least as of several days ago. Perhaps he was aware of Shadow's lethal intentions. Perhaps she'd even been apprehended or killed. Or she could be biding her time for the right opportunity.

*I am powerless to do anything about it.* All she'd learned hadn't prepared her for arcanir bonds and navigating the politics of a slave-holding House in Sonbahar.

She rested her palm on her unsettled belly. Whatever it would take, she would be free of this place and find her way back to Emaurria. To Jon.

"Come to me tomorrow," Samara whispered. "I'll give you some ginger for your nausea."

Rielle turned to her on the mat and smiled. "Thank you," she said softly. "Chamomile usually helps, but..." She twirled a finger at their surroundings. No chamomile for her here.

Samara shook her head, a rustle against cloth. "No, Thahab!" Even hushed, her voice was insistent. "Chamomile isn't safe for your child. Ginger..."

*Child?* The rest of her words faded.

There was no way. No possible—

Well... Not *entirely* impossible, but...

She frowned, rubbing her belly, tracing back to her last moonbleed, but her thoughts stumbled. The last she could remember had been just after Melain. Three months ago?

Three...? Divine, no, it couldn't be. Absolutely could not—

She curled tighter. In the midst of everything since Courdeval, she hadn't had time to consider her absent moonbleeds. She caressed her belly.

Three months. Three months and no moonbleed. Three months since... Jon. Since that passionate eve of battle she'd spent in his arms —and the morning. She hadn't taken her nightly dose of queen's lace that eve, or the night after when Shadow—

Samara was right.

In her heart, she knew it.

A child.

She shook her head, a smile sweeping across her lips. Could it be? Jon's child.

She inhaled quickly, fighting her broadening smile. Divine... A *child.* She hadn't planned on a family so soon, but... she hadn't planned on Jon either. And his love had embraced all the shadows in her life and kissed them into brilliant light.

A soft calm blanketed her.

It would be all right. It was all right.

She spread her fingers over her belly. This child was welcome. A surprise, but a joy. She'd teach her all about magic, the natural world, the invisible things that were everything, and Jon—

She blinked away the wet happiness in her eyes, closed them. His smile, warm, loving, and his open arms, wide enough for her and a family of their own. She opened her eyes. Yes, he'd be happy, too.

A distant whimper—a slave in the far corner.

A slave...

Trapped in House Hazael, her child would be born into the stuff of nightmares. "What am I going to do?"

Soft warmth covered her hand—Samara's comfort. She climbed onto Rielle's sleeping mat and wrapped a consoling arm around her. "You will keep your child safe, stay out of trouble—"

A clink of bottles and laughter interrupted the soft breaths and snoring in the room. Samara froze mid-sentence.

A few women gasped, cried. Squeals and whimpers rolled in from the farthest rows and inward.

A shiver rattled her spine. She poked her head out and peeked past her feet to the rows beyond. Two men swaggered between sleeping mats, rolling women over, grabbing at their faces and breasts, moving on. She squinted in the dark, discerning a burst of black hair covering the face of one and—a star tattooed on his neck.

Guards.

No. No, no, *no*. She curled up closer to Samara and, huddled together, held her gaze. *Pass us over. Pass us over.*

Clumsy footsteps neared, but she didn't look, couldn't. *Pass us over…*

A hand gripped her shoulder and pinned it to the mat. She stared up into the face of the guard she'd seen on the way to Samara. He looked down at her and winked.

Tremors started at her limbs and worked inward until she quaked all over.

"No," she said, shaking her head, but he grabbed her arm.

"This is the one," he said to his friend. "Not working now, is she?" He dragged her up, but Samara locked her arms around Rielle's waist.

The guard yanked her, but Samara wouldn't let go and was dragged along.

Rielle clawed at his arm with her free hand, grappled with his fingers, thrashed in his grip. He whipped around and slapped her.

Her face snapped to the side. On fire with pain. Her jaw radiated—

She twisted and stared at Samara, no words coming even as she begged for something, anything—

"Stop!" Samara shouted, her chest quivering like a rabbit's but her feet planted squarely on the floor. "You must stop this instant, guard!"

Every face in the room awoke and alighted upon Samara. The guard, too, froze in his steps as bidden and faced her, scowling.

"You dare, *ahabadah*?" he bellowed, throwing Rielle aside to advance upon Samara.

"No, please—" Rielle grabbed at his arm, but he shook her off. Divine, Samara was only a girl, only—

Samara raised her chin. "This slave warms Zahib Farrad's bed. You risk Zahib's displeasure with this act."

The guard grabbed Samara's upper arm. "You lie, ahabadah, or else she would be there now."

Samara thrust her chest out and stared him down. "You know who I am, guard. If I lie, Zahib will give me the lash. This slave has the childbearing sickness and was too ill to attend him this eve. I'm treating her myself."

The guard's face tightened, his eyebrows drawing together, but he remained still. At last, he pushed Samara away. "If you lie, you will feel the lash, ahabadah. Keenly."

Her stance rigid, Samara didn't waver. "So be it, guard."

For a moment, all the air was sucked from the room. Not a single breath needled the silence until the guard turned to leave and beckoned for his friend to follow. When their steps faded from the servant quarters, Samara's shoulders slumped.

She backed toward the wall and leaned against it, then raised her wide-eyed gaze to meet Rielle's.

"What have you done, Samara? You will—"

"You and your baby are safe," Samara said, her voice hoarse. "At least for tonight."

Rielle moved to lean next to her and slid down along the wall until she landed on the floor, wrapping her arms around herself. Samara had risked her own safety. Tomorrow, there was no telling what she might face.

But tonight, they were still here together. Safe.

She closed her eyes, and everything escaped—the fear, the shame, the relief. It rolled down her cheeks as she cried into her knees.

Samara knelt beside her, an arm outstretched. "I don't know what will happen tomorrow, but..."

She didn't finish her words, cut off by a sob, and Rielle leaned into her, burying her face in Samara's shoulder. Cautiously, Samara embraced her, and together, they wept.

"You will have to avoid this place tomorrow," Samara whispered. "In the slave quarters, he might... come looking for you."

This is what life would be like at House Hazael? Biding her time as a scribe was entirely different from living in constant fear and, perhaps, torment, until Jon arrived.

And once he did, would she be full with child, attempting an escape? Her months in Sonbahar had been grim, and despite the compassion of Samara's sacrifice, there was now the very real possibility of never getting out.

She would never become a magister, avenge her family, or change anything.

Shadow would never pay for her treachery.

Jon would be assassinated.

And their child would be born a slave.

And by the Divine, what had this merciful girl done? Samara had saved her from the guard tonight, but tomorrow, when the lie came undone, this girl would pay for it in blood.

"Thank you," she said. "I don't deserve your kindness."

"Karak is a hateful man, Thahab. He could have harmed your baby," Samara said, and several women crowded closer. "As much as we can, we protect our own here, especially the children."

Murmurs of agreement wove in from the women around them, their faces sunken but their eyes earnest and unwavering; she hadn't even begun to understand the depths of this life's despair, but these women were unbroken by sheer force of will, by union, by sisterhood.

"Thank you." She nodded, the rawness inside softened by Samara's warmth. These women risked their wellbeing and lives to protect those who needed it most, their strength greater than pain, greater than fear.

Samara gave her a squeeze. "Come."

She pulled Rielle to her feet, and they crawled into Samara's sleeping mat. Cuddling close to Samara, she curled up. It had been a long time since she'd slept in the embrace of a friend, warm and safe.

Starlight still shone through the cage of the lattices, glowing on the floor. She stared through it at the stars, as she did every night, the ghost of Jon's embrace closing around her.

But tonight, she couldn't sleep, not after the night's events. A four-teen-year-old girl couldn't suffer for her sake. Tomorrow, she would have to find a way to spare Samara the lash for her brave intervention, if such a possibility existed. She'd have to talk to Farrad.

She stroked her belly. *And then we find a way to endure until your papa comes for us.*

# CHAPTER 17

*B*rennan sucked in a relieved breath. Twelve days had passed before the port city of Harifa was finally visible from the KPV *Gorgon* in the morning light. It was a cityscape of tall spires, white cylindrical buildings, and brightly colored tents. The bustling docks came into view, where a throng of workers, sailors, merchants, and travelers filled every space. It wasn't long before their scents hit him in a chaotic wall of odor.

Faster would have been better, but the square-rigged Kezani caravel had made good time, considering that many vessels took fifteen days. The voyage, however, had been unbearable, as the *Gorgon,* the only vessel immediately departing Suguz directly for Harifa, was a spice trader's ship. He had spent the entire trip with a headache from the cargo's overpowering aroma.

When he'd asked for directions to the slave market, the captain of the *Gorgon* hadn't hidden his disgust, a rare reaction for a Kezani businessman.

Brennan disembarked and made his way south through the city, squeezing between the endless congestion of people, past the outskirts of the sprawling market to the area populated entirely by a coalition of slavers. They had adapted an old horse breeder's compound of stables and pens into a slave market.

His detour to Suguz had cost him precious weeks during which Rielle had likely suffered. He couldn't fathom what her condition would be now. There were suspicions that he could not bear to acknowledge, could not bring himself to consider... suspicions for which, if she had indeed suffered, he would never forgive himself.

If he didn't find her here, there was no telling where she could have been taken, nor under what circumstances.

Yet a voice of hope whispered delusions of blind optimism and would not be silenced: What if she had freed herself? What if she was here? What if today they were reunited?

People eyed him warily; his feet had sped him to a run. The Wolf's doing.

The slavers would never deal with him if he showed up panicked and desperate. As he neared the compound, he focused on slowing to a walk and gathered his composure until his breath was slow and steady before he finally entered.

The main office was the closest tent to the market—and with good reason: the slave compound stretched on as far as the eye could see, and business was better when it was convenient to potential customers. Inside, only one hawk-faced slave trader was present when he had expected a group and, at the very least, guards. The slave trade in Harifa must have been safe indeed, if such bold conditions were common.

"*Marbahen,*" the merchant greeted in Harifa's dialect of Standard Nad'i.

His years of visiting Xir as a boy were already serving him well—he understood most dialects of Nad'i, and the High Nad'i that Father had insisted upon Kehani and his tutors teaching him was understood by all but the simplest of commoners in Sonbahar, even if it was spoken only by the elites.

"*Sabeh al qir,*" he replied, bidding the merchant good morning in High Nad'i. Choosing his words carefully, he told the merchant that he wanted to buy a slave, an attractive woman with golden hair from the North, and asked whether the merchant had any.

The merchant replied in the negative, that he didn't have any, and that the last one had been sold about a week ago.

Sold.

Brennan drew in a deep breath and held it. The Wolf raged.

*Not yet.*

He knew exactly how to proceed—naturally, bribery—if he could only master his baser instincts.

"That's a shame," Brennan replied casually. "I heard that this market had the best selection. My father vacations in Xir at around this time every year, and I had hoped to have his favorite kind of woman waiting for him," he explained, sparing the merchant a crestfallen glance. "Do you recall who purchased the last one?" He reached for his coin purse just as the merchant was about to shake his head. "I am prepared to pay whoever bought the slave double her market value, and I'd be very grateful for your assistance." He tipped the purse and poured out several golden Sonbaharan araqs onto the table.

The merchant's eyes fixed upon the coins, and as another araq dropped onto the pile, he opened his mouth. "I believe there were a few pleasure houses from Xir that purchased several women, a fair-haired one among them," the merchant said, his gaze never leaving the small mound of gold.

Pleasure houses.

He clenched his teeth, feeling the Change starting in his hands and mouth, waiting on the merchant's further words. Far away, he heard the voices of three men chatting, the breeze, and the din of the market's shoppers and merchants.

"House Afzal, House Fakhri, and House Hazael, I think," the merchant added, bemused.

*Afzal, Fakhri, Hazael.*

*Afzal, Fakhri, Hazael.*

*Afzal, Fakhri, Hazael.*

Again and again and again until he was certain he would remember those names for the rest of his days. The Wolf snarled, louder, closer to the surface, anxious, hungry.

Finally, exposing his teeth in a wide smile, he leaned in.

"Allow me to express my gratitude."

He grabbed the man's face, covered his mouth, and twisted his head from his body, relishing the red spray of the motion with an exhalation.

His nostrils flared to breathe in the thick smell of blood.

He dropped the head. It bounced off the corpse and rolled across the ground in the tent. His eyes followed its path, then fixated upon the body.

The raw abundant flesh and seeping fresh blood.

Primal urges spooled within him. His control wavered. His mouth watered. The Wolf's snout battled to emerge, his teeth turning sharp and lupine. He crouched over the body before he even realized it, his face hovering just above the pool of blood.

He longed to lose himself in it.

He covered his mouth with his clawed hands. The Wolf craved—

He gagged. Each day was worse than the one before. His control was at its limit. Even knowing that, he could barely hold back.

*Rielle,* he reminded the Wolf and himself, a desperate plea. *Rielle.* She was one thing they agreed on. The one thing they both needed.

With all his might, he drew away from the body until he stood at his full height once more, inhaling deeply, still eager to breathe in the smell of a fresh kill.

But he took a step back.

And then another.

And another.

The Wolf had begun to recede, and as soon as it did, he exited the tent, more determined than ever to find Rielle... and with her, his sanity.

# CHAPTER 18

Jon gazed toward the horizon as they took the eastern route back to the Kingsroad. The Nivos snows coated the fields and hills that rolled far beyond his line of sight and faded into the steel blue of the afternoon sky. The white-dusted red peak of a small monastery reached high up in the distance, nestled among the snow-covered thatched roofs, smoking chimneys, and sandy clay walls of a tiny village.

If they hadn't routed the mangeurs before Espoire, what would have happened to this settlement?

He combed his gloved fingers through his white destrier's immaculate mane. The mangeurs were but one of the Immortal threats, and the cost to defeat them had been enormous. He'd left Courdeval with two hundred and seventy men and women, and he was returning with one hundred and two, a mere fraction. Even before the battle, three hundred and sixty-three lives had already been lost.

And now, after the battle, the number had climbed to five hundred and thirty-one.

Five hundred and thirty-one who would never see the afternoon sky again.

The crisp wintry air chilled as he inhaled deeply. The battle was over, but the war was far from won.

The viscounty of Costechelle faced a harpy invasion. Aestrie reported spirits wielding ice magic. Loud, eerie howls had converged around Maerleth Tainn. Villages went dark. People disappeared from the roads.

The ranks of the Emaurrian military were depleted, and if the county of Bisclavret was any indication, so were local knights and soldiers. The Order tried to maintain stability, but paladin numbers were dwindling—and considering losses, recruitment suffered. And the Emaurrian Tower of Magic wouldn't intervene but for payment.

Clouds rolled across the steel-blue sky.

He needed to bolster the Crown—strengthen the military, not just with numbers but with diversity, skills and abilities of all kinds. Mages. Paladins.

What if mages, regardless of their religion or affiliation with the Divinity, could swear fealty to the Crown, work for a commission? What if paladins didn't have to swear the Sacred Vows? What if women were welcome among their ranks?

What if mages and paladins could work side by side?

But the Order maintained stability, and the Tower was a dangerous threat if provoked. He couldn't afford to risk either. Not now. He would have to bargain from a position of power. Power that the Earthbinding would afford him. If it worked, he'd be one with the land. When he finally began testing the waters with the Proctor about integrating the Tower into the Crown, any threat from the Divinity might be mitigated by Earthbound abilities.

And if he won over the Tower, he could bargain with the Order from an even stronger position.

All of it relied on the Earthbinding, blasphemy and infidelity. If he became one with the land, his inner state—if his will was strong—would be reflected in the land. If he were happy, at peace, Emaurria would prosper.

Happy...

There was only one thing in this world that would truly make him happy. Rielle.

He stiffened. Derric had tried to dissuade him from pursuing marriage to her, but if she were with him, he'd be happy. And if he were Earthbound, his happiness would mean Emaurria's prosperity.

He smiled. The Earthbinding wouldn't just be for Emaurria's sake. There was no way Derric, the rest of the Grands, Parliament, or the Houses could stand in the way of their marriage. Not if it directly translated to the land's benefit.

Where marriage was concerned, this was his best chance at a political checkmate. If he became Earthbound, he could ask for her hand, with the Grands, Parliament, and the Houses inevitably agreeing, not just for his sake, but for that of the land.

Whether she'd accept his proposal, on the other hand...

He held a breath and exhaled lengthily. The Earthbinding... He didn't want anyone else. Ever.

And when she returned, when she learned of it, it would hurt her. The very last thing he'd ever want to do. He sighed. Was coupling with one stranger too high a price for marriage to one's beloved? Would it frustrate the purpose entirely?

And if Rielle had made that choice? If their places were exchanged?

Pain radiated from his jaw. His hands numbed. He lowered his gaze to the reins, gripped in the vise of his fists. If Rielle were in his place, doing what he was about to do... It would hurt. It would cut to the bone. He popped his jaw and relaxed his hands. But he wouldn't ignore the greater good nor punish her for choosing it.

Would she do the same?

It couldn't matter anymore. The world had broadened far beyond the small circle he shared with Rielle. Although he'd vehemently objected to the Earthbinding for months, when faced with threats like the mangeurs, he couldn't any longer. Not in good conscience. If Pons and Olivia agreed it would work, and that it would help his people, save lives that conventional means couldn't, then the decision was made.

It would be a ritual, nothing more. No emotion, no love, no relationship. Only his body borrowed for the kingdom's sake.

"What's on your mind, Your Majesty?" Pons' voice.

Jon eyed the discolored snows of the road. "The Earthbinding."

Pons nodded, looking out at the horizon. "Have you changed your mind about it?"

"I've had to." Jon swallowed. "When we return to Courdeval, would you see to the preparations?"

A sharp intake of breath. Barely noticeable. "Yes, Your Majesty."

Hooves crunched the snow into submission. Pons would prepare for the ritual. It was going to happen.

A stiffness settled in Jon's neck. As a mage, Rielle would see the necessity of this. And he'd spend the rest of his life making it up to her, if she let him. "How well do you know Rielle?"

Pons lowered his gaze and smiled. "Better than she thinks."

"Really? It seemed, when we first met, you weren't fond of her."

"Did it? Let me tell you a story." Pons cleared his throat. "Before I had my éveil, Derric and I were very... close. My parents wanted to separate us, marry me to the neighboring farmer's daughter, which was problematic for a multitude of reasons. We argued, and... I had my éveil. I didn't mean to, but I hurt them... And they disowned me."

Some families, especially those who followed some sects of the Terran faith, shunned magic. He himself hadn't trusted it much before Rielle. "I'm sorry."

"They were too small hearted to accept me as I was, Your Majesty. I found my true family among the mages." He smiled sadly. "When I went to the Tower and Derric to the Order, I eventually became infatuated with my master. And, despite what you see now, I was once rather comely." He winked.

Jon laughed under his breath. "I don't doubt it." Pons' deep laugh lines meant he'd been jovial as a young man. Happy people drew others in easily.

"My master and I fell in love. I never asked, but he wrote me favorable reports, requests for commendations, and the like. And when we were discovered, I was the reason for the rule applied to Leigh and Rielle."

Jon raised his eyebrows. "What did the Divinity do about you and your master?"

He sighed. "The Grand Divinus wanted to move me to Magehold, to separate us, but all my friends were here, in Emaurria. My master went to Magehold in my stead. He became a magister and served in the Magisterium until he died, about twenty years ago."

"I'm sorry."

Pons shrugged. "He loved me. And he sacrificed for me. There could be no insinuation of favoritism or corruption." He took a deep breath. "When Rielle came to the Tower, she had gone through... a traumatic éveil... but she took to her innate magic easily, natural as breath. But like me, she struggled with battle fury, and like me, she'd been parted from her first love. Only hers was..." He shook his head. "I sympathized with her. But after she faced some disciplinary action from Magehold, for her sake I couldn't afford even the appearance of partiality. Because her achievements were suspect, to legitimately earn her place, she would have to work twice as hard, against adversity, difficulty, to deflect any accusation of nepotism. Her place earned many times over. I treated her more harshly so her achievements couldn't be disputed. If she succeeded, it would be on her own two feet, and not because of any sort of favoritism."

Tough love. In order to ensure she'd be well received professionally, he'd distanced himself.

"So yes, I know her well enough, Your Majesty."

"About the Earthbinding..."

Pons tilted his head. "What the Earthbinding requires... It isn't love. It is a separate matter. She'll understand the reasoning. She will outwardly accept it, tell you she forgives you, and tell herself she forgives you... but for some time, it will quietly haunt her, eat away at her, unless your love overwhelms the hurt."

His love would overwhelm the hurt. It had to.

# CHAPTER 19

*D*rina stowed her spyglass in her pocket, smiling in the darkness of a cozy rented room in Azalée, with the savory rosemary scent of roast lamb, the evening meal, lingering in the air. Tonight, the service entrance to Trèstellan Palace experienced unusual activity. Dancers, players, heaping carriages of food and wine...

Tonight was the eve of the Joyeuse Entrée. It had to be.

She changed into her white leathers, a hue not unlike the snow atop the Triumphal Arch's ashlar masonry. She sheathed her dagger in her boot, filled her waterskin, and packed some bread, then gathered the supplies she'd recovered from the weapons cache she'd buried. A heavy crossbow and four arcanir-tipped bolts. She grinned. Its worth equaled a home of her choosing in a place like Alcea or Orchidée.

Working for Evrard Gilles had come with its fair share of perks.

She stowed the crossbow and the bolts under her white cloak. With a final glance around the dark room, she shrouded herself in shadow, opened the window, murmured an aeromancy incantation, and jumped.

The wind carried her down. Her booted heels landed softly on the snow-covered cobblestone. Through shadowed alleys, she picked her way across Azalée, over its wall, and through Orchidée to the

Triumphal Arch, keeping out of the full moon's light. Well past midnight, nary a soul walked the Courdevallan streets.

When she arrived at the arch, no one was about, but she had to be sure. *"Mother earth, grant me your sight, / Show through your eyes, reveal all life."*

Small masses of anima—stray animals, vermin—meandered the streets, and two forms tucked into the dark cover of the arch.

A couple of lovers.

She kept to the darkness until they left, arm in arm.

She sighed. She and Marko had been inseparable, would have spent their lives never out of each other's sight. When at last she'd see him in the Lone, she could bring him a gift of justice. Payment for his life's sudden end. Something to show for the lengthy years apart, alone, broken. A head to roll for shattered dreams.

She stared up the hundred-and-fifty-foot monument. It marked the victory that had immortalized the Farallan dynasty. And now, thanks to its keen vantage point, its last living heir would die for *her* victory.

One Kezani mage was worth a king's life. Marko was worth Jonathan Dominic Armel Faralle's life.

*"Wings of wind, great and soft, / Take me high, bear me aloft."* Repeating the incantation, she soared to the top of the Triumphal Arch. When she ceased the repetition, she landed with a soft crunch in the snow. Quickly, she flattened herself to the arch's surface. Up so high, the winter wind bit, but the heavy snowfall this year provided ample concealment.

No one would think to study the top of the arch, and even if someone did, she was well cloaked to match the heavy snow. And should anyone look too intently...

*"Mirror of dreams, master of deception, / Mask my form, hide me from all perception."* An illusion spell from the Magisterium. If anyone searched with nature sight, she wouldn't be found, but once she revealed the arcanir-tipped bolt, the charm would be dispelled.

Its cost was immense, but her anima was still more than half bright, and after the shot, she would need only enough for an aeromancy spell and a shadow cloak to escape to an abandoned residence in Orchidée, where she had stored supplies.

If she'd calculated well, the king would enter Alcea before noon. And then he would die.

~

JON REINED in his eager destrier outside the walls of Courdeval beneath the blinding midmorning sun. He stared at the snowy northern gate, through which he would soon enter the city with Olivia, Pons, Perrault, and three squads of his Royal Guard, including Raoul and Florian. Four squads of knights also joined the Joyeuse Entrée, along with a company of paladins and a company of Emaurrian soldiers, interspersed with performers of all kinds to make this parade a massive spectacle.

He, perhaps, the biggest spectacle of all. Dressed in his dark modified arcanir armor—polished to a blinding shine—and a priceless Zeharan-red cloak lined with ermine fur, the golden Emaurrian crown atop his head, he felt like one giant ornament.

Above him, servants bore a fine baldachin made of luxurious brocade, richly patterned in deep blue and embroidered with golden winged serpents. The Farallan coat-of-arms, a dragon clutching a laurel leaf and a rose, coiled around a four-paneled shield, an ivy leaf in each panel. His white destrier, extravagantly barded, complemented the ostentatiousness. He shifted uncomfortably.

Next to him, Olivia hid a smile behind her hand—or tried to. She rearranged on her side-saddle.

"I feel ridiculous," he grumbled, flexing his neck.

She didn't bother hiding her smile anymore and nuzzled the miniver of her gray cloak. "Oh, come on. You won a great victory. Your people want to celebrate you."

" 'Celebrate.' " Five hundred and thirty-one people had died to the mangeurs. Paladins didn't celebrate after victories; they thanked Terra, prayed, and honored their fallen. He clutched the reins tightly. "Right."

A horse stamped its foot to his left, barded in white. In the saddle, Pons was decked out in a fine white velvet overcoat and matching trousers, the ensemble trimmed in gold, his gleaming chain of office about his shoulders under a fine black cloak.

Pons breathed deeply. "Your Majesty, you want many great things for your people. Safety, security, prosperity. To accomplish those things, you need their faith, their support, and their loyalty. And this is how you get it—by marking what you've done for them, giving them cause to remember you, to value you."

Shoring up support. Right. Jon shrugged, reluctant to agree even if Pons spoke true.

Pons continued, "You're not celebrating a victory paid for by five hundred and thirty-one lives"—as Jon's eyes darted to him, Pons raised his eyebrows—"you're solidifying support so that bloodshed can be avoided in the future."

To avoid rebellion. Revolution. To dissuade usurpers with tenuous claims thinking his rule weak. All of that would mean bloodshed, and preventing it would save lives.

"The kingdom cannot withstand infighting when the real enemy wears no human face, Your Majesty," Perrault added from behind.

Right. Yes. He knew that. Needed to focus on it. The Immortals were the enemy, and Emaurria couldn't fight them while fragmented in every way. He looked over his shoulder. "Thank you, Captain. Wise words." When Perrault inclined his head, Jon turned to Pons and Olivia. "Thank you all." He looked ahead again, staring at the northern gate.

Espoire was saved. The march of Bisclavret would recover. The mangeurs were dead. There was relief in those truths.

And if he could earn the kingdom's approval, he could continue to do his all to protect it and spare his people future harm.

"It's been difficult to see past our losses," he said with a deep breath, "especially with the reminders so near."

They all glanced back at the trophies from the battle: the heads of the mangeurs, prepared for display, for burning in the square outside Azalée.

"A necessary horror," Perrault said. "The people must know exactly what we face... and what we have defeated."

The people had to see with their own eyes that the reports were true.

The Master of Ceremonies, a brightly clad plump oldster, gathered everyone into position and signaled the trumpeters. Horns called the Joyeuse Entrée to begin.

A squad of mounted soldiers bearing pole-arms and shields led the procession, followed by a troupe of festively attired performers carrying baskets of flower petals, wrapped confections, coins. Behind them, riders on specially trained horses, dancers, fire-breathers, marching musicians, honored paladins and soldiers from the battle. And then Jon and his entourage, the Royal Guard, one hundred and sixty-eight caparisoned horses for all those who'd lost their lives in the battle, and more basket-bearing performers and soldiers with horse-drawn carts displaying the mangeurs' heads for all to see. More guards and some musicians brought up the rear.

The shadow of the northern gate passed over him as they entered the city, its Chardon District, its small homes adorned with flowers, carpets, tapestries. People lined the main thoroughfare, cheering and chanting his name, faces bright as they captured the bounty tossed to them.

Horns blasted, musicians played a lively tune, petals rained over the procession, children laughed and scrambled for the confections and coins, some civilians shouted, others screamed, some cheered his long life and good health.

Countless people filled the streets, pressed together, a tight river of paladins, soldiers, and performers winding through them. Tight quarters, a cacophony of sound, a kaleidoscope of sight.

A little boy waved from atop his mother's shoulders in the densely crammed bazaar of Dandelion. The entire market teemed with people. Farallan banners hung from tall buildings, fluttering in the wind.

Jon smiled and greeted people from time to time. Servants rode up to him with baskets of coins that he handed out.

Before the siege, Courdeval's population had totaled just under 300,000 people, and it might have stayed much the same, if his eyes didn't deceive him now.

The streets tightened in Violette District, full of middle-sized homes and the working class, who studded the thoroughfare as far as the eye could see. Massive tapestries hung from roofs, depicting the victories of old led by the Farallan dynasty. When the route opened up to a small square, a stage along the route featured a scene from a duel between an actor garbed as a crowned paladin and one as a Crag Company general.

The paladin-actor leveled his sword at the general on his knees.

Blatant propaganda. He rolled his eyes to Olivia, who only smiled knowingly.

The crowd cheered and applauded.

The parade continued into Alcea District, where the marked uptick in luxury shone in the scale and grandeur of the homes owned by the rich merchant class and the nouveau riche. The lavishness of the decorations increased—more flowers, bigger banners, more intricate tapestries. The crowds on the streets tightened ever more, lines of spectators pushing in on the procession, cheering, screaming, grinning, shouting, trumpets blaring, music soaring, the roar in the background—

Another tableau, wedged among the crowd, featured a winged woman in dazzling white silk, golden waves of voluminous hair falling to her hip, a wreath of laurel upon her head. Terra. She was handing a wrapped bundle to an elderly high priest at her feet.

Was it...?

Olivia eyed him and nodded toward the scene.

The Goddess handing *him* to Derric. Terra have mercy. Blasphemy? "Have the Master of Ceremonies reprimanded," he grumbled to Olivia.

"King Jon the Giantslayer!" the crowd shouted. "Long live the king!"

Surreal. Pressure pushed in, air fled, tapestries, high walls closing in. It was too much. He smiled and nodded, hand on Faithkeeper's hilt, staring ahead, up a hill covered with crowds, the Triumphal Arch peaking beyond. Almost to Orchidée, then through Azalée, and to Trèstellan...

Only a bit farther.

He distributed coins and greeted Courdevallans as the procession ascended the hill, glancing to Olivia.

"Almost there," she mouthed.

*Almost* couldn't come quickly enough.

She urged her horse closer and leaned in as they crested the hill. "You look comfortable."

"Right at home among dense crowds cheering at me," he said through a tight smile. "Why wouldn't I be?" They'd have much to discuss tonight—about the mangeurs, the Earthbinding, the ridiculous tableaux, everything.

Chuckling, she nudged his arm.

Something in the sky gleamed.

A glowing white veil of magic sprang before him. Olivia tumbled out of the saddle and into him.

A sharp cry.

They fell to the snowy cobblestone, dotted with red. A horse screamed, others shying and bucking. The baldachin came down, heavy brocade blotting out the sun and sky.

Jon rolled over Olivia, braced over her, avoiding the bolt impaling her shoulder.

Hooves came down around them.

Magic rippled above. A repellent force-magic aura. Pons.

Jon shifted to get his arcanir clear of Olivia. Red soaked into the shoulder of her gray cloak. Blood. "Healing?"

A line formed between her brows. She shook her head.

Arcanir poison.

"Commander Garreau! Take your squad to the arch and capture the archer immediately," Perrault bellowed.

"Yes, sir!" A dozen horses broke away from the procession and pushed through the crowd. Or at least tried.

Olivia looked up at him from the snow, heaving swift breaths.

"You're all right," he whispered, surveying the wound. "Stay with me, Olivia."

She nodded, pallor claiming her face. Jon removed his cloak and pressed it around her wound.

Servants scrambled to lift the baldachin. Royal guards apprehended and calmed horses. Raoul shouldered his way through, followed closely by Florian.

"Jon—" Olivia stammered, fading. "Water..." She licked her pale lips and blinked sluggishly. "Belladonna..."

Belladonna? He searched her face. "Poison?"

She inclined her chin.

"Your Majesty!" Raoul tried to help him up, but Jon brushed him off, scooped up Olivia, and rose.

"Sodalis!" Jon called.

All paladins within earshot turned to him.

"You four"—he tipped his head to the men surrounding him—"assemble the physicians in the palace infirmary immediately. Tell them to prepare for belladonna and arcanir poisoning."

"Yes, Your Majesty!" They saluted, then departed. The baldachin stiffened into place, horses and men cleared from around them. Stillness settled over the procession and the crowd.

With the help of another paladin, Jon set Olivia atop his destrier, then mounted behind her. Too out in the open. They had to move. Fast.

A servant handed him the reins.

He made for the palace, with servants, paladins, and soldiers scrambling into place around him.

# CHAPTER 20

*P*anting, Drina darted into the abandoned home in Alcea
district, where she'd stashed clothes. She hastily changed
into the middling gown—a russet-brown cotton frock and a beige
cloak to match—and picked up her apothecary's satchel.

Neatening the clothes, she peeked outside. The paladins hadn't
caught her trail yet, but they would. She hurried out, following the
well-trod paths in the snow to the main thoroughfare, where people
still gathered in the streets, collecting coins and wrapped sweets. The
crowd buzzed with rumors—of the assassination, the king's romance
with the Archmage, the baffling heads of the Immortals.

She forced a faint smile and bent to pick up some coins. She'd
had one shot. One shot to kill the king, and the meddling red-haired
strumpet had ruined the whole thing. Thrown herself in front
of him.

It had been the perfect moment—the king distracted, the crowd
watching him, the Royal Guard watching him, everyone watching him.

But for one meddling woman.

She'd acted fast—too fast—and ruined the entire plan. *Fortune shits
on this day.*

The idiot paladins wouldn't find anything they could trace. She still had her anonymity and access to the palace, courtesy of Claire Gouin and Countess Vauquelin.

A new plan. She needed a new plan.

The king, for his newness and the kingdom's weakness, was surprisingly well guarded by the Order. Too well guarded this time.

She needed to catch him alone. In private.

She raised her eyebrows. The means were simple, as an apothecary with access to the palace; she could get to the king's rooms. On a night when the Royal Guard, when the whole of the palace would be distracted.

A night like Veris.

Smiling, she made her way to Peletier's. Yes, Veris.

STARING AT THE MARBLE TILE, Jon sat in the palace infirmary, chin in his hand. Terra have mercy, Olivia could have died, and might yet.

An assassination attempt. Someone had just tried to kill him. In public.

If someone wanted him dead, then he had to be doing something right. Many had a stake in his rule, but just as many, if not more, had a stake in his downfall. And that of the kingdom.

It wouldn't fall. He wouldn't allow it. He wouldn't ignore anything in his power to strengthen the kingdom. Not anymore. Not when it emboldened enemies to hurt those he loved.

Movement echoed in Trèstellan's massive infirmary, its vinegar scent faint. Beneath the rib-vaulted ceilings and canopies, a dozen screened-off wards divided the infirmary, the largest in Courdeval. Of the dozen wards, only one was in use today.

Someone pulled aside a curtain. Olivia lay in a bed, a nurse bringing a cup to her lips.

He sprang from the chair and headed to her side.

A heavy woolen blanket, down comforter, and immaculate white sheets covered her up to her waist, and from there on, she wore a white cotton gown, bandages padding her right shoulder. The gauze only barely shrouded a dark red stain beneath.

A sheen of sweat coated her frowning face, her red hair moist and plastered to her head. The nurse raised another cup to her mouth, and she drank greedily.

He took her hand.

Her eyes met his. Dilated. "Jon... you're... here..." Her voice broke, faint, weak.

The nurse, an older woman, bowed to him. "Your Majesty, she's been given an antidote to the belladonna poisoning and should recover within a couple of days. The arcanir poison may take longer."

He nodded, more than familiar with arcanir poison himself. Its nullification of healing magic made recovery difficult.

"Made from a... a bean, and things." Olivia's unfocused eyes sought his with a modicum of success.

The nurse handed him the cup, patted his arm, and moved to the next ward.

Olivia smiled weakly, breathing irregularly. "You can thank me now... Jon."

He sat on the bed next to her and leaned in, glaring at her. "You idiot."

Her brow furrowed. "I think you mean 'hero.' "

"No, I mean 'idiot,' " he bit out, sitting up. "What in Terra's name were you thinking?" He scowled at her wound. "You could have died." He slammed the cup on the nearby table.

The faint smile lingered on her lips, but it slowly faded. "You're my king," she croaked. "I owe you my loyalty."

He canted his head and rested a hand on her arm. "Olivia."

She managed a watery grin. "Besides, if I let my best friend's soon-to-be husband die on my watch, I'd always regret it."

His eyes widened, then he blinked, slowly. A laugh burst from his mouth, and he covered it. "What am I going to do with you?"

"Retain me as Archmage and reward me with a handsome raise?"

"Done."

"Learn to cast a repulsion shield?"

He winced. "Done...?" He eyed her peripherally.

She drew in a lengthy breath. "Don't do the Earthbinding ritual."

He shook his head. "Olivia..."

Her eyes locked with his, deep, determined, unwavering. "We can continue fighting conventionally. I know we can. And Leigh might get us those Immortal hunting squads from Vervewood."

He heaved a sigh. Vervewood couldn't protect an entire kingdom. And neither could his armies, nor the paladins, not on their own.

"And we still don't know what it'll do to you. For all we know, it could kill you. It could destroy your mind. It could madden you."

Pressure built up in his chest, and he clenched his mouth shut, turning away from her. She wanted to bait a fight? Now? "And the previous Earthbound kings?"

"Who knows what kind of preparation they underwent? There has to be a reason they stopped doing the ritual."

He shrugged. "Lack of necessity."

She narrowed her eyes. "Who happily surrenders power because it isn't needed? There is no such thing as having too much power."

"Isn't there?"

"Spare me the semantics."

He sighed. Someone had just tried to kill him, and it was the least of his worries. The Immortals were strong—too strong for Emaurria to survive much more conventional warfare, especially so depleted. Unless he sacrificed himself for the sake of the land, there might not be an Emaurria to survive. He'd barely convinced himself to do what needed doing, and he didn't need Olivia to break his will now. "If you weren't lying in a hospital bed, I'd reprimand you."

"Lying is unbecoming, Jon."

He pressed his lips together, but a smile emerged anyway. "And to think, mere months ago, you were calling me 'Your Majesty' and standing on ceremony."

She narrowed her eyes. "Don't change the subject. The Earth-binding asks much. I don't want you making those sacrifices, risking your sanity, your *life*."

"You think I do?" But his actions spoke plainly. Cold. Reasoned. Dishonorable. While Sir Jonathan Ver rolled in the grave, King Jonathan Dominic Armel Faralle was alive and well. *Doing good* had changed so drastically it was barely recognizable.

She raised her eyebrows and scowled at him.

"It's not as simple as all that, Olivia. Not anymore. The Rift demands a price. And I won't shirk that price while the rest of the kingdom pays and pays and pays. It's not who I am."

"And if you die?" She blinked sluggishly.

He'd been asking himself the same question since battling the mangeurs. "I intend not to."

"And if you do?"

He exhaled a long, slow breath. There was only one hope. "Then I die trying to save this kingdom."

"And what if you don't?"

He shut his eyes and pinched the bridge of his nose. "What do you want me to say, Olivia?"

"That you won't do the Earthbinding."

He wanted nothing more than to do exactly as she suggested, but then what? Would soldiers and paladins continue dying to the Immortals? Would small, depleted Vervewood's hunting squads protect an entire kingdom? Should he just give up on the love of his life and marry one of the suitresses?

The Earthbinding offered hope. Hope that he could turn the land against Emaurria's enemies himself.

There was nothing else. Nothing else but slowly chipping away at everything he had left to offer. "Not all men are destined for easy paths. A king's life must be defined by duty, not ease. You know this."

She heaved an exasperated huff and shook her head. "Any man can change his cards. Destiny isn't set, or else no one would ever transcend the circumstances of his birth." Her eyes locked with his. "You would have been a dead prince. I would have been a fishmonger. Rielle would have been a duchess."

He clenched his teeth bitterly. "I lost the right to change my cards the day I accepted the responsibility of being king."

"Don't you want—"

He rose. "What I want must bow to what I must."

A man cleared his throat. Jon looked over his shoulder.

"Your Majesty," Tor said with a bow, then offered Olivia a warm smile.

"Tor," she greeted softly.

Tor approached and crouched near the bed. "Praise Terra you live." He took her hand.

She blushed.

"Thanks to you, he"—Tor tossed his head toward Jon's direction —"is alive and well." Tor grinned.

"Catching bolts with my flesh is one of my greatest talents," Jon joked. "Next time, let me handle it."

"My former squire brings up a good point." Tor gazed at her, his hazel eyes dancing.

She smiled. "And the assassin?"

Tor sighed. "Still at large, unfortunately. Derric has increased the guard at the gates and the walls. Could the Guardians increase the wards in His Majesty's quarters as well? Just in case the assassin gains entry to the palace."

Olivia nodded. "I'll issue the orders forthwith."

Tor squeezed her hand. "You took quite a fall, from what I heard."

She smiled. "His Majesty broke that fall... albeit with less-than-pillowy arcanir armor."

Tor laughed. "Well, then perhaps it's for the best that I asked your household to prepare your rooms for your recovery, if that's not too forward."

"Not at all. That sounds perfect."

Jon cleared his throat. "I'll leave you both to it." He glanced at each of them, then shot Olivia a knowing smile. She inclined her head.

Tor rose and bowed. "Your Majesty."

With that, Jon took his leave, striding to his quarters. The burning of the mangeurs in the square had gone on without him, and so could the feast. He'd face the Grands—and his suitresses—tomorrow.

Perhaps their nations would continue detente, if he could manage to stay balanced on the knife's edge.

At least long enough to perform the Earthbinding.

# CHAPTER 21

*R*ielle leaned on her elbows over the stack of news articles in the third-floor solar. The morning had been translation after translation, but the words on the page meant nothing. Her child. Samara. Farrad. The lash. The thoughts circled like wolves and gave her no peace.

The best thing she could do for her child was to escape—easier said than done—but saving Samara was a different challenge entirely. No matter how much she thought about it, there were few options but to throw herself at Farrad's mercy and beg him to let her take Samara's place. Even to protect her child, she couldn't let a young girl suffer.

Perhaps for coming forward, Farrad would be merciful. It was her only hope.

Farrad was in negotiations with another House today and wouldn't return until late in the evening. Or such had been the word at the slave quarter this morning. She would hurry through her work, then make her way to his quarters. And face the inevitable.

In the soft glow of the early sun, she shuffled through the last of the news reports: ships destroyed by mysterious creatures, a drought in Hongo, a Pryndonian princess arriving in Emaurria.

Emaurria?

She blinked.

*Her Highness, Princess Adelaide Breckenridge of Pryndon, arrives in Emaurria's capital city of Courdeval, as the latest of the region's most eligible ladies, for the courting pleasure of the King of Emaurria, His Majesty Jonathan Dominic Armel Faralle.*

She read and reread the scrap of paper.

*Eligible ladies.*

*Courting pleasure.*

*His Majesty, King Jonathan Dominic Armel Faralle...*

And that was all. The last news of the day. No other papers. No word on whether he was...

The paper crumpled. She wrung it in her hands, trying to squeeze out one more paragraph, one more sentence, one more word.

When had Adelaide arrived? How long had she been there? If a princess was there, then Jon was—

No.

She had to finish. The sooner she finished, the sooner she could speak to Farrad. The sooner she could ensure Samara's safety.

*Work...* The text before her blurred, and she blinked, dipping her quill in an inkwell to translate the Pryndonian tongue into High Nad'i.

Breathing deeply, she peered at the paper. Empty.

Jon wasn't coming.

She set down the quill and raised her chin, staring through the lattice at the blank sky.

A rustle, and she glanced down at her hand. Her fingers clenched the paper again. She loosened her grip.

Every night, she'd thought of Jon. Called out to him. Waited for him.

He wasn't coming.

She squeezed her eyes shut. Jon loved her, had felt a duty to keep her safe. The only thing that would prevail over that duty would be a greater one. To the kingdom.

He'd chosen the kingdom over her.

She braced against the desk. Of course he would. As he should. He owed a duty not just to one woman, but to a nation. Of course he couldn't come after her, not as the king of Emaurria.

She hadn't really even expected it. No, to expect it would have been foolish. She pressed a palm to her belly. *And he doesn't even know about you.*

Of course he would court princesses. A king had to marry high for the good of the kingdom and from beyond its borders—especially when the previous king had married from within. Of course. She had known all that. Like her, Jon was confined—not by tangible bonds, like hers, but by the bonds of royal duty. Of course.

Then, why—?

She dabbed at her wet face with her upper robe. She had known it all and tucked it away in her mind. Seeing the unforgiving truth on paper was another matter.

The realities of his position—no, the realities of their relationship —were harsh. Jon wasn't coming for her, and he would soon marry. Both as duty dictated.

Allowing herself to rely on him before hadn't been easy, but it had felt right. Now... Now that he was so much more to so many more people, she couldn't rely on him anymore. It wasn't even fair.

She wrapped her arms around herself. *It's all right. I'll get us out of here. Whatever it takes.* She smiled tightly.

After a few deep breaths, she dipped the quill in the inkwell again and transcribed the news. News like any other. Translated words. Nothing but strokes and ink. Nothing but.

As soon as it was done, she trudged into the hallway and handed it off to another house slave. Finally out of her hands.

The rest of the day bled into Aina's unfinished project. Willful denial was a great motivator. Anything to keep her mind busy. She was close to finishing a compilation Aina had entitled *Healing Poultices*. The sun had risen to high noon, but just a little more. The moon had risen, but only another line...

Ihsan didn't stop to question her remarkable stamina as the hours flew by, but brought her some goat's cheese and flatbread at midday and a meat pie when the sun set. More food than she ever received at the slave quarters.

When she finished transcribing the final recipe, Ihsan was nearly asleep at her seat, experimenting with a healing spell that treated the symptoms of the Wasting, a disease yet without cure. Rielle nudged her awake.

"Yes, yes." Ihsan came alert. "What is it?"

"I've finished the book of healing poultices, Zahibi."

Ihsan flipped through it silently. "I see that you added an index. Very helpful." She closed the book and swept a palm lovingly over the cover. "Take it down to Samara's desk. She'll make sure all of the required ingredients are ordered in the morning."

Rielle took it and began the long trip from the third floor down to the apothecary; from there, she would make for Farrad's quarters immediately.

The villa was quiet this time of night, with nary a servant stalking its dark halls. Empty. As she followed the sparse light of the sconces to the first floor, only the sound of the indoor courtyard's fountain accompanied her soft footfalls.

There was no one outside the apothecary. She unlocked the door and found the room dark and unattended. Too late? She bit her lip.

The open door admitted light into the room from the hall, however dim, and she crept to Samara's work space. Scattered among the jars, envelopes, books, and papers, were pouches of black tablets. Sen'a.

She swallowed.

Of course it would be available here. In a house of pleasure. Complete, entire, consuming pleasure.

A chill racked up through her limbs. The dissonant twang of need. One small dose, and for a few hours, she could forget being a slave, forget the news she'd read earlier, forget it all, and melt. Dissolve into blinding pleasure, into nothing, into a blankness free of any thought or worry.

She blinked.

No.

Not now.

Not ever again. For her baby's sake. For her own. The sooner she left the apothecary, the better.

She left the book on the table, by the wall of full shelves, covered jars lining their length. The apothecary was well stocked. A heady mixture of scents competed— cinnamon, vervain, and primrose among them. She followed the middle shelf to its end, jars oozing the smells of their contents, even through their fabric covers. Wormwood and belladonna—poisonous if used in certain ways—and the key in her hands felt weightier.

Why did Ihsan trust her with access to poisons?

The belladonna jar's cover was slightly open, and she reached out to close it.

Arms closed around her body.

A flame cloak—No—the sting of arcanir—

Glass broke and books fell.

Coarse stubble brushed her cheek, and soft hair tickled her ear. She shivered.

"House rumor says I have claimed you." Farrad. His soft, serene whisper stilled her. "The golden-haired one."

She swallowed. "Zahib."

He drew in a slow breath, tightening his hold. "I can't say I have had the pleasure."

*If not for these arcanir shackles, you'd be scorched.*

But there could be no magic, no argument, no combat. She needed a favor from him and, chained with no status, had no way to force his hand.

His arms breezed away. She faced him and dropped to her hands and knees. It was all she had. Perhaps if she begged his forgiveness, his mercy, Samara could be spared the lash.

"Zahib, it was all my fault. Samara had no part in it. If anyone must be punished, let it be me." She brought her forehead so low it nudged the tile floor. *Divine, please spare me. Spare me.*

He dropped to a knee. Pressed two firm fingers below her shoulder. Urged her to rise. "Your gesture is appreciated, but unnecessary."

Unnecessary? She glanced up, wincing—would he strike her?—but he only studied her with evaluative dark eyes, raven's wings against a midnight sky, endless, bottomless, unfathomable. "I don't understand, Zahib."

He rose and held out his hand, looking like a sultan in his Zeharan-red knee-length thiyawb, richly dyed and cinched in at a fit waist.

Cautiously, she took his offered hand, her palm smoothing against his callused skin, and there was something familiar about him. She let him pull her to her feet.

"Samara is an intelligent girl," he said, still holding her hand. "She has a soft heart, but she does not interfere like this often. She likes you. And you seem to be worth her liking."

She bit her lip, her head throbbing. This was the man who had strangled a woman, who had killed another man before her very eyes. A killer, but... a murderer? Who was she to believe, Ihsan or Samara?

"I—thank you, Zahib," she replied, embarrassed as her hand moistened with sweat.

With a smile, he released her.

"Samara," she whispered. "If there is any punishment to be had, let it be mine."

He raised a dark eyebrow and offered a bemused smile. "Are you so eager for punishment?"

"No," she replied, fidgeting, "but if there is any... I don't wish anyone else to suffer on my account. Especially not Samara."

He took a step toward her, and she mirrored in retreat until her back met the wall. There was nowhere else to go. Her jaw quivered, and she brought her teeth tightly together.

"You are loyal." Gently, he neared and reached for the twine binding her braid and shook it free. Curling locks of her hair around his fingers, he arranged it over her shoulder.

"I won't have my own daughter lashed for her courage," he said, playing with her curls. He was so near, the coolness of mint tea hinted on his breath. "But I do wish to know the truth of the rumor."

The truth of the rumor?

"I—" *House rumor says I have claimed you,* he'd said. The dark skies of his gaze met hers, and she looked away.

*The truth...* Did he claim her? He was letting her decide.

Her thoughts descended to her belly, and the life that grew there.

If she said no, what would happen tonight, when she eventually had to return to the slave quarters, unable to protect herself? Would the same guard return? Would another?

How many nights of uncertainty would she bear before something endangered what now mattered most?

Her turn to study Farrad. House Hazael's zahib in his grandfather's stead, no one would dare cross him as Samara had demonstrated with mere mention of his name. A master duelist, he would answer any slight with deadly response.

Her heart dropped. Could she—?

His protection could ensure her child's survival—and her own— until she could find a way to escape this place.

But could she willingly share this man's bed, betray Jon, for the sake of her child's safety? And her own?

Or could she gamble with both her life and her child's for the sake of fidelity to the man she loved, here of all places, where lives came and swept away with the sand?

Before her stood her means of survival—a powerful man, whose embrace was her only viable survival strategy.

Farrad grazed her jawline with a curious finger. Her heart raced, but she ignored the tightening in her chest. There were no easy choices to be found here.

*When the enemy takes your sword, you must draw your dagger.* Without magic, this was the dagger left to her, if she'd but pick it up.

"Everything in this house is yours for the taking, Zahib, including me," she said.

With a slow shake of his head, he traced her lips. "I have four wives, willingly married, and have had many a lover seek my bed. There is pleasure in free will, but none to be found in 'taking.' "

She shivered. He wanted her to choose him. Of her own free will.

There was little freedom in her choices, but she did have the power to set her course here. With a trembling hand, she reached for him, brushed her palm over his Zeharan-red thiyawb, over the hardness of his abdomen, and up to the firm muscle of his chest. Strong. Powerful. Safe.

This was *wrong*. All *wrong*.

He held her gaze, unmoving as her touch explored.

*Wrong.*

She stepped toward him and lifted her chin, floated up to his mouth, brushed his lips with a trembling whisper. *Wrong.* He threaded his fingers through her hair at the back of her head and claimed her waist with a secure arm. *Wrong.* His lips met hers with equal restraint, dreamlike in their slow teasing against her own. *Wrong.* They shared the same minty air, kissing, breathing, speaking the old language of man and woman. *Wrong.*

"Tell me your name," he breathed against her mouth, "that I may know what to call this mirage." He kissed her softly.

Tremors rattled in her arms, in her chest, everywhere, and she fought to still them.

"Thahab," she whispered, snaking her quivering arms around his neck.

Everything about this was *wrong.*

No, not everything. She had spared Samara the lash.

His hold tightened.

Spared herself and her child the dangers of the slave quarter.

His body was flush against hers. Scorching.

Perhaps with some maneuvering, she could spare herself further enslavement here.

His mouth covered hers.

Secure an escape.

His tongue sought hers.

With position came power.

He broke the kiss, his gaze sweeping her face. A brush of night-black wings. A crease on his brow. Searching dark eyes.

She would find every bit of power that came with Farrad's embrace.

"Thahab," he repeated, savoring each syllable. He stroked her cheek and pinned her to the wall.

# CHAPTER 22

*J*on nocked an arrow, drew his sixty-pound recurve, and aimed for the center of the target two hundred yards away. The twang of the bowstring, and the arrow hit.

Just right of center. He sighed.

A chorus of soft clapping erupted from the suitresses. No doubt succumbing to pretense as he did.

Raoul snorted.

Jon side-eyed him. "Something funny?"

Raoul straightened. "No, Your Majesty."

The shot or the audience? Both, probably. When he'd arranged to have his bow restrung and scheduled time at the range, he hadn't invited anyone. All he'd wanted was a quiet hour to himself.

Someone had just tried to kill him yesterday, and the assassin remained at large. Parliament had stalled on acknowledging his legitimization, which delayed an official coronation. Valen had not yet returned with word on the courier. And Pons was still gathering what the Earthbinding required.

All of that, on top of the burdens of ruling, had begged for quiet diversion.

But here they were.

*Subtle hint noted, Derric.*

After an attempted assassination, Derric had happily invited women from all over the region to come take up the bow right here in the courtyard. Either the suitresses were well vetted or Derric was willing to risk his king's life for the sake of courtship.

He grunted and eyed the wall of Royal Guard lining the rim of the snow-covered courtyard. Other than their palpably increased presence, talk of the attempted assassination had become scarce among the courtiers, buried by word of the Veris Ball. And even here, at the archery range, the hot topics were gowns, dances, and jewelry.

Despite the thick blanket of snow, the weather was quite mild for a winter's morning, but he cupped his mouth and warmed his fingers.

"Cold fingers?" Raoul murmured, raising a brow.

Jon huffed under his breath. Just like old times at the monastery. "I bet you I hit center in two shots."

"What's on the table, sire?" Florian asked, raising a brow as he rubbed his hands together.

"How would you like it if I train inside tomorrow? Reasonably close to a hearth?" He grinned.

"Very, ridiculously much," Florian answered.

Raoul grunted—it was more than he usually said. "And if you win, sire?"

Jon's grin turned wicked. "You two teach some of the ladies to shoot," he murmured. *And take some of the pressure off me.*

Florian smirked but nodded, as did Raoul, who looked like he'd just eaten a lemon.

Jon forced a smile for his audience—as was expected—and followed with a second arrow and a third.

He lowered his bow. Both hit the center, earning a louder bout of claps. He begrudgingly indulged the spectacle, turned to the group, and bowed dramatically for full effect. He raised his head.

"Ladies, I invite you all to join me and enjoy this *unusually good weather* with some archery," he declared, with all the charisma he could muster. "Florian and Raoul"—he cocked his head toward them—"have graciously offered lessons."

Excited giggles and giddy whispers spread among the ladies as they headed toward the variety of bows—shortbows, recurves, and even a couple longbows. All of the suitresses had been accounted for on the day of the parade, or he'd wonder at a few of these sharpshooters.

"Was hustling part of the training at Monas Ver, sire?" Raoul grunted, his eyes dancing.

"Call it a hobby." He clapped Florian and Raoul each on the shoulder before they headed toward the bows.

A whisper of wind hissed—an arrow flying.

Lady Kaia Jorunsdottir of Skadden held a longbow. His eyes followed the trajectory to the target, where a heavy-grain arrow was embedded in the bull's-eye.

He whistled under his breath. The longbow—similar to the paladins' style—had a one-hundred-pound draw weight: handling it was no easy task.

He stopped next to her while she nocked another arrow. Her eyes darted to him briefly and then away to her shot. As she exhaled, she loosed. Both of their gazes locked onto the arrow as it thudded into the target, just shy of the bull's-eye.

"Good shot," he said. Did Derric know if she had any skill with a crossbow?

Kaia turned to him. "Your Majesty is too kind." She bowed her head. "My homeland, Skadden, is an unforgiving place. We women train in combat, or we die."

He went rigid. Although Skadden bordered Emaurria to the north, little was known of it, since its warbands mostly fought amongst each other and very rarely ventured south. But apparently their entire population was armed to the last person.

"Then the women of Skadden are wise... and strong." And they'd be an asset to any ruler—currently Kaia's mother, Erle Jorun Strand, whose territory outgrew that of all the other warlords combined.

Flushed, she pressed her lips together. "Thank you, Your Majesty."

He inclined his head. Every able-bodied person in a kingdom ready to serve—no dead weight. No outside organizations to refuse orders or withhold their aid.

Beyond, Magdalena and Yumiko ably used recurve bows. Not surprising. Magdalena carried herself confidently, as warriors did. And

Yumiko came from Kamerai, where archery was commonly practiced by women for sport.

Ahead, Florian demonstrated the use of the shortbow to Alessandra, Farai, Nadiyya, Salma, and Adelaide, earning *oob*s and *abb*s. At least he was talking to someone other than him or Raoul, or any man, for that matter. Life at court was an... adjustment, to say the least, for paladins.

Melora ably used a shortbow, beaming at him as he walked past. So King Odhrán had arranged for his daughter to become an expert archer.

At the end of the line, a dark-haired woman stood, holding a recurve bow at her side, looking out in the direction of the target. Nora.

He followed her gaze outward. Two arrows lay in the snow between her and the target. She gave him a self-conscious shrug.

"Good morning, Lady Vauquelin," he greeted, keeping his distance. "I didn't expect to see you here." Derric wouldn't have invited her. Perhaps she genuinely practiced archery?

"Good morning, Your Majesty." She fixed him with a pleasant look, her mysterious hazel eyes not unlike her brother's. Her dark hair fell unbound, tousled by the wind against the contrasting white fox fur of her cloak. "After all that happened yesterday, I had hoped for some diversion, but I'm afraid archery is not one of my talents," she said with an embarrassed half laugh. "I never quite learned to shoot."

That wasn't unusual. Many nobles chose to educate their daughters in the arts and entertainment—singing, dancing, flower arranging, needlework, playing musical instruments—and left other skills by the wayside. He'd taught pages and squires at the monastery and could, without a doubt, get her to hit the target. She was making the same mistakes he'd seen countless times.

He approached her. "Show me your stance."

With a heavy sigh, she turned to the target, nocked an arrow, and drew the bow. All wrong. He took a step, then paused abruptly.

"May I?" he asked, and she nodded.

He moved behind her. "Since you're shooting a right-handed bow, you should place your left foot down range, not your right."

She exchanged her misplaced right foot for her left but didn't space them far enough apart.

"Shoulder-width apart for stability," he added, and she pulled her right foot back.

"Rotate your feet parallel to the shooting line," he whispered, and she did so. "This is the basic square stance."

Taking a step back to view her posture, he shook his head. "Try to stand up straight." He extended his arm and rotated her chin over her right shoulder.

"Keep your chin over the shoulder of your bow arm." He checked lower—her hips were out of position. He gently moved them until they were tucked under her upper body.

"When setting your hips, try to flatten your lower back for even more stability." A spicy floral scent infiltrated his nostrils. "Your center of gravity is too high. Try to relax and lower your chest and ribs down toward your stomach."

She exhaled and did as he instructed.

He moved to push her shoulders down a bit. "Keep your shoulders down—that's it."

He reached around and adjusted her hold on the arrow. "Hold the shaft close to the nock behind the fletching"—he manipulated her grip —"and let it rest on the arrow rest. Then, rotate the shaft until the hens are oblique to the bow and the cock is perpendicular to it," he explained, referring to the feathers of the fletching as he rotated the arrow.

"Now snap the nock of the arrow onto the bowstring." He moved her delicate hand to do the task. Setting her hand in a three-fingered grip on the fletching, he helped her fix upon the target just above nose level and moved her elbow.

He drew and loaded, anchored, moving her body to transfer the draw weight of the bow from her arms and shoulders into her back, and aimed. "As you release, your bow arm's shoulder should remain stationary and your chest widened, as if taking a deep breath. Allow the bowstring to leave your hand and follow through."

She loosed the arrow. As he watched it fly, the unmistakable softness of her backside pressed into him. The arrow hit the target, and she giggled.

A quick study.

She turned her head and leered at him. "I appreciate the lesson, Your Majesty," she said, her voice low and lilting. She shot another arrow expertly, hitting the outer rim of the bull's-eye. "Your hands-on style is quite effective."

He raised his eyebrows. A quick study indeed... So quick, she'd learned before he'd said anything.

She laughed throatily, her amusement reaching her eyes, and hid a toothy grin. "I'll try to remember how you recommend handling the shaft." She briefly arched a shapely eyebrow for full effect.

Chagrined, he raked his fingers through his hair, and then *laughed*. More than he'd laughed in over a month.

Nora Marcel Vignon was not to be trifled with—she was a master of her own game. She'd judged him well and sprung a trap tailored to his vulnerabilities.

No, he wouldn't underestimate her at their next meeting. They exchanged a look that he imagined many a fox and hare had exchanged.

"She fancies you," a feminine voice taunted softly.

A brazen comment. He twisted around. Nearby, Alessandra sauntered toward the bows. He gawked at her, but she kept walking.

Behind him, someone cleared her throat, and he turned.

Melora held out her bow. "Um, I could use a lesson, too."

Looking down at her hopeful face, laughter bubbled up, but he suppressed it—somehow. Aislinn grasped Melora's arm and shook her head.

The sound of rapidly approaching footsteps closed in.

Eloi, looking particularly rushed. "Your Majesty." He paused a moment and caught his breath. "The Grand Master wants to meet with you in your study."

A raise. Eloi, for his blessed good timing, would get a raise.

And if Derric was calling him away from this, then it was definitely important—Derric prized nothing above "securing the line." If someone had told him a year ago that Derric would insist so aggressively that he take a woman to wife, it would have been unbelievable.

"Tell him I'm on my way." He cocked his head to Florian and Raoul, who began to extricate themselves from the suitresses.

Eloi nodded one too many times, bowed, and left.

Nora's coy smile reached her hazel eyes. Speechless, he was about to blurt out a good-bye, when she bowed. "'Til next time, Your Majesty."

He gave her a nod before she departed, the winter sunshine catching in the luster of her dark hair. Clever, beautiful, bold—he needed to guard himself around her.

She disappeared into the palace, and he faced his guests. "Duty calls yet again. Please enjoy yourselves as long as you like, and I hope to see you all at dinner." He inclined his head and received a response of bows and curtsies.

As he turned to leave for his study, Melora heaved a disappointed breath.

What important matter did Derric want to discuss? Tor already briefed him daily on the state of military affairs in the kingdom. Although the mangeurs hadn't re-emerged, the Immortals were an ever-present problem. Perrault had laid out his logistical concerns clearly—the paladins were not a sustainable force to defend the kingdom. Paladin Grand Cordon Guérin had concurred.

And today he'd signed an appropriations proposal to hire a small mercenary force to guard the Kingsroad. He had also given Tor, as Constable of Emaurria, broad latitude to redetermine enlistment incentives for the Emaurrian Army. It would be some time, too, before enough soldiers could be promoted from within and trained into the depleted Royal Guard.

Maybe Valen had returned with news? Or perhaps Parliament had finally acknowledged his legitimization? That'd be a sunny day in the Lone.

When he finally reached his rooms, Derric awaited in the study, his tall frame straight and regal, silhouetted against the window.

Jon closed the door. "What is it?"

Derric turned to face him. "How are the ladies?"

Jon circled around his desk and pulled out his chair. "Adequately diverted. That's not all, is it?" He seated himself and motioned for Derric to be seated.

He took the cue. "Jon," he began.

If Derric was reasserting his familiarity, the news had to be bad.

"The lords of Parliament are yet stalled on acknowledgment of your legitimization."

Of course they were.

Sighing, he leaned back in his chair. Since the lords had returned to Courdeval, they'd done nothing but gradually press a thorn into his side. Although Duke Faolan Auvray Marcel abstained, along with his entourage, Viscount David Orfevre Fernand of Costechelle, an elderly miser who commanded the favor of numerous lords, had been the sharp tip of that thorn.

They'd begun with complaints about the funeral costs for the Faralles—even his parents and the king—and had continued with selfish requests and petitions accomplishing nothing but their own interests. He had mostly ignored them in favor of ensuring the security of the kingdom and its people, but action on such matters didn't seem to earn their attention or approval. "What are the numbers?"

Derric shook his head. "Thirty-four yeas, eight nays, and forty-four abstentions."

There were, then, at least thirty-four nobles who actually cared about the common good. And so many abstentions meant the lords hesitated to cross their more influential peers... or him. He would work with that. Possibly. He sighed. "Duke Maerleth Tainn?"

"Abstaining."

Of course he was. "His brothers?"

"Marquis Forel abstains"—that would be Desmond Auvray Marcel —"and Viscount Lanvalle stands with you."

If Viscount Aidan Auvray Marcel stood with him, it was Tor's doing. But that still left ten abstentions or nays he had to convert to yeas. He needed to find a man of influence to press. "Viscount Costechelle?"

"Abstaining." Derric pursed his lips. "You will have to hold a lit de justice."

Meet with Parliament himself? Trying to compel them to act?

Derric continued, "It will cow the recalcitrant lords and impose your sovereignty."

Viscount Costechelle wouldn't hinge his entire plan—and there most certainly *was* a plan—upon a single meeting. Jon shook his head. "It will accomplish quite the opposite, if they mean not to obey."

"Then they will be arrested for treason."

"A fine start and end to my reign," Jon replied with no small amount of sarcasm. "Destabilizing the Houses. Moreover, the simple fact of my attendance will demonstrate Parliament's power to compel my appearance." Coming like a dog to heel whenever Parliament held out? It hadn't worked for King Marcus.

Shaking his head, Derric looked off to the side. "Then... a lettre de cachet?"

The logical next move. A signed and sealed order... a lettre de jussion commanding Parliament to act, joined by Pons' signature and seal as Lord Chancellor.

Far too moderate a measure for that lot. "A lettre, too, may be ignored."

Derric hesitated and gave him a grim look. "Darker routes, then?"

Jon drew in a slow breath. Without Parliament's acknowledgment of the legitimization, there would be no coronation, and the matter of succession would remain unsettled. For the stability of the kingdom, there was little he would not do.

And if he failed, he'd be powerless to do what needed doing, slave to the lords' selfish desires.

No, he couldn't afford to lose face to Parliament's drama. His actions now would set the tone of his relationship with the Houses for the rest of his reign. He needed to have the appearance of control, which would fail if Parliament was in a position to reject any of his actions. Yet he needed to maintain stability, which meant that arrests, executions, and assassinations were off the table.

Bending influential members of Parliament was his best option. Demonstrate to the rest of the Houses and to Emaurria that he commanded respect.

Duke Maerleth Tainn was out of the question—too affluent to be bribed and too insulated to be threatened.

But Viscount Costechelle could be bent. The means would set a precedent. A bribe would mean a never-ending and ever-growing demand for coin, and an evergreen source of blackmail. But a threat... a careful but real threat... Its judicious use here could ensure future compliance.

Threatening innocents was against the Code.

Jon rubbed his chin. Could a king continue playing by a paladin's rules? It was wrong, sinful, unethical...

But those were burdens to *his* honor, and against the burdens of the kingdom, weren't they wanting? If he had to do wrong to do right, wasn't that his responsibility now as king, no matter what it made him?

He drew in a deep breath and grimaced. "I... I want you to ask Paladin Grand Cordon Guérin to pull paladin defense from the viscount's castle in Costechelle. They are, however, to maintain defense of the city."

The color drained from Derric's face. "Costechelle has been battling a harpy invasion for the past two weeks. If we pull the paladins from the castle's defenses, the viscount's family and household could be killed."

"I know." To a paladin, it would have been unconscionable. Unthinkable. Leaving people helpless in the face of imminent death. It *was*.

But Viscount Costechelle left Emaurria helpless in the face of imminent death. And if needed, its king would have to cut the finger to save the hand.

If the viscount bent, he would influence other lords to join him. And if he didn't, well... He'd be broken, and the consequences might serve as a lesson to the other lords. The more vulnerable among them would either surrender or seek support from the strong. Either way was better than deadlock.

Ruling a kingdom wasn't the same as keeping the faith. As a paladin, he'd prioritized the Terran faith and its tenets above all else, but as a king, he could afford those voluntary shackles no longer. And neither could his advisers.

No matter what it cost him.

Derric blanched. "Raphaël will never agree to it."

Jon only stared him down. "He will if he wants to keep one of his paladins on the throne." He rose. "Talk to him, then send the viscount word that the paladins at the castle must reinforce the city to protect its citizens, and that he should make arrangements with a private force. Have a dove ready to deliver orders to the paladin commander there, and await word from Parliament about the viscount's vote before reestablishing defense of the castle."

If the viscount chose to ignore the consequences, then he would seal his own fate.

"Mercenary forces are exhausted," Derric reminded him. "If he does not comply, there will be casualties."

"And how many more will there be if we must repel challenges to the Crown due to his obstructionism? Has all of this been for nothing?" He lowered his gaze.

How far would he have to go to secure the interests of the kingdom? The sacrifice and dishonor accumulated—but his duty was absolute.

And failure would mean... It would mean that all he'd sacrificed, every dark deed he'd done, would have been for nothing. He had to succeed. After so much sin, there was no other choice now. "We will see if the serpent still bites when presented with its own tail."

Derric gaped at him.

A knock on the door.

"Enter," Jon called.

The door opened, and Pons entered. "Your Majesty," he greeted, then shared an affectionate look with Derric.

Jon nodded in greeting. "What is it?"

Holding up a scroll, Pons said, "Everything is in order for the Earthbinding, but there is still some preparation for Your Majesty before we travel to the Vein. You must fast for a fortnight from sunrise to sunset, and purify your body."

The time for the pagan ritual had come.

# CHAPTER 23

The weak winter sun had reached its zenith in the pale sky, the glitter of its rays modest on the never-ending snow cover outside the forest's edge. All seemed as it had always been. Leigh looked at the rest of the riders. If Vervewood lay within, it did not look any different from the outside. He'd seen this woodland many times, traveling to Melain or Courdeval, and had never suspected the ruins of an entire elven civilization resided within. Perhaps it was time for a new pair of specs.

Elven civilization or not, the sooner he met with this Narenian Sunheart and negotiated the peace, the better. Then he'd bring his wayward former apprentice home. No matter what Jon said, Marcel could only be trusted to pursue his own selfishness. And that would come into conflict with Rielle's wellbeing. It was as certain as the wind was cold.

He sighed. Too much damn time on the road. It was cold, and snowy, and void of wine and whores, and cold. The Divinity was rotten to the core, but at least Pons knew better than to send him on back-to-back missions. Knew that a month or two indoors kept a wild mage a little less... wild.

"How much farther?" he grumbled.

"Not far." Ambriel Sunheart led the way. Although the captain had been quiet for days, his silent stares had become longer, intense, pensive. Perhaps one tangible perk of being on this mission.

Well, the captain's *tangibility* was yet to be certain.

Mostly, he pretended not to notice the looks. Then, on occasion, he met them unequivocally. His reactions puzzled the handsome captain. Good. Leigh hid a smile.

As they entered the forest, his skin warmed, his energy refreshed; he took a deep breath, his body, by all signs, awakening. Warming. Invigorating. How curious. The air hung heavy, dense, but it did not weary; rather, it revitalized. Although faint by comparison, it was like becoming one with the earth's anima at the Vein where he'd become a wild mage, a sort of rush of refreshing energy. He looked around. The light-elves' stiffness relaxed, yet the Emaurrians seemed unaffected.

"It is a prophet's connection to the earth that allows him to sense where its magic is strong," Ambriel said.

Leigh turned to him, but Ambriel did not face him—he merely stared ahead, riding through the trees, his horse's hooves crunching on the moderate accumulation of snow. But his lips twitched.

Connection to the earth... He hadn't awakened at the forest's edge. The earth had. Two months ago.

He bowed his head and pulled his hood. The Rift hadn't only awoken the Immortals but the very earth, too, then? Or had the light-elves done that?

Ambriel led them to a narrow path. Despite the forest's distinct new feel, there was still no sign of an elven civilization. Leigh surveyed the forest ahead. Trees. Plain damn trees.

But something was amiss. The snow cover lessened the farther in they traveled. And the longer he stared, the stranger the sight of the trees lining the path became. Change. Were they changing? He looked down the narrow path, but it widened. The trees, they... bent around it, curving in a natural embrace as far as his eyes could see. He gasped.

Whispers and sharp breaths rippled through the Emaurrians, even the gigantic Sir Marin.

"Vervewood welcomes you, Ambassador," Ambriel said loftily and smiled.

"Geomancers?" The magic was subtler than he'd ever seen, if so, but he had to know.

"Magic? No, Ambassador."

A familiar two-note song came from the trees. A chickadee. The male sang the song in isolation, when away from other chickadees, especially its mate. A familiar sound from Ren, his home in Kamerai. But here, in Emaurria? He scoured the canopy for the songbird.

At last, he found the small, round bird, its shining black head and bib a stark contrast to its white-and-beige body. The chickadee ruffled its feathers, inspected him, and flew to land on his arm. The bird hopped, bit by bit, to his wrist, and examined him expectantly.

"Is this... actually happening?" Leigh asked, his tone quiet and even, for fear of startling the bird.

"He's come to greet you," Ambriel said.

Greet...? The chickadee eyed him, turning its head this way and that. If he remembered his tales right, there was a good chance he was about to burst into song and be kissed by a prince.

The bird flew away and landed on a branch, resuming its two-note song.

Leigh blinked and tried to find his tongue. Minutes passed. Or hours. "That... doesn't usually happen."

"There's a certain allure to the unusual." A gleam in Ambriel's eye. Seductive. Brief.

Yes, the unusual certainly did bear an allure. "I concur," he answered, lending his voice the unmistakable low tone of interest.

A corner of Ambriel's mouth turned up, then he looked ahead. They crossed a lengthy bridge of melded wood, like greenery grown together, over a ravine surrounding a large plateau. Leigh followed Ambriel's line of sight.

So much green. His jaw dropped.

Across the bridge, ironwoods, tall and straight, stretched toward the heavens, standing equally spaced like sentinels of the forest. But their branches—fine, reaching—intertwined in arches, circles, and winding patterns.

Between two ironwoods, spaced farther apart than the rest, a majestic arched bough bridged them high in the canopy. An intricate design not unlike the lattices of Sonbahar decorated the space above, its art not dense like that of Sonbahar but natural, easy, flowing. In the center, a beautiful, circular symbol graced the design, capped by another glorious arch.

Light flanked the beauty of this living panel of trees, bright, serenely so. Through the arch and farther ahead, a massive trunk figured in the open woodland, as thick as ten ironwoods grown together. But rather than stretch toward the heavens, its wood split, braided around itself, bloomed into a verdant crown in the center. And there, at its heart, a massive crystal glowed with a golden light, touched by the sunlight streaming through a rare part in the canopy, absorbing the radiance and illuminating all around it.

It was... the source of serenity. Breathtaking. Divine. "Was this... always here?"

Ambriel hesitated. "When we... awakened, the Tree of Light had grown around the Gaze, but we asked it to bloom."

Asked? He jerked his chin at the odd choice of terminology. "You mean 'spelled'?"

"No."

"You... asked... a tree to do something?" Leigh challenged, raising an eyebrow at the captain. "As in, 'Excuse me, tree. Could you please open up?' "

"Not I. A tree-singer."

Tree-singer... His mind conjured images of elven bards singing to trees for favors. What could one ask it for? Shade? Wood? Relationship advice? "And it... complied?"

Ambriel bobbed his head toward the Tree of Light. "What do your eyes tell you, Ambassador?"

Leigh scowled, but then again, he himself had never been merciful with slack-jawed bewilderment either.

As they passed by the Tree of Light and the Gaze, they came upon an overlook and a wide stair descending below. But beyond the edge—

A sea of trees—no, buildings—no, trees—formed a city. Hollows too perfect to be natural formed in thick ironwood trunks; stairs wound around them; doorways and balconies and windows figured, not carved or drafted but sung? Small crystals not unlike the Gaze hung from winding branches.

Boughs bridged the tree-structures, connecting nearly everything high in the canopy. Clear water flowed from a waterfall flanking it all, parting the woodland realm with a gentle system of sun-dappled streams. Grass grew green and thick, a lush verdant bed, paying no mind to the season.

And, above it all, a harmony so beautiful it might have floated down from the heavens.

"Are you all right, Ambassador?"

Leigh wiped the moisture from his eyes. Blinked. It was all still here. "I've never seen anything so... magnificent."

"My heart warms at your praise of Vervewood's view, but there is still much you have not seen." Ambriel surveyed him through long, fair lashes.

"Show me." Leigh tore himself away from the scene to face the captain.

Ambriel gave a cordial nod, then led their party down the wide stair into Vervewood and, presumably, to Narenian Sunheart.

# CHAPTER 24

*R*ielle reached out next to her in the massive bed, brushing her arcanir-cuffed arm against the smoothness of the sheets. Farrad was already gone—the sun had only begun to rise, but he often left early to practice the sword. She rolled over, her bare back against the luxurious bedding, and stared up at the bed's gossamer white canopy. How many days had it been? Or had it been weeks?

Every day, she worked in Ihsan's solar from the early morning hours until long after the sun had set, and then she came here, to Farrad's quarters, where she worked long into the night to keep herself and her child safe.

She stroked the fine cotton sheets. The conditions certainly had improved over the slave quarter, and the constant fear took a nightly reprieve. Farrad had been passionate, protective, and perhaps, in his own way, affectionate. She was his lover, but more than her surrender, he sought her ear. Every night, he recounted the day's events, talked through problems, shared plans. The workings of House Hazael had opened to her, split like the bed curtains.

Mornings were always a negotiation with herself. *Unfaithful. Disloyal. Inconstant.* How could she share her heart with one man, but a bed with another? If Jon knew...

Across the black canvas of her eyelids, she could see his face, the line between his brows, his squeezed-shut eyes, a shake of his head. His back as he turned from her. His figure fading into the distance.

She wasn't here by choice. She wasn't free to leave. Jon would understand that, wouldn't he? A man could be reasonable...

But love wasn't. He would *understand* the confines of her prison, sympathize perhaps, but could his love endure this? Knowing she'd been with another man?

She shook her head. Love was unreasonable. Love didn't survive disloyalty, no matter the excuse. Nothing would ever be the same. But this was survival.

She smoothed a hand over her belly, caressing it like she did every morning. It remained flat as it had always been, perhaps even more so since she'd been off the shores of Emaurria, but she could nonetheless feel her child, a fullness inside of her, the indescribable feeling of, even now, somehow never being alone. Samara had guessed that it could have been conceived no earlier than some three and a half months ago.

Jon's child. She lowered her gaze but smiled to herself. Regardless of whether she and Jon could be together, the child in her belly had been fathered by the man she loved.

And their baby couldn't be born here, into the hands of slavers. If she could escape, if she could make it back to Emaurria... It was too soon, much too soon, but he'd be happy to be a father. Overjoyed. He would love this child, raise her, protect her, guide her.

*Her.* Rielle bit her lip. When had she decided their child was a daughter?

"What's your name, sweet?" she whispered, caressing her belly. What would it be like to hold her own daughter, to nurture her, to watch her grow up?

She remembered Mama singing as she brushed her hair, untangling curly locks full of prickly rose-bush leaves and honeysuckle, grass, hay, and mud. Some mothers would have scolded little girls who climbed, hid, rolled around, and came home looking wild. But not hers.

*Nature is in your blood, Rielle. It calls to you, and you answer.*

Rielle smiled. *I miss you, Mama.*

"Sylvie?" she offered, short for Sylviane, like her mother. The name of a strong, kind, wise woman.

No objection came. Would Jon like it?

It was a good name. He'd love it. Sylvie. Sylviane Lothaire. With Shining Sea eyes, his eyes, and her laugh, and prickly leaves in her hair.

Rielle let the grin linger a while longer. She had a long day ahead of her. Here in Farrad's quarters, her relief at momentary safety hadn't tempered her desperation to escape, and she had to keep looking for a way out. Sylvie would not be born to slavery. In a few months, it might be too difficult, and after Sylvie was born, perhaps impossible.

And she had Farrad's favor now, his protection, but for how long? He'd taken many lovers, and how would she know when her time would pass? And... what would happen to her then?

She had to escape *soon*. Now. While it was still possible.

Tonight, after completing her work in Ihsan's solar, she would take the long way back to Farrad's quarters and evaluate her options for escape. Even in arcanir cuffs, there had to be a way.

Her stomach had the audacity to growl at her. She sat up. A breakfast tray already awaited on the bedside table with a silver dallah of coffee; it still steamed. A fragrant stack of freshly baked flatbread heaped upon the tray, teasing her nose. Around the bread, small bowls of white goat cheese contrasted with gleaming black olives. A thick yogurt cheese filled yet another dish, glistening with olive oil.

Before she'd become Farrad's lover, she had seen such breakfasts for the Hazaels or guests, but never for herself. It was a far cry from the porridge or beans and lentils of the slave quarters, a very tangible benefit of her new status. Since Farrad had taken to leaving her here in the mornings, she'd always wrapped the remaining food and brought it back to the slave quarters later to share. And so she would do today.

She swept aside the diaphanous bed curtains and reached for the dallah, uncovering the metal flap on the long spout's crescent-shaped beak to pour herself a demitasse of coffee.

She grabbed a piece of flatbread, tore it to pieces, and helped herself to the feast, rushing. Her meal might have been fit for a distinguished guest, but she, here, most certainly wasn't one. She had work to do.

Hastily, she washed and dressed and hurried to the slave quarters to hand off breakfast, then to the third-floor solar. Ihsan, dressed in a beautiful indigo thiyawb, already awaited her and greeted her with a quirked eyebrow.

"You're late," Ihsan said flatly, not looking up from her work. "Perhaps my brother's attentions are going to your head."

"I apologize, Zahibi." Rielle bowed low. "It won't happen again."

"See that it doesn't." Although Ihsan's voice had a hard edge, something like a smile emerged on her face. Not a smile, exactly—a twist of the lips.

Rielle hurried to her workstation and gathered up the stack of news and correspondence. She spread a new roll of paper, dipped her quill in the inkwell, and began translating.

Although Ihsan was aware of her new arrangement with Farrad, she'd made no negative comment. Well, nothing more than general irritation.

The day Rielle had arrived at House Hazael, the feud between the siblings had seemed so deep-seated, and she such a point of contention, but neither Ihsan nor Farrad had shown any of the same rage since the new arrangement. Farrad was pacified, but Ihsan? She hadn't so much as sniffed in complaint. It was unusual, and something didn't fit.

Rielle paused, letting a black droplet fall back into the inkwell. She'd watch, pay attention, but in the meantime, she had a mountain of work ahead of her.

The hours passed in boredom, scribbling translations, until she came across a piece of news from Emaurria: Parliament had yet to confirm Jon's legitimization. She narrowed her eyes. Of course the elitists of Parliament would hesitate in confirming Jon. They wanted something—they usually did—but with Jon as king, how likely were they to get it?

Ihsan glanced over, and as nonchalantly as she could, Rielle continued and moved on to the next piece of translation. The day dragged until her hand ached and the daylight dwindled.

Once she'd finished, she stood from her stool and put away the books Ihsan had left out, taking a moment with some of the tomes on magic. These past few weeks, she'd been practicing the ritual for a forbidden sangremancy three-level ward. It required three perimeters of the caster's blood, which could be activated with a word—*Yol.* Perhaps it would someday prove useful against Shadow... and the irony of defeating her with a spell learned here, of all places, would be fitting.

She was reading about flame-cloak destabilization in a pyromancy book when Ihsan's voice carried from far back among the bookshelves.

"Thahab, come here moment."

In all her days working here, this had never happened. Called to the back? She took wary steps toward the source of Ihsan's voice, thoughts racing.

Swallowing, Rielle rounded the bookcases to find Ihsan in the dark, sitting at the window, the lattices open, gazing out at the starlit night sky. She gestured to a chair opposite her.

Her chest tight, Rielle moved as bidden.

For a long while, they sat, the sweet scent of jasmine wafting in, coupled with the cleanliness of crystal waters, the freshness of the palms. The silence lengthened until the calls of birds, the soft foot-steps of patrolling guards below, and the rustle of trees in the night wind became almost deafening. Beyond the window, the lush grounds, and the walls of House Hazael, the city of Xir glittered, a sea of sparkling gold against the black velvet night. Out there, free women lived—mages, warriors, sisters, mothers, lovers, daughters—living as they pleased, somewhere that guards didn't threaten them and arcanir shackles didn't exist.

And somewhere beyond the shimmering city, across the scorching desert and the Bay of Amar, her homeland lay waiting, soft cool earth patiently expecting her homesick feet. And, she prayed, Jon.

"What would you do," Ihsan's soft voice broke the quiet, "if I told you I would like to free you?"

*Am I... Is this a daydream?* Rielle's gaze darted over, and Ihsan clearly sat next to her. A master of this house had spoken those words? Given the chance to escape this frightening life? To reunite with Jon, Olivia, Gran, Brennan, Leigh, and everyone else she loved? To have her free-dom? To bring Sylvie into the world away from this place?

It had to be a dream, but even if it was, she would grasp the chance with both hands.

"Anything, Zahibi," Rielle whispered in reply.

Even in the dark, Ihsan's eyes were grim. "I hoped that would be your answer." She leaned in and tucked a lock of Rielle's hair behind her ear; Farrad liked her to wear it unbound. "Your knowledge of High Nad'i was not the only reason I chose you. The day of the auction, I reached out to you in resonance. I know you are possessed of strong magic and a deep anima, and that is exactly what I need."

Looking into Ihsan's eyes for some hint of what she wanted, Rielle could find nothing. "I don't understand, Zahibi."

Ihsan took a deep breath and leaned back, then blew it out in a long, wistful exhalation. "I wish to see House Hazael in honor," she said, "with no slaves... but paid servants in every position. Grandfather had always planned to do it, but nearing death, with Farrad whispering in his ear about fortune, the family name, legacy, and so on, his determination has wavered," she explained. "Mine has not. I, however, cannot realize this vision unless I am House Hazael's scion."

That left only one answer. "You want Farrad dead."

Ihsan's brow creased. "For Aina, for the countless others he has brought to violent ends—yes. I want to see him dead. And you are in the perfect position to make it so."

The perfect position. Rielle raised her eyebrows. Aina had been in the perfect position, too, hadn't she? To try to kill Farrad? The perfect position for his hands to close around her neck and strangle the life from her body.

Then this was how she had died, a pawn moved by Ihsan, a sacrifice in Ihsan's grand game to win her family's empire.

A sacrifice...

She need not be. A master mage of the Divinity of Magic, she was a quaternary elementalist, manipulator of fire, water, earth, and air. Without her arcanir cuffs, she could bring down all of House Hazael, reduce it to rubble, to dust, and killing one man would be child's play.

*One man. Farrad.*

Her heart softened, and her shoulders slumped. The only reason she sat here now, unharmed, was because of him. In all their nights together, in all he'd told her, he'd never mentioned his plans for the future, nor his support of slavery. No manipulation of his grandfather. It didn't seem like him.

Samara's father... an honorable man—

*Who owns slaves. Who owns me.*

No matter how kind he seemed to her, his kindness was, by circumstance, impossible. A person who didn't find fault with owning other people could never be kind. Could never be honorable.

A person who didn't find fault with owning other people was a person she could kill.

But she had been gullible before, and vowed never to be gullible again. How could she trust Ihsan's word? "What do you wish me to do, Zahibi?"

The chair cushion rustled as Ihsan faced her. "Every year, Farrad has a massive celebration for his birthday." Ihsan pulled up the coverlet and propped her head up with her hand. "He invites all the nobles, and he drinks, celebrates. The party rages on into the wee hours—with everyone, the guards included, partaking to excess. He always takes his current favorite at the end of the night to his chamber. This year, he will do the same, and that woman will be you. There, alone with him, you will kill him." Ihsan's face was expressionless, but almost... placidly so.

Rielle frowned. How could it be possible? How had Ihsan known Farrad would choose her as his lover?

*She is mine.* Ihsan's words echoed in her head from that first day at House Hazael. Farrad's intensifying look, scorching as the desert sun.

Had all of that been to spark Farrad's interest? She assessed Ihsan with new eyes. Whatever game the woman was playing, she was a master.

But even if Farrad took her to his chamber that night, how could she kill him? Her robes would afford her no privacy to hide weapons. She'd have no use of her magic. She'd have no means. "But—"

"The day of the party, I will replace your arcanir cuffs with false ones." Ihsan took her hand.

*False arcanir cuffs.* She would have full use of her magic.

"And then, I will leave town on business. You will do as he asks all day and all night until he takes you to his chamber. Then you will kill him, and anyone who gets in your way, and then you will leave this place," she said. "I will bribe a guard at the West Gate to give you passage and araqs for your journey, wherever you go—it is best if I do not know where, Thahab. I will return, mourn my dearly departed brother, and Grandfather will name me the scion of House Hazael. I will free every slave here and bring House Hazael into honor when his time comes."

Stunned, Rielle gaped at Ihsan. "You trust me not to kill you the moment you remove the arcanir cuffs?"

Ihsan nodded. "You have suffered here. I know this. But I also know that you have reason to live"—she eyed Rielle's belly—"and without my help, you will not make it out of Xir alive. The Divine Guard on the wall will overpower you."

How many mage guards were there? Perhaps a dozen? Were they all enforcers? No wild mages among them, surely. With the element of surprise, perhaps she could—

"Killing me, without a plan of escape as I will provide, would grant you, and your unborn child, a most certain end. Word would get to the gates long before you could."

Rielle hesitated. Just how long had Ihsan known about her child? Her mind searched back to the stable, the auction, and... Ihsan's examination. A scribbled note. Had it been then? A strong mage with an undeniable reason to live and escape... Power and desperation.

It had all been planned, from the beginning.

And Ihsan had been right. About everything. "Correct, Zahibi."

Ihsan gave her hand a squeeze.

"May I ask... what happened to Aina?"

A silence settled over Ihsan. "She... She wasn't a mage." Her voice was low, barely above a whisper. She looked away, her face shrouded. "But you are. You'll survive this, make it out in the chaos of the party. I know you will."

Aina hadn't been a mage... Well, Farrad knew nothing of her magic, of her reputation at the Tower. All he knew was what he saw. A woman. A slave.

"Are we agreed, then?"

Agree to have her arcanir removed, and for the reward of her freedom, kill a man who owned people?

"On my honor, yes, Zahibi," Rielle replied in earnest. It would be five days until Farrad's birthday, and she had precious little time to prepare. And she would need to hide her intentions from him until then.

"Good. Then go to him, Thahab, and keep him content. Do everything he asks for five more days, then in the confusion of the party, you'll go free."

Rielle nodded and rose, inclined her head to Ihsan, and departed for Farrad's quarters. Every night, he ordered a lavish supper that he shared with her as he relayed amusing bits of news; they shared his luxurious marble bath; and he plied her with kisses, massage, and pleasure into surrendering to him.

Once she set aside her guilt and her lack of meaningful choice, a part of her enjoyed his company, and but for his status as the heir to this vile empire, she might have been sorry to have to kill him.

Might have.

Taking the long way to Farrad's quarters, she tried to assess the options laid out before her. Could Ihsan be trusted? Her plan had been carefully constructed, but had she revealed the whole of it? Her reason, wanting to see House Hazael in honor, was worthy, if true, but it lacked the urgency to prompt the murder...

However, if Ihsan was offering her freedom from arcanir, she would gladly accept—but plan for the worst case. If anyone tried to apprehend her after Farrad's killing, she needed a proper escape plan.

Five days.

If Ihsan could deliver on her end, in five days, she would kill Farrad abd Nasir abd Imtiyaz Hazael.

In five days, she would be a free woman.

# CHAPTER 25

*D*eep in the heart of the royal lands outside of Courdeval, amid the snow-covered trees and grass, a large, verdant patch of grass somehow persisted despite the winter. On a summer day, to a non-mage, it might not have looked or felt anomalous.

But therein stood a massive, circular stone structure. Whether it was natural or constructed by some ancient beings, Jon couldn't fathom, but at its center lay a Vein. Wild magic.

Now, in the dead of winter, the stark white framed its power with unerring clarity, even in the scant light of torches and the gibbous moon.

His mind had filled to capacity with concerns the past few days. Armies, whether of the Order or the Crown, would not be enough. Vervewood's hunting squads would not be enough. And marriage—it was his last resort. The Earthbinding would have to work. It would protect the kingdom, as kings were supposed to do, but it required much. Much more than he had been prepared to give. Yet Pons' historical accounts of the flourishing land after kings became Earthbound convinced him beyond any reasonable doubt.

None but kings and their elite had ventured here to perform the ritual for centuries, if not millennia. And it felt *warm*. The silken robe and ermine-trimmed cloak he wore felt all too heavy here, hot despite the season.

The drum and the shroud of night eased his troubled mind. And here, he could think of nothing but the vibrations shaking him to his core, resonating with his anima. He closed his eyes, focused on the hum, attuned himself to it. Every part of him grew lighter even as it filled with life itself, until he felt weightless.

"Your Majesty," Pons' voice interrupted from outside the circle, "as I warned earlier, do not reach out to the power here in resonance. It would end badly."

"I'm not." The power reached out to *him*. Nonetheless, he pulled his attention away.

The Earthbinding had required a fortnight's fasting and bodily cleansing in waters blessed in the name of the dead gods. But here, he and each of the ritual's participants shared wine of Emaurria's grapes, vines, soil—touched by the starlight, night, moonlight, and firelight. Pons, Olivia, a chanter, two drummers, and the servant who summoned him to dinner every evening—he did not even know her name—partook of it with him. None but they would witness this sacrament, this blasphemy, this legend, this ritual. But his kingdom would know soon enough.

*The mythos of the Earthbinding can prove stronger than its true effects,* Pons had said, and there was wisdom to his words, based on historical accounts. If it could possibly be true, who would challenge a king powerfully bound to the land? What force would dare invade it, if its king could sense every change, affect an enemy army by will alone? And history had treated the Earthbound kings with respect.

He took in his surroundings. The stone formation created a sacred circle, like the ouroboros Rielle had identified in the Moonlit Rite. Here, he was to address the dead gods, undisturbed by outside forces. Their ways long lost, their names long forgotten, would they listen to his prayers? Did these deities still stand watch over the lands of their bygone worshippers?

A platter featuring four small mounds of soil lay just outside the circle, next to a pouch of moonstones. A white doe stood calmly, tethered to a nearby tree. A painted box concealed its contents. A water carafe stood free on an altar, its clear glass catching the beams of light.

Peering into his chalice, he watched the wine's dark surface. There would be no return from this ritual. In the eyes of Most Holy Terra, he'd be a blasphemer, a heretic calling upon false gods. But the day he'd climbed the twelve steps to sit upon the Emaurrian throne, he'd left Jonathan Ver, his soul, and his concerns below. Left behind, secondary, as he'd ascended to his new name, his realm, and its needs.

He stared at the reddish-purple darkness, then brought it to his lips and drained it. No return.

Pons' face maintained an appropriately contemplative frown. Next to him, Olivia stood in a black velvet gown, her eyes downcast, but as he looked at her, she raised her gaze to meet him.

Gleaming, anguished eyes. Pleading eyes. *Don't do this*, they said. *You can still refuse.*

Something in him fractured, and he offered her a half-hearted smile. *Thank you for caring about the man in me. His heart. His soul. Thank you for seeing more than the kingdom's blade.*

That's what he'd become, hadn't he? A blade to be drawn for the kingdom's sake, to be bloodied, to be tarnished, to be broken if needed. To be wielded coldly, pragmatically, for a blade was only a blade; it had no soul, no heart; it was only a tool, to be used in fulfillment of a purpose. Never to be considered, nor cared for, nor loved. Nor free.

Tears welled in her eyes.

*Thank you, Olivia.* But he shook his head. There was no turning back.

She covered her mouth, nodding once, twice, again, before lowering her gaze once more.

He glanced back at Pons, whose hardened expression left as little room to argue as there was to turn back. Jon dipped his chin in silent assent.

Pons clasped his hands. The unnamed woman came and took the chalice from Jon's hands, then left him alone in the circle once more.

Taking a deep breath to gather his composure, he hoped he'd remember all the words. There would be no second chances. He stepped to the center of the Vein, the cool grass caressing his bare feet. Revitalizing energy climbed through his body.

At the center, he turned his face up to the heavens, raised his hands on either side of him, palms facing upward.

"Hear me, Ulsinael, Lord of the Stars!" he called, in a deep, booming voice. "Hear me, Rathenis, Lady of the Night! Hear me, Nenarath, Lady of the Moon! Hear me, Firenith, Lady of the Flame!" He invoked all the gods overseeing the Earthbinding. "Turn thy holy visages away from thy Chosen's enemies. Listen not to their prayers. Accept not their offerings. Enemies of the land seek, by evil means, to bind the hands of thy Chosen. Most Divine of the Heavens, hear thy Chosen!"

He stared at the night sky's constellations, at the astral manifestations of the dead gods, willing them to hear his prayer.

"Hear thy Chosen, Ulsinael, Lord of the Stars!" Pons said. Jon's gaze at the sky remained unbroken.

"Hear thy Chosen, Rathenis, Lady of the Night!" Olivia said.

"Hear thy Chosen, Nenarath, Lady of the Moon!" the unnamed woman shouted.

"Hear thy Chosen, Firenith, Lady of the Flame!" a chanter called out.

Jon bowed his head in reverence and closed his eyes, surrendering to the raw drum beat.

"Hear thy Chosen, Ulsinael! He bares himself to thy light!" Pons said. Soft footsteps entered the sacred circle, drew closer until they stopped.

"Most Divine of the Heavens, hear thy Chosen," Jon said. "Ulsinael, Lord of the Stars, I bare myself to thy blessed light."

At that, the heavy, ermine-trimmed cloak fell away as Pons removed it. And then the silken robe.

Skyclad, Jon listened to Pons' retreating footfalls, keeping his eyes closed. Never in his life had he felt more exposed, but there was no room to feel, only to do what was necessary.

"Most Divine of the Heavens, hear thy Chosen!" Jon called out. "Rathenis, Lady of the Night, I submit to thy holy darkness." This time, quieter steps closed in. Olivia's. She rubbed him with soil from all corners of his kingdom, starting with his face and working her way down. She coated his neck, shoulders, back... He couldn't help but open his eyes.

A mortified part of him wanted to jump out of his skin, but he forced himself to stand his ground, to accept the contrition of this moment. Hers had to be much worse, and he'd beg her forgiveness later.

When she finished rubbing the dirt onto his feet, Olivia pressed her lips together and stood. She glanced up at him but once. A world of unspoken words stormed in her gaze, but at last, she gave a supportive nod and left the sacred circle.

His heart beat irregularly, but he focused on the next prayer.

"Most Divine of the Heavens, hear thy Chosen!" he called. "Nenarath, Lady of the Moon, I receive thy silvery touch." He held out his hands, his palms an empty cup.

The chanter, repeating words of a dead tongue to the beat of the drums, entered the sacred circle. She deposited moonstones in his cupped palms, cold and smooth against his skin. He closed his eyes, said a prayer to Nenarath, and returned them to the chanter. They would be dispersed to every corner of the kingdom. As the chanter left the sacred circle, Jon stared at the flame of a torch behind her. He watched it burn, raw, ancient, like the fire of passion.

"Most Divine of the Heavens, hear thy Chosen!" he shouted. "Firenith, Lady of the Flame, I cleanse myself of evil with thy righteous inner fire. I cast it beyond thy chosen land to curse my enemies."

The unnamed woman entered the circle then, clad in a luxurious, rabbit fur-trimmed cloak, the drum beat much too unforgiving for her delicate way. Her fawn hair flowed unbound behind her, decorated with a wreath of night-blooming jasmine, grown from this land. She fixed her chestnut-brown eyes, wide and gleaming, upon him.

His heart pounding, he watched her, too, his breath catching. He didn't know her name, but tonight, she was the land. Emaurria.

"Most Divine of the Heavens, hear thy chosen!" he called. "Bind me to the earth!"

She cast off the cloak. Naked beneath, she met his eyes shyly. Terra have mercy, he wanted nothing more than to pick up her cloak, wrap her in it, and send her back to the palace.

But that was not what duty required.

She approached, taking slow, uneasy steps. Unwilling to let her bear the burden alone, he moved to the close the gap, meeting her halfway, in the circle's center. He tried not to look at her nakedness, but could feel her gaze upon him, and so, out of respect, he focused on her face, her large eyes.

A trembling hand reached out and found his chest, over his heart. Slowly, she pressed her fingers into his flesh, the dirt of his land marring her immaculate skin. His skin barely contained his nervousness.

He couldn't do this.

He had to do this.

The drums beat on, no slower, without stopping, relentlessly. He gazed up at the moon, a man beneath it as billions had stood before, with a woman beneath it as billions had stood before. Her hand slid up his chest to his shoulder, then glided over its curve and down over his bicep to his forearm until it joined his. She raised his hand to her breast, pressed his palm into her supple flesh. Rising on her toes, she curled her fingers around the back of his neck, wove them through his hair, urged his mouth down to hers.

His heart sped to bursting.

Run. He wanted to run. But his body wouldn't cooperate.

Her lips—small, fine, and delicate like the rest of her—found his. As their kisses deepened, he knelt with her and lowered her gently to the bed of supple grass. Her hold was tight. Firm. Needy.

There was no turning back now.

The sweet smell of the flowers in her hair mingled with the deep scent of earth in his nostrils. Beneath him, she winced, but a second later, she opened her mouth in a silent gasp. He imagined the moon above them watching a man and woman lying beneath, lying as billions had lain before. The ancient, primal beat of the drums filled him up until the surrounding winter spun, until his head swam, until torchlight played on her face in mystical illusions, and the beat took him, took his body, hers, immortal rhythm beneath an immortal moon, the ancient music of the night played fierce and hard, vigorous and raw, driving, driving, and driven at last to stunning end. He heard his own shaky exhalation in the quiet from afar, her soft cries, and he blinked at the distant world beneath him as it faded to torchlight playing on her flushed face.

Relaxation claimed his body, and he held her as she trembled. She covered his hand with hers, stroking his fingers as her breath slowed. Calmed.

At last, he rolled onto his back next to her and stared up at the black heavens, their darkness impossibly wide and deep.

This most intimate of moments hadn't been for strangers, for other women, but for the one he loved. That intimacy was now gone. Forever.

And the woman, hadn't she imagined her first time with a man she loved? A man who'd love her, who'd be there for her? He stared at the black sky, but no answers came. He'd taken something from this woman. Something he hadn't wanted to take, that she shouldn't have had to lose.

But the bond was consummated.

She sat up next to him and, with Pons' assistance, rose. He wrapped her in a cloak, handed her a cup of wine.

When Jon sat up, he planted his feet on the ground, rested his elbows on his knees, stared at his hands. Dirty. Like the rest of him.

He let his hands fall atop his elbows and rested his forehead on his arms. *A separate matter.* He'd allowed sex to become a separate matter from love. He clawed at his chest, at the painful hollow forming there.

The Laurentine signet ring wasn't there. Removed. For this.

When Pons led the woman away, Olivia tarried a moment and rubbed her upper arms before opening the painted box, retrieving a dagger in its scabbard, and leading the white doe into the sacred circle. Her footsteps stopped, and Jon raised his head. She held out the dagger to him hilt first.

His fingers brushed the crossguard. Wetness streaked her face, her eyes reddened beneath a determined frown. So many wrongs tonight, so many sins, and it wasn't enough. With this blade, he was to kill innocence, if he could muster the resolve.

It was all too much, too far for Jonathan Ver, but this... this was for his kingdom. He couldn't falter for the sake of his own morality.

He pulled the dagger free of its scabbard. Rising to his knees, he regarded the animal before him, her skin a pure white. His manner gentle, he reached out to touch her. Her flesh rippled at the contact, but her breathing slowed, relaxed.

Still petting her, he plunged the dagger deep into her heart. She gave a distressing cry and fell to the ground.

Something pure had been destroyed tonight. Something beautiful. Irretrievably.

Olivia dropped the doe's lead, left the sacred circle, took something else out of the painted box—a black opal. Gesturing over it, she whispered an incantation.

Indignity, cruelty, infidelity. Blasphemy. Betrayal of his goddess, his love, and himself. This would cost him all that he cherished, all that he loved, all that he was.

The Earthbinding demanded much. Too much. But he had to finish.

Returning his attention to the sacrificed doe, he dipped his fingers into her blood, pulled them out, and spilled the blood to the north. He repeated the action for the other cardinal directions, an offering to the dead gods, requesting them to protect the land on all sides. When he finished, he used the dagger to skin the doe.

It had been months since he'd skinned an animal, but his hands hadn't forgotten. Something familiar to do, something he could lose himself and his dark thoughts in. Careful, methodical, he completed the task. He lay his new ceremonial dagger next to him.

Olivia brought the opal into the sacred circle, deposited it into his bloodied hands, and walked away.

He gazed up at the sky, holding up the gemstone, blood running down his arms. "Most Divine of the Heavens, hear thy Chosen! I confine the evil of my enemies in purity, that they may do thy chosen land no harm," he said and placed the black opal inside the doeskin, then wrapped it. It made the perfect confinement for evil and impurity, being pure from the outside while holding the symbolized evil inside.

Olivia took the doeskin containing the opal and sewed it closed. She placed it at the circle's center.

He put his hand on the sealed package. "All evil threatening my land, I, Chosen of the Most Divine of the Heavens, order thee to depart."

When Jon held out his hands above the doeskin package, Pons approached with a water carafe and poured. Jon washed his hands, transferring all lingering impurity to the doeskin package. Pons picked it up; it would be taken beyond Emaurria's borders to protect the land.

It was time. Were the dead gods alive once more to hear him? Cleansed, consummated, suppliant, he would be bound to the earth now, or he wouldn't.

He stood, looked at the sky, held out his hands to his sides, palms facing up. "Most Divine of the Heavens, hear thy Chosen!" he bellowed. "Enemies of the land seek, by evil means, to bind the hands of thy Chosen. Accept not their offerings. Listen not to their prayers. Turn thy holy visages away from thy Chosen's enemies. Hear me, Firenith, Lady of the Flame! Hear me, Nenarath, Lady of the Moon! Hear me, Rathenis, Lady of the Night! Hear me, Ulsinael, Lord of the Stars!"

He stared at the night sky's vast constellations, at the astral manifestations of the dead gods, willing them to hear his prayer. Weariness slowly took its toll; he blinked as the torches became flame-red wisps and the ritual's participants no more than silhouettes against the firelight.

"Hear thy Chosen, Firenith, Lady of the Flame!" the unnamed woman cried.

"Hear thy Chosen, Nenarath, Lady of the Moon!" the chanter shouted.

"Hear thy Chosen, Rathenis, Lady of the Night!" Olivia called.

"Hear thy Chosen, Ulsinael, Lord of the Stars!" Pons shouted.

Exhausted, Jon broke his gaze from the sky and clasped his hands. Had he been heard? Would he be Earthbound?

Rielle would never forgive him. He would never forgive himself.

His mind barraged, all grew dark as he collapsed.

# CHAPTER 26

Crossing a desert should have given Brennan time to think, but all it had done was sharpen his resolve to kill. Every step, every stride, his mind seized on new and worsening fates Rielle may have suffered. He'd found strands of her hair, but that meant she was in trouble, far more than she'd ever been. As he made his way into Xir, no matter which House had her—Afzal, Fakhri, or Hazael—he was ready to destroy anyone and anything that could have hurt her.

In the vast emptiness he'd traversed, there had been some comfort in liberating the Wolf. He'd given his rage free rein, a step closer to making peace. When the Wolf had finally exhausted himself, he'd begun to plan.

Since all three Houses were pleasure houses, the best course was rather simple: visit and request fair-haired slaves. Unless she was someone's private concubine, he would find her—and even then, he would smell her on her *master.*

A growl rumbled deep in his throat, and he tongued the edges of his teeth. Yes, he had something special in mind for that possible circumstance.

He would make use of Father's reputation and rely on the Houses' certain desire to please Duke Faolan Auvray Marcel. That would gain him entry and impeccable service. If all went well, no one would be alive to tell the tale; it was an unfortunate circumstance, but he was willing to do far more.

First, however, he headed to the one place in Xir where he could set the stage for his plan: Father's villa. After sidling through Xir's narrow streets in the dying twilight, he ignored the villa's massive, metal-studded, wooden door. Instead, he listened for the guards within, crept around to the back, and once he'd exposed his claws, scaled the wall.

The villa's garden was just as he'd remembered. Among the heavy-laden lemon trees, myrtle shrubs grew everywhere, their five-petaled white flowers star-shaped pops of light in the gathering dark. As he stalked toward the shade of the lemon tree pergola, he breathed in the strong, resinous scent of terebinth shrubs—with their tiny, reddish-purple flowers—that overpowered all the others but that of the white rockroses.

Kehani had brought them from her village and planted them in the garden herself when Father had moved her in. Over the years, the white blooms—bearing a conspicuous, dark red spot at the base of each petal—had conquered the garden, growing everywhere light could find. Labdanum, the highly aromatic resin coating the rockroses' leaves, dominated the air.

At last, he ducked under the pergola, making his way to Father's room. Just below the window to his quarters, he climbed the wall, opened the window's lattice, and sneaked inside. The heady scent of ambergris stirred him, but it was solitary; there were no humans.

Quietly, he shut the lattice and moved aside the satin and velvet brocade drapes. The room was dark; it hadn't been used since the year before. Father would be arriving soon, as he always did, to winter with Kehani. While wintering with his mistress, Father planned to force *him* to marry, regardless of Rielle's decision, which was as certain as day giving way to night. To some other woman.

Well, Father would soon know his view on the matter.

The room was ornamented with grand furnishings—typical of Father—and featured a tented canvas ceiling, carved wooden chests, ornate statues, and a massive bed swathed in fine, white linens. Plush, tasseled pillows decorated in deep blues, yellows, and white added the woman's touch that could only be Kehani's.

Above the bed—he grimaced—was a massive portrait: Father, Mother, Nora, Una, Caitlin, and him. Father had commissioned two of them three years ago. So this was where he'd shipped the second one. No doubt Kehani *adored* that. Brennan scrutinized his own image—it was remarkably close, although the artist had given him an unusually devious expression.

Across from the window and through the interior latticework was an open-air inner courtyard, its formal sitting room on the ground floor. Brennan caught the tease of mint tea being served somewhere close. He moved to a nearby room with water to drink, wash, and shave, then returned to Father's room to dress. Although he'd needed to pack light—very light—Father's similarity in size would ameliorate that circumstance. Striding naked to the wardrobe, he threw it open and perused his options.

Delicate footsteps came from afar. Brennan knew Kehani's gait well. Grinning, he chose a luxurious white shirt, a black velvet doublet, and leather trousers, then tossed them onto the bed. It seemed that, like him, Father preferred Emaurrian attire over Sonbaharan, even if his wardrobe contained a small section of thiyawb.

Kehani walked in, flanked by guards, and gasped.

He flashed her a sly smile.

"Brennan," she whispered, waving off the guards. As they left, she took a few steps closer, her eyes darting from him to the portrait and back again. "Is it really *you?*" she asked, in Standard Nad'i. Her black-as-night eyes traveled over his body.

"Who else would dare raid Faolan Auvray Marcel's closet?" he asked in reply, in High Nad'i. Leisurely, he dressed while she watched.

Six years his senior, she was still as beautiful as he remembered. At home, she wore her hair loose, in cascading black waves. She was small, so very small, slender and, he guessed, light as a feather. She moved to light an oil lamp, and her flowing white gown trailed her every movement. And Great Wolf, Father left her to wilt here alone most of the year.

Her puzzled face gave away the words her position didn't allow her to ask. Although she lived in the villa, it belonged to Father, and Brennan was his heir. She could scarcely ask why he had come and why he hadn't used the front door. Brennan sighed.

"I'm meeting a friend to take in the city for a few days," he explained. If he had to bring Rielle back to the villa, then at least his story would make sense. "I would have come by the front, but you know I dislike fanfare."

Kehani smiled. When he was a child, they'd often grumbled to one another about the ostentatious displays Father insisted upon. "I welcome you," she said, and when he finished fastening his doublet, approached. She glanced down between them and back at his face. "Come. You must be ravenous."

Brennan wanted to raise an eyebrow but allowed himself only a tilt of the head and a mischievous smile. "Voracious."

Kehani held his gaze for a moment, then donning a pleasant expression, gave a nod and led the way to the inner courtyard's sitting room. He savored her scent, topped lavender and her own personal, comforting smell. It had been long, too long, since he'd visited. The last time he'd come, he'd been fourteen.

The servants brought wine and a salad of shredded carrots, chopped parsley, fresh garlic, and lemon juice, seasoned with oil, cumin, cinnamon, paprika, and cayenne. As the spice bloomed on his tongue, so did memories of his boyhood years. How he'd missed the place.

"The resemblance is uncanny." She watched him eat. Stared.

"Don't be ridiculous." Brennan moved on to the chicken couscous, isolating the flavors of saffron, turmeric, and ginger. "I'm not my father."

Kehani grinned. "I met your father when he was just a few years older than you are now. You look so much like him." Her gaze lingered.

Brennan shrugged. "What he and I share in common is a very short list."

"Not as short of a list as you'd think." Her gaze fluttered to him, a brief tease. She was attracted to him. He could use that.

The smell of the pastilla, an elaborate meat pie of shredded squab in crisp layers of werqa dough, wouldn't go ignored any longer. Brennan helped himself. The savory lemon-onion sauce married with the cinnamon sugar sprinkled on top in delicious harmony.

"No wonder Father returns heavy every year," Brennan commented before his last bite. "You should hear what the Maerleth Tainn weapon-master barks at him while sparring in the spring."

As she prepared a pot of mint tea in her elegant fashion, she chuckled. "Faolan says the same, but it never curbs his appetite."

Reclining to rest on an elbow, Brennan eyed Kehani's delicate hands as she served him mint tea. "Perhaps he and I do share... a lot more than I thought."

"Would that please you?" A dark look in her eyes.

"As much as it would please you." He sipped his tea, relishing the stiffening of her posture and the gentle flush of her cheeks. "Kehani..."

She cleared her throat. "Yes?"

"Would you"—he smiled briefly at her, raked his gaze over her form—"do something for me?"

Her throat bobbed. "What is your desire?"

Brennan let out a lengthy exhale, then took another sip of tea. "House Afzal."

Her perfectly shaped dark brows drew together. "I'm sorry?"

"A reservation. For tomorrow."

Her eyes widened, then she bowed her head and nodded. "If that is your wish."

"And House Fakhri, and House Hazael."

"When?"

He grinned broadly. "Tomorrow." So many pleasure houses in one visit would be tight, but he wouldn't be there for the entertainment.

"Three Houses? All in one night?" she asked, raising her eyebrows. She batted her eyelashes. "That's an ambitious night."

"I'm an ambitious man."

Her breath caught. "And tonight?"

He drank his tea, letting his heavy eyelids drape his gaze. "I'm open to suggestion."

"Perhaps it's time to retire. I find when I blow out the lamp, the night answers."

"Does it?"

"If you leave the drapes drawn, keeping out the light, yes."

The drapes drawn? The lights out? He could have swallowed his tongue.

It had been months since he'd bedded a woman. But this one... This one... presented distinct advantages. If he could control Kehani, he'd be free to do as he pleased here. Whatever was necessary. If she objected, he had only to tell Father, who had an abundance of mistresses but only one son.

He took a deep, relaxing breath. "I'll have to remember that."

"I hope that you do," she said, inclining her head. "Goodnight, Brennan."

"Goodnight, Kehani." He watched her leave, finished his tea, then headed upstairs to his father's quarters. The room was still dark but for the one oil lamp. Tomorrow would be a long day, but if fortune favored him, he'd find Rielle. He drew the drapes.

As he undressed, he hoped the fair-haired woman the Harifan slave trader had mentioned was indeed Rielle. It destroyed him to hope for such a thing, but when the alternative was no lead on Rielle whatsoever, it was the better of two terrible options.

*I will find you.*

He sat at the desk to write a quick letter to Nora about his whereabouts, sealed it, and marked it as outgoing for when the servants cleaned the quarters tomorrow.

At last, he blew out the lamp and went to bed, his mind still racing with thoughts of the next day.

Less than an hour later, the door creaked open, and when he smelled Kehani, he didn't stir. Dropping a thin garment on the floor, she approached the bed and, with a feather-light touch, pulled the cover from his naked body. Her mouth trailed needy kisses from his chest down.

He'd seen it in her eyes earlier—desire. Wilting in the desert alone had ill-suited her, and even days away from Father's arrival, she yearned for connection. The longing spoke through her eager fingers, her anxious lips. The heavenly sound—it teased the Wolf within, flirted with danger, maddened him.

She did as she pleased and then dismounted him.

Afterward, the Wolf's madness faded. He didn't say a word as Kehani found shaky footing on the floor, leaned against the bed for a moment, then gathered her garment and staggered out of the room. She closed the door softly behind her.

She hadn't lit a lamp, nor said a single word. Perhaps she'd thought it an anonymous encounter, just a woman, just a man, that he'd never be able to say with certainty it had been her and not a servant. A grin broke free. Being a werewolf had its advantages.

Spent, he melted into a sated relaxation, rolled onto his side, and drifted off to sleep.

~

RIELLE STIRRED AWAKE.

Farrad's quarters were still dark, and she reached her hand out next to her to feel the bed. His warmth was still there, but he wasn't. The stars shone through the lattices, and their familiar comfort flowed into her.

Quick steps came from the doorway to the hall, and she squinted to see through the sheer bed curtain. Farrad's strong form strode past the bed and to the desk.

He threw a piece of paper onto its polished surface, thumped his palms down, and leaned over it, taking deep, calming breaths. The starlight illuminated the hard muscles of his bare back, rigid in stark relief.

She'd never seen him frustrated like this; few things unsettled him. As her mind wandered to Ihsan's request, Rielle swallowed. Had he somehow found out?

She lay still, unmoving, her pulse quickening as the quiet length-ened. If he meant to kill her, bound in arcanir as she was, her only choice seemed death. She tried to slow her breaths, her gaze darting about the room for something, anything, she could use to defend herself. His rapier hung, sheathed, over the chair by his desk, too far for her to hope reaching, and requiring too much skill for her to successfully wield. On the bedside sat the near empty bottle of wine— of everything, it seemed her only option.

She surveyed him. Although he'd beat the desk in frustration at first, now he hung his head and his shoulders slumped. Disappointed?

If he knew about the plan to kill him, he would act. A duelist, a swordsman, his fighting instincts were sharp. If he were threatened, he wouldn't keep his blade sheathed.

What was it, then?

It had to be something else. Something that had caused him grief, not anger.

Gambling on her guess, she slipped from the bed, her feet cushioned by the thick rug beneath, and padded toward him, shivering at the night's coolness against her bare skin. When she reached the far side of the desk, he turned his head slightly but didn't look up. He hung it again, weighed down completely.

She extended a hand and let it rest between his shoulder blades, firming her touch to rub him gently.

He exhaled a relieved sigh, leaning into her touch. A night breeze swept in through the lattices, and he straightened, turned, and gathered her in a warm embrace. His fingers threaded through her hair, soothing her more than she liked; it reminded her too much of Jon.

She pushed the thought aside. She couldn't muster the ferocity to fight for her survival while drowning in guilt. There'd be time enough for that later.

"What is it, Zahib?" She rested her chilled cheek against the heat of his chest.

His fingers tugged gently, teasing a shiver from her.

"The burden of being Grandfather's heir weighs heavily tonight, upon me and upon you." He hesitated, but did not continue.

She peered up at him. "I don't understand, Zahib."

He cupped one of her cheeks in his hand and searched her eyes in the dim ambient light of the stars. "You call me Zahib, golden one, but I have no power here. I am no more than the palm, and my grandfather the wind."

A tremor shook her. What burden weighed heavily upon him, and upon her? Her mind presented a dozen terrifying possibilities. Was she to be sold? Was Sylvie? Did Imtiyaz want her working as a House pleasure slave?

She shuddered and dared not entertain these thoughts any longer.

"Please, Zahib." She pressed her fingertips into the hard flesh of his biceps. "Unburden yourself to me."

He raised her chin and kissed her, a light brush of his lips against hers, so soft it felt like a parting kiss.

Was it?

He pulled away but held her chin raised. "The son of a very important shafi here in Xir is coming to this House tomorrow. Grandfather has made it clear that no expense be spared to please this man. His father's influence, in no small part, keeps this House rich."

What was the problem? She shook her head.

"He enjoys young, exotic women—fair skinned, fair-haired, fair-eyed women among them, and I am looking at the only one of age in this House."

Her knees buckled. She staggered away until she hit the bed. She reached out to feel for the bedding before settling into it. "I am to be... given to him?"

Like some favor, she'd be presented to a stranger, for his amusement, for his pleasure. An object, reduced to three qualities—fair skin, fair hair, fair eyes.

Perhaps she'd evaded a night of violence in the slave quarters that night, but it had finally caught up to her. One more sacrifice to bear before she and Sylvie would be free.

She gazed up at Farrad, struggling to keep the tears from her eyes. He bridged the distance between them and knelt at her feet, then took her hands in his on her lap.

"If I could spare you this indignity, this suffering, I swear upon the Divine that I would."

She licked her lips and shook her head, looking away from him. The man for whose protection she had betrayed Jon couldn't protect her at all, and she'd been a fool to believe he could. Few could be trusted to truly place another's interests above their own when it mattered. And Farrad, heir to the slave-owning empire, could never be trusted to place anyone's interests above his own.

"You think I wish to share you with any other man?" he asked, his voice firm, deep, biting, as he squeezed her hands.

She snapped her gaze to his. "Then why are you doing this?"

"This order comes from above, from Grandfather. My hands are bound."

Her gaze descended to her own wrists, cuffed in arcanir.

"Poor choice of words." He rose and smoothed the hair on her head. "Were I truly the zahib of this house, this would never happen. I would see you—"

"But it *is* happening." She brought her feet up onto the bed and gathered her knees to her chest, bowing her head to hide her face from him.

"Yes," he said softly, distantly, "as long as Grandfather lives, I can do nothing to stop it." He put an arm around her, and as much as she wanted to push him away, she gave in and pressed her face into his neck, taking what solace she could.

Two days. If she could hold out for two more days, all of this would become a memory, a distant memory, one she could forget after some weeks, months, years in her own bed, among all she knew and perhaps even friends. She would love her child, raise the next Marquise of Laurentine, and these few months would be no more than sand carried away on the whispering winds.

Farrad climbed into bed with her, and she curled into him, watching the stars as she always did, and allowed herself to selfishly steal comfort from this man she would, in two short days, kill.

# CHAPTER 27

When Jon awoke in the comfort of his bed in Trèstellan Palace, he lay awhile with his eyes closed. His mind was quiet, but just beneath lay a new consciousness. Like the smell of red wine in his room, the feel of luxurious bedding, the sound of soft breath, and the taste of a parched mouth, he now perceived a thousand new sensations. Something strange in the forest outside of Courdeval... A freezing of the River Mel up north... A darkness near the Emaurrian Tower... And vivid life near Melain—Vervewood? And if he focused, he could single out an individual spark of nature, moving, living, breathing —a wild mage. Leigh.

But it wasn't like the night of the ritual, myriad impressions assaulting him all at once, overwhelming him, shutting him down. No, now it had all faded into the background, along with everything else he could perceive, unobtrusive unless he chose to focus on something in particular, like a taste, a sound, a touch, a smell, a sight.

He opened his eyes. Morning sunlight streamed into his bedchamber. Next to his bed, Tor sat in a chair and watched him, worry etched into his face and his broad shoulders hunched.

"Sacrilegious rituals and black arts," Tor mumbled with a sigh, then leaned forward in his chair and handed him a cup of water. "How are you feeling, Jon?"

"Less like my head will explode." Jon sat up and drank deep. On the windowsill outside the glass, snow piled high. In his bedchamber, flower arrangements covered every available surface. "Where did all this come from?"

"The suitresses wish you a quick recovery." Tor smiled.

The winter land offered no flora, so he imagined the royal greenhouses were a great deal emptier. Jon's mind numbed at the thought of returning to his everyday dance with deception and dishonor. The Earthbinding had exhausted him and demanded too much, but at least it had been honest. "How long was I out?"

"Two days."

Two days? Two days of work gone, two days of petitions, letters, negotiations—his head pounded, and he grimaced.

"You gave us quite a scare. Olivia said you were showing no physical symptoms, but that your mind was in a state of chaos, and you'd need time to recover. She said there was nothing for it but patience as your mind acclimated. Praise Terra, you've woken."

*Terra.* He winced. All his life, he'd worshipped Terra, served Terra, believed Her and Her pantheon to be the only gods, the *true* gods.

He'd performed the blasphemous ritual, and... It had worked. His prayers to the dead gods had worked. If the only gods in existence were Terra and the rest of the Eternan pantheon, then why had a blasphemous ritual to the dead gods worked?

Ulsinael, Rathenis, Nenarath, Firenith... They existed. His changed state confirmed Their continued existence. *Gods above, you heard me.*

But Terra had touched his life. It was as certain as night turning to day. Terra had to exist, too. She had to.

What did all of it mean?

"Do you feel any different?"

In every way. And not just from the ritual. He took in a deep breath, extending his perception to frost melting in the canal, hoof beats vibrating in the ground, wolf howls flowing through the forests. "I can feel the land—every boon, every harm, every anomaly. The Earthbinding worked."

"Thank Terra for that," Tor said, sitting up, "since Derric has announced you Earthbound to all the kingdom."

Never letting an advantage go unpressed... That was Derric.

Tor took a sip of wine, his face crinkling as he winced. "I have no idea how a ritual to the dead gods worked—and I don't think I want to know. What can you do with it?"

Good question. Jon sighed. "I don't know. I can... see things. Sense other places." He frowned. "But Pons and Olivia made it sound like it would be... more."

Tor set down his goblet and folded his arms. "Perhaps you could try to focus on a threat? See what you can do?"

With a nod, Jon closed his eyes.

He imagined the room around him... The down comforter, the four-poster bed, the rug, his weapons on the table, the silk drapes and their crystal ties catching the sunlight, the windows... And then the cool, crisp air chilled his skin. The brine of the sea filled his nostrils. Waves beat against the cliffs like his own body, and he ascended a rocky slope, the soft shrubs tickling, the dust texturing his entire body, to the darkness of a cave. Moist, moldy air inundated him, and then he was high up, black feathers catching spare sunlight below him. Large wings, long hair, human bodies clad in black robes, clawed hands, talons for feet... and human faces with too-wide mouths exposing the sharp teeth of a carnivore. Harpies.

His body was taut—no, completely rigid. Closer. He had to get closer...

He couldn't move toward them. Like stone, he was—

Stone. *I am the stone.* A copper vein in the rock. Entombed. Contained.

He traveled through the stone, circled them, moved below them. One stirred, raised his head, and stared at the ground. Scowled. Snarled.

He reached out, but nothing happened. Nothing moved.

He was the ground. And could no more fight the harpy than the ground could.

Nothing. It had been for nothing. He roared, shaking the pebbles and dust, and the other harpies awoke, searched.

He withdrew, back through the cave, down the mountain, off the cliffs and into the air, and he remembered his bed and himself in it. And opened his eyes.

Tor jolted upright in his chair. "Are you—"

"Worthless," Jon snarled, scrubbing a hand over his face. "It's worthless."

Tor moved to the edge of his seat. "What? Why? What happened?"

Nothing. Nothing had happened. That was the problem, his failure. "I can do no more than see and sense."

What had the Earthbinding been for? Was this all there was?

Tor rested a hand on his shoulder. "You've only just awoken. Don't surrender yet. Pons and Olivia will shed some light on this. You'll see."

On what? They hadn't even known what the Earthbinding would do. They still probably didn't. It had been a shot in the dark, and they'd hit nothing. Jon sighed.

Tor squeezed his shoulder. "This will cheer you up... Parliament confirmed your legitimization. Your coronation will be a few weeks after Veris."

So his deplorable machinations with Melletoire and Costechelle had succeeded. He wasn't sure whether to be disgusted with himself or celebrate. It seemed a common dilemma for him these days. "That's good news, at least."

"Well, it's not all good news," Tor said slowly with an uneasy grimace. "Caerlain Trel is repelling a pirate attack. While our navy is recovering, Silen has sent a flotilla of caravels and secured the coast and trade routes from Silen and Kamerai."

Emaurrian ship-builders worked hard to meet the navy's quotas, but not fast enough. Even one geomancer could make a dramatic difference in the navy's recovery, but Jon hadn't made overtures to the Divinity about it yet. There were questions of Rielle's whereabouts and Leigh's actions to consider before continuing diplomatic relations with Magehold.

But he had discussed creating an Order of Sages that welcomed the kingdom's hedge witches into training for the Emaurrian military. It would be some time before any of them would be fit for duty.

Moreover, thanks to King Macario, he was fulfilling the promise he'd made at the docks months ago—with the trade routes secured, ships would be sailing into port all along the coast, and even into Courdeval. There would be work at the docks again.

"Please send King Macario an extravagant gift of thanks." Although his navy needed recovery, the kingdom's coffers—and his own—certainly didn't.

"Already done," Tor answered. For a while, he remained frowning, his dark eyebrows drawn.

"Good." His mind wandered back to the ritual. He'd been with another woman. And for nothing.

Tor cocked his head, his eyes probing. " 'Good,' you say... And yet you look troubled."

No matter how well he learned to hide his expressions, Tor could always see through him.

"I know you feel the ritual hasn't accomplished much—"

"It's not that." Jon crossed his arms.

"Are you still feeling ill? Do you need to rest?"

"No." Jon paused and took a deep, slow breath. "You know I'm in love."

Tor nodded and folded his hands together.

"The Earthbinding... required a coupling." Jon sat higher in the bed, folding over the covers, and shook his head. "I'm in love with a woman, a missing woman, and while she's gone, I betrayed her with another." He pressed his eyes shut. "It's shameful. Dishonorable. And when I finally see Rielle again, what will I say to her? I can't lose her."

His elbows on the chair's armrests, Tor brought his folded hands up to his stubbled chin. "Tell her the truth," he said. "All of it. She might, in time, forgive you. She might not." He let one of his hands fall. "But you have not sullied your honor. Duty and circumstance left you few options, and this sacrifice, for its potential reward, was difficult but not unconscionable. To deny its occurrence when you speak to her, to give into deception, that would be dishonor."

"I would never lie to her. I just don't know how to say it."

"What matters is *that* you say it. You can't build anything on an unsteady foundation."

He should have expected Tor's advice would be to do the right thing and accept the consequences. It was something Jon had been trying to live up to all his life. Even now. But what was right had changed so much from his days as a paladin.

"Sometimes," Jon said, "duty calls for actions that dishonor the Sacred Vows."

Tor shook his head. "We are bound by them no longer." He picked up his wine goblet and held it out pointedly; he no longer held to the Sacred Vows either. "As a king, your duty is now to your kingdom first and to all else second. It is your path. Because I know you, I know you will sometimes despise yourself for it, but you must do what needs to be done. Unlike the well-lit path of a paladin, it is a shadowed path you walk now, the winding road traveling dark corners at times. And when you cross that darkness and punish yourself for it, know that I am here to tell you when to stop."

Jon nodded. As difficult as it was to accept, he would do what he had to. "What about Valen? Is he here?"

"He sat with you all through the night and is sleeping now," Tor replied, digging in his pockets, "but he asked me to give you this."

Jon opened the wax seal. Inside, the note said simply in Valen's rounded script: *No luck.*

The only link to the person responsible for the regicide, the siege, everything—was in the wind. With a sigh, Jon folded the note back up. "And Olivia?"

Tor grinned, and it reached his eyes. "She's... I... What a remarkable woman."

Jon canted his head. *Remarkable woman...* He raised an eyebrow and smiled. "Yes, she is."

Tor cleared his throat. "The paladin you asked to have discharged —Derric had it pushed through. All that remains is the knighting ceremony."

Sir Edgar. Good. If the assassin was still about, and the courier's master, then Olivia might need his help again.

Quick footsteps came from the antechamber. Derric hurried through the doorway. He was pale, with dark circles under his honey-brown eyes as they examined him.

"Praise Terra." Derric motioned to a servant, whispered something in his ear, then moved toward the bed. Derric took his hand, checked his pulse at his wrist, pressed a palm to his forehead; suddenly, he felt like a sick eight-year-old again. "How do you feel?"

"I'm all right. Promise." He met Derric's worried gaze until it became a nod.

Jon relayed what he'd told Tor, and Derric clasped his hands, looked above, and murmured his thanks to the Goddess.

It was the dead gods who had granted him an ancient boon. Were Derric's thanks misplaced?

"I will pass this information on to Olivia," Derric said. "Perhaps she can find out more about your possible... abilities." Gently, Derric seated himself on the bed, his eyebrows drawn together and his head bowed. The lines in his face deepened. "There's something else."

Tor rose. "He's only just awoken, Derric," he said. "Let him rest."

Meeting Tor's hard gaze, Derric shook his head. "This can't wait."

When Tor seemed about to argue, Jon interrupted, "What is it?'

"Princess Alessandra," Derric said. "I have it on good authority that she is considering leaving court."

Jon pinched the bridge of his nose and drew in a deep breath. After completing an ancient ritual, he'd returned to playing a wooing game. As much as he wanted to tell Derric to let her leave if she wanted to, being Earthbound didn't resolve all of Emaurria's vulnerabilities. In fact, he didn't know the full extent of what it *did* resolve. His kingdom still needed the protection of alliances, foreign soldiers, and the period of detente a royal courtship afforded. At least until Leigh could nego-tiate a favorable agreement with the light-elves.

"What do you need me to do?"

"We are in a sensitive position. Our forces are spread thin handling the Immortals, and until the alliance with the light-elves is ironclad, we must keep Silen in play," Derric replied.

"On that, we are agreed." A small, intricate scabbard lay on his desk. The ceremonial dagger from the Earthbinding.

Derric paused, indulging a troubled frown. "I think you should grant her a private audience and do whatever is necessary to make sure that she stays, but it is your decision."

The words cut deep. Jon threw aside the white covers, prompting

Derric to rise, and left the bed. He rubbed his chin, annoyed at the two days' growth. When he reached the washbasin, he splashed his face and stared into the mirror.

Alessandra's departure would not only mean the withdrawal of Macario's much-needed flotilla, but also the beginning of the entire courtship maneuver's collapse. If she didn't believe she had a chance of becoming queen and left, it was only a matter of time before the other ladies followed suit.

Perhaps she even knew that, knew all it could cost him and Emaurria. Perhaps she was indignant at being a pawn here, and that was the reason behind her sudden urge to depart. But even if all that were true, Emaurria couldn't risk the loss.

*He* couldn't risk the loss. "I'll do it. Arrange the private audience," Jon said, preparing to shave.

"I will," Derric answered, meeting his eyes in the mirror. "You'll meet her in the Grand Library in an hour. I'll order you a bath."

"My thanks."

At that, Derric inclined his head and left. Some movement came from the other room, and soon, a couple servants trickled in to draw a bath. Tor lingered, anchoring a hand on his hip.

After all he'd learned about Silen, the late Prince Robert, and his wife Princess Giuliana, Jon had no illusions about what it would take to convince her to stay.

"What kind of man does it make me?" he wondered aloud.

"A man may do as he pleases, but a king does what he must," Tor answered.

Jon looked at the man in the mirror. Perhaps someday he would be familiar again. But not today.

~

IN THE MORNING LIGHT, Rielle stacked the books the Sonbaharan Tower of Magic had requested. Her hands shook, and she couldn't tell if it was from fear or excitement or equal parts of both.

She followed Ihsan's instructions and worked under a veil of calm while within, anxiety and fear waged an anxious war of attrition. There was still so much risk involved in the plan, even if most of it was solid. Ihsan had shown her the false arcanir cuffs—which looked indiscernible from the originals—and had walked her through every part of the plan.

However, there were still a couple matters left outstanding. Although she had plotted a path of least resistance out of the villa, she would have to fight at least a dozen guards, two months out of practice with magic. She was a formidable mage, but even formidable mages needed practice. What time she could find, she used to read Sonbaharan tomes on elemental magic. They detailed some unique spells she hoped to incorporate into her repertoire.

Ihsan had also provided her with critical information on Farrad. He had a single sigil somewhere on his body, in addition to being a capable warrior.

If the sigil protected against elemental magic, then she would fail the assassination, but it was a risk she had to take. Ihsan promised to give her a poison-tipped hairpin for precisely that case. She would have to wait for the moment in which he would be most vulnerable.

And after that, the guard at the West Gate would know her, give her a purse of gold araqs, and let her pass to buy a camel and travel for the nearest port.

When she finished stacking the books, she scrawled a quick note to give to the head of the house slaves. The sooner the books left House Hazael, the better. As she worked, she steadied her hand and tried to combat her anxiety. Tomorrow would be Farrad's birthday— and the party that would end his life.

And tonight, she would have to bear the attentions of a stranger. The price of freedom was steep.

She folded the note and left the solar. She made her way down the stairs, and no sooner had she set foot on the landing when crisp footsteps sounded down the hall.

A house slave, flanked by a group of others. "You are summoned by Zahib Farrad."

Her stomach rolled, and with difficulty, she swallowed. It was time to prepare for the shafi's son. There would be no refusal, no excuses, no escape. Just submission. She had to be as obedient as possible until Farrad took her into his chamber the next night.

She nodded, her hands shaking, and followed. The slaves led her not to the pleasure house room she'd expected but to a bath. They swarmed her, their movement a disorienting blur as she tried to make sense of all being done to her.

Hours later, she trudged to the entertainment hall. Bathed in saffron, she wore a lavender crocus flower in her hair, a living ornament. Gone were her simple two-piece house-slave robes, replaced by the extravagant regalia of a pleasure slave decked out for entertainment: a top entirely covered with jewels, beads, and golden coins, and a skirt of blue silk slung low on her hips and secured with a thick sash of gold mesh and clinking coins that sounded with her every movement.

A jeweled chain had been woven into her partially pleated hair, the remaining thick curls unbound and saturated with pomade until they shone like the gold adorning her body. Heavy earrings dangled from her ears, and a multi-strand necklace with hundreds of golden coins weighed down her neck and chest, jingling as she walked. Matching bracelets, a belly chain, and anklets added to the excess.

A spectacle. One so heavily adorned, it seemed impossible to move. But the cacophony of metallic sounds accompanying her every barefooted step proved otherwise. She'd have to ask Farrad's permission to wear something simpler tomorrow, for comfort—and so that her escape efforts wouldn't alert everyone within a fifty-foot radius.

As she reached the doors to the entertainment hall, two men escorted her in. Her every noisy step turned heads.

The massive space was decorated with lush rugs, detailed tapestries, and silk canopies slung from the ceiling. Several stations of large cushions and waterpipes spread throughout the room, separated with standing sandalwood lattice screens or tapestries. Well-dressed male patrons lounged everywhere, with mostly female entertainers and pleasure slaves, but some male dancers and servants in attendance. Guards lined the room, standing at attention with impeccable form.

It appeared idyllic, a place of bliss and relaxation, when beneath it all shackles bound half the wrists in this room, half the wills, and money had changed hands.

Sensual music joined the haze of smoke in the air. Farrad approached in his Zeharan-red thiyawb, scowling, and grasped her arm.

"Forgive me," he whispered, his grip on her upper arm soft. His regal bearing was more rigid tonight, his face hard. He turned to the slaves escorting her. "Take her to him," he said sternly. "Accommodate his every request."

Farrad departed before she could reply. No, he hadn't wanted this, and it pained him. But she couldn't let that deter her from what had to be done tomorrow.

The slaves urged her ahead to one of the semi-private areas. If she was lucky, maybe the patron would drink himself to exhaustion and leave her be. She hoped.

Her escorts finally stopped, and she couldn't bear to look at the man. But as was proper, she bowed in his direction, where he was seated and smoking a waterpipe.

"I am Thahab," she said, introducing herself as his *almutifi* tonight. If she didn't please him, Imtiyaz could have her lashed, beaten, sold —killed.

Malaise stirred in her stomach. She had to do this. Tears threatened to surface, but she bit them back. No one would see her cry tonight.

*Just get it over with.*

She just had to entice him, hurry it up, and then scrub her skin raw in the bath. Get clean again.

Fighting the unease, she closed her eyes. Notes feathered on her skin, vibrated inside. Music. Good. It would help keep her mind off what she had to do.

She opened her eyes.

*Brennan.*

Her breath caught in her throat, sending a ripple of shock up her neck that forced her mouth open.

The boy she'd grown up with, her fiancé, her former enemy, her werewolf thrall, her ally, her friend. *Here.*

His skin was darker than its usual bronze, and he was somehow leaner, which defined the musculature beneath his deepest-green thiyawb all the more. His gaze locked onto hers with smoldering focus.

The moment the beast's wildness blazed in those hazel depths, she gave Brennan a disapproving look, grateful she had her back to Farrad. If he suspected she knew Brennan, this would all end disastrously.

Suppressing her shock, she let the drum beat in, and her body knew the rest, winding, curving, bending to the music's whims.

Brennan's amber rebellion burned, intensified to a raging anger, and Great Divine, if he couldn't get himself under control, he'd get himself killed. She tried to connect to him through the bond to no avail—the arcanir.

Divine help her, *the arcanir*. He could kill everyone here, and she wouldn't be able to do a thing about it. There were innocents here, like Samara somewhere in the house, but a massacre would bring every mage and warrior in Xir upon them. The zahibshada would level the city before allowing the escape of two murderers to weaken him. They'd have no hope of leaving the city.

It had to be her way.

All she could do was lock eyes with him and pray he understood.

For one very long moment, she wasn't sure whether he would obey her wishes, but then, he took a puff of the waterpipe, the wild blaze fading a measure before it vanished. He breathed in deep, glaring, and when his eyes went cold, she neared him and blocked him from Farrad's view, dancing just within arm's reach.

She wove in close enough to feel his scorching body heat as he breathed out smoke. For her sake and his own, he needed to keep it together.

His nostrils flaring, he inhaled deeply. While she moved, she stole glances at him, her gaze trailing his changed body. He watched her examine him with interest, smoking the waterpipe, his eyes narrowed.

He scrutinized her thoroughly, beginning with her face and making his way lower. With a modest lift of his eyebrow, he stared at her belly, his breathing slowing.

She needed to talk to him, but there was no way to do it here.

Brennan licked his lips, giving her an idea. She leaned in close, stealing the chance to press her lips to his cheek and whisper, "Grab me."

She danced away. From beneath his eyebrows, he mustered as lustful a stare as she had ever seen. He grabbed her hips with blazing hands and followed their gyrating motion for a moment before drawing her in and pulling her down.

Planting her knees on either side of him, she straddled his lap, raked her fingers to the back of his head, and pressed his face to her chest, isolating her rotating hips. He inhaled, long and deep, and then his breath heated between her breasts.

When his sultry lips met her skin, she shivered, and something inside her responded. One of his palms made its way up her back, coaxing her closer, while the other weighed down her hip until her core was flush against him.

*Divine...* She trembled. His mouth traced from her chest to her collarbone—making her gasp—and up her neck, before at last, his lips found hers.

The heat of his lips seared against her own, unbearable and irresistible at the same time. When his tongue sought hers, she opened to him, drawing on his mouth and waning from it like breath itself while her hips moved against his in pulse-pounding rhythm. Something throbbed inside her, and she pressed harder against him.

He gasped, throwing his head back—just the opening she needed. She kissed his neck, lightly sucking, and moved up to his jaw, near his ear.

"Ask for a private room all night. We'll talk when the guards leave," she whispered, then redoubled her attentions on his neck toward his shoulder.

He met eyes with one of the Hazaels' managers, gaze speaking with the imperious nonchalance he'd been born to. The man approached.

"A private room for the whole night and two bottles of your finest wine," Brennan said in High Nad'i, hissing as she nipped his shoulder.

Soon, a small escort of servants and two guards arrived. Brennan rose, swept an arm under her knees, and hoisted her up into his arms.

Divine, some part of her had wondered whether she'd ever see him again, and here he was, in the flesh. As he followed the servants, she let herself feel him—his heat, his breath, his skin against hers—the nearness of him. His presence here was as though her world had walked into her nightmare to remind her of reality. Tears pushed to the surface, but she held them in. Barely.

The walk felt much longer than it actually was, and when they were finally shown into the room, it had nothing more than an enormous, lavish bed. The two guards took up posts in the hall on either side of the doorway, their backs turned to the open latticework. Despite being a "private room," it offered little privacy in actuality, but at least it was away from Farrad's scrutiny.

Brennan laid her on the bed and joined her, perched on his knees to throw off his thiyawb while two servants hurried in with wine and other items. She had seen Brennan naked before many times during his Change, but as she looked up at him, disrobing, it was different than any other time.

Even in a situation like this, trying to steal a moment to speak, she was struck by his beauty. Her gaze traversed the vast expanse of his chest, following its lines, enthralled by every inch of his bare body. He was all hard muscle, lean and rippling, like a wild animal, an apex predator, and yet in his soft eyes and his slow movements, there was no threat, no danger, but care. His eyes never left hers, fixed in inquisitive concentration, waiting for any sign from her to stop.

He would find none. The guards waited for her work to be done, and then they would leave, replaced by a patrol through the hall for the night.

Since her humiliation at Tregarde, she hadn't fathomed being in bed with Brennan, and no matter how beautiful he was, she didn't want him that way. She once would have preferred torture over bedding the man who had so wronged her.

But what choice was there? She needed the guards to leave to discuss her escape. And there was only one way to accomplish that.

It would be over soon. She could shut out her heart, shut out her mind, be somewhere else until it was over. For weeks, she'd been with Farrad, and if she had managed that, she could manage this. She could.

Her heart heavy, she reached up to touch him, her palms gliding over his rising and falling chest. He peered down at them, observing her exploration with a patience she had never seen in him. Her palm settled over his heart, its beat quick but strong, the flesh there hard and taut like the rest of him.

If she shut out their past, thoughts of the man she loved, and everything but his body and hers, she might accomplish this without weeping.

When she met his lustful eyes, she slowly nodded her permission just as the servants exited, the guards still visible on the other side of the lattice.

Brennan raised one of her feet to his lips and kissed his way up her leg as she unhooked her bra. When it was off, he descended to her and kissed her collarbone while she unfastened the sash that held her skirt in place—the final article of clothing guarding her honor—or what remained of it.

If it had to be anyone other than Jon, then she had some small amount of comfort that, even if she despised the thought, it was Brennan, by her permission, and not some stranger. It would end in her freedom, with Brennan's help, and that was what mattered most.

He lavished her breasts with attention, tantalizing with his tongue until her entire body awakened to need against her reluctance. As his hand slid up her thigh and over her hip to grip it, she tried to let the sensation of his touch dissipate any other thoughts she had left.

*Jon... Divine, Jon...* Her eyes watered, and she closed them.

His lips returned to hers in soft but eager kisses; she grasped a fistful of his hair and pulled him closer. The sooner this was over, the better.

Her head swam while he acquiesced to her urging and deepened his kiss. His tongue played against hers at first, teasing longer and deeper strokes until she writhed beneath him. They needed to finish before whatever held her composure broke. Her frantic hands pulled, clutched, grabbed—doing anything and everything to bring him closer. He obliged, devouring her mouth with hungry kisses while she angled her hips up to his.

He throbbed against her, but he didn't move to enter her. When she reached between them, he grasped her hand and buried his face in her hair, his breaths hot and harsh against her head.

"We'll try to be convincing," he whispered, his voice nearly inaudible, "but if you want me to stop anything I'm doing, pinch me."

*Convincing?*

Then he didn't intend to—

Great Divine—she'd never expected...

But they could pretend, if they were careful.

He rose to his knees and pulled the sheet up over his backside to his hips. She tried not to look at his bare body, but she peeked. He caught her, his eyes dancing for a vain moment; then he descended back down to her, covering their lower bodies with the sheet, a portion slipped stealthily between them.

Facing her with an intense look, he waited—for her agreement? Her chest heaved with nervousness, but she nodded, and his body visibly contracted with purpose. Through the sheet, his hard length pressed against her, his heat blazing between them. Gasping, she clutched a fistful of bedding while he moved in perfect time.

Great Divine, it had no right to feel this good, this act, this betrayal, this necessity, but the rising pulse of pleasure in her lower body would not be swayed by reason.

Her hips rose to meet him, the tension building at her core, and his pressure was just right—enough to please but not to hurt, pleasure just out of reach. His eyebrows drawn, he forced out a harsh breath, and he must have longed for entry, for tightness, for release—her former enemy, her wolf, her loyal wolf. Whatever else he was, he was loyal to her. He was here.

She raised a hand to wrap around his neck, her fingers digging into his flesh, part pretense and part primal, bringing his mouth down to hers. Groaning, he kissed her in a greedy assault, plundering her mouth with a ferocious urgency, and Divine help her, she wanted to give him all he sought, everything, as her conquered body writhed against him.

A cry escaped her lips—the throbbing between her legs peaked, pulsed to rapture, and it spread to her hips, her belly, her entire body, until she wanted to weep in submission to the sensation, to crumple in shame but be no more than the pleasure vibrating in her core and everywhere. Intensity etched into his face, he curled over her and forced out a rough breath, finding his release in body-quaking spasms. Mesmerized, she watched the pleasure dominate his face, her craving lower body contracting at the sight.

Was this what it was like to make love with Brennan Karandis Marcel, even this pale imitation? Had everything gone differently three years ago, would this be her life? The moment fell like nostalgia, a loose anchor plunging ever deeper into vast, unknowable depths until lost.

She closed her eyes and shivered at the wetness of the sheet between them.

With an exhilarated breath, he collapsed next to her, his arm draped over her belly and his face turned to hers. For some time, he didn't move but to breathe, hard and fast at first, then slowing and deepening. She lay, intertwining her fingers with his, taking solace in this anomalous moment in the long nightmare that had been her enslavement.

It was both troubling and confusing. No matter the reason, tonight they had crossed a line that could never be uncrossed.

The telltale sound of retreating footsteps sounded from the hall. The guards had left.

"I'm sorry," Brennan whispered.

She glanced at him, at his overbright eyes. She believed him. For years, he'd been torturing her, hurting her, begging her to break the curse, but the broken look in his eyes—she believed it. "You had the opportunity to take me, but you didn't."

When they'd entered the bedchamber, she hadn't expected anything else.

"Of course not," he murmured. "Although I would relish the opportunity to make love to you... not here, and not like this." He sniffed. "And don't take tonight as any indication of my usual performance."

She smiled despite herself. "Wouldn't dream of it."

"Now tell me everything," he said gravely.

With a grim nod, she whispered it all into his ear. She told him of Shadow's scheme, of her connection to the pirates who had attacked Laurentine, of her threat to kill the man she loved. She told him of the *Siren* bearing her to Harifa. She told him of the slave auction, of Ihsan, of being a scribe, and of Farrad... And then she told him of Ihsan's plan.

"You needn't suffer any longer. I'll break you out." His fingers squeezed hers.

"No... They know your identity and could easily find me later if you're noticed. And there's a company of guards here... even you couldn't survive that."

"You're wrong. I know—"

She couldn't risk rebellion. "Please," she said, "let me handle this my way. If I succeed, no one will ever come after me, and you won't take any risks. It's the best of all options. If I fail, then please, by all means, save me from being executed."

Silent for a moment, Brennan finally rolled his eyes. "So you're going to kill Farrad?" he whispered.

She nodded.

"Fine, stick with the plan. I hate that bastard." A crooked grin tugged the corner of his mouth.

Farrad wasn't all bad. Maybe if she revealed Ihsan's plan, he'd somehow secure her freedom.

Or he'd have her locked up.

Or worse.

She didn't know him well enough to accurately predict his response, and she couldn't risk Sylvie's life on a guess.

"Tomorrow night, I'll be waiting just outside, under the pomegranate trees in the courtyard. You had better show up."

"I will. I promise." There was another question on the tip of her tongue, but she hesitated. If she didn't ask, she would regret it. "Tell me of home."

He rolled over onto his back, then paused, his body rigid. Listening for spies?

He reached into his clothes on the floor and handed her a folded note; he must have deemed it safe enough. "Immortals are emerging all over the kingdom, but the paladins seem to have the situation under control. Last I checked, your former master was locked up in the arcanir dungeon for thwarting the rite. We also suspected he might've had a hand in your disappearance, but it looks like that wasn't the case."

Of course not. She hadn't expected Leigh to stand against her, but she'd understood it. But this? Never.

While she examined the smooth paper in her hands, Brennan continued. "Olivia is a capable Archmage and seems to have recovered.

She's indispensable right now, decoding ancient texts to find out how to handle these Immortals."

That sounded like Olivia. Rielle smiled.

And that left the mention of only one person. She rubbed the folded parchment with reverence.

"Jon asked me to give you that when I found you." Brennan's voice was hollow.

Her heart weighed heavily. When she would tell Jon about this, she couldn't guess his reaction. Her fingers trembled as she opened the note, her gaze drawn to the fine slope of his script.

*Rielle,*

    *I pray this letter finds you well.*

    *By now, Brennan has found you. I am told that as king, I am the most powerful man in the realm and can do anything, yet I find many things I cannot do, chief among them leaving. I am told that, just by entering a foreign country, I could start a war.*

    *I have faith in Brennan to find you, to do what I long to do but cannot. Trusting that faith is the only way I am able to stay and function here, when everything else in me demands I find you.*

    *I don't have the words to ask your forgiveness for not being there myself. In truth, I don't expect it, and I wouldn't deserve it. But I will await you here, your love or your indignation, forever if I must, so if nothing else, allow me the favor of looking upon your beloved face at least one more time.*

    *I love you.*

    *Yours,*

    *Jon*

Tears streaming down her face, she read the letter several times before Brennan snatched it from her grasp and covered her mouth. He cocked his head toward the hall, then hid the note among his clothes on the floor.

The patrol was coming, but all she could think about was Jon. He hadn't ignored her. Hadn't abandoned her. When she returned to Courdeval, she would tell him everything and beg his forgiveness.

Lying on his side, Brennan faced her and pulled her into his arms, an embrace not unlike that of a sleepy lover. His breath slow and steady, he seemed at ease, but the stiffness of his alert muscles hardened against her.

The patrol walked by, the guards' footfalls sounding from the hall. As they passed, the tension lost its hold on Brennan's body; the safety and warmth of him relaxed her to a state she hadn't experienced since the eve of Monas Amar with Jon.

It was the familiarity of someone she knew. That was it. He'd come for her when no one else had.

But... How had he found her? She hadn't thought to ask earlier because of the bond's usual possibilities, but it occurred to her that he hadn't been able to rely on it.

"Brennan," she whispered, and he nudged her head softly. "How did you find me?" Her eyelids grew heavy.

"I'll tell you after the party." He kissed her neck softly, his lips a hot brand upon her skin. "Get some sleep tonight. I will watch over you."

With a tired nod, she wrapped her arm around his and cuddled closer, catching the twinkle of the starry night sky through the lattices. She wished she could stop this moment in time and never wake to the nightmare of morning.

# CHAPTER 28

Tugging his shirt sleeves nervously, Jon headed for the Grand Library. After his bath, his valet de chambre had selected an ensemble that *presented his physique to best advantage.* Chagrined, Jon shook his head. His valet had the unique ability to make him feel like no more than a very fashionable doll. He wore the tailored black leather doublet that had garnered so much attention a few weeks ago, a crisp white shirt, and fitted black trousers tucked into his riding boots. It had been some time since he had felt so on display—since Bournand. Since his time with...

He couldn't even think her name. Not now. Thinking her name would somehow make her witness to this betrayal, and as reluctant as he'd been before, imagining her reaction would make him abandon this course altogether.

*Macario's flotilla. Emaurria needs Macario's flotilla. The flotilla...* Repeating the thoughts kept him walking.

He had taken some time to think as he'd washed and dressed. With a heavy heart, he had agreed with Tor's words. *A king does what he must.*

*A separate matter.*

He heaved a breath. For the sake of her father's flotilla, he would convince this princess he might marry her. He would make her laugh, make her smile, make her forget all of this was a maneuver. He would play the part his Camarilla tutors and lessons had been preparing him for, that of the consummate suitor, for as long he needed to.

For the sake of his kingdom, he would deceive and pretend, and hate himself, and keep doing it anyway.

Two guards snapped salutes as he approached the Grand Library's massive double doors.

He walked in. Alessandra stood in the center, wearing a red brocade gown that emphasized her slender figure, flanked by a tall window aglow with the afternoon sunshine. Upon his entrance, she turned her head and viewed him in profile. Her waves of dark hair were gathered in artful coils, secured high, with flowing ringlets guiding the eye to her breasts and exposed back.

"Your Majesty." She curtsied.

"Princess," he greeted with his most pleasant expression.

She allowed him to take her hand, and he brushed it with his lips.

"You came." He held her hand a little longer than custom dictated. In her other hand, she held a book entitled *Masters of Sileni Architecture.*

"It is a brazen woman who would ignore a king's invitation." She looked out at the snowed-in courtyard through the window, then spared him a sideways glance.

"And yet you decided to come."

She shot him a quick smile. "I should be offended, Your Majesty."

"But you're entertained. A singular, if brazen, woman."

Alessandra pursed her lips. "I see you." She scrutinized him with her chestnut-brown eyes. "You are charming, Your Majesty, and light-hearted... but only on the outside." Her gaze fell to his chest, right where, beneath his clothes, he wore the Laurentine signet ring. "Your heart belongs to another, and you're suffering terribly." She was silent awhile. "You're a worthy man, Your Majesty, in many ways, but I don't wish to continue vying for your heart, when only its ruin is available."

*Macario's flotilla.*

"A ruin, am I?" How had she seen right through him? But his role here and now was the gallant, not the confessor. He squinted and forced a rueful smile. "You wound me, Princess."

Alessandra looked him over and gave a little shrug. "A very handsome ruin, but a ruin, nonetheless."

*Emaurria needs Macario's flotilla.*

He moved a step closer and leaned in. "Silen's history is full of builders." He tipped his head toward her book.

"A ruin is much easier to rebuild when it is abandoned," she said, but her chest heaved quicker breaths. She glanced away, her gaze wandering back from time to time as she feigned interest in something beyond the window.

"Should I take that to mean you're afraid of challenges?" He cocked his head.

Mouth open, she eyed him and set down the book. "Is your tongue as skilled in all else as it is in verbal sparring?"

*The flotilla...*

Crossing his arms and leaning against the window frame, he replied, "Telling you would reveal the answer in the most unexciting way."

Her eyes shone. "Then show me," she said, her voice an octave lower.

*It is a separate matter.*

He swept her up and pinned her against the window, eliciting a soft gasp, but she lifted her chin, lips parted. He claimed her mouth, crushing her lips with his own, his hands gliding down her body to her waist.

He shut out everything else and focused only on what he could feel right this second. The suppleness of her lips. The soft give of her body. The spiced argan scent of her hair. The subtle sweetness of her mouth. The mounting urgency of her breaths.

And she wasted no time, slipping her fingers into his doublet, unfastening, while her tongue sought his.

When she splayed his clothes open, he grabbed her and lifted her; her legs fastened around his waist, and her eager mouth took his once more. He moved to a table, threw all its items to the floor with a sweep of his arm, and lowered her to the surface. Raising her chin to expose her neck, he trailed kisses from her jaw to her collarbone while she tore at her gown's laces.

*A separate matter.*

After he threw off his doublet, he lifted her high enough to grab the back of the gown and force it open, eliciting a gasp with each rip of the brocade. With trembling hands, she wrenched the bodice down.

Terra have mercy—

A soft commotion came from the other side of the doors.

"Your Majesty—" Olivia's muffled voice from the hall.

*Praise Terra.* But he held Alessandra's gaze and exhaled forcefully. "Not now," he called out.

Alessandra raked her fingers through his hair, urging his face to hers. She assailed his mouth, devouring it with unrestrained need.

"It's urgent!" Olivia shouted, and then a "Don't touch me," presumably to the guards. "It's about the spiritualist!"

*The spiritualist...*

*Rielle.*

Olivia had managed to get the spiritualist here. He could finally get some answers about Rielle. He paused.

"Don't you dare stop," Alessandra hissed.

*Rielle.*

"I wish I didn't have to, Princess," he lied, breathing heavily over her. Well, not entirely a lie. Lust raged through him, demanded satisfaction, and he struggled to rein it in and regain control over his own body.

It was *not* a separate matter. The reward lust alone offered was illusive, a mere scrap of kindling compared to the wildfire of love. And he wouldn't betray Rielle again—not unless he had no other choice. The Earthbinding weighed heavily enough already. There had been pleasure of the body in the act itself, but then a coldness, a shame, afterward. Regret. Remorse. Burying the man he had been—the man he wished to be.

No, this was pretense, no more than it needed to be, until duty demanded utter sacrifice.

At last, he sighed and pulled away. "Just a moment, Archmage Sabeyon," he said, careful not to address Olivia by her first name in front of Alessandra.

Staring at the ceiling, Alessandra huffed, dragging her bodice up over her breasts. Quickly, he stuffed his shirt into his trousers and picked up his doublet. Alessandra hopped off the table and took his hand, rising on her toes to kiss him—passionate, deep, needy.

She pulled away and breathed against his lips. "You'll think of me tonight."

With that, clutching her bodice to her chest, she faced him. He held out his doublet for her; she put it on, draping one side over the other, and with a feline smile, walked away, her gaze lingering for a moment before she turned to the door.

His eyes followed her, and at the sight of Olivia scowling in the doorway, he sobered. Attired in a black velvet gown, her hair in a long, red braid adorned with a golden circlet, she appeared elegant, if stern. She exchanged a narrow look with Alessandra in passing, a brief but bitter smile flashing on her face; Alessandra must have grinned at her to elicit such a response.

The princess left, and Olivia turned her attention to him as he fastened his shirt.

"I would say I'm sorry to interrupt," Olivia said as she approached, looking him over with a glare, "but I'd rather not lie."

A grunted half-laugh escaped his lips. "Tell me what you truly think, Olivia."

"I think you're being an idiot," she said, and when he raised his eyebrows, added, "Your Majesty."

He cracked his neck. "An idiot?"

None of this was ideal, but the necessity of keeping Macario's flotilla here—by Alessandra's favor—had required a certain amount of lip service.

Her gaze flickered lower, then she looked away. "You did ask me to tell you what I truly thought."

"By all means, enlighten me on my idiotic ways."

Rolling her eyes, Olivia shook her head and turned back to the door. When she moved toward it, he followed. "I don't think you can handle hearing it."

"I wouldn't have asked if I couldn't." His chest tightened as they walked down the hall, flanked by his guards, to meet with the spiritualist. Finally. He felt the rumble of a winter storm on the edge of his consciousness and ignored it.

Olivia kept her gaze on the floor ahead of them. "You're betraying who you are, and for what? To keep that tart of a princess from retreating back to her palace because she didn't get to bed the king? What are all these dark deeds for? Who cares?"

"I have to care, Olivia. It is by dark deeds that this kingdom survives."

"Forget about dark deeds. You're about to secure an alliance with the light-elves, Your Majesty."

A vein pulsed in his arm, and he flexed his fingers. "And does the entirely landlocked queendom have a navy to protect our coast from pirates?"

Olivia let out a frustrated growl. "You're complicating matters."

"No," he said, louder than he'd intended, "you're simplifying them. And the question is why." He inspected her through narrowed eyes.

"Because I'm trying to help you avoid making a huge mistake, Your Majesty."

Jon clenched his hands. "Are you?" he asked, his muscles tense. "Or are you just meddling?"

Olivia stopped in the middle of the hall, her gaping face frozen, and she shivered. "I can't believe you said that."

Neither could he. He anchored a fist on his hip and palmed his forehead, rubbing it. This was quickly getting out of control. The cost his actions required haunted him, but the cost of inaction would haunt him more. He didn't need that choice between a bad option and a worse option shoved in his face, not by Olivia, not by anyone—but she didn't deserve his bitterness.

"I have never loved a man like I loved James," she murmured, her voice uneven. "And you, my king, looking like him, laughing like him, reminding me of him every single day... and yet making one bad choice after another... must be some kind of punishment."

He met her livid green eyes. "Forgive me. I... I don't know what's come over me."

Olivia's intensity faded. "It's who you are around those royals, Jon.

That heartless, cocky, devil-may-care king—whoever he is—is slowly taking over."

The king was taking over, and the kingdom needed him. And Jon couldn't stop him.

No... he *wouldn't*. The man he'd been was already buried. "I appreciate your concern—"

With a dismissive wave of her hand, she rolled her eyes.

He took her waving hand, and she jumped but did not pull away.

"No, Olivia, I really do."

She looked away for a moment, then glanced back, her cheeks reddening.

"I shouldn't have snapped at you, and I'll mind that in the future. But there will be things I'll do that you won't approve of, and although I'll be glad for your counsel, if I do not heed it, you'll accept that."

Her shoulders slumped. "I understand."

With a temperate nod, he released her. After a moment's quiet introspection, she continued down the hallway, and he followed the path to her study.

A shiver worked its way down his spine, but he took a deep breath and composed himself. The spiritualist would have answers. Rielle was alive. And gods above, when he learned where she was, king or no, he'd go after her.

Olivia opened the large, azure-blue doors to the Magic Library. It was immense, housing thousands of arcane tomes in dozens of languages. The colorful spines lent the quiet place a bright cheer, some wear revealing the age of the knowledge contained within—some as old as a thousand years or more, carefully preserved both by magic and conventional means. Tufted armchairs and great, carved tables awaited research and leisure, bearing the images of beasts once thought to be no more than myth.

As they passed by a massive cedar table, he ran a finger along the ornate dragon carved into its surface. Before the Rift, this had been the kind of dragon Emaurrians could imagine in their country. Carved. A work of whimsical art.

There had been reports now, however, of large airborne-creature sightings, dragons among them. And he's seen one himself by the Brise-Lames.

*Let them stay aloft.* And away from his people.

Olivia strode to her study at the end of the room. Numerous shelves of jarred powders, fluids, and various substances trimmed the room. A long table bearing alchemical contraptions spanned its length, all manner of alembics, retorts, ambices, and cucurbits of glass, metal, and ceramic set in various stages of experimentation. Books, papers, and models filled almost every available space. And, in the middle of it all, an elegant desk, with books stacked a dozen high and a collage of papers obfuscating its wooden surface. Beneath his booted feet, a green-and-gold geometric-patterned Sonbaharan rug softened the room, a conspicuous burn mark blackening the edge nearest the alchemy station.

He looked around the room but found no one else present. Perhaps he and Olivia were early, the spiritualist yet to arrive.

Olivia rounded her desk and sat down with a sigh. She scattered the papers, then singled one out. With an expectant smile and brows raised high, she held it out to him.

He examined the note. "A list of items to prepare, an arrival time..." His teeth clenched. "You could have given this to me at any time, but you chose to interfere in the Grand Library?"

She crossed her arms. "Aren't you glad I did, before you did something you'd regret?" she asked, her voice lofty.

Regret? If Alessandra left and Macario withdrew his flotilla, if pirates ravaged Emaurria's coast and killed hundreds or thousands, *that* would be cause for *regret*.

Fuming, he crumpled the page. There were so many things he wanted to do right now that he'd *regret* later. He nodded tightly, holding back the sharper things he wanted to say, and glared at her. "Spare your judgment. I have enough of my own."

The smile disappeared from her face. He turned to leave.

"Did Sir Jonathan Ver ever imagine he'd have to prostitute himself for the greater good?" she asked his back.

"It doesn't matter," he replied, stopping at the doorway before he left. "Sir Jonathan Ver is dead."

# CHAPTER 29

The morning heat of House Hazael had never been so sweltering. Sweat coated Rielle's back, her waist, her hair. She opened her eyes, blinking away the light streaming through the latticed windows and the white gossamer of the bed's canopy, then looked down at the muscular arm around her.

It was her werewolf who'd heated the bed to sultriness.

She rolled onto her back and glimpsed his slumbering face, light and shadow from the latticework casting an intricate pattern upon his deep-bronze skin. The sun's radiance caught in his long lashes, in the shine of his short, dark hair. At times like this, he looked like no more than a beautiful man, but as she surveyed him, she could see the Wolf inside—the dormant power, the calmed beast, the quiescent darkness. The danger just beneath the surface made his beauty bewitching, a pleasing contradiction; countless lovers had fallen under its spell.

Her gaze traveled from his contented face down his powerful, naked body, covered only with the sheet that had separated them the night before. A flood of memories flowed through her—the way he'd watched her while smoking the waterpipe, how he'd looked for permission to touch her, how he'd kissed, how he'd moved...

And how he had respected her. Despite the circumstances, despite everything, he'd found a way to make the pretense seem real when he could have—

He stirred, and she blushed, embarrassed by where her gaze rested. She cleared her throat and melted back into the bed, into him, into his arms. He pulled her in tight, burying his face in her hair. Tucked into his embrace, she relished the smoothness of his skin and the hardness of his flesh. He held her close. So close. She felt safer than she had in months.

His cool breath on her sweat-soaked flesh made her shiver, her skin taut.

"I don't want to leave here without you." He kissed her ear. "Not for a day, not for an hour." He pressed his soft lips to her neck.

"Shh." She hadn't expected anyone to come for her; Brennan's appearance had been a jolting and amazing surprise, and now that he was here, she couldn't fathom him leaving.

But he had to. Just not at this moment. "Don't speak. Not yet."

He nuzzled her. "Why not?"

She closed her eyes, taking hold of his arms to pull them tighter around her. "Speaking means we're awake, and I don't want the night to be over yet."

Morning meant returning to the villa at large, to being no more than a slave. She wanted the safe, soothing night with him to last. But already, the arcanir cuffs stung her wrists back to her depressing reality.

"Let me take you from here," he said. "We can leave right now and never look back."

It was a beautiful dream, but a dream was all it could be. They would never make it out alive, and even if by some small chance they did, the Hazaels would link her to Brennan and seek vengeance upon both their Houses. "We can't."

"Why not?"

"I told you last night."

The rumble of a growl served as his objection, and then he left the bed.

She sat up to follow him with her gaze as, entirely nude, he retrieved a tray from the hall and brought it to the bed. Her stomach growled, and she couldn't decide whether to look at his pleasing form or the enticing offering he carried.

Complementing the usual baked flatbread, white goat cheese with black olives, and thick yogurt cheese with olive oil was an array of sweets rounding out the feast—sugary cheese pastries soaked in syrup, and spiced fritters.

Brennan looked at her with an expression not unlike pain as he set the tray upon the bed, then offered her a demitasse of aromatic coffee. What was that look? Bewildered, she accepted the coffee, eyeing the food hungrily while she sipped. He seated himself next to her and rested a hand on her thigh.

"Eat," he said. "Please. I can see your bones."

She turned to him then, and although he averted his gaze, she could see the dullness in his eyes. She'd eaten well as Farrad's lover, but for months before that, she'd starved. She held out her arm and noted the protrusion at her wrist, the visible line of her forearm, and her bony elbow. She became aware of her own nakedness, and could—just barely—identify her ribs.

Carefully, she set the demitasse down on the tray and covered herself with the sheet, then feasted on breakfast. She stopped only to sip the coffee, its bittersweet taste enhancing her meal, then turned to the pastries. Their sweet cheese was a revelatory thrill, and the fritters, so like the beignets in Emaurria but flavored with saffron, cinnamon, and cardamom.

When she'd eaten her fill, she rested her hand on her knee, holding her sticky fingers away. He hadn't moved. Why wasn't he eating?

"Aren't you hungry?"

With a dark look, he grasped her hand. Gasping, she watched him bring her fingers to his lips. She wanted to tell him to stop, but as he took her fingers into his warm mouth one by one, the words died in her throat. His body came to life with arousal, and she swallowed.

Whatever had happened last night—the *not*-lovemaking—had changed something between them. She wasn't sure what, exactly, but it was difficult to look at him now.

"Delicious." He placed her palm on his thigh. The moment he did, her fingers couldn't help but press into the firm flesh there.

She took off an earring and pressed its point into her palm until a bead of blood appeared. His eyes flashed from hazel to the Wolf's amber as he watched.

His control. He hadn't asked for her blood, but he needed it, had needed it for months, and they'd both be safer tonight if she gave him her blood. It wouldn't provide him with anything until her arcanir cuffs were off, and then, their bond would return—she hoped.

She held her palm out to him, and he accepted it with both hands, raised it as he dipped his head down to kiss it. His lips met her skin first, then the warm, wet pressure of his tongue. A shiver rippled over him as he pressed harder, perhaps trying to coax out a little more of what he needed so much.

Something inside her unfurled, throbbed, and she closed her eyes, allowing in only the sound of needy breaths, the feel of his mouth on her flesh, the smell of sweet syrup.

Her eyes met Brennan's as he slowly lowered her palm. What hid in their hazel depths? Desire, restraint, sorrow, frustration? Perhaps even...

Voices came from the hall. Their time together was quickly coming to an end.

He rose to dress. Every second watching him meant one second nearer to his departure, home slipping away from her grasp, and her chest hollowed at the thought. She wrapped her arms around herself.

She wouldn't break. She wouldn't cry. She would kill Farrad abd Nasir abd Imtiyaz Hazael and leave Xir and Sonbahar free.

The hospitality staff approached their room. Dressed, Brennan leaned in, took her face in his hands, and kissed her.

Although some part of her wanted to resist, another surrendered to him completely. The syrup and her blood still on his lips, he tasted sugary and coppery when his tongue slipped into her mouth; hot, wet, and urgent, his sweet violation coaxing desire from her perfidious body.

When he began to pull away, her lips brushed his once more, reluctant to part. Once he left, she might never see him again.

"I will wait for you, hidden in the courtyard. Be merciless. Be safe. Come to me," he whispered to her lips before drawing back. Her face in his hands, he looked at her one last time, moisture welling in his eyes, then tore himself away.

She stared at the empty doorway. As much as she had, at times, cursed the bond, cursed her lot, and cursed him, Brennan Karandis Marcel had claimed a place in her heart. Forever. He had tracked her all the way to Sonbahar, and some part of her knew it wasn't just for his monthly control or for the sake of possibly breaking his curse.

Brennan loved her.

Since the night he'd given her the choice not to marry him in Melain, she had known it in her heart. And he'd come here to free her, to take her back to Emaurria, back to Courdeval, back to Jon.

Her face buried in his pillow, she breathed in the spice of his scent and stretched out across the bed to look at the floor. Jon's letter was gone. Brennan had taken it with him.

Her spirits fell, but he'd done the right thing—if it were found on her person, her identity would be revealed, Brennan's complicity, and perhaps, a weakness of the new Emaurrian king.

Still, she yearned to read Jon's words again, to see his script again, to feel him near again. Every day away from him, her heart ached all the more. To see his face, to melt into his arms. She wanted to tell him how stupid she'd been, all that she'd done, to beg his forgiveness. If he'd but have her, she'd rejoice.

*Make no mistake—he will ascend the throne and forget you between the thighs of many women. Then, he will wed a queen or a princess as kings do.*

Shadow's words on the *Siren* still haunted her. It was true that she could not hope to marry a king, especially not when the kingdom had so few allies. But she didn't care about marriage. She cared about Jon and their daughter. About being together in any way they could.

She got out of bed, dressed in the entertainer's garb, and headed to Ihsan's solar. As soon as she arrived, Ihsan's head perked up from the table. Her gaze traveled the length of her body, and she covered her mouth. "Thahab, I—"

Rielle held up her hand and shook her head.

"Are you injured?"

"Let's just forget last night," Rielle said. In the event that Ihsan was less than forthcoming about her entire plan, better she not suspect anything about Brennan.

Ihsan looked her over but nodded. "Come." Ihsan rose and gestured to the door. "It is a fateful day. It is time to prepare."

At that, Ihsan led the way to her quarters. Once inside, she shut the door and locked it, then approached the trunk at the foot of her bed. From it, she pulled out a box and touched her hand to it. It glowed a faint white and opened.

The false arcanir bonds lay within, the ones she'd seen a couple days ago. Very dangerous in the right hands. Her hands. "And the brand?"

"Disturb it. It is like any other rune—disturb its pattern, and it will not work," Ihsan explained. "Cut through it a few times and do *not* heal the wounds with magic until you can get a runist to alter the design to something innocuous."

Doable. She glanced down at her wrists. "What about—"

Ihsan pulled out a pair of keys.

"How did you get those? I thought only the overseer had them."

Her eyes downcast, Ihsan answered, "Grandfather has them, too. I... borrowed them."

With that, Ihsan met her eyes and held out a palm. Rielle presented one wrist, then the other, and just like that, the arcanir was gone. Closing her eyes, she engaged the bond and sensed Brennan—not far, he bristled with impatience somewhere, but interest surged back to her through the connection. He knew she was free of the arcanir. Good. A surge of power flowed through to him—control, enough of it that he could safely conceal his beastly nature.

She examined her own palms, her own hands, her own wrists, anew. Gesturing, she clad her flesh in a flame cloak; it sparked to cover her fingers, then traveled up her hands and arms until her entire body shone radiant with fire.

The light reflected in Ihsan's dark, gleaming eyes, which smiled as surely as her mouth did.

～

WHEN NARENIAN SUNHEART RECEIVED HIM, Leigh had struggled not to stare. The elven ruler was tall, with a large but slender frame, platinum blond hair falling straight and long past her hip. Her face was all angles, but refined with soft lips and sharp, silvery eyes, evocative of starlight and so unlike those of her people. Perched regally on the Treeburst throne, she was flanked by the imposing swirl of wood backing the massive bench she sat upon, easily as tall as three men. Atop her royal head, she wore an earthen crown, the likes of which only a tree-singer could have created.

Those all-knowing eyes had a coldness to them, less like a sage and more like the shelves of scrolls a sage's knowledge came from. Cold, yes, but also hard to read. Jon wanted Immortal hunting squads and information to help Emaurria survive the upheaval of the Rift, but they had yet to learn what Narenian truly wanted. There was no way it was merely food, clothing, and friendship.

The reception had been formal and brief, with Narenian sparing a few words and a nod to acknowledge him and his guards. Ambriel had then led him to a tree, and up a stair winding around it, to the hollow where Leigh was to board. And he'd been left there for the night without fanfare. The paladins guarded his door in shifts, their own quarters nearby.

In the evening, he'd felt a strange presence reach out to him briefly but had otherwise remained undisturbed until the talks had begun the next day. Narenian spoke Old Emaurrian herself and did not require a translator. They'd finalized matters of language learning, embassies, information exchange, food supply and cultivation assistance, and Immortal hunting squads, but some finer points remained.

Today, at a grown—not built—table, Narenian maintained her royal poise, but the intimidating grandeur of the Treeburst throne was absent. Upon the table, too, was a token of compromise—not elven fare but Emaurrian, food the party from Courdeval had brought. Times in Vervewood had to be dire indeed to entertain an outsider with donated meals. The distant song of the tree-singers lulled, ever-present here.

But the show of level footing, compromise even, led Leigh to question what Narenian wanted. Power rarely negotiated from an appearance of weakness. The elven queen readily gave the thrill of victory—and it meant that soon, she would ask a deceptively small price.

"When we awoke, the plant life my people depended on for food was absent," the queen said, breaking Leigh's musing. Perceptive.

He met her ghostly silver eyes and grinned. "I wondered about traditional elven foods."

The queen's gaze adopted a faraway quality. "Just as we took care of the land, the land took care of us. Our tables were once laden with its gifts—fruits, vegetables, meats, fish—but we did not use the fire as you humans do. Our food is pure, unchanged, preserving as much of its nutrition as possible."

"Raw?" Leigh asked. His own native Kamerai was known for its raw fish dishes. "Some human cultures eat this way, but not exclusively, to my knowledge." He looked at the table, full of cooked vegetables, grilled meats, stews, breads.

"I am certain that, after this, there will be some demand for Emaurrian cuisine," the queen said with a smile.

Ambriel shot her a look from across the table. Indeed, some among the light-elves were already developing a taste for things Emaurrian.

Leigh suppressed a grin and returned his attention to the queen. "You mentioned some plant life being absent. If you have samples, however minute or deteriorated, a geomancer could spell new growth." *Is that what you want? Your world as you remember it?*

Whatever she wanted, perhaps he could find a way to stack even more support against the Divinity while he was here, too. Since the Rift, a whole new world of potential enemies to the Divinity had awoken. He smiled inwardly.

The queen stiffened. "Truly?" She drew her eyebrows together. "Perhaps there are some preserved specimens."

"Shall I order them found, Your Majesty?" Ambriel asked.

"At your leisure, brother."

If he could hinge the elven alliance on the acquisition of mages, perhaps Jon could be swayed to break the Emaurrian Tower away from the Divinity. His new reign was the perfect time to offer new terms to Emaurria's mages, and if the Divinity bristled, he had the paladins to withstand a conflict. It wouldn't be a complete victory, but it would be a start.

And with the Immortals killing and destroying, Jon would no doubt be more receptive to uprooting the status quo. The Emaurrian Army and the paladins alone weren't going to keep the land safe, not from all the Immortals. Hopefully Pons was right about the fantastical Earth-binding, and not just day-drinking and talking rubbish.

"Tell me more about the journey here," Narenian said.

To what end? Leigh was certain the queen had already heard the tale in a private briefing, had already asked the pertinent questions. Ambriel recounted the story of the wyvern, describing the battle in more detail than Leigh remembered, emphasizing Leigh's bravery and power. The other light-elves at the table listened with interest but not shock, showing their approval with slight nods.

"I thank you, Ambassador Galvan," Narenian said. "It seems my scouts returned whole, thanks to you."

Flattery. Leigh lowered his head magnanimously.

"Before the Sundering, when our time broke, there were others like you," Narenian said, taking a sip of water. "Do many humans still harness power from the Veins?"

"On occasion, although few succeed."

Ambriel sat a little straighter at that, his focus intensifying.

"It was so during our time," Narenian said. "But the few humans who did succeed became linked to the earth, capable of drawing upon its magic."

Unsure of what to say, Leigh simply listened, glimpsing Ambriel's intense expression.

"Although we desired a closer bond to the earth, no elves ever succeeded in such an endeavor," Narenian revealed. "Have your human scholars come to understand the Veins better?"

Narenian wanted wild magic for her own people. For herself.

Leigh met the queen's gaze squarely. "Unfortunately, the volatile nature of the Veins makes research difficult, and any research that is done is the property of the Divinity of Magic." *And you want that property. To get it, you'll have to stand against the Divinity.*

"Yes, I understand that your mages are not under your king's rule? It was not this way during our time."

"The Divinity is a newer religion, claiming power over all mages, and thus, over many lands, through international treaty," Leigh answered. If the light-elves would but side against the Divinity, so much could be simplified.

"We were aware of a goddess and her pantheon, but an even newer deity has claimed worship among the humans," Narenian reflected. "In any case, it seems that our gods still hold some sway."

The dead gods. He carefully controlled his face. Besides these light-elves, who still worshipped them?

Narenian folded her hands in her lap and leveled an even gaze at Leigh. "I will be forthright with you, Ambassador," she said. "Your king is Earthbound, and we hold with the land. An alliance is certain, if that is your wish. Language, plants, research, supplies, troops and so on are negotiable, but we are a reasonable people."

Leigh remained silent but stunned, not only at the announcement of an alliance but also at the news that Jon was Earthbound. Had the strange presence he'd felt earlier been Jon? "Forgive me, but how do you know?"

"The trees have spoken," the queen answered firmly.

The trees... had... *spoken*. He suppressed the urge to sigh. Still, her confirmation made too much sense not to believe. "That is wonderful news."

If it really was true, then he couldn't wait to discover the power such a ritual conveyed. He'd been wrong, and Pons had been right, and probably not day-drinking. His loss.

If the Earthbinding truly *did* grant power over the land, then he'd never been happier to be wrong. More power outside the Divinity's hands—independent of them—was a good thing.

"However," Narenian said, her countenance paling, "the Immortal beasts were problematic before the Sundering, and even with human magic, I question whether they can be defeated. We can spare few hunters currently. Some, but not many." An unnerving pause. "The humans used the Sundering to sever the Immortal beasts' souls from their bodies. That may be the only solution now, as well—only this time, our race means to remain."

The other light-elves stilled; some even gasped.

Baffled, Leigh didn't even bother to hide his reaction. Humans could seal the Immortals away again? "How?"

"The blood of every Immortal to be sealed was collected and used in a rite at the Vein in Amaranth—a place you now call 'Courdeval.' Beyond that, I do not know," Narenian said.

A sangremancy ritual in the Lunar Chamber. It had to be. But without more information... "Then that knowledge is lost," Leigh replied.

"I do not know, but I know who does," Narenian said. She paused, her starlight eyes glimmering.

"Who?" He was on her hook, but it didn't matter. The answer was worth it.

"Before I share that with you, I will need an assurance from your king, on his honor, that we will not be among those sealed."

"I am certain he will agree, but I will have to discuss the proposal with His Majesty."

Narenian displayed a faint smile. "Your party brought doves, did they not? I will need a vow witnessed by Aiolian Windsong." With a motion of her finger, a light-elf woman with unfathomably deep eyes and too-tight braids nodded, her face as expressive as a stone wall. "There's one more thing."

"Yes?" Leigh asked.

"We will need a dragon mage."

Leigh frowned. "What is a dragon mage?"

"The dragons were the first race to practice the magics—they *were* magic. They possessed all fourteen of them."

"All fourteen of..." Leigh gaped. "All fourteen schools of magic?"

Narenian nodded.

*Divine's tits.* "Pardon me, Your Majesty, but where do we find a dragon mage?"

She pierced him with her gaze. "We will make one."

# CHAPTER 30

*J*on looked over his hand of cards at Alessandra, who scrutinized her own with pursed lips. The morning light played on the brocade of her pink dress, and in the luster of her long, dark curls.

He had two cards—a king and a heart—and if he could get rid of both, he'd win. She had three cards herself.

That evening in the Grand Library had proved to be but the first of many spent in the company of Alessandra. Derric encouraged asking for her hand, while most of the Grands supported at least fostering a closer relationship with her, something to suggest King Macario's support wasn't a waste.

Praise the gods, nothing had gone so far as that evening in the Grand Library, but it was only a matter of time, wasn't it? She'd either want to know their relationship was going somewhere, or she'd want to move on with her life. And he could hardly blame her.

But he had other things on his mind. If Olivia was to be believed, he'd be meeting with the spiritualist soon, and then—

A servant approached and refilled their wine—small stature, fawn-colored braid, chestnut eyes. The woman from the Earthbinding.

Straightening, he raised his eyebrows, but she only behaved as she always did, gracefully pouring, bowing, silently receding. *Manon*, Pons had called her recently. She was still here? Serving in Trèstellan?

But then, was she to lose her position for her willing participation in the ritual? That wouldn't have been right either.

Alessandra's throat clearing broke his thoughts, and across from him, she arched a brow. "Someone you know?"

*Gods.* "I—She's..."

A smile played around her mouth. "Don't bother."

Was this it? The collapse of his efforts with her? "Princess, I don't—"

"Alessandra," she corrected, crossing her legs, holding her cards over her chest, and then eyeing him as if she were about to burst with laughter.

He cocked his head.

"I hardly expect celibacy from a king." She shook her head. "And you're adorable, all flustered and nervous about being caught."

Adorable? He frowned. "You don't expect..." He couldn't even bring himself to repeat the words.

She gave a languid shrug of her shoulder. "We're not married, and even then, couples have arrangements."

Arrangements. She'd accept mistresses, lovers...?

She peered at her cards. "Do you have a heart?"

He frowned again, and she nodded toward his hand.

"Oh," he breathed, looking down at his cards. He did have a heart, and he pulled it out and handed it to her. "But unless you have a king, I win."

She drew another card and, grinning, pulled one free and revealed it to him in the palm of her hand.

A king.

"So you do have a king," he said, and laughed quietly to himself.

"Is that a promise?"

Jon waited in his study for the spiritualist to arrive, staring at his Sodalis ring as he twirled it on his fourth finger. His life as a paladin was over now, but still, he couldn't bring himself to retire its badge. It had graced Rielle's finger once, and that short while had infused it with something so very different than belief in Terra, adherence to the Sacred Vows, or commitment to service in the Order. Somewhere in this ring was a promise made between lovers, a vision of their future—a fading image on the horizon, disappearing ever farther into the distance the harder he tried to reach it.

Was there a place, outside of past and memory, where those two lovers could live out their lives, as they'd planned? Would he ever again hold the only woman he'd ever loved? Would he ever see her again?

He covered the ring with his palm, rubbing it as an ache formed in his eyes. He glanced out the window. The sky was clear but gray, the world beneath it a land of snow and ice. A southerly wind picked up the snow powder and carried it downwind. His mind followed it, his heart longing for just a glimpse of where she was, wherever she was, to see her alive and safe.

Opening his awareness, he searched for her, stretched the limits of his mind, the shores and borders of Emaurria. Nothing.

A knock echoed from the hall.

"Enter." Jon stood and looked at the door expectantly.

Raoul walked in and bowed. "The Archmage, Your Majesty."

"Send her in."

Raoul bowed, then left. Jon raised his hand to his chest, where the Laurentine signet ring rested, hanging from its cord. Tension rose inside him, hardening his every muscle.

Olivia entered and bowed in perfect form, by all signs recovered from their heated exchange a couple days before. She didn't support his courtship of Alessandra, but since that day, she'd kept her objections to stony silence and smoldering frowns.

"The spiritualist has arrived on schedule," she said.

"Did you..." His throat dry, he swallowed. "...find out anything yet?"

"No." She bowed her head. "I thought it should be you."

As much as he longed for some answer to hold on to, his heart pounded at the thought. "Together, then." He touched the Sodalis ring. "When can we meet with him?"

"Now, Your Majesty."

He stiffened.

"He awaits you in your solar, with his tutor." She watched him with uneasy eyes.

For a moment, he braced his fingers on his desk to gather his composure. *Now*. Some answer looming in the vague future had been one thing, but *now* was entirely another.

Olivia didn't move.

"Let's go," he said, at last.

She nodded, and as he left his study and proceeded to the solar, she followed in silence.

Inside the solar stood a slender young woman with a boy. The woman had short, curly, dark hair that caught the sunlight shining through the stained glass. The boy with her, swimming in his mage coat, appeared no older than ten.

The young woman curtsied, and the boy bowed.

"Good day, Your Majesty," the woman said, her voice tremulous.

"Please rise." Something about her face caught his curiosity, and he approached her. When she visibly swallowed, recognition dawned. "You are..."

"Master Mage Erelyn Leonne, Your Majesty." She inclined her head and shifted her tawny brown eyes. "Your Majesty, um, defeated me in the Emaurrian Tower's courtyard."

*The cantor.* She'd had a beautiful voice that night, but his sigil tattoos had protected him from the negative effects of sound magic. A brief memory of striking her flashed in his recollection, and he grimaced. He never enjoyed raising a hand to a woman, regardless of the circumstances.

"Forgive me, Master Leonne. My behavior that night was inexcusable."

Her eyes rounded, she raised her chin and shook her head. "Not at all! I tried to use magic on you, Your Majesty! It is *I* who should beg *your* forgiveness—"

"Then you're both sorry," Olivia interrupted, shooting Jon a peeved look. "Water under the bridge." She shrugged and gave a forced smile.

On task. Jon turned back to Master Leonne. "Thank you for coming."

"It is my honor, Your Majesty." Master Leonne put her hand on the boy's shoulder, who looked up at her uneasily. He was all too young to be a mage, but the éveil could sometimes come early.

Olivia took a few steps forward. "Although Francis is a spiritualist, Erelyn is a cantor. She is knowledgeable about spirit magic, and her abilities help soothe him. Together, I think they should be successful."

When Master Leonne gave an optimistic nod, Jon directed her and the boy to a sofa, then took a seat opposite them in an armchair. Imparting her quiet support, Olivia stood beside him, despite the available seats in the room.

In just a moment, he'd know where she was. He'd know where Rielle was, where to look, and bring her home.

"If he doesn't know the person," Master Leonne began, "he'll need something of theirs as a focus."

Olivia's note had said as much. When Jon reached for the signet ring, Olivia laid her hand on his shoulder and shook her head. Instead, she took off her bracelet—a plain silver chain with a small mermaid charm, her mother's—and handed it to the boy.

A test. Jon watched with interest.

The trinket in his palm, the boy stared at it, then glanced at his tutor.

"You can do it, Francis. It's all right." Master Leonne hummed a soft tune.

When she smiled her encouragement, he looked back at the bracelet and closed his eyes. Slowly, he took on a violet glow, wisps of magic swirling around him like glimmering smoke. "A woman, older, with kind eyes and red hair?" His voice, despite its childish pitch, harmonized eerily.

"Yes," Olivia whispered.

When the boy opened his eyes, his irises were purple. "She lives, far to the west. A cold wind blows in from the sea, but the cottage is warm. A cat jumps onto her lap. She sews a cloak." He blinked, and the violet glow disappeared. Hanging his head, he puffed short breaths.

Master Leonne put her arm around him, and the boy calmed. She looked from Jon to Olivia and back.

"My mother," Olivia explained. "And that is most certainly what she's doing." She squeezed Jon's shoulder and nodded toward the boy.

Jon pulled the chain, along with the ring, over his head and handed it to the boy.

"The ring, Your Majesty?" He looked up at Jon hopefully.

"Yes."

The boy handled the object with care, piling the golden chain into his palm with the signet ring. Master Leonne sang, and when the boy closed his eyes, the same violet aura surrounded him. He squeezed his eyes tighter. "A blond woman, beautiful, with eyes the color of the sky?"

His spine stiffening, Jon said, "Yes. That's her." His breath came short and quick, his heart thundering. Every muscle in his body went rigid as he awaited the boy's next words.

The boy opened his eyes, his irises glowing purple, widening. He shook his head.

Unable to move, Jon stared. His face tight, he questioned whether he'd seen correctly. A shake of the head. Breathless, he stiffened as a sudden coldness hit him at the core.

"Francis?" Master Leonne asked, pulling the boy closer.

The boy pressed his lips together, his face blotchy. "Reborn..." When he squeezed his eyes shut, tears burst from them, and he buried his face in Erelyn's chest.

Blanched, she looked up at Jon, her eyes wide.

"Reborn," Jon repeated, breathing raggedly. There had to be more than that. There had to. "What does that mean, 'reborn'?" He turned his gaze to Erelyn, who remained silent but unsettled, holding Francis close. "What does it mean?" he demanded.

She flinched. "It means—Your Majesty, it means..." Her eyes teared up. "Great Divine, I'm sorry, Your Majesty, it means—"

Master Leonne's brows knitted together, and she shook her head. "Anima absorbed back into the earth, repurposed to grow—"

Before the pressure could break through, Jon sprang from his chair and strode to the window. The light assaulted his aching eyes.

It couldn't be. It just couldn't.

Terra have mercy, it had to be a mistake. Black storm clouds rolled in, suffocated the sun, ghosts of lightning haunting their dark shroud.

His palm went to the Sodalis ring, covering it, feeling it—the tangible promise. Together. They would be together.

"That'll be all," Olivia said behind him, her voice quivering. Footsteps retreated from the room.

Some part of him broke. He braced his hands on the stone window sill, pressed the rough texture into his palms, leaned into it. Rough and painful. Reality.

"Jon." Olivia's delicate tone made him shudder.

"No." The word tore out of him, hoarse and stubborn, even as grief took its unrelenting hold. Thunder rolled. "No." Gods above, even as he repeated the word, the thrashing inside broke through.

He whirled around, grabbed the table next to him, and threw it aside. The crash of wood called to the violence inside him pushing against his inner barriers. He swept a row of books off its shelf, ripped it from the wall, broke it against the stone, flung the pieces.

His hands needed to destroy, needed to break, needed disorder—the whirlwind inside demanded its due. Magic came to his hands, animated his surroundings, hurled them in myriad directions in loud crashes. All around him became a chaotic blur.

A tightness seized his chest, and he grabbed at it, the pain.

It squeezed. His heart thudded, pounded, heavy.

"Jon?"

The room tilted, and he doubled over, tearing at his chest.

"Jon!"

Guardsmen rushed into the room, but Olivia shuffled them all out but for Raoul, who held him as everything spun, as needling agony tore into his chest.

Olivia knelt next to him, her palm stealing into his shirt against his skin. The faint warmth of her magic filled him.

Wildly, he looked around him, at everything, but there was nothing left—disorder, parts, shattered pieces of a life that had waited for the woman he loved to complete it. Pain deepened at the back of his throat, a hoarse hollow gaping.

Everything in the solar lay broken, and his breaths only came in gasps and wheezes. Raoul's hands held him steady, his ice-blue eyes wide.

"My life... for Her will," he breathed, speaking the final words thousands of paladins had spoken before him.

Raoul shook his head, then swore. "With honor and valor, you have served," he replied, his voice breaking.

"Her voice... calls... me," he hissed, grasping at his chest, at its unforgiving tightness.

Raoul's eyebrows drew together tightly, his eyes wild beneath them. Drops hit Jon's face. "Answer with pride... son of Terra," he whispered.

Jon squeezed his eyes shut. If it was time, he could die faithful.

The pain didn't ease. Gods, he deserved it. All this time, he'd fought off thoughts of Rielle, memories, trusted her rescue to Brennan, and she'd been—she'd been dying. Somewhere far from here, she'd breathed her last, and he hadn't even known, hadn't been there, hadn't...

A blinding white light flooded his field of vision, and he reached out for her hand.

Warmth ebbed away the pain. Slowly.

It abandoned him, and something else, something sore, flowed into its void, rising, shoving to the top. The soreness pushed from the inside out, his chest aching at the expansion, his heart faltering in a merciless grasp that squeezed and squeezed.

He blinked his eyes open, and a blurry Olivia was shouting, both of her hands on his chest.

He drew in a breath, and another, and another. The world began to come into focus, ghosts superimposing over reality.

"Don't you dare die, Jon," she screamed. "Don't you dare, don't you even dare. You give up, and I'll never forgive you, never, never—"

"Olivia," Raoul bit out, shaking her arm, and nodding toward him.

The floor was hard against his back, shoulders, and head, and he looked up at them both, catching his breath.

*Rielle.* Blessed Terra, he'd only seen her a couple months ago. Held her in his arms. He would never have believed it.

But the boy—Jon had seen the test and the magic before his very eyes. The obliteration of hope. The end of a life. *Her life.*

Olivia sobbed quietly and wrapped her arms around him, pressing the Laurentine signet ring against his chest.

He'd promised Rielle he'd return it to her.

He'd promised.

OLIVIA FALTERED in Edgar's arms, sapped of the strength even to walk. She couldn't feel her feet. He braced her in the hall, slung her arm around his neck, and finally gathered her up and carried her.

"Come, Your Ladyship," he said softly. "I'm not officially your guard yet—not until His Majesty knights me—but Raoul and Florian summoned me. Not a moment too soon, either. I'll take you to your room so you can rest." His moss-green eyes were soft.

*Your Ladyship.* She'd been fretting over forms of address while Rielle... while Rielle had been dying.

Hot tears rose anew. She covered her mouth and squeezed her eyes shut.

And Jon—Jon had nearly died, too. Divine, had no healer ever seen his heart? Seen the defect?

He was fit, healthy, so perhaps no one had ever thought to check, but now that he'd shown symptoms... now that...

She covered her mouth, but tears rolled down her cheeks.

She could relieve the symptoms, but she couldn't heal the heart he'd been born with. "It's too cruel," she whispered.

Rielle was gone, and he—he had two, maybe three years at most before it would kill him.

"Hm?" Edgar asked, close, mercifully close.

She shut her eyes and rested her head against his chest. Losing both Rielle *and* Jon? Life couldn't be so cruel. The Divine couldn't be. Terra couldn't be.

Edgar opened the door to her quarters and rushed to her bedchamber, where he laid her upon her bed. Although the curtains were open, hardly any light illuminated the room; the sky had darkened from gray to black. None of the red shades in his maple-brown hair showed.

She curled up tightly, gathering her pillow, and pressed her face into it. Soft light brightened the room, her bedside candle as Edgar lit it. A thick knit blanket covered her—Mama's—and the bed sank as Edgar sat next to her.

He took her hand in his. That warmth, that comfort, was too much.

What had happened to Rielle? Where had she been the moment she'd... Had she been alone? Without a friend, family...?

"Your Ladyship..." Soft, soothing.

"I left her to die," she cried out between sobs. "She came to save me... and I left her to die."

Edgar squeezed her hand. "You didn't know. You couldn't."

No, she hadn't anticipated the abduction, but she should've known. In a palace teeming with Crag Company mercenaries, she should've known...

She shook her head. "It's my fault..." Tears soaked her pillow. "It's my fault, and..."

Edgar swept her wet hair off her face, tucked it behind her ear, stroked her head gently. "It's not your fault, Your Ladyship. We all make our own choices, and your friend did, too."

She closed her eyes. "You don't know..." And she couldn't even tell him about Jon. Not without telling Jon first.

Edgar leaned in. "It is said, 'And the blackwood trees shall part, and such a light will pour forth, and at its center will be all the righteous who've come before, and the Most Holy to wipe every tear from your eyes, for there shall be no more crying, nor pain, nor death, for the earthly things will have fallen away.' "

He spoke of heaven, at the heart of the Lone. Divinists and Terrans alike believed in its existence... Rielle had, too. Sniffling, she blinked. "Do you think it's really there, Edgar? Heaven?"

"Of course it's there. It is written." He glanced at the window. "They say the Immortals came from the Lone. And if the Lone exists, so must its center."

Was he right? Would she see Rielle there someday? Would Jon?

Her heart felt as black as the sky beyond her windows, but with Edgar's words, perhaps a little lighter. He gave her a soft, sad smile, and the corners of his eyes crinkled. He was trying to make her feel better, but it was a lost cause.

Her best friend was dead. And another friend was dying.

She rubbed her cheek against the pillow's soft, wet cotton, fresh tears still streaming from her eyes. They were supposed to have spent Midwinter together. She and Rielle would have stayed up together like they used to, sharing the stories of their lives, laughing together, happy. They would have shared the new magic they'd learned, and talked about the latest volume of *Court Duelist*. They would have gossiped and teased one another...

But they'd never see each other again. Or laugh. Or talk. Just like James, and Anton, Rielle was gone. And Jon had but a couple years to live.

Edgar stroked her cheek. "Tell me what you need, and you'll have it. Just please... I want to—"

The door opened, and Edgar turned sharply. "Lord Constable." He rose and bowed.

"Sir Armurier," Tor greeted as he entered, carrying himself with that easy elegance all Marcels seemed to be born with; everything about him, from his hazel eyes to his deep-bronze skin and dark hair, even his ability with a blade, declared his lineage as one of Maerleth Tainn's distinguished sons. Although he wasn't lord of any lands, his name alone was invaluable. It was no wonder that many of the court's ladies fawned over him, with his kind heart, unwavering honor, and ruggedly dashing looks in his early forties.

She and Tor had been spending more and more time together recently, and he'd begun courting her in earnest. He knelt at her bedside and took her hand. "I came as soon as I heard. I'm so sorry."

She nodded, and he kissed her forehead and then lightly brushed her lips with his. "Is there anything I can do? What do you need?"

She shook her head.

He glanced over his shoulder. "You can go, brother. I'll stay with her."

His face tight, Edgar bowed. "Yes, Your Lordship."

Tor turned back to her, and Edgar's look lingered on her a moment before he departed.

She sniffed and eyed Tor. "Jon needs you."

Tor raised her hand to his lips and kissed it. "Derric's with him. And I'm here for you."

She shuffled over on the bed, making room, and he sat, holding her hand. "I don't want to be alone," she whispered.

He kissed her fingers, then slowly lay next to her. "You never again need be."

She clung to him, let him take her into his arms, rested her face against the burgundy tiretaine of his doublet. Rielle would never again know the embrace of a loved one... She'd lost too much, and Olivia had lost too much, and loss was the everlasting way of things. It hurt too keenly, and would keep hurting, and she never wanted to lose again.

Tor's arms were safe. He was a Marcel, well insulated, and a warrior —skilled, a survivor. Not a royal. No one out for his head.

She wept, buried her face in his chest, and resolved never to let go.

Whoever did this—

She'd find the one responsible. The Swordsman. The one responsible for James. For Anton. For Rielle. For Jon. Even if it took weeks, months, years, or lifetimes, the Swordsman would never take anyone away ever again.

# CHAPTER 31

*R*ielle cringed, dread slithering in every part of her body. Today was the day. The day she'd kill Farrad. The day she'd win her freedom.

The thought should have comforted her, but no matter how she rationalized, she had spent weeks sleeping beside the man whose blood would stain her hands tonight. Her only comfort was her unobstructed connection to her anima—in the false arcanir cuffs, she could feel her magic once again. She could *use* her magic again, even if she dared not until tonight.

The army of slaves and servants preparing her had waxed her skin bare, bathed her in saffron, painted her with henna. They'd adorned her hair, decorated her with jewelry, applied makeup. By the time they had dressed her in the jeweled red silk top and skirts, she'd almost felt relieved.

Barefoot, they led her through the lattice-framed hallways out to the courtyard, the marble cool beneath her feet. Her attire's adornments clinked softly as a provocative tune of drums, cymbals, tambourines, and oboes intensified.

Against a sapphire-blue evening sky, the courtyard glittered with decorations, bursting with vibrant color. Cushions, ottomans, silk hangings, and dazzling blush-colored lilacs and lavender crocus flowers festooned the space to excess. Fire braziers lit the extravagance while brightly dressed guests mingled, laughing and chatting, momentarily sated by fine drinks and waterpipes. Slaves led diamond-collared animals on golden chains—leopards, cheetahs, lions, and others she had never before seen outside of drawings.

Several tiered tables graced the outer rim, food saturating every available surface in dizzying arrangements. Tall poplars lined the court-yard's perimeters like verdant soldiers watching the revelry with disinterest.

Although the lilacs' aroma hung heavy in the air, another smell—smoky but slightly sweet—overpowered it. Her escorts came to a halt and donned face masks. Before her, on a lower level from the guests, lay a stunning, writhing heap of scantily clad beautiful bodies on floor cushions—whimpering, moaning, heaving. Party favors for later, trapped in a crowded purgatory, fumbling hopelessly with smoke-induced need.

Firm hands held her in place while a censer swung before her, an orb of intricately wrought silver, trailing crimson smoke.

*Ithara.*

She bucked against the hands keeping her in place, angling her face away. *No. Sylvie—*

She held her breath, but one of her escorts held her nose through her thrashing until she breathed in, coughing, wheezing, fighting every breath. Would it hurt Sylvie? She drew her eyebrows together, eyes watering.

*A doctor. We'll see a doctor as soon as we break free of this place.* Healers worked for the Sonbaharan Tower, and visiting one was as good as getting caught. But doctors weren't bound to the Tower.

Everywhere she looked, censers of smoking ithara studded the slave platform—around, beside, and even hanging from the wisteria-wrapped pergola overhead; there would be no relief, just the blur, the haze, the desire.

The music muffled until it became but a faint tune timed by the pounding of her own heart, the blood surging inside, the unwanted pulse beginning. The disordered array of rhythmic bodies before her blended until it became a fleshy sea, its tide of pleasure flowing in sensual waves. Harmonious and discordant, each body engaged others differently, yet in the same acts... she watched it, apart, hypnotized by the motion...

Then she drowned in it.

Push and pull. Arms, legs, hands. Pleasure rippled from a thousand points on her body. Push and pull. She closed her eyes and shook her head, trying to recall when her escorts had left, when she'd lain down. Push and...

The heat, its rise and fall, rise and fall—it lulled. She closed her eyes...

Her eyes fluttered open. On her back, she blinked as her head moved, her feet moved, but above her, no hanging wisteria, but sky—lovely, open, midnight-blue sky.

On both sides of her, women shifted like snakes, and so did she, her spine and limbs curving to the provocative beat of the music. When she turned her head, gleaming dark gazes watched with interest, surrounding her, a wreath of vividly thiyawbed guests. At last, she found the darkest gaze, a familiar one, fire burning deep in those endless black pools, waiting to consume.

"I want you to feel every second tonight." Farrad's mouth appeared to savor the taste, curling upward, anticipation falling from his lips in languorous words. Another drag on the waterpipe.

Wrong. Something felt wrong.

But she only writhed, only moved, only danced.

The weave of the rug rubbed beneath her feet... Time hurtled forward—with a flourish, the sheer red scarf flowed at her back, following the sensual undulation of her hips, her belly, her ribs, her chest, her shoulders, her neck, her head. The music played on, the drums beckoning to her body while she moved. Heat from a brazier warmed from behind her, although a chill breeze fondled her skin through the haze.

All around, the floor cushions waved with bodies—guests with slaves, taking their pleasure, a sheet of silk flowing in the wind. Somewhere in the distance, an animal roared, primal ferocity splitting the heady lust of the night. She hadn't forgotten how she'd conclude it, but the animal call fanned her determination.

Her cuffs slid up her arm as she moved. False arcanir. She found Farrad, caught glimpses of his pleased countenance as he reclined in a luxurious violet thiyawb draped over his honed body.

She would kill him.

Forcing helplessness into her expression, slack face and large eyes, she danced on, but Farrad abd Nasir abd Imtiyaz Hazael would meet his end tonight—at her hands.

With a relaxed curl of two fingers, he gestured to his stiff-postured guards. Right away, they approached her from behind, raised her to her feet, and helped her inside. Around a bicep, she had a clear view of Farrad sauntering behind her, smiling. His gaze never left her, every second of its persistence a pang of guilt for what she had to do.

Had to do.

She looked at her bright-red silk skirts, juxtaposed with her bare flesh. A swath of blood, and she'd be free.

Her gaze wandered to the inner courtyard through the intricate latticework. There, at its center, the fountain flowed, cool constancy pouring over the white marble—the water calm and clear but in motion. After tonight, her life would return to its former state; after one last firestorm, the past would wash in and pervade once more—a life of magic, work, motherhood, and if she was fortunate, love.

But first...

Her attention meandered back to Farrad. Carefully controlling her expression, she regarded him with desire for the last time. It brought a pleased smile to his face.

A shadow darkened overhead; the guards had brought her through a doorway. Farrad's quarters, where she'd spent so much of the last few weeks.

She saw it with new eyes. The enormous, sturdy canopied bed with sheets of purest white dominated the space. Detailed mosaics graced the walls in dark violet, lively green, and soothing crème, brought together in some pattern. She'd seen it every day for weeks, and yet, she hadn't allowed herself to analyze it, consider what it meant. A flower of some sort?

Farrad strolled into her field of vision and faced the mosaic walls, his hand arcing in a grand gesture.

"Beautiful, isn't it?" He turned to her for a moment and raised a cup. "It's called 'moonflower' here, although northerners sometimes call it 'demon's trumpet.' An ominous name for a flower, wouldn't you say?"

She stared at the mosaic until she saw not its luxurious tile, but a field of soft, crème-colored flowers blooming in the night beneath the moon's radiance, swaying on green stalks tinged with violet. Their beauty drew in the eye, only the dark omen of violet betraying their poisonous nature.

Moonflower.

Heat flushed in her face and spread through her body.

"Some among my people have used its essence for certain... specialized purposes. A small amount can relieve pain." He paused to remove his dark-violet thiyawb, exposing his warrior's body. Without magic, she would have had no hope of defeating him. "A large amount can cause death."

Her pulse raced, and the flush of her skin escalated to heat. *My hairpin. Is it poisoned with concentrated moonflower extract?*

"A carefully controlled amount, however," he said, approaching her, "can create unbelievable pleasure. Moonflower intoxication produces a complete inability to differentiate reality from fantasy—delirium. Fever, racing heart, and visions. The blown pupils it causes can render one intolerant to light for days thereafter," he said, crouching to lift up her chin and examine her eyes. "But it's worth the pleasure."

"My... child..."

"You needn't worry. All will be well."

She blinked sluggishly. He drank of the cup, then brought it to her mouth. She tried to push it away, but all she managed was a whimper. He tipped the cup into her mouth, and the bitter liquid ran down her throat and her neck, soaking into her top.

"You will love it. A rare pleasure, and we will enjoy ourselves greatly tonight."

Time blurred, and then her pulse sped as the fever rose; Farrad began to fall out of focus before her. Moonflower intoxication. She had to kill him. If she was to leave before the intoxication overpowered her, it would have to be soon.

He undressed her in soft pulls of silk, exhaling slowly with every pull, grazing fingertips against her skin as he stripped her bare on the immaculate-white sheets.

With her hands next to her, any spells she attempted would be visible. As soon as he'd notice, he could kill her.

He drew a finger across her chest, and she shivered. "Let yourself relax, Thahab. For once." His teasing voice became distant. "Tonight, and every night hereafter, you are taken care of."

He pinned her and slowly descended to press his lips against hers, a soft kiss that sent ripples of pleasure through her body. He lavished her with his attentions, leaving her gasping.

*Wait for the moment when he is most vulnerable.*

Divine, the thought of killing this man made her chest tighten, but she couldn't succumb to mercy now.

"So quiet," he whispered, his voice a low rasp. "Are you not pleased?"

A palm slid over her belly, trailing pleasure as it swept across, then lower.

She squeezed her eyes closed, shutting out her doubts. Tears threatened to leave her eyes, but she forced them back. With all her might, never had she wanted to pull on her bond with Brennan as she longed to now, but with all of the guards surrounding House Hazael, he would never make it in and out unseen, and if he were caught or recognized, this nightmare would follow them both to Emaurria.

No, with her anonymity here, it was up to her to win her own freedom and find her own way out. No tears. She focused on the rhythm of Farrad's breathing, biding her time until the opportune moment.

No—she couldn't risk being pinned beneath him.

She opened her eyes, reached for his stubbled face, and urged him down to kiss her. He obliged, and she pressed against his shoulder. When he rolled over, she climbed atop him, her bare skin pebbling at the night breeze.

His palms ascended her bare thighs to her hips, and as he threw his head back and closed his eyes, she planted her palms on his chest—one over his heart.

A single ice spike, and it would be all over. *Do it. It's the only way.*

His touch traveled her back, her chest, and slid down her arms to brush over her cuffs.

His brow creased.

She gestured the spell.

His eyes flew open, and he jerked away.

The ice spike materialized, burst from her spellcasting hand, and went through his arm. Nothing happened. He glowed with a faint black aura that disappeared as quickly as it came.

*Magic.*

Reality or fantasy?

*The sigil.*

He grabbed for her arms, and she clamped her thighs tightly around him. With one hand, she iced over the entrance into the room until it was four feet thick. He rolled her off him, but she hooked her leg around his and dragged him to the floor.

She drew upon the natural stone in the room, destroying the detailed artwork to encase his legs, but he grabbed her neck and pinned her to the floor next to him.

"Even you?" he bit out. His eyes brightened beneath a scowl, and the fire she cast from both hands affected him not at all.

*Sigiled against the elements.*

"An augur foretold my destiny," he hissed. "Death by elemental magic. I know my stars, and I made certain to be sigiled against them."

The corners of the room darkened. Guards called out on the other side of the door and pounded upon it. They would soon enter. She had precious little time.

Her magic wouldn't affect him, and short of reducing all of House Hazael to rubble—including herself—she couldn't kill him. She'd failed.

"But you, Thahab, of all people? Poisoned against me?"

*Poison. The hairpin.* As his hold around her neck tightened, she thrashed her arms above her head, eyes fixed on his, and reached for the long pin. As soon as it came to her hand, she buried it in his chest.

He released her, and she scrambled away, gulping mouthfuls of air, but he pursued, ripped the pin from his chest, and stabbed it into her side. She screamed, yanking it out immediately.

He collapsed to the floor, writhing, wincing.

Grabbing her side, she murmured the healing incantation to close the bleeding wound. But she slurred the words, and the spell faltered.

*Focus.* The poison would kill him, and she needed to flee before whatever trace amounts remained could affect her.

"What did Ihsan promise you?" He sat up and covered his wound, dark blood seeping through his fingers. "Freedom? Freedom for the whole House?"

Ignoring him, she picked up his violet thiyawb and hurriedly put it on. The pounding on the frozen door grew louder.

The color began to drain from his face. The poison working. "You foolish woman. Ihsan wants to sell this House's slaves. She's kept Grandfather living just until she can kill me and inherit it all. And she won't let you live. That woman is ruthless and leaves no loose ends."

It was fortunate, then, that she hadn't relied on Ihsan's trustworthiness.

His jaw clenched, and his eyes turned glassy. "It is *I* who... planned to free you once I inherited the power to do so."

Empty words.

"If you don't believe me, look at the parchment on my desk. I had the documents drawn up today and planned to show you in the morning."

The ice blocking the door began to crack, but his words froze her in place. Was it true?

Sylvie. She couldn't think about him now; she had Sylvie to think about.

Mumbling the incantation again, she rushed to the desk and grabbed the parchment there. A man in his position might say anything to avoid death, but she hadn't the luxury to believe fanciful tales nor the time to read them. After all of this, she'd see this parchment was nothing at all and feel vindicated.

She tucked them into the thiyawb and moved to the latticed

window to open the latch and steal a glance below, clutching her injured side. It had healed some, but still bled.

Good enough. It would have to be good enough until she got somewhere safe. While voices called all around the property, no one appeared directly beneath Farrad's window.

She turned back to the quarters and, with a sweep of her arm, ignited a swath from one end to the other, sparking flame near his feet. Nothing would be left of him when all burned and collapsed upon him, sigil or not.

The flames reached up to the ceiling, igniting it in a blaze that spread above.

With a last look at his wan, hardened expression, she wavered. "You were kind to me. I hated the idea of killing you, but I hated enslavement more."

"Blood for blood." Pale as death, he looked away at the door's cracking ice.

What if he wasn't lying?

No, he had to die, and he would; if the poison didn't take him first, the fire would.

At last, he went limp. The poison had worked. Ihsan wouldn't have given her anything less than deadly. Farrad abd Nasir abd Imtiyaz Hazael was dead.

*Samara's father.*

*Shit.*

If Farrad hadn't been lying, if Ihsan truly intended to sell all of House Hazael's slaves, then Samara would be sold.

The ice covering the door cracked to the floor. Rielle drew in a sharp breath. She couldn't leave here without Samara. She had to find her.

Biting her lip, she looked outside, at the grass in the darkness below, and used her magic to raise a small circle of earth in a pillar up to the window. When it reached her level, she jumped onto it, the window slamming shut behind her. She gestured for the earthen dais to descend.

When she reached the ground, she made for the cover of the

nearby colonnade. The pomegranate trees. She had to get to the pomegranate trees.

She looked around to gain her bearings. No stars out tonight—the sky was dark. Too dark. Her head spun. The slave quarters, the barracks—

The barracks, a square outbuilding.

Where Vittoria had been killed. Where countless women had been hurt and killed.

A haze closing in from all sides, she focused on the barracks, channeled blazing power in both hands, cultivating fiery orbs on either side of the building. Fixated on it, she clasped her hands together.

Fire engulfed the barracks. As she pressed one orb into the other, a raging inferno consumed the building, a scorching orb trapping all inside. Distant shrieks, agonized screams, and dying throes writhed in the humid air.

She held the spell, staring at the burning, the scorching, the destruction, through the screams and roar of fire. The barracks withered to black, collapsed, and still she willed the flames to consume. Not a single survivor. Not even one. Cleanse House Hazael. At least this one place.

"There!" a voice rang out.

Snapping in the voice's direction, she threw an ice spike.

It pierced a guard's chest.

Blinking through a smoky blur, she glanced at the barracks. No, the glowing embers that had once been the barracks.

No more tarrying. With the barracks destroyed, the other slaves had a chance, one she prayed they'd take. She would head for the pomegranate trees, where Brennan promised to wait for her. Together, they'd find Samara and escape.

She fled, the ghosts of moonflower essence slowing her down to a limping crawl, but Farrad was no more.

She was free.

# CHAPTER 32

*T*he scent of Rielle's blood carried on the wind long before the shouts of the guards alerted Brennan to her movement. He'd stayed hidden among the dense pomegranate trees, as promised, but as the coppery smell hit him, his body ached to go. If she was hurt, she might need his help.

*She'd use the bond.* But that thought did nothing to quiet his nerves. He paced beneath the sweet canopy, fallen fruit crunching beneath his feet while the enemies' calls increased in volume and number.

Orders or not, promise or not, he had to go to her. He stripped off his clothing, listening to discern the content of the shouted orders. He began the Change, shifting to full Wolf. With any luck, the Hazaels would have no reason to link him to her disappearance or track them to Emaurria. After tonight, Rielle would be safe.

Under the cover of night, he darted across the lush courtyard, keeping his movement quick and low to avoid notice. He pulled on the bond to no avail; instead of moving toward the pomegranate trees, Rielle moved away. Following her direction, he avoided the shuffling squads of guards, crept in the shadows, then darted to the colonnade. Blood and burning flesh mingled with jasmine in the air as he sidled along the wall.

There, nestled amid the copious jasmine, Rielle crouched, clad in the thiyawb of the upper class, mouthing some words to herself. A healing incantation. She hadn't seen him yet. Several charred bodies lay in disarray around her.

Careful not to startle her, he approached. A short distance away, he paused in the dark and waited until the vicinity cleared of running slaves and fleeing guests before Changing back to his human form.

He grabbed her from behind, covering her mouth with a palm, and dragged her into cover with him. She screamed into his hand, her body afire with magic—a flame cloak spell.

At times like this, he didn't rue his werewolf nature.

But the spectacle would draw attention. He angled to show her his face, and the flame died, if not the screaming. He realized then it wasn't from terror but pain. The side of her thiyawb was bloodied.

Ever the fool, he'd drawn that side against him. He pulled away with care, until her muffled screaming ceased. Only then did he uncover her mouth.

Shaken, she turned to him. "Is it really you?"

She reached out. Her hesitant fingertips brushed against his lips, her hand rested against his cheek, and her thumb pressed into his chin. "Brennan?"

"It's me," he hissed, glancing at their surroundings.

Something was wrong. No, several things. Her heart raced, faster than he'd expected. Her eyes—even in the night, he could discern her blown pupils.

Drugged. Badly.

"I won't be tricked again." She laid her palm against his chest, closing her eyes in concentrated silence. After a moment with his beating heart, she opened them, apparently satisfied with his reality. "It's really you."

"Of course it's me." He tried to keep the edge from his voice. "What were you given? Ithara?" The scent had carried earlier.

A slow nod.

Ithara created and amplified desire, distorted pleasure to the limits. He'd partaken before, even if his beast blood did not allow the effects to linger. Ithara couldn't be all that was wrong. "What else?"

At her side, she buried a hand beneath her thiyawb, the faint glow of magic and whisper of an incantation evidencing her healing. A sluggish blink, and she slumped onto his chest, into his lap.

"Moonflower," she slurred, fading. "Can't heal it..." Her cheek burned with fever against his stomach.

*Moonflower*. She lived, so it wasn't a lethal dose. But now her doubts about reality made sense.

"You came for me," she murmured against his skin. "Farrad is dead... Samara... We have to find... Samara..." Her voice drifted off.

Voices came from the gardens. He gathered her up and hid behind a pillar.

A squad of guards shuffled through the colonnade, pausing at the charred bodies, and just before they could move past, he swept her around the edge to avoid being seen. The whole property teemed with men searching for an intruder, and soon, the city would be swarming with slave hunters and mercenaries looking to cash in a bounty. Their time was running out.

He waited until the squad rounded the corner, then kept to the cover of trees and bushes as he carried her back to where he'd left his clothes. Although his items were nondescript, if they were found, Rielle's escape would be linked to an accomplice and perhaps, eventually, to his own departure from Xir.

Finally, the shadow of the pomegranate trees' canopy shrouded them. He navigated around a rappelling spider and laid Rielle gently upon the ground. He found his clothes and dressed quickly, his attention on the guards fanning out to search the property. One of them made his way toward the pomegranate trees.

Brennan froze. Instinct dominated as he took cover behind a massive trunk, listening to the cautious footfalls of the approaching guard. Nearer and nearer the stranger crept, far from his comrades, his gait alert. There would be but one chance to get this right without making a sound.

The steps slowed near the tree Brennan hid behind, but they continued. A pomegranate fell from above and thumped upon the ground. The guard turned. Opportunity. Brennan sprang on him from behind, covered his mouth, and put him in a hold, keeping him there until the guard passed out. Killing him—without magic, anyway—would only alert the guards that she'd had assistance.

After camouflaging the guard in some nearby bushes, he slunk back to where Rielle lay. Although she was quiet, her fever had not abated, and she slept fitfully. It was a wonder she hadn't been heard already.

Climbing the ten-foot wall was their only option, and it had to be now, before the missing guard attracted investigation. Brennan slung her over his shoulder.

When the shouting was distant, he Changed to his man-beast form, as much as he could in such little time. He scrambled up the wall and over, smothering a yelp from Rielle as she jostled awake. On the other side, he Changed back to man and, holding her against his chest, strode toward Father's villa through the night streets of Xir.

The nausea that came with Changing too often hit him heavily, but he stifled the urge to vomit and proceeded. Rielle nuzzled his chest, wriggling in his hold; now that she was awake, the ithara's effects reigned over those of the moonflower.

"Brennan," she whispered. "I need... You have to save her from—"

Taking a deep breath, he tried to ignore the intoxicating smell of her blood, but the rare treat caught his Wolf's attention and held it, ceasing the imbalance that made him sick. Instead of balancing, he now had to control the force of his wolfish urges.

She bunched the fabric of his thiyawb in her trembling hand, going rigid against his arm. He quickened his pace.

A dark thought he'd been willfully ignoring invaded his mind then—the scent of the man on her, mingled with her blood. Farrad abd Nasir abd Imtiyaz Hazael had dared to harm her, had done unspeakable things to her. If she hadn't killed that demon herself, Brennan would have relished the task.

Although she had recounted the events of the past few months to him, the telltale changes in her heart rate had spoken volumes of the account's alteration. Whether out of shame or indignity, she hadn't told him everything. And those secrets tore at his soul. What she had endured at the hands of her tormentors—would he ever know? If he could ever bear to know. These streets would run red with blood.

Lamplit stalls and small groups of revelers dotted the dark city street. A passerby scrutinized him for longer than usual, and mustering a congenial expression, Brennan muttered some excuse in High Nad'i —his wife falling asleep at a party. The old man smiled and nodded, looked away, kept walking, his pulse normal. His reaction had spared his life.

"We're not married yet," she whispered, with a soft chuckle. She rubbed her face against his thiyawb.

*Yet.*

The delirium of ithara and moonflower drugging must have been affecting her more than he'd thought.

"It hurts." Her voice no more than a whimper, she contracted in his grasp.

Urgency tightened his body. "We're almost there," he replied, his breath catching for a moment. When, exactly, he'd fallen in love with her eluded him—When she'd relived the fire at Laurentine? When she'd nearly killed herself to force his hand? When their parents had arranged their engagement? When they'd forged the bond?

It didn't matter anymore. No matter when or how long, he loved her.

Whatever that meant.

"Brennan." She squirmed in his embrace.

The villa was in view. "Almost there." He held her closer, attempted to comfort her.

"Not that," she replied weakly. "Samara... We have to go back for Samara."

He pressed his lips together. "We can't. If we go back there, we're—"

"You don't understand!" She squeezed his arm. "She saved me, and—"

"We're not going back, Rielle."

The smell of salt assaulted his nostrils. Her eyes watered. Great Wolf, she wept? She wept... "Is she a slave?"

She nodded. "An apothecary. A young woman."

"I'll have my father's mistress purchase her, whatever the cost."

After a moment, she nodded weakly.

In the distance, he heard no more shouts. "I think we lost them—"

"My brand," she blurted. "My slave brand. They'll find us... You have to destroy it..."

Slave brands were tattooed into the flesh, usually the small of one's back. To destroy it would be— "You can't possibly mean—"

"Claw it... Break the rune." Her eyes fluttered open and closed.

Brennan charged toward the villa, knocked on the doors, and when they opened, stormed past the startled servants.

"Run a bath and build a fire in my quarters," he commanded one, who disappeared right away. He turned toward another. "Fetch a healer—"

Rielle struggled in his grasp, thrashing. "Healers work for the Sonbaharan Tower."

"No healer," he repeated. "A doctor," he instructed the servants, who nodded and rushed away.

Rielle didn't want to risk exposure. He understood. But her healing skills were limited, and he didn't know what to expect beneath the bloodied thiyawb.

A stunned Kehani rushed down the stairs in her robe, her cascades of black hair trailing her, flanked by a chambermaid.

"Brennan, what is the meaning of this? Who is this woman?" She gestured toward Rielle with a wisp of her silk robe.

"My betrothed."

"The Marquise of Laurentine?" Kehani's eyes widened. "What is she doing here? Where is her entourage?"

"She and I will be leaving before dawn." He proceeded up the stairs to the bath. "She will need some clothing... toiletries..."

"Is she all right? What's happened?"

Pausing on the same stair, Brennan looked down and regarded her squarely. "No. More. Questions." He turned his attention to her chambermaid, a leaf trembling in the wind. "Prepare all that Marquise Laurentine will require for five days' travel. Now."

The maid could have waited for confirmation from her mistress or serve the heir of the man responsible for her wages. She chose the latter.

He turned back to Kehani, whose narrowed eyes were fixed upon him, bold for a little woman over a foot shorter than him. She didn't like him ordering around her household.

He didn't care. "You—and your household—are to tell no one she was even here. No one. Not even my father."

Kehani gave him a moment's blazing look but nodded; he didn't need to voice the threat they both well knew. If Father ever discovered he had been here alone, Brennan could tell whatever story he wanted. Kehani had seduced him. The truth.

And he was certain that although he wouldn't be Faolan's favorite child, there would be no question whom his father would choose and whom he would cast off. And Kehani had to know that, too.

When Brennan continued up the stairs, Kehani didn't move nor speak. He readjusted his hold on Rielle and looked straight ahead. A firm hand could buy expediency, if not friends. He'd exhausted his favor with Kehani.

The bath was ready when he arrived in his rooms. Two nervous maids lingered; he dismissed them with a wave. As soon as they left, he carefully peeled off Rielle's bloodied thiyawb, thankful its dark-violet color had camouflaged the stain before Kehani, and set aside some bloodied parchment. He didn't need her or the servants gossiping about Rielle's state. The less they knew, the better.

He threw the garment onto the hearth.

Beneath, she wore nothing but drying blood and fresh bruises.

When he hadn't blinked for some time, his eyes began to water. His mind rejected consideration of what she'd suffered this night, even as his entire body contracted to the point of quaking. He drew in a sharp breath and lowered her into the warm bath.

Upon contact with the water, her eyes flashed open, then fluttered as she rolled her head to the side and moaned. "Where am I...?"

Despite the question, she rested her head against the tub and closed her eyes once more.

"You're safe." He pulled her forward and gently washed her back. The scar of a puncture wound marred her side, just below her ribs. He washed and rinsed her hair, then gently rested her head against the tub once more. Remembering the washcloth that had sunk to the bottom, he reached for it, but she caught his arm and drew in close, shifting uncomfortably in the water.

Her mouth nearly upon his ear, she whispered, "I need... resonance."

He drew his eyebrows together. "The one thing I can't give you."

As a werewolf, he had no magic and could never share resonance with her, could never provide her with the nourishment her anima needed. Even if, by some miracle, she agreed to be his, he would never be able to give her all she required. It darkened his thoughts. "If you asked for anything else, I..."

Her wet grip on his arm slid down its length to his wrist beneath the water and, at last, to his hand. She sat up in the tub, facing him squarely, her pupils so dilated only a blue rim remained of her irises. Looking away, he washed her quickly.

"I don't feel... well." She trembled.

"The doctor is on his way." He wrapped her in a towel, carried her to a chair, and dried her off.

He dressed her in a large tunic and tossed the towels away.

Eyes wild, she swallowed and rubbed her upper arms. Uncomfortable. She was uncomfortable.

He carried her to the bed and gently laid her down. Curling up, she buried her face in his pillow. When she closed her eyes, tears escaped them.

What had she suffered? How much? If he considered it, his reaction would only make things worse. He stroked her hair and kissed her forehead before stepping away to change. "Everything will be all right now."

He stripped off his blood-stained clothes and tossed them into the fire. Once he'd washed, he toweled off and dressed beneath her watchful, drugged-black gaze.

Things had changed between them. Although she must have seen him naked a thousand times, something had shifted between them. More than the ithara, more than the moonflower, their usual relationship had gone and would never return.

She rested a hand on her stomach.

A lot had happened. Too much. The child in her belly, the dagger in his heart. She'd smelled sweeter; her heart had beat faster. He hadn't raised the subject, and she hadn't either; if it had been conceived during her enslavement, it only would have added to her anguish.

He grabbed some gauze from the cabinet near the washbasin. "Roll onto your stomach."

She complied, resting on her elbows to watch him as he approached the bed. Once there, he took hold of the tunic's hem, hitting just above her knees, and raised it until he reached the curve of her backside. She rose off the bed, enough for him to continue to her back.

He raised the hem, sweeping his palm over her curves until he exposed the brand on her lower back. Shaped vaguely like a blooming crocus, it had to be the rune to which she referred. He caressed it, disliking the thought of marring her skin.

But he Changed his fingers to claws, and her flesh quivered beneath his touch.

"Are you ready?" He grazed her skin with the tips of his claws, and she stiffened, pressed her chin into the pillow.

"Yes," she replied, muffled, and with merciful quickness, he slashed through her brand, deep enough to scar. She was rigid beneath him as he pressed the gauze to it, but she already moved to heal it, only enough to scab over the wounds. Her anima had to be dark. And he could do nothing to help her.

When he Changed his claws back to fingers, her blood remained, thick, warm, and aromatic on his fingertips. He raised them to his nose, inhaled deep, then lowered them to his lips, a hair's breadth away from his mouth.

"Brennan."

He glanced at her back. She held out the bloodied gauze to him.

His gaze lowered to his bloody fingertips, and a shudder rode his spine.

Once before the full moon. Once only. A drop, and no more. And he had already gotten this month's control from her that night in House Hazel. He only ever took what he required, never more, never for—his lip curled—pleasure.

Horrified, he snatched up the gauze, wiped his fingers, and went to wash his hands.

He'd already gotten his control this month, so why did her blood tantalize him now? He looked in the mirror, a glimmer of wolfish amber in the reflection's eyes.

The Wolf was still there.

His eyes widened.

It would take some time before he'd feel like himself again, in control, completely.

Two servants arrived at the door, with an older man in a long, sandy-colored robe, his shoulder-length black hair streaked with gray.

"Doctor," Brennan said, forcing a calm he didn't feel. He took the man's hand. "Please." He gestured to the room. "She's poisoned with ithara and moonflower essence."

The doctor rushed in, and Brennan dismissed the servants and closed the door. As he watched the doctor tend to her, his thoughts turned dark. When she returned to Emaurria, what would happen?

Although things between Rielle and himself had changed, she still loved Jon. She'd still read that letter with stars in her eyes. But would she still bind herself to him, even barred from becoming no more than his mistress?

And the child she carried—would she decide to bring it into the world?

He stiffened. *What if it's his?*

Of all things, that would be catastrophic. She'd never let go of Jon, then—and a former paladin with no family... He'd never let her go either.

After a thorough examination, the doctor cleaned the blood from his hands and opened a small vial; Brennan breathed in—telar leaf oil, used to counteract ithara. It required very careful dosage.

The doctor opened Rielle's eyelid and carefully deposited two drops in one eye and the same in the other. Then, he retrieved a tincture, opened it—passionflower extract, concentrated, a strong sedative—and squeezed a dropperfull under her tongue. He finished up and approached Brennan, gesturing to the hall. Brennan accompanied him out and shut the door.

"The healed wound to her side caused internal bleeding—and she's suffered a rare complication with ithara," the doctor said softly. "I've done all I can for her, and she will improve with time, but... she's already begun the bleed. I'm sorry."

A sudden coldness chilled Brennan to the core. "The bleed?"

He crossed his arms, covered his mouth, and inched open the door. Rielle lay on her side, curled away from them, her breath even and soft —asleep.

"Yes. The child is lost," the doctor said softly.

Lowering his gaze, he fought a pain in the back of his throat. "What about a healer?"

Rielle hadn't wanted a healer for fear of contact with the Sonbaharan Tower, which would record everything meticulously and lead the slave hunters right to them.

Not even he could hope to stand against all of Xir's mages. She'd be recaptured, tortured, executed.

But if it were her decision, if she had to choose now, would she—

"Even if a healer were here, there would have been no hope. I'm sorry."

He gently shut the door and stared at his feet. He clenched a fist so tight his knuckles cracked. "What should I do?"

The doctor's soft eyes looked away toward her direction, and he bowed his head. "She will be in pain, and she will bleed. Do not lie with her for a fortnight." He searched Brennan's eyes. "Treat her gently, kindly, and hold her."

He nodded somberly. If she allowed it, he'd do all that and more, for the rest of their lives.

He handed the doctor a coin pouch heavy with araqs. This doctor had saved Rielle's life, and for that, he would live. "For your work and your silence."

The doctor wavered, blinking, but his fingers closed on the pouch. He inclined his head and disappeared down the hallway.

Brennan reached for the door but paused, gathering his composure. What would he say to her? What could he possibly say to make her feel better?

Steeling himself, he opened the door. After dousing the candles, he sat on the far side of the bed. She lay where he'd left her, curled into herself, frail, alone. His fingers reached for her, but he closed them, fighting a chill.

She shivered.

He looked away, pawing a hand through his hair. A monstrous tightness formed in his chest, devouring, growing, filling.

The room's darkness closed in on him, wrapped him like a robe, and he breathed in deep, slow, then moved next to her, wrapped his arm around her, and buried his face in her wet hair. Beyond the scent of the lavender and olive oil soap, the salt of her dried tears lingered.

"Try to get some sleep. We must leave before dawn." He held her long into the night, wide awake.

# CHAPTER 33

*J*on wiped the sweat from his brow, then resumed striking the practice dummy with his sword. The day had been gray but clear of snowfall, and he'd been training relentlessly since dawn—with the sword, the glaive, the bow, the sword again. Better that way. Better to keep his mind on drills than—

Now, the dimness of dusk began to shadow the training yard. He'd sparred with all of his guards until he'd exhausted them. Perched on the sidelines, they pretended not to watch. He didn't need a partner, nor anyone. As long as there was a practice dummy, he'd work with that. And when there were no more, he'd shadow-spar.

Cut, block, return to guard. Cut, block, return to guard. He repeated the drill, repeated the strikes, repeated the pattern. Cut. Chips of wood splintered and flew from the practice dummy. Block. It would soon need replacing. Return to guard. But keeping his body occupied, staying focused on training, repelled the impact of reality a small measure. Cut. That small measure kept him standing.

A large chunk of wood broke. He'd lost count of how many dummies his squire had replaced today. Block.

"Time for a new one," Tor said from behind him.

Return to guard. Giving the dummy a once-over, Jon answered, "This one still has some limbs intact." *Not for long.* Cut.

"The audacity."

Block. Jon rolled his eyes. Return to guard. "Don't you have a kingdom to run?" he asked as he struck the dummy once more.

"That's my line, Your Majesty."

"Yes, well," he began, getting in another hit, "as Derric so bluntly pointed out, my 'unstable emotional state' might affect my decision-making. 'Unfit to rule.' " Cut. It hadn't been his own decision to take time off. Block. No, it had been the High Council's *strong suggestion*— after Olivia had told a vague story, he was sure, *for his own good.*

Return to guard.

Derric himself had called him "unfit to rule," and Tor had temporarily taken over managing the kingdom. Jon cursed under his breath as he sundered off one of the dummy's arms. He was about to call for his squire, but Tor stepped into his path with his sword drawn.

Jon transitioned to sparring with him.

"Many of your people lost loved ones during the siege." Tor lunged.

Jon parried and followed with a riposte. "I'm aware."

A parry and counter-riposte. "Even burdened by the shroud of sorrow, they work for you, fight for you."

Jon blocked. "Set aside my grief and see to duty. Got it. Thanks for the talk." Vexed, he broke away, but Tor pursued. Instinct took over as Jon raised his guard.

"Feel it," Tor said, with a few quick cuts that Jon met. "Don't try to fight it indefinitely. Let it in. *Grieve.*" A descending strike.

Jon blocked again. "That's not what we do. In the field, we—"

"We're not in the field." Tor renewed his assault. "You're blocking —prolonging a losing battle. But this isn't combat—this is grief. You need to take the hit." Tor struck his shoulder, then Jon broke Tor's guard and leveled his sword at his former master's neck.

*Let it in...* He heaved breath after ragged breath. "What if I..." He paused and lowered his sword. "What if I can't recover?"

"You can." Tor took a few steps closer and laid a hand on his shoulder in support. "You will."

Could he? Could he let in the darkness that had been pushing against him, and live to see it someday dissipate? He swallowed. In the field, paladins acknowledged bad news about loved ones and grief, but reminded themselves that worry and grief were useless emotions. Surrender to them made a person unfit for duty. Useless to his unit— worse, a liability. There was time enough after a mission to let in worry and loss.

But a king... A king was always on mission. There was never a time to let in weakness, to surrender to anything that might cripple his fitness to perform his duty.

It was antithesis to all he knew, but at the moment, Tor's judgment was far worthier of trust than his own.

*Let it in...*

With a nod, Tor sheathed his sword. "There's something else."

"What is it?" Jon handed Faithkeeper off to his squire, accepted a towel from a valet to wipe his brow, and accompanied Tor toward the palace, flanked by Raoul and Florian. Bit by bit, the late-winter chill slowly overpowered his heat.

"A message from Vervewood. Our ambassador says the light-elves want you to swear an alliance vow according to their custom before a light-elven witness."

According to their custom...? More blasphemy. A tightness formed in Jon's chest. They headed into the heart of the palace to his quarters. The wall sconces and candelabra already lit the halls with soft light. Courtiers bowed and whispered greetings, and he returned them lifelessly as he had a thousand times. "What does this 'vow' involve?"

Tor shrugged. "The witness will come with instructions."

He tugged his rolled-up sleeves down. Instructions. Just what would he have to do now? Buttoning his cuffs, he closed his eyes and breathed deeply. He'd become no more than a blade to be wielded whenever the kingdom required.

And if it at last broke him, what little remained, at least it would all be over. An end. A peaceful end. No more pain, no more loss, and the blackwood trees would part, and such a light would pour forth... And at its center, Rielle, waiting, smiling, hand reaching out for his.

He opened his eyes and sighed. "If it means peace and ridding this land of the Immortal threat, I'll do what is required."

They reached his quarters, where Raoul and Florian relieved the two guards from their posts.

Tor squeezed Jon's shoulder reassuringly. "It's not just 'what's required,' it's life going on. Remember her, give her the thought and respect she deserves, but remember yourself, too. It won't always be like this, Jon. I promise. I know these last few months have been tough, but peace is in sight."

Life didn't just go on. It couldn't. If it just went on and returned to guard so soon, she'd never mattered, and the loss of her had never mattered.

When Gilles had killed Bastien, he hadn't replaced him, forgotten him, moved on. He'd suffered, remembered, and vowed justice.

He squeezed his eyes shut and shook his head. Life didn't just go on. It couldn't.

He pulled away, and Tor's face went slack; he was only trying to help. Jon sighed. "I know you mean well, but I don't want to hear this right now."

Tor nodded and waited in the quiet hall, the only sound the distant footsteps of courtiers. His subjects. And beyond them was a city and a kingdom relying on his ability and willingness to protect them.

Such as by forging alliances. Which this vow would allow him to do.

"I'll swear the vow. Whatever they want. It doesn't matter anymore." Just as he was about to enter his quarters, Olivia turned into the hallway and strode toward him. He shook his head, but she only walked faster, touching Tor's hand as she approached.

"We must speak," she said to Jon.


JON RUBBED HIS FOREHEAD, trying to process all she'd just told him. "Are you sure?"

Olivia tightened her clasped hands in her lap, brushing them over her black dress. "Yes. There's something wrong with your heart, and it can't be healed."

He raked a hand through his sweat-matted hair. "Why is it only surfacing now?"

She shrugged weakly. "Queen Alexandrie struggled with heart problems much of her adult life, but I wasn't her healer. I suspect you inherited the condition from her."

*Her.* His mother.

"You've led a fit, healthy life until recently, and then there was the Earthbinding, which has been a huge strain on you and may have provoked this, and then there was the stress of... of..."

The love of his life dying.

Olivia lowered her gaze. "Now that your symptoms have surfaced, things are going to get worse. You might have more of these episodes, and one of them will kill you."

He'd already made his peace, said his final words to Raoul. "Two to three years, you said?"

Her lower lip trembling, she nodded. "If you sleep well, rest, try to stay fit and healthy, it may be on the longer side. Obviously no sen'a or trux, and the less wine and spirits, the better." She rubbed her arms. "I'll do all I can, Jon, but I can only heal your symptoms. You'll need to be near a healer for the rest of your life."

For two to three years.

He tossed some kindling on the fire and watched it char.

Since taking the throne, everything in his life had burned. His honor, his faith, his love. Now his future. Ash lost on the wind.

And what did it mean for Emaurria? What could he do for the kingdom in two to three years? "What about the Earthbinding?"

Olivia blinked. "I hadn't considered it, but it's possible the land may sustain you for some time—"

"No." He shook his head, huffing a breath. "Will this negatively impact the land?"

Her mouth fell open. "Oh, Jon..." She just stared at him with sullen eyes. "I'm not sure. There's little in the histories to help build a hypothesis, but we'll find out."

So they would learn the answer in the worst way possible. He covered his face with his hand.

A forsworn paladin bastard as king, who could barely survive a couple of years, and might possibly leave the land in worse condition than he'd found it—at best.

Emaurria deserved better. But there was no one else.

"What are you going to do?" she whispered.

The only thing he wanted to do was go back. Go back to Melain, to a blissful moment, and fight time until it stopped, until it gave him a lifetime there, with Rielle, together and happy until they were old and gray, and died in their bed, surrounded by fat grandchildren. She would live, and he would live, and they'd need nothing else but each other.

But even then, even in those bright days, that had never been possible. This death sentence had always lurked inside of him.

He sighed. "I need time to think. Right now, I..." All he could think about was her.

Olivia rose. "Take all the time you need. I won't tell a soul."

"Thank you," he said quietly, turning back to the fire, watching it burn.

~

As Leigh headed for the tree hollow that housed his quarters, Ambriel accompanied him up spiral steps winding around a trunk and onto a narrow bridge grown high over most of Vervewood.

A dragon mage. If Narenian was to be believed, a dragon mage could complete another Sundering, which could rid the world of the Immortal beasts, of this entire catastrophe... that he had wrought.

A dragon mage... could be made. But how? She'd dodged all attempts to follow up on the question. If the light-elves had any records here—as unlikely as that was—he'd need to find out.

After dinner, the sky had darkened with nightfall, but the Gaze-like small crystals suspended from branches illuminated the dark with small bursts of glowing starlight.

Reflections played in the quietly humming rivers weaving through the land.

Ambriel's eyes caught the shine of a nearby crystal, and his skin took on a silvery cast. Decked out in Emaurrian fashion—a white cotton shirt unbuttoned to the chest, a forest-green velvet overcoat, fitted black breeches, and boots—his fit physique stood in stark relief.

The light-elves took their time crafting their own clothing. They could take forever... Hopefully.

Ambriel met Leigh's gaze with a coy smile. *The captain.*

The *captain* was becoming a distraction. An all-too-tempting distraction.

Leigh cleared his throat. "So how does one become a dragon mage?"

Ambriel breathed a slow, lazy breath. "In resonance, you and your partner fill one another, but that is not the only option." Ambriel looked him over, devoured him with those golden eyes. "You may also draw from your partner, draw until you take everything."

Leigh's mouth dropped open. He swallowed. "That would lead to fureur. I can't imagine anyone would choose it."

"Contact with arcanir removes the choice, and prevents fureur."

Draining an arcanir-bound mage of anima? Leigh frowned. "But once anima has been extinguished, it cannot be relit."

"Correct."

That would mean... the ability to unmake a mage. If such a possibility had existed, it had become lost in history's faded pages. Or... kept quiet by the Divinity.

Shaking his head, Leigh continued trudging, but Ambriel was no longer at his side. He looked back.

"We've arrived at your quarters." Ambriel stood before—indeed—the entrance to the tree hollow.

Leigh approached him and stopped a couple feet away beneath a glowing crystal. "This... drawing from a partner, taking. How is it done?"

His head bowed, Ambriel took a step forward, a smile playing on his lips. "I am no mage, Ambassador. I am familiar with... similar things, but not when it comes to anima." When he raised his chin, he was only inches away.

Illuminated, beautiful, powerful. A god, some facet of Solis come to earth, impossible perfection among mere mortals, there to be worshipped, adored, feared.

The waterfall splashed, soft play in the night.

Heat pooled in Leigh's lower body. His breathing slowed. "Show me."

A brief raise of his eyebrows, and Ambriel leaned in, eyelids falling heavily.

A rumble shook the landing—a horn blow reverberating through the sultry air.

Ambriel stiffened, snapped toward the Gaze. Shouts and calls rippled throughout Vervewood.

Leigh followed his line of sight. "What is it?"

"A raid." Ambriel's mouth pressed into a grim line. He took off across the nearest bridge, and Leigh chased after him. The rickety wood stretched high above land and waterways. Perhaps looking down wasn't the best course of action.

"Who?" he called out as they ran.

Every soul in Vervewood was in motion—on the bridges, the steps, below.

"Dark-elves," Ambriel bit out, fleet footsteps descending the spiral stair. At the bottom, they pushed past armored elven women bursting out of a doorway.

Inside, armor and weapons lined racks. Ambriel hastily donned leather armor.

"What are the—?" Leigh waved his hand toward the commotion. Someone pushed him aside to grab a longbow and arrows.

"Dark-elves," Ambriel repeated, fastening a wooden chestplate with a grimace.

Leigh batted Ambriel's hands aside and made quick work of it while Ambriel chose a weapons belt and arms.

"We light-elves dwell in and worship the light, the sun, the moon. The dark-elves dwell in and worship the dark." Ambriel clipped a sword and a dagger to his belt, and grabbed a kite shield, a short bow, and an arrow-filled quiver.

Leigh finished with the chestplate and eyed the wood grain. "Wood? *Really?*"

Ambriel flashed his teeth briefly in an expression too vicious to be called a grin. "Ironwood. As strong as your human metals, but light." He strode outside, where an entire forest of elves trickled toward the Gaze through the sea of trees, the women armored, carrying bows, swords, shields. The massive crystal refracted silvery moonlight, blessing the surrounding soldiers with an otherworldly glow.

"How do you know it's the dark-elves?" Leigh ran to keep up through the lush grass and over an intricately grown bridge. They ascended the wide stair.

"This isn't the first time," Ambriel hissed through gritted teeth.

A heavy feeling weighed in Leigh's stomach. He ducked his head as he kept up. So the elves hadn't been entirely honest. They offered a new ally with one hand and a new enemy with the other.

The elves formed ranks, Ambriel finding his place in the front and barking orders in Elvish.

Bows aimed at high targets. Leigh's gaze climbed the ironwood trees embracing Vervewood. Arrows flew.

High up, hooks dug into branches, trailing ropes that went taut. From the other side of the wall of trees, dark figures ascended—three, ten, no... More. Arrows plucked them out of the sky. Severed ropes.

A hand-axe whirred by. Buried in an elven chest. Blood gushed.

Ambriel nocked another arrow.

Two hand-axes flew toward them. Leigh cast a repulsion shield, repelling the two weapons. Sparking, they fell harmlessly to the ground.

He spread the shield wide, providing cover for the archers, then channeled attractant force magic in his free hand. Scanning the ironwood canopy, he plucked dark figures from the branches one by one. They flew, screaming, to their deaths.

Bones crunched. Flesh squelched. Blood sloshed.

Screams erupted from Vervewood. Light-elves dragged away toward the trees by a few dark-elf survivors. Channeling repellent magic, Leigh hit each of them with force-magic shoves, pushed them together, then—with a closing of his hand—crushed them together into a bloody paste.

Not a muscle moved.

A susurrus rippled through the light-elves, whispers and mutterings a tide.

From the ironwood branches, ropes hung limp. Not another soul emerged.

Voices reclaimed the hush, sharp orders and questions, desperate calls. Ambriel lowered his bow and returned the arrow to its quiver. He eyed Leigh, brows drawn, and gaped.

Leigh patted his shoulder. "Now, where were we?"

DRINA STOWED her entry papers in her apothecary's satchel as she headed past the service gate and into the palace. A second delivery of wild carrot powder, red raspberry leaf tea, and chasteberry... Lady Vauquelin must have been pleased with the first. Keeping her pleased would remain a priority, at least until the king met his fate.

The morning light shimmered through the massive windows, motes of dust dancing above the gleaming marble floors, where fashionable high-heeled slippers and glossed leather boots clacked past. Great hearths housed great fires, warming through the late winter chill, and she paused to heat her palms on her way to the stairs and Lady Vauquelin's quarters.

Shifting her satchel, she knocked.

The door opened. A freckled young woman smiled and bowed her head. Primly, perfectly. Vassal nobility, no doubt. A lady-in-waiting. She offered a polite greeting. "My lady is currently indisposed. If you would be so kind as to wait, she will be along presently."

Drina nodded, and the lady-in-waiting held the door and invited her in, ushered her to a seat in the salon. Drina sat and accepted black tea and a small plate of glazed petits fours. The lady-in-waiting busied herself arranging a bouquet of lilies while voices carried in from the bedchamber.

"Who are they?" a woman's mellifluous voice trilled. A stranger's.

"His Camarilla tutors," Lady Vauquelin said softly. "They take a turn around the Winter Garden once a week."

"Companions?"

"Of course," she replied. "But you mean are they his lovers?" A pause. "No, no. He was innocent but months ago. Perhaps, contrary to rumor, he still is. He wouldn't know the ways of the game; his advisers were wise to procure tutors on such matters." Another pause, then a soft huff. "Perhaps if they were both women. But a man and a woman? No, not for him. I daresay he's much more traditional."

"*Too* traditional?"

A haughty laugh. "Don't be ridiculous, Chantal," Lady Vauquelin cajoled. "Look at him... Dark, gloomy, lifeless. Broken. Perhaps once, he might have had the will to remain steadfast, but no more. He is ripe for joy, vulnerable, and so unaware."

"You're utterly wicked." An excited giggle from Chantal.

"So perfectly wicked." They both laughed. "But he needs *someone*. Every man does."

"On the subject, is your brother coming to court?" Chantal asked.

A puff. "We have more important concerns than my wayward brother."

Chantal whimpered dejectedly. "Is it so contemptible that I would like his strong arms to comfort me while my husband handles these trade negotiations?"

"Your life is stable. Take care upsetting that stability, my friend." Another pause.

"Don't worry. No one will take Vauquelin from you and your boys, Nora. The new king doesn't seem the type."

The soft sound of a kiss. "Great Wolf bless you, Chantal." A lengthy, contented breath. "Shall we meet for tea later? I have appointments."

Drina straightened on the sofa.

A pair of delicately slippered feet soon padded across a rug to click across the floor. A young woman appeared, a little over five feet tall, slender but shapely. Her chocolate-brown curls tumbled in a cascade down her back, but her most striking feature was her classically beautiful porcelain face, with bright, youthful sage-green eyes. She was easily one of the most beautiful women at the Emaurrian court.

She glided through the salon, sparing only a mere imperious glance before exiting the quarters.

Another set of footsteps, and Lady Vauquelin entered bearing a gown over her arm, a heavy sigh relaxing her shoulders.

"Melanie," she said, and the lady-in-waiting inclined her head. "Take this back to the dressmaker. The embroidery is unimpressive. Tell him I want his best work by the Veris Ball, and that my father sends his regards."

Veris...

The night Drina had raided the chambers of the Master of Ceremonies, she'd discovered a dance suite for the Veris Ball. The king would dance with many women, perhaps even seduce one, and he'd end up in his quarters, where amid the commotion over the ball, she'd end him. To be killed at the end of such a night, with a lover in his arms—

Drina resisted the urge to grin. How perfect it would be for that bitch Favrielle to discover her man lost to another woman *and* to this life. How deliciously perfect.

Melanie accepted the dress and bowed. "Yes, my lady." She took the gown and disappeared.

Lady Vauquelin's hazel eyes settled on Drina. "You're early."

Drina tapped her satchel and suppressed a grimace. She'd arrived midmorning, as agreed. She plastered on a simpering smile. "Apologies, Your Ladyship."

Lady Vauquelin waved her hand dismissively and seated herself primly in an armchair off to the side, settling her red silk robe over her legs. "I trust you've brought all I've ordered?"

"Yes, Your Ladyship." Drina opened her satchel and unloaded the packages. Veris was one month away... She would have to guarantee her return to the palace. An inducement would work. "Is everything working to your satisfaction?"

Lady Vauquelin raised a perfectly arched eyebrow and sighed, reclining in her armchair. "Despite all my preparations, I cannot avoid the fact that a man is required."

An open admission? "I can't imagine Your Ladyship would have any difficulty in that regard." Drina looked her over for effect.

Lady Vauquelin smiled. "No. Not usually. My uncle has promised to help me get this man's attention, but he's proving... a challenge."

"There are tools that may assist in any man's... surmounting." When the lady merely raised her eyebrows, Drina continued, "An aphrodisiac lip balm. It has only recently been tested and sold, but I have heard when worn in very close proximity to a man, it has the power to madden him with need." A perfect inducement.

Lady Vauquelin bolted upright in her chair most ungracefully. "And you can procure this balm?"

Drina drew in a slow, contemplative breath and tilted her head. "I do know the apothecary who formulated it. I could reach out to him if Your Ladyship should—"

"Please do." She crossed her legs. "When would it arrive?"

"In a month, perhaps."

The lady shook her head, dark curls bouncing. "No. Not soon enough."

"It would be imported from Pryndon. Quite a distance away... And I'm certain few, if any, other Emaurrians have procured it."

Exclusive. A woman like her would need to have it.

Lady Vauquelin narrowed her eyes. "I must have it."

Drina smiled. "Then you shall, Your Ladyship."

The lady rose, red silk billowing about her delicate form. "I will see you in a month."

A month from now, on the day of Veris. Another set of entry papers... and another path to ending the king.

Drina rose and bowed. "Thank you, Your Ladyship."

# CHAPTER 34

*A*n arm tightened its grip on Rielle's waist, a man's breath in her ear. Her entire body went rigid, her pulse thrashed in her ears, and Divine, there wasn't enough space here, not enough room—

A tremor shook through her, and the man beside her stirred.

"Rielle," came the voice. Brennan's.

She opened her eyes. A massive bed and tasseled pillows in deep colors. Satin-and-brocade drapes. A tented canvas canopy. Not House Hazael. Somewhere else. She drew into herself and thanked the Divine, despite the cramps assailing her stomach.

Brennan pulled away, then gently rested a palm on her shoulder. She quivered.

"Are you all right?" he asked.

"Just fine," she replied, with forced cheer. Last night, she'd dreamed of him holding her, and when she'd awoken, he *had* been holding her. *Fine...*

But her head pounded, and her stomach, and her side, and her inner barriers rusted for the lack of anima. She felt hollowed somehow, caving in. Her gaze wandered next to the bed, where a pile of bloodied gauze and cloths lay.

An injury... Where? She pulled her knees in tighter, shifted. Then felt the rub of the gauze against her skin, beneath her.

*No*...

Her palm descended to her belly. It was no different—smooth, unmarred—and yet...

Her eyes watered, and she closed them. Strong arms enclosed her.

She shook her head. It couldn't be. It couldn't.

Just yesterday, everything had been fine. She'd been four months with child.

A smoky haze, a poisoned pin, Farrad bleeding, dead... Fighting guards... She moaned. So much injury, so much blood...

Too much.

Too much blood, cramping, pain, and Sylvie—*Divine, Sylvie*—

Gone.

Her chest filled and filled and filled to bursting, and she gasped for breath, tried to inhale, but there was no room.

She'd lost Sylvie. Her child, Jon's, four months along, and... she was gone.

No, she couldn't be, couldn't—

The tears flowed, heavy and stinging, and she couldn't stop them. Wouldn't. Pain seized her body and squeezed, and her chest was tight enough to implode. She pressed her fingers into the flesh of her chest until pain bit, deep and penetrating, spreading, sprawling, opening and hungry, singing a ravening call to the elements, to her magic, a choir of anima rising to hum, deafening and soothing—

A clamp on her arm. Brennan.

"Rielle," he said, and he grabbed her shoulders, shook her. "Great Wolf, Rielle—"

A flaming bed, fire blazing up the satin-and-brocade drapes, canvas in ashes and crumbling—

Brennan grabbed her face, squeezed her cheeks. "Rielle, stop this! Now!"

Heat seared from her hands up her arms, flame licking her skin—

"Jon!" he shouted. "What about Jon? He's waiting for you, isn't he? Are you going to leave him alone?"

*Jon.* She inhaled, smoke and ash. *Jon*...

Her heart ached, held, embraced, crushed. Jon... No, she couldn't leave him. Wouldn't. She loved him. Needed him. And he needed her, needed her to tell him about Shadow...

To live. To survive...

The flames cloaking her arms faded, died.

She met Brennan's eyes, the tempest there, and her vision blurred. "Why her?" she whispered between sobs. "Why her and not me?"

He pulled her into an embrace, stroked her hair softly, rocked her gently.

Great Divine, of all the things taken from her here, not her child, too. Not to the Hazaels, not to this place. Why did the Divine take her? Of all life, an innocent who had not even begun to live?

"How?" She croaked.

Brennan's hold tightened. "The doctor did all he could," he whispered, "but it was... too late."

*Too late.* A hollow widened in her throat, and she shuddered violently.

She closed her eyes, trembling against him. She was here, with Brennan, alive and free, but at what cost? The price for freedom had been steep. Sylvie had paid, and she had paid, and Jon had paid, and Farrad had paid, and the guards had paid, and she would pay for the rest of her life.

And Samara...

She gasped. "Brennan. Samara—We need to go back for her."

"You barely got out alive," he said hoarsely. "We're not going back."

She stiffened. "Yes, we are. I'm not leaving her there—"

"I told you last night, I'll have Kehani buy her."

Buy? She winced. If Farrad was right, Ihsan would be selling the slaves. And if he was wrong, she'd be keeping them. Either way, someone could make an offer and try to buy one. Someone like Kehani. "She will?"

"Yes," he whispered, pulling her closer. "I'll make sure of it."

*And I'll make sure of it.* "Have her sent to Trèstellan, to me or to Olivia," she said. "I want to see her free."

"Yes, as you wish."

She glanced out the latticed window. It was still dark, although there was a glimmer of light on the horizon. The dawn was imminent.

It would be a day unlike any other in four months. A lonely, hollow day... but she was free. She pulled away to look at him.

"Brennan," she said softly, "thank you... for saving my life."

He lowered his gaze and nodded. "You didn't need me... All I did was carry you out."

She shook her head. "No. Without you, I'd still be there, and... worse."

He chewed his lower lip, and then the bed shifted as he stood. "I know this has been a horrible night and day, but..."

Every moment they spent here, they risked capture. Her gaze lingered on the bloodied gauze until it blurred.

Shadow, and this place, had robbed her of Sylvie, and had robbed her even of the time to mourn, and yet greedily awaited more. Her capture. Her death. Brennan's. Jon's. Her heart broke for time, but there was none to be had here. No more. Blinking, she raised her teary gaze to Brennan's and nodded.

The grim line of his mouth shifted to a brief, comforting smile before he stalked about the quarters. "The servants brought some things for you."

The splashing gave him away at the washbasin. She sat up, her limbs not quite feeling like her own. Her fingers trembled. Her anima was dark—very dark—but there was nothing she could do about that now. The healing had been costly. She looked at her bare thighs, just below the hem of an unfamiliar tunic. Bloodied.

Jumping from the bed, she peered down at her legs, wincing as her cramps spiked.

Brennan was at her side instantly, reaching out to steady her.

A wave of weakness doused her right away, setting her legs trembling, and she closed her eyes, rubbing her face with a sweaty palm.

Her gaze rested on the bloodied gauze and cloths. The cramps doubled her over, and she wept, and damn it all, she couldn't stop.

The blood... She had to see this, every day, for days, weeks, Sylvie's death, until...

Taut, Brennan reached out but stopped and clenched his fist. "I don't know how—" He broke off. "Tell me what to do, Rielle. Please. Tell me what I can do."

The tears wouldn't stop, and she sobbed uncontrollably. How had she allowed it to happen? Why? Divine, how could this have happened?

"I'm sorry," he said. "I never—"

"I'm fine," she said, wiping away her tears. She wasn't fine, but she couldn't bear to talk about this any more, to stay here. The desert awaited them, and the Bay of Amar, and Courdeval, and...

Jon. Great Divine, *Jon*. How would she be able to face him after this? How could she tell him that she hadn't been able to keep their child safe?

Her hand went to her forehead, and she rubbed it, rubbed her face as it twisted.

"We have to go." Sad eyes roved over her.

Forcing a nod, she glanced at him, then toward the balaustine-red thiyawb and matching halla hanging on a hook. "Is that for me?"

"We should discuss—"

"I'm fine, really," she lied, her breaths shallow as she reached for the thiyawb.

Brennan remained silent.

Her breath caught. She could never lie to him. He'd know by the beat of her heart. He knew now. She wrung the garment in her hands.

"I'll find us some food while you get dressed," he said cautiously. "I'll send a maid up to help you with your hair."

She reached to touch her hair, finding it a tangled mess. All that mattered now was getting out of here and to Courdeval before Shadow could take away another person she loved.

IGNORING the throbbing tangle of emotions inside him, Brennan rushed down to the kitchen. The harsh desert sun would dawn in an hour, and both he and Rielle needed to be out of the city by then. He could already smell the white-bean wayfarer's soup cooking; as a boy, he'd always eaten it with Father the day they departed Xir.

In the kitchen, several women flitted around. "Breakfast," he demanded.

"Zahib," Cook said, inclining her head, "we will bring breakfast to you and your guest forthwith."

With a shrug, he thanked her; she'd been there as long as he could remember. Unable to resist the scent, he grabbed a flatbread and left the kitchen. As he passed the inner courtyard, he spied Kehani having tea, her dark waves unbound over a flowing, emerald-green thiyawb. For all her indifferent airs this morning, he could hear her heart race as he strode past.

"The news has already spread all over the city," she called out to him. Foolishly running her mouth. Recklessly.

Clenching his teeth, he approached. "Keep your voice down." He tipped his head toward his quarters.

Kehani raised her eyebrows. "Farrad Hazael is a well-regarded man, Brennan. He is known for treating his wives and children well, for being a fair businessman, a respectable duelist. All of Xir and the zahibshada himself are looking for the slave responsible for this." She tipped her head toward his quarters.

"She is no one's slave," he seethed, keeping his voice low. "A woman of noble birth, *my* betrothed, was abducted and sold into servitude. No one takes from a Marcel." When Kehani froze, speechless, he continued, "And you're misinformed about the man. Any man who could subjugate someone—"

"A *slave.*"

"—cannot be called 'well regarded' by any stretch of the imagination." He suppressed a growl.

"To them, she is no more than a slave. Be glad they do not know her true identity." Kehani took a deep breath. "For all your time here and your Sonbaharan blood, you still do not understand our ways."

"Our *ways?*" He scowled. Father understood Sonbaharan *ways,* all too well, and that was what was wrong with him. "I don't want to understand *ways* that make such atrocities acceptable."

"Brennan," she said, in that smooth, sincere way that had always reached him as a boy. "I do not say this to anger you but to educate you. I see what you have gotten yourself into. And I want you to be aware of the danger. You might leave Xir today, but Xir will not leave you. Ever. Every shafi, nawi, and even the zahibshada himself will not stop looking for the one who dared touch such a man. It sets a dangerous precedent."

He turned away. "I don't plan to be found."

"Just promise me you'll take care," she said, her shaky tone laced with worry. "The ire of every influential man in Xir is not something you should ignore."

"If they even think of touching what's mine, it is they who should fear *me*."

"Your father is the same way." She met his gaze squarely.

Ah, an effort to threaten him should he reveal their dalliance to Father... Brennan almost admired her boldness, attempting to play her weak hand. "Yes, he's very protective of his *family*."

Duke Faolan Auvray Marcel would favor a mistress over his only son and heir the day the sun neglected to rise. And she well knew it.

Her gaze narrowed, but she smiled and sipped her tea. "I sent my maid to attend your fiancée."

No taste for defeat—a subtle cue to go. "Thank you." He paused. "There's something else I need you to do."

She heaved a lengthy sigh. "I'm hardly surprised."

"There's an apothecary slave at House Hazael, a young woman by the name of Samara. I want you to buy her through intermediaries and have her sent to me at Trèstellan Palace."

She raised dark eyebrows. "You would involve *me* in your crime spree? I don't plan to risk my head for—"

"No one would dare touch you, and you know it." He peered at her. "I'll reimburse you, naturally, plus a handsome fee for your efforts."

She finally nodded.

Just as he turned to leave, she said, "You could have told me why you were here."

"I didn't want to implicate you." *Or risk you trading secrets for favor.*

"You already have."

"It would be best if you slept through last night, and no one heard or saw a thing." He didn't need to add the threat of outing her to Father.

Her black-as-night eyes locked with his, she smiled. "Isn't that what happened?"

W HEN THE SUN peeked over the horizon, Rielle had already exited the hateful walls of Xir with Brennan. Her hands trembled—anima withdrawal. At her wrists, the false arcanir cuffs occasionally showed past the deep-red sleeve of her thiyawb; she and Brennan hadn't had time to remove them. Maybe he could break them later.

She squinted; even with her gaze downcast, the light still tormented her sensitive eyes, and her cramping stomach had to be the worst pain she'd ever felt in her life, even through the herbs the villa's maids had given her.

Between the western Altaef Mountains and the eastern Siddi range stretched a low, flat desert. Sand dunes disappeared into the horizon, the shape of never-ending round bellies veiled in honey-brown shrouds whipped about by the wind. The voices of shifting sands whispered secrets lost in time, in the endless, stark wilderness. Here, in this otherworldly place, she was no more than a red drop in a sea of sunburnt gold.

They made north to Gazgan, a small port town west of Harifa. They'd left the villa with a large breakfast that Brennan had insisted she eat on the way. A fried egg in olive oil with a wedge of creamy cheese and black olives, which she'd eaten with the flatbread and a mix of cumin, sesame seeds, and salt. With it, she'd had a soft, tart goat cheese and a spicy white-bean soup flavored with onion and garlic and served with olive oil and cumin. A *massive* meal. The soup had been heavy, but now, hours later, she was thankful for it, even if the harsh stink of camel made her nauseous.

She'd never ridden a camel before, but Brennan had advised her, all the while carefully keeping his distance. They had left through Xir's West Gate, and just as Ihsan had said, the guard on duty had met her eyes, asked whether she'd dropped something, and when she'd said yes, handed her a pouch of gold araqs. And she was out of the city, as promised.

*Ihsan...* At last, Rielle mustered the courage to take the bloody parchment from her thiyawb. Farrad's parchment. She unfolded it.

Release documents. She blinked and reread them. And again. It was... just as Farrad had said.

A shudder shook her, and gooseflesh pebbled her skin. Had he been telling the truth? About everything? If she had just waited, done nothing, would he have seen her freed? Her and Sylvie?

Her fingers shook. Sylvie would have lived. Her daughter and Jon's, alive, well, growing up. If she had just—

A soreness formed in her throat and lungs, and even in the desert heat, cold iced her flesh. That future was beyond her now. That sunlit day would never dawn.

If only Farrad had told her... Could she have stopped to listen to him? Or would she have been dead for it?

But knowing what little she had, the killing and the escape had seemed her only options. Seemed.

When Brennan urged his camel closer, she looked at him. As soon as the sunlight assaulted her eyes, she regretted it. Her ribs squeezed, and her skin tightened.

"You know, Emaurria's probably covered in snow right now," Brennan said, with a pleasant animation to his tone, a lilt, one she hadn't heard in years. "Remember that one year when your family was at court for the winter, and Father and I returned from Sonbahar early? We built a massive snowman in the courtyard."

"*You* built a massive snowman in the courtyard," she replied, with a chuckle. She'd been no more than six when eleven-year-old Brennan and his father arrived for a visit at her family's Courdevallan villa, Couronne. The snow had fallen late and heavy that year, and she'd goaded Brennan into helping her build a snowman after she'd exhausted her brother Liam's patience. Brennan had obliged.

"At your behest," he argued cheerily.

When she'd remarked with concern that their snowman would be cold, Brennan had taken off his cloak and swept it around their creation.

"When you shed your cloak, I don't think I'd ever seen your nanny so upset." She laughed.

" 'Foolish child! You'll catch cold!' " he imitated with a hoarse falsetto. Indeed, his nanny had chased him around the courtyard with the cloak until his father had come to scold him. "You know, she was able to convince my mother that I still needed a nanny for another year after that," he intimated, "considering my recklessness."

"Not a lifetime?" she joked, and Brennan nudged her.

She stiffened, realizing what he'd done; he could be very charming when he wanted to be. "Thank you. I needed that."

"I like to see you happy." Brennan had made her laugh countless times as a child, but after their falling out, she had never expected him to do so again.

Despite her aching pupils, she wanted to see his face.

"Damn." He paused, going very still. "We're being followed."

Staring at her hands, she heaved a sigh. It had been too much to hope for a clean exit. Perhaps the guard hadn't known he was helping a murderer escape. "How many?"

"I count about a dozen." He hesitated. "Gazgan is a two-day trip by camel. On horses, they'll catch us."

Then their pursuers would catch up with them sooner or later. She and Brennan could wait for them to close in, stop and fight, or hold out for more advantageous conditions. "At nightfall, we'll ambush them."

Brennan shook his head vehemently. "*We* will do nothing. At nightfall, *you* continue on with the camels, and *I'll* ambush them."

"Brennan—"

"You can't fight in your condition."

Her condition. Ill. Empty. Childless.

No, lacking anima... Her anima did regenerate on its own, albeit slowly.

"You can't stop me." She eyed him in challenge, despite the pain of the sunlight. "There's no way I'm letting you fight a dozen men while I run and hide," she said, unflinching beneath his hard gaze. "I know my limits."

"Stubborn woman," he growled, amber eyed, too much of the Wolf clawing through to the surface. His camel bucked but didn't throw him.

Before Sonbahar, before House Hazael, she'd been a stubborn, formidable woman. She could be herself again. With a decisive swallow, she ignored her tingling fingers and toes. Battle awaited.

# CHAPTER 35

*L*eigh healed a gash in an elven warrior's arm, mouthing the incantation while his eyes traced Ambriel checking on the other patients. The dark-elves had attacked without warning and penetrated Vervewood's defenses easily. And without mages, Vervewood had no wards, no advance notice—even their scouts had been picked off before they could sound the alarm.

When would it end? How? The dark-elves lived below ground, behind obscured entrances and beneath layers of arcanir-infused rock. Nothing short of full-scale war or natural disaster would defeat them.

He moved on to the next patient, another young woman, with a crushed pelvis. Shaking his head, he crouched and healed her, too.

Would a race who attacked without cause, both warriors and civilians, accept peace? Would they bind themselves to terms?

Ambriel stood over the dead—nearly a dozen shrouded bodies—with his hands on his hips, a grim line chiseled over his brow. The celestial voices of the tree-singers carried on the wind, and far behind Ambriel's stoic silhouette, the ironwood canopy grew dense, boughs spreading and rising, weaving into a labyrinthine lattice. Greening. A wishing wreath to keep safe all within.

Leigh sighed.

The young woman clutched his arm and smiled warmly, despite the blood in her hair and the lingering trails of tears from her eyes. "Thank you," she whispered, in barely discernible Old Emaurrian. "Thank you... for... saving us."

Softness bloomed in her soft oak eyes. He smiled, gave her an encouraging nod, and rose. The makeshift infirmary housed perhaps two dozen wounded, who now rested in recovery. If he hadn't been here... How many more would there be? His gaze shifted to the shrouds. And how many more dead?

*Saving us.*

A peaceful people. They didn't deserve this.

"May we speak?" Ambriel approached, lips pursed.

Leigh nodded and followed him out from under the shaded makeshift infirmary and toward a grown spiral staircase up a thick old oak. Near the top, a hollow awaited, and Ambriel entered, unstrapping his weapons belt, unfastening his armor. His quarters?

Leigh brushed a palm over the smooth wood of the walls, glancing over the softly glowing Gaze crystals strung from slender twigs. The floor beneath his feet rustled, gave way—a plaited wickerwork rug, pliant and warm. The splash of water came from the other end of the hollow, where Ambriel washed his hands and face over a vessel. He lingered over the water's surface, watching.

"So much suffering," he whispered, his voice a deadened monotone. "Now you know why we need your help."

He and his elven host had been remiss to mention a war when they'd arrived in Trèstellan.

Leigh rested his back against the wall. "Not just food and clothes."

The silence claimed the space between them. Ambriel's broad shoulders slumped as he gripped the edge of the table before him. "Not just food and clothes."

Leigh sighed. "You know Emaurria is already engaged in conflicts with countless Immortals... and international relations are... not looking bright."

Jon was a capable warrior and a perseverant man, but his game with those suitresses couldn't last much longer. And then, bereft of allies, Emaurria would face threats from the sea and land on its own—unless he succumbed and married into an alliance. Taking on another war to gain a weakened ally was poor strategy.

Ambriel pinned him with an unwavering gaze. "That's why you mustn't tell your king about the dark-elves."

Leigh quirked an eyebrow. "You want me to let the people of this kingdom blindly enter a war?" He sighed, and Ambriel lowered his gaze. "Sympathy is a line, not a circle."

Ambriel moved to a chair and motioned to another opposite from him. "It wouldn't be as detrimental as you think."

Leigh sat, but didn't relax.

"Your king is Earthbound. He has immense power, but he doesn't know it yet. He wouldn't even know how to use its full strength, but we could show him. We could teach him."

"And how will that help?" Leigh crossed his arms.

"The dark-elves could not withstand the wrath of the land itself."

"How? The arcanir—"

Ambriel shook his head. "It's not magic, *dreshan*. He is one with the land. It is nature, pure and raw. He is its will."

Even so, Jon had been no mage before the Earthbinding, and becoming the will of the land after would not come easily to a man accustomed to power in the form of a blade. "If he's so powerful, why keep the dark-elves a secret? Surely you can convince him?"

Ambriel's eyes hooded. "Would he believe us? Humans do not trust easily—"

"Should we?" Leigh tilted his head. "You want to lie to him, to the entire kingdom. Do you think that inspires trust?"

"No, but—"

"And what about me? Were you planning on telling me about the dark-elves?"

"Eventually."

Leigh narrowed his eyes until Ambriel sighed and held up his hands.

"No." He slumped back in his chair, leaning his head against it and staring up at the Gaze crystals. The soft glow cast a silvery light on his alabaster face, starlight on white marble. "What if he or his advisers refuse to help?"

Leigh brought his chair closer, dragging it noisily along the floor. Golden eyes fixed on him.

"*I* want to help."

Ambriel looked away, then his brows drew together. "A wild mage..."

Leigh nodded.

"But your kingdom—"

"Surely the dark-elves attack humans, too."

Ambriel shook his head. "They attack and raid anyone with supplies, but they want the Gaze crystal."

"Why?"

Ambriel's eyes widened. "Surely you've noticed most of our people are women?"

Leigh huffed under his breath. Indeed, the vast majority of the elves were women—their warriors, and most everyone else. But presented with the fine view of the captain before him, his thoughts hadn't lingered on the gender distribution of their population. "Why?"

Ambriel shrugged. "It was before my time, but it is said that when we began conquering peaceful civilizations, our gods forsook us. Cursed our people to obscurity." His fingers tugged the towel from the table, a soft white fabric. "Do you know what this is?"

"A towel?" Leigh answered flatly.

Ambriel chuckled softly. "No... It's linen and cotton woven together."

Leigh sighed. "And...?"

Dancing eyes met his. "They used to be pure linen, but our weavers changed them. These... They're more resilient. Stronger for the blend."

Leigh frowned. "Is that the obscurity you speak of?"

With a nod, Ambriel rose. "Our gods wished for our race—the elves—to fade into humanity. Become one, lose ourselves, our essence, to become stronger together. More resilient."

Clearly, that hadn't happened. "What went wrong?"

Ambriel folded the towel and set it back on the table. "Our queens didn't wish us to disappear. Our society changed. Each man was required to sire a son. Women became our warriors."

"But you're—"

Ambriel scoffed, and a wry smile claimed his face. He clasped his hands behind his back and looked out at the night sky. "I'm the queen's failure of a brother, who loves men." He glanced at Leigh airily, his smile set in place, then looked back out.

"Is that unusual here?"

Ambriel exhaled lengthily. "No. But I cannot life-bond until I sire a son. And I've sired thirteen daughters."

Leigh's jaw dropped. *Thirteen daughters? Thirteen children?* He gaped about the hollow. Where—?

"We're a long-lived race." Ambriel's grin broadened. "My sister has long since life-bonded them to other royals among the light-elves."

There were other light-elf settlements than Vervewood?

And Ambriel had adult, married daughters? He appeared no older than his thirties. "Just how old are you?"

Ambriel's lips twitched. "Before the Sundering, I was beginning my three-hundred-and-twenty-second year."

"Three hundred and twenty-two?"

Ambriel nodded.

And how many years had passed since the Sundering? Leigh shivered.

"But I digress." Ambriel moved to a console table bearing a water carafe and cups. He poured two. "All elves are subject to the gods' forsaking, even the dark-elves, *especially* the dark-elves. We each have an abundance of women among our kind, but the dark-elves can hardly even conceive children. Even before the Sundering, they were fading."

Was it really the gods' forsaking? But what else could it be?

"But they, too, rejected the gods' will. Instead of venturing out into the human world to blend, they have decided our Gaze crystal grants us good fortune, and that their race will be saved if they kill us and take it for themselves." Ambriel handed him a cup.

"Would it?"

"Of course not. We, like all light-elves, found the heart of life in the forest and settled there. Removing the Gaze crystal would destroy Vervewood, and it wouldn't save them. But they won't listen."

"So, for them... It is a matter of survival. They won't stop." Leigh accepted the cup, his touch lingering on Ambriel's fingers.

"No, they won't. And we don't wish to be raided to extinction." He crouched next to the chair, covering Leigh's hand on the armrest with his own. "So you see why it is imperative your king agree to help us."

Lying to Jon and leading the Emaurrian people blindly into war was out of the question, but that wasn't the only option. "What do you have that Emaurria wants?"

Ambriel shrugged. "We can hunt the Immortal beasts—"

"Because you know more about them than we do."

Ambriel's eyes widened. "Knowledge?"

"You know what the Earthbinding can achieve, and how to accomplish the Sundering. How to make a dragon mage. All that knowledge has been closed to us, lost to us. But you have it."

Ambriel shook his head. "If your king wanted to know these things, we are not the only source."

"The only source to extend the hand of peace." Leigh took a drink.

Ambriel squeezed his hand. "You didn't have to tell me this, but you did."

It was a statement, but a question nevertheless hid within: why?

He returned the empty cup to Ambriel. "Our alliance will be mutually beneficial. I want to see it... consummated."

Ambriel smiled, the illumination of the Gaze crystals catching on his blond lashes. He rose. "As do I, *dreshan*. As do I."

JON REMAINED IN HIS CHAIR, staring into the hearth, his room dark but for the flames.

Two days had passed. Or four. With the constant snow, day and night didn't matter.

The snowfall continued, having never stopped since it started days ago. A tray of food sat next to him, untouched. His valet had laid out clothes, unworn. Jon stayed in his tunic and braies, robed, the blanket from his vast bed wrapped around his shoulders. Faithkeeper lay on a nearby table, sheathed for days.

The cycle had become his new state of being. Pain ripped through him at night, and the emptiness that came with dawn left him hollow during the day. Inside, silence echoed from silence, a void reclaimed by pain come nightfall.

Letting it in... This is what came of letting it in.

He rose and laid another log upon the fire. It could have gone out. It should have. But when he watched the fire, it didn't hurt as much.

It felt like *her*.

The sight of her back as she'd left the Lunar Chamber... It was the last memory he had of her. The last time he'd ever see her.

Gods—Terra, her pantheon, the Divine, the dead gods, any who listened—a devout Terran should not have prayed to them all, but he had, for any of them to bring her back. Any of them.

He curled his fingers into a fist. Never. He never should have left her side. He should have followed her to the dungeon, to the ship—wherever she had gone after the Lunar Chamber. The moment she'd gone missing, he should have left to search for her, and never relented.

But he'd ignored her. The woman he'd had the audacity to say he loved.

And now she was dead.

He drank his wine—he'd lost count of how many cups he'd had. It was always one less than he needed. The sharp edges of pain, grief, anger, frustration—wine blunted them, blurred them. No wonder everyone outside the Order had always partaken. And what did it matter if it took a day off his life, a week, a month?

He glanced out the window, at the heavy snow falling, and watched it awhile. His land lay buried beneath the weeping cold, with no end in sight.

*Unfit to rule.*

Derric's earnest instruction to recover for the sake of his kingdom meant nothing. Land, titles, gold, jewels, power, status—it was worthless, all of it, worthless. It could buy not another second of life for her. Not a moment. When he couldn't keep the woman he loved safe, what hope was there for an entire kingdom? He'd lived his entire life for others, had asked for nothing, ever, had hoped for nothing for himself.

Until her.

And now she was gone.

The wine did nothing to numb him.

Faint voices came from the hall. He'd commanded his guards not to allow even a single visitor to enter, lest they wanted to spar with him again. They had their orders.

But he listened anyway.

"Your Majesty," one of his guards called. "Constable Marcel and Lord Chancellor Olivier demand an audience."

*Brave of him.* Jon sipped his wine. But few men could turn away a warrior of Tor's caliber and the former Proctor of the Emaurrian Tower of Magic.

"Send them in," Jon called back, staring into the fire.

Tor's sure gait and Pons' sweeping steps filed into the bedchamber. Tor dragged a chair from nearby and set it between Jon and the hearth. With a harsh exhalation, Jon scowled at him, but Tor's hard expression didn't waver, his hazel eyes fixed. Determined as always. While Jon stared Tor down, Pons folded his large frame into the other armchair, his full head of gray hair looking unusually frazzled. The space beneath Tor's eyes had darkened.

"How is Your Majesty feeling?" Pons asked carefully.

Jon looked away from his former paladin-master to Pons and took another sip of wine. "Why do you demand an audience?"

"We have received word from Ambassador Galvan. Nearly everything is in order for the elven alliance." Pons straightened in his chair and gave a good-natured nod. Usually cautious in his speech, today he seemed even more so.

"They'll sign a pact to side with Emaurria against the Immortals and any other threat to this land," Tor added.

*Which the light-elves would like to continue inhabiting.* It was common sense. If ever there were a time to oust them, now—while they were weak and ill equipped—would be advantageous. But if they were content within their forest and prepared to follow Emaurrian law outside of it, then he would hardly turn away an ally. "And what do you need from me?"

Pons and Tor exchanged a look.

"That's why you're here, isn't it? You need something."

"There's something else... The light-elves, along with other Immortal races and beasts, had their souls severed from their bodies in the last

Sundering," Pons said. "It's what petrified them. They know how this was achieved—the blood of every Immortal race was collected and used in a ritual by humans. It seems that the original ritualists betrayed them."

Jon raised his eyebrows and drank deeply of his wine. It was gracious of the light-elves not to seek revenge, but they were in no condition to, regardless.

"They believe this treaty will be mutually beneficial, but... considering the humans' betrayal last time, they require your personal assurance that it will not happen again—that you will be faithful to one another—and then a treaty signed with Queen Narenian." Pons clasped his hands.

Jon shrugged. "Of course. I'd never condone betrayal of a peaceful ally. Tell them that if they want my assurance, they have it." But it wasn't so simple. If the light-elves learned the value of his word, they might not expect him to adhere to an *assurance*. With a sigh, he faced Pons. "You realize I'm an oath-breaker?"

"Jon," Tor cut in. "They have a rite. The vow I mentioned to you before."

"Of course they do," he shot back, turning to his former master. "I don't care."

The light-elves worshipped the dead gods, and he'd already learned the nature of what the dead gods required of their supplicants. The Earthbinding still felt raw. He glared at Tor.

Pressing his lips into a thin line, Tor swallowed, then took a deep breath. "Jon, I know you're in mourning. I feel terrible asking you to do this, and there's been little time for you to accept that the marquise—"

Jon tore away from the armchair, pressure mounting to bursting in his face. Fight. Gods, how he wanted to fight.

Tor knitted his eyebrows together and looked away.

Hadn't Tor been the one who'd advocated letting it in? To take the time to recover? And now, what? The first sign of difficulty, and they were here to ask him to set aside his grief and return to his duties.

He would have been better off before, keeping it out, focusing on duty—

He threw the blanket to the floor, grabbed his cup, and moved to the snow-covered window. The cold radiating through the glass bit a little deeper. He slammed the cup on the windowsill.

Booted footsteps clicked behind him. "I wish you could take all the time you need to bear this loss," Tor said, with firm articulation tempered by softness. His paladin voice. Gods. "You deserve no less. She deserves no less. However... while I can manage some day-to-day affairs in your stead, I can't be king for you, Jon."

In the cup, the dark red wine roiled, still disturbed from when he'd placed it. Only one thing would still it—a purge. Consuming the bittersweet violence until the cup was empty.

"Don't you feel it's time to start getting back into routine?" Pons offered.

Jon stared into the cup. "I don't feel... anything."

A long silence.

"Well, if you change your mind, we've arranged a meeting with their witness, Aiolian Windsong, in two weeks," Pons said.

Jon picked up the cup and finished what remained of the wine. "Leave me."

With a few brief words of acknowledgment, both of them made their exit. Jon trudged back to the armchair and sat with the blanket before the hearth once more, staring into the empty cup.

It had been months since Vindemia, but at the bottom of the cup, the bonfire still burned. Rielle sat, a knee tucked in to her chest, firelight reflected in her golden hair. She turned to him with a beautiful smile, happiness shaping her eyes to half-moons. Fire, cider, and love warmed all corners, and with her in his arms, he couldn't have felt the chill that night, or any other.

That night, indignation, love, and desire had surged in him, filled him to bursting. He'd never felt so... alive. Never.

And now... Now, he didn't feel anything. His thoughts and his heart were always elsewhere, and there was nothing left here.

Another cup of wine. He gulped it down. And another. The burning down his throat was sweet, sweet relief, and yet so far from... from what he wanted. He refilled it.

Had she... she felt this way, with the sen'a? To feel more than every
—everything, and then far—far from it all?

He blinked sluggishly.

Yes, he wanted to know how she'd felt. See through her eyes. Know
this part of her, wear it... a blood ritual turned brand, a handfasting by
scar to... her.

He palmed at his eyes, blinking away the blur.

The fire had nearly... died.

He blinked again and glanced at his cup. Emp—empty again. Too
much wine.

Distant giggles... from the hallway.

Shouts... from the guards. A shriek.

Who dared—dared intrude on him now? He gripped the armrest.
The commotion continued. Throwing off the blanket, he rose, his
vision hazy for a moment, and stalked—staggered—to the door. He
just wanted to be alone. Would—would say that to anyone bold enough
to try to ignore—his wishes.

He grabbed for the door handle—damn it, the wood, the wood, the
metal at last—and yanked the door open, stumbling into the hall.

Everyone on the other side froze. Two guards—Raoul and Florian.
Raoul reached out for his shoulder and steadied him, looking him over
in grim assessment.

Nora raised her chin to meet his eyes. Her fluttering eyelashes
swept like great black wings... enormous and all-encompassing...
fanning a cool breeze over his face, once—twice—thrice—

A cool breeze on his face. Now, just for one moment...

She wore her dark tresses unbound and a black silk robe tied
closed. Improper, especially for a lady of the Houses.

"Your Majesty," she greeted, curtsying, while Raoul and Florian
rushed out apologies.

"Lady... Vauquelin." He waved off the guards and caught himself on
the doorjamb. They returned to attention at their posts while he
peered at Nora's pert expression. The hour was late. Very late. "What
are you doing... here?"

A coquettish smile teasing her lips, she batted her great black wings and cleared her throat. The vibration throbbed through his skin and beneath, humming through his blood.

"Word around the palace says you could use a friend," she said, "so here I am."

He gawked at the dark-haired, hazel-eyed beauty, the hazy aura around her, shadowy, soft.

*Nora.*

Her silk robe was black with a vine pattern that grew and grew and twined around her figure, beneath her—breasts, and around, sprouting leaves and thorns... and leaves. It slipped from her shoulders, revealing a dark-red nightgown that... left nothing, *nothing* to the imagination. Shadow and sheer dancing, appearing, disappearing.

She rose to kiss him, her lips supple against his as she threw off his robe. Mmm. He took a few steps back into his quarters and meant to push her away but found his arms wrapped around her. Tight. Silk swept against his skin, rippling a pleasant shiver.

She kicked the door closed behind her, her palms gliding over his back, firm and languor—languorous in their touch, tracing paths of... ecstasy over his flesh. Good. It was good. Her skin's softness against his, like... like lying in a field of feathery dandelions...

Her tongue invaded his mouth, sensual but urgent, sweet like... honeyed pear, and he seized the comfort of it with thirst, now, more and more. Good... good. She pulled away, only enough to slip the tunic over his head, and led him to the bedchamber.

# CHAPTER 36

When darkness blanketed the desert, Rielle followed Brennan toward an oasis that would be the halfway point on their journey to Gazgan. She couldn't see a thing now, but a candlelight spell would give her away as a mage. Too risky. If their pursuers were tracking them, at the very least, her magic could remain a hidden advantage.

They stopped on the way in, and with Brennan guiding her, she laid down a few fire, earth, and air runes. If they were lucky, their pursuers would be thrown off their mounts, hurt, or even killed on contact. A shiver shook through her; the air had gone cool with the sun's departure.

Once she finished, Brennan tethered the camels to a date palm and tended them, then made the telltale strike of steel against flint. She followed the soft noise in the dark, reached out until she touched his shoulder, then lit the tinder with a mere spark of magic in a covered fire pit. The flash of brightness assaulted her eyes; she recoiled.

He covered her hand with his. "You should conserve your anima."

"It's nothing." Her innate elemental magic darkened her anima little, unlike all the non-innate healing she'd done the night before.

And it looked no different to an observer than a natural spark. She slipped her hand free.

"Thanks to our pace earlier, we have about three hours until they're upon us," he said. "You could get some sleep, some food..."

"I'm fine. I can't imagine getting much of either until we handle our problem." She peered at the supplies he had next to him and grabbed a bedroll and a blanket. "I will, however, enjoy any time not spent on a camel."

He grinned, then turned away. "I'll alert you when they're near."

With a whisper of thanks, she moved to the other side of the fire and laid out her bedroll and camel-hair blanket. She burrowed into it. Perhaps it had been her loss, and everything here in Sonbahar, but Brennan had been so strangely careful in his treatment of her. He'd once been very kind, loving, considerate as a youth. For nearly a decade, however, he'd been callous, threatening, vulgar.

But he was returning to his former self. Was this his true self, then, or were both facets part of the same man? As good as he was to her now, would it last?

She shivered in her bedroll under the blanket, and he came to bed down next to her. The silence remained unbroken while he sat and stared into the fire with a ruminative frown—at least until her teeth chattered. He peered at her, eyes narrowed but a corner of his mouth curling upward.

"Even with all of that"—he gestured to her blanket and bedroll—"you're cold?"

"I'm—"

"Fine?" he offered.

She scowled at him. Perhaps her brave face hadn't been as convincing as she'd hoped.

"Do you trust me, Rielle?"

Trust? Such a question usually hid another. She looked at him. What could he possibly want?

"Well?"

"Yes," she answered in exasperation. "With my life."

"Then let me warm you up."

She froze, restlessness coiling in her legs, her arms, her whole body.

"Nothing untoward," he said. "I promise."

*Nothing untoward.* She breathed deeply. Everything they'd done in Sonbahar had been untoward; there was little reason to believe this would be any different. But she couldn't help but want to believe him. Or perhaps her shivering body just wanted his warmth.

She nodded, but he didn't move, just sat there, eyeing her.

A shiver shook her. "All right."

Of course he'd made her say it. She rolled her eyes.

He lifted the blanket and eased into the bedroll. At contact with him, she went rigid, but slowly, the tension dissipated as he slipped completely inside. She settled into the curve of his arm, hesitating before she rested her cheek on his chest... So warm. All of him was so *warm.* Cuddling closer, she drew a leg across his thighs, drawing her entire body flush against his.

He wrapped her in his embrace, doing no more than breathing while her shivers began to subside. He smelled of camel, sweat, and his usual spice, but somehow, Couronne's lush courtyard ghosted across her closed eyelids, verdant green grass and a white drive, the wrought-iron-clad double doors. With a deep breath, she relaxed. His warmth seeped into her, a slow wave flowing through her body to every corner of her being, until even her very fingertips thawed and rebelled, rubbing his chest softly, testing the firmness of the flesh beneath his thiyawb.

She stopped. "Maybe this isn't such a good idea."

Brennan blew out a breath. "Do you think Jon would want you to be cold?"

"No." Not that it mattered. Lying wasn't an option. Not anymore. Never again. Upon her return, when she'd tell Jon everything, any love he still had for her would be forever changed. Once she told him about her decision to become Farrad's lover, her night with Brennan at House Hazael, and losing their child, he would never look at her the same way again. No matter how much she loved him and needed him.

Every time he'd look at her, he would be reminded of all these things. If he never wanted to look at her again, she'd deserve it.

Her lip trembled, but she bit it.

Killing Shadow. That's what she'd have to focus on. Shadow, who'd caused all of this, most of all, Sylvie's death. If not for Shadow, Sylvie would still be alive, and for that injustice, she had to pay. She had to die. Suffer as Sylvie had suffered.

Brennan rubbed her shoulder. "I won't cross any lines, Rielle. Not unless you ask me to."

"I won't," she said, but she snuggled closer. If she was honest, the thought didn't fill her with revulsion as it once had. Something had changed in him—he'd become... more like he'd once been. A friend.

Although she expected Brennan to argue, he didn't. He simply lay there, stroking her shoulder and arm in a hypnotic back-and-forth motion, lulling her to slumber as she watched the stars.

BRENNAN OPENED HIS EYES. Darkness still shrouded the desert, but hooves pounded the sand beyond the runes. Nearing.

In his arms, Rielle slumbered, cheek to his chest, wrapped around him like a willowy vine. He smiled despite himself. After all they'd been through, he'd never imagined this outcome. Rielle, comfortable in his presence—comfortable enough to hold him, to be close, to be vulnerable? It was intimacy he didn't deserve and had proved himself incapable of cherishing once, but he cherished it now.

She loved Jon. Of that he was certain.

But she'd opened her heart to him; he was certain of that as well.

And a dozen warriors were coming to kill her. Soon, they would be upon the runes, and that's when he'd have to strike.

Doing his best not to disturb her, he slipped from her embrace and settled the camel-hair blanket upon her. She shifted, but didn't wake. A rare peace claimed her face, a peace he'd see prolonged, if he could.

Disrobing, he gazed out into the desert, catching the sweetness of the palms and dates on the night breeze, the musk of the fox and the mice scurrying about in the cold, and invited the Change to full wolf.

A muzzle burst from his mouth, fur from his skin, a tail, and claws emerged from his fingers. He dropped to all fours, lupine pads meeting the sand. He glanced at Rielle, still sleeping.

*Be safe.*

His look longed to linger, but he tore himself away and stalked among the scattered tufts of weeping lovegrass toward the runes. He lowered himself among the cover of a tamarisk's slender branches and ample foliage, and stared out at the band of warriors closing in. The night breeze carried in the scent of man, horse, and Xiri steel.

He couldn't discern their weaponry at this range, so he waited.

Silhouetted against the starlit sky were lances, bows, sabers. Four lancers, two bowmen, and six swordsmen, but these weren't just any warriors.

Hisaad. The elite raiders serving the zahibshada. Trained to ride since before they could walk, they knew nothing but horse, blade, and tactics. Their raids were legend.

Brennan swallowed. Victory would be hard won.

A cloud of dust swirled in the distance. The hisaad rode in at a canter, wearing out the horses, pounding the sand, and didn't slow at all as they neared the runes.

Brennan went rigid, muscles hardening as hooves tore up the desert.

Flames burst from the sand.

Wind cut in a spire.

A pit opened in the earth.

The world's fury unleashed. Rielle's.

Horses and men screamed. Flesh singed, and the coppery tang of blood flooded the air. He kept low to the ground in wait.

Two hisaad burned. One blew apart. One tumbled into the pit.

A bowman deftly maneuvered his horse around the abyss, flanked by unfettered fire and storming winds.

Now or never. Brennan leaped for the bowman.

The bowman turned and shot an arrow into Brennan's chest. He closed his jaws on the bowman's unarmored face and tore him from his horse. He crushed the man's head between his teeth.

Horses closed in, an arc abutting the flames. Weeping lovegrass caught fire, spreading, smoking. As a lance lunged for him, Brennan leaped away through the fire. Seven hisaad remained.

There'd be no retreat. He was the last line before Rielle, and her anima was too dark to defend herself with.

A lance burst through the flames, narrowly missing his shoulder, and disappeared. He shifted to man-beast and broke off the arrow in his chest with a wince.

When the lance lunged again, he grabbed it and swept it to the side.

A thud hit the ground—the lancer. Brennan spun the lance, jumped through the flames, and pierced the man's face into the sand.

Pain bloomed in his shoulder. A saber lodged there.

Two more flashed in his periphery.

He grabbed the swordsman's arm and slid beneath the horse, his superior strength pulling the rider along. Snarling, he yanked the blade from his shoulder and buried it where the armor gapped, into the swordsman's armpit, deep into his chest. Then he rent it free with a spray of blood, taking momentary cover behind the horse.

He clutched his hemorrhaging shoulder. Two lancers, two swordsmen, one bowman. And then she'd be safe.

A bowstring snapped. With a flash of claws, he beat aside an arrow as hooves closed in behind him.

Agony ripped through him. He staggered forward. A lance. He stared down in disbelief.

*Rielle...*

The slash of a saber for his neck, and he raised the blade he held to parry. He craned forward, with searing pain, and plunged his blade into the swordsman's horse. Deep in the chest. It shrieked, reared, and tumbled to the ground.

The lancer who'd pierced him urged his horse into motion, and Brennan with it. Dragged through the dust, he grabbed the lance protruding from his abdomen and tried to pull himself off it, wood and metal abrading his flesh, his blood seeping from the wound and pouring down his body while his legs thrashed across the unforgiving sand. Skin ripped away, flesh tore, bones cracked—his teeth clenched against the unrelenting assault of pain.

At last, he was free of the lance.

He fell down, inhaled the sand. It hurt to breathe.

Hooves beat the ground.

He struggled to rise, but the severed muscles in his shoulder, chest, and abdomen wouldn't cooperate. Kneeling was the best he could manage. Sand caked his blood-soaked skin.

Flames consumed the world around him. Fate thundered in on four legs.

He pushed from the ground, staggered, collapsed. Knees—

Not even he would survive beheading.

He stared into the abyss. Alone, in the middle of a desert. It wasn't quite how he'd imagined it.

The bloodied lance charged for him again.

*Not yet.* He fell to the side and grabbed for the lance. He tried to sweep it back, but his shoulder failed him.

A swordsman dismounted, closed in, and lunged for his chest. He caught the saber, released the lance, and swept a low kick, taking the man off his feet.

He plunged his claws beneath the mail shirt and dug deep, raking through the man's entrails. A gurgle began his slow, excruciating death.

Two lancers, one swordsman, one bowman. And then she'd be safe. Only—

He tried to brace himself with the saber, pushing down against the pommel, burdening his unsteady legs.

A sharp piercing in his back—between his shoulder blades—an arrow rippling pain. He lost his grip on the saber and grabbed for it.

The lancer charged once more.

He twisted to evade—thundering hooves behind him—a point tore through his shoulder and pinned him to the ground. A lance. The second lancer.

Sand. He tried to rise. Couldn't.

Tightened his grip on the saber.

*Rielle...*

Boots hit the ground. Three blades whispered free of scabbards.

*I...*

A saber plunged through his other shoulder, anchoring him. A knee settled on the small of his back.

He caught the sheen of the dagger in his periphery, firelight consuming the steel. Sharpness broke into his skull at his temple. Plunged. Agony burned through his head.

And then all was dark.

A LOUD RUMBLE sounded in the distance. Rielle jolted awake, feeling around for Brennan. The night was so dark it was nearly black, but the ever-watching stars offered some scant light. Her gaze darted about wildly.

He was nowhere to be found.

She searched the ground until, finally, smooth fabric slipped beneath her fingers. Brennan's thiyawb. She raised it to her chest and looked out into the distance.

A fire burned, a growing light among the black. Her runes.

She clutched the thiyawb tighter. Brennan had gone into battle. Alone.

Her heart raced as she scrambled out of the bedroll. Magic? Her anima hadn't brightened much—she could cast a few spells, and that was it. No healing. And if she wasn't careful, she'd go into fureur, tap into her life force, and cast spells until dead.

But Brennan was out there. She wouldn't abandon him. Something... She had to do *something*.

Smoke filling her nostrils, she broke into a run toward the fire. A couple highly destructive spells were her best option. There'd only be one chance—maybe two. And to kill them all, she'd need her enemies clumped together.

Bait.

She tried to pull on the bond.

There was nothing.

Cold swept through her, chilled. She shuddered and looked inward. The part of her anima devoted to the bond was free. No bond.

Her foot slipped in the sand, and she stumbled but caught herself.

No bond.

*Brennan—*

*No, you're all right.*

A fire blazed ahead—the rune's explosion had caught some tufts of weeping lovegrass. Horses shuffled in the distance. A few runes lay dormant to the left.

She ran faster. Bait. But it couldn't be obvious.

The flames silhouetted a small tree—a tamarisk. She darted toward it and allowed herself to trip with a yelp.

Sand filled her nostrils as she rolled. *Come and get me.* Huffing, she rose.

Hooves pounded the sand. Four riders.

She scrambled backward, ducked behind some weeping lovegrass. With a twist of her fingers, a fireball sparked to life. Twirling it in her palm, she built it. The riders staggered and closed, almost alongside the dormant runes.

It was still too small; it had to be big and distracting. She waited as long as she dared.

She threw the fireball just to the right. A crack, a whoosh. Sand and flame flew, exploding in dust and sparks. They veered to the left. One rider caught fire.

Sleight of hand.

With her other hand, she raised a wall behind them. Sand hardened and rose into stone. Fifteen feet tall, curving for twenty feet around them. Flame blocked their front and right. The runes blocked the left.

Three riders made for the quickly closing gap between the runes and the wall.

Too late.

She drew in her fingers, drawing the wall's stone to collapse toward them. A rumble shook the sands, an explosion. Fire and wind burst from the runes. Horses screamed. Men shouted. The grating of stone against stone abraded the air.

Eyes wide, she stared ahead, her breath coming fast and harsh. Tremors racked her body.

Had any lived?

In an instant, she looked inward. Her anima dangerously skirted fureur.

She blinked it away. Unable to spare the cost of an earthsight spell, she staggered to her feet and scanned the desert before her in the light of burning grasses.

Nothing moved. Only the crackling of fire disturbed the quiet.

*Brennan.*

She crept through the ruins, the burning brush, and the carnage, searching the ground for him.

A fallen horse, wisps of black mane fluttering in the wind. Just past it, she could see the hilt of a saber and most of a lance. Plunged into the ground. Plunged into...

Her breath caught. She scrambled toward the horse, her terrified gaze descending along the blade of the saber until she found where it met with flesh. A man's back.

Brennan's back. Through his shoulder.

A lance through his other shoulder.

An arrow in his spine.

A dagger in his head.

In his head. A dagger in his head.

She cried out, covered her mouth. Couldn't stop the tears from coming. Ran to him and fell to her knees. Her hands shot toward him but paused just over his skin. Was he...?

She placed her palms on his back, sticky with blood. He was cold. There was nothing—

She shed her thiyawb and covered him, rubbing his arm through the cloth. Warm him up. She had to warm him up. Just a little warmth, that was all. That was all he needed.

Just—

Only a little, and—

A sob tore from her throat. She gulped it back.

She brushed his hair away from his face. Glassy eyes. She gasped.

"No." Choked, the word barely emerged.

Her ankle pulled out from under her.

She fell to the ground, dragged. A tight, painful grip.

A man, trapped under a horse, pulled her. Scrambling, she kicked at his face and grabbed wildly. No magic. She couldn't use magic.

Divine. He was at her knee.

Her hand found a hilt, and she pulled through the resistance. Even before it was free, she knew from where it came. Brennan.

The man seized her thigh with both hands, nails breaking the skin.

She lunged forward and grabbed for his wrist. Yanked back. His wide eyes froze open.

A dagger slash—the eye.

He screamed, rolled his head to the side. She plunged the blade into his neck. His hands instantly released her.

She scrambled away. The man gasped, gurgled, but she turned from his dying throes to Brennan.

Still. Unmoving. Fingers trembling, she closed his eyes, the softness of his eyelashes tickling her skin. Making her shiver.

*Divine, please.*

She sniffled and dragged an arm across her face. The bond hadn't returned. It had never left her like this before. He had never...

The weeping lovegrass next to him burned. Close. Closer.

If she didn't move him, he'd burn, too. Anchored to the ground by the saber and the lance, he'd need them removed. She stared at the arrow embedded between his shoulder blades.

When he'd been pinned here, he had to have known it was his end.

But he hadn't pulled on the bond. Hadn't called out.

He'd... died.

*Brennan, you—* She rubbed her lips together and shook her head. Hot tears burned in her eyes, rolling sticky warm trails down her face, robbing her of the strength to move him, and she couldn't stop the sobs that wracked her body. He'd allowed himself to die here to protect her. Hoped he'd bought her enough time.

Her entire body shook.

*Brennan...* Why did he? There was nothing in it for him. He could have run, could have lived. Even without his monthly control, he could have at least survived.

He'd wanted something from her. She laughed sickly, tears bursting forth with renewed force. That's what she'd told herself for so long. But here he was, the selfish wolf, the cruel man, the manipulator, dead. For *her* sake.

To save herself, her child, and Jon, she'd agreed to assassinate Farrad. And she had. For her actions, the warriors had been sent after her, but Brennan—

*Brennan* had paid the price.

She'd killed Farrad, and Brennan had died for it. Blood for blood. She exhaled bitterly.

A nearer tuft of weeping lovegrass caught fire.

She wouldn't leave him here. Not like this. She'd move him or die trying. Grunting with effort, she pulled out the arrow.

She struggled to her feet and grabbed the saber hilt. After one pull, it wouldn't budge. *Please, please... just, please... Come on...* Weeping, she yanked at it until it was finally free, then threw it aside.

He didn't flinch.

Didn't move.

Only lay there, absent, no pain, no... anything.

Her lower lip trembled, but she bit it into submission.

The lance was even worse, but it, too, at last came free.

A firm hold on his wrists, she painstakingly dragged him to the cover of the tamarisk, her arms and legs numb. She collapsed to her knees and onto her chest, the air oomphing out of her lungs as her face met the sand.

Crying, she dug her fingers into the ground. Tried to pull nearer. Huddled close, rested her forehead against his. Full of sand and tears, her eyes burned, and she shut them. Surrendered.

He'd loved her.

He'd loved her, and now he was gone.

# CHAPTER 37

Olivia crumpled the message in her hand. "Why didn't you deliver this to His Majesty?"

"Apologies, Lady Archmage. His Majesty's guard said he was indisposed."

Indisposed? She shut her aching eyes. She'd cried for days; Jon was still in mourning and she'd only just told him about his heart, but the kingdom relied on him. He couldn't afford to be "indisposed."

She waved off the messenger. The young man bowed and left her salon. Silence and the blush of the early-morning sun reclaimed the room.

She reached behind her for an armrest, and when her grip closed around the familiar damask, she surrendered to the chair.

The light-elves of Vervewood were being raided by another tribe of elves, the dark-elves of Stonehaven.

She smoothed her black wool gown, busying her anxious fingers. The alliance hadn't even been sworn, and already it threatened to fall to ruin. Leigh had written in no uncertain terms that the light-elves would gratefully offer information on the Sundering, the Earthbinding, and dragon mages in exchange for Emaurria's assistance.

Emaurria already struggled for breath beneath a never-ending assault of Immortals, and now this?

But if Leigh's words were true, Stonehaven threatened all. Better to handle a fledgling enemy early with an ally than to wait while the enemy grew strong on conquest. Jon would see reason.

She pushed to her feet and shook out her skirts. See reason... Tor had assured her of Jon's agreement to swear the elven oath. That meant he had already improved, if only a little.

It was time to speak with him. Together, they'd support one another through Rielle's death and work to find the one responsible. They would keep the kingdom safe, and it started with this alliance.

Clutching the message, she strode out into the hall and toward the king's quarters. Jon hadn't faced the messenger, but he would face her.

In these early hours, she passed rare faces offering cordial greetings, courtiers going about their normal days. None of them knew Rielle was gone, nor the depth of her loss or Jon's. None of them knew Jon had but a couple years to live. The kingdom lived on, breathed on, unaware.

Someone would have to tell the Duchess of Melain, Rielle's great-grandmother. Olivia knitted her eyebrows together. She would make the visit if Brennan didn't return soon. The duchess deserved to know, to be told in person, and there were arrangements to be made, contingencies, and...

She swept the wetness from her cheeks and took deep, calming breaths. It would not do to meet Jon in tears. Surely he was barely managing on his own and would not need a reason to falter.

At last she arrived in the royal wing and before Sir Raoul and Sir Florian, who stood sentinel, if with a ghostly pallor and sickly sheen.

She greeted them, earning lifeless greetings in return. "Are you quite well?" She glanced from one to the other.

Sir Raoul scowled at his partner, then sighed. "Yes, Lady Archmage."

Even as he said so, his ice-blue eyes dulled. She pressed her lips together. Was some fever spreading through the palace? "Honesty, Sir Raoul, is a virtue. If you are ill, I am—quite conveniently—a healer."

He grimaced. "It is not that, Lady Archmage."

"Very well." She tipped her head toward the door. "Is His Majesty in?"

Sir Raoul's gaze darted to Sir Florian. "He is... indisposed."

Did Jon suffer this fever as well? Had he taken ill? It could worsen his condition. "Divine, you two! I am the Archmage, yes, but a healer first. If His Majesty has taken ill—"

Sir Raoul shook his head and opened his mouth when one of the doors opened. He and Sir Florian stood to attention.

Laughter exited the king's quarters first, quiet and girlish, and then Nora Marcel Vignon in a man's brocade dressing gown, her dark shimmering locks disheveled, her face-paint smudged.

Olivia gaped, eyes widening, her chest taut as thread on a loom. A woman? A woman had been in Jon's quarters, and—by the look of her—had spent the night?

Nora's hazel eyes met hers, and a little smirk stole onto the beautiful woman's face. Smug. Victorious. With a flutter of her long lashes, she glided away down the hall.

Olivia's vision blurred before she remembered to blink. Her mouth had gone dry, and she brought her lips together once more, her gaze scrabbling toward Sir Raoul.

His eyes went soft. Sympathetic. "Lady..."

Paper crackled in her hand. She stormed through the open door.

"Lady Archmage!" Sir Raoul's voice bellowed behind her.

She didn't stop, striding through the antechamber, the study, and into the bedchamber. The indignity, the disrespect, the *callousness*—

She shook her head. "How *dare* you—"

A set of gloved hands gripped her arm, and she thrashed free. In the massive four-poster bed, Jon sat bare chested, the sheets over his lap, elbows on his raised knees and his head in his hands.

"Lady Archmage," Sir Raoul scolded, "you cannot—"

Jon raised a hand and waved the words away dismissively. "Leave us," he mumbled.

She yanked her arm back and stared a hole through Sir Raoul's face. He pressed his lips into a thin line, bowed, and exited. When the door closed, she stalked to the side of the bed and threw the message at Jon. It hit him in the shoulder.

He didn't even flinch. The sour smell of old wine rolled off him.

"What the *hell* do you think you're doing?" she shouted at him. "The kingdom is on the verge of war, and you're—"

He shot up and bolted from the bed, shoving her aside as he ran to the garderobe and vomited.

Puffing a sharp breath, she poured a cup of water, then headed to the washbasin and grabbed a towel. She held the towel out to him.

"Why, Jon?" She shook her head. "Why?"

Coughing between dry heaves, he palmed his mouth before he grabbed the towel and wiped. "Olivia—"

She snatched the towel away and handed him the water. He eyed her lifelessly, and she turned away from him and searched his quarters for clothes. She found braies on the floor and threw them at him. "I told you to avoid wine, to rest, and this is what you do? Are you *trying* to die?"

"I don't need to... explain myself to you," he rasped, then took a gulp. And another.

Don't need to explain? She could have struck him. "I'm your healer! It's my mission to keep you alive and well." His health was her duty. "And we only just found out about Rielle two days ago! This is how you honor her? How do you think she would feel, knowing you did this? How can you even claim to have loved her? I don't even—"

"It's over," he said quietly. The cup thumped on wood, and he moved to the washbasin and splashed his face. He shook out his hands, leaning over the basin, staring joylessly into the mirror.

Her back hit the wall, and she shut her eyes, leaned her head against it. Every time she visited the abbey, beheld James' gisant, a part of her begged for release from this prison, to be reunited with him. The world was lonely now, and thin; in those moments, if she couldn't have the perfect world he'd existed in, she didn't want any world at all.

But that part of her gave way to reality, to the sunlight dancing on the marble floor, to life continuing to beat its steady pulse. Friends, family, nature and its beauty. Destiny, future. Ripples of good that would flow from her into everything and everyone else, ripples that would not exist without her.

She opened her eyes. Jon hadn't moved, staring into the ghost of a man that stared back at him in the mirror. Caught staring into the abyss inside of him, he would never see reality, the sunlight dancing... None of it.

She approached him and gently took his hand; he didn't resist, and she covered it with her other. She squeezed his hand, and his eyes shuttered. "You still have time. Do you see nothing beyond these bars you've forged for yourself?"

His eyes met hers in the mirror and for a moment focused, then he lowered his gaze and pulled his hand away. "You said something about war."

She sighed inwardly and paused. Numbness. That was what he wanted.

The destruction in the solar after meeting the spiritualist—that was the violence that churned within him, and he would have it stilled. By any means necessary. Wine, women—and who knew what else? If he would not respond to love and support, then it was up to him to decide when he could bare his heart again. And she—and everyone—would be there for him when he did.

She retrieved the message from the bed, then handed it to him. "Vervewood has been attacked by Stonehaven. They seek Emaurria's aid in exchange for knowledge."

He scanned the message, then closed his eyes and breathed deep. "If what he writes is true, then Stonehaven is a threat to all. And we cannot allow a peaceful civilization to be destroyed. Not while we have the means to prevent it."

Bracing on the washbasin, he stared into the mirror, through it, intensely. His eyebrows drew together, tight, determined. Knuckles whitening, he shut his eyes again. "I see them... Hundreds near Vervewood. Stronger. With prisoners. Humans, elves, others... Werewolves."

She jerked her head back. Werewolves? She'd gotten reports of them around Maerleth Tainn. Was this a second pack?

Jon struck the side of the basin with a palm. His eyes shot open. "I can see them, but I can't do anything more. I can reach out to them, almost touch them, but that's it. What was the point of this ritual if that's all I can do?"

She paced to the balcony doors facing the city. "You can see your enemy. Know their whereabouts, their numbers. That's a great asset."

He huffed. "So we can see our doom before it destroys us."

"Leigh also wrote that they know more about the Earthbinding. Perhaps you're not as limited as you think."

"Perhaps." A low, monotonous voice belied the hope of the word. "Call the council to a meeting. We're going to war."

JON RUBBED the fine grain of the lacquered table in the High Council chambers. They'd been at it for hours and were no closer to a solution for the violence the light-elves faced from Stonehaven.

"The light-elves of Vervewood came to us in bad faith," Derric said. Dark circles had settled under his eyes; he had added some of Jon's duties to his own to help Pons. "They knew they were under threat and withheld that information, trying to trap our kingdom into an alliance. They disrespected our king. We can't trust them—or any Immortals. They see us as inferior, a tool to be used. Our best options are human alliances. At least we can navigate them more easily."

"We've been crawling in the dark," Tor said, staring down Derric across from him. "The light-elves have knowledge we need to survive in this new world. If we must fight for that—and by doing so, save a peaceful people—then so be it. We must make a good-faith effort to do what's best for everyone."

Auguste shook his head, stroking his pointed gray beard. "At what cost? The light-elves do not speak our language. How do you propose we fight by their side? Language learning has been slow"—a glare at Olivia—"and without communication, we are fighting this war unilaterally." He folded his hands and turned to Jon. "Our ambassador is already learning their secrets. We won't need the light-elves. Let them fight their own battles. If they prove themselves strong enough to survive, then we'll give them the choice of an alliance or annihilation. And if they lose against this Stonehaven, they'll have weakened our enemy, and their culling will be all the easier. One hand washes the other."

Olivia scoffed, her narrowed eyes glinting. "I have yet to see Leigh turn his back on the greater good. If you think he will simply plunder an innocent people of their secrets and then leave them to die, you do not know the man."

"He is a wild mage, isn't it so?" Auguste raised his eyebrows. "Surely he has the power to take care of the matter, then."

Olivia tilted her head to eye Jon, her lips pursed tight. One of these days, she would grab Auguste's pointed beard and give him the thrashing of his life.

Jon fought the twitch of an emerging smile.

"Even a wild mage is not without limits," Pons interrupted. "His capacity for destruction is great, but if there is any arcanir involved, he will be at a disadvantage. And he is limited to two spells at a time like any other mage. He is only one man." No replies came. "We should continue researching the Earthbinding. Perhaps we may yet find answers?"

Olivia sighed. "I and my clerks have been working on it, but our library is limited when it comes to ancient texts, and Trèstellan has the most impressive magic library in the country."

"So we fight their wars for crumbs of knowledge?" Derric fixed an earnest gaze on her, and Olivia folded beneath it. "That's not an alliance. That's extortion."

Valen rapped the table with his large knuckles. "That's not at all what the message said."

"Then you haven't read between the lines." Derric raised his chin.

Valen's massive shoulders slumped, and his jade-green gaze shifted to Jon. Did he still feel subordinate to Derric?

Jon nodded to Valen. "If you have a solution, Lord Chamberlain, let's hear it."

With a loud sigh, Derric leaned back in his chair.

"We know Vervewood needs assistance in dealing with this Stonehaven, whose raiding shows they are already our enemies as well," Valen said. "And clearly, Vervewood knows we need information. But they have not suggested we fight their battles in order to obtain it."

"That is *exactly* what they've suggested," Derric interrupted, but when Jon shot him a glare, he threw up his hands and pressed his lips together.

"There is the oath ritual upcoming," Valen continued. "They withheld the true state of their situation, so why not ask them for information on the Earthbinding as a show of good faith? They know we pursue the Sundering, to seal off the worst of the mindless beasts and monsters, and that to accomplish it, we'll need a... dragon mage," he said, blinking rapidly. "Knowledge of the Earthbinding doesn't help us accomplish that goal. But it can help us help them."

"An emissary?" Olivia offered.

Valen nodded.

Rubbing his chin, Jon leaned back in his chair. Asking Vervewood to send an emissary to teach them about the Earthbinding would be a safe but valuable overture. And Vervewood could still keep its knowledge about dragon mages until the alliance was finalized.

Derric objected, and as the council debated the merits of Valen's suggestion, Jon studied his own hands, tired of all the squabbling. A naked expanse spread before his mind's eye, soft curves and languorous motion. Kisses, caresses, pleasure in excess—the night unfolded through a dreamy haze that had existed then and only clouded even more now.

It had felt good. The feeling of utter emptiness, allowing sensation to rule for a time and exiling the haunting echoes of his mind. Surrender to wild abandon that left behind not only who he was but everything. Absolutely everything.

He had heard tales of hollow men destroyed by loss, reduced to ruins shadowed by grief, dead to the world. Men who had allowed emotion to strip them of their strength and, worse, their honor. Lesser men. Honor was the very essence of a man; how could anyone allow his very essence to be torn away by the loss of one person?

But now he knew. He knew the destruction of each of them, their ruination, their shadows, their death. Intimately. He knew why they abandoned honor, why they allowed their very essence to be torn out. He had once been impaled by a sword that should have killed him; and when he'd thought of death, he'd thought of that sword piercing his flesh, releasing the red ebb of his life. But he knew better now. There was death that had nothing to do with a blade or blood—death of the soul. Theirs had died, and his had died, and they were hollow, and he was hollow.

But he still had work to do. And he would devote the remaining years of his life to the kingdom, to service, to doing what was necessary.

He straightened and studied each expectant face at the table. "We will proceed with Valen's suggestion." He turned to Olivia. "Lady Archmage, would you draft a message and have it sent to me?"

She nodded. "Yes, Your Majesty."

"Good." He rose. "If there's nothing else?" Without waiting for answers, he said his goodbyes and exited the High Council chambers.

In the hallway, Manon waited for him, her fawn-haired head bowed. "Your Majesty—"

Olivia entered the hallway with Tor and shot him a look that could kill, her gaze shifting between him and Manon.

He shook his head and shrugged, and as Olivia left, over her shoulder she mouthed a word that seemed very much like *bastard.*

He sighed and turned back to Manon, heading toward his quarters, and she accompanied him, quickening her pace to keep up with his strides. He slowed. "What is it?"

She cleared her throat. "It's Princess Alessandra, your Majesty. She wishes me to tell you that she's tired of your silence, and that she demands—"

"She couldn't send a note?"

Manon bit her lip and reddened. "She insisted that *I* be the one to deliver her message."

He sighed. Did Alessandra think he was too busy having an affair with his servant? That this was the reason he'd avoided her? "I'm sorry. I interrupted you. Please continue."

"Yes, sire. She demanded that you meet her in the Grand Library immediately." Manon paused and inclined her head. "That's all of it, sire."

He thanked her, and she returned to her duties. And it seemed he was to return to his.

~

Jᴏɴ ᴇɴᴛᴇʀᴇᴅ ᴛʜᴇ Gʀᴀɴᴅ Lɪʙʀᴀʀʏ, exchanging greetings quietly as he made his way to the remote back corner, where Alessandra had tucked herself away on a small sofa with what looked to be the eighth volume of Clément Hardelin's *A History of Emaurria*.

As he sat across from her, she said, "I was just wondering if you were coming."

Of all the suitresses, he liked Alessandra most; sharp, bold, wise beyond her years. And unapologetically sure of herself. There was nothing enjoyable about deceiving her or leading her on, or in this case, ignoring her. "It's been a rough few days."

"So rough," she said, closing her book, "that you couldn't spare a moment to write me a note." Her placid gaze settled on him, and she blinked. She set the book aside. "What could possibly have been so rough?"

*I have three years to live, at most.*

*The love of my life is dead.*

Neither of which he could tell her. Or... at least not about his heart. Not yet, anyway.

A few people moved about the library, some nestled in chairs, reading. No one seemed to pay them any mind.

He dragged his armchair closer to her, and she followed the movement with curious eyes. "Do you remember when you called my heart a ruin?"

Taking her lower lip in her mouth, she looked away. The afternoon sunlight gleamed in her eyes, then she bowed her head. "Yes, I remember."

"It has... become a memorial," he said quietly.

Her hands clutched her olive-green skirt in weak fists. She opened her mouth, then closed it.

"Before I became king, I was in love with... She was the love of my life." He looked beyond her to the window, where snow gently fell in the courtyard. Sometimes he'd imagined taking morning strolls in it with Rielle. This place had become duty and nothing else, but with Rielle here, it could have been a home, at least for whatever time he had left. "She's been missing for months, and as... king now, I couldn't go search for her. A few days ago, I found out she died."

After a long moment, Alessandra made to clasp her hands, but didn't. "I... I'm sorry," she whispered, meeting his gaze briefly. "She was the one you'd been holding out for? The reason for this whole courtship maneuver?"

So she'd seen through it all. "Everyone kept telling me she and I could never marry. But I would have moved mountains to make it happen. She and I both could have. And we would have done it. She's amazing, strong, determined—" He flinched. "Was." He leaned forward, bracing his elbows on his knees, and rubbed his face. "When I found out, I needed some time. A lot of it. But all I got was a few days."

"I'm sorry," she whispered. "The crown is heavy. Sometimes too heavy." The quiet stretched. "What are you going to do?"

A question he hadn't yet asked himself.

As much as he wanted to, he couldn't ignore his responsibilities. The kingdom was under assault from every angle by the Immortals, and it needed alliances, defense, protection. It needed stability and wise rule. Something he couldn't deliver on his own—not now, and perhaps not ever.

Parliament and his advisers hounded him for a queen, heirs. And that time was running out.

Rielle was gone, and he wouldn't love again. Perhaps it was time to consider giving in to Parliament's demands, to choose a queen fit to rule, wise, and to deliver the stability the kingdom hoped for. To lock in an alliance. All before he died.

Or at least to take one step forward before all the suitresses returned home.

"I need a queen who can halve the burden of rule," he said, and raised his gaze to hers.

A corner of her mouth briefly turned up. "Is that an offer?"

"Are you interested?"

She took a deep breath and crossed her legs. "My brother, Lorenzo, is going to be king of Silen someday," she said with a contemplative smile. "It's the last thing he wants. But I... When we were growing up,

I was hopelessly committed to saving everyone I could. I remember finding some noble children harassing a stray cat, and I threw rocks at them until they left it alone." A half-laugh.

That seemed like her. Bold, fearless. A touch violent. He smiled back.

"They didn't dare strike me back, of course. But I would never rule Silen—that was my brother's destiny. And it was a commonly held belief that I'd never rule anywhere. The court called me 'the Beast Princess.' You see, I had *curvatura* of the spine as a child, so they called me deformed, ugly, fated to be a burden to my father, and later, to my brother. No suitable husband would want me, and an Ermacora—even a deformed, ugly Ermacora—could not be wed to an unsuitable husband."

A terrible thing to do to a child. He sat up and looked her over. There was nothing deformed or ugly about her; she was stunning, really, with her slender, shapely figure, dazzling dark curls, and vaguely feline facial features. Classically beautiful, even.

She gestured to herself. "As you can see, I grew out of it, but by the time that happened, most suitable men were already married or betrothed, and here I am, an old maid." An amused chuckle. "And *still* the Beast Princess... just no longer because of my looks, but my 'brazen behavior.'"

"Do you still throw rocks at bullies?"

She laughed under her breath. "If they deserve it. I grew up being laughed at, excluded, so I found other ways to make myself heard. And in Silen, that is more the purview of men."

He'd heard that in Silen, women were relegated to the household, the ballroom, and the bedchamber, but never the stateroom. "You can be as brazen as you wish here. I welcome it."

She leaned back against the sofa, smoothing her hands over her gown. "You might spark a mass immigration of Sileni women, Your Majesty."

"And would you be the first?"

It could be her.

Why *not* her? If he had to choose *some*one, why not Princess Alessandra, vanquisher of bullies and savior of cats?

King Macario's flotilla already defended the coast, and Alessandra herself was capable and eager to rule. He wasn't looking for love, and neither was she, or at least didn't seem to be. It didn't matter what he wanted anymore; perhaps it was time to be pragmatic and do what was necessary.

"Are you asking me to be your queen?"

"Yes," he said, and her eyebrows rose. "I know it's sudden, and not at all romantic, and you deserve better—"

"We both know this isn't a love match."

He nodded. "Perhaps we could spend some time together until Veris, and... unless you form the desire to throw rocks at me, we could then set things in motion?"

He would tell her the whole truth before the ball, and if she still agreed, then the kingdom would have what it needed. And... in two to three years... he could leave Emaurria in her hands, couldn't he?

With a pensive smile, she nodded. "That sounds reasonable."

He stood from the armchair. "Care for a walk in the courtyard tomorrow?"

# CHAPTER 38

The late-morning sun beamed the searing desert heat onto Rielle's skin. Her head tucked into the crook of Brennan's arm, she stared at the tamarisk's slender branches swaying in the wind. Small leaf scales enshrined tiny twigs, and like little evergreen feathers, they fluttered softly.

Or perhaps she did.

She glanced at her fingers, trembling, fluttering like the leaves in the wind. Anima withdrawal.

She had nothing left. One last spell that would take her life.

The fires had died in the night. None of the defeated warriors had moved. All dead.

How many hours had it been? Ten? Twelve?

She pulled Brennan's cold arm tighter around her and blinked away tears. The day moved on, but she couldn't. She couldn't bring herself to move at all, no more than she could stand the thought of leaving him here alone.

He'd loved her.

Proud, conceited, stupid wolf. She bit back a sob. He should have let them come. He should have run. He should have stayed alive.

But he was gone. She chewed her lower lip, fighting the urge to weep. It didn't matter. The tears came whether she fought them or not. She wanted to be with him, stay until the Great Wolf himself came and claimed him, forever if she had to. He would have wanted her to leave him here, to go home to safety, so his sacrifice wouldn't be wasted.

But he didn't get to decide.

If fortune favored her, there were still two camels at the oasis. She wouldn't have to leave him. He wouldn't have to be alone. She would take his body home to Emaurria, where he belonged, interred with the rest of the Marcels in the family crypt beneath Castle Tainn. He deserved no less.

She struggled to rise, but could do no more than brace herself on an elbow before she collapsed again. The desert wind beat against her face and whipped her hair into her eyes.

Couldn't even rise. How would she get to the camels, let alone put Brennan on one? She wiped her eyes, streaking sand and grit into them. "Damn it!"

The wind howled its deafening response.

"Damn it!" she shouted, louder this time, and as the words tore through her, she gave into them, surrendered the fight, and screamed. She knotted the thiyawb she'd covered Brennan with, gripping it so fiercely her fingers ached. Hadn't the sands taken enough from her? Her freedom, her dignity, her child. Not enough?

*Brennan...*

He'd loved her once. She'd hurt him. He'd hated her. But he'd never stopped caring. In his own twisted way, he'd still been full of passion, just as Gran had said in Melain. All her life, as long as she could remember, he'd been a force, a howling wind she couldn't ignore, whether for good or ill.

And now there'd be nothing. Not his love. Not his hate. Nothing at all.

She rested her cheek on his abdomen, stretching her arms across him. Her palm pressed to his warm hip, heated by the desert sun.

Warm...

Sucking in a sharp breath, she raised her cheek and crawled higher to press her ear to his chest. An act of desperation. But she had to try.

A thump.

Trembling, she looked inward for the bond. *Please, Divine, please. I'll do anything. Please.*

A shudder rattled her, and she convulsed. As she peered inward, the last of her anima had been claimed. None for her use, not even one last spell.

The bond. It was there. The bond had reclaimed the last of her anima.

The bond was there.

*He* was there.

*Brennan.*

She gazed at his face. Color enlivened his features.

"Brennan." She grabbed him and shook him.

Nothing.

"Brennan!" She shook him again. "Brennan! *Brennan!*" she screamed, her voice thundering over the howl of the wind.

BRENNAN SHIVERED. Cold. So cold. He'd never felt so cold in his life.

*"Brennan!"* Her voice echoed through the endless dark.

Through the spiky grass, he staggered with his hands out until his palms found something solid. Rough. A tree? No scent. He could barely breathe, his entire body shaking. What was this place? Was he dead?

He could feel everything here, but see nothing.

And he heard *her.*

*"Brennan!"* Her voice resonated through the darkness, quaking through the ground beneath him. A ripple splashed at his feet. Some sort of swamp. He swept his hands around him, catching the tips of the spiked grasses that came up to his thighs.

Her voice came from everywhere and nowhere. He stared through the darkness, looking for something, anything but black.

He wrapped his arms around himself, rubbing them against the cold of this place, which bit so much deeper than the bone.

There was nothing here. Even his eyes, his Wolf's eyes, couldn't perceive a thing. The yawning hole of death, Nox's Maw—was this it? Was this forever? The Lone?

He shook, tremors consuming every inch of him, and not from the cold.

*"Brennan!"* Her voice screamed so close, almost at his ear, and he reached all around him.

Nothing.

He shouted, pressing his head between his hands. His breaths came short, shorter, and he fell to his knees in the water, gasping.

The world was black. And that's all there was.

He closed his eyes.

He didn't want this world and its endless dark. He kept his eyes closed. Rielle. He imagined Rielle. She'd been five years old when he'd first seen her, twirling on the grassy cliffs outside Laurentine under the vast cerulean sky, a red rose in her golden curls.

That silly child was to someday be his bride. Someday be the Duchess of Maerleth Tainn. He'd laughed.

"Are you laughing at me, Lord Brennan?" she called, still twirling.

He looked at his parents, who were in deep discussion with Marquis Laurentine and his wife.

"I'm talking to you!" Rielle shouted. She added a little hop to her twirl.

"You caught me, Lady Favrielle."

"I know why you laughed!" she replied in a singsong voice.

He raised an eyebrow. "Why is that?"

"Because you're *afraid* to look silly!"

Another laugh exploded from his mouth before he could catch it. What a bold little child.

"Mama says to face your fears. Face your fears, Lord Brennan!" she giggled. "Mama says it's good!"

Holding in a toothy grin, he cautiously strolled onto the grassy cliff. Was he actually considering this? Indulging the teasing of a twirling little girl?

"Come on!"

Great Wolf help him, he twirled.

Now he imagined her as a young woman of nineteen at Tregarde three years ago, kissing him in the rooms he'd had prepared for her. He'd chosen every detail of her trip to Tregarde, telling himself it had all been to humiliate her.

But he'd known everything she liked. Every detail. From her allergy to strawberries to her addiction to custard tarts and sugared almonds. And he'd imagined the joy it would all bring her. Maybe she'd finally love him. Maybe she'd never abandon him again.

Her lips were warm, firm against him...

And then the hurt flooded in.

She couldn't abandon him if he abandoned her first. With finality. So she'd never hope again. So he never could.

*I love you, but you hurt me.* The words were impossible. His mouth couldn't form them. They were strong, and he was too weak for them. Afraid.

He couldn't love her then.

If he could take back that moment in the Tregarde kitchen, take her in his arms and tell her he loved her and he was sorry, throw out every last cackling guest and swear them to silence and respect upon pain of death—no matter her reply—if he could take it all back...

He imagined her nestled in the crook of his arm at the oasis in the night. He should have told her then. Should have told her a hundred times. A thousand times, no matter her reply. "I love you."

Light assaulted his eyes. A field of white blinded him until a shadow shielded his face.

Teardrops landed on his cheeks. He blinked. And found her face.

The bluest sky on a clear day. Her eyes, red rimmed and watering. Sparkling tears fell from them, off fluttering blond lashes, sunshine radiant through the golden corona of her tangled hair, and she smiled. He'd never seen anything so beautiful.

"You're alive," she whispered.

Alive.

He looked up at her, trails of wetness soaking into his ears. Alive.

He could breathe. Sucked in deep, quick, irregular breaths. The sand gave way beneath him.

Sonbahar. He was in Sonbahar with Rielle. Alive.

She beamed at him.

The hisaad—they hadn't—and she was—

He wrapped his arms around her, letting happy laughter burst free, rolling with her in the hot sand, and she laughed with him. Great Wolf, she was all right. And he was alive to see it.

"I'm not afraid to twirl," he said, his voice a low rasp. He stopped flat on his back, Rielle lying in a heap atop him.

"Hm?" She raised her head and met his eyes, her own bright as summer.

He wouldn't die without her knowing the truth, with the most important words he could ever speak bottled by fear in his chest. Not again. Not ever. "I love you."

She blinked, and her eyebrows rose. Soft pink bloomed in her cheeks. "I..." she whispered, glancing away, a faint smile enchanting her lips. "I'm glad. That's probably not the answer you want to hear, but..."

He drew in a deep, slow breath. He hadn't said it to elicit a response.

But of all the things she could have said... "As long as it's not 'I hate you, Brennan. Please go die,' which would be no worse answer than I deserve"—he watched her mouth fall open—"I can hear it."

She closed her mouth, but as she looked away and shook her head, a smile fought its way out.

He loved her. And she knew. Whether she embraced his heart or broke it, she knew it.

She lowered her head to his chest and hugged him. "Just please don't ever die again. I don't think I could bear it."

He wrapped his arms around her. "I'll try not to."

Singed death intruded upon his nostrils, and after a time, he craned his neck to look around them. Burnt tufts of weeping lovegrass mingled with dead horses and hisaad bodies. They were still in the middle of the battlefield.

How much time had passed while he'd been... dead? He stroked Rielle's skin—her arms were bare. She only wore a sleeveless chemise, pants, and boots, but the balaustine red of her thiyawb peeked out between them.

She'd covered him with it, like a blanket, as if she'd thought he'd be cold without it. Somehow, the thought warmed him. "We need to get to Gazgan," he whispered to her, smoothing her windswept hair.

"I know," she mumbled against his chest. "It's just... I can barely move."

When he looked her over, she trembled. Anima withdrawal, and still bleeding. He was healing slowly... And probably hampering her natural regeneration. "I'm sorry."

She shook her head. "Don't be. You're alive."

He strained to sit up, and she shifted aside to let him. His head pounded. A splitting headache. He raised his fingertips to his temple and—the roughness of a scab there, where he'd been... stabbed. At times like this, he didn't hate the curse.

The ache in his shoulders was even worse, and he didn't even want to know what they looked like.

"Take it easy," she said. "You look like you've been—"

"Murdered?"

She hissed. "Through hell."

He struggled to his feet and handed her the thiyawb. Blushing, she took it without meeting his eyes.

His nakedness embarrassed her now. He suppressed a grin.

Chaos littered the sand. Every shrub in the area but for the tamarisk had been reduced to cinders, along with some of their attackers. What had she faced without him? His gaze darted to her, curled up on the sand, clutching the thiyawb close. "Why didn't you run away? Hide?"

She shrugged.

He took in the blackness surrounding them. There had to have been an abundance of fire. "Right," he mused. "When you see fire, you run toward it. Of course."

She swatted him with the thiyawb, and he dodged, laughing. A little teasing might get her on her feet.

She scrambled to rise, then faltered and caught herself. Quickly, he braced her.

Her assessment had been unfortunately correct. She really could just barely move.

As they made their way to the oasis, she sighed. "You're back from the dead, and *I* need *your* help just to walk."

Because he was draining her through the bond. "I'm only on my feet because of you. It's your last strength keeping me standing."

She opened her mouth, but then only nodded.

They picked their way through the grasses to where their supplies lay. He eyed his clothes, but drenched in blood as he was, he couldn't dress quite yet. He lowered her softly to the blanket, and when she was seated, he headed for the water.

"Where are you going?" she called after him.

He grinned. "I have sand in unspeakable places, Rielle. There's no way I'm getting on a camel until that changes."

Her gasp only made him chuckle quietly to himself. He washed quickly, dressed, and then picked through the hisaad's belongings. He gathered what he and Rielle might need, prepared the camels, and helped Rielle mount hers.

Gazgan wasn't far. They could make it there by morning, if they made good time.

~

BRENNAN MOUNTED HIS CAMEL, and they headed northwest. If luck was on their side, they'd make it there and depart for Emaurria before word could arrive from Xir about Farrad's killing. If no more hisaad pursued them.

The heat bore down on them ruthlessly, and although she blinked sluggishly, he felt increasingly better, which meant she had more anima to spare. Her anima slowly brightened... But she'd need to find a resonance partner in Gazgan to brighten fully.

He exhaled a long breath. The thought that he could never give her resonance had perched on his mind ever since she'd moved to the Tower. And of course she'd taken a mage as a lover. *A mage* could give her resonance.

They weren't a perfect fit. They never would be. But whatever she needed, she would have.

Silent, she looked his way from time to time, her eyebrows knitted together. Did she doubt he still lived? Did she think he would go limp, fall dead at any moment?

When she looked at him again, he turned to face her, his eyes trained on her until she met them.

"What?"

"I'm fine," he said, not wanting her to worry. "I'm more concerned about you."

She waved him off. "My anima is slowly brightening. It's helping."

Even aside from her anima's dimness, the scent of her blood carried on the wind; she still bled from losing the child. Xir, and the desert, had pushed her to her limits. "When we get to Gazgan, we'll need to find you a resonance partner." He lowered his gaze. They didn't have a week or two to wait before getting her back to her full power.

"I thought all the mages in Sonbahar reported to the zahibshada?"

"They do. Although Gazgan's zahibshada maintains it as a free city —no slaves—if word has spread from Xir about a fugitive accused of killing a shafi, you won't be spared." He looked out at the horizon. "But Gazgan is a port city. Many foreigners come and go. And I don't doubt some are mages."

"It's a gamble."

"Your inability to use magic is a greater gamble. We'll be careful. I'll make sure whoever it is doesn't report to the zahibshada."

She glared at him. "You mean... kill them?"

If that's what it would take. He shrugged.

"Brennan—"

"As a last resort," he shot back. "We'll see."

"Let's not pick anyone who might need killing, all right? I don't want any more deaths on my conscience. Enough people have died already."

"Who, Farrad?"

She looked away.

"Who cares if he's dead?"

When she turned to him again, tears welled in her eyes. Tears. For the man who'd kept her as his slave? He steered his camel closer to her.

She'd spent months at House Hazael. Whatever the man's faults,

she'd shared his bed. Killing a lover, no matter the motive or justifica-
tion, couldn't be easy. "If it's complicated—"

She swept a thiyawb-clad arm across her face. "He..." She took a
deep breath. "He said that he, and not Ihsan, planned to free House
Hazael's slaves. He said Ihsan's concerned with legacy. She doesn't want
to see the House diminished, while he can't... *couldn't* bear to see his
daughter be a slave anymore. I... I may have done a horrible thing,
worse than I'd even imagined."

Brennan swallowed. If that was true, she hadn't just killed a good
man, she'd mistakenly destroyed House Hazael's slaves' best chance at
freedom.

"He was good, and I..."

"Didn't know."

She turned to him, eyes wide, cloudy.

"You wouldn't have made the same decision if you'd known ahead
of time, right?"

She pressed her lips together, then slowly shook her head.

"You were deceived, and you took your best chance at freedom.
You can't blame yourself for what you didn't know."

"It's still my responsibility. I have to do something about it. I will."

"You're not exactly in any position to, right now." He fixed his eyes
on the distance. At the edge of the horizon, he could just make out
scattered lights. They would be there within the hour.

Her shoulders still slumping, she brushed a hand over her face and
smoothed her hair away. "What?"

He nodded toward the horizon. "I see it."

Her eyes shone in the fading light, fixed upon that distant sight,
and slowly, a hesitant smile spread across her face. Her gaze brightened
then, teary, as she beamed.

An ache formed in his chest.

Her human eyes couldn't possibly see the city at this distance, so
what was it she saw? Freedom? Home? An end to the nightmarish life
she'd been forced to live in Sonbahar?

The longer he watched her face, the more painful his ache became.
Jon. She saw Jon.

The look in her eyes was love, and she'd see him again at last.

He lowered his gaze to his hands, where he held his camel's reins. All he'd done since Courdeval had been for her benefit, undoubtedly, but for his own, too. Unable to accept her rejection, he'd been weak before. He'd hidden his soft vulnerability with sharp edges. Edges that had made her bleed.

But he was strong now, strong enough to try to win her hand, to do whatever he needed to do for the woman he loved. True strength. He wanted to have it for her. And for himself. He *would* win her hand.

He looked at her again. Tears rolled down her cheeks as she smiled at him, tucking wisps of her windswept golden hair away.

And he smiled back at her.

In the twilight, they arrived in town, and the salt was thick on the air. A bay breeze swept in, heartening after so long inland. Colorful buildings lined the coast, variegated warm shades of summer, and Great Wolf willing, there would be a vessel bound for Emaurria.

Rielle wilted in the saddle next to him. The temptation of a soft bed was strong, but instead, he led them to the docks. The priority was getting home.

A few ships sat in port—trade cogs, a few caravels, and a carrack. One of them had to be headed for Emaurria, even from this small port city. Someone would know.

People still shuffled about the docks, and he paused next to some sailors loading a cog and asked after the dockmaster.

The men gladly offered direction and pointed to a well-lit building just a few paces away.

Inside, the dockmaster, a man thiyawbed in indigo, cordially checked for departures to Emaurria. After a brief glance, he frowned.

"No passenger ships to Emaurria. No trade ships to Emaurria," he said in High Nad'i.

Weary, he stood loosely, shoulders and hips relaxed. He looked in Rielle's direction. By the window, she touched a globe wistfully, tracing the Emaurrian coastline.

Brennan leaned in closer to the man. "Nothing at all?"

"With all the Immortals—the sea serpents, mermaids, and such—there are fewer ships crossing the bay. But let me look again." The dockmaster raised his eyes and winced. "The only departure is the *Liberté,* tomorrow—"

Brennan stood taller. "Perfect."

"A pirate hunter." The dockmaster looked back to Rielle.

Brennan suppressed a wince himself. A pirate hunter? Certain vessels were allowed by a sovereign nation to combat piracy, specially outfitted to attack pirate vessels. Pirate vessels like the one that had borne Rielle from Emaurrian shores. But their work was dangerous. Although they often defeated and captured pirate vessels and their cargo, any fool with a ship could seek pirate-hunter privileges from a sovereign.

"The *Liberté?*" Brennan asked.

The dockmaster nodded. "Captain Verib has been hunting for three years and has seen remarkable success."

So this captain was either smart and would continue to survive— until he came across someone smarter—or he was lucky, and his luck could run out with them aboard.

But they didn't have any other options. And Rielle was, after all, a quaternary elementalist. Her mastery of hydromancy would help mitigate the risk—

If they could find her a resonance partner.

He held back a grimace. "Would the captain take us on?"

The dockmaster drew in a breath. "For the right price."

Brennan nodded and thanked him. The man drew up a message for the captain and sent his messenger. Rielle looked up from the globe and raised her eyebrows.

He approached her and wrapped an arm around her shoulders. "The only departure is a pirate hunter, tomorrow morning, but he might take us on."

She shifted in his embrace.

"How are you feeling?" he whispered.

She rested her head against him. "Exhausted."

"We'll find lodging as soon as we get word."

She nodded against him. While the dockmaster did his work, they examined maps and looked out the window at the ships, and although they desperately awaited word, he felt light on his feet.

Her nearness soothed him. These past few days had been difficult, but Rielle's close proximity had been a healing balm. It felt right, her being close to him. Natural. And how many years of this feeling had he tossed aside in his weakness?

But it was temporary. Soon, they'd be back in Emaurria, and she— she would go back to Jon.

*And I'll go back to...*

Being alone. He swallowed, resisting the urge to push the thought away.

That wasn't his fate; he would win her heart. He loved her, was best for her, and she would see that.

The messenger returned and handed a letter to the dockmaster, who read it and nodded to Brennan with a slight smile. For a small sum, they could be on their way to Courdeval tomorrow.

Brennan handed the man payment, and then he and Rielle departed. They mounted their camels and headed into the town square.

"We're going home," she whispered, her voice quivering and breathy.

He looked out into the thinning night streets. If he did nothing, everything would soon be as it was. But if he was to claim her for his own, he had the length of the voyage to show her his true heart and hope she saw worth in it.

# CHAPTER 39

rina shifted her apothecary satchel on her hip and took a deep breath as she crossed Trèstellan's inner bailey, crunching through the snow. The clouds were obfuscating the early dusk. The days had been a steady gray, with little to no wind, and nightly snowfall that froze to ice by morning. She could set her clock by the predictability of the weather. Had this anything to do with the announcement that the king was Earthbound?

If this was the extent of that power, it was nothing.

Ahead of schedule, Lady Vauquelin had summoned her yet again. The aphrodisiac lip balm would not arrive for another month, but the summons had been cryptic.

*Perhaps she finally got her wish.*

The shadows of birds crossed the shimmering snow. A peregrine falcon chasing a small pigeon. Did this bird of prey now know that *it* was the pigeon?

The awakening of the Immortals had meant the awakening of dragons, but there had been no confirmed sightings... until rumors had spread after the Battle of Brise-Lames. The soldiers and paladins there had seen a dragon. Doubtless they had all been shaken to the core.

How did mankind even begin to defend against such a thing? What hope did armies have?

But dragons were real.

And if dragons were real, then the Bell of Khar'shil was real as well. A sangremancy ritual to summon a dragon... to destroy any enemy.

Jonathan Dominic Armel Faralle would die, but if she didn't leave Courdeval with his death in hand, she'd take his flesh or blood and no less. The bell would be perfect, but if it didn't work, she'd still have her pick of sangremancy spells to end him.

*A certain end, one way or another. Marko, you will rest well avenged.*

Footmen opened the palace doors, and she made her way through the glum halls, where even the once-constant patter of courtiers was now sparse; they gathered around the hearths in lifeless conversation.

At last she arrived at Lady Vauquelin's quarters.

Melanie answered the door with a quick smile and gestured her in, smoothing the wrinkles from her plain pink frock. "My lady awaits you in the salon."

Inside, Lady Vauquelin paced, dressed in an exquisite crimson velvet dress trimmed with gold embroidery. A fine garment. Melanie moved to a console table and arranged a massive bouquet of marigolds.

Lady Vauquelin turned her head, gleaming dark tresses bouncing. "Mistress Vaganay! Finally you arrive." Wide-eyed, the lady rushed her to the sofa and seated herself.

*Finally?* Drina suppressed a scoff. Upon receipt of the summons, she'd gathered her satchel and left the inn immediately. "Forgive my tardiness, Your Ladyship."

Lady Vauquelin waved a slender hand. "Yes, yes, all's forgiven if you can deliver what I need."

Drina ducked out of her satchel's strap and leaned forward. "Anything Your Ladyship desires."

A grin from ear to ear. "You do not disappoint, Mistress Vaganay."

Good news. "Then you've had success."

Lady Vauquelin crossed her legs and relaxed in her seat. "Of a fashion. Melanie?"

The young maid started, a few marigolds dropping from her hands. "Yes, my lady?"

"Tea." Lady Vauquelin closed her eyes and sighed.

"Yes, my lady." Melanie disappeared, leaving the flowers on the table.

"They're from him," Lady Vauquelin said through a smug little smile. She gestured to her dress. "This, too."

A grateful man? Or a guilty man? The marigolds suggested the latter. "Then everything has gone well."

The lady took a deep breath and exhaled lengthily. "Not everything. I need... something that could impair judgment."

Impair judgment? He was being cautious, then. "Wine?"

Lady Vauquelin shook her head. "Not enough."

"Ithara."

The lady's face lit up. "Yes... Ideal." Her eyes took on a wistful glaze, staring in reverie, and her mouth followed in haunting, a ghost of a smile.

Had the man she meant to impair not been Favrielle's love, he could be pitied. Manipulated, hunted, run directly into the wolf's waiting maw. Although if he was indeed cautious, perhaps he hadn't entirely taken leave of his reason.

"You can acquire it?"

Although the Emaurrian Crown had reluctantly allowed sen'a through its borders, Sonbahar's ithara was illegal and spread from one shadowy hand to another, an expensive guilty pleasure secreted to the pockets of the rich and desperate. Yes, she knew such shadowy hands and could procure almost any treasure.

But this was Nora Marcel Vignon. Daughter of Faolan Auvray Marcel, Duke of Maerleth Tainn, who had an open door to Sonbahar and all its treasures. Why not ask him?

The woman's leg bounced, her lips pursing, twitching. Self-conscious?

*Naturally.* She must trick a stallion to stud, an embarrassment she would not dare voice to her father. Or perhaps he did not know or approve of this scheme. Did she need protection her duke father could not provide? No longer provided?

Or protection *because* of her duke father?

"Well?" The lady straightened.

"Forgive me, Your Ladyship," Drina replied, and a little crease marred the lady's smooth brow. "I searched my memory for certain merchants, and yes, I do believe I can acquire what you need."

A smile, blindingly white and wide, dominated Lady Vauquelin's face. "Splendid."

Porcelain rattled as Melanie arrived with the tea and served them.

"When?" Lady Vauquelin lifted a cup to her lips and took a soundless sip, only the slightest shift of her delicate throat betraying her.

"A few days, at the very least." Before the lady could open her mouth, Drina added, "I shall need the time to devise a scent to camouflage the ithara. Unless you are unconcerned about its detection?" She drank some of her tea. Honeyed. Spiced.

Two perfectly sculpted eyebrows rose. "Brilliant suggestion, Mistress Vaganay. Your intelligence belies your station."

*Thousand thanks, haughty bitch.* "You honor me with your praise." She smiled thoughtfully and inclined her head.

"Soon, a new Court Alchemist will surely be appointed," the woman crooned, setting down her tea, her grin flashing a dazzling brilliance, "and you should make a magnificent assistant."

Assistant?

*Before a scream could leave your lips, I could relieve your body of your head.*

"I have some influence with the Crown now, and I'm confident I could see it arranged." She practically glowed as she grinned.

"Splendid, Your Ladyship!" She chuckled softly. "I should like that very much." She straightened. "I should go and send the necessary letters, Your Ladyship, by your leave?"

"By all means." The woman stood from the sofa with a toss of her shining locks.

"You shall hear from me soon." Drina stood and bowed. "A pleasure as always, Your Ladyship."

And she took her leave of the luxurious quarters. A couple of servants strode past in the hall.

The lady would have her weapon. She seemed a weakling, vulnerable, a pretty flower to be admired with little depth, but in the shadows of her petals hid a ruthlessness—poison. Strength. Like beautiful rosy-pink foxglove, stunning to see, but known as dead man's bells. Without a husband and turned away from her powerful father, Lady Foxglove did not recoil from shame and indignity if it meant attainment of her ends. Better to blush once than to pale a hundred times.

*If the ends are worthy, all means are utile.*

And if the lady attained her end—Drina smiled—it would but sweeten the vengeance. The death of a lover would be a sword through Favrielle's heart, but the knowledge that her lover strayed *and* conceived a lovechild? A second blade. A third. Drina grinned.

At last the hall was empty, and she cast a shadow cloak over herself and crept to the dark wall.

Now it was time for the true work to begin. On the night of the Veris Ball, her blade would finally taste king's blood.

A good plan included not only entry but escape. For that, she'd need a schedule of guard postings and rotations. At the changing of the guard, she'd make her exit. She planned to live to savor her hard work.

Cloaked in shadow, she made her way to Trèstellan's east wing, where Guard-Captain Lambert Corriveau's office was located on the ground floor. Guards strode in and out, clad in shining armor and Trèstellan's sapphire-and-white tabards. She angled around a wall.

Voices neared from behind.

Whisper-quiet, she crept across to a statue, taking cover behind the massive plinth. Two guards passed toward the guard-captain's office. They would enter and soon leave.

Opportunity.

She abandoned her satchel, then moved from shadow to shadow in the sconce-lit hall and took up position in the corner next to the door. Muffled conversation carried from the office for some time, followed shortly by footsteps, nearer and nearer.

The door opened wide.

One guard left the room. Another.

Drina slipped in toward the dark, the door shutting behind her. She crouched next to a cabinet.

Two candelabra lit the office, and Corriveau slumped over his desk, massaging his grayed temples. Thick brows furrowed, he stared at a paper, closed his eyes, breathed slow and deep. Such targets were butter to the knife, and were she here to kill him, his life would have earned its cost many times over.

Not tonight. Between now and Veris, as little had to change as possible. Nothing, preferably, for the sake of stability.

The high-backed chair scraped at last. His gaze settled on her.

She froze. Swallowed. Her fingers twitched over her boot, where her soulblade was sheathed.

To his eyes, she would be nothing more than shadow, camouflaged in the darkness cast by the cabinet.

He headed toward her.

She tensed, her fingers grazing the pommel of her soulblade.

Closer, closer—but no, he went to the cabinet. A drinks cabinet.

She suppressed a relieved sigh as he poured a glass of brandy, drank it down, and poured another. With a turn to the windows—they faced the gardens—he sipped the second glass. Slowly.

Last year, in the office of the General of the Blackblade mercenary company, she had crouched for seven hours, waiting for the general to abandon a document long enough to steal it. The name of a pirate captain and slaver who could not be bought. One without heart. Whose word was iron.

Pity Faolan Auvray Marcel's machinations hadn't planned on a hidden heir. He hadn't reached out to her about assassinating Jonathan Dominic Armel Faralle, but he would hardly complain about a dead king, least of all when it would likely lead to the reestablishment of the Marcel royal line.

Corriveau drained the dregs in his glass, set it down, and moved to his desk. He pulled out a key, unlocked a drawer, and arranged various documents within. He locked it, doused the candles, and made his exit.

Finally.

His footsteps faded in the hall until silence reclaimed the office. She headed for the desk. The locked drawer.

She grinned.

Magehold surely missed its skeleton key. She seized the thong around her neck, pulled up the recondite artifact, and inserted it into the lock. *Open.* She turned the key.

Unlocked.

Correspondence, orders, complaints, rotations. For the next couple of months. Including Veris.

And just like that—entry and exit. For a royal assassination.

In their room for the night, Rielle bathed while Brennan sat facing away from her at the table, eating. A lot. She smiled.

As she washed, her hand shook like a novice over her first healing spell, but she ignored it. They'd asked around the inn about mages, but the innkeeper said they all stayed at the zahibshada's palace or the barracks, where even foreign mages were welcome to lodge, brighten their anima, and learn. Of course.

Brennan had thanked him and said they'd visit there tomorrow, a wise answer to deflect suspicion. And then he'd sent a message to the captain of the *Liberté*, asking whether there'd be another mage aboard for resonance.

No word yet. She'd have to keep her trembling under control.

After rinsing her hair, she left the tub and toweled off. In their packs she found a floor-length crimson chemise that had to be a night-gown. Ostentatious, but she put it on. It was soft, at least.

Smoothing its fabric against her body, her palm lingered over her belly. Her flat, empty belly.

The pressure behind her eyes pushed.

It would pass. It always did. It would pass.

Her fingers shook, and she fisted them, forced her hands to her sides. She raised her chin, took deep breaths, blinked and blinked and blinked until it passed.

She still bled, but less and less, and the painful cramps had less-ened. Her body was recovering, even if nothing else was. But she couldn't afford to give herself over to grief. Not now, not yet, not until Jon was safe and Shadow was dead.

She wasn't alone. Brennan was here. She could talk to him, keep her mind occupied. Worry about the resonance partner she sorely needed. And definitely not think about what he'd said to her in the desert.

"I'm decent." She stepped out.

Brennan continued eating, making quick work of a heaping plate, but the table was...

There had been enough food for a small army, but there was enough just for her now. She hid a smile and sat.

He glanced from his empty plate up to her. "What?"

She picked some of everything for her own plate. "Nothing."

He leaned back in his chair and crossed his arms, eyeing her with a crooked smile. "Clearly it's something."

Ever since his first Change, he'd eaten like a... Well, like a wolf. But it had been so long since she'd sat down to an intimate meal with him and actually watched him. She took a sip of her mint tea. "I'd forgotten how much you eat."

He huffed a breath, his hazel eyes gleaming. "Watching my figure?" He held her gaze.

Her face warmed, and a shiver shook through her frame. He was attractive and he knew it. Half the women in Emaurria knew it. She did, too, especially after their night at House Hazael.

But this wasn't about that. She lowered her eyes and drank her tea silently.

"You care about me," he said, his voice low.

Gulping, she tried not to choke on the tea and set it down while it trailed down her chin. Of course.

An amused smile was his reply.

Of course she cared, but it was even more than that... It was—

There was a knock on the door, and she heaved a sigh. Thank the Divine. She grabbed for a napkin and blotted her chest.

"Enter," Brennan called, not taking his eyes off her. No small favors, then.

A serving boy shuffled in and handed him a small folded note. Brennan paid him, and the boy left.

Brennan opened it and read. "Well, can you make it through tonight without resonance?"

She nodded. "What does it say?"

He handed it to her. "That there will be a mage aboard. The captain. And the quartermaster has made it clear that the captain would be happy to oblige a beautiful mage needing resonance."

She raised an eyebrow at him, her cheeks afire. "What exactly did you promise him?!"

He chuckled. "Definitely not *that*."

Scoffing, she read the note herself. "Why does it say 'beautiful'?"

He shrugged. "I might have said 'my beautiful wife requires resonance.' Or something." He shrugged again and looked away.

*Wife.* He'd presented them as a married couple... all too close to their lengthy history together. Had things gone a little differently, today they would have been married for seven years.

But who would her husband have been? The sweet boy she'd once fallen in love with? The vengeful spurned lover of just months ago? Or the mature man before her now?

And after all the lies and deception, could this newfound maturity of his—such as it was—even be trusted?

*He died for me.* His sacrifice had ended the confusion. Completely. No, she could harbor no more doubts. If he wanted to ensure his survival by breaking the curse, getting himself killed did not achieve that. Not unless he'd known he'd reawaken.

She held in a breath. Had he? Could he have known?

"What is it?" He leaned in.

"Just wondering what to do with this new you."

A mischievous smile tugged at his mouth. "Love me."

*Mature.* "Idiot."

He leaned back in his chair and threaded his fingers together behind his head. "What's there to do? I was a complete asshole, for which I can never sufficiently apologize, but I realized why. And how stupid I was. And I want to make amends." All traces of mischief had vanished.

"That simple?"

"That simple."

*Never sufficiently apologize.* Indeed, his coldness since she'd joined the Divinity would have been forgivable, if not for that exercise in malice that was Midwinter at Tregarde three years ago. And the constant threat and violence with which he'd treated her since. There were acts that words could never excuse. And a Marcel did not apologize.

She turned to her lamb, prune, and almond tagine and ate quietly. "You haven't, you know."

As he cleared his plate, he raised a brow and swallowed. He swabbed his mouth with a napkin. "Haven't...?"

"Apologized."

An intense glare speared her, but in the stillness, that intensity slowly abandoned his face. A quiet clinking, and he looked at her hand. The fork in it hit the plate as she shook. He inhaled a contemplative breath.

She set down the fork.

He shot up from his chair and rounded the table, took her hand, and knelt. Softly, he caressed her knuckles, her fingers, and brought her palm to the side of his face, where he kissed it gingerly. Her mind went blank, and ethereal fingers curled around her nape, coaxing a shiver.

"I know I have no right to ask your forgiveness, so I won't... but I *am* sorry." He lowered her hand and held it gently. "If I could take it all back, I would."

A Marcel did not apologize. "You're not just sorry because you want the curse broken?"

He shook his head and sighed. "I don't even care about the curse breaking anymore."

And grapes had grown on the willows. She eyed him warily. Words were easy, and this didn't make up for that public humiliation at Tregarde. She wasn't sure what ever would. But if he'd had a change of heart, truly changed, she wouldn't ignore that either. "This really isn't some sort of ploy?"

"I understand if you don't believe me. But I'm taking you home to Jon. And I'm going to back off. Give you all the space and distance you want from me." His hazel eyes were soft, sincere. Rare. "I won't interfere. Not unless you wish it."

Wish it? Her? She straightened in her chair. "Well, I won't."

"That's fine." He rose and looked toward the bed. "Come on. We have an early start tomorrow."

She nodded and made her way to the other side of the bed. Across its vast expanse, he stood and watched her, just as she watched him. An ache took form inside her, shifted in an imperfect vessel. It didn't belong. This look shared between them was a lost future, a forgotten dream where this was normal.

Lost. Forgotten.

"I am not sleeping on the floor." He anchored a hand on his hip. "So don't even ask."

Shaking her head, she climbed into bed. "Nothing untoward."

"I didn't offer, did I?" He blew out the lamp and then joined her.

"I'm just making that clear." She wriggled closer but slammed her arm down between them.

He scoffed. "The arm barrier is clear. Crystal clear."

"Shut up," she whispered, and yawned.

"You first." A smile laced his voice.

Brennan was sorry... *and* didn't care about the curse breaking?

Blinking sluggishly, she snuggled against the pillow and faced the window, catching a glimpse of the starry sky.

She'd been gullible before and believed ludicrous words, believed them because they had fallen from Brennan Karandis Marcel's coveted lips, and the price for that gullibility had been hard, brutal, cold. A lesson. And it had smarted.

His words were as ludicrous now—more so—but the lesson's smarting had faded. Just a little bit. Despite the hardness, the brutality, the coldness before, she wanted to believe these words now. She wanted to believe them because they fell from Brennan Karandis Marcel's...

# CHAPTER 40

By the light of a Gaze crystal, Leigh recorded the last bits of oral history he'd learned of the dragons. He paused only to knot his long hair at his nape and sip the tisane of blackthorn, hawthorn, and mountain ash the light-elves so favored. It was magnificent, if one enjoyed bitterly astringent notes too far removed to be called *flavors*. Personally, he'd have much preferred using the blackthorn sloes to make gin.

Ah, gin. And wine. Necessities so ubiquitous everywhere so as to be considered expected—that is, not *considered* at all—but the light-elves defied expectation. Tragically.

He dipped his quill in the inkwell. The dragons had once been the dominant civilization and had welcomed all to their cities, great centers of learning. Visitors stayed in towers—towers he, and the Divinity, knew all too well. The dragons' seat of power, Khar'shil, was destroyed by the ancient wild mages after betraying the last dragon king, Nyeris, and binding him to a bell, of all things. Bound, to be summoned with purpose and banished as desired by the keepers of the Bell of Khar'shil, he could be called to appear at Veris, a magical time of equal day and night.

Bound... Summoned... Resurrected. Dark, dark sangremancy.

Leigh removed his spectacles and leaned back in his branches—tree-sung seat—whatever.

Once upon a time, before he'd opened the never-ending box of dreams and horrors, the assertion of resurrection would have been ludicrous. But the ludicrous had become real, and if any impossibilities yet existed—or did *not* exist... he could never decide on the semantics—he would never again be so foolish as to name them.

This secret knowledge of the light-elves could not be made public, and if any tomes yet existed containing it, better they remain forgotten and undiscovered. Any fool who might have rung the Bell of Khar'shil with the right ingredients and ritual could have unleashed an ancient power—if not for the Sundering. But now, with the Rift, it could be done... with the power of this page.

He shook his head. It seemed as though the world had expanded, but it had always been there, vast, only shrouded. The Rift had torn open that shroud, revealed the vastness for all to see. Peoples who wanted survival and peace, or death and war. Alliances or feuds.

The Rift had torn open that shroud.

No... *He* had.

Footsteps plodded behind him. Metallic. Armored. Paladin.

"Ambassador." Sir Marin paused before him and lowered all that bulk he called a chest into a bow. "Word from Trèstellan." He held out a small missive in the rolling plain of his palm.

Leigh accepted it. "Thanks."

Sir Marin nodded, the slightest crease on his middle-aged brow betraying his worry.

With good reason. This one piece of paper could mean war for the entire kingdom.

As Sir Marin left the hollow, Leigh tore open the missive. He quickly read through the pages of finely sloped script—Jon's.

No hot-headed rush to battle. Naturally.

It was the light-elves who had begun to treat in bad faith, withholding the true state of their security. Or lack thereof.

In exchange for the elven oath ritual, Jon wanted an emissary sent to court to advise about the Earthbinding. Favorable terms... for the Emaurrians.

Ingenious, really. The demand that Jon participate in an oath ritual —rather than be taken at his word to remain a loyal ally—might have translated to a perception of Emaurria in a weakened position. Or so the posturing would have indicated.

But Jon—or his Council—had correctly read the martial situation as desperate. Emaurria had options in choosing an alliance, but the light-elves faced imminent annihilation. Disparate stakes.

And yet the offer was fair. The Emaurrians and the light-elves remained united in defending against the Immortal beasts preying upon the populace. And with the light-elves holding the requisite knowledge about the Earthbinding and the Immortals, those bargaining chips remained to compel Emaurria to assist in defeating the dark-elves. This alliance would be the best thing for both parties.

Jon had once been a paladin. Certainly he'd not let innocents simply die. Paladins had a poor stomach for injustice.

And finally: *Once diplomatic options with the dark-elves have been exhausted, Emaurria shall openly commit to an entente to act with the full force of our military should the dark-elf queendom known as Stonehaven commit an act of war upon either Vervewood or Emaurria.*

Pages with diplomatic parameters. Leigh memorized them and then burned them.

He was to treat with the dark-elves.

Ambriel would not be pleased, but Emaurria needed the truth of the matter directly.

Leigh sighed. And Jon trusted him to learn that truth from the queen of Stonehaven.

"Guard," he called. There was always at least one paladin posted at the entrance to his hollow.

Sir Marin strode back in. "Ambassador?"

"Would you be so kind as to ask after the captain for me? It seems we have some pressing matters to attend to."

"My orders are to guard you, sir."

Naturally. Stick in the mud. Or, in Sir Marin's case, *branch* in the mud. *Trunk* in the mud. Divine's tits—*tree* in the mud.

"Very well." Leigh rose, pulled his hair free of the knot, and left his spectacles upon the table. "Then guard me as I call on the captain."

"Yes, sir."

He strode past Sir Marin and made his way to Ambriel's tree hollow. It was time to draft a message to the prickly queen of the Stonehaven dark-elves...

And determine whether Emaurria would take peace by quill or by blade.

~

WATCHFUL THROUGH EARTHSIGHT, Leigh waited in the frosty clearing beneath the waning moon's light, surrounded by a squad of paladins. Nearby, Sir Marin peered into the darkness like a wary hound. Well, in his case, mastiff.

As the wind blew by, the fur of Leigh's hood tickled his cheek. In this third month of Ventos, the sensible wind would have merely breezed by, teasing the grasses like a bard among maidens at a wedding. But the sensible wind, it seemed, had extended its holiday in the sensible world of yesteryear, along with the grasses and the thaw.

He kicked up a bit of hardened snow. Patience had never been one of his strong suits. And these dark-elves—making him wait—tried his very thin iteration of that suit.

*It's a massive risk to go*, Ambriel had said after the dark-elf queen had replied favorably. *Dangerous.*

He'd be meeting with the queen's Quorum—her inner circle of warriors. Dark-elf queens came from the Quorum, challenged sitting queens who fell short of their duties. Single combat. Only one of the Quorum or another ruler could issue the challenge.

If the queen was fierce, her Quorum were just as intimidating.

*I inhale risk and exhale danger*, Leigh had replied as he'd left with his paladin guards. It had been the correct answer, honest and unquestionably suave, but the look in Ambriel's eyes as he'd departed had been... mournful.

The light-elves faced constant threat from the dark-elves, that much was certain, but how many of the dark-elves were there? In a war, how many Emaurrians and light-elves would die? Could the losses be avoided with some diplomacy?

If there was risk, someone had to take it. Even if it didn't end with peace, he would at least have some reconnaissance to share with Cour-deval—and Ambriel.

Besides, as Jon had written, the kingdom couldn't go to war without first *attempting* peace.

Even if Ambriel had considered it a suicide mission, there'd been no other option but to go. At least one man.

And yet, here he stood, surrounded by paladins.

"I don't understand it," Leigh murmured in Sir Marin's general direction. "You really didn't have to come along."

Sir Marin grunted but didn't divert from his stare into the dark. "And you didn't have to save those innocents."

The light-elves in the attack? "It was the right thing to do."

Sir Marin's eyes half-mooned in what passed for a smile. "Then you do understand, Ambassador."

Ah, paladins. Sir Marin was here for far greater reasons than Jon's orders or—a half-laugh escaped him—the Order's orders. These paladins were here for right.

Leigh swept off his hood, tossed his hair. They may have stood common ground, yes, but he would do so *in style*.

A dozen forms closed in, bright figures of luminescent anima in the darkness of the forest. Careful. Predictable. They wouldn't arrive without scouting the surrounding area for light-elves.

And they wouldn't want to meet in an open area that could be attacked.

It seemed he and the paladins were to go on a trip.

"Do not fight unless they draw first blood," Leigh hissed to the paladins. "We're about to be ambushed."

While the paladins stiffened, Leigh dispelled his earthsight. They couldn't risk all-out war because of some jitters among a small group.

Several lithe forms materialized from the brush, clad in black leather armor from head to foot. In the slit of shadow between hood and mask, only the hint of honey-hued eyes reflected the moonlight.

The paladins didn't move.

One figure took a few wary steps forward, a shallow, white-hot scar slashed across her lavender nose. "Ambassador?" A harsh, thickly accented voice, undoubtedly feminine. And speaking Emaurrian. Surprising.

Leigh inclined his head.

Those honey-hued eyes narrowed nearly to disappearance. "I... Captain Varvara." She traced from her belly to her mouth with a black-gloved hand. "All you... and we."

He nodded, and she mirrored his gesture, then motioned to her squad. They advanced, withdrawing black shrouds.

"Ambassador—" Sir Marin began.

"Do not resist," he answered, as Captain Varvara herself shrouded him. He sucked in a sharp breath, but it tasted—

He frowned, taking a step forward only to stagger and knock into the dark-elf bracing him.

There was a musty sort of—

*Divine's tits.* He swayed, the blackness of the shroud becoming his own.

# CHAPTER 41

*A*rms crossed, Olivia stood in Jon's study, waiting for something to happen. They'd been practicing force magic since lunch, with nothing to show for it. That seemed to be the way of things for her lately, given the investigation about the courier. But she'd be damned if she failed to teach Jon a repulsion shield.

The Faralles' magic learning had been her responsibility; Jon's magical ability was her responsibility. At the very least, he had to learn how to defend himself.

Jon repeated the repulsion-shield gesture, his fingers out, spread properly, but nothing happened. Growling under his breath, he loosened the collar of his deepest-blue doublet, then raked his fingers through his hair.

In moments like these, he reminded her so much of James, and afternoons they'd spent debating legislation, the kingdom's latest hot topics, and sharing their ideas. His determination, his intensity.

He tried again, to no effect.

She opened her mouth, but he clasped his hands behind his back and strode past her to the window, his lips pressed in a firm line, as if they held back an invasion of frustrated words.

Slowly, she approached him and paused next to him, looking out at the snow-covered roofs of Courdeval.

"This isn't working, Olivia. I'm just not cut out to be a mage."

"That's not true," she replied. "You've managed some magic before, such as—" Such as in the solar, when the spiritualist had told him about Rielle. She cleared her throat. "I have faith in you, but... you have to focus."

He glared at her. "I *am* focusing."

"No, you're not. And no amount of glaring is going to change the truth."

He held her gaze for a searing moment, then sighed and looked back out at the city. "Tell me again."

About focus. He'd asked her several times, and she'd always obliged. "Magic doesn't come from your hands, but the rune you map with a gesture. Casting spells requires focus... threading your anima into a shape, into words. With shapes, you can draw a rune physically, or you can visualize it and map it with your hands. A repulsion shield's rune has five points that diverge from a center... and you map it by spreading your fingertips. Are you visualizing it?"

"Yes," he grunted.

"No, you're not. You're too busy thinking about other things."

He eyed her peripherally, but his lips resumed their firm guard.

"Once you've learned the spell, you can train yourself to cast even despite distractions—improving your focus—but as a novice, you'll never learn unless you clear your mind." She didn't have to ask to know what his thoughts were. His mind was wandering, and she couldn't blame him. His life had been upended; how could he *not* think about that constantly?

It had only been a few days since the news of Rielle, and he'd... taken a new lover. And just this morning, he'd met with every suitress to kindly inform them he was formally courting Princess Alessandra Ermacora of Silen.

She'd seen him with the princess, walking the courtyard together, arm in arm, and riding horses on the palace grounds. She'd seen the jeweler, the florist, the pâtissier, and the chocolatier leaving Jon's quarters, as he'd selected gifts to send her. With everything else on his mind, he was now entangled in a courtship—additional stress.

"You don't have to push yourself so hard, Jon. If you need time, take it. The other Grands and I can handle the extra work, and marriage will still be there when you're ready."

His eyes closed as he exhaled lengthily, then bowed his head. "Can you do the oath ritual for me?" he demanded, barely audible. "Can you meet with Parliament for me? With the Grands? Can you marry for me? Continue my father's line for me?"

She swallowed and looked away.

"You can't," he said, straightening and breathing deeply. "Tor wanted me to grieve... take the time. But he also once taught me that a blade cannot be wielded by two masters. If I allow grief to rule me, duty won't. And I don't... have the luxury of indulging it, not for longer than I have already, nor even *as* long as I have."

As he watched the city, there was a certain vitality missing from his Bay of Amar eyes, a spark she'd seen in James's gaze. Hunger for the future. For life. They had turned cold somehow.

This wasn't a life anymore. This was survival until he could accomplish what duties he felt beholden to fulfill.

"Nothing has ever hit me this hard, but I have to fall back on my training," he said. "Losses will occur, but whatever you feel, you must complete the mission."

Setting aside his feelings? Like what he was doing with Nora? It didn't have to be that way. "But this—whatever this is, with Nora, isn't it—"

"Not up for discussion." Tight-lipped, he scowled at her.

"Jon—"

He stalked away from the window and toward the bedchamber. "Magic lesson's over for today. That'll be all, Olivia."

She followed. The drapes were wide open, had been for days; at least what he was doing had brought him out of darkness, but he didn't need to debase himself. "I'm not just the Archmage, Jon. I'm your friend. Talk to me."

He grabbed his sword from a nearby table, along with a small kit, and dropped into an armchair by the fire.

"Ever since Spiritseve," he said, removing a whetstone, "when I go to bed, I keep thinking about all the things I could have done differently. *Should* have done differently." He began the slow scrape of stone against metal. "And since the... news, it's only gotten worse. I can't sleep, I can't rest, can't function. I count the stars at night just to get a couple hours' sleep. It's eating me alive." The slow, methodical scrape went uninterrupted. "I know you don't approve, but when I'm with Nora, everything else gets shut out. For a few hours, I can just be... empty. I can survive." He looked over his shoulder at her with those cold eyes. "Is that what you wanted to talk about?"

Her heart sank. "But maybe if we just talked about those things you wished you'd done differently—"

Another scrape. "Talking about it won't change that I didn't go after her. There's no point."

"Changing things isn't the point," she said, heading closer to the fire. "Talking about it might alleviate your burden."

"It hasn't in four months."

When she moved to sit, he froze, sword and whetstone in hand. She remained standing. "Are you angry with me?"

He looked into the fire. "All of this would be easier if you stopped insisting I fight what must be."

Easier? Her mouth fell open. Did he honestly believe that making a mistake meant his happiness had no more value? His dignity? His well-being? "You'd like that, wouldn't you? To throw yourself down an endless hole, punish yourself, with no one extending an arm to save you?" she shouted at him. "To let yourself be dirt because it's easier and it's only two or three more years, right? Right? You'd love that, wouldn't you? Wouldn't you?"

"I'll keep practicing, Olivia," he said quietly, his voice a low, lifeless monotone. "I'll work on clearing my mind. Tomorrow will be different."

He wouldn't even engage her about it anymore. "Someday, you're going to look back on this and wish you'd taken the time. Wish you hadn't dishonored her memory. And you'll remember this conversation, and how I tried to tell you."

He didn't reply, and she stormed out of his quarters and into the hall. Never in her life had she screamed at King Marcus. Never. But here she was, acting like an angry sister with Jon.

This was unprofessional of her, and if he so chose, he could dismiss her over it.

Maybe it was his love for Rielle, or maybe the moments she'd seen James in him, but she couldn't stand by and let him destroy himself, all just to be some shell of a king, even if he *was* dying. *Especially* because he was dying. Wasting a few months or a year was terrible but not disastrous when there were decades more. But for him? These would be the last years of his life, and he'd spend them already dead.

The kingdom didn't just need a blade to wield; it needed a righteous, honorable, good man to lead them. A well man—emotionally. And Jon wasn't well. *That* was where his duty lay—in becoming well again, to go on and to lead his kingdom. Not in going through the motions, suppressing everything just to *complete the mission*. Down that road was the complete loss of his self and his will to live.

And as much as he didn't want her to, she'd find some way to save him before it was too late—not just his emotional wellbeing, but his heart. His *life*.

Jon sluggishly blinked his eyes open, squinting at the predawn light—no help at all to his pounding headache. He wanted to rub his forehead—but his arm was trapped under a head full of long, dark hair, wisps sprawled over her bare skin.

A fire crackled in the hearth, dying but still in its throes. Smoke puffed, and above it, Rielle smiled coyly.

"That's her, isn't it?" Nora's soft voice rasped. She squeezed his hand, intertwined her fingers more tightly with his. "The Marquise of Laurentine. Looks like her."

"It is." He didn't look away from the portrait.

A fingertip softly stroked his knuckle. "Rumor says you loved her."

"I do." He met Rielle's eyes in the portrait. *Love me at your peril.*

"Why isn't she here?" she whispered.

He tensed. "Because she died," he said under his breath at last.

Nora rested her head on his shoulder. "I'm sorry." She rubbed his chest softly with her bronze-skinned hand, a shade darker than his. "I can see it troubles you... Perhaps you should have the portrait removed."

Removed?

Remove her... He swallowed. That was what he was doing now. Removing her... from his heart.

That wasn't what he wanted. This hollowness, this numbness, kept him functional, but what did that mean, when the person responsible for her death still walked the earth? Whoever had hired Gilles.

Rielle was gone, but she needed justice. And he needed it, too. More than anything.

When Brennan returned, he'd return with answers. The circumstances of her death, perhaps a name, something to help bring her killers to justice.

Those piercing sky-blue eyes of hers pinned him. *What are you doing for me, Jon? Leaving me to rot while you console yourself with a new lover?*

A pressure formed in his chest as he met those eyes that saw right through him, their disappointment, their judgment.

The knights and paladins searching for her were never going to find her, and he hadn't done a thing more for her sake. Nothing.

*Did you ever even love me, Jon?* Her voice ghosted in his head.

He couldn't just sit on his hands. She deserved more. So much more.

It was time to revive Olivia's investigation.

"Will you marry Alessandra?" Nora traced a heart on his chest.

Marriage was inevitable, and he was responsible for the stability of the kingdom, with only a couple years to secure it, and Alessandra was intelligent, well bred, shrewd, bold. A fine partner for any man who wanted one. "If she'll have me."

He extricated himself from bed and stretched as the first pink rays of the dawn filtered through the curtains.

Nora chuckled behind him. "If she won't, she's a fool."

Nice of her to say, but it wasn't true. He didn't have much to offer any of the suitresses, not really. They were here out of obligation, just like he was.

Outside the windows, the snowy rooftops stretched far, to the bay, a land frozen in winter, in time, with no thaw in sight. He rubbed his chest.

In a little less than two weeks, he'd have to swear a ritualized vow not to betray a peaceful civilization.

The world had come to this—his honor and goodness suspect, doubted, but for a rite. Vervewood didn't know him, didn't know his reputation, the rigidity of his honor, but... Neither did he. No longer. The Code of the Paladin that had defined his role then could never hope to keep a kingdom safe and peaceful now. Whoever he was now, the paladin he'd once been no longer spoke for him. He couldn't.

Everything in him wanted to cling to the Code, its righteousness and familiarity, but that was selfishness.

Continuing the investigation—eliciting answers by whatever means necessary—was the right course of action now, while he was still alive to see it done. No matter how dishonorable it would soon become.

JON STRODE to the Royal Warden's office with his guards and Eloi, Olivia trotting alongside him.

"Don't do this!" She grabbed his arm, but he brushed her off. Servants walked by without a second glance.

Prisoners had been sitting in the dungeon for months, and to what result? One dead end after another? If the Order couldn't find answers its way and Olivia couldn't find answers her way, then it came to him to do what needed to be done. To seize justice for the kingdom, his parents, and Rielle.

"The paladins won't agree to this!" she hissed. "Torture?"

He huffed. "We're not so benevolent as you imagine. We're practical." Paladins can and did torture criminals in the field, when their guilt was certain and their information could save lives.

"Not on this scale. Not so... severe."

Indeed, the mass torture of untried prisoners—physical, psychological, emotional—was anathema to the Order of Terra. And repugnant to him. But needed. Not only for Rielle's justice, but the kingdom—he couldn't leave a queen and an heir behind while his family's murderer remained at large. He needed to assure their safety and survival as best he could before it would be... too late for him to do anything anymore. "It's not up to them. I am thankful for the Order's assistance"—Raoul and Florian behind him performed their duties honorably—"but this is still my kingdom. And my dungeon."

She leaped in front of him, her face contorted in a snarling frown. "They tortured *your father!*"

He stopped. His mouth hung open, but he quickly shut it. "Yes, they did. And he gave me up, didn't he?"

Olivia raised a hand, but immediately curled it into a fist and lowered it. "How dare you—"

"That's how Gilles figured out who I was, right? Why paladins around my age were assassinated on the roads?"

The Duchess of Melain had passed on that news last autumn, when he and Rielle had been staying at Melain. It hadn't made sense at the time, but it did now.

Olivia gaped at him, the tightness abandoning her face, and she averted her gaze. "He... He wouldn't..."

"How did they manage that, I wonder?" He eyed her, how her shoulders curled inward, and—his father hadn't been the only prisoner Gilles had kept. His father's lover stood before him, and a man like Gilles wasn't stupid enough for coincidence. "Better to give me up and save you right then and there, right? I could take care of myself. Better than you could, locked up in arcanir in the dungeon, at Gilles' mercy." That was the least cruel explanation he had.

He couldn't blame his father for it. Choosing between the well-being of his lover, locked and helpless in a dungeon, or the identity of his son, a presumably capable paladin far away? If put in the same position, he might have chosen the same.

When Olivia met his eyes, her own were big and overbright. She pressed her lips together.

Yes, his father had loved her. Dearly. But his confession proved her wrong about this plan. Jon proceeded around her down the corridor.

"Jon," she called. "Are you going to be... just like Gilles?"

Gilles? He was nothing like Gilles.

Gilles had tortured and killed for profit, for personal gain. He'd used torture and death for nefarious purposes; yet, to fight without those weapons was to fight with an arm behind one's back.

*I can't do that anymore.* The Order's idealistic means were their own ends, but he needed to capture a murderer. A traitor. And he was running out of time. He didn't need honor; he needed victory. Justice. The traitor's head. Maybe then—

Maybe then... "I am going to take justice for this kingdom. I am going to punish the one responsible for all of this." *And be the king Emaurria needs, even if it means abandoning everything I believe in. Duty is sacrifice.* Without waiting for her reply, he continued down the corridor.

The Royal Warden was in his office, sitting at his mahogany desk, and upon Jon's entry, rose. He bowed from the waist as Raoul and Florian took up posts at the door. "Your Majesty."

His name was Gustave Alis, a silver-haired former guard captain from Aestrie who still clung to armors of formality and duty. Tor had recruited and hired him, praising the man's discretion and perfectionism. Gods willing, he'd been correct in his assessment of the man.

"Good morning, Lord Warden." Jon cocked his head to Eloi, who handed over documents.

Gustave looked them over. "This is..."

"A full pardon." He sat at the desk and motioned for Gustave to join, which he did. "I want there to be no misunderstandings about the importance of this matter, so I am here to personally deliver it."

"A pardon for"—Gustave fixed gray eyes on the documents—" 'any and all crimes committed under Emaurrian law in the pursuit of evidence, whether actionable or not, regarding the principal who retained the services of the Crag Company, by which the regicide of...' "

"Yes." Jon ran his fingers over the armrest of the chair—a serpent's face. "Carte blanche to solve one of the worst crimes in our history."

Gustave met his eyes with utter calm. "My guards include paladins."

"You will also find there orders transferring all paladins from jail guard duty, as well as permission to request any new guards as are required from Guard-Captain Corriveau, and blank requisition orders signed by me."

Gustave rubbed his bristly chin, shuffling through the papers. He nodded. "As you wish, Your Majesty."

Jon stood, and Gustave mirrored. "You will report daily, directly to me. Your authority is unfettered where these prisoners are concerned, with exception to efficacy, as judged by me. Do not fail."

Gustave bowed. "You can trust me, Your Majesty."

"I will await your report tomorrow afternoon." With that, he left the Royal Warden's office and headed for his lessons with his Camarilla and history tutors and dance instructor. A ridiculous way to spend the rest of the day, but the Grands insisted. Perhaps if they knew those lessons were a waste?

He sighed.

Here, Olivia's wariness was well received; torture made no distinction between the innocent and the guilty. As a paladin, he could have never contemplated such a thing, not unless he was personally certain of the prisoner's guilt, and even then—

He shuddered.

But his personal preferences could not control his rule. He could not ignore the needs of a country for the sake of his own concepts of honor and goodness. A king's soul darkened to keep his kingdom in light. And that was his only role now, all that mattered.

He would get justice for his kingdom, his family, and Rielle, even if he had to cut through flesh and bone to do it.

# CHAPTER 42

The early dawn set fire to the turquoise coastal waters of Gazgan. On horseback, Rielle shielded her eyes, squinting as she looked out at the many single-masted dhows lining the docks, the few caravels, and a large square-rigged three-masted ship with a fore-castle and aftcastle outfitted with cannons. No fewer than two dozen gunports figured along the upper deck, wider than the weather deck—an extreme sloping tumblehome design for peerless hardiness—with heavier guns on the lower deck. It outclassed anything she'd ever seen built in Laurentine's shipyards.

It had to be a frigate. Silen had begun building such ships years ago, but she'd only seen a couple herself. Designed for escort, they protected wealth-laden prizes. They were second in size only to the new ships of the line, whose firepower dwarfed that of the frigate, sacrificing maneuverability. But only a couple had been built, far away in Pryndon, last she'd heard from Hugues Naudé, Laurentine's steward.

Brennan's lips parted. "Incredible."

"So which one's the *Liberté?*"

Grinning, he tipped his head toward the frigate.

Her mouth fell open. *That?* They were sailing on that monster? "Is there a war that I'm not aware of?"

He huffed an amused laugh. That sound... It made her smile.

She frowned. Strange. She'd always loved it as a child but, in her nine years at the Tower, had come to rue it, as it had often trailed after comments at her expense. But now, it had whispered its way back into her good graces. She narrowed a critical eye at him as they reached the *Liberté*.

He flinched. "Are you going to tell me why you're giving me the evil eye?"

"It's not the evil eye!" She pursed her lips while he shook his head. "And anyway, how did you know? You didn't even look this way."

He grinned crookedly. "Your usual *perfect* stealth amazingly faltered."

Poking fun at her? She dismounted, and he removed their packs.

"I can feel when you look at me," he said as he set them down.

Her feet stopped. He could... *feel* when she looked at him? She pulled the halla lower over her brow. Could he always feel it, then? Whenever she looked at him?

He leaned in and raised her chin, his hazel eyes unabashed. "Every. Single. Time."

She looked away, straining against his hold until he let her go with a deep sigh. Did he mean to make her so uneasy?

The sun brightened in the sky, its fiery hues slowly golding.

He handed off their camels to a merchant and then talked to the *Liberté's* quartermaster, a black-haired rakish man, no older than his mid-thirties. By his angular face and stiff carriage, a Pryndonian.

Relishing the cool breeze, she closed her eyes and breathed in the salt air, the smell of fish, wood, and oil. It smelled like home, lacking only the freshness of the coastal grass or the effervescence of wintry air. Laurentine was a seaside march, its castle looking out over the endless turquoise waves of the Shining Sea, and every morning had been a brilliant blue, bright and hopeful, refreshing. Being near the water had always reminded her of Papa and Mama.

He took her hand, and she jumped. His hold was warm, firm but not tight, just enough to feel secure. He'd always had a quiet confidence about him, and as a girl, she'd never doubted his ability to protect himself, his family, or her.

She hadn't needed that, not since her éveil, but the thought was still a comfort.

His breath warmed her ear. "Married couple, remember?"

A shiver shook her, and her skin contracted with gooseflesh. All this nearness and familiarity was too much, a dangerous habit to get into, but yes, how could she forget their convenient disguise? She nodded, and they boarded the ship.

Laurentine had made a fortune in shipping, shipbuilding, and fishing, and she'd been around ships all her life, but the *Liberté*'s size and grandeur belittled any she'd ever seen. Wide-eyed, she craned her neck to look at the top of the mainmast, then glanced from bow to stern. It had to be over one hundred feet long—maybe one hundred and forty, with a fifteen-foot draft.

A young sailor wearing an eye patch showed them to the lower deck, the berth deck where the crew slept, and directed them to an empty area where two crewmen secured a hammock and blanket and deposited their packs next to a bolted-down chest. After thanking them, Brennan stowed their belongings in the chest, locked it, and pocketed the key.

The young sailor—no, the boy—couldn't be older than seventeen; he had long, dark hair tied in a long tail, and stood just smaller than her own five feet ten inches. How had he lost his eye? Had there been no healer?

"Once we set sail, Captain said to stop by his cabin." The boy threw his head back, throwing a wisp of hair off his eye patch.

She'd been staring. Her chest fell. "I'm sorry," she whispered.

The boy shook his head and offered her a smile. "It's all right. Lost the eye in a knife fight on the streets of Zehar when I was nine. I'm used to it by now."

Her mouth dropped open. Knife fighting at nine?

He straightened. "If it earns me a second look from a pretty woman, it's not all bad." He gave her a wink. "Not often we have a woman aboard... Usually, it's just us and the mermaids. I'm Zero. What's your name?"

Brennan huffed a half-laugh. "Out of your league," he murmured, with a glimmer of amusement in his eyes.

Grinning, Zero raised his hands, inclined his head, and nodded to Brennan, whose eyebrows peaked; then he took his leave.

"Brazen boy." Brennan rested a hand on their hammock and tested its stability. "I like him."

She smiled. "Me, too."

He patted the hammock. "Well, shall we test it further?"

With a swift swat at his arm, she clenched her teeth. "Could you please just"—she hissed—"behave?"

He gave her a blank look. "I meant lie down for a bit."

She shook her head, planted her right leg in the hammock and spun into it onto her back.

All of this familiarity and proximity played tricks on her. It had been years since she and Brennan had fooled around—to catastrophic effect—and that night in House Hazael had made touching him, kissing him... feel like it had all happened yesterday.

Did time heal all wounds? Was that it?

Some part of her had opened to him, welcomed him, despite their history. Not fully, but had she forgiven him?

It was all happening far too fast. Far too much at once. She needed to go up to the weather deck, take in the fresh air, the sea, the sun, and the sky. Reacquaint herself with the beauty that was so reminiscent of home.

Brennan rested a hand on her knee. "So do you want to rest or go watch as we disembark? I know you didn't sleep well last night, but then again, I know there is little you love so well as the sea."

"You know me too well."

"We've known each other a long time. The window from your bedchamber in Laurentine overlooked the Shining Sea." He squeezed her knee. "Come on. I can tell you're in no mood to rest."

Indeed, she wasn't. No part of her would rest comfortably here. She needed to be back in Courdeval. With Jon.

Brennan had come all the way to Sonbahar to find her, had died for her, and she would be forever grateful—but falling into old delusions of feelings long destroyed would be a mistake, for a multitude of reasons.

She had to get far enough away from him to forget how handsome he was. And how good he smelled. How warm he felt... And to remember the ordeal that had been the last ten years of his wrath.

But when he offered her a hand, she took it, allowing him to help her out of the hammock. The crew bustled in the midst of various tasks, and Brennan led her around them and up onto the weather deck.

Main sails furled, sailors scrambled on every part of the ship. It teemed with activity. Brennan warmed her shoulder as he leaned against the railing next to her. Beyond the white sails, yellows and golds gave way to light cerulean in the skies, where not a single cloud dared intrude on the brightness. The sun had woken steadily and would soon beat down on them with all its might. But until then, the morning was cool, eased by the winds, and the turquoise waters of the Bay of Amar glimmered with gold.

Back on the Sonbaharan coast, Gazgan bid adieu with a wave of sandy-colored buildings and the dazzling golden domed roofs of the Temple of the Divine and the zahibshada's palace. Across the bay, tiny dhows bobbed on the sun-dappled waves, their lateen sails loosed as they sailed to deliver their cargo.

There was beauty in this land, beauty Sylvie would never see.

She crumpled, blinking heavily. No, time didn't heal all wounds. It couldn't.

*I will see you again someday, Sylvie.*

The city faded to nothing more than a small dot on the horizon.

Her hands shook, and she clutched the railing tighter. She looked inward. With her anima bright enough for only a few spells, she'd need the resonance the captain of this vessel had agreed to provide.

Captain...

*Captain Sincuore.* The name intruded, uninvited. She shivered. Her time aboard the *Siren* had been a bone-chilling mix of abuse and amnesia. And they both made her go rigid. She clenched a fist.

*A red stain.* She'd promised herself that day on the *Siren*. Someday, Captain Sincuore would be no more than a red stain. Just like Shadow, who'd suffer as Sylvie had suffered.

"What's on your mind?" Brennan didn't look over from where he leaned against the railing, his gaze fixed on something in the distance.

"My enemies."

A touch of wolfish amber gleamed in his dark eyes. "*Our* enemies."

She stiffened and faced him. "It's not your—"

"The moment they acted against you, it became my concern. And so shall it remain, until their blood goes cold." He flashed a rictus grin, predatory.

His intensity was unadulterated. Unstoppable. And his interest in her survival was undeniable. She nodded.

He straightened and offered her his arm. "Come. Let's go see the captain, as promised."

There was no other choice. Circumstances required a visit. She took his arm, and they headed toward the aftcastle cabin. Brennan raised his knuckles to knock, but then quickly shuffled her aside.

The door flew open, boots pounding onto the deck. The quarter-master strode across the quarterdeck to the main deck and down the hatchway.

She looked after him and leaned in toward Brennan's ear. "A disagreement?"

"Must be. That's the quartermaster—Sterling. But it doesn't concern us." After a moment's hesitation, Brennan led her into the open captain's cabin.

A well-muscled, six-foot-tall man stood silhouetted against the square-windowed quarter gallery, holding a bottle of wine. His long straw-blond hair was bound in a chaotic knot at the back of his head. Broad shoulders tapered to a lean physique clad in a gray cotton shirt, black waistcoat, black trousers, and knee-high leather boots. A rapier with an intricate swept hilt strapped to his belt and a dagger sheathed at his back, he looked every bit the warrior she expected to captain a ship like the *Liberté*.

He took a drink. "Stand there all day if you want, Sterling," he said in accented Pryndonian. Emaurrian accent. "We're going after that ship."

He thought his quartermaster had returned?

Brennan cleared his throat. "Captain Verib."

The captain turned, sighed, and set down his bottle. "Ah, the passengers Sterling took on." His voice was low, business like, and more refined than she had expected of a pirate hunter.

As he met her gaze, his face went slack and his light-blue eyes widened.

Sky-blue eyes... like an Amadour.

Like Mama.

"Rielle?"

Her heart stopped. "Liam?"

ON HIS KNEES, Leigh rattled the arcanir shackles. Arcanir. It always had to be arcanir. Why couldn't they be silver shackles? Gold shackles? Something shiny, fashionable, and not quite so... stinging.

With a sigh, he raised his eyes to the woman seated on the vast stone bench at the end of the great hall, a tomb of intricately carved blue-gray stone, geometric patterns angling in etchings.

The woman wore the same black leather armor from foot to—well, chin. Unlike Captain Varvara, this woman wore no black mask over her light-blue face nor hood over her head of gleaming short white hair. She spoke calm words with hard edges in a deep, self-assured voice.

Next to her stood a hooded and masked black shadow. "Queen Matryona... you... welcome."

A harsh, thickly accented feminine voice. Captain Varvara.

Sighing, he staggered to his feet as best he could in shackles. He cleared his throat and slowly raised his hands to his chest. "Thank you. I'm Leigh Galvan, Ambassador of—"

"*Leighgalvan,*" the queen repeated, narrowing her golden eyes. When she'd opened her mouth, she'd revealed her sharp, pointed fangs.

"No, Your Majesty." He shook his head. "Leigh. Galvan. Ambassador to His Majesty, King Jonathan Dominic Armel Faralle of Emaurria."

A soft half-laugh echoed down the hall. "*Matryona u Terezila u Nadeva u Vasilisa, Koroleva Kamenila Khevena, Okhotniza Glubinu, Pavi T'my.*"

His mouth dropped open, and another laugh—deeper, throatier— echoed. He straightened. "Leigh."

She waved a claw-tipped hand. "Matryona."

Well, progress was progress.

The queen murmured something to Varvara with a wild-eyed excitement. Even when she was calm, that same wild-eyed excitement menaced beneath the surface.

"What... you... things?" Varvara asked.

He frowned. They weren't going to make much progress in broken Emaurrian.

She motioned around the great hall. Stacked books, some bottles of wine, statues of well-built warriors.

He shook his head. How to explain what Emaurria desired? "Outside," he began, pointing up, "dragons. Wyverns."

Varvara didn't answer.

He tried again in Old Emaurrian.

"I understand," Varvara replied in Old Emaurrian.

A sigh of relief demanded exit, but he denied it. They understood each other, but this was still a negotiation. "We have dragons, wyverns, giants, and all manner of dangerous Immortals unleashed upon the land. Our king would acknowledge your territory and offer trade in exchange for joining forces against the beasts."

Varvara murmured to the queen, who quickly replied. "Our territory needs no acknowledgment. We do not need trade. And the beasts in the sky realm do not stalk our deep."

Fantastic. He needn't have bothered coming.

"We could, however, assist your king if he would assist us."

"What kind of assistance do you require?"

"We would take the light-elves prisoner."

Prisoner. They wished to imprison—enslave—the light-elves? The light-elves, who'd already shown him hospitality? Ambriel?

It was repugnant, and would be no less so to Jon himself. "Emaurria is a free kingdom, where slavery never has nor will exist."

Varvara translated.

A huff, then an expressionless face as the queen dictated her answer. "We are not Emaurrian," Varvara said. "The light-elves are our oldest enemies. They know there hasn't been a dark-elf child born since two centuries before the Sundering. The Deep has turned away from our offerings. And yet, they would selfishly keep the Gaze crystal to themselves while our people are destroyed. We shall not allow that. We must acquire the favor of the gods." Her deep, cold voice echoed across the stone hall.

Ridiculous. Prehistoric races waging wars for the favor of long-forgotten gods.

If they had a low birth rate, perhaps they suffered from a disease? "Our people practice advanced medicine. My king could send some of our physicians to diagnose the cause of the infertility." After Varvara translated, he added, "And I do not speak for the light-elves, but they have not attacked you. They do not desire war." *So stop fighting each other and rebuild your civilizations.*

As Varvara translated, the queen arched a brow. "They do not?" Varvara translated. "Then it is because they are weak, and ripe for conquest. This negotiation is over. Deliver your king's answer within three days."

Weak. Ripe for conquest. "No, that's not it at all—"

Varvara strode from her post at the stone bench and pushed him back.

"Wait." He stood his ground, despite her strong hands. "Your Majesty, surely you know by now that our king is Earthbound."

Varvara flinched, easing her hold on him, and translated. The queen paused for several breaths, then bit out a harsh answer. "This changes nothing," Varvara grumbled.

He stumbled and turned to face a massive doorway. She marched him out of the hall and down a sparsely lit corridor.

"That can't be all." He strode with Varvara toward—wherever they were going.

"It is." Her stony voice betrayed no more than her uncompromising bearing.

"So you want to keep fighting? Dying?"

Her gait didn't falter. "I will do as my queen commands."

"Even if the light-elves would agree to stop fighting? To establish peace? If our physicians could help your people?"

They moved through another doorway onto an elevated walkway. Above, a mauve glow radiated from... mushrooms? Below, blue- and purple-skinned dark-elves forged and sharpened weapons, some wearing little more than rags. The putrid stench of a tannery infiltrated his nostrils. What animals existed down here to skin? On second thought, he didn't want to think about it too much. "This is what you want for your people? Perpetual war?"

"It is very simple, mage." Varvara pushed him through another doorway. "There will never be peace. They have something we both require. We cannot both possess it."

"And is war and death better than going out into the world?" Ambriel had mentioned the gods' desire for the elves.

She puffed and looked away. "You lack understanding. Such a thing would end our people as surely as war and death. It is surrender. But we still choose to fight the end."

Then they truly believed they could win. Destroy the light-elves and steal the Gaze crystal to sustain their civilization. Or at least expect it to.

"And what about the people you imprison? They have families, friends, their own people. You feel no remorse?"

"Spoils of war." She shoved him through another doorway into a dark room. Utter obscurity, but she proceeded with a confident gait. "Before the End Curse, it was not we but our men who fought. Who took spoils of war. We watched. We learned. And we fight and take as they did." She moved away from him, footsteps receding. "A wolf does not take pity upon the hind."

He opened his mouth, then closed it. In the dark ages, women were taken as spoils of war—as wives, concubines, slaves. Some countries still allowed such practices. And this ancient race, wise for vastly many more generations before humans, did the same.

Footsteps neared.

He squared his shoulders. "It was wrong then, and it's wrong now. The only difference is that you have the power to right it."

"I do not. My queen does, and her decision is law."

And only a member of the queen's Quorum or another ruler could challenge her to single combat to the death... and potentially save Stonehaven. "You can disagree, can't you? For the sake of your people? Aren't you part of her Quorum?"

She ran a lavender-skinned finger along the scar across her nose, and her honey eyes met his, intensified, as if she were about to speak.

The musty shroud went over his head once more.

He fought the weakening, but his knees trembled and surrendered anyway as he slipped from reality.

$$\approx$$

LEIGH SQUINTED in the bright sunlight of the radiant dawn peeking through the ironwood trees. A silhouette shaded the brightness. Ambriel's head.

Back in Vervewood, then. "How long?"

"A few hours." Ambriel leaned forward. "They used a signal fire."

"Is everyone accounted for?"

"Yes. The dark-elves kept their word."

At least there was that. The party had been returned, and the dark-elves could keep their word. For better or for worse.

*I do not speak for the light-elves, but they have not attacked you. They do not desire war.* He fought the urge to palm his face. What idiocy had possessed him? Hope? Optimism?

*They do not? Then it is because they are weak, and ripe for conquest. This negotiation is over. Deliver your king's answer within three days.*

These people, these cultures, were foreign and mysterious. And he had no business negotiating diplomacy. He was a mage, not a diplomat. His skill lay in destruction, and he'd been tasked with securing peace?

*And yet, here we are.* Because only mages still used Old Emaurrian.

Queen Matryona would be waging her war—the only question was when. Her offer was unconscionable, but he had to write to Jon. "Pen, paper, and dove?"

Ambriel gestured to someone who departed quickly.

"Thank you." And he had the dubious honor of notifying Ambriel of the imminent danger facing his people. "You might want to prepare your defenses." When Ambriel drew his brows together, Leigh sighed. "Matryona has taken your tendency toward peace for weakness. She expressed an intention to capitalize on that."

Ambriel closed his eyes and exhaled slowly, lengthily. He did not deflate; it was not hope that escaped him. He blinked sluggishly. No, a sort of weariness. "We are already prepared. And we will send your king the Memory of Vervewood, our priestess Aiolian Windsong, as emissary."

He'd met Aiolian. Behind her stone-wall face sat two all-knowing ancient eyes. He shivered. There was an eerie quality to her, like being in a room with the moon or the stars. But colder, quieter, and more distant. Another shiver. "Very nice... I'm sure she'll stare him into submission."

Ambriel didn't waver. "You're going with her."

Folly! Sitting up, Leigh shook his head. "If I go with her, who's going to protect you from the dark-elves? This is ridiculous."

Ambriel straightened, his fair hair catching the sheen of morning. "We will stand on our own until you return. Your help has been greatly valued, but we will survive. Your king will learn we face imminent war with the dark-elves... and you are uniquely needed at his ear, to convince him our cause is worthy, as you have seen for yourself."

He had a point.

Aiolian's stony visage certainly wasn't going to win any sympathy. No, the situation called for someone who had been here, seen and heard all he'd needed to win Emaurrian hearts and minds. And he was it.

"Very well. I will go and return victorious. My king won't tolerate Queen Matryona's behavior. He was a paladin once, a devout servant of Terra. And Terra abhors the suffering of the innocent." If Jon insisted on wagging the righteous finger of justice so much, the least he could do would be to occasionally poke a tyrant with it.

But would he take on another war?

Ambriel held his gaze. "Your arrival has been the saving grace of our people."

Leigh scoffed. Saving grace? He'd botched the whole of this. "Any other diplomat would have—"

Ambriel took his hand. "No other."

# CHAPTER 43

*R*ielle covered her mouth, swaying with the deck as the
*Liberté* bobbed on the waves.

Her brother—her *living* brother—rounded the desk and rushed
toward her. Her own feet refused to move, and her knees buckled.
Brennan's grip tightened on her arm, bracing her, but he let her go just
as Liam pulled her into an embrace.

Tears burst from her eyes and streamed down her face, dampening
the smooth cotton of his shirt.

How could this be? She pressed her face to his solid chest, breathed
in the salt on his skin and the wine on his breath, closed her eyes and
absorbed his warmth.

It was him. Liam. Her brother.

"You're alive," she whispered, but no more than a mangled sob
came out.

He stroked the back of her neck softly. "Something like that."

Alive. He was alive.

For nearly a decade, she'd believed her entire family dead, but here
was Liam, somehow alive, when all of Laurentine had burned. Two
years her senior, he'd be twenty-four now.

She pulled back to gaze up at his face. A shadow of the fifteen-year-old she remembered still lingered in the planes of his face, the same slightly upturned mouth, light blond lashes, thick eyebrows. He sported a rugged golden stubble now, but she still recognized his prominent jaw and cleft chin beneath.

"How is it possible?" she whispered. When he only looked back at her with searching eyes, she reached up to touch his face. "I watched Laurentine burn... and no one... no one else... escaped."

He drew in a breath and held it, his muscles stiffening. Why?

"I'll tell you everything," he said finally. "Let's sit." He led her to one of two tufted chairs before his desk and seated her. After rounding the desk once more, he eyed Brennan coldly. "You too, Marcel."

Brennan hesitated but stalked to the second chair. He waited until Liam sat before he did.

Liam leaned forward, elbows on the desk, and cracked his knuckles. He nodded to the bottle. "Wine?"

Before she could answer, he poured her some. But he didn't afford Brennan the same courtesy. She raised an eyebrow.

Liam took a drink. "You're married?"

"No," she answered at the same time Brennan said, "Betrothed."

Brennan leaned back, posture relaxed but jaw clenched. "You have a problem?"

Icy eyes stared him down to the sound of knuckles cracking. "I may have been gone for nine years, but I wasn't dead. I heard what you did to my sister."

"I'm right here," she growled. "And is this really more important than how you're alive?"

Brennan sneered. "So... what? Are you going to thrash me now? Have me flogged? Throw me overboard? Make me walk the plank?"

Liam grinned broadly, a smile so bright it would have been handsome had it reached his eyes. "Oh, I trust my sister to handle her own enemies. She's a Lothaire."

"And what does that mean?" Brennan shot back.

Two chairs fell as Liam and Brennan leaped to their feet.

She glared at Brennan, clenching her jaw so tight her teeth cracked.

Brennan's gaze dropped to hers. The tension fled his body. He swallowed. "I—spoke without thought."

She stared down at the white knuckles of her fist. The urge to hit him slowly subsided.

She dropped her head in one hand but covered Brennan's arm with the other.

Slowly, he righted his chair, moved it closer to her, and sat.

If she were honest, the Lothaires—her parents included—had been masters of the game, their web of spies and gossips working intrigues in their favor. She, however, had left the Houses and all their machinations behind after what had happened at Laurentine.

The House of Lothaire was no longer feared, and she, its scion, was no more than a cautionary tale told to young debutantes eyeing handsome lords.

*Its scion.*

She looked up at Liam. Morning light shone in his golden hair. "You—you're the Marquis of Laurentine. The rightful lord of our House."

He folded his hands together and met her gaze unequivocally. "I am Verib, captain of the *Liberté.*"

"But—"

"Liam Amadour Lothaire died nine years ago." He exhaled deeply. "And he's not coming back."

She leaned forward. "Why not?"

Shaking his head, he looked away. "I don't want it. Any of it."

Being the lord of Laurentine came with money, status, influence, power...

But he didn't want the duties that came with it, did he? Ruling the march, collecting taxes, being called to court, swearing fealty to a monarch, a political marriage, securing heirs?

Any of it. She rubbed her lips together and lowered her gaze. He didn't want any of it...

He'd been alive all these years, and if he knew about what had happened at Tregarde, then he had clearly known she'd lived. And he hadn't returned. Hadn't written. Hadn't given her a single word of his own existence.

"Any of it," she repeated softly, and raised her eyes to his.

The intensity of his gaze gave way to softness, and he looked into his bottle of wine, swirling it absentmindedly. "I can't go back."

She slapped the armrests. "Why didn't you tell me you were alive?" She fought back the tears welling in her eyes. "I could have kept it a secret, if that's what you'd wanted."

The soft lapping of the waves pervaded, accompanied by the gentle creak of the bobbing *Liberté.*

Liam glanced at Brennan. "Leave us." When Brennan only eyed Rielle, she nodded her permission.

Brennan didn't look away, his carriage completely relaxed. At ease. He rose, gave a slight inclination of his head to Liam, and left the cabin. Even after he'd closed the door softly, she still looked the way he'd left.

What was so private that Liam wouldn't say in front of Brennan?

"Do you trust him?" His wine in hand, Liam rose from his armchair and moved back to the gallery windows, resting an arm against the frame above him. The daylight played on his face and in the shining hues of his hair.

"I do." Brennan had died for her.

"You shouldn't." He took a drink. "A man who's betrayed you once will betray you again." The hoarseness of an old wound laced his voice.

What had happened to him? In nine long years, she couldn't fathom what he might have gone through to end up captain of this ship.

But he didn't know Brennan. It was true enough that Brennan had betrayed her, but he'd matured since then. Become a new man. "People change."

Liam grinned bitterly. "No. They only think they do."

She shook her head. "What happened to you?"

"You remember Mama's bower? How it jutted out over the cliffs, overlooking the Shining Sea?"

She smiled. They'd all spent many cheery days there. "Of course."

"One of the marauders was torturing me in there when the fire started." He stared out at the bay. "He'd bound me in arcanir and tied me to the bed with ropes, but when he ran out of the room, I was able to pull a hand free... and then freed myself. Only by then, the fire had become unstoppable. The castle was falling apart, and so was the hall right outside the door. I looked back at the window. I had no choice. I jumped."

Her mouth fell open. "You jumped from that height?"

He drew in a long breath. "Bound in arcanir, it was either that or burn to death." He exhaled slowly. "There was only one chance of survival."

The terror he must have felt in that moment... The choice of burning to death or jumping and hoping not to hit the cliffs or the rocks, not to land hard enough to break his bones...

*And it was all because of me. And my éveil.*

What would he think if he knew? She looked him over. Did he know?

No, she didn't think he did. And she couldn't tell him, not now, not when she'd only just gotten him back.

Someday.

"I awoke aboard a Sileni merchantman that had escaped the harbor. I introduced myself under an alias, joined their crew... lost a fight with some pirates, and ended up sold at fifteen."

Enslaved. "Oh, Liam..."

"They can never catch Northerners, you know? The Skaddish. They fight to the death, every last one of them. But a few of us Emaurrians take after their pale looks. And the Sonbaharans love that." He set down the wine.

*Thahab. Golden one.* Farrad's voice echoed in her mind, and she shivered.

"House Abdal's zahib saw fight in my eyes and decided it'd be interesting to see how my life would end. Before I ever took to the seas, I spent five years in Harifa as a gladiator."

*Divine—*

*No...*

She'd only suffered for months what he'd suffered for years—and worse than she had. The masters of Sonbahar invested heavily in gladiators, who earned their keep winning purses and attracting clients seeking pleasure, women and men, which the gladiators had no say in accepting or rejecting.

And Liam had suffered *that* for five years. His life on the line, his pride ignored, his choices taken away. All that time, he'd been abused, and she hadn't known at all.

She rose and cautiously joined him at the windows. The waters were almost clear now, in the brightness of the morning sun. She folded herself into him, rested her cheek against his chest. "I'm so sorry, Liam."

She told him about her own past four months here, and although he went rigid when it came to Shadow, Sincuore, and House Hazael, he wrapped an arm around her. Held her. For a while, he remained quiet, holding her and looking out with her.

She nuzzled his chest. "If you had a ship, I wish you'd come home."

"Home?" He pulled away and crossed his arms. "To do what? To be forced to bend the knee before a king? Forced into a marriage? Forced to play politics?" He narrowed his eyes and nodded toward the bay. "On the seas, no man lords over me. Never again. I'm free. And I'm never submitting again."

"You could have told me you were alive. A courier. A letter. Something."

"Better that no one knew I was alive. Including you."

Was returning to be Marquis of Laurentine truly that terrible a fate? Yes, he'd have to run the march, appear at court on the king's whim, swear fealty, marry, and secure heirs, but he'd want for nothing. As Marquis of Laurentine, with no arranged marriage in effect, he'd have his pick of brides. He'd have money. Power. Influence. "You want nothing to do with Laurentine?"

"No, I don't. Not with any of it."

"Including me?"

His eyes widened, and his arms slowly fell to his sides. A sullen gray faded his expression, and he rubbed his mouth. "It's true that I didn't come back and I didn't write. But I didn't stop caring." He raised his gaze to hers. "I followed news of you. I knew you'd had your éveil and had gone to the Tower. I knew what that beast of a Marcel did to you. I knew you'd denied him your hand and were making a future for yourself."

He'd gotten news of her and denied her the same? She bit back sharp words. "And knowing this about me comforted you?"

"Most of the time."

"Yet you denied me the same comfort. Instead, I thought I'd—" *Killed you.* "I thought I'd lost you. I thought you were dead. I didn't even deserve a scrap of comfort, news of you."

His mouth thinned to a white line. "I couldn't—I can't go back."

"Why not?"

He paced the cabin. "I just can't."

She stomped her foot. "Why not?"

He slicked back some stray wisps of blond hair and shook his head. "There... There'd be questions."

"So what?"

He grabbed the armchair Brennan had been sitting in and leaned over its back, braced against it. He hung his head. "Was I to tell them I'd run from Laurentine? That I was too scared to come back?"

"You were fifteen!"

"And that I'd been sold into slavery?"

"It wasn't your fault—"

"And then take all their judgmental looks, their pitying glares, their whispers about what happened to me? Moved like a pawn in the arena, treated like a thing, barely even human, rented out every night?" His voice cracked, hollowed. "With everyone knowing all that, with the truth laid bare, could I ever be a man among the Houses? Would they ever see me as anything more than a..."

*Victim.* The Houses set upon weakness like vultures and took power mercilessly. What little influence Laurentine had retained after the fire, it had lost with her humiliation at Brennan's hands.

But it didn't matter. She stormed toward him and grabbed his shoulders. "It doesn't matter."

He glanced at her, eyes bloodshot. "What?"

She squeezed his shoulders. "It doesn't matter. Who cares what the Houses think?" She searched his eyes and the growing curiosity there. "We're Lothaires. If anyone says anything, we'll destroy them."

He frowned.

"Any tongue dares speak against you, and we'll make sure it trembles at the thought next time."

"How?"

She raised a hand next to her face, smiled slyly, and snapped her fingers. A flame sparked to life there. "The options are many, dear brother. I hold with fire."

In his eyes, the flame glowed, danced, grew as he straightened. "We can't stop them from talking."

"It is precisely their talk that will give us the opportunity to demonstrate our power. We will duel. Let them talk. Let them talk, so they might see their words burn."

The flame flickered in his eyes. Her hand shook. She extinguished the fire and made a show of dusting off her hands. Her anima was dim, but encouraging him was worth every last bit.

He sighed, but a smile spread across his face. "You've become strong, little bee. Stronger than I ever could have imagined."

Weakness had reduced her to ashes, so much so she had nearly wanted to cease existing, but it was only from those ashes that she could rise anew. Leigh's betrayal, being sold into slavery, losing her child... These things had been painful, each worse than the last.

But she was still standing.

That pain hadn't destroyed her. And if the pain hadn't, the Houses had no chance.

Liam eyed her trembling hand. "You came to me for resonance."

She sucked in a breath. That had been *before* she'd learned Captain Verib was her brother.

"I'm the only mage aboard, besides yourself."

She sighed.

He rolled up his sleeves and looked around the cabin. "All right. Where do you want to do this?"

There was the captain's chair, the armchairs—

She looked at the captain's chair and the desk before it. "Why don't you sit in the captain's chair, and I'll sit across from you on the other side of the desk? We'll join hands."

He squinted contemplatively, then nodded. "Best of all options." He sat in the captain's chair, cleared the desk, and rested his arm on it.

She took a seat across from him in Brennan's armchair. Hesitantly, she reached for his hand.

His large, rough palm closed around her own, its warmth comforting. She offered him a smile. He returned the expression, despite the tightness in his face. He closed his eyes, and so did she. The pull was strong, drawing her toward him, and she pulled back, the connection stretching to its limit until it caught, tight, solid, unbreakable.

THE SUNLIGHT against Rielle's closed eyes wasn't as bright as it had been—was it the late-afternoon sun? A part of her didn't dare open her eyes, not yet, not until she knew her dream had been real. That *Liam* was real. Here. Alive. "Liam?" she whispered.

He groaned. "How did you dim so much anima? Did you destroy an entire damned city?"

She cracked an eyelid. "Something like that."

Indeed, it was late afternoon. It had taken much longer than with Jon.

*Jon.* Just the thought of him flooded her with warmth. Remembering his arms around her, the need of his lips against hers, the love in his eyes—it made her empty hands ache. She needed him, and...

He was marrying someone else. She'd go to Courdeval to find him betrothed or already wed... And what? Wish to become his mistress? Was that all that remained for them now, a wisp of a grander dream their hearts had dreamed together?

No, love could withstand anything. Their love could.

Her chest tightened, compressed. She couldn't think of that now. What mattered first was getting home, warning him, dealing with Shadow, making her suffer for what she'd caused.

Liam stared off to the side, wisps of straw-blond hair shrouding his face.

She stiffened in her chair. "Thanks."

He held up a hand and waved her off.

She braced on the desk, her knees weak. After a moment to gather her composure, she made for the cabin door, but paused before it. "Liam... I know what you said, but just think about it. If you spend too much time worrying about what others think of your life, you'll miss your chance to live it as you truly wish."

He didn't raise his head from the desk, but he didn't need to. He'd heard her. Now if only he'd listen.

With a sigh, she headed out onto the quarterdeck. Crewmen eyed her, winked, whistled. Heat blazed in her cheeks. Great Divine, they thought—?

She took a deep breath. Let them think. It didn't matter. If he cared to reveal who she was, he could explain what had really happened.

She strode to the hatchway and picked her way down the ladder. Her and Brennan's hammock had been in the corner, and when she looked there, he jolted straight, alert, and then stalked over to her.

He wrapped an arm around her and led her away from the full-moon eyes of the crew. He closed the door to a room—so stocked with barrels that there was hardly any space to move. The powder room. A small porthole allowed a ray of sunlight for the dust to glitter in.

"What?" she whispered.

Brennan grabbed her shoulders, near enough that cinnamon, cypress, and the heady scent that was so uniquely his filled her nose. She breathed it in and shivered.

Divine, he had no right to smell so good.

"The whole crew thinks you... We boarded as husband and wife, and now, they think—"

She laughed softly. "Perhaps we should set them straight."

He sighed. "What, and tell them you're his sister?" he hissed. "Because that would be so much better. Offer every man aboard your identity to make it *that* much easier for the Hazaels to track you down." He narrowed his eyes, but his nostrils flared.

He breathed. Deep. Eyed her.

His hands moved down from her shoulders along her arms, firm, hard, and fell from her elbows to her waist.

A pulse of need made her gasp. She took a step closer, the heat of his breath warming her head. When she closed her eyes, she was back at House Hazael, in bed with him, beneath him, and his heat seared her skin, his grip firm on her hip, that crease of pleasure on his brow—

"The resonance," he whispered, his breath a soft chill in her hair, sending a shiver down her spine. "Does it always make you…"

"Yes," she said, looking up at him.

A low breath hissed from his lips. His eyelids descended heavily, and his fingers pressed into the flesh of her waist. His warm hands sent a frisson through her body.

Her breathing shallowed. There was not enough air to take in, not enough in the room—were the walls closing in?—and Great Divine, it was hot, like a desert at noon, and she just wanted to fan herself—did that porthole open?—the thiyawb was much too stiff, her hair pulled back much too tight, and by the Divine, she wanted him with every fiber of her being.

*It's the resonance.* The resonance had readied her body, and it sought satisfaction.

Without a doubt, she desired him, had desired him since that night, but this wasn't her will making a choice, but the aftereffects of resonance. He was attractive, she had needs, and he was here.

She pressed wary fingers against his chest. "Brennan—"

He stiffened, then smiled, ease relaxing his features. "Jon. I'm well aware."

Yes, she loved Jon, but… it wasn't only that. Brennan was *not* one night's pleasure; he was so much more, would always be so much more, and never approached lightly.

And the long history between them made any deeper involvement inadvisable, undesirable, no matter how her body reacted to his; she couldn't read him, would never be able to read him, and never fully trust her heart when it came to him. He was dangerous. He would always be dangerous. Allowing herself to fall for him, even a little, would only ever end in tragedy.

A few days more. She could hold out a few days more.

# CHAPTER 44

*J*on eyed the neat stack of missives on his purple-
heartwood desk, right next to his Old Emaurrian
language-learning books. One letter bore the elegant
scrolls of Leigh's hand.

He tore it open and read:

*Met with Queen Matryona of Stonehaven. She offers assistance in quelling the
Immortals in exchange for Emaurria's help in subjugating the light-elves.*

*Explained reservations. No change. The queen cannot be reasoned with and
demands answer within three days. Her captain shows some hesitancy but
remains loyal...*

*Captain Sunheart mentioned the dark-elves have a custom that allows a
queen to be challenged in single combat, but only by a member of her Quorum or
another ruler. She is renowned as a fast, capable warrior, feared, and Queen
Narenian doesn't consider herself Matryona's match...*

*I may have an angle on a member of her Quorum, but if not, that option
remains in the event of battle...*

He tossed the paper onto his desk, leaned back in his chair, and
loosened his cravat. Blinked.

Ever since he'd ascended the throne, the kingdom had been in a constant state of war. And would so continue.

"Raoul," he called.

The hall doors creaked open, deliberate footsteps clicked nearer, and in the doorway to the study, Raoul bowed. "Yes, Your Majesty?"

"Summon Paladin Grand Cordon Guérin and the High Council to meet tonight." His answer to Queen Matryona's offer would require preparations. Extensive preparations.

"After the opera?" Raoul asked.

The opera. Right. He was taking Alessandra to see *Il Cuore Spezzato* tonight, her favorite. He'd invited the company from Caerlain Trel especially for her.

"Yes," he answered. "My thanks, Raoul."

"Your Majesty," he replied gruffly. "If... if you ever need someone to join you in the practice yard, I don't mind." His ice-blue eyes were unwavering, his face set.

He didn't just mean sparring. He meant a sympathetic ear. A kindness... a gesture of friendship.

Jon grinned. "You'll live to regret that, my friend."

Raoul shifted on his feet. "Fairly certain I already do."

They shared an amused look before Raoul bowed. "I'll have your clerk alert Paladin Grand Cordon Guérin and the High Council, Your Majesty. By your leave?"

Jon nodded, and with that, Raoul left.

And so Queen Matryona would have her answer. Emaurria would be ready for the repercussions.

He stood and headed for his privy wardrobe to change for tonight.

Faithkeeper was displayed on the wall, four feet long from pommel to tip. He grabbed the scabbard and drew the double-edged arcanir blade, which had been with him since his vows at eighteen. The cruciform hilt had a straight cross-guard, the quillons ending in knobs, and the hand-and-a-half grip, covered with leather and wire wrap, had felt always a part of him, but now, apart. The worn, moon-shaped pommel, a Terran symbol, had often provided him comfort, his palm seeking out its familiarity at his side whenever he'd been troubled.

With Faithkeeper in hand, he'd personally see the queen's unconscionable plans ended as he had so many evils before, even if it cost him his life this time.

The elven oath ritual required allies swearing loyalty to each other's bloodlines. If he died, the light-elves would remain beholden to his blood heir.

Which meant...

He closed his eyes and exhaled a slow, defeated breath. It meant he'd need a blood heir before he died. Before this war was fought.

An heir... a child of his own.

Since Vindemia, when Valen had spoken to him of—he smiled faintly—*a bounteous clan*, the thought had returned from time to time. Marrying Rielle, a handfasting as she smiled at him. Huddling together in bed, holding their first child on a quiet morning. Chasing their children in the gardens, laughing with them, watching them grow up as he and Rielle grew older, hand in hand, facing their life and the kingdom's needs together.

A hollow formed in his throat, and his eyes watered.

Gods, it had all been reduced to that, and only that—a *thought*. Never to be. She was dead, he was dying, and that future was like the wind. A faint whistle, a howl that haunted his days, but one he could never touch, never hold, never chase and laugh with.

And now he had to face the prospect of bringing a child into this world, only to leave her fatherless shortly after her birth.

Cruel. Irresponsible. And yet what the kingdom demanded of him. If Alessandra agreed, they'd conceive an heir and she'd remain regent until their child came of age. And he would swear all the necessary oaths, make all the necessary alliances, to ease the burden of rule for them both after he was gone.

He'd tell her all of it before Veris, and pray she agreed.

With a sigh, he sheathed Faithkeeper. To face the dark-elves, his blade wasn't enough. Nor the Order's, nor the army's.

He looked inward, imagined his weapons, armor, and clothes about him. The silk drapes and their crystal ties, the windows letting in the muted afternoon sunshine... The chill wintry air bit his skin, the crisp scent of an ironwood forest, and deeper in, lush foliage brushed his skin. Below him, two-legged figures traversed soft ground latticed with waterways, among them a figure so bright it shone like a star.

A wild mage. Leigh.

Reaching toward him did nothing; he could scarcely move but to sway just slightly. A tree. He was a tree.

He strained to bend, to approach, but leaves merely fluttered on the boughs. Not close enough. Nowhere near close enough.

He pulled back, past the soft foliage, through the forest, into the cold air. Windows figured in his vision, letting in afternoon light to dance on silken drapes and in crystal-adorned ties, and then he saw himself, standing amid weapons, armor, and clothes.

With a gasp, he staggered back until he hit a wall, and gulped in breaths, wide eyed and shuddering.

What good was this power? The power to be a stone, a tree, immovable, useless? He slammed the wall with a tight fist.

Useless. Without that emissary to teach him, it was useless. And without it, he was only a blade, and useless, too.

But if the light-elves were right—if there was more to being Earth-bound—perhaps that was the key to victory against the dark-elves. In a few days, he'd swear the elven oath ritual. With the emissary's knowledge would come not only victory against the dark-elves but true power. The power of the land. The power to attract allies... and to survive without them, for this generation and the next. Freedom.

But if, on that day, the emissary didn't arrive, neither would victory, power, nor freedom.

A soft knock came from the hall, and he called out permission to enter.

Soft footsteps clicked, and then Alessandra stood in the doorway to his bedchamber, a fan folded in her hand. She was dressed in high fashion, a purple gown with a plunging neckline, and her dark waves were bound high, with some ringlets over her shoulder. "Are you ready?"

The opera. Right. He pinched the bridge of his nose. "I'll get changed, and we'll go."

She cocked her head, holding his gaze with a knowing look, before she gave him a sympathetic shake of her head. Tossing the fan onto the bed, she glided across the room to stand behind him, her gown swishing as she moved.

Her hands settled on his shoulders, and she rubbed firmly, deeply. "Is it the pirate attacks again?"

He and Alessandra had been tracking the pirates' movements along the western coast and staying in contact with her father's flotilla. "No, it's the dark-elves. We may soon be going into battle... *another* battle."

"Is Vervewood worth it?" she asked, her hands still working miracles in his muscle.

"We need the knowledge the light-elves have, but even if Vervewood weren't worth it, Stonehaven's queen is a slaver." And that would not be tolerated.

"Then all we can do is prepare. You're already doing all you can, and there's no sense in worrying too much about what's to come." Her hands rubbed lower, finding tense spots and relaxing them. "Is there anything I can do?"

Besides battle plans and preparing troops, he still had yet to learn repulsion shields, or master the Old Emaurrian he'd need to communicate with this Aiolian Windsong when she arrived. "Not unless you want to study Old Emaurrian with me."

A soft laugh. "You'll be jealous when I'm better at it than you."

"Is that a challenge?" Smiling, he turned around, and her hands settled on his chest.

She arched a brow, her chestnut-brown eyes gleaming. "Done."

She wasn't in love with him, nor he with her, but they would be the best of friends. He could feel it.

Since the news of Rielle, his nights with Nora had been like the breath of life, and he cared for her, but they'd both known it wasn't more than diversion. They'd both known he would have to marry one of the suitresses, and likely Alessandra.

And Alessandra—brilliant as she was—was no one's consolation prize. She deserved a strong, capable man who'd love her well, and he'd thank the gods if she settled for him.

"If we're going to the opera," he said, eyeing her hands on his chest, "we should leave, Alessandra."

She held his gaze, searching his eyes, and the quiet in his

bedchamber settled about them like velvet, heavy, smooth, warm.

"Aless," she whispered, as her palm slid up to his cravat, pulling it loose as she rose on her toes and kissed him, softly, slowly. They breathed the same air for a moment before she drew a small measure away, holding his gaze.

She let the soft silk slip from her hand to the floor.

"No opera tonight," she whispered, taking his hand and leading him back to the bed. "Tonight, you relax, give me a taste of what a lifetime of being your queen would be like, and then I destroy you with my superior Old Emaurrian skills."

He followed her, and his lips found hers again; she was beautiful, and his body knew these steps, even if his heart wasn't in it.

"Destroy me," he breathed between kisses, as he unbuttoned his shirt. "Do you want to spend a lifetime doing that, Aless?"

She laughed as she reclined onto the bed, her voluminous purple skirts blooming around her. "We'll see after tonight. No pressure, Your Majesty." She smiled softly.

Only the fate of his kingdom rested upon it. No pressure. None at all.

He joined her, clearing his mind of everything but the present.

"THE STARS," Rielle cried, stirring in the arms around her. Beneath the looming darkness. Amid many breaths and bodies. Too many. Together... in chains... made to sleep in small, cramped, too-tight stalls —*No.* "I need to see the stars."

Darkness blanketed the crew deck, only patches of moonlight glimmering through the hatchway and portholes, illuminating crew dozing in hammocks.

"Rielle." Brennan's voice, soft and warm against her ear. "It's a bad dream. Just go back to sleep."

A bad dream... Yes. She was free now. The stable and the ship that had brought her there were in the past. Past. The warmth and the quiet beckoned once more. She shut her eyes. Cold arcanir shackles chilled her wrists—

But not anymore. Not anymore. She squeezed her eyes shut tighter.

Brennan hugged her gently. She shifted in the hammock until she came face to face with him. She'd known his face—its prominent aristocratic features, as cruel as they were handsome, and the hazel eyes that could lure a smitten girl into endless depths—long before the stable and the ship. The same face now kept those demons away. A talisman, even beneath the coarse growth covering his chin and jaw, beneath the long, dark lashes shading his gaze.

He'd saved her. Even with her magic, her knowledge, her experience, she would have never escaped House Hazael alive without him. And she had escaped. Perhaps repeating it to herself would make it feel real someday.

She traced a finger along his stubble. Real. Here. And yet, when she closed her eyes, the shackles she'd once worn were still real, too.

"Come," he whispered. "Let's head to the weather deck."

She drew her eyebrows together.

"To see the stars." Smiling in the lambent glow of the night, he glided over her from the hammock, then helped her out of it.

Her hand in his, he picked a way among the hammocks and led her up the hatchway to the main deck.

On the quarterdeck, Liam stood at the wheel, his straw-blond hair silver in the moonlight; he held a spyglass to his eye.

She dashed to the starboard gunwale and stared out into the darkness. The sea lapped against the *Liberté*. On the rolling midnight-blue surface, the silvery moon shone like a pearl.

Far into the distance, two tiny lights flickered.

"Another ship," Brennan murmured. "Liam's found whatever he's been looking for," he whispered.

The ship Liam had said he was chasing. Her grip tightened on the railing. "Battle."

"Battle," Brennan agreed.

Liam collapsed the spyglass, his eyes enchanted with a green glow. Earthsight—an incantation, since he was a pyromancer. The glow fled, dispelled. He nodded grimly. "To your posts!"

Boots thudded across the deck and up the hatchway. Crewmen climbed rigging.

"Extinguish aft and stern lanterns! Loose topsails, gallants, royals!" Liam's voice bellowed over the bustle. "Gun crews at the ready!"

Crewmen opened gun ports and positioned cannons on the upper deck while relaying orders.

"We've got the wind of her," Liam said to his ship's master.

But he hadn't ordered any men to mortars. Why not? He could easily cripple another ship from afar with his stock.

A hand covered her own. Brennan's.

"What do you see out there?"

His werewolf eyes would see more than hers would.

"A ship about eighty feet in length." He squinted. "A... partition on the main deck."

Partition? A slave ship.

"Orders?" she called to Liam.

His mouth gaped, but he closed it. "Get to safety. The hold. Now." He narrowed his eyes.

There was no way she would hide in the hold while everyone's lives were at stake. "I'm a quaternary elementalist," she hissed back, and the men around her slowed. "I'll turn the very sea to your aid."

Crewmen paused around her, looking to their captain.

Liam swore. "Wait for grapnels, then do battle as you will." He turned to his ship's master, but snapped back. "Do no damage to her upper or lower decks. And do not sink her."

She stood to attention. "Understood."

Liam nodded to Brennan. "And you—"

"Stay by her side," Brennan said.

Liam nodded, then held up his hand. Everyone around hushed.

The quiet hung heavy aboard the ship, a growing presence, its weight burdening her shoulders and—the crew shifted—theirs, too.

Flapping, from afar. The unmistakable loosing of sails. Liam's eyes blazed. "Chase cannons! Load chain shot! Tear through those sails!"

A hiss, and cannon fire boomed, thundering from the aft.

"Twelve-pounders at the ready!"

A whirring cut the wind.

"Brace!"

Brennan pulled her to the deck, covered her. Iron crunched

through wood.

"Sight the muzzle flash!" Liam bellowed. "Double shot to the aftcastle!"

A barrage of cannon fire became a cacophonous storm. Discord crushed through the hull. Crewmen shouted and screamed. And above it all, Liam barked orders that his officers relayed.

The sanctuary of Brennan's arms encircled her, firm and unrelenting, and she leaned into him. If they could survive the initial onslaught, she would see the slaver's crew dead.

The storm of shots lessened in interval.

Foreign shouts and screams called in the distance. Neared.

"Captain!" Zero shouted to Liam. "They're dumping cargo!" Lightening their load for speed.

*Cargo.* They were throwing *slaves* overboard. *People.*

"Deploy the boats!" Liam shouted over the noise. "Grapnels!" he yelled. "Master Aryn, take the helm!"

She peeked over Brennan's arm. Liam made for the boarding netting and climbed.

"Brennan," she whispered.

He pulled away, enough to look out over the gunwale. Past him, crewmen heaved ropes, pulling in the hooks grappled to the slaver's railing. Roars rippled through the *Liberté,* deafening and terrifying all at once.

The slaver's rigging burned—Liam's magic. Atop the slaver's aftcastle, a dozen hands readied bows, and men filed onto its poop deck. She craned her neck to peer at the crow's nest, where archers picked targets.

*Damn it.* Here, she and Brennan were easy targets; and she wouldn't hide behind him. *Time to light them up.*

Weaving an aeromancy spell with both hands, she scrambled toward the stern and angled around an eighteen-pounder. She shadowed the sky with black clouds. Next to her, Brennan stood sentinel, scanning the slaver.

She held the storm in her left hand and directed it with her right, calling the lightning to an enemy raising a sword to Sterling.

A bolt split the sky. The enemy shook and sizzled. Singed, he fell.

Sterling glanced over his shoulder in the man's direction before parrying a cutlass blow.

She called lightning to man after man—

Brennan swatted something before her. She fell back, her focus— and her aeromancy—dispelled.

An arrow thudded into the deck behind her.

"Arcanir," he snarled.

She looked back at the ship. Where had it come from?

"There, behind the wheel." Brennan leaned in and pointed. The tip of a bow limb peeked out of cover.

From high up, something glinted in the moonlight—

Another arrow, from the slaver's crow's nest. Brennan reached.

It penetrated his hand. Blood spattered the deck and her face. Brennan's blood.

Hissing, he pulled the arrow free and snapped the shaft in half. The sage-tinted arrowhead clattered to the deck.

He looked back at her. "We have to get you to safety."

The crow's nest archer readied another shot. They needed to move. Her gaze darted about the deck for cover—the captain's cabin.

"Come on!" She jumped over splintered deck beams and raced up to the quarterdeck.

She threw the heavy door open and pressed her back to it. Brennan rolled into cover after her.

An arrow thudded into the other side of the door.

She peeked around the edge. If she aimed for the crow's nest archer, the wheel archer would target her—and vice versa.

Swords clanged, men screamed and shouted, and flames crackled from afar.

Brennan leaned in. Amber gleamed in his lethal eyes. "I'll handle them."

There were no other viable options. She nodded. "I'll cover you. Try not to die."

He grinned broadly, a playful wink topping the look of pure confidence. She smiled in return as he rounded the cabin door. She'd cover him. Hydromancy. Ice. She conjured a shard of ice in her hand. Guided by her magic, it would find its target.

One arrow cracked into wood. Then another. She peeked out from cover. The crow's nest archer ducked behind the mast.

The wheel archer—just visible. A clear line of sight. She threw.

The ice shard sped to its target, narrowly missing a running *Liberté* crewman—Zero. She winced, but it found its target in the wheel archer's knee.

"Yes," she hissed to herself. Her gaze darted to Zero fighting near the slaver's gunwale—and an enemy lighting a fuse. To a twelve-pounder. Aimed at her.

She tumbled into the captain's cabin, scrambling for the gallery windows.

A loud crash, and splintered wood pelted onto her. The shot had gone clean through the cabin, blowing the door off its hinges in the process.

If he reloaded, he'd be aiming closer to the stern. She crawled across the cabin, through a broken window, and swung down onto the stern balcony.

On the water, people aboard an overburdened pinnace rowed for the port side of the *Liberté,* no doubt for the boarding netting. Others clung to flotsam, struggling to stay afloat and alive.

She called the waves to help the pinnace along and sent out candle-light to the farthest person, so he wouldn't be missed or forgotten.

But there, beneath the candlelight, was darkness. Black water. She squinted. No, a shadow.

The size of a ship. Bigger than the *Liberté.*

"Get to the ship!" she screamed out over the water. Dozens of people struggled, their limbs bound in shackles. Her own wrists chilled, making her shiver.

Any hydromancy spell to draw them nearer could also attract what-ever was beneath the water's surface.

Shuddering, she scrambled to the starboard corner, scanning the slaver wildly for Brennan. Finally, she found him high up in the crow's nest, imprisoning the struggling archer in a hold.

"Brennan!"

His face immediately snapped in her direction. His preternatural hearing.

"There's a shadow!" She pointed out to sea.

He shook his head.

"In the water!" She looked back out there. Great Divine, whatever was beneath the surface, she needed to get everyone out.

Brennan threw the archer to his death and began the long climb down the mast.

What could he do about a massive sea creature?

Cannon fire made her flinch as shots blew past.

Spelling a waterspout or a maelstrom would hurt the people afloat... And she couldn't target it while it was underwater. She had to think of something else.

Scare it away. In case it didn't work, she moved her candlelight spell farther out to sea—and then fed its fiery glow with two hands, building it, spinning it, growing it.

The candlelight grew until it illuminated the dark waters like a thousand candles.

The clangor of battle quieted. Faces turned to the light. And the shadow moved below it.

A chill shook her and froze her in place. It wasn't working.

Massive tentacles surfaced and wound around the giant candlelight spell, sweeping through its ethereal glow.

"Kraken!" The call rippled through a dozen men.

*Kraken.* And she'd actually drawn this nightmare closer.

But it was distracted by the candlelight... Vulnerable. She had to do something.

"Hands to stern chasers!" Liam bellowed.

Both hands devoted to the candlelight spell, she would only have a moment to attack the kraken before it disappeared back under the surface. *You want fire? I'll give you fire.*

A fireball.

Dispelling the candlelight spell, she cast a fireball, as large as she could manage in an instant, and sent it flying.

Flame illuminated the monster and only singed a tentacle. It struck the surface, sending floating survivors away.

Another tentacle shot out and struck the surface.

And another.

And another.

Panicked screams rose from the water.

One halted immediately. Disappeared. The man vanished beneath the water.

She grabbed its railing and clenched it. No. No, no, no.

She'd only succeeded in making the monster angry. The survivors from the slaver wouldn't live to taste freedom unless someone did something.

While the kraken remained underwater, she couldn't target it.

*Underwater.*

That was how she had to defeat it. She threw off her thiyawb, down to her chemise and linen pants. Her hands tightened around the railing.

"Rielle, stop!" Brennan's voice thundered behind her.

She jumped, streamlining her body into a fine point. Her feet broke the water.

She surfaced and swam toward the last position she'd sighted the kraken. If she could just get beneath the surface, even a flame cloak—if cast with strong enough will and destabilized—would cook the creature alive.

Amid terrifying screams and tentacles slamming the surface, people swam past her toward the *Liberté*. Cannon blasts roared from the ships.

A splash broke the water behind her. Brennan. He surfaced and gulped air.

One stroke after another. She was marquise of a coastal march. She'd been raised on the water, swimming and diving since childhood. If anyone could handle this, it was she.

"Stop this madness!" he shouted.

"Go back!"

There was no one else. The only other mage present was Liam, who had to lead his crew through this and captain the *Liberté*.

Finally out far enough, she submerged and cast another candlelight spell, a firefly against the night. The creature would seek her out.

Pressure seized her waist. A tentacle. Serrated chitinous rings cut into her flesh. Breath bubbled from her nose. Her entire body trembled.

The water reddened.

*Not yet.* She needed to be close enough to kill it.

Water pushed against her, resistance as the tentacle pulled her. She held the candlelight before her, aching eyes fixed on her destination.

A massive mouth. A sharp, chitinous beak to tear her to pieces.

Shuddering, she dispelled the candlelight and closed her eyes. The azure pool of her power—her anima—consumed her inner vision. She gestured the flame cloak, willing it to its maximum intensity. Brightness radiated from the other side of her eyelids.

The pressure abandoned her waist. Water pushed and pulled.

She opened her eyes. The flame cloak blazed to thirty feet in every direction, boiling the water to bubbling opacity.

There—not far—a singed, injured tentacle flailed and vanished.

Now or never.

Her own magic wouldn't hurt her. Using both hands, she pushed the flame cloak's intensity past its limits, destabilizing it.

It burst.

Everything went white. An explosion flared over fifty feet in every direction.

Fixed on the kraken's last location, she swam toward the surface as the darkness of the depths reclaimed the water once more.

A massive broken shadow sank below, descending into the black.

Dead... Was it dead?

Her chest tightened. Air. She needed air. She craned her neck up to look at the surface, some thirty feet up. She swam, kicking her legs.

Fires glowed on the surface, some hundred feet away. The ships.

A sharp pain stabbed her chest from all sides. Agony. Twenty feet.

Faster. She had to—

Swim faster—

Darkness closed around her.

Weakness.

Her lungs squeezed, wringing.

Not like this.

Lights. Tiny lights shone like stars in the depths. They grew, rushing toward her, glowing white, beautiful. Heavenly.

Fifteen feet. She sucked in a lungful of water.

# CHAPTER 45

*B*rennan swam around some flotsam toward the glow of magic. The little fool—was she trying to get herself killed? What was she thinking?

Smoke, black powder, burning wood and silk, blood, and the overwhelming smell of salt water filled the air. Shouts rang behind him, a chaos of men's screams.

"Kraken! All hands to guns! Blast that thing out of the water, or we're all dead!"

Whose voice rose above the din, he couldn't tell. The captain of the slaver? Someone from the *Liberté*?

The glow of magic beneath the water enlarged, a fiery sphere swelling, and swelling, destabilizing. *Great Wolf, protect her.*

He cut through the water, cannon blasts sounding behind him. Iron hit the surface, and he gulped air, dove, eyes fixed on the massive glowing fiery sphere amid the depths.

Agony shot through his back. Bones crunching. Air bubbling out. Blood.

It—

She—

No breath. A vise squeezing out barbs of pain. Darkness closing in. Fading. Had it been a cannon shot...?

Closing around him—arms. Up, up, up—

The surface. The night sky on fire, licked by orange flames, breaths like shallow, needling agony.

"Don't you die, Marcel," a voice hissed in his ear. Liam's. "She'll kill me if you do."

She. Rielle.

*She's underwater. Go after her. Save her.* Words he wanted to say, but only wheezing came out.

They came under the shadow of the *Liberté.* Several pairs of hands reached out from the boarding netting.

"Take him." Liam let him go and turned back toward the open water.

"Captain." A grim voice. Sterling's.

"You have the helm, Sterling. If I'm not back in—"

"We're not leaving you, Captain."

A moment passed, and then the rhythmic splashing of a fast swim.

As the darkness narrowed his field of vision, he had the vague sensation of rising, ascending through the air, his eyes meeting a flame-licked sky that blackened and blackened.

Wood met his skin. A groan ripped out of his clenched mouth. Pain radiated outward and up and through—

*Find her, Liam. Find her.*

GASPING FOR BREATH, Rielle coughed, spewing water on the sand. She grabbed her belly, wincing at the pain there, the wetness coating her arm. Blood. A soaking-wet shirt covered her.

*"Sundered flesh and shattered bone, / By Your Divine Might, let it be sewn."* Liam.

A warm glow soothed her, soft and light. Liam's magic. She opened her eyes and found knees beside her. Liam kneeling over her. Only the waxing moon lit the dark, its faint glow a glittering blanket.

"You—" She coughed, rasping. A small, iridescent scale slipped from her chest and into her hand.

He brushed hair and sand from her face. "Look," he whispered.

She glanced past him. Constellations glowed in the water, tiny stars shining in the dark. She tried to sit, and Liam helped her up.

Not constellations. Not stars.

*Eyes.*

People peeked out from beneath the water's surface, their eyes shining with luminance. One sat nearby, half on the sand and half in the surf. Water whispered from the woman's hips and—

No. Fins?

Iridescent scales shone in the faint moonlight, clad their bodies from hips to... fins.

"They saved us. Mermaids." Liam slowly helped her into his shirt, guiding her arms into it, and the soaking wet fabric clung to her skin.

She'd burned the kraken. And everything within a fifty-foot radius. Her mouth fell open. Liam. She ran her hands over him.

"Are you all right?" she rasped. "Did I hurt you?"

"I'm fine," he whispered.

A song bewitched her ears. A beautiful vocalization, almost like whales singing, from the mermaid in the surf.

In the soft moonlight, the mermaid's hair reflected a radiant light green. She held a curled fist to her chest and leaned in, repeating the soft, warm song. Its notes embraced, comforted. She blinked, flickering the stellar glow of her eyes. She extended an arm toward her people in the water, the dozens of them.

A harmony of her vocalization came from the water. Passionate. Heartfelt.

Tears rolled down Rielle's cheeks, and she dabbed at them with a wet sleeve. She couldn't understand what the mermaids said, but the song wrapped her in love and kindness, warm and soft.

Rielle brought a hand to her chest, holding the scale, and curled a soft fist there, like the mermaid. She and Liam were alive thanks to their kindness. "Thank you," she whispered back hoarsely.

The mermaid hummed a lilting note, her lips curved in a smile, and she inclined her head. Another soft harmony followed. As a wave receded, she receded with it.

Rielle reached for Liam's hand. The water's constellations flickered, dimmed, and faded into the night.

Such stunning radiance...

The kraken. The kraken had been drawn to her candlelight spell. Its glow.

The glow of the mermaids' eyes... Had it preyed on them?

She turned to Liam, who watched the waves with a wistful gaze. "You came after me."

"I should've known the fires would draw the kraken." He lowered his gaze. "You saved us all."

That was one way to put it. She'd nearly gotten them all killed.

"I suppose now I can't shrug off my men's stories about mermaids." He drew in a lengthy breath. "You know, it's said that mermaids give away a scale to a rare lucky few, and if you sing to it underwater, mermaids will hear it and come to you."

A precious token. She'd treasure it.

The Rift had returned the kraken to this realm... But the mermaids, too. She blinked, looking out to sea. "Did you free everyone?"

He nodded. "As best we could."

There were no ships in sight. Blackness stretched in every direction. How far had they gone? Last she remembered...

She stiffened. "Brennan."

Liam hugged her and held her close, but she pulled back, forcing him to meet her gaze.

"Tell me."

"Rielle... He was..." His voice died. "He was hit by cannon fire."

A shudder rattled her bones. He'd be all right... Wouldn't he? She looked inward and pulled on the bond; he pulled back, but faint, distant.

He was alive. But had they left him out at sea?

She trembled. "Did you save him?"

Liam took a deep breath. "My crew pulled him aboard, badly injured. I fear the worst." He softly moved her dripping, sandy hair from her shoulders. "They told me you'd jumped into the water, and I came after you."

He'd come after her, not knowing whether she'd live or die. He hadn't abandoned her to her fate.

She hugged him. "Thank you... But how will your crew manage without you?"

With a soft chuckle, he pulled away. The moon shone in his eyes. "You vastly underestimate Sterling. He'll look for us come dawn."

Smiling, she nodded. If Brennan was aboard, Sterling would have no trouble finding them here.

Here. Where was here, anyway? How far had the mermaids taken them? She looked around. They were on a tiny island, no bigger than fifty feet long, with a few palms clustered at one end. Would it still be here at high tide?

"Come," Liam said. "Let's get a fire going." He rose and held out a hand to her.

She took it, and they made their way toward the palms.

~

BLINKING AWAY THE RAIN, Jon looked out across the land of the Vein, its untimely lush greenery the bridge between him and the elven host. The thaw had come, chasing away the winter, but the heavens remained a dreary gray, interrupting only to weep from time to time. Leigh, Tor, Pons, and the rest of his High Council crowded nearby, witnesses and the visible remembrances of duty, along with Aless, whose solemn presence conveyed her support.

When his eyes met hers, she inclined her head and pulled her gray fur stole closer. They'd been inseparable the past few days—and nights—and although she hadn't asked it of him, he'd have to end things with Nora. It didn't feel right otherwise, especially since he and Aless would wed soon—if she agreed after he told her everything.

The wind howled by, billowing his cloak back toward the Bay of Amar, an old way, a past way, too far behind and too small for the king in him to dare seek.

Across from him and past the standing stones, the elven emissary stood at the tip of her squad of guards, clad in an Emaurrian cloak, her hair woven into tight braids that made her stern face even more severe; the length of her locks was a shock of white-blond down her back, riffled by the wind like a bright-hot fire. She looked him over across the distance with a head-to-foot appraisal.

"Aiolian Windsong," Leigh supplied, whispering in his ear. His platinum-white hair was half-plaited in the Vervewood style. "Behind her brick-fortress face is the light-elves' wealth of wisdom."

"Wisdom she will share?" Jon hissed in reply, his gaze unwavering.

Leigh sighed. "That *is* the agreement."

Aiolian and her guards had refused refreshment upon arrival; their instructions were to swear the oath before taking any solace.

And so, here they were, in the rain, hungry and staring at each other.

Another thud as the cleaver came down, and the huntsman finished butchering the stag. Blood pelted the earth as he shook off the blade.

A fresh kill to bind a pagan ritual oath. He sighed. Whatever was required. Olivia looked up from the flesh and at him, her eyebrows raised in a question.

He nodded to her, and she, in turn, nodded to the drummers, who began their beat.

"We're ready," Jon said to Leigh, who inclined his head and moved to stand just outside the circle of standing stones.

Aiolian strode to the circle and cast off her cloak into the hands of her guards.

He, too, moved to the circle and cast off his own cloak, which his valets accepted. He set foot inside, the grass cool against his bare feet, and she followed.

The drums beat louder, or deeper, vibrating, pulsing like resonance, but he resisted the call, resisted the incomprehensible power that called to him here. He walked to the center and held out his arm in greeting.

She clasped it. "Well met, King Jonathan Dominic Armel Faralle of Emaurria," she said in Old Emaurrian.

"Well met, Priestess Aiolian Windsong, Memory of Vervewood," he replied in Old Emaurrian. Hopefully the words he'd practiced with Aless were right.

"Today, I come as my queen, Narenian Sunheart of Vervewood." The grim line of Aiolian's mouth remained even as she spoke.

"I understand."

With a nod, she released his arm.

He held out his left palm, and she intertwined her fingers with his, formed a cup; Olivia entered the circle and placed the warm, bloody stag's heart in their hands, then exited and distributed the rest of the stag's parts around the standing stones. A circle of flesh.

Four months ago, the thought of standing on a Vein with an elf, holding a freshly killed animal's heart, surrounded by its flesh, swearing a heretical oath, invoking pagan gods—the very thought would have leashed his footsteps to the nearest monastery, begging for blessing, pleading to be sent to Monas Tainn's sanitarium to take the Fifth Vow of silence and the Sixth Vow of enclosure.

Droplets of rain fell on his skin, myriad and unremarkable, like myths coming to life, like blasphemy, sin, and heresy; like tragedy, blood, and living death. He exhaled lengthily. The outlandish things that become familiar.

When Olivia finished the ring of binding, he met Aiolian's eyes. Now or never.

"Hear us, Anaruil, god of suppliants! Hear us, Ririnith, glorious goddess, mother of all! Hear us, Urrenael, devourer of flesh!" He invoked the elven gods overseeing the oath ritual—not Terra. The dead gods. The dead gods he prayed now lived again. "Come, with friendly spirit, and listen to our oath!"

Aiolian repeated the invocation in her native tongue, soft sounds like leaves rustling, a breeze through the tall grass, a stream whishing by.

He shivered. "Let the sun, the sky, the rivers, and the mountains bear witness to our oath. Let all of you here today bear witness to our oath," he called, and the crowd answered. She repeated, and the crowd answered.

He closed his thumb over the heart. "Queen Narenian Sunheart of Vervewood, I, King Jonathan Dominic Armel Faralle, swear my whole-hearted loyalty to you and your heirs, to turn over any traitors found plotting against you or your family, to punish any assassin of your line, and to be a friend to your friends and an enemy to your enemies, in perpetuity." He covered the stag's heart with his right palm.

Aiolian's moon-silver eyes locked on his. "King Jonathan Dominic Armel Faralle, I, Queen Narenian Sunheart of Vervewood, swear my whole-hearted loyalty to you and your heirs, to turn over any traitors found plotting against you or your family, to punish any assassin of your line, and to be a friend to your friends and an enemy to your enemies, in perpetuity." She covered his hand firmly with her right palm.

"Let this oath become one with me, as bread and wine, and pass on to become one with my sons and daughters," he called, and when she repeated, they raised the heart in unison, each took a bite. A drop. They split the heart and devoured it. He chewed the raw, soft flesh and swallowed. Another drop.

He fought back a heave and swallowed. "If my oath be broken, let my sons be pursued by your avenging furies. I swear these things to you, before Anaruil, Ririnith, and Urrenael, in good faith or else lie clothed in earth, my kingdom devoured."

An ancient page from one of Olivia's books sprawled before his mind's eye, a great wolf's maw devouring a king, his people, his land, consuming all, taking all, Urrenael of the elven pantheon, cunning eyes, sharp teeth, fur black as night, appetite as deep as the Shining Sea itself.

He blinked as Aiolian repeated the words.

"Let all of you here today bear witness to our oath," she called, and the crowd answered. He repeated, and the crowd answered. "Let the sun, the sky, the rivers, and the mountains bear witness to our oath. Hear us, Urrenael, devourer of flesh! Hear us, Ririnith, glorious goddess, mother of all! Hear us, Anaruil, god of suppliants!" She invoked the gods, and he repeated, his gaze falling to his bloodied hands.

Olivia broke the circle of flesh and entered with cloaks for them both. Jon nodded his thanks and aimed a cordial smile at Aiolian. A flicker of pleasantry, then the grim line of her mouth returned like a change of the guard defending a fortress.

"Come," he said, tipping his head toward Trèstellan. "Let us celebrate."

Aiolian narrowed her eyes and called out to her people.

"Finally!" Leigh said, clapping him on the back. "By all the gods, living and dead, tell me there's gin."

He forced a smile. *Celebrate*, he'd said, but no part of him wanted to laugh and make merry. He wanted to learn the secrets of the Earthbinding immediately, and secure the safety of his realm—and Vervewood.

Now that he'd sworn his loyalty to Queen Narenian, her emissary would reveal all, and he'd finally become what his people needed him to be.

❧

As the dawn brightened the sky, Brennan paced the quarterdeck. Rielle pulled on the bond, and he still felt it. She was alive, and she needed him.

Sterling stood at the wheel, his sharp brown eyes fixed on the horizon. His short sable hair wisped in the southerly wind.

Brennan sighed. "Can't this ship go any faster?"

Sterling's face remained emotionless. "We're full sail with the wind at our stern. If you find eight knots too slow, Lord Marcel, you're welcome to try swimming."

Brennan rolled his eyes. Great Wolf spare him slow, giant ships, the open water—in fact, sailing altogether. The Lothaires may have been built for water, but the mountains were where he belonged.

"And you will have to share how you were able to take a cannon blast to the back and survive, let alone pace my deck and insult my ship."

"I told you. I have a healing rune on my foot." He'd had the healing rune tattooed onto the sole of his foot for precisely this reason. His rapid werewolf healing would need explanation—lest someday he be suspected of being something other than human.

"I've never seen a healing rune work like that."

Brennan scanned the horizon, searching the direction from which she'd pulled on the bond.

Smoke.

He gripped the railing and squinted. There, in the distance, grayish-white smoke rose into the reddened sky. Would humans be able to see it? He could wait. Perhaps the quartermaster would catch sight of it.

"Are you certain this is the right direction?" Sterling asked.

"I told you. I saw her swim that way."

"They could be anywhere." Sterling reached into his coat for a spyglass.

*See the smoke.* Brennan's grip on the railing tightened. The wood creaked under hands fighting the Change.

Sterling collapsed the spyglass and nodded to Brennan. He took a step closer to the railing. "Hoist gallants, royals! Land dead ahead!"

Cheers erupted from the crew, and a renewed energy invigorated their work. Brennan fixed his gaze upon that distant smoke, damning his eyes for their inability to decipher anything on the tiny island. The grayish-white smoke meant living wood and foliage. Palm trees.

Was she all right?

The night before, as the iron had broken his body, he'd seen a flash of white-hot light in the bay's dark depths. Pyromancy. Rielle.

And that light had been the last of her he'd seen before pain and darkness had claimed him.

When he'd awoken—a stiff surprise to all the crew—Sterling had told him Liam had gone after her.

Then Rielle's stranger of a brother had done what *he* hadn't been able to do. Brennan suppressed the lick of jealousy abrading his chest. But the tightness there didn't subside. *I should've been there.*

*As she's been for me.*

For a decade now, Rielle had been there for him, answering every moon to grant him control. She could have locked herself up in that Tower of hers, made access very difficult and conspicuous for him, but she hadn't. As much reason as he'd given her to hate him, she'd protected his secret. Protected him.

And time after time, he'd failed her. Failed to come in time to Laurentine nine years ago. Failed to set aside his own hurt and fear three years ago.

*No more.*

He would be there for her. When she needed him, and not just when she called, he'd be there for her.

He left the quarterdeck for the main, and headed to the fore, all the way to the ship's prow. The dawning light had brightened to day, setting the turquoise waters aglow with sunshine.

Even with the wind against him, he could smell the smoke now, see the fire on the small island.

And two figures.

He sucked in a breath.

*There.* He wanted to shout it to the crew, but he bit his tongue. The foolish anxiety nearly eclipsed his survival instincts.

Great Wolf, he wanted to jump from the ship and swim for that close-by shore.

Knot by knot, she became clearer. The waters had peeled away the pretense, woken the rawness inside her. Her hair had escaped its braid and flared around her head like a great golden mane of wild curls. She wore a billowing white shirt that fell to mid-thigh.

Waving, she opened her mouth wide—shouting—still too far away to discern. But relief glittered in her face, in her smile, her half-moon eyes, and appled cheeks.

Next to her, Liam waved, bare to the waist, his own blond mop of hair tousled by the wind. He put an arm around her, and they shared a smile.

When Sterling finally deployed the pinnace, Brennan could have jumped from his own skin. His foot tapped the wood as he rowed, and it wasn't long before he abandoned the oars and cleared the side to rush through the knee-deep water.

*Rielle.*

She ran to him, jumped, and threw her arms around his neck. The scent of smoke, sand, and seawater flooded his nostrils as he breathed her in, enveloped her in his embrace. He ran his hands over her—over her back, her shoulders, her neck, her head.

"Are you all right?" He repeated the question, repeated it again and again through all her nods. He held her tighter, closer, his palms finding her real.

"I'm all right," she said at last, her voice a relieved rasp below his ear. "Liam said you'd been injured…"

"I'm fine," he whispered, and pulled away to look at her.

Her fingertips strayed from the nape of his neck and into his hair. She raised her face to his, her sky-blue eyes locked on his, and she heaved breath after breath through parted lips; he wrapped her in his embrace, bowed his head closer to hers, her full lips mere inches away. His heart stopped, and he dared not breathe. *Rielle.*

Each exhalation, sweet with date fruit, passionate and eager, coaxed something deeper from him. Something dangerous.

The whoops and calls of crewmen came from the pinnace, and she drew away, enough to just hold his gaze for a moment before blushing and looking away.

*Don't look away.* He drew his eyebrows. *Don't ever look away.*

Grinning crookedly, Liam trudged through the surf and clapped him on the back. "To the ship. You'll have plenty of time later to remind yourselves you're still alive." He tilted his head toward the pinnace.

Rielle kept her reddened face turned aside and wouldn't meet his gaze. She cared for him, and that was enough for now. He took her hand, and they boarded.

*Reminding ourselves we're still alive…*

He took one last look at the island, at the embers of the extinguished fire already being swept away by the wind.

# CHAPTER 46

*J*on pulled back his presence from the rose bush in the gardens below and hissed. It was near midnight, and he'd accomplished nothing.

Aiolian muttered something in Old Emaurrian, too quiet for him to hear, even if his nightly language lessons with Aless had worked wonders in comprehension.

"You're still perceiving as a man would," Leigh said. "Would you at least attempt to do as she says?"

Jon eyed him and grunted. "I'm still *perceiving* as a man because I *am* a man." He grabbed the goblet on the stone balustrade, drank, and stared out into the night.

"Can't you just be a rose bush for a moment?" Leigh leaned his back against the balustrade while Aiolian glared at him peripherally. She murmured something to him, then sighed and strode past Raoul and Florian back into the great hall.

"What did she say?" He did catch *hopeless human* and *small mind* in there, but not much else.

"You don't want to know." Leigh exhaled lengthily. "I know you're a novice at this, so you won't come into your full power overnight. But

I'm leaving tomorrow, and achieving some progress would be a good parting gift. You need to do the meditation like she said."

He puffed. "What, imagine I'm some bush while the kingdom demands action?"

"The kingdom needs its Earthbound king at full power."

Jon sighed. Leigh was right.

Spending hours each day, imagining himself as a bush, a tree, a mountain, a river... What it would be like? The answer to moving mountains wasn't haunting the mountain; it was *being* the mountain. No, the *life* in a mountain, the anima. That there even was life in a mountain was news to him, but now he had to *be* it. He'd been a human all his life and now had work to do in learning to become everything else.

But supposedly, if he could abandon his human perception and learn what it meant to be the anima in a bush, a tree, a mountain, a river... then he could learn to control them, imbue them with his will.

Just not nearly fast enough. If only he'd had the power months ago—

"You're worried about her," Leigh said.

Gods. If only he knew.

"You should be," Leigh added grimly. "When she returns and finds out you've been fooling around, you're going to lose her."

Jon straightened. "I—"

"Don't even bother denying it. I've seen enough secret lovers to know you and the Sileni princess are"—he cleared his throat—"*close.*" Leigh glared at him peripherally. "Not sticking to the Code much anymore now, hm?"

Jon sighed and bowed his head, staring into the gardens below. "I have to wed one of them. She's a wise choice."

"And Rielle?"

He and Olivia had decided to wait to tell Leigh until after the peace with Vervewood was negotiated. No doubt he would abandon everything to find her... to find her body.

*As I should have done.*

He shook off the feeling. Brennan would find her. He had to. She'd find her eternal rest here, in the soil of her homeland.

"The cost of being king. Having the power to protect and save countless lives, but at the cost of love, joy, honor... self."

Leigh stared into nothing for a long moment. "When she returns, *you* must tell her. The entire truth, direct from you. She's no stranger to duty, and might put up with you anyway." A lopsided grin appeared and faded just as quickly. "But if she finds out any other way, you *will* lose her."

If Rielle were alive, he would have ended things with Nora, prayed Aless would release him from his word, and begged Rielle's forgiveness. He would have moved mountains to marry her, and she'd have helped him. He would have brought the Tower and the Order under the Crown, as he'd planned, but much sooner. He would have unified every willing Immortal race in the land. He would have made the need for a political marriage unnecessary.

To be with her, even for three years, for three months, even three *minutes*, he would have done anything, or died trying.

But that was past him now. She was gone.

Leigh patted his arm. "No sense in worrying about it now. Why don't we focus on the Earthbinding? Just *try* to make some progress tonight. I'll wait with you."

It would be a long wait. But if Leigh was being supportive, it was a once-in-a-lifetime opportunity.

With a sigh, Jon closed his eyes, pictured the enormous balcony off the great hall, Leigh, Raoul, and Florian, the stone balustrade, the chill spring air beyond and below... Bare branches and thorns, roots spread into the hard earth. Feeder roots, small and fine, into large anchor roots, stable and strong. Emerging up, the hardy rose shank, thick to the bud union, where basal canes scaffolded, others sprouting from the bud eyes—and redundant canes that would be pruned. Weakness cut away to preserve strength.

Old wood recently cut away, part of the shank opened up to air circulation. Cool air kissing vibrant life, a slow-moving stream spreading to every stem, spirit. He could feel it in his veins, follow it to a cane, push it to a petiole of seven leaves, toothed like a serrated knife, and a bud, anxious for life, and he let it free, encouraged it, and hope bloomed. He drank in the sun, relished it with every fiber of his being, until the wind shook through his leaves.

He swayed but did not break, and shadows interrupted the blessed light, tall, dark shadows.

People?

People... He remembered his own face, up there on the balcony, past the air and the stone balustrade, next to Leigh and Raoul and Florian...

He gasped.

"Jon!" Leigh shook his shoulders, and Olivia covered her mouth with a hand while Aiolian said something to her. Raoul and Florian crouched next to him, a squad of guards behind him.

Bright light assailed his eyes—noon sun—and he blocked it with his arm, a heavy fur falling off his shoulders. He was on the floor, covered in furs. At noon.

Olivia rushed to him and knelt, resting a hand gently on his arm. "Are you all right?"

He nodded. Last he remembered, it had been evening, and he and Leigh had been talking on the balcony... "How long was I out?"

"All night and all morning," Leigh grunted.

Aiolian arched a brow and said something to him, about the gardens?

Leigh frowned. He really wasn't the best of translators.

"What is it?"

Olivia beamed next to him. "In the gardens... A single rose is blooming."

HEART RACING, Rielle fidgeted with the clasp on her cloak, tightening the knot. The snow-covered bright white stone of Trèstellan Palace came into view, a shining jewel at the crown of Courdeval.

Warmth radiated against her arm—Brennan standing sentinel at her side. The stark white palace neared, and she shivered.

Brennan covered her gloved hand with his own. She eyed him, unsure of what to say. *Thank you.*

He gave her hand a gentle squeeze.

She owed him her life. And so much more.

Silence lingered over the soft roll of waves. He gazed at the white-gray sky and sighed. "What's the plan once we dock?"

She'd planned it for months now. Jon had to know about Shadow as soon as possible, and telling him would necessitate revealing her own arrival.

And yet, if the world knew she was alive and well in Courdeval, a serpent like Shadow, who had so relied on her continued suffering, might be tempted to strike, swiftly and fatally. And Jon couldn't be placed at risk.

Incognito. It was the only way to return to Courdeval.

"I can't be here as myself, Brennan," she whispered. "But I need access to the palace, and to Jon."

He blinked. "Mine." He cleared his throat. "My access—you could blend in among my liveried household. No one will pay you a second glance."

At Trèstellan, no noble would question a servant. Beneath their notice... It would be an ideal disguise.

He leaned against the railing, intense hazel eyes fixed on the vast expanse of blue. "I'll send him a message." He looked her over. "And a messenger."

The perfect plan. As a messenger, seeing Jon...

The look on his face when he'd see her... She smiled. He'd been waiting four months, and his letter—

That *letter.* She melted. He'd been as worried about her as she'd been about him. When they were finally reunited, the confessions, the problems, the threats would wait one day. A single day, until she relearned the circle of his arms, the calm waters of his sea-blue eyes, the deep notes of his voice. Then she'd tell him everything and pray he'd forgive her.

Their love could overcome anything. His love had helped her make peace with herself, become whole again after the mess she'd been from her éveil. He'd helped her save herself, and everyone she loved, from fureur, and her power was now completely under her control. All that had happened since, once she told him, he'd forgive her with time, wouldn't he?

And given the news she'd translated, he'd had to entertain suit-resses from all over the region. What had he been duty-bound to do? Court them, perhaps even—

She swallowed. No. It had only been four months. He would never betray her, no matter how much she didn't deserve his loyalty.

If he still loved her, they'd figure it all out. It would work. It had to. When she closed her eyes, she could still smell the lindenwood and smoke of him, still feel his breath on her skin, his whisper against the crown of her head. Even the memory of his embrace warmed her.

"He's a lucky man," Brennan whispered, his deep, husky voice choked, "our king." He watched the sea, eyes glazed.

"You're too kind."

He shook his head. "Selfish." He didn't look up. "I'm a selfish man, Rielle. Very selfish. But less so now than I have ever been."

"No." She touched his arm and rubbed it softly. "I finally recognize you again, Brennan." When he turned to her, she smiled. "The boy I loved so well... You are finally the man he was always going to become."

He covered her hand with his and gently stroked one of her fingers. "A couple years too late." But before she could answer, he straightened and cleared his throat.

Ignoring the hollow in her throat, she pulled the knot on her cloak tighter. For two weeks, she'd leaned on him for support, for comfort, and he hadn't pushed. Hadn't pried.

But she'd been cruel. When the ship's pinnace had come into view, when Brennan's eyes had met hers, there'd been nothing in the world she'd wanted to see more. Him, alive. With her. And the power of that had pushed her past a boundary, a firm boundary, stupidly and hopelessly.

She'd wanted to kiss him. Wanted to. But hadn't.

Brennan had been good to her, been there for her when no one else had. Their pretense at House Hazael, pretended passion, had readied her hands to him, readied her body—forced a familiarity that yet lingered, all the more pronounced in their continued close proximity.

He was attractive, always had been, but more than that, she cared for him now, *loved* him, even if she wasn't *in* love with him. He meant a lot to her, and there was no denying that anymore.

"Furl all sails!" Liam shouted. "Bring her in steady, boys!"

Courdeval. They were docking. She glanced at Liam. If she didn't talk to him before—

"Go on." Brennan gave her a nudge. A sort of weariness had settled into his expression, a crease between his brows, but he still offered her a smile and nodded toward the quarterdeck.

She inclined her head and, boots clicking, headed up to the wheel, shrugging deeper into her cloak as the chill wind blew past.

Before she could ascend the ladder to the quarterdeck, Liam tipped his head toward his cabin. "Sterling, you have the wheel."

"Aye, Captain," Sterling answered with a puff of breath on the cold air. He strode to the wheel and took it with articulated procedure.

Liam offered her his arm. She laced hers through it and allowed him to lead her to his cabin. He escorted her to one of the tufted armchairs.

Rather than rounding the desk, he drew the armchair next to her closer, unfastened his wool overcoat, and settled in. "I—" he began, just as she said, "Liam—"

They shared a smile. He leaned back in the armchair and gestured for her to continue.

"I want to see you again." She reached for his hand. "I want you to come home."

He intertwined his fingers with hers and gave her hand a squeeze. "This ship is my home. You know that," he answered softly. "But I want to visit you, too."

"Do ship captains get vacations?"

He raised his eyebrows. "Shore leave."

"So you'll be here a few days?"

He nodded. "We need to resupply, and the crew need to cut loose after..."

He didn't need to say it.

"How will I know where to find you?" she asked.

"You can send me a message here, and it'll get to me. Also, the

*Liberté* makes berth in Gazgan, so if you ever wish to correspond, that would be the best place to send me mail."

"Will you?" she asked. "Correspond?"

He left the chair and took a knee at her side, clasping her hand in both of his. "Of course I will."

For nearly a decade, he hadn't. She wouldn't hope that he'd start now.

He brushed her cheek with a finger. "Don't make that face, little bee. Please." When she glared at him, he stuck out his tongue, and she smiled. "I didn't want you to... pity me."

"I don't. I wouldn't." She shook her head vehemently. "I... I love you. I've missed you."

"I won't abandon you again, I promise." He stood and kissed the top of her head. "Well, aside from literally abandoning you when we leave port."

She gave him a shove, but he evaded.

"You won't be rid of me so easily." He plopped back into the armchair. "When we come to Courdeval, we usually stay at Claudine's in the Dandelion District. If it's still open, that's where we'll be."

Someday, she'd have to tell him the truth about Laurentine. About their family. What she'd done. There was so much he needed to know, very little of which she was brave enough to tell him now. "Before... Sonbahar, I was the king's lover. I haven't seen him in months, but I will tonight."

Liam's eyes widened. "Then, Brennan...?"

"Just friends."

He scoffed. "You two are fooling yourselves." She opened her mouth to argue, but he cut her off. "The way he looks at you... He loves you. And the way you look at him... You love him, too."

Her mouth dropped open. "Liam—"

"I'm not saying I approve." He held up his hands. "You know I don't. But don't lie to yourself. Never to yourself."

Her and Brennan? It was—

It was...

She lowered her gaze. Some part of her did love Brennan. What they could have been. But that part only dealt in embers and ash.

"The king." Liam exhaled a long breath. "They say he's a good man —strong, pious, honorable, fair."

She smiled. "He makes me want to be a better person. I only hope I live up to it."

"A paladin, I hear?"

"Former."

He winked at her. "Well, Emaurrian politics will not welcome him gently."

Parliament was a nest of spitting vipers, and the Houses were worse. But Jon would have to learn to manipulate politics—perhaps he had already.

But Jon was Jon. Despite navigating Emaurrian politics and the demands of his crown, he'd still inherently be the same man she'd fallen in love with.

A call came from outside.

"We've docked." Liam stood and pulled her up from her chair and into an embrace. "Take care, little bee. I hope we meet again soon."

She wrapped her arms around him and absorbed his warmth for a moment. "You're alive."

He laughed softly. "Yes. Yes, I am. Keen observation."

"I just had to remind myself," she said, pulling away. "You take care, too, brother." With a loving smile, she exited the cabin and disembarked with Brennan.


THE CARRIAGE RIDE into Azalée wasn't as long as she remembered. Although the city appeared restored—with only some buildings still bearing the visible signs of siege—people didn't crowd the streets. Perhaps the biting cold kept them inside.

Unusual weather. She couldn't remember a time when the capital had been so frigid in spring. Sitting next to her, Brennan rubbed her hands between his own; the heat of his blood brought some life into hers. She could have heated them with pyromancy, but she didn't want to draw attention to herself.

Passersby gawked at the carriage window, but sunken deep into her cloak's hood, she wouldn't be recognized, even with her fiancé. The golden brown of her tan skin, lingering from the Sonbaharan sun, certainly helped.

She and Brennan stopped at an inn, where he sent for servants and livery from Victoire, his family's villa. They ate, drank, and bathed hastily, and when the servants finally arrived, she couldn't wait to throw on the clothes—finely made trousers and a coat in crimson and gold, a crisp white cotton shirt, and polished black leather boots. She braided her hair simply, plainly, and then spun for Brennan.

"Do I look the part?" She held out her arms.

He drank from a snifter of brandy and looked her over, his gaze meandering up her legs to her face. He set down the brandy. "You do."

"Good. Let's go." She cocked her head toward the door, and her stomach growled.

Brennan nodded to the table laden with food. "Not until you eat something. You haven't eaten since this morning, and I'm not sure half a bowl of fish stew counts."

Although she wanted to jump out of her own skin, she plopped into a chair and idly dipped a point of crusty bread into her bowl of potée, pushing around pieces of bacon, carrot, and parsnips. What was food to her, when she was about to see Jon again?

But just over a month ago, she'd been in arcanir shackles, starving, every day a fight for survival—hers and... And Sylvie's.

Freedom had come at a high cost, an unconscionable sacrifice that any good woman—any good mother—

She winced. The long nights since House Hazael had heard her quiet sobs, collected her tears. She'd mourned, and blamed, and rued, and regretted. And Shadow would pay for it all, for everything, and then there would be some measure of justice.

And Jon... He'd been here, didn't know, hadn't—

She shook her head. "Do you think he'll forgive me for losing our child? And... for being Farrad's lover?"

He kept the silence for a long moment, then slid the empty snifter aside to his pile of cleared plates. He folded his hands on the table. "You did what was necessary to survive. There's nothing to forgive. If he doesn't see that, he's a fool."

With a spoon, she submerged the bread in the potée and held it there.

"And if he didn't know you were with child, then nothing good will come of telling him it's lost."

She flinched. "I won't lie to him."

"Sometimes a lie is kinder. He can't change what happened. Neither can you. He'll only feel guilty that he wasn't there, frustrated that he couldn't do anything, angry for revenge. But it's done. Do you want any of that?"

Bubbles escaped the submerged bread.

"No," she whispered. What she wanted from him was forgiveness, understanding. Lifting the burden weighing so heavily on her heart.

"Then don't tell him."

But it wasn't just about forgiveness. She'd been reckless, seized the first chance of escape, and Sylvie had died because of that. Because of her.

Perhaps some wounds never healed.

But didn't Jon deserve to know he'd had a child? Didn't Sylvie deserve life in her father's memory? Not telling him would be cruel to him and Sylvie both, and selfish to the extreme.

"If you lost a child, wouldn't you want to know she'd existed?" she whispered. "Even if it hurt?"

His eyes widened, amber flashing like lightning before he looked away.

That was answer enough. She gently removed the spoon, and the bit of bread floated to the top of her bowl.

She'd tell him. Once they dealt with Shadow, she'd tell him everything, and they'd bear the loss together, and honor Sylvie's memory together.

The sooner she saw him, the better. She lifted the bowl to her mouth and gulped down the soup. When she pushed back her chair, he stood, grabbed it, and pulled it out for her.

He held out a hand and, when she took it, helped her to her feet. The city beyond the foggy window had darkened to twilight gray as the sun turned its back.

"Let's go."

He gave her hand a squeeze before he released her. "Now that you've silenced that growling hound you call a stomach."

Smiling, she reached for her cloak and put it on while Brennan gave word to his servants. Out the window, she could just barely make out the battlements and turrets of Trèstellan in the dark. She sucked in a shaky breath and shook out her jittery hands.

It was time. Tonight, she would finally see him. She would finally see Jon.

# CHAPTER 47

*B*rennan wrapped an arm around Rielle in the carriage. The cold had frosted to a savage freezing; even clad in the strandling-lined wool cloak he'd procured for her, she still trembled. Even his own considerably hot blood had chilled.

These moments, enshrined from the world and time, could prove to be the last he'd have so closely with her. She was returning to the arms of the man she loved. And the king, if he had any sense, wouldn't let her go again for any price.

He took her leather-gloved hands in his and rubbed them. She wriggled closer and rested her head under his chin.

Great Wolf, it was a foolish ruse, holding her here, holding her close, a deception that quieted the clamoring fear in his chest. He would lose this. He would lose her. The king would never let another man hold her like this ever again.

He squeezed his eyes shut.

And she... She had finally taken down her walls, allowed herself to be vulnerable with him, accepted him into her heart. Let him in. The Duchess of Melain had been right. *Love her. Love those she loves.*

He'd told Rielle not to concern herself with him. Given her cause to think he'd made peace with it all. She'd believed him, or this nearness of hers would have been bitter. Bittersweet. No matter what she believed, her nearness would always be welcome, in some way. Welcome, but unlikely ever again.

He'd regained her trust, her love, her friendship. He'd regained nearly all he'd stupidly lost. Only to lose her to Jonathan Dominic Armel Faralle.

He puffed a warm breath on her hooded head, and she moaned softly.

There was nothing to do but either continue vying for her favor or lose her gracefully.

He wanted her to love him, to choose him. Even looking at her now, he saw her wearing a Maerleth Tainn signet ring, her belly full with his child and heir. The woman he loved. His wife. Mother to his children. The daydream's beauty dazzled with enough shine to keep him captivated for a lifetime.

The carriage jostled.

A daydream was all it could ever be.

He'd made it clear he wanted her. If she'd wanted him enough in return, there had been the entire trip from Xir for her to make it known. But she hadn't. And wouldn't.

If he continued vying for her, he'd only force her to push him away. If she loved Jon, she wouldn't tolerate a threat to that love. She'd push away another suitor.

But she wouldn't push away a friend. No, as her friend, he could stay close to her. Never as close as he wanted, but closer than he could be if he pursued her overtly. He rested his chin lightly on her head. As a friend, he could keep her in his life; he could stay in hers. He'd watch over her from a distance, keep their monthly meetings. And someday—perhaps someday—she might break his curse.

Yes, he would gracefully abandon pursuit of Rielle. He would let her go. But in the absence of the flame of requited love, hope would still provide a glimmer of light. And he could subsist on its radiance.

The carriage stopped. They had to be at the Noble Gate to Trèstellan Palace. He'd fulfilled his vow to the king, and to himself. He'd brought her home.

He pulled aside the curtain and presented his documents to the guards.

They inspected the interior and let him through. "Welcome back to Emaurria, Your Lordship."

He nodded. "My thanks. May the night be kind to you."

"And to you, Your Lordship."

The carriage rolled to speed again, hurtling toward the palace. He reached for his waistcoat's pocket, where he'd left the folded and sealed message Rielle would take to the king. It read simply, *Found her in Xir. She couldn't wait to see you.*

The carriage pulled to a halt, jostling as the footmen dismounted and opened the doors.

He rubbed Rielle's arm through her cloak. "We're here," he whispered, the words a reluctant rasp. It had ended too soon. All too soon.

Shivering, she smiled up at him. "Good. I can't wait to get out of this cold. It's as if the world will never be warm again."

"It will." *For you. I promise.* He exited and assisted her out of the carriage.

Despite the freezing air, he breathed in deeply, staring at the white stone palace walls and the ornately carved door before them. Nowhere else to go but through.

EVERY HAIR on Rielle's body stood on end while she waited for Brennan and his household to settle him into his quarters. Apparently, the Royal Guard needed to be certain a noble was in residence before they allowed his messenger access to the king.

At least they were being careful with his life, trying to shield him from potential assassins.

But once the Royal Household and the Royal Guard knew Brennan had returned, no one would doubt his liveried messenger moving about the palace with a message bearing his seal, even to the king's own quarters.

Warmth flowed through her body. For four months, she hadn't seen the man she loved. But tonight... She stood, nerves electrifying her body.

While the servants flitted about Brennan's luxurious quarters, she paced, tapping the wax-sealed paper against her palm. As soon as Brennan's chamberlain returned with word, she would go.

Arms crossed and clad in impeccable black velvet, Brennan leaned against the window frame in his bedchamber, eyes fixed on the city. "Have you ever seen it this cold before?"

"Never."

He narrowed his eyes. "Strange."

The cold was unusual, but weather could be unpredictable. An elementalist could have been responsible for a chill here and there, but over all of Courdeval for so long? And to what end?

The door opened, and she jumped. *Finally.*

A kitchen maid brought in a tray with a decanter of red wine, along with goblets, bread, butter, some cold cuts, and jam. "Sorry, Your Lordship. It's after dinner. I can have Chef fix you a hot meal, if you like?"

Rielle deflated.

Brennan smiled warmly and inclined his head. "My thanks. A bottle of brandy, and I'll be fine for tonight."

"Yes, Your Lordship." The maid bowed and exited.

Rielle buttered a piece of warm bread, her mouth watering. At the inn, she'd neglected to eat more than a few sips of potée, despite Brennan's urging. Too nervous to eat. But here, there was nothing to do but wait and eat.

As the comforting flavors danced on her tongue, she could have whimpered. Emaurrian partial rye and fresh, unsalted butter. It had been so long. So very long.

"That good?" Brennan asked from the window, an amused lilt playing in his voice.

"That good." She popped another piece in her mouth. Just like old times at the Tower. She'd always eaten well there—perhaps a little *too* well. She laughed under her breath.

"So"—he walked over and poured himself a goblet of wine—"you'll need about three loaves a night for a few weeks to look like yourself again."

Pursing her lips, she kicked out at him, but he evaded. "I wasn't that large!"

"Soft," he whispered, his hazel eyes darker than usual. "You were soft." He poured her some wine.

As she reached for it, she examined her bony hands and wrists, her thin arms. Sonbahar had taken a lot. Starvation could do that to a person. "Don't worry. Bread, butter, and I are quite fond of each other, and I expect we'll spend a lot of time together"—she took a drink —"with our good friend, wine."

He cocked an eyebrow, huffing a half-laugh into his goblet, then grabbed some bread himself, piling cuts of smoked duck atop it. "You need to bolster your strength. Does your... 'friendship' extend to smoked duck?"

Having finished her third slice of bread, she licked the butter off her thumb and helped herself to some meat. "Well, there's no such thing as too many friends, is there?"

He pulled out a chair and sat, eyebrows raised.

A gentle rap sounded at the door.

"Yes?" he called.

His chamberlain entered. "My lord, the Royal Guard and the Royal Household have been notified of your arrival, as requested."

Brennan stared at his goblet, swirling it slowly. "And the king?"

"In his quarters, my lord."

Brennan took a drink. "Thank you, Gerard."

"My lord." Gerard bowed and quietly shut the door.

Then...

Frozen, she raised her eyes to Brennan's. "Does that mean...?"

He nodded and drank again. "Yes. You can go to him now, if you wish."

Jon. She could finally see Jon.

She leaped from her chair and gulped down the rest of her wine, then darted to the mirror to check her face, hair, and teeth. It wouldn't do to see him for the first time in months with butter smudged on her face or crumbs in her hair. She smoothed some stray curls, tucking them back into her braid, and ran her index finger over each eyebrow. Her teeth, since washing them at the inn, were clean.

"Quit worrying," Brennan murmured into his goblet. "You look fine." He gulped some wine. "As fine as you can, anyway, before your angles round out again—"

She glared at him, but he only grinned back crookedly. Trying to set her at ease? She rushed to him and threw her arms around his neck. "Thank you for everything, Brennan. I don't know if I'd be here without you."

He swallowed a mouthful of wine and patted her shoulder. "Go."

After dropping a kiss on his cheek, she dashed to the door and out.

She walked through the halls with the letter in hand, her official documents from Brennan tucked into her shirt. With every step, her heart pounded harder and harder, until it became an ominous drum thumping in her ears, a march guiding her footfalls. She would see him again. In minutes.

The unusual cold had permeated the castle walls, the hearths and sconces doing little to keep it at bay. She puffed warm air into her hands from time to time, reminding them of heat once more. They'd thaw. Probably.

Although she was liveried in Tregarde's crimson and gold, the Royal Guard—paladins, judging by their behavior—stopped her more frequently the closer she approached the king's quarters. She found herself nodding through each conversation, repeating the same few words, and taking visual cues about how to respond as her heart, its anticipation, and its longing drowned out all else. How many more faces, how many more moving lips and demanding hands would she have to engage before finally seeing him?

With a forced smile, she tore herself away from yet another guard.

At last, the tall double doors to the king's chambers were in sight. As she approached the guards posted outside, she beamed and murmured a cheerful excuse that it was her first time at the palace while they inspected Brennan's seal.

She stared at the ornate doors, and for a moment, they disappeared: Jon would stand on the other side, looking back at her with relief and love and joy. He'd take her into his arms and say he'd waited four long months for this moment.

Divine, she'd missed him. His smile, his warmth, his teasing. Had he looked out at the sky, night after night, with longing, as she had? Had he held their most precious moments together close to his heart, as she had? Had he lain awake every evening until he pictured the face of his lover, as she had?

One of the guards asked her a question, and she watched the unyielding lines of his face as he spoke; she couldn't hear a word. Her heart, beating so loudly in her ears, began to slowly quiet, but some strange mix of sounds...

"...an official correspondence, but..." The guard's lips kept moving.

From behind the doors, breaths, loud and ragged—

"...not possible..."

A woman's moans—

*Not possible.*

"...to wait or leave the correspondence with..."

A man's voice she... knew, but it couldn't be—

"...but His Majesty is currently... indisposed," the guard finished, lowering his gaze.

*His Majesty...*

*Jon.*

It couldn't be.

It just couldn't.

The sounds assailed her in a fierce series of blows that only began with her ears, every moment harder, heavier, harsher, filling her up, pushing aside everything else, crushing all inside, leaving no room for—

*No room—*

She couldn't breathe.

She gasped, trying to catch her breath as the mess inside fought its way out. A million stars exploding, a sky collapsing—

"Mademoiselle?" the guard asked with some concern. "Would you like to wait or leave the correspondence with me?"

From the other side of the doors, the woman cried out his name.

She tried to swallow the lump in her throat and noticed a nearby tapping sound; her head lowered until she was faced with her own foot, shaking erratically—*anxiously*.

Not another minute. She couldn't stand here another minute.

Get away. She had to get away.

Wordlessly, she handed the letter to the guard, forced a quick smile, and spun to leave, the hall ahead a blur.

She walked, trying to shut out everything, but the unwanted sounds continued—whether from his quarters or in her head—and they chased her every speeding step.

*Keep walking. Just keep walking.*

She tried to stay upright, staring at the blurry end of the hallway. Her exit from this torture. With every movement, the emptiness in her chest widened.

*A few more steps. Only a few more.*

Once she rounded the corner, she braced herself against the wall, bringing a hand to her chest as if to hold it together, but to no avail—it would break, it would crumble, and it would unravel the very fiber that held her together.

The gasps, the cries, the moans—her legs moved faster. Away. One foot in front of the other, she ran, muffling her mouth with one determined palm.

She had to escape, had to forget—

Great Divine, how she wished now to never have done this, never to have hoped—

She stumbled and fell to a knee. It had been foolish. All of it.

Pushing off the floor, she ran, ran, and ran, her feet taking her as far from him as they could. Passersby balked, but she didn't care. She ran until her legs turned leaden, too heavy to keep moving, to keep fighting.

Finally, a door—*the* door—Brennan's door.

But why had she come to *his* quarters, of all places? What words of comfort would he offer? Wouldn't he rejoice in this, of all things?

But the door opened, and there he stood. His hazel gaze was earnest. Clear.

She swallowed and bit her lip, shaking her head as no words would come, and he took her in his arms, and it was so much comfort, too much—his warm body against hers, his strong arms holding her in their loving embrace, his stubble brushing her forehead.

Whatever had kept her strong and standing for the past months failed her now, collapsing upon itself. Her knees buckled, and she slipped in his embrace, but he caught her.

"I got you. You're all right." His voice, despite its reassurance, choked.

There was no more holding back.

She rested her wet cheek against the velvet doublet covering his chest. "He didn't... wait for me." An unfamiliar voice, broken, shrill.

He squeezed her, groaned. The rumble of his voice vibrated from his body against hers, and she closed her eyes, focusing on his warmth, on his breaths, on him.

"Stay here tonight," he whispered, and she nodded against his chest, breathing him in, cinnamon spice, cypress, and familiarity.

He scooped her up and carried her to his bedchamber, where he lowered her gently to the bed and nestled her under the covers. He climbed in next to her, wrapped an arm around her and held her together.

# CHAPTER 48

*T*he sun's morning rays warmed Jon's skin. He'd slept too long, hours past dawn. It had been a long night.

Outside the window, snow layered the sill. Gods, not again. It was nearly spring—much too late for snow. He had to get a handle on his power.

Despite his nakedness, sweat coated his skin. A fever. No, a fire. It burned inside him.

He peered at Aless asleep upon his chest, not a care in the world. After Leigh had left Courdeval, thoughts of Rielle had reclaimed him, haunted him.

He rubbed his face. If Aless agreed to marry him after he told her about his heart, they would announce their engagement in a matter of days, and they might be married by the end of summer. And he still had yet to formally end his affair with Nora, although he hadn't seen her for a while. She deserved more than just being pushed out of his life; she deserved a meeting face to face.

But another time. It could wait.

He slipped from the bed. Aless could sleep all day if she wished, but he had a list of tasks that could take weeks. The Lord Warden would be reporting soon on the interrogations, as he always did in the afternoon.

He washed and dressed, the final piece the black leather doublet his valet had left out. Perhaps he'd open the windows in his study to make the leather bearable.

On his way to his dining room, he passed the mirror and caught a glimpse of the man reflected there. Dark, tired, angry. He raised a hand to the bristly stubble on his jaw. Two weeks' growth. Rough, like a ranger. He huffed. The men of the Houses sported beards. So could he.

He didn't know the man in the mirror, but he was beginning to. This man in the mirror didn't think dark thoughts anymore, but he wore them; he filled his days with work and his nights with distraction; he kept the land safe. Stable. Kingdom and country first. All else second.

He could do that—for the rest of his life, couldn't he?

Manon and another maid brought in breakfast. He thanked them, grabbed his mail, and sat with a cup of black tea. He sorted through the endless invitations, letters, petitions—

A note with a wax seal. Tregarde's seal. Brennan.

He dragged in a deep breath as his heart hit the floor. There had been no way of getting word to Brennan. Sooner or later, he'd return to Courdeval. He had to. Perhaps his mission had finally led him to her final...

He clenched a fist. Whoever was responsible for her death—no matter who—would suffer for it. Greatly.

He tore open the note.

*Found her in Xir. She couldn't wait to see you.*

Wide-eyed, Jon reread the note six times.

*She couldn't wait...* His chest pounded. He pinched the bridge of his nose.

*She couldn't wait to see you.*

He breathed raggedly. *Found her in Xir.* He rubbed the note between his fingers, the fibers harsh against his skin. *Found her in Xir. She couldn't wait to see you.*

He sucked in a breath and lowered the note to the table with a shaky hand, letting it rest light as a feather. He stared at it there, next to his tea.

The note was real.

Rielle was alive?

He looked around the room. Books, shelves, walls, drapes, window, a snowy Courdeval... Not a dream.

Somehow, he was even warmer.

Rielle was *alive*.

He bolted from his chair.

Rielle was alive! He grinned. How was it possible? Never mind that —where was she? He grabbed the note, rushed to the door, and burst out into the hall.

Raoul and Florian came to attention. "Your Majesty," they greeted.

Jon held up the note. "When did this arrive?"

Raoul scrutinized the seal. "From Tregarde, Your Majesty?"

"Yes."

"Late last night," he answered, shaking his head. "The messenger looked like—"

"Never mind the messenger." Jon rested a hand on Raoul's shoulder. "Tell me, my brother. Is Tregarde here, in Courdeval?"

Raoul glanced at Florian, who nodded.

"He's in his palace quarters, Your Majesty," Florian answered.

Praise Terra. Jon grinned broadly. "My thanks."

Both Raoul and Florian saluted, then followed him in escort as he rushed to Brennan's quarters with eager steps.

Terra have mercy, Brennan had returned. He was in the palace. Had he brought Rielle here? Was she in Courdeval?

As he passed courtiers and guards, he hastily acknowledged bows and salutes and greetings. Was she here in the palace? Or in the Lothaire villa, Couronne? Victoire, perhaps? Was she all right?

Terra help him, he had endless things to tell her, to beg her forgiveness for—but she was *alive*. Everything else didn't matter.

At last, he arrived at the door to Brennan's quarters and knocked right away. Knocked again. No answer. If the man wasn't in, he'd break down the door. He raised his hand again, but the door opened before he could knock.

Brennan.

His eyes widened as Jon embraced him. Florian and Raoul took up posts on either side of the door.

"You found her." Jon pulled back, holding Brennan's shoulders. He'd never been happier to see him—and owed him *everything*.

Nodding, Brennan opened his mouth, then closed it. He hesitated.

Jon rushed past him and into the antechamber, his eyes sweeping the room. Bursts of sunlight. Red velvet drapes. A subtle flower print on the upholstered walls. The air sizzled, electrified.

"You did find her?" He turned back to Brennan.

"I did." Brennan lowered his gaze. He wore only loose lounge pants fastened with a drawstring and a matching silk robe that hung open from his heavy shoulders. Spiritless.

Why wasn't he happy? Was Rielle hurt? Had something happened to her? Jon grabbed him. "Is she injured? Tell me." He searched Brennan's face. "Terra have mercy, Marcel—"

Brennan inhaled, pressing his lips together. "She's not injured."

Jon shook his head and squeezed Brennan's shoulder. "What's the matter, then? Is she here? Speak."

Brennan's eyes bored into his, a dark-wooded forest, too dense, too thick, too deep. He looked past Jon at the door to the bedchamber.

"Wait here." Pulling away, Brennan gathered his composure, and then he marched to the door, his black silk robe trailing after him.

Jon looked after him, a frown settling in his face. She was in Brennan's bedchamber?

Stiffening, he watched the door as Brennan opened it, entered, paused, and then closed it.

Together...

Could they be... together?

But he had no right to expect anything else—he'd betrayed her in every possible way. While he'd stayed behind, Brennan had gone after her. And yet, it was a thousand bricks on his shoulders.

He moved as close to the door as he dared, then stilled.

"His Majesty is here to see you." Brennan's muffled voice, slow, cautious, came through the door.

Jon didn't move, didn't breathe, would never move, never breathe, unless he heard her answer.

"No," came the low reply, barely audible.

*Rielle.*

It was *Rielle.*

He stared at the crystal doorknob. The only thing between them.

*No.* The voice had been hers, but... lifeless. What had happened to her?

He glared at the door. Was Brennan going to try to keep him from seeing her? He could try. He would fail.

Waiting a foot from the door, Jon squared his shoulders. The door opened.

"She doesn't—"

He shoved Brennan aside. Before Brennan could recover, Jon rushed past him and into the room.

Terra herself couldn't have kept him out.

On the bed, she sat curled into herself, smaller than he remembered. Frail. Fully clothed, she wore a red-and-gold brocade coat, white trousers, and polished black boots. In bed. She raised her eyes to his.

Cold and bloodshot.

She pressed her lips together in a thin white line. Her teeth clenched, she fisted her hands and constricted her arms around herself, squeezed, and pulled her knees in to her chest. Contracted until her muscles trembled. Those cold, bloodshot eyes narrowed on him.

His heart threatened to leap into his throat. What had happened to her? Had someone dared hurt her? He rushed to her side, reached for her. "Rielle—"

"Don't touch me!" she screamed, scrambling away. She fixed him with a hateful glare.

His mouth fell open. "What?" he breathed. "Are you—"

"Get away from me!" she shouted, bunching up the sheets, clawing them in tightening fingers.

What—

He stood rigidly, willing himself to stay apart from her.

Brennan came in, rubbing his chest. Had the werewolf poisoned her against him? Was that it? What had he told her?

"Your Majesty—" he began.

Jon stalked toward him. "Not. One. More. Word," he seethed, "or—"

"Don't you *dare* speak to him that way!" Rielle shouted at him, her voice the fury of storming waves crashing against the cliffs.

Every bit of fight drained from him as he turned to face her, unable to blink for his bulging eyes, unable to swallow for the pain in this throat.

"Brennan *came* for me. He brought me *home*. He was... there for me"—she clenched the sheets tightly, a smoldering stare fixing on nothing—"while you—" She clipped her words, grimaced, and shook her head.

Jon's arms fell to his sides. The pain in the back of his throat sharpened.

She met his eyes, a maelstrom staring into his secrets and sins. "—forgot me."

He inhaled a sharp breath but couldn't fill his lungs. It was all wrong. Everything. "No, Rielle, never—"

She shook her head, those tempestuous eyes storming for him and him alone. "Betrayed me."

*Betrayed.*

Terra have mercy, she knew.

She *knew.*

He staggered toward the bed and grabbed one of the bed posts for support.

"Rielle," he choked out, "let me explain—"

"Don't even try to deny it!" she screamed, her slight frame shaking but immovable.

Terra have mercy, she *knew.* He had no idea how, but this never should have—Gods, she deserved more. More than to learn of his shame in the most painful way possible. If only he could have told her himself, begged her pardon—"Rielle—"

For a moment, she just glared at him, glared until that tempest became unbearable, and then she lowered her gaze. "I... heard you."

*Heard...* He waited for more, watched her face, but nothing else came. Silence. He lowered his gaze. Shimmering cloth. Red and gold.

*Red and gold.*

Tregarde's colors. Red and gold.

Livery. Red and gold. Tregarde's—

*The messenger.*

He dropped to his knees, caught the side of the bed, and brought a hand to his forehead.

*She couldn't wait to see you.*

Terra have mercy, she'd come herself. Last night, she'd come to his quarters herself. She'd heard him with Aless. She'd *heard* him.

She'd come back from the dead—from a distant land, from months away—back to him, and she'd come... She'd come to that.

He raked his fingers through his hair, and it was all he could do to shut his eyes and pray this was some nightmare. That he hadn't, through his own faithlessness, hurt her so deeply. Irreparably.

A choked sound. Muffled. Quickly suppressed. Hers.

Terra have mercy. Not this. He wanted nothing but to comfort her, but it was the only thing he couldn't do. She didn't want him near. Couldn't stand his presence. The hollow in his chest widened.

"I'm sorry," he pleaded. "I thought you were—"

"Get... out." The words, soft and quiet, crushed him.

She hated him.

She didn't want to see him.

She never wanted to see him again.

"Get out!" she yelled.

He staggered to his feet, until his back hit a wall. A thousand pins pierced his chest, and he grabbed at it, fisting the leather of his doublet.

"Get out, get out, get out!" she screamed, the unbroken mask of her face cracking. Wavering.

Anything but—

From the corner, Brennan rushed to her, knelt at the bed by her side. He took a handkerchief from the nightstand and handed it to her.

She grasped it and wiped her face. "Brennan, this place, I can't—" she whispered to him, her voice breaking.

Brennan gathered her up and swept her out of the room. The door to the hall slammed shut.

Silence shrouded the room, reclaimed the empty space, and Jon. Snow piled outside the window, casting its darkness.

Rubbing the agony piercing his chest, he thumped his head against the wall, wincing at the pain, struggling to breathe. He deserved it, and a lot more. That look on her face—when her composure had broken—stared deep into him, into darkness, and through, a sword of truth, of judgment, of righteousness. And its sting was sobering. Cleansing. Burning through the lies and sin like a hungry fire. For that look of hers, for the anguish he'd caused, he accepted the pain. And more.

Through blurred eyes, he looked out at the room, where in one moment he'd had everything and, in the next, had lost it all.

OLIVIA FOLLOWED the guard through a doorway into a room with red velvet drapes and upholstered walls. Something wrong with the king. Something they needed her for. She clenched at the brocade of her dress.

Divine, it was his heart. He'd had another episode, and would she get there in time to—

The guard opened an interior door and held it. Taking cautious steps, she peered inside.

A bed, its sheets mangled, and then, on the floor...

Unmoving, Jon sat, his back against the wall, staring into nothing, his face blotchy, his eyes... red. Breathing ragged.

She dropped to her knees and grabbed for his wrist, then pressed a fingertip to his skin and gestured a diagnostic spell. Her presence entered him and traveled his heart, his lungs, his stomach, his liver, his kidneys, his brain, his eyes, the many pathways of life in his body—all in an instant. She urged the blood backed up in his lungs outward, flowing through to the rest of his body.

He gasped a breath, clutching her arm as his eyes widened.

She withdrew her psychic presence. "Jon?" she asked softly. "Do you feel better? What happened?"

When no answer came, she looked him over. He was clean and

properly dressed. As he exhaled, something crinkled in his doublet. Paper?

"May I?" She eyed him, waited awhile, then unfastened his doublet, and there, between it and his shirt, was a message. On the back was a broken wax seal—Tregarde's. A message from Brennan?

Her heart raced, but she opened it.

*Found her in Xir. She couldn't wait to see you.*

Found her? Rielle?

*She couldn't wait...*

Rielle was alive?

She grabbed Jon's shoulders. "Rielle."

His Bay of Amar gaze flowed toward hers.

"Is she alive, Jon?" She shook him gently, and he blinked—once, twice, three times. "Is Rielle alive?"

He braced a palm on the heavy-pile rug and lumbered to his feet. Several slow breaths later, he held out his hand to her. "Yes, Olivia. She's alive."

She gasped. Alive... Rielle was alive.

They'd been wrong—how?—but it had never been such a blessing.

She took his hand, let him pull her to her feet, and embraced him. "That's wonderful news."

"It is," he replied, his voice low, sullen.

She pulled away. "Why aren't you..." Behind him, the tangled sheets... The tangled sheets on the bed took on new meaning.

Brennan's quarters. These were Brennan's quarters. Jon had come here, must have found—

"Great Divine," she breathed, stroking his cheek with a sympathetic palm. "I'm so sorry."

He took her hand, bowed his head, and frowned. "No... It's..." He swallowed. "She returned, came to my rooms, but I..." He drew in a ragged breath. "In the morning, I read the message and came here." He met her eyes, his own reddening. Haunted. "Olivia, she knew everything."

He straightened, his pained gaze on the rumpled bed.

Knew everything...

She closed her eyes, her shoulders slumping. Rielle had come to see him and found him with a lover. After all these months away, she'd returned to find he'd moved on. Betrayed her. Become someone else entirely.

She had to be—

A shiver shook her spine. "Where is she, Jon?"

He shook his head. "Promise me you won't tell her about this." He placed a palm over his heart. "Promise me."

JON BROUGHT down Faithkeeper again and again, and although Raoul parried and blocked, he receded with every strike. Finally, Raoul lowered his sword and shook his head before wiping his pale brow.

*Next.*

Jon turned on Valen, who tossed him a glaive. One of his favorite weapons, aside from the long sword. He held out Faithkeeper to his squire, who quickly took it and stepped clear, then felt for the flat side of the glaive's seven-foot pole to properly angle the eighteen-inch blade at the tip.

Facing Valen, he took up a ready stance, and they sparred glaive to glaive.

A crowd of exhausted guards and soldiers ringed them in the practice yard. If they were tired, then they were out of shape and needed the extra practice.

"We've been out here for hours," Valen said between strikes. "Are you going to open up about what's really bothering you?"

Jon lunged with renewed vigor, but Valen parried. "Shut up and spar."

Valen jerked his head back but continued the exercise.

Good. Jon lost himself in it, nothing but muscle, weapon, memory, and reflex. There was no sense in talking about it. Anything anyone could possibly tell him, he'd already told himself.

He'd betrayed her. She hated him. He deserved it.

His attacks struck faster, harder.

He wasn't sure how he could ever meet her gaze again, but then, she never wanted to see his face again anyway, so at least his shame had its head.

One blow after another after another, and Valen's face contorted— he was shouting.

"Jon!" he yelled, over and over again, before he finally caught the pole of Jon's glaive.

A madness surged through his body, wove through his arms, coiled and clenched in his hands. They didn't want to stop moving, stop striking, and neither did he.

The ring of guards and soldiers around him and Valen had turned tense, with most standing alert, some even appearing to hold their breath.

He closed his eyes for a blessed moment. Terra have mercy, he was losing his mind. His men were here, watching his descent into madness. *Some king.* Sighing, he opened his eyes, released the glaive, and held up his hands with a forced smile. "Maybe you're right—a break is in order."

He could almost feel the collective sigh of relief as Valen handed their glaives off to a waiting squire while another brought them two towels. Walking back toward Trèstellan, Jon swept one over his face and slicked his hair back as his muscles relaxed.

"Florian told me some of what happened," Valen said from next to him, toweling off his sweat-soaked arms and thick bear-brown hair. "What are you going to do?"

He'd been asking himself that same question since Olivia had left this morning for the city.

He wanted to plead for Rielle's forgiveness, find a way to make it up to her, to ease the anguish he'd caused her, but how could he do that when she wanted nothing to do with him?

"It's not about me," he replied grimly. "It's about her." The distance she wanted broke his heart, but he'd broken hers, so what right did he have to ache? "She wants nothing to do with me. She wants space. And that is what she will have."

Valen grimaced and shook his head. "What will that solve? What you did was faithless, weak, disloyal—"

Jon glared at him, for all that he deserved those words.

"—callous, and wrong, but you did have your reasons. Nothing that excuses what you did, but at least she'd have some explanation, instead of believing that as soon as she was off these shores, you found the next best woman to take her place."

Terra have mercy, how he'd wanted to explain. To tell her a spiritualist had declared her dead, that he'd wanted to drown in grief, that his duties had demanded otherwise. That he loved her more than life itself, and without her, had become a sad, weak fool who'd made the worst choices he could have possibly made to go on without her. That at the first test of faith, he'd failed miserably.

"An explanation would be for me," he answered, "to alleviate my own burden. She doesn't want to hear anything from me right now. And I'll honor her choice. Someday, if she ever sees fit to see me again, to speak to me again, I'll tell her everything."

Valen sighed, and through double-doors held open by footmen, they entered the palace, flanked by Florian and Raoul. "The woman you love is *alive*. Even if she doesn't forgive you, you're not even going to *talk* to her? You have that kind of patience?"

Patience. That was what these past four months had been about, hadn't they? If he'd only been patient, waited on word from Brennan, instead of succumbing to anxiety and forcing answers, perhaps he never would have made such massive mistakes. He would have had to tell her about the Earthbinding and Manon, and that would have been difficult for them, but would she have hated him?

No, as difficult as it would have been to overcome, she would have understood. But this, with Nora and Aless? Never. She'd never understand, and why should she? He deserved her hate.

"Yes, I do," he said. "I'll wait as long as she needs me to." Even if she never forgave him. Even if she never wanted to be together ever again. He'd ask Aless to release him from his promise to her. He'd end things with Nora. He'd take no other. He'd have the patience now that he should have had these past four months—but this time, to beg her pardon. Being together again was impossible after what he'd done, but maybe there was a chance he could alleviate the anguish he'd caused, at least some. "Hopefully she'll speak to me again someday."

Valen huffed. "Until that day, I guess I sacrifice myself in the practice yard."

Jon rolled his eyes as they were about to part ways. "As if you have a choice."

Valen barked a half-laugh before striding toward his quarters.

Jon headed for his own. He'd have to wash the madness off, because he had a long day ahead of him, beginning with recalling the knights and paladins searching for Rielle, and then his late-afternoon walk with Aless... and praying for her mercy.

# CHAPTER 49

Through the parting crowd, Leigh strode to the Treeburst throne, flanked by a squad of elven guards. Each face wore variations of the same masks—curiosity, doubt, fear. These people were strangers in their own land now, and had left their fate in the hands of a foreigner. No surprise that they weren't at ease.

He didn't turn his head this way and that, but he glanced over the many faces for Ambriel's. The visit to Courdeval hadn't been long, but in a way, it had been *too long*.

Narenian perched upon the throne like a sleek cat, her sharp, silvery eyes sighting him like a nocked arrow.

Ten feet away, he stopped and bowed. "I bring news, Your Majesty."

"You are welcome, Ambassador Leigh Galvan," she declared, her regal voice loud and strong. "You may speak freely."

The crowd stilled and quieted, only the faint rustle of leaves in the breeze daring to interfere.

"King Jonathan Dominic Armel Faralle has sworn the oath ritual with you through Emissary Aiolian Windsong." A susurrus of soft gasps. "It is done. And I have returned with the negotiated alliance agreement. Once it is signed, Emaurria will be your sworn ally."

The starlight of Narenian's eyes shone a measure brighter, just briefly; she nodded and stood, her back perfectly straight, a tumble of long platinum-blond hair gleaming behind her. Chin raised, she searched the crowd, a faint smile playing on her lips. Measured. "My loyal subjects, tonight we celebrate our new bond with the Emaurrian people. May it continue to grow and prosper."

Soft clapping rose in unison, filling the space with the sound of relief to accompany the many pleased faces.

But not his own. Where was Ambriel? Had the dark-elves attacked again? Or had the light-elves launched an attack of their own?

He wasn't one to quail in pursuit of his own ends, not unless he bore the crushing weight of the greater good. Like relations between two countries. He sighed inwardly.

The crowd closed in, a cacophony of questions and compliments enveloping him.

Quickly, he forced a smile and nodded agreement to those around him. Indeed, Vervewood was one step closer to an alliance, and when the alliance would at last happen, his work would be done here.

But the thought didn't please him, gave him no relief.

Amid the crowd near the throne, a fair head peaked above the rest, a hardened expression meeting his probing. Ambriel.

Such a tepid reception? Hardly worthy for a messenger of peace. Not every Kamerish-Pryndonian former-magister wild mage made peace between Emaurrians and a civilization of myth. He exhaled and arched a brow at Ambriel.

He'd returned victorious. Surely that had to count toward some reward?

Ambriel failed spectacularly at hiding a grin.

Narenian raised her hands, and the clapping faded. "Let us gather tonight, when the first star takes to the sky. Let us all take part in this momentous occasion." She turned to a member of her household. "See that it's done."

The woman bowed and quickly departed.

At that, Narenian seated herself upon the throne once more. "Ambassador Galvan, you and Emissary Aiolian Windsong have served Vervewood admirably."

He shook his head. "I have merely done as bidden by my king, Your Majesty."

"Nevertheless." She regarded him with a hint of a smile. "You have earned our respect and are welcome among us. Please enjoy all Verve-wood has to offer, with our sincerest blessing."

He raised a brow. All Vervewood had to offer? He glanced at Ambriel, who was doing a fantastic job at not facing him directly. Was Narenian offering her blessing?

"I..." He straightened. "Thank you, Your Majesty. I'm honored."

She let her smile free and nodded, then dismissed him. He receded three steps and turned away, heading for his quarters with a bounce in his step. Victorious hero, queen's honored guest, and celebrations of his accomplishments: these were not new features in his life, but they never lost their luster.

But he hadn't looked forward to a celebration this much in years.

He spotted the tree with the cascading root and ascended the winding stairs to his hollow. Such a small space, but upon his entrance, the tiny Gaze crystals within twinkled a starlit greeting, and the wood felt familiar and welcoming beneath his booted feet. His bed waited, and he threw himself into it.

Someday, this could be a comfortable life. A happy life.

But everything had gone well. Emaurria and Vervewood were allies, and Stonehaven would soon know. As vicious as Queen Matryona had shown herself to be, it would be the height of arro-gance to attempt an attack now and make enemies of all surrounding her.

And if she entertained such madness, perhaps one of her Quorum would invoke the single-combat rule. Perhaps Varvara would, for the sake of her people.

As much as he didn't mind killing here and there if it suited the greater good, *an entire race* of people, ones who perhaps disagreed with their misguided leader, was another matter. Lives came and went with the wind, but entire civilizations? On such a grand scale, decisions had to be weighed all the more carefully.

But the détente was a blessing. Surely by now, some diplomats in Courdeval were learning Old Emaurrian and making good progress. He wasn't needed here anymore, and Jon would send someone else. And he would leave Vervewood.

And look for his vanished former apprentice. Someone had to teach her a lesson, after all—he grinned—and no doubt His Majesty would have other priorities.

THE SUN WAS SETTING when the pan flutes and singing began; Leigh made his way to the feast, weaving through clusters of laughing celebrants and servers bearing earthenware jugs of spirits. Smoke and the aroma of roasted pork carried over—the humans sharing their cuisine, or just tired of eating only raw foods. And who could blame them?

Silhouetted against the reddish-golden glow of dusk, Narenian sat at the head of a long trestle table adorned with colorful dishes and greenery. She languidly sprawled over her chair, gaze resting on her consort as she laughed with Ambriel.

There was so much to tell him, more than could be said in one night. But chief among all things, goodbye.

Ambriel's gaze caught his, and Leigh offered a grin. Smoothing things over, hopefully.

"The hero graces us with his presence at last." Ambriel raised an earthenware mug to him.

Narenian motioned to a place at her left, and Leigh joined them on the bench, exchanging pleasantries. One cordial evening, at the very least, should mark a momentous occasion like this. He feasted with them, chatted, laughed, listened, made merry, and the celebration was enjoyable, or should have been, but for the words he had to say tonight when he could get Ambriel alone.

"You received correspondence today, *dreshan*." Ambriel broke into his thoughts.

"I did?" It had to be from Courdeval. Was something amiss already? "Is it urgent?"

"It could be."

Narenian smiled into her goblet and waved them off. "Go. Attend to your *urgent* matters."

Leigh pressed his lips together and eyed her, but rose along with

Ambriel. Was *everyone* aware of all that was unsaid between them? The nosy light-elves could use some diversion. Theatre. Opera. A brewery. Maybe a hobby or two. Perhaps then they'd stay out of each other's dramas and make up their own.

Ambriel cocked his head toward a steep set of stairs grown into a massive trunk—the royal quarters?—and Leigh followed him up, looking out over the elves and humans crowded below, firelight reflected in a sea of platinum-blond-haired heads, and the dappling of human brunettes and redheads. Chatter, laughter, and song carried past like a happy breeze.

Vervewood was a small enclave in Emaurria, but if the future someday looked like that, would it be so terrible? Humans in Verve-wood and elves in Emaurria, sharing food and wine and words? Sharing their lives, even?

He followed Ambriel into an open room with a large pillow-laden bed on one end, two savonarola armchairs and a wide table bearing a map and a jug on the other end.

Ambriel snatched a wax-sealed message from under a map marker and presented it. He gestured to one of the armchairs, then approached the open-air balcony overlooking the interwoven water-ways and the cascading waterfall.

Leigh ran a finger over the dried blue wax. The Farallan dragon. He cracked it open.

> Rielle is alive and back in Courdeval.
> I am sending you a replacement to train. An Amadour.
> Back to being a rose bush.
> J.

Leigh exhaled a relieved breath through his nose and folded the message. *That's my girl.* She was a survivor, and he'd trained her himself, made sure of her skills himself. And he'd never doubted her return.

They'd have to get together soon over some port, so she could tell him about all the fools who'd gotten in her way and how she'd crushed them.

*Alive and in Courdeval...* Well, he couldn't ask for better than that, could he? It said all he'd hoped for.

And yet what it *didn't* say spoke volumes. Back from where? And why not "alive and well"?

And where was all the pathetically romantic gushing? Betrothal, a royal wedding, the nine planned heirs, and thirty-odd grandchildren?

Perhaps Jon was a conservative writer, even if he'd walked around with stars in his eyes for months. Or maybe Rielle had found him with his princess, and burned them both to a crisp.

And what about Marcel? No mention of him. Had he brought her home, or had she returned alone? Or worse, had she brought *him* home?

Leigh frowned. When had she returned? He'd only just left Courdeval.

"On your brow, there is a line I don't like the look of." Arms crossed, Ambriel leaned against the table, all bulk and muscle and exuding sexiness and—

"Just thinking."

"Ah"—Ambriel turned to the table and poured some spirits into his cup—"then you should stop."

"Because you don't like the look of this line?" He pointed to his forehead.

Ambriel handed him the cup. "Is there a better reason?"

Shaking his head, Leigh brought the cup to his lips, then took a drink. "This line and I are very well acquainted... We've been nigh inseparable for years now. I regret to inform you that we're something of a package deal."

Ambriel dropped into the armchair next to him, and together they looked out at the waterfall. Laughter and song carried from below. "It's a new world, *dreshan*. Bigger and heavier than the old. You cannot carry it. At least not alone."

Another drink, and Leigh sighed his surrender. "Very well. At least not tonight." He set the empty cup on the floor, then frowned again.

"Empty cup, empty words?" But there was a smile in Ambriel's voice.

Leigh raised an eyebrow at him. "That word—*dreshan*. You call me that sometimes. What does it mean?" *Foreigner*, probably. Or *mage*.

It was Ambriel's turn to sigh, but he clipped it with a half laugh. "It is an Elvish word. Something like 'adored one.'"

*Adored one?* "But—I heard you say it weeks ago, after Stonehaven attacked."

Ambriel rose. "Pity you didn't speak Elvish."

Was that why every set of lips in Vervewood gossiped about them? "And you knew that."

"And here we are." Ambriel spread his arms, wide and inviting, his lips curved in a confident smile. With good reason.

Leigh stood, turned, clutched the back of the armchair, staring into the shadows. It wasn't as much a victory as Ambriel believed. "I'm not a good man, Captain."

"Neither am I." Ambriel's firm, deep voice, and then a soft step. "Your people have never seen a light-elf, a dark-elf, a mermaid, a dragon. But it is a 'good man' that is the myth. At least the way your people think. A good man never does anything wrong, isn't that the idea?" Another step. "But we are all our deeds. Good and bad. And there is not a man under the sun who has done only good."

And he'd thought his *own* hope had been in short supply. Leigh clutched the armchair tighter. "Then none of us are good?"

"None." The word warmed the back of his neck, soothed its way down his spine with a pleasant shiver. "And none of us are bad either. But that doesn't matter." A soft touch began at his knuckles and firmed as it rose up his arm, radiating pleasure and heat and anticipation.

"Then what does?" he whispered, unwilling to speak up, to move, to even breathe for fear of interrupting that touch.

"That you want to be good." Up his biceps to his shoulders, fingers and palms melting tension and pressure—

He exhaled loudly, tossing his head back... onto a waiting shoulder. His back pressed against warm hardness, Ambriel, solid and strong behind him, long arms that wrapped his body, and fingers that tilted his mouth up.

A hot whisper against his lips. "What do you want to be tonight, *dreshan?*"

"Yours."

A deep rumble of a laugh, and Ambriel led him to the bed.

# CHAPTER 50

*R*ielle stared out at the sliver of the bay visible through their room's window at Claudine's. The dull morning sun had risen to its highest, and her gaze hesitated to stray from the discontented waves.

Jon had betrayed her. Been with another woman. Just the thought made her shudder, made her fists clench, made her want to scream and yell, but... "The worst part about it is that I don't even have the right to be angry. He's done no worse than I have."

She'd been Farrad's lover.

A clink. Brennan setting down his brandy. "You had no choice. He did."

Did he? From the moment he'd told her he was king, she'd known his obligations. She'd spent the past few months translating news of him and his suitresses. He was getting married, wasn't he? He'd chosen one, of course.

Even knowing that, the thing that filled her head had been... the sound of him with... another woman, and even when he'd found her, *that* had been all she could hear.

"You were in an impossible situation. A choice between dying or suffering, between greater and lesser odds of survival. You can't be blamed for pursuing life."

Pursuing life. Isn't that what Jon had done? Instead of sitting around and waiting for her to return, *if* she returned, he'd chosen to go live his life. Turned the page from her chapter in his life to something new.

Beyond the diamond-grille window, Courdeval was a muted gray. Freezing rain had drenched the city all morning.

The door creaked open behind her, and Liam entered with a thin smile, his mess of straw-blond hair secured in a knot at the back of his head. He held up a hand in greeting. "Still planning to head back to Trèstellan?"

"I have to." Given all that had happened, she'd neglected to tell Jon about Shadow. And those words couldn't come through a message that could be intercepted. She owed him that much.

And leaving it like this... She'd made a spectacle of herself. Wept, shouted.

She pressed her lips together. The calm thing to do would have been to meet him, cool and poised, and tell him she wished him happiness in his new relationship, and that should he ever require the assistance of an elementalist, he'd have to look elsewhere. Then smile sweetly and leave.

The *calm* thing to do. But right then, calm had been about as possible as flying.

Now was her chance to leave things differently, try not to be a sopping mad mess, so it wouldn't nag at her the rest of her life.

With careful steps, Liam approached her and gently rested a hand on her shoulder. "I hate to see you like this, all because of this... *king.*" He spat the word with snarling disdain. "Forget him. Forget all of it. Come with me on the water and take it out on some pirates."

Brennan sighed through his nose. "Don't be an idiot. She's not going anywhere."

Liam jerked his head. "Did I ask you?"

She shook her head. "Liam, I know your heart's in the right place, but—"

Brennan rose, his brow chiseled with a scowl. "Do you honestly think she's going to walk away from this and run like some coward? Like *you*?"

Liam clenched the hilt of his rapier. "Let's have this discussion outside, Marcel, and let our blades do the talking."

She spun to face them. "Win or lose, do you think either of you dying will *improve* matters?"

Chest puffed, Liam stared at her blankly.

"Liam, I know you mean well, but Brennan's right. I could never just leave. Not until I speak to Jon and kill Shadow, at least."

Liam clenched his jaw, but when he glanced in her direction, he deflated and sighed. "Sorry. I just—you're sad, and I feel like I can't do anything."

"You can't." Brennan curled a fist and cracked his knuckles. "This is for her to resolve."

Resolve... She couldn't even begin to think how.

Time? Distance?

A return to routine, maybe. And the Tower. That was where she belonged, where she could forget Jon, what he meant to her, her love for him, how he'd hurt her.

"What are you going to do?" Liam asked her.

She sighed. "I'll tell him what he needs to know, then I'm going back to the Tower."

Brennan's upper lip curled. He hated the Tower, of course, but she'd always found comfort there. It wasn't always easy to live there, but she knew what pains awaited in those white-marble walls, and she could bear those. This... this was different. Being in the same room with Jon had clenched her heart like a vise, and being in the same city surprisingly didn't feel much better.

Someone knocked at the door. Liam opened it a crack.

"Visitor," Claudine said gently, smoothing her frock with nervous hands. Managing an inn with an iron hand, she was nevertheless clearly unsettled by whoever it was who'd arrived.

It couldn't be... could it? Jon? Would he have followed her here? Her heart beat faster, battering against her chest. She wanted to run, hide, get as far from here as—

"Would he be so bold," Brennan began, "and so incredibly stupid?"

"A man?" Liam straightened, squaring his shoulders. Great Divine, if it *was* Jon—

"A woman. Said you knew her."

Brennan rubbed his face. "Thank you, Claudine. I'll be right down." His sister, maybe?

Claudine was closing the door when footsteps clicked up the stairs.

"Is that the room? Stand aside, Madame," a woman's voice said.

Her heart leapt. *Olivia.*

PAST THE MIDDLE-AGED INNKEEPER, Olivia entered the room, and there she was, Rielle, liveried in Tregarde's red and gold.

"Olivia." Her eyes wide, Rielle closed the distance between them, her frail body so much less than it had always been. Rielle's arms were around her before she could reply.

*Alive.* Rielle really was alive. She hugged her back, tears pricking her eyes.

When Jon had told her, she'd believed it, but the spiritualist's words had seeped into a part of her and pooled, so deep that nothing but these arms could reach. "Are you—"

"I'm fine." Rielle pulled back and grinned, her sky-blue eyes lively, intense. "I am, now that you're here."

"What happened to you?" Olivia whispered. Where had she been? Was she all right?

A man cleared his throat. Tall and tan-skinned, he stood with his arms crossed, his messy blond hair knotted at the back of his neck. He wore a rapier at his side, and worn leather boots that had seen far too much ocean water. He had to be a sailor, for at least a handful of years in his... nearly three decades?

His face—Divine, he was handsome, in a rugged way—was familiar, his eyes a sky blue she knew all too well.

"Aren't you going to introduce us?" he asked Rielle, his voice deep, gravelly.

Eyebrows high, Rielle slowly smiled. "I was going to, but Olivia doesn't have time for ship captains gallivanting about... Are you a ship captain? Or... or is there some *other* identity you claim?" Her eyes sparkled, and next to her, Brennan covered his mouth, his own gaze gleaming.

The blond man rubbed his chin and scowled at Rielle before sweeping a graceful bow before Olivia. "Captain Verib of the *Liberté,* my lady, at your service."

She inclined her head. He had to be an Amadour. A cousin of Rielle's, perhaps? "Well met, Verib."

"The pleasure's all mine," he said, those sky-blue eyes locked with hers.

Handsome, yes, but Rielle was right. She *did not* have time for ship captains, especially when her best friend was back from the dead.

Brennan clapped him on the back. "Let's leave these two to catch up. I'll buy you a round."

Verib hesitated before nodding and leaving the room with Brennan.

Rielle took her hand and led her to the bed, where they both sat.

"Tell me everything," Olivia said, "from the very beginning. What happened on the night of Spiritseve, after we parted ways?"

Rielle heaved a sigh, fell back into the pillows, and bit her lip. She began a tale of the past several months' events, spoke of how Shadow had abducted her, sold her into slavery on the order of some mysterious client; she described the ship and its captain, the chaotic mess of images that was her memory aboard. The long torment of the market slave stables in Harifa. The violence, the death, the inhumanity. The lengthy trudge across a desert to a new nightmare.

She spoke of the other women there, sisters of circumstance, and a brave young apothecary, and a master with an offer. Of her pregnancy, Jon's child. A *child.* Brennan's arrival, her drugging, the assassination. Losing her child, Great Divine. Fleeing Xir, nearly losing Brennan, crossing the Bay of Amar, battling a kraken, being saved by mermaids. Helping to free a slave ship. How she'd longed to see Jon. How she'd found him.

By the end, Olivia lay crumpled, her head in Rielle's lap. A sickly heat spread in her stomach. Too much. It was all too much. "If only I had stayed with you—"

"Then you might've suffered with me. Or worse. It's good that you didn't."

*Suffered.* Rielle had been abducted by a vengeful enemy, kept prisoner on a pirate vessel, and sold into servitude. She'd discovered herself with child and clung to a master to survive. She'd nearly died and had lost her child escaping... Had nearly lost Brennan... And had come close to drowning while battling an Immortal.

"Needless to say, this doesn't go beyond you and me," Rielle added, tucking a lock of Olivia's hair behind her ear.

*Doesn't go beyond...?* "You're not going to tell him?"

"I will," Rielle said, "but after this nightmare with Shadow is over. And it has to be me."

All that Rielle had suffered... Jon had to know the price Rielle had paid to save her, him, and Courdeval on Spiritseve, that he was a father. Share in her grief. He'd never want Rielle to bear the sadness of their baby's death alone.

Here she was, between the two of them like a wall, holding Jon's heart problem on one side, and their baby's death on the other, keeping truths from them both. But they were truths Jon and Rielle needed to share with *each other.* "I understand."

She squeezed Rielle's hand. "Jon sent countless knights and paladins to look for you, but you'd vanished without a trace. I have no idea how Brennan found you."

"He knows me," Rielle said softly, "far better than I thought he did. Than I expected him to."

There was a quiet affection in her voice, a gentleness, that hadn't been there before whenever she'd spoken of Brennan. "He's changed?"

Rielle nodded. "You have no idea how much."

*Do you love him?* The thought formed in her mind unbidden, but she couldn't ask. Wouldn't.

Olivia shook her head. "I know it looks very bad, but both Jon and I thought you were dead. A spiritualist told us so. And Jon, when he found out... he didn't take it well."

Rielle rose and went to the mirror, but she dropped her gaze, didn't look at her reflection. "He thought I was dead?"

"We all did," she replied quietly. Surely that would ease things, to know grief and pressure had driven him to this, and not boredom or disregard for her feelings? Even so, Jon had been foolish and didn't deserve her forgiveness, but Rielle didn't deserve to hurt like this either.

"Olivia, I *heard* him in bed with another woman." Rielle's watery gaze locked with hers. "Even if he thought me dead, even if he had a thousand valid reasons, that night is not something I can just erase from my mind."

"Talk to him," she said. *Let him tell you he thought you were dead, and that he's dying.* "After what you've meant to each other, and everything you've been through, you need to hear him out. Understand why he reacted the way he did. And maybe, with time, things will get better." *Whether you're together or apart.* "All wounds heal with time, don't they?"

With a sigh, Rielle nodded. "Perhaps so, but... we have a bigger concern right now—Shadow trying to kill him."

Shadow—she was alive? *She* was the one who'd been hunting Jon all this time?

Rielle flitted about the room and collected some clothes, then she stepped behind a screen and threw off her Tregarde livery. "She won't stop until he's dead or she is. Increase his guard. Lay down wards."

"We're already doing that, but with the Veris Ball coming up, it couldn't hurt to check again. To do more. She might strike then, in the thick of all the activity."

Rielle was silent a time, only the sound of clothes rustling as she changed. "Stay vigilant," she said. "And there, on the desk"—a note lay there—"if you can get that to him and get me an audience tonight, I'll talk to him."

Olivia raised her eyebrows. Then she was willing to forgive him after all? "You will?"

"About Shadow, yes."

But not about anything else. "Rielle—"

"After Shadow is dealt with." Rielle stepped out from behind the screen, an ankle boot clicking on the floor. "I promise. But right now, I just... I can't think beyond the sound of... *them.*"

It was a lot to take in. If she'd been in the same position with

James, even if she sympathized with his reasons, purging such a thing from her mind would take time.

It wouldn't be perfect. Nothing ever was.

But Jon had fallen far from perfection. Very, very, *very* far. He'd succumbed to doubt when he should have had faith.

With her irresponsible oversight of the spiritualist, she'd only pushed him down the wrong path, but he was still the one who'd taken it, one willful foot in front of the other. The person he was now could never be a good partner in life, not until he redefined how the man and the king would keep peace inside him.

Perhaps it was for the best that Rielle was taking a step back, at least until they could find a way forward, whether together or apart.

"I understand," Olivia said, rising. "I'll head back to Trèstellan and expect you at...?"

"Midnight."

～

BRENNAN WAITED on the stairs until finally, the lithe woman left Rielle's room, her head of dusty-red hair bowed as she tightened her moss-green velvet-and-rabbit-fur cloak. One of her slender, pale hands bore a recondite ring set with a misty emerald jewel. The Ring of the Archmage.

*Olivia is Rielle's friend.* She had been, long before becoming Archmage.

He hadn't eavesdropped on their conversation—Rielle deserved better—but that didn't mean he wouldn't find out what had happened. And Olivia would tell him.

She approached the stairs, and when her green gaze landed on him, she gasped. "Brennan."

Arms folded across his chest, he met her wide-eyed glance with unwavering adamancy.

"Let me walk you out, Olivia," he said, hitting her with the full effect of his deep, aristocratically apathetic voice, and all the practiced allure that had unsettled a legion of women before her. He flexed his arms, straining the crisp black cotton of his shirt, as she joined him in the stairwell. "So, do you think the king deserves her sympathy after he betrayed her?"

"That's up to her." She scowled at him, her face set. "And he didn't mean to betray her."

Interesting. "Did he neglect to mention his lover to you?" he asked as they strolled down to the landing.

She heaved a sigh. "I know, but... he didn't mean to betray her."

"He didn't wait."

"He believed she was dead."

"He didn't wait."

She slammed a palm on the wall. "A spiritualist told him she was dead!"

The pub went quiet, and the crew of the *Liberté* stared at them for a moment before Brennan grinned and escorted her to the door. He opened it for her, and she walked through.

"A spiritualist?" He laughed, escorting her toward the stable. "A spiritualist who clearly lied. And the fool believed it, all too readily."

"Jon didn't think—"

He raised his eyebrows. " 'Jon,' is it?" He chuckled coolly. "I admit a grudging respect. Just how many lovers *does* he have?"

With a glare, she pulled up the hood of her cloak. "It's not like that. We bonded over Rielle, and we're friends. That's all."

Her pulse was even. It was the truth. "Like I care."

She hissed. "*His Majesty* didn't think the boy would have any reason to lie."

"The boy?" Brennan frowned.

"The spiritualist."

Great Wolf. If it was—"What was his name?"

Olivia scrunched her face. "The boy's? Why?"

"What. Was. His. Name?"

She shrugged. "Francis."

Great Wolf. But he had to know. " 'Francis' what?"

"Francis... I don't know!" she spat. "When I asked my friend Erelyn, she said he could do it, and that was all."

"Erelyn Leonne?" He held his breath.

Olivia nodded. "How do you know her?"

Erelyn Leonne. Master Erelyn Leonne. His nephew's magic tutor. Francis's magic tutor. Francis Marcel Vignon, the future Count Vauquelin. Nora's son.

Nora, his sister, who had so fawned over the king when he'd been Tor's squire. Nora, who had recently lost her husband in the siege and scrambled for some security, to keep the king from appointing a steward to manage Vauquelin, and perhaps to insulate herself from Father's ceaseless grasping for power.

"You idiot." The people in the street paused a moment before resuming their walking.

"I don't take kindly to being insulted," she bit out through gritted teeth as she looked around.

"The truth is often unkind." He continued to the stable. "Let me tell you what an idiot you are. You had the king in a vulnerable position, grappling with the question of whether his beloved was alive or dead. Naturally, you couldn't watch him suffer, *so you decide to help,*" he said, with mock sweetness. "So what you did was... You brought in the only spiritualist anywhere near Courdeval, and because your friend was his tutor and the boy was, merely, a boy, you didn't question his name."

"He was a child." She glared at him. "What did it matter?"

Nonchalant, he continued. "Do you know my sister, Countess Nora Marcel Vignon?"

Olivia blinked. "Countess Vauquelin. She's, um"—she lowered her gaze—"she and the king—"

"Fuck," Brennan supplied. "Yes, I assumed." He sipped his wine. Yes, Nora had always possessed the boldness to pursue anything she desired with all the restraint of a hurricane. "Did you know she has two children?"

Olivia frowned. "Two children..."

"Two sons. Nora has two sons, my nephews. Henry, age six, and Francis, age nine." While she remained frozen on the cobblestones, he continued. "Francis had his éveil recently, when his father was killed, and revealed himself a rare mage. A *spiritualist*, would you believe it? Nora retained Master Erelyn Leonne to tutor him."

Olivia's mouth dropped open, but no sound emerged.

"So let me tell you what an idiot you are. You had the king in a vulnerable position, grappling with the question of whether his beloved was alive or dead. So you brought in a child spiritualist, whose mother coerced him to lie to the king, and she benefited from the lie and ended up in the king's bed. Which cost him the only woman he's ever loved. Which has led to him, and your best friend, suffering right now." He held the stable door open for her. "So yes, Olivia. You are an idiot."

She curled a hand into a fist, but he didn't move. "I'm an idiot," she called out to him.

A stable boy eyed her as he exited, but he didn't dare linger.

Brennan tilted his head toward the stable, and Olivia entered, where he helped her with her horse.

The king hadn't been forced to bed other women, so most of the blame rested squarely with him, but Olivia wasn't blameless. It was Olivia's ill-procured assistance that had convinced the king Rielle had died. It was the king's sincere belief that had driven him to grieve and, likely, to balm that grief with whatever remedy presented itself. And Nora would have been a very persuasive remedy.

That had destroyed Rielle and, in turn, destroyed the king. And their relationship.

Olivia, and her negligence, bore at least some responsibility.

And yet... A part of him couldn't ignore that Olivia was to *thank*, at least in part, for the opportunity that might soon present itself. Thanks to her, Rielle might soon be unfettered by promises and love to Jon. Free. Free to love another man.

Perhaps, even, to love *him*.

For that, he owed the woman a debt, however small.

# CHAPTER 51

*J*on gave Aless a somber smile as she arrived in the gardens for their late-afternoon walk. So much had changed, and yet, on the surface, everything appeared the same. But after today, it wouldn't.

As easy as she was to talk to, this conversation would present a greater challenge than an entire day of sword drills, glaive sparring, even Olivia's repulsion-shield tutoring.

As she approached, he offered her his arm. She wrapped a white gloved hand around it, her white cloak a stark contrast against his dark blue.

"I trust you're well?" he greeted.

Smiling, she shrugged. "I will be, after you dazzle me with the story of why I haven't seen you all day."

He lowered his gaze to the path, leading her slowly past the manicured hedges to the wisteria arbor. The stone pillars were strong enough that the wisteria didn't crush them as it grew and spread.

Never in his life had he thought he'd need to have this conversation. Ever. But here he was. Life wasn't done challenging him.

"My principal secretary was gone for four months, and he just returned from Sonbahar," he said, gesturing to a bench and assisting her as she seated herself. He sat next to her, and they looked out at the gardens and the distant couples and friends strolling.

"Brennan Karandis Marcel," she said, intertwining her fingers with his. "Is that right?"

He nodded. "When I couldn't leave to look for... *her*, Brennan offered to do so in my stead, and I agreed. After the Archmage and I consulted with a spiritualist, we realized he was looking for... her body."

She gave his hand a gentle squeeze.

"Aless," he said, meeting her chestnut-brown eyes, "he found her *alive*."

Those eyes widened, and her lips parted for a brief moment.

"I don't know how it's possible, but I saw her with my own eyes in the palace."

She nodded, licking her lips before she pressed them tight. "What are you going to do?" she asked softly, gently.

Rielle had recoiled from him, thrown him out, fled from him. He'd betrayed her trust, and she had every reason to hate him.

But she was alive, and he loved her, with every fiber of his being. He'd be with no other woman, even if that meant being alone for the rest of his short life. Rielle didn't deserve the hurt he'd caused, and she certainly didn't deserve any more. If she didn't want to see his face again, then he'd bear that righteous penance, and not carry on as he had before. No matter the consequences.

Or that was what he *wanted* to do.

"Aless," he said, stroking her hand slowly with his thumb, "I know we plan to announce our engagement at the Veris Ball. I made you that promise." She searched his eyes, but he pressed on. "But I'm here to ask whether you would find it in your heart to release me from it."

She looked away, her gaze wandering over the wooden wisteria vines twining around the arbor's stone pillars.

When she looked back to him, she smiled, leaned in, and brushed her lips against his in a warm, lingering moment. "I release you from your promise," she whispered, a hair's breadth from his mouth.

If there was anything that could unsettle her, he didn't yet know it. "Thank you."

With a sage nod, she pulled away and looked back out at the gardens, folding her hands in her lap. The breeze played with a few of her gleaming, dark locks. "It's a rare thing, Jon, and you're fortunate. If the love of your life isn't dead, then you need to try to win her back."

There was no winning her back. But he could try not to hurt her any more.

And for this, he'd have called Aless amazing if he hadn't already known it. "I won't forget this, Aless."

"No, you won't." She grinned, but it soon faded. "I know you've sent all the others home. I'll buy you as much time with my father as I can." She stood, and he rose with her. "The joy in life is measured by the boldness with which it is sought. Love her forever, Jon, because if she rejects you, you've lost your chance with me. And I'm too good to give you a second."

He met her sanguine smile with one of his own. "Should you ever need anything, Aless, you will always have a friend in me."

She inclined her head, then walked away, chin held high.


JON STARED at the oak tree in the courtyard. "It's not going to work."

Aiolian swept her knee-length overcoat aside. Coolly placing her palms upon the table, she glared at him. "As I've said, Your Majesty, you must not be the tree, but the anima *within* the tree."

Sometimes he wished Aless hadn't so diligently studied Old Emaurrian with him. "I've no talent for magic."

She shook her head. "You *mages*"—she spat the word with a distaste many a paladin would admire—"have learned to manipulate anima into magic. But raw anima isn't magic. It is life."

"And how does that help me?" He was in no mood for this, or anything. Later this evening, he'd have to meet with Nora and formally end their affair. After all she'd seen him through the worst period of his life...

Aiolian sighed. "Project your presence into that tree."

"But how will I—"

"Your human ears will still hear me, even if your presence is there."

With a grimace, he closed his eyes and pictured the solar, its wood-paneled walls, granite fireplace, its peaked windows; the warm sunshine alighted upon his face, the cool air raised the hairs on his skin, and the freshness of new leaves flowed into his nostrils. Below, couples walked among the manicured trees and shrubs.

He extended his arms, wiggled his fingers—and there was but the slightest tremble of the leaves, a breath of the slightest breeze.

*You do not have arms, legs, or skin, Your Majesty,* a stern voice whispered. Aiolian's. *You have branches, a trunk, roots, bark.*

He imagined what it would be like to be covered in bark, the wind hitting its dry roughness, rigidity—

*You aren't only the tree, but its will,* she said. *You are threads of life through every fiber of its being. Be the anima within it, and everything in the land shall bend to your will.*

Be the anima? Easier said than done. He'd somehow become the anima in a rose bush, but he couldn't remember how.

He'd never seen anima before. Threads of life? What might that look like?

Silky strands of starlight... glowing silver white... shimmering, twinkling. In the furthest reaches of his branches. Below them, on the ground over his roots, a bright figure strode toward the palace. Olivia?

He leaned in, and a great groan rumbled through the air. Creaks, a gnawing whine.

She froze and gazed upward.

*Olivia,* he wanted to say, but wind rustled through leaves.

*Pull back,* Aiolian's voice said again.

Pull back? He frowned, a creak and crisp abrasion. Like bark against bark. He shook his canopy.

*Pull back. You are a man. Remember your body, remember the tree, the courtyard, the palace, the solar. Pull back.*

A man. He flexed his hands, branches that shook in the wind. Branches. The tree. The courtyard of manicured greenery. The sunshine warm upon his face—the peaked windows of the solar, the wood-paneled walls, the granite fireplace—

He gasped, snapped his eyes open, clenched the armrests of his chair until the wood groaned.

Crouched next to him, Aiolian rested a hand on his. *"Always* remember yourself. Some part of you must always remember. Do not let yourself inhabit the land completely, or—"

He nodded. She didn't need to say the words. If he forgot what it was to be a man, he'd ever remain a tree.

A quick descent of cold—wet—on his lip, and he dragged a wrist along his mouth.

Blood.

He inhaled, rubbed at it, and pulled out his handkerchief.

Aiolian lowered her gaze, blinked slowly. "Your human mind isn't accustomed to such labors. Perhaps we can attempt to have a healer present, but this is a thing untested with your human *mages*. Until then, you must practice gradually, on smaller living things—a flower, a shrub—with less dramatic exercises. Eventually, you will be able to do more without hurting yourself."

An ache pressed against his forehead, and he rubbed it. "Thank you."

She nodded and stood, then inclined her head. "It is why my queen sent me, Your Majesty."

He stood with her. "Together, we will accomplish great things, Emissary Windsong."

"It is my hope." She glanced at the door. "Shall I call a servant to assist you?"

With the blood. "I'll handle it myself." He inclined his head to her. "Good day to you."

"And to you, Your Majesty." She returned the gesture.

Satisfied he'd wiped most of the blood away, he headed for his quarters, flanked by Florian and Raoul. He stuffed his handkerchief back in his pocket. Projecting his presence would come at a cost, but if Aiolian could be believed, it was like any physical labor. With practice, skill, and time, he would reach some level of competence.

If he could survive.

He nodded to the courtiers who greeted him in the palace halls and at last arrived at his quarters.

Raoul and Florian stood to attention and saluted. "Your Majesty, Countess Vauquelin awaits you in your quarters," Raoul said lifelessly.

He nodded. Perhaps the sooner he spoke with her, the better.

The antechamber, dining room, and study were empty; Nora had to be in the bedchamber.

The metallic scent of blood invaded his nostrils, and he headed straight for the washbasin. As he washed his hands, he looked over his shoulder at the woman sprawled on his bed like a queen in a bright-red gown.

"I haven't heard from you in almost a week. So here I am, to remind you of why I'm unforgettable." Her smile stretched, then a line formed between her brows. "You're covered in blood."

He splashed his face. The cool water soothed his aching head, too —a measure. "Don't worry—it's mine."

A half-laugh. "That makes me worry more."

He toweled off, and a knock echoed from the hallway. "Yes?"

"Archmage Sabeyon, Your Majesty," Florian called.

"Send her into the antechamber," he called.

"Yes, Your Majesty."

Jon faced the bed and Nora's arched brow.

"She can't wait?"

He huffed his amusement. "I'd ask you to make yourself at home, but..."

With a deep breath, she leaned back into the pillows, stretching out her legs under her gown's skirts. "I *am* at home."

And that would make their talk all the more difficult; Nora had done nothing but keep him company, help him escape the horrors of reality when he'd believed Rielle dead. She'd been a friend to him and an ally, not just a lover. She'd done nothing to merit being cast aside.

But the woman he loved was alive. Whether Rielle forgave him or not, he wouldn't carry on as he had any longer. "I'll not be long."

He left the bedchamber and shut the doors, then the study's doors, and at last, those of the dining room, until he turned to face the antechamber.

Olivia shed her cloak and laid it on the sofa. "Jon—good, you're here."

He gestured to the sofa, and she sat.

"Did you see Rielle?" He seated himself next to her.

Raising her eyebrows, she bowed her head and fidgeted. "I, um... I did."

She looked up at him briefly and then away.

So she'd met with Rielle. And, by the looks of it, whatever she'd heard hadn't been good.

He scrubbed a hand over his face. Terra have mercy, he couldn't help but see Rielle's red-rimmed eyes anew, her anguished face. Brennan carrying her out of the room. *Get out, get out, get out!* The last words she'd said to him.

He dropped his head in his hands.

She hated him. Never wanted to see him again. Whatever she'd told Olivia would hurt, but he deserved it.

He folded his hands together. "How was she?"

Sighing lengthily, Olivia pulled at the brocade of her dress. "She wants to meet with you."

His spine straightened. Meet with him? She wanted to see him again? "Where is she? I'll meet her right away."

Olivia shook her head. "She'll be coming here. Tonight. Midnight."

He stood, raked a hand through his hair, paced the antechamber. "Florian," he called.

The hallway door opened, and Florian poked his head inside. "Yes, Your Majesty?"

"Talk to my chamberlain. Have him arrange a late supper, tea and custard tarts"—Rielle's favorite—"and an intimate ambiance"—but not here; he didn't want to suggest the wrong expectations—"in the Grand Library. Midnight."

Florian paused, then nodded. "Yes, Your Majesty."

"That'll be all."

Florian acknowledged him and shut the door.

Bowing her head, Olivia bit her lip. "Jon..." she said gently. Too gently. "It may not be as you—"

"I know." He strode to an armchair and dropped into it. "She wants to see me again. I'm glad for it, and I don't presume a thing more."

She bobbed her head, rubbing her lips together. "There's something else."

Terra have mercy. Something else... He didn't want to hear it.

Rielle was coming to see him, and there was *something else.*

*Someone* else.

Brennan. She loved Brennan. A soreness formed in his throat.

"It's about the spiritualist," she whispered.

Frowning, he leaned in.

"I'm so sorry. I... made a mistake," she said hoarsely, her eyes watering. "The boy. Francis. He's... the heir to the county of Vauquelin."

That made him... *Nora's* son.

Rigidity climbed his muscles until he could hear the blood rushing in his ears.

"It's all my fault," Olivia blurted. "I should have been more thorough, but he was just a boy, and his tutor was my friend, and I was so eager to learn anything about Rielle, I just..."

He leaned into his chair, forced his head back, and stared at the ceiling. Nora's son was the spiritualist. Had told a lie.

The tears, the difficulty... The boy hadn't *wanted* to lie. He'd *had* to.

All this time, Nora—the same Nora sprawled out on his bed right now—had played him. She'd brought her son, a spiritualist, to court, the only one of his kind in the kingdom, perhaps, aside from Donati. And she'd known Rielle was alive.

*Why don't you have her portrait removed?* she'd asked.

If anything should be removed, it was Nora. Out of his bed, out of his room, out of his life.

*All this time—*

And what, had she hoped to insinuate herself into his good graces through this deception? Surely she'd know Rielle would return someday. Or she'd been desperate enough to gamble on the odds.

No... Nora Marcel Vignon did not risk without a plan. She couldn't have hoped for marriage, but—

A child.

He jolted upright in his armchair. Terra have mercy, was she—

No, no, he'd been careful; he'd used the sheath, just as his Camarilla tutors had taught, despite her insistence to the contrary.

The notion of being tutored in such matters had, at the time, seemed ridiculous, but he was grateful for it now. Having grown up a bastard, he would never take the conception of a child lightly, especially when he wouldn't live long enough to be a true father.

But if she'd schemed in order to—

He clenched his fists so hard his knuckles cracked.

*Terra have mercy.* He took deep, cleansing breaths. He wouldn't talk to her like this. Not until he calmed down. Not until he knew his own strength again.

"Forgive me," Olivia whispered. "I should have checked—"

"Yes, you should have." Despite the brusqueness of his answer, it did no good to blame now, no matter how angry he was. Olivia had gone far beyond her duties in serving the kingdom and helping him; if she'd erred, it was because he'd overburdened her. He sighed. "I'm sorry. You didn't deserve that."

She kept her head bowed.

"Thank you for telling me." He rose and cracked his stiff neck. "A lesser person would have kept such knowledge hidden."

She raised her head. "I would never have forgiven myself. My mistake has come at a high price to two people I love very much."

Mistake. Unintentional. He knew that.

He'd once blamed Leigh for Rielle's disappearance—wrongfully. Despite Leigh's guilt in thwarting the rite, he'd no more caused Rielle's disappearance than any other circumstance leading her to the capital. All the blaming had done was cost Leigh his freedom when he could have been useful—

*And keep me from facing my own guilt.*

He wouldn't make the same mistake with Olivia. She'd been involved in the situation, but she hadn't caused it. That guilt lay squarely with Nora.

He offered Olivia a hand.

She took it, and he helped her to her feet.

"You've been a great friend to me, Olivia," he said. "This kingdom —and I—wouldn't be here without you."

She flushed and pulled away. "I hope all goes well tonight. If you'd like to talk tomorrow, I'll be in the Magic Library."

He nodded. "My thanks."

Her cloak in hand, she smiled warmly and took her leave.

All that mattered now was earning Rielle's forgiveness, if such a thing was possible.

And dealing with Nora.

All this time, Nora had been playing him for a fool. Scheming. Lying to his face. Smiling at him in bed while harboring deception in her heart. Balling his fists, he turned back to the dining room door, opened it, then crossed his quarters to the bedchamber's door.

Nora still lay sprawled in bed, grinning up at him, but her grin quickly faded.

"We're done." He strode to his privy wardrobe, unfastening his doublet, and sorted through his clothes for something to wear tonight.

"What?" Nora rose and knelt on the bed, sat back on her haunches. "Why?"

"How about treason?" he answered through clenched teeth.

Her mouth fell open, and she paled. Good.

"She's alive after all." She raised a languid shoulder. "I saw my chance, and I took it."

Not a shred of guilt. He crushed the fabric of an overcoat in his grip.

He shouldn't have expected otherwise. "You used your son to lie to me."

She pursed her lips playfully. "Did I?" she asked mockingly. "Novice mages, especially children, are so unreliable. It's difficult to know what they'll say or do."

Already planning her defense. "And yet, when there's an arrow in the target and you're holding a bow, there's an obvious conclusion. One your judge would see clearly."

The levity faded from her expression. "You wouldn't try a widow, Your Majesty, surely? You'd have mercy?"

He pulled away from the clothes, straightened, and regarded her through slitted eyes. "You have my mercy, Nora," he bit out, "unless word spreads of what happened. Then you will force your own arrest." Despite his poor judgment, he couldn't have others deciding he'd be easy to manipulate, nor lenient with treason.

She opened her mouth—

"You're no longer welcome at court. Leave within three days."

Her eyes narrowed. "And if I stay?"

"You *won't* have my mercy." Shoulders squared, he stood unmoving, gaze fixed on her. If she meant to test him, she would learn just how dedicated he was to following through on his word. Even if she had been his lover. Even if she was a widow.

She lowered her gaze to the floor.

A moment passed, and just when he'd decided to dismiss her, she left the bed, smoothed her gown, and bowed. "By your leave, Your Majesty."

As she exited, he leaned against the doorjamb. Nora was leaving court. Aless would be as well, and his stalling tactic was on the verge of collapse.

And yet... Rielle was alive. Here. And meeting him tonight.

She'd suffered too much because of him, and hope of reconciling with her was lost. But whatever else happened, he loved her and he had to stop hurting her.

Even if she wanted nothing more to do with him, tonight he'd give her the one thing she'd wanted more than anything for as long as he'd known her.

# CHAPTER 52

The Great Bell chimed half an hour to midnight before Rielle woke and sat up from her short rest. Perhaps her eyes wouldn't be so sore anymore.

Next to her, Brennan lay face down on the bed, but he jerked awake and raised his head to look at her.

She held up her hands, and he rubbed his tired face with a palm. All day, he'd watched her as though she might break. She'd already done that once, and didn't plan to dwell on it. Nothing would come of more weeping and wailing; reality was what it was.

And yet, having a friend near, Brennan near, had been a comfort she'd needed.

She looked toward the window.

There wasn't enough time to take a carriage to Trèstellan. She'd have to ride. Squinting in the dark, she tried to decide what to wear; Brennan had brought what things she'd had on her mission to Monas Amar. Something among those would have to do.

A cotton shirt, a dark-blue brocade vest, wool trousers, and a skirted black leather overcoat, long and lined with wool. She stepped behind the screen and hastily changed.

As she laced her boots, a rustle came from the bed. Brennan rose, his form silhouetted in the ambient streetlight from the window. He pulled on his overcoat and met her at the door as she threw on the strandling-lined crimson wool cloak he'd gotten her.

"What are you doing?" she whispered, rushing to braid her hair.

"You're leaving," he answered. "Where you go, I go."

Overprotective. She rolled her eyes but headed into the hall and down the stairs, then outside.

In the street in front of Claudine's was a massive snowman wearing a cloak. A sharp sound somewhere between a gasp and a squeak escaped her throat, and her hand reached up to press a fingertip to the snowman's carrot nose.

The door opened behind her, and she spun to face Brennan, who grinned broadly.

"You did this," she said, her voice quivering.

He shrugged. "It's not nearly as fun without my nanny chasing me around with the cloak, is it?"

She laughed and turned back to the snowman, his walnut-shell eyes and smile. She touched one and traced the smile across.

"I would've used coal, but that would've been stolen in about a second."

Shaking her head, she suppressed a chuckle. The snow had been slowly melting, and he'd used the last of it to make this. To cheer her up? "When did you—"

"While you were sleeping."

"Why?"

"Aside from being fun?" He walked past her toward the stable, but eyed her over his shoulder with a half-smile. "You know why. I wanted to see you smile, and... Well, what I want, I get."

As soon as she realized she was beaming, she pressed her lips together, but the upturned corners refused to obey.

With a smirk, he entered the stable, and she followed, walking backward to eye the snowman for a minute longer.

With jittery fingers, she saddled a horse. What had gotten into him? Had these past years just been some nightmare possessing the Brennan she used to know? This wasn't the same man who'd maliciously shamed her, far from it. He'd hurt her deeply once, but now... Now...

She couldn't think about who he was now. Not right this moment. Not until after tonight.

Brennan wasn't the only one who'd hurt her deeply.

She sighed. Would Jon try to explain? Could she even bear to hear any of it? Perhaps he hadn't done what he'd done with *malice*, but he'd hurt her, too. And this morning had been... Divine, she'd *shouted* at him, wept, lost complete control of herself.

*Not fureur*.

No, thanks to Jon, she'd made peace with herself four months ago. She felt love, rage, and grief, and she owned it, was strong enough to own it, instead of curling up while a shadow self took over.

Shackled in arcanir, she'd had four months to feel the power of those emotions and to take ownership of them. She was whole, and that was in great part due to his love and guidance.

On the night of Spiritseve, Jon had loved her. It was as certain as her beating heart. And her disappearance wouldn't have changed that overnight. Every moment they'd spent together since Bournand had proved his love.

And some spiritualist had made a mistake and declared her dead. What had happened when he'd heard those words? In her time at House Hazael, if one of the many pieces of news she'd translated had declared him dead, what would she have done? With no room to grieve as she'd planned to save herself and Sylvie, might she have distracted herself with something, too?

The bay stallion nipped her elbow. She yelped and tried to calm him.

"Sorry," she whispered, taking better care in his saddling.

Brennan made quick work of saddling his horse but waited to give her a leg up.

"Thank you, Brennan. You didn't have to do that." She smiled faintly. It wasn't fair to him. None of this was. "And you don't have to watch me. I'll be fine."

"All the same," he answered, "until that bitch is dead, I'm coming with you."

*That bitch.* Shadow. He worried Shadow would hurt her if he didn't come along.

As much as she wanted to protest, she wouldn't turn away his help.

"All right." She urged the stallion out of the stable and toward Trèstellan, shivering at the biting cold outside.

THE GREAT BELL chimed midnight when she and Brennan made it to his quarters. A sealed message from Jon waited there, asking her to meet him in the Grand Library.

"I'll wait for you here." Brennan laid his cloak over a chair.

She hugged him and kissed his cheek before she thought not to. He raised his eyebrows, but to his credit, he quickly smiled.

"Go," he whispered.

The message in hand, she shuffled through the halls as quickly as she dared, presenting the message whenever stopped.

Tonight, at least, couldn't go as badly as last night had.

Finally, she made it to the Grand Library's ornate gilded doors. Jon's guards stood outside and, when she showed them the message, opened the doors for her.

A dazzling abundance of candles illuminated the vast library, splendid floral arrangements bountiful with red roses gracing the enormous tables at the center. Floor-to-ceiling windows faced the courtyard, frosted but for the steamy pane before Jon.

He leaned against the frame, dressed in finely tailored black tiretaine wool and cotton, his arms crossed, biceps straining against his sleeves. His eyes, fixed on something in the courtyard, bore none of the verve she so vividly remembered. They were subdued, and perhaps now, so was he.

He glanced her way and straightened as the doors closed. The radiance of the candlelight cast a warm glow on his bronze skin.

"Rielle," he said, deeply, hoarsely. A world crept in the shadow of that one word.

She bowed.

He winced but gestured to two high-backed chairs at the end of the long center table, one at the head and one to its side. When she approached, he helped her out of her cloak and pulled out the closer chair for her, then seated himself. She took off her gloves.

For a moment, he just looked at her, eyes sullen beneath a creased brow. "Are you well?"

*Well?* A small part of her fractured at the question—there was no *well* after what had happened. Not even close.

But she silenced that small part and nodded. "Brennan said I'll need to eat about two loaves of bread a night for a few weeks until I look like myself again."

Jon crossed his arms and covered his upturned mouth pensively with a finger. "He's not wrong." He nodded toward a platter of cakes and tea service on the table. "Help yourself."

"I don't plan to make up all the difference *now*."

He laughed under his breath while she poured herself some white tea and helped herself to some spiced custard tarts, her favorite. Not a coincidence. She took a sip of the tea—jasmine—with an inward grin. He tried to put her at ease. It was working.

For a moment, he watched her warily, then poured himself a cup.

Straightening, she set hers down. "I don't want to waste your time, so—"

"You couldn't, even if you tried." He set down his own cup. "Where have you been?" He nodded to her hands.

Her golden-brown, tan hands. She sighed. "Sonbahar."

He leaned back in his chair and rested his ankle on his opposite knee, tracing a soft circle on the table with a finger.

Her eyelids fluttered closed—she remembered the softness of his touch on her skin the night before Spiritseve, camped on the Mor Bluffs—and fluttered open again. The night they'd conceived Sylvie.

He raised his eyebrows. Awaiting further answer.

She cleared her throat. "And then we, um, took a ship home."

A faint line deepened between his eyebrows. "You were in Sonbahar, and then you took a ship home." He took a deep breath. "That's it?"

She shrugged. "I killed a kraken and met some mermaids."

"Rielle—" He frowned and shook his head, his bearing hardening.

"Tell me what happened. Don't you have any idea how worried I've been?"

She stiffened. *Worried.* He hadn't sounded *worried* in his quarters last night. "I had some idea, Your Majesty, yesterday."

His eyes blazing, he raked his fingers through his thick hair. An anguished gesture. Pained. "I thought you were *dead*." He clenched his fists, then crossed his arms again, keeping them tight against his chest, as if they'd betray his will. "I died a slow death waiting for any news of you. *Any.* And I had no reason to believe the spiritualist Olivia procured would lie—"

The rising pressure boiled over. "So you gave up?" The question choked out of her.

"It had been nearly four months. When the spiritualist told me you weren't among the living, Terra have mercy, but yes, I believed him." His eyes shone, a violent tempest raging in his sea-blue depths.

He looked away and dragged in a deep breath. "I should have come after you myself."

A thousand times. She'd thought a thousand times that he was coming after her. In the dark, in the cold, in the heat. In danger. In humiliation. In fear. She'd held on to that thought. That she needed Jon, and he was coming for her.

But a fragile part of her, a selfish part, had always wanted to come first for him, above everything and everyone. And it was that fragile, selfish part that couldn't ignore him setting her aside, even for the sake of a kingdom.

Yet he couldn't have put her above the entire kingdom. She knew that. Deep down, she knew that, but she'd still wished it. She'd sold herself dreams and delusions, tranquilized herself with a fanciful tale of a man who loved her coming to save her. It had been naive, pathetic, but it had been hope when she'd sorely needed it.

Rain tapped against the massive windows, washing over the frost, blurring it.

A deep frown settled into Jon's face, holding back, holding in. For a while, he stared into nothing with searing intensity, before taking several deep breaths.

The rain eased.

She stared at the window, doubting her own eyes. Uncanny. "It's strange, but the rain..."

"I am Earthbound." His voice, deep and hoarse, rang hollow.

Earthbound. She and Jon had talked about it in Bournand—but not in real terms. According to legend, the Earthbinding was a ritual performed at a Vein by a king, a ritual that would bind him to the land to influence its health, prosperity, and strength.

*Bound to the land. Jon and the land are one.*

Courdeval had been freezing, colder than she'd ever remembered. Frigid.

She stared at Jon, her mouth falling open. Was that how he felt? Cold, detached, without warmth of feeling? His heart frozen to its core?

"Losing you was"—he shook his head—"waking death."

She? She was... the reason?

She slumped in her chair, but Jon bolted upright.

"No," he breathed, his eyebrows drawn together. "No, please. Don't think it. Don't think it a second more." He reached across the table before he caught himself and pulled back his hand, slowly curled his fingers inward. "It's my responsibility to master myself, to become what this land needs me to be. No one else's."

She glanced at his tense hands. Would they feel the same as she remembered? Warm, strong, a little coarse, firm on her body, safe, secure... wrapped around her own hands, so perfectly, like they belonged there.

Divine, she loved him. Loved him so much it hurt. All she wanted was to go back to before all this, before that night outside his quarters, before Spiritseve. But that was impossible. "What do you want from me, Jon?"

"I want you to be happy."

She looked away.

The moans and cries from his quarters haunted her.

"Too much has happened," she whispered, her voice breaking. The pain of that night hadn't dulled. And he hadn't come to her rescue, or Sylvie's. Had grieved her loss, if it could be called such, with a lover, no matter his reasons. She just wanted to scream at him and thrash him and cry, but what would that do?

It would still hurt. Maybe it would always hurt. Or maybe it would be as Olivia had said—all wounds faded with time.

He leaned in. "I... I have a few things for you."

She tilted her head. What could he possibly...?

He reached around his neck and raised a necklace bearing a ring. A signet ring. Hers. He held it out to her, letting it hang from his grasp, and she held out a palm for him to drop it into.

The Laurentine signet ring, engraved with the rose encircled by a chaplet of honeysuckle, was warm in her hand. Jon's warmth. She rubbed its band softly before donning the necklace over her head, pulling her braid out over it.

He then removed a ring from his hand and placed it on the table in front of her. The Sodalis ring.

"I can't accept this," she whispered. He'd given it to her once in Melain, with his love.

"Accept it, free of any conditions."

"Jon—"

He shook his head. "It's yours. I've only held it for you in your absence. Please."

She reached for it and placed it over her thumb, the only finger it wouldn't slip from easily.

Finally, he slid some parchment toward her from the far corner of the table.

"What is this?" She read the script.

"A grant of your petition to dissolve your marriage contract."

Her lips parted, but her breath caught. How often had she prayed, even aloud to Jon, that the new king would grant her petition? And here it was, the freedom she'd so longed for.

Freedom.

She'd no longer be promised to Brennan, and he no longer promised to her. She would be free to marry someone else, or no one at all, if she so desired. And he would be free to find a new bride.

She swallowed. Just five months ago, she'd hated Brennan so fiercely that she would have done anything to dissolve the betrothal.

But since Xir...

Since Xir, he'd been a new man. Kind, sincere. Loving. Honorable. He'd become the man she'd always imagined he'd someday be, back when she'd been just a girl. The kind of *husband* she'd always imagined he'd be. The man her parents had wanted her to marry. The man Gran wanted her to marry.

Whenever she looked at him, she didn't see hurt, pain, or past sins. She saw a man who'd sacrificed his own life to save hers. A man who'd searched for her across seas and deserts. A man who'd built a snowman just to make her smile. An ally, a friend, a loved one... a good man, one who didn't have to marry a royal, marry for the kingdom's sake, only with Parliament's approval.

She raised a palm to her chest. *Do I want to marry Brennan?*

Holding her breath, she dared consider the thought. Not today, not tomorrow, but... someday?

Someday, she could wed Brennan.

Brennan, who'd set his entire life aside for the past few months just to find her, to protect her, to help her. Who'd put her first.

She didn't want him to find a new bride.

For his part, Brennan had admitted he loved her. And it was no secret to her that he wanted the curse broken.

A lump formed in her throat. After losing her child in Xir, she couldn't even fathom the notion of ever having another, but...

Someday, the hurt wouldn't be so near, the grief so keen, and maybe she could... bear his child and break his curse forever.

She loved Jon, but she wasn't ready to commit to abandoning Brennan. The most she could ever be to Jon would be lover, mistress. He could never marry her, but... Brennan *could*.

If she had to choose between love and marriage, which was the right choice?

Or would she someday... fall in love with Brennan?

Her brows knitted together, she rested a hand on the parchment.

She didn't have to decide now.

"Thank you for this, Jon," she said softly, pushing it away, "but it won't be necessary."

His neck corded, he gave her a bleak stare. "You and... him?"

The lump in her throat thickened. "I... We'll see."

A muscle twitched in his jaw. "You know why he wants you."

She leaned away. "He's changed."

" 'Changed,' " he repeated bitterly. "You think he'd so quickly abandon what he was willing to kill for?"

"It's more than that," she snapped. "He loves me. I won't just—"

Jon's mouth went slack. "You really believe that." The color drained from his face, and he pulled back. "No... *you* love *him*."

She jolted in her chair and shook her head. "I didn't come here to talk about Brennan."

His eyes widened beneath furrowed eyebrows. "Are you in love with him?"

"What right do you have to ask me that?" Divine's flaming fire, her eyes were watering again; she bit back tears.

Glaring at her, he crossed his arms again.

A small sound escaped her throat, something she didn't recognize as her own voice. "Jon, until last night, nothing but the thought of being with you again—" *Kept me going.*

The intensity of his glare faded only a measure. "Then you'd accept the papers, wouldn't you?"

He'd stayed here while she'd suffered, while Sylvie had *died*. She'd returned here to find him in bed with another woman, and now he demanded she placate his jealousy?

He sighed. "I'm sorry... I... I have no right." He scrubbed a hand over his face. "All I've managed is to do and say all the wrong things, when—"

She shook her head. "I came here to tell you there's an assassin plotting to kill you." She lifted her chin, holding in the pressure behind her eyes. "It's Shadow, one of the Crag Company's mage captains."

Jon tightened his crossed arms. "The Crag Company is destroyed."

"She isn't. Shadow was the one who"—she took a fortifying breath—"abducted me the night of Spiritseve."

His tautness faded.

"On the ship to Sonbahar, she told me her husband was one of the attackers I'd killed in Laurentine a decade ago. And that she was taking her vengeance. She said because I killed the man she loved, she would kill the man I..."

He opened his mouth, but no words came.

The silence stretched too long. Strained. "If she finds out I've returned, I think she'll feel compelled to act. And she has a soulblade spelled to kill the one I love most, with just one cut."

"Are you sure... it's me she'll be after?" he asked gently. Carefully.

She pinched her lips to keep them from trembling. She did love Jon, no matter how badly she tried to feel otherwise, no matter that she couldn't imagine being together again. It was hopeless, but it was the truth, and one she wouldn't deny. Shadow would have no reason to suspect anything about Brennan, and in any case, it seemed difficult, if not impossible, to kill him.

She nodded. "And I want to help stop her, but I'll need a plan."

Waiting around for Shadow to try to kill Jon again was no plan at all, but tracking her down wouldn't be so simple either.

"I think she's already attempted to kill me once, then," he said, looking away. "Olivia saved my life."

She smiled faintly. That sounded like Olivia, all right.

But that meant Shadow hadn't been idle.

He pressed a fist to his mouth. "I'll have to discuss it with my High Council, but instead of waiting for her to strike again, it might be best to draw her out at a time of our choosing."

There was logic in that. Luring her in, trapping her, at a time of *their* choosing. "When would that be?"

He raised his eyebrows and shrugged, then sucked in a breath. "Every year, the palace hosts a Midwinter Ball, but this year, obviously, it was canceled. My advisers and I decided to host a ball for the end of the Terran spring festival of Veris."

"When?"

"In five days." He sipped his tea. "If your return would compel her to act, then in a couple days, we could let it be known you've returned. I could escort you to the event, the Champion of Courdeval back from afar, as my special guest. If you're right about her, she won't be able to resist."

"Escort me?" Was this some ploy to smooth over what had happened? And *Champion of Courdeval?* What was that about?

"I understand if you don't wish to." He lowered his gaze. "I understand if you want nothing to do with me ever again."

Seeing him now hurt. Sitting here, looking across the table at him, knowing what she knew, hurt. And it probably would for the foreseeable future.

But she wouldn't leave him to be killed by Shadow. "I want to help stop her. Let's do this."

He eyed her doubtfully. "Thank you."

She nodded, and then the silence pervaded until he poured himself another cup of tea. "Where are you staying?" he asked. "Olivia wouldn't say."

"Claudine's, by the docks. I couldn't trust staying at Couronne without word spreading of my return."

"Claudine's," Jon repeated. "Can I send you correspondence there?"

"If you want to. I'll let you know when I move to Couronne."

The Great Bell chimed two. Two in the morning. She started. When had the time flown by? She took another bite of her custard tart. "I'm sorry. I didn't mean to keep you."

Jon slid the teacup and saucer away. "You haven't. I'm not even tired." His eyes fixed on hers. "You should stay here tonight."

"Thank you. But I think I'll head back to Claudine's." Putting on her gloves, she rose, and Jon rose with her. She reached for her cloak, but he took it for her and wrapped it about her shoulders, then leaned in to tie the front.

Linden and woodsmoke. She breathed deeply, his scent taking her back to cool nights camped under the stars, dancing at Vindemia in Bournand, days spent abed in Melain.

His eyebrows drawn together in determination, he made her knees buckle. She grabbed the chair for support before she made a fool of herself.

"There," he said quietly, his voice an octave deeper than usual. He swept her braid over her shoulder, his fingers lingering at her neck, his thumb stroking a delicate line from her ear. She leaned into his touch, her lips parting in a soft exhalation, and his fingers brushed along her jaw to her chin.

Moans echoed in her head. From his quarters.

Her blood running cold, she pushed away from him, wrapped her cloak about her, held a quivering hand between them. "Don't."

He gave a slow, disbelieving head shake, his mouth falling open as his arms fell to his sides. "Are you—"

She backed away toward the door, trembling. This had been a mistake. She should have just told him and left. "Don't."

He held out his hands. "Tell me—"

"Don't touch me," she snapped, heaving ragged breaths. "Ever again."

He knew she loved him and that she needed space. He knew that, and he'd ignored it. She needed to leave. *Now.*

With a long, pained look, he lowered his arms. "I'm sorry I—"

"No." She reached the door, scrabbling for the handle behind her.

"Forgive me," he said gravely, but she wouldn't hear another word. Couldn't. She threw herself out of the Grand Library and, ignoring the puzzled guards, fled.

If she opened her heart to Jon now, even a little bit, while nothing was resolved between them, he would rend it wide open. She'd never recover.

A mission. Until Shadow was dead, this—he—could only be a mission. Nothing more.

# CHAPTER 53

*J*on paced his bedchamber, raking his fingers through his hair. How had the night deteriorated so quickly?

Rielle had recoiled from him. *Recoiled.*

He dropped into a tufted armchair by the hearth and threw his head back, staring up at her portrait. A nineteen-year-old Rielle looked at him, her chin raised, smiling coyly, challenge gleaming in her sky-blue eyes. A woman in love.

How had he misread her so disastrously? Yet again.

When he'd wrapped her cloak about her shoulders and leaned in to fasten the closure—on account of her gloved hands—her eyes had shone, softened, darkened. She'd breathed deeply, slowly—a lingering touch at her neck as he'd swept her braid over her shoulder. She'd leaned into it. Her lips had parted. She'd exhaled softly.

He'd traced a gentle line along her jaw.

In that moment, he'd felt it: she still loved him.

And then she'd broken away. Recoiled. Pushed away from him with an anguish he'd never seen. *Don't.*

She'd held a hand between them, as if she'd feared he'd force himself on her. *Don't touch me. Ever again.*

He dropped his gaze to the fire, the consumed embers there, nearly snuffed out.

Cold. So cold. He'd never felt so cold in his life. He kneaded his chest with the heel of a palm but hardly felt it at all.

He dropped his head into his hands, rubbing his forehead with his fingers. She couldn't bear his touch. Couldn't stand him. Would never forgive him.

He threaded his fingers through his hair, pulling at it as he raked his hand through.

The woman in the painting smiled coyly at him. A woman in love.

He hissed in a sharp breath. Nineteen-year-old Rielle. Three years ago.

She *had* been in love. With Brennan.

*Thank you for this, Jon,* she'd said, pushing the parchment away, *but it won't be necessary.*

She wanted to marry Brennan.

Slumped in the chair, he watched the flames with morbid fascination. It had all burned. All of it.

He wanted to lay his heart bare to her, give her everything he was and ever would be, for her to do with as she willed, for as long as he lived.

*Don't touch me. Ever again.* She didn't want him. It was over. He'd lost her.

He gazed at the portrait once more. This was a different Rielle than four months ago. He'd hurt her with Aless—and gods, he still had to tell her about Nora, and Manon—but that wasn't all.

What had happened to her in Sonbahar?

She'd told him very little... that Shadow had abducted her, that she'd been on a ship to Sonbahar.

An enemy wouldn't have sent Rielle to another country to go free.

She'd been sold.

He dropped his head in his hands once more, raking fingers through his hair.

Her shaking hand between them, as if she'd feared he'd force himself on her. *Don't touch me. Ever again.*

A hollow ached in his throat. Terra have mercy—

What terrors had she suffered in bondage?

Heavy, cold shackles. Dark, cramped quarters. Shouts and rough hands. Hits, lashes, pain, pain, pain.

A silenced voice. A dead voice. A caged will. A broken will. The woman who'd stared Flame in the eye and fought him herself, who'd plunged a shard of glass into her flesh for his sake—his love, his forever, unrelenting and fierce—

Chained.

Clothes and shoes and dignity stripped away. Brands and blurted prices. Wrists held down. Barked orders. Compliance or agony.

He covered his mouth with a clenched fist, his entire body going rigid, his gaze unwavering from the embers. Even now, even after everything, all he wanted was to go to her, plead with her to tell him everything, to unburden herself, and to let him help her in any way he could.

*I'm most helpful to her here, leaving her be.* That was the reality, painful as it was. This plan to catch Shadow would, at least, give him a chance to see her, perhaps alleviate some of the hurt, if he didn't stumble in the attempt.

He rested his chin on his hand, stroking the day's growth there with a thumb. He breathed a long sigh, blinking heavily.

That anguished face... Terra have mercy, he could never hurt her like that again. No matter how willing she seemed, he'd never touch her with love again, ever. Not unless she initiated, which would never happen.

BRENNAN LAY IN BED, his face buried in Rielle's hair, smelling of her usual rose oil and her own scent. The early morning rays peeked through the drapes.

She'd rushed into his quarters in the middle of the night, answered none of his questions, and curled up in bed. When he'd cautiously lain next to her, she'd wriggled closer until her back rested against his side, and had fallen asleep.

Sometime during the night, she'd moved to rest her cheek on his chest, where she lay now.

She loved him. He loved her. She loved another man more. But she slept right here in his arms.

She'd trusted Jon. Loved him. And he'd abused that trust, hurt her deeply. And now she needed to put herself back together.

He understood that. But this was the most confusing relationship he'd ever had in his life. What was it that she wanted of him?

He had to get her out of the palace, away from Jon, somewhere she could think clearly, *breathe*. While she was here, seeing Jon again, she was under his influence; while he plied her with charm and favors, she'd never realize how flawed his love had been, how weak he was, how bound by his new role, that he'd never be able to put her first. That even if all this had happened again, the king still wouldn't have come for her.

That influence was strong. Overwhelming.

*And I can't even breathe a word of it to her, or she'll just think it's jealousy.*

No, she had to come to the realization herself, and abandon her feelings for the king. It was the only way.

A lock of hair lay over her eyes, and he stroked it away. If she didn't know what she wanted of him—or worse, if she wanted nothing— asking her would only force her to realize it.

Even if this was an illusion, a mistake, he didn't want it to end.

Her eyes fluttered open, and her palm slid across his abdomen, slowly with increasing firmness. He shivered, and she looked up at him, blinked sluggishly.

"Divine!" she gasped, extricating herself from him and sitting up. "I'm so sorry. I didn't mean to—"

"You are always welcome." *To everything I have. To everything I am.*

She covered her mouth, glanced at him and away again, and blushed. Those golden-tan cheeks of hers reddened beautifully. Because of him. He grinned.

"Could we go back to Claudine's?" She flattened the halo of wispy hair at all angles from her braid.

Away from the palace? It was as though she'd spoken his mind. "Of course," he replied. "When?"

She stood and smoothed her rumpled clothes, her gaze landing on a spot on the floor across from the bed. Where the king had stood.

"As soon as possible." She crossed the bedchamber to the wash-basin. "I don't want to be here another minute more than I have to. We should've left last night, but I..." She splashed her face.

He sat up and left the bed. "We'll go." He approached her and rested a palm on the small of her back while she dried her face with a towel. She gazed up at him. "Why don't you wash up and change, and I'll tell my household to prepare our horses? We'll eat, and we'll leave."

A warm smile spread on her lips, then she nodded and embraced him. Drawing his eyebrows together, he wrapped his arms around her, too, rested his chin atop her head, buried his nose in her hair, inhaled the intoxicating smell of her.

"You've been unbelievable, Brennan," she whispered.

Unbelievable? He fought a smile.

"You've done nothing but help me, fight for me, protect me, support me. You've asked me for nothing, demanded nothing," she said softly into his chest. "Don't think I haven't noticed. You've set aside your entire life these past few months. And I'm grateful."

*Life.* What had his life been before these past few months? Managing Tregarde and Calterre, a whirlwind of court functions, seducing the most promising of each year's debutantes, casting them aside when he tired of them, tranquilizing himself with upscale brothels and mundane games of intrigue, victories that didn't truly satisfy. Running the nights away in the forests when the Wolf grew restless. Visiting Maerleth Tainn, Mother and his sisters, training in Faris and the rapier.

Aside from spending time with his family, had that even been much of a life? After the past few months—fighting across Emaurria, the Kezan Isles, Sonbahar; defeating bandits and mercenaries who'd wanted to destroy the kingdom, pirates and slavers, hisaad; coming to Rielle's aid, becoming her friend, and... more. Spending his days and nights with her. Sailing across the Bay of Amar. Waking up with her in his arms—

*This* was life. Everything before had merely been passing the time.

And now, he could imagine this every day. Having her close, loving her. Living in the same home, sharing the same bed, the same life. A marriage. Children. Joy. And the curse broken.

Just a year ago, it had seemed so impossible a dream that he'd convinced himself he didn't want it. Her. Any of it.

But he could smell the sweet truth. See its happy sheen. Hear its quiet breathing. Feel its softness beneath his hands.

"You don't have to thank me," he whispered. "I haven't done anything I didn't choose to do."

She pulled away, licking her lips, and smiled warmly. "Still."

Her smiles and embraces were gratitude—gratitude that he didn't care to think about when her body was against his, when her smiling face filled him with warmth. But she desired him, loved him, at least in some small way, and she hid those feelings beneath thanks.

Perhaps she knew it; perhaps she didn't. Someday, she would have to unearth her love and desire.

But he wouldn't push her. He had waited a decade for her, and if she needed his patience, he would wait until she was ready.

His hands slid slowly to her hips, then he let her go. "All right. I'll notify my household. There are fresh clothes in the armoire."

She nodded. "I'll freshen up and meet you in the antechamber."

He left her to it and yanked the bell pull by the bed. When Gerard arrived, he told him to have the horses saddled and ready for departure within the hour, then the man left.

Brennan headed into the antechamber. Among the full spread of breakfast, the kettle was still hot, so he poured himself and Rielle some black tea, adding two sugars to hers just as she liked.

He drank his tea and listened to the sounds of her getting ready in the bedchamber—the splashing of water, the shuffle of steps, the soft creak of the armoire door, the swish of fabric and rustling as she changed, the quick strokes of her hair brush.

A morning song, one he'd gladly hear every day of his life.

He set down the teacup and stared out the window. Another gray day, dreary and cold. But it didn't matter; things were looking up.

She soon exited the bedchamber, fresh faced and impeccably dressed in her usual attire of shirt, vest, trousers, and boots, her hair braided anew, and it was his turn to get ready.

Within the hour, they'd eaten and were riding back toward the docks, cloaked to hide their identities as best they could. He scanned their surroundings and listened for anything out of the ordinary, but there was no sign of the bitch that had taken her. In a city as dense as Courdeval, tracking her would be difficult.

But there was a lot of talk and activity. Azalée's usual bustle had exploded—the words on everyone's lips today being *Veris Ball.*

Rielle urged her horse through the crowds, on occasion using her earthsight, without sparing any attention to the idle chatter or business. These things didn't often interest her—she'd shunned court for years—but she ignored all around her with a willfulness that suggested more than disinterest.

Reluctance.

He faced forward once more, carving a route through the dense streets. Was she going to the ball? Had the king invited her?

She wasn't pleased with the king, that much was clear, but there was something else.

No doubt an invitation already awaited him at Victoire, if he deigned to go. Which, if she was going, so would he. No Master of Ceremonies in his right mind would snub the heir to Maerleth Tainn.

At last, they made it to Claudine's. After stabling their horses, Rielle headed to the melting snowman, rested her hand on him for a pensive moment, then went inside. At the front desk, she retrieved—

Mail.

Together, they proceeded up to the room they shared. After tearing open the seal—the king's seal—she read the letter and plopped onto the bed, spreading out like a lily pad on the covers.

She waved the letter and held it out to him.

*I've made arrangements with my household to ensure our plans unfold as we discussed. Proceed to Couronne, and send word. Every eye in Azalée will see our preparations for the ball, and every tongue will move on the subject.*

*Yours,*

*J.*

The short length of the note and plain phrasing was almost cold, but it wasn't on the king's end. No, he very carefully used *our, we,* and that closing.

The brevity and plainness was for her benefit. Her comfort.

Their plans... What did they entail?

Brennan read the note again and returned it to her. She folded it up and shoved it into her vest.

"You're going to the ball with him."

She faced him with a frown. "No." She blinked. "Well, yes. But not for the reasons you think. We want to lure Shadow out at a time and place of our choosing. I'm going to let it be known I've returned, and he's going to find every opportunity to bring the subject to everyone's lips. He's announced a very public midnight walk in the Trèstellan gardens after the evening's dancing. Open, dark. She'll know I'm back. And she won't be able to resist trying to kill him with me right there."

The plan had merit, at least the lure. "So you're the bait, but what ensures that she won't kill him... and you?"

She grinned, broadly, deviously, like a she-wolf ready to devour her prey. "Sonbahar wasn't entirely a waste of my time. I learned about sangremancy wards there... And I'm going to set a trap."

"I should be there."

The hungry grin faded. "You're welcome to come. I won't turn away your help, if offered."

He sat next to her. "To you, my help is always on offer."

She smiled. "Anything in particular? Maybe a snowman army?"

He laughed. "I could... keep watch from afar until she attacks, and then help take her out. And... if she's smart, she'll scout the grounds and perhaps even the palace for vulnerabilities. I could do a sweep of the gardens, the great hall, and... the king's quarters, to make sure she hasn't set any traps herself." Trying way too hard to remain relevant. He suppressed a grimace.

"Good thinking. I'll let Jon know, so you'll have the proper permissions in Trèstellan." She rummaged through her packs, pulled out paper, a quill, and an inkwell.

"Now?"

"Yes." She spread out her supplies on the nightstand. "And I'm going to let Davina know I've returned."

Davina, Couronne's chamberlain and acting steward. The letter would give the villa's household some time to prepare for their lady's arrival.

She scribbled two notes, heated the wax with a fiery palm, and stamped them with her signet ring—on a long chain around her neck. Newly reacquired...

From the king. Next to it on the chain was the familiar Sodalis ring the king had claimed her with at Melain. So he'd made a gift of it to her.

But she didn't wear it on her hand. She rejected his claiming.

He suppressed a smile. "When do we leave?"

She sprang up and opened the hallway door, looking this way and that before calling a maid. Once the girl took the letters, she shut the door. "*We* don't."

He grimaced. "Rielle—"

"It can't look like a trap." She took his hand. "Jon is supposed to be courting me, winning me over, showering me with gifts. We're supposed to be lovers going to the ball together."

He clenched his teeth but maintained a facade of calm.

"And how would it look if you're staying there? Everyone knows you're my fiancé. My fiancé and my lover spending the night at my villa will look—"

He grinned despite himself. Many a tale he'd read—the dirty sort— had started with a similar line.

She swatted his arm and pursed her lips. "I can't afford to give Shadow any reason to suspect the trap."

Heaving a sigh, he shook his head. "If she's as clever as she's been so far, she'll suspect anyway. You're courting danger." But Shadow wasn't the only threat. "And the king will only use his proximity to you to try to regain your affections while you're alone, vulnerable. Do you really want that?"

She narrowed her eyes. "Being alone does not mean being vulnerable."

He grunted. "You know what I meant."

She huffed a breath. "Yes, I know. I've considered it, too. But the reasons he and I aren't together are many. One night of acting at

Couronne isn't going to change any of them. And it's our best bet to root out Shadow, both for my safety and his. Do you really think it would be better to wait for her to strike when we least expect it?"

He rolled his eyes and turned away. Of course not.

And he didn't have any better ideas. He gathered some of his clothes and stuffed them into a pack. "But I'm still taking you there. If she's on the road, waiting for you, then I'm not letting her get her chance."

She raised her eyebrows but blinked her objections away. They made quick work of packing their things, and after she asked that their packs be sent to Couronne, they headed to the stable.

She saddled her horse while he saddled his.

To draw Shadow out, she and the king would have to appear the reunited couple—happy. Irritatingly happy. And Rielle returning to Couronne with her fiancé and openly staying there together would fly in the face of that appearance.

He understood it, but he didn't have to like it.

He gave her a leg up into the saddle, and she pulled up the hood of her cloak. "I'll see you to Couronne, then I'll go to Victoire and see you at the Veris Ball in a few days. If you need me, just pull on the bond, and I will come to you."

"Thank you, Brennan."

He nodded and urged his horse from the stable and out onto the cobblestone avenue, pulling up the hood on his own cloak. No sign of the shadowmancer bitch. A part of him prayed she was waiting to ambush them on the road. At least then he'd rip her throat out and save Rielle the trouble of playing pretend with the king.

Rielle followed after him. For nearly four days, he wouldn't see her —the longest time apart since he'd found her in Xir.

But if it meant capturing Shadow, it would be worth the sacrifice. If fortune smiled on the bitch, Rielle would be the one to kill her.

If not... Shadow would wish she'd never been born. A rictus grin split his mouth. Oh, yes, she would suffer. Greatly.

# CHAPTER 54

Throwing off her hood, Rielle dismounted her horse and headed toward Couronne. It had been over a year since she'd stayed. Although the rain had turned the beautiful greenery to mud, the grounds were still well kept. The villa's steeply pitched roof, its highest peak at the center, overlooked the streets of Azalée.

Sided with white stucco, the villa's blackwood half-timbering contrasted beautifully, so much like Laurentine's barns and silos, which used white pines. A jettied first floor, abundant with mullioned windows, hung over an ample, pillared front portico.

She removed the Laurentine signet ring from her chain and placed it on her finger.

Two grooms hurried through the mud to her and took her horse when she'd traversed half the way to the villa.

Couronne's blackwood front doors opened, and Davina burst out. Her curly gray-streaked sable tresses wrapped in a tight bun, she glided across the grounds, her petite form quicker than she looked. "A sight for sore eyes! Welcome home, my lady!"

Davina hugged her. They'd always been thick as thieves, and Davina was almost as motherly as Mama had been.

"Davina," she said warmly. "How have you been?"

Davina pulled away but held her, looking her over. "I've been worried sick! Since the Battle for Courdeval, rumors have abounded, and I've inquired as to your whereabouts everywhere—"

Rielle smiled. "I'm fine."

"—and now you write me saying, 'I'm coming to Couronne shortly, and the king will be visiting.' *The king*!" Davina shook her head. "All the preparations to be done—when is he coming?"

Rielle shrugged. "Today?"

"Today!" Davina's eyes bulged, then she turned to the grooms, who stood by gawking. She swatted at them. "You two! What are you doing dawdling about? The king is coming here. The king!"

They exchanged glances and shrugs. "Will he be visiting the stable?"

"Probably not," the other offered. "Why's the king coming?"

Davina smacked his arm. "Don't ask why! Just go make sure everything is in perfect order!"

They bowed, tugged the stallion's bridle, and made for the stable. Davina laced her arm through Rielle's. "Now, tell me all about His Majesty..."

She let Davina lead her into the villa and answered her myriad questions about Jon—his habits, his preferences, his disposition, his personality, acquaintances, everything. So much— she knew so much about him, more than she'd even thought she'd known. And since coming back, she felt like she didn't know him at all.

Just when she'd thought the questioning over, Davina only instructed her maids and footmen to make preparations, then resumed with questions of the past year as she drew a bath and laid out fresh clothes. *Appropriate* clothes. Davina had kept the wardrobe up to date and fashionable.

Rielle answered what questions she could without divulging Brennan's secret, Liam's survival, her plan with Jon, or her own tragedies. For her part, Davina didn't pry and instead focused on brighter moments.

"It's all true, then?" Davina hesitated, but Rielle didn't stop her. "The rumors about Melain, the king's fondness for you, the...?"

"Affair?" Rielle supplied, and Davina drew in a slow, deep breath. Word had spread of her mission and its many details, then. "Yes."

"It is said that the king fell in love with the Rose of Laurentine, and that she left him—left him with naught but grief."

Rose of Laurentine? She resisted the urge to gag. As if she were some flower waiting to be plucked. And without the whole truth of the past four months, the ill-informed rendition had colored her relationship with Jon a much different shade than reality.

"Something like that," Rielle whispered.

"My lady, do you... love him?" Davina asked softly.

"Yes." Unfortunately. But what had her love meant to him if he'd believed the false declaration of her death, if he'd so quickly turned to another woman to forget her? How special could she have been, really, to be replaced so easily?

And the way he'd manipulated her last night... He had to know how hurt she was, even if she was still in love with him. How could he have used that love to try to force closeness? The divide between them couldn't be bridged with caresses—nor with kisses, embraces, and love-making. She needed to give him the truth of what had happened in Sonbahar—all of it—just as his truth of taking a lover had been bared to her.

Then, once they saw each other clearly, maybe it would be as Olivia had said: the wounds would fade with time. Maybe she could sit across from him without hurting. Maybe they could at least be friends again.

Davina washed Rielle's hair in the tub. The rose scent filled the chamber. "Do you think he'll ask for your hand, my lady?"

She shivered, curling into herself. Not something she could picture.

He couldn't, anyway, even if he wanted to. Just as the Houses needed his approval for their marriages, so, too, did he need Parliament's approval for his own. And with the land in turmoil, no marital alliance from the previous generation, her disastrous reputation, the Marcels' prior claim to her hand, and Jon's status as a bastard—albeit legitimized—there was no way they'd approve. There was no reason for them to approve. She could offer nothing—no alliance, no armies, no power—but trouble.

And there was no way she'd agree either. Not only because of the mess between them, but because she'd only be weakening her own country.

But Davina—and everyone else—needed to believe she and Jon had hope. "Perhaps if word spreads of his visit here, the circumstances, we could win the people over."

"I'll see to that," Davina said, the grin clear as a bell in her voice.

"But even so... I don't think it's possible," she whispered. She'd spent the past four months believing their love could overcome anything. But she couldn't see how this wound could possibly heal.

"If you love him, he may yet live up to that honor," Davina replied, rinsing her hair. "And if he doesn't, love is its own end, isn't it?"

Rielle inclined her head and offered Davina a faint smile.

As much it had hurt to learn Jon hadn't waited for her, their love was still precious to her. Even now, even with all the hurt, even if they wouldn't be together, he'd still been the love of her life.

But how much could love truly withstand? This had to have been too much. Far too much.

Davina finished readying her, dressing her in a crimson brocade gown, embroidered with gold-threaded roses along the neckline and trim, with flowing split sleeves and open lacing down the front revealing teases of an ivory silk chemise—and jeweled crimson slippers to match. While Davina tamed her tresses with pins, Rielle placed the Sodalis ring on her thumb—more acting—and searched through her recondite satchel for the tiny bottle of immortelle Jon had given her.

The cluster of yellow blooms remained vibrant.

"What is it, my lady?" Davina paused.

"The first gift he ever gave me." She thumbed the round glass bottle with nostalgia. "The flowers are immortelle. He had cut this cluster outside Monas Ver when he was a paladin, because it reminded him of home. When we fell in love, he... gave it to me."

*Perhaps home can be with you*, he'd said. She sucked in a breath and closed her hand over the bottle.

"That's beautiful," Davina whispered, her gaze in the mirror roving to the Sodalis ring on Rielle's thumb.

Jon had given more of himself than she'd ever expected; he'd sacrificed his calling, his family of paladins and priests, his only personal possessions, life as he'd known it. And it hadn't been just to bed her. He could have had that in Bournand, even before then, or with any other woman, but that hadn't been what he'd wanted.

Her hand gently brought the bottle of immortelle to her chest. Always. That had been what he'd wanted, what she'd wanted. A perfect love, together, always. Her eyes teared up.

She tied a small white ribbon around the bottle's neck, then bound it to a two-foot-long golden chain from her jewelry box. She fastened it around her neck and tucked the tiny bottle into her décolletage. Hidden away.

Could she do the same to their love? Hide it away, deep in her heart, where it could slowly fade, as it should?

A job. A mission. That was all she could allow herself with Jon for now.

The doors to the bedchamber opened.

"My lady, there are deliveries for you," a maid announced. "Many, many deliveries."

Rielle's palm darted to cover the bottle of immortelle, and she looked out the window onto the cobblestone avenue, where many of the Houses' servants and some lords and ladies had gathered to gawk.

She closed her gaping mouth. Large horse-drawn carts of imported tea, exotic fruits, and delicate desserts and confections... Enough geomancy-grown immortelle to fill several of Couronne's rooms... Four dozen bouquets of three dozen red roses, their arrangements so massive that each vase required two people to carry...

When the day faded, two barded palfreys were delivered—Pearl and Onyx—sleek and shining to perfection, and a large box stamped with Madame Marlène's seal, the Houses' most celebrated dressmaker and tailor.

A gown. On such short notice, there was no way Madame Marlène could have completed a new garment. Or if she had, it would cost a fortune.

Four assistants carried the massive box onto the Couronne grounds, flanked by others carrying smaller boxes.

A ripple wove through the crowd. Another carriage stopped before Couronne, heavily guarded—a mage, bowmen, pikemen. A footman opened the carriage door, and a well-dressed older man emerged, head held high. He bore a medium-sized finely wrapped box clad in gorgeous white satin and tied with a sapphire-blue ornate bow. Laurent's, known across the kingdom for its stunning jewelry.

Another man, younger and lithe, well dressed but not so well as to outshine the first man, followed suit, bearing a stack of three small satin-wrapped boxes with sapphire-blue bows.

Jon had written that every eye in Azalée would see their plans for the Veris Ball, and every tongue would move on the subject.

He wasn't wrong.

Davina gave her a knowing look.

"I am blessed with His Majesty's goodwill," Rielle said, tempering the fullness rising in her chest with a soft sigh.

Davina approached her and looked out the window as a winery cart pulled up, then she rested a hand on Rielle's arm. A slow smile brightened her face. She nodded toward the window. "Well, all of Azalée—and Courdeval—now knows his heart."

An artful pretense, and no more. Rielle's grip tightened on the immortelle, but she forced a smile. "So do I."

OLIVIA EXHALED a relieved breath as Lydia unfastened the laces of her golden-yellow ball gown. It was beautiful, and well worth the inability to breathe.

With the courier in the wind and no way to track down Shadow, there was little else to do but work and prepare for the ball. And better to get her gown out of the way now before her magic lesson with Jon —*still* working on the repulsion shield.

A knock came from the hall, and she bade Lydia pause.

"Enter," she called, looking down the suite of rooms to the doorway.

Edgar entered and placed his hand over his heart, but his moss-green eyes looked her over. "Forgive the intrusion, Lady Archmage, but the Lord Constable is here to see you. Shall I let him in?"

So wooden. Over the past month, he'd been a perfect guardsman, with none of the youthfulness she'd seen in Kirn... and she missed it.

She smoothed her gown. "Please. Send him in."

"As you wish, Lady Archmage." With that, he disappeared through the doorway.

*Lady Archmage.* The implied distance made her wince inwardly. Hadn't they become friends?

Tor entered, eyebrows raised as he gave her a once-over and a nod of approval. He grinned and clasped his hands behind his back. "Is that...?"

"My gown for the Veris Ball," she replied with a smile, dismissing Lydia to lay out her emerald-green Archmage's robes. "Do you like it?"

He approached, his tall, large frame clad in a burgundy velvet overcoat that lent his hazel eyes a certain brandy warmth. "That's putting it lightly, my dove."

Heat rose in her cheeks.

He brushed her lips with his, and she melted. He smelled like a forest—cypress and moss and a revitalizing mint. "Do you have a moment?"

For him? She nodded.

He took her hand and led her to the nearby sofa, where he seated her gently and sat next to her. "I know you're a Divinist, but my brother invited me to spend Ignis at Maerleth Tainn, and I was wondering if you'd like to join me?"

A pleasant shiver pebbled her skin. Ignis? That would be in a little over a month. And he wanted to take her to meet his family? "I—I'd love to."

Grinning, he dipped his head, blinking with long, dark lashes. Divine, he was handsome. "Good, because I'd like to introduce you to everyone."

*Why?* She wanted to blurt out the word, not because she didn't know the reason, but because she wanted to hear him say it.

"Olivia, I haven't loved a woman in decades, not since before my vows, and I think you're wise, strong, determined, smart—someone who makes me want to be a better man." He squeezed her hand. "I'm serious about you."

"Serious?" Commitment. Marriage.

"Very." He searched her eyes with a soft smile, a sort of quiet affection, and she wrapped her arms around his neck and shifted to sit in his lap, drawing away only to kiss him. He held her steady.

Torrance Auvray Marcel, nobleman, Lord Constable, and a good man, was serious about *her*.

"Care to show me how serious?" she whispered in his ear.

He straightened and cleared his throat, his hands slipping to her waist. "Olivia, it's been a long time. A very, very long time."

Smiling, she shook her head—he was only in his early forties, perhaps a decade and half older than she, not some oldster. "And you're not eager to make up for lost time?"

He barked a laugh and looked away. "As wonderful as that sounds, it's not the most important matter between partners. Let's take things slowly, and we'll get there."

Slowly? What kind of torture was that?

James had loved her early and often, met her hot blood with his own searing heat.

But Tor was Tor... No doubt the transition from paladin to freedom was a massive adjustment, with many shocks along the way. And she didn't want to add to them... overly much.

She kissed him lightly and stood. "All right. Slowly it is."

"Good." Mirroring her expression, he rose, too. "Olivia, I know you're good friends with the Marquise of Laurentine. My niece told me she's returned."

His niece—Nora.

"Yes," she replied, frowning. He wanted to talk about Rielle?

"She'll be staying close to Jon, won't she? Leading up to the Veris Ball, during, after?"

"I—yes. Why do you ask?"

He took her hand. "He's family to me. I know he has the Royal Guard and us, but... I think she'll protect him. And she can stay by his side, unlike us."

*Stay by his side?* "I don't know. I'm not sure they're going to stay together."

His eyebrows drew together. "But he loves her. Through and through and through. All those months—"

"I know."

"Then—"

"It's not that simple." She pulled away. "When she returned, she found him with another woman. It may take some time to mend, if at all, and even then…"

He lowered his gaze, his eyes turning dull as he stared at the floor. "Sometimes the people we love cause us pain, but it doesn't mean we stop loving them. It means we try to help them, no matter how difficult it is."

"I hope that's what happens, but she's been through a lot, too. And since she's returned, he's only added to her pain." She turned around, presenting the back of her gown. "Unlace me."

A soft intake of breath, and his fingers went to work. "There are so many evil forces in the world. We have to be there to support the ones we love."

The Marcels had to be a tight-knit House to produce someone like Tor. She smiled. "And am I among those?"

IN HER EMERALD-GREEN Archmage's robes, Olivia entered Jon's quarters.

"In the study," he called out to her. By the distracted sound of him, he was buried in paperwork.

He sat at the desk, his big frame crowding the chair, his booted feet on top of the purple heartwood surface, crossed ankle over ankle. With a furrowed brow, he scrutinized some papers. "Basilisks attacking villagers on the outskirts of Caerlain Trel," he said, without looking up. "The count's forces are still depleted after the pirate attacks a couple months ago. He requests assistance."

Every day brought some news of Immortals causing chaos and destruction, but her *family* lived in Caerlain Trel. "How close to the city?"

"Not enough to worry yet," he said, lowering his legs and setting the papers down. "But we can't leave the villages to ruin either. I already have Tor looking into it."

Her most promising lead was a spore that caused hallucinations in Immortals, but the tome she'd translated said it came from moss in the "sky realm." If there was such a place, she didn't know it.

And her search for a cure to Jon's heart problem had proved fruitless. But perhaps some of their new allies would have answers? Once the alliance was stable, perhaps she could convince Jon to allow her to write to Leigh about it?

Jon set the work aside, meeting her eyes with his tired sea-blue gaze.

"You did remember your magic lesson, didn't you?"

He blinked and raised his eyebrows, his mouth curving. "That was today? I thought it was tomorrow."

She crossed her arms. "It's today, tomorrow, and every day thereafter until you finally cast a repulsion shield." Which was long overdue.

He leaned back in his chair, by all signs hoping his staring contest would win him a reprieve.

It wouldn't.

A knock.

"Enter," he called out, without looking away.

Typical. She rolled her eyes.

"Eloi, Your Majesty," Raoul's gruff voice declared.

"Send him in." To her, he said in a low voice, "Come on, magic can wait *one* more day, can't it?"

She shook her head. "It's waited too long already. Just cast the shield, and then we'll talk."

He heaved a sigh in surrender.

Eloi walked in, tossing his head and displacing some of the blond locks obscuring his eyes. "Word from the merchants, Your Majesty."

Jon's smile turned into a broad grin as he accepted the papers, and he unfastened the collar of his sapphire brocade doublet and the first two buttons, revealing more of the crisp white shirt beneath. "Bring the rest as they come in."

"Yes, sire," Eloi said with a gangly bow before he left the study.

The broad grin didn't waver as Jon reviewed the papers, half-laughs under his breath occasionally punctuating the silence.

When she cleared her throat, he looked up at her and opened his mouth.

"Wait, don't tell me—he delivered some amazing secret strategies to cast a repulsion shield." She narrowed her eyes.

Wordlessly, he handed her the papers. Delivery notes for expensive foodstuffs, massive quantities of flowers, jewelry, horses, couture—"I hope you don't expect to win back her affections with gifts."

He stood. "Of course not. I don't expect to 'win back her affections' at all. But that doesn't mean I can't try to lift her spirits a bit with this charade. Can you imagine the look on her face? I can see her surrounded by boxes, baffled and speechless, a little smile, and—"

"It's going to take more than a bunch of things to 'lift her spirits,' Jon," she said. His relationship with Rielle seemed to be in such a precarious position, and he was hoping *things* would fix it?

"I know," he said, sobering. The grin faded. "Olivia, I can't change what I did here, or what happened to her in Sonbahar. I know that. And that hurt might stay with her forever. It's not something I can fix, but if I can make her smile, even once—make her happy for a minute, a second—I want to try."

She raised a brow. Maybe she'd rushed to conclusions. If he was managing his expectations, perhaps there was a chance... "Just... be careful. I don't want either of you to get hurt."

Jon offered her his hand. "Olivia, when you love someone, hurt is part of the bargain."

Taking his hand, she stood from her chair and nodded. "Well, I can't do anything about that kind of hurt."

"No shields for that," he said with an amused huff. "I'm just glad she's alive."

"Me, too." She moved a few steps away and smoothed out her robes. "And I think we're getting close to you finally casting this. Just a few more sessions, maybe, until you get it. Then we can move on to more exciting spells."

"Exciting." He straightened and took up a ready stance. "Right."

"Focus."

He nodded and held out his arm, his fingers spread out in the repulsion-shield gesture.

"Remember, visualize the repulsion shield's rune and map it—"

A translucent blur the size of a full-length mirror appeared in front of him, and he held it, brows drawn.

"Good," she said quietly, approaching with slow steps. She cast a reversal spell on herself to immediately heal her next injury, and she reached out toward the translucence.

"Olivia," he warned.

"Stay calm." She reached until she encountered resistance, then she pushed against it, pressing more of her weight into it, until she used her full body weight.

The shield held.

He'd done it!

Grinning, she stepped away and clapped. "Very good. Now, remember, to dispel it, you can simply break the gesture, or stop visualizing the rune."

With a nod, he pulled his fingers into a fist, and the repulsion shield vanished, and she dispelled her own magic. For a moment, he stared at the space the repulsion shield had occupied, then at his hand as he flexed his fingers. Finally, his gaze rose to hers, and a slow smile claimed his face.

He closed the distance between them and drew her in with a one-armed hug.

She leaned her head against him. He'd finally found his focus. The more he practiced, the easier it would come to him.

But something had shifted, and Rielle's return wasn't a coincidence. The heavy burdens he'd been carrying all these months had finally lifted just enough.

"You're the most difficult student I've ever had," she said, "and I've taught children."

When he laughed and pulled away, she rested a hand on his shoulder. "No, you did well. It's not easy to start learning magic so late."

"Is that... is that *praise*?" he teased, heading to a nearby table. "Such a rarity is cause for celebration, I think." He poured himself a drink from the carafe. "Do you want some water?"

Not wine? Her heart leapt.

# CHAPTER 55

Fingers brushed through Leigh's hair, smoothing in and down to the tips in lengthy, languid strokes. The solid warmth next to him was Ambriel.

And they'd had a night to remember.

"You're awake." There was a smile in Ambriel's normally grave voice, in the lilt of his words.

"Shh," Leigh replied. "No, I'm not. Because if I'm still sleeping, we don't have to move."

A soft chuckle. "We *are* in the queen's bed, but there are perks to being her brother."

Leigh cracked open an eyelid. "Commandeering her sleeping quarters?"

"Getting *away* with commandeering her sleeping quarters."

Grinning, Leigh rolled onto his back, eyeing Ambriel propped up an elbow next to him. A layer of the stern-faced soldier had faded away to reveal more of the smiling lover beneath.

Well, *of course* he was smiling.

Ambriel lowered his head and kissed him, his warmth melting away any morning lethargy. "Good morning, dreshan."

*Dreshan.* Adored one... yes, he could get used to that.

Distant screams came from below, followed by a massive commotion.

Ambriel sprang from the bed and to the overlook. A moment's glance, then he was hastily donning his clothes.

"What is it?" Leigh sat up.

"An attack." He tossed Leigh's clothes to him. "Hurry."

Ambriel was already down the stairs, half-dressed, when Leigh threw on his trousers, boots, and belt, and darted after him, putting on his shirt and overcoat.

Where there had been feasting the evening before, there was now bustling activity. Quartermasters distributing armor and weapons from carts, officers barking orders—

Ambriel caught a chainmail shirt and a halberd—human armor and weapon—and hurried on. "Get me archers!" he shouted to the other officers. "Now!"

"They hit the armories first, sir!" one called back.

Divine's tits. Leigh chased after Ambriel, down another flight of stairs to the vast expanse of Vervewood below.

The dark-elves' earlier attacks had been reconnaissance.

A battle raged in the glen. The light-elves and paladins ringed the invading dark-elves, whose numbers kept increasing. Up high, in the ironwoods surrounding Vervewood, hooks and ropes continually supplied invaders.

"The trees!" Ambriel bellowed. What few bows there were targeted high.

Leigh cast a repulsion shield in a massive dome over the light-elves, as many as he could cover. Nothing and no one would get through.

For a moment, a lull descended over the battling forces. Arrows bounced off the repulsion shield, and dark-elves snarled as they fought for entry. What few dark-elves trapped inside were quickly slaughtered.

Holding the repulsion shield in one hand, he anchored threads of his magic into the invaders in the ironwoods with the other.

Then pulled.

All those rooted flew toward the repulsion shield, drawn by unseen ropes. He gestured the anchor spell into an attraction ring outside the repulsion shield, yanking in all those outside of it.

Dark-elves littered the edge. Trapped against attraction and repulsion, their bodies were slowly pulled apart.

Screams rent free. Blood burst into the air, bounced off the repulsion shield to spatter the ground in a dark circle. Gasps from within the repulsion shield rippled through the light-elves as every last intruder outside of it was eviscerated by magic.

He dropped the attraction ring.

Up in the trees, a tall, slender figure stood on an ironwood bough, holding her rope. Her hood was down, a white-hot scar across her lavender nose. Varvara.

"Don't be a fool, Varvara!" He shouted to her in Old Emaurrian. "It doesn't have to be this way." If she'd only challenge her queen to single combat, all this could be avoided. Lives saved. Entire settlements.

Her eyes were wide, wild, staring at the circle of corpses. That stunned gaze slowly wandered to him, then with her rope firmly in hand, she leaped from view.

Quiet permeated the glen, and not a single soul dared ascend to the ironwoods.

He dropped the repulsion shield.

The crowd around him recoiled, giving him a wide berth, whispering to one another.

The whispers had always followed him. An enforcer. A wild mage. Brutal. Violent.

But they were alive. Alive to say whatever ignorant things they were saying.

He sighed through his nose and turned back to the stairs, the crowd falling aside in waves as he waded through it.

"Where are you going?" Ambriel called after him.

"The alliance has been triggered," he called back without turning around. "It's time to send word to Trèstellan."

# CHAPTER 56

*R*ielle followed the commotion and moved to the window once more. After days of gifts, there couldn't be any more. Innumerable flowers, extravagant gowns and shoes, priceless jewelry, wine, cakes, fine silver, perfumes, all the latest books, exotic potted plants—if there remained any other gifts under the sun to give, she couldn't imagine them. And Jon was finally arriving tonight, all part of the ruse to make the Veris Ball irresistible to Shadow.

The twilight cast the district's white-stucco villas and walls in a soft golden glow.

The crowd hadn't dissipated, had appeared every day to witness the spectacle. As a merchant's carriage disappeared, a beautifully adorned coach-and-six surrounded by mounted guards came to a halt before Couronne, the carriage a gorgeous carved masterwork of gilded wood and elaborately painted panels, harnessed to six immaculate white steeds.

Fit for a king.

Her chest tight, she couldn't tear herself away. Two coachmen opened the carriage doors, while a third rolled out a red carpet over the street to Couronne's drive.

Jon emerged, cloaked in ermine-trimmed black velvet, riding boots shining to a high gloss, a massive blade strapped to his belt. Faithkeeper.

Chin held high, shoulders back, and standing tall, he looked every bit the royal. Regal. Two paladins guards and a small squad escorted him up the drive.

He glanced up at the window, catching her eye just before he disappeared from view toward the door.

She stumbled from the window but caught herself. Divine, he was here. *Here.*

Outside, the crowd had grown larger; he could have instructed his coachman to bring the carriage up the drive, but he hadn't. He'd wanted to be seen—seen arriving at his alleged lover's home for the evening. For the night.

A frisson rattled her bones. He would be spending the night here.

All an act. All part of the plan. Nothing more.

Davina stood at the door. "My lady—"

Of course. She couldn't fall to pieces now; she swallowed and nodded, taking deep, slow breaths to regain her composure. Jon was here for their plan, to spend the night and give cause for rumor about an affair, all of it to culminate on the night of the Veris Ball.

Indeed, the entire day had brimmed with bliss—gifts, preparations, a dramatic arrival. The *appearance* of bliss.

If Shadow desired her despair, then she would be unable to resist the lure at the ball.

Rielle followed Davina downstairs and past the two paladin guards, their visors up—the same men from...

From *that* night.

One looked away, and the other lowered his gaze.

They remembered her, then.

Her legs weakened, but she drew herself up. *The mission. Think of the mission.* She was here to eliminate the threat to Jon's life. What had happened that night didn't matter right now. The heavy look in their eyes didn't matter right now.

Head held high, she entered the great hall.

A valet removed Jon's cloak and took away his black leather gloves. Jon's gaze swept the great hall—its ten-foot windows, six crystal chandeliers; the grand arched mahogany hammerbeam roof, celadon-paneled walls and wood trim engraved in honeysuckle vines; a table that sat four dozen; the high-backed chairs upholstered in white shadow-striped silk; and the ornate marble floor, with massive tiles a former marquis had ordered inlaid with a design of the blooming red roses his lady had loved so well.

When Jon finally faced the door, where she stood, his eyebrows rose. He inclined his head. "Rielle."

A pleasant shiver stroked her back. Her name. She'd always loved her name on his lips. Even now, it seemed, against her will.

"Jon." She inclined her head, then neared him, fully aware of the attentive servants meandering the hall, the guards posted everywhere, even Davina. When word spread of this night, it needed to be of a warm, affectionate reception—a loving welcome that crowned a day of loving gestures. Convincing.

She held out her hand.

For a moment, a spark lit in his eyes, a brief pause before he accepted her hand and brushed his lips over her knuckles in a whisper of contact.

Her skin tingled, a soft touch that feathered over her body.

A charming smile swept across his face. *Well met, Favrielle,* he'd once said, in a memory close enough to be this very moment.

She gasped softly, her heart racing as memories of their introduction in the Tower rushed in. His charisma had been sizable then and suspicious, but over the course of the two months thereafter, he'd shown his genuine sincerity, offered it with the charm she'd so doubted at first, and now she knew it for what it was. His true self.

His grasp loosened on her hand, but she curled her fingers around his, urged him closer. Convincing. She had to be convincing.

His lips parted, but he pulled her in, took the invitation in stride; her palm came to rest over his heart as his hand found her waist. The rise and fall of his chest staggered, irregular. Nervous.

Her heart raced. Just days ago, she'd told him never to touch her again. Now a part of her, attached to months ago, wanted him never to stop.

She met his eyes, their searching and their banked fire, their uncertainty and their passion. Restraint. Without some greater sign from her, he would do no more. At her wish, he would do no more. It was what she'd demanded.

But her eyes watered. She leaned in and closed them, raised her chin.

Body stiffening, she waited—stupid, stupid, stupid—and began to open her eyes when his hold on her tightened, his palm gliding to the small of her back; the light above her faded into dusky relief as he eclipsed it, and his soft breaths warmed her mouth before his lips met hers in gentle embrace.

All the tension in her body relaxed in his hold, the intimacy of his kiss a heat that melted all objection.

Every ounce of strength fled her body, and she collapsed against him, the feel of him welcoming, inviting, home; he pulled her in, holding her close, so close she could feel the erratic rise and fall of his chest, his heart beating irregularly against her breasts, the tautness of his stomach.

Wetness glided down her cheeks, but she didn't care. She drew away only to return, tasting his mouth, eliciting a sultry exhalation that took her back to days and nights spent abed, intent on learning the limits of loving fascination. To no end. Even now. His lips played against hers, asked, entreated, and nodding, she opened to him, welcomed him into her mouth, met his soft tongue with hers.

Her mind slid into Bournand, into Melain, into sultry nights making love to him long after she'd spent the energies of her body, ravenous for his passion, her need insatiable, never able to get enough of him. The hours enjoying his gentle curiosity spread before her, laid into deep slumber in the loving circle of his arms and mornings when they exchanged smiles in the shy light of the rising dawn.

The moans echoed in her heart, in the dark hall outside his quarters, where she had heard the last breaths of a love that had surrendered in her absence.

Eyes open. She looked at him, forced herself to look.

That love still lingered in his eyes, shrouded in mist. Haunted. But his love wasn't enough now, not if he could do what he'd done in her absence. She needed something more, something he could never give...

A happy life together, the two of them wed and loyal to each other, an impossible spell to clear that terrible night from her memory.

He raised a slow hand and brushed a tear from her cheek.

"I've missed you," she said.

A ghost of a smile disappeared as quickly as it came. He lowered his gaze and swallowed. "So have I. Every day, every moment." His breathing turned heavy, belabored.

Her heart softened. If he, full of love, had believed her dead—if he'd shattered—

The moans. The breaths.

No, no, no.

Divine, would that night always taint what they'd had? Would she always see him through their haze? Always be haunted?

"Would you join me upstairs?" She intended to motion toward the door, but—

His hand still gripped hers. He'd never let go.

His gaze dropped to their joined hands, and he released her. He gave her a slight nod and followed her from the great hall, escorted by his guards.

Upon sight of a smiling Davina, she paused. "Please have His Majesty's luggage brought to my chamber."

"Yes, my lady," Davina acknowledged with a bow, and quickly departed.

Her fingers running along the honeysuckle vines carved into the banister, she led Jon up to her chamber, where his guards did a sweep and then took up posts in the hall as she and Jon entered.

He closed the door behind them, and the tension in his face and shoulders slowly dissipated. He nodded toward the balcony over-looking the courtyard, and she agreed. They headed outside.

Night had already fallen. The musky scent of earth lingered on the cool air, sweetened by the freshness of new greenery.

Jon leaned against the stone balustrade and looked out toward the flickering lights of the night. "I'm sorry you had to endure that." He paused. "All of it."

"It's not your fault." She joined him, closing her eyes as a breeze blew past.

"If you want to call this off, I—"

She shook her head.

Quiet, he slowly straightened and gazed up toward the waxing gibbous moon. "We imagined it all so differently, didn't we?"

In Melain, full of love and hope, they'd planned on Faolan Auvray Marcel becoming king, or a complete stranger. They'd bet their lives on her not marrying Brennan, on Jon securing a knighthood, on the future king granting them permission to wed someday.

And now, Jon *was* king, had the power to break her betrothal contract with Brennan, and yet hadn't the power to marry an Emaurrian noblewoman. Nor the privilege.

"Things were different then." She straightened, too.

"I was different then."

Yes, he was right; he had changed. Although he'd always borne burdens, the weight he bore now crushed, and he'd become someone else. Someone who could succumb to weakness. Someone who could leave her to die. Who could betray her.

But some of his old self still remained, locked in the depths of this unsettling new him. His kindness. His generosity. His passion. He'd changed, yes, but she still saw the man she used to know buried deep in the black heart of this king.

"I received your gifts," she said, trying to lighten the mood a little. "I'm not sure the entire city saw."

He huffed a half-laugh. "Then I fell short of the mark."

"Madame Marlène's? Laurent's? Whatever the mark was, you obliterated it."

He chuckled. "There are perks to being king."

*King.* The word encompassed the entirety of the wall between them. "How is it? Being king?"

He rubbed the back of his neck. "It's like... being the air in a room too full of people."

"I'm sorry."

"I'm not up to the job, and I'm not sure I'll ever be." He shrugged. Donning a soft, sad smile, he turned to her. "What do you wish of me tonight?"

"I thought we might have dinner up here and then retire. As long as we're found in bed together looking scandalous when the chamber-maids come in, I think our work will be done."

Shadow hated her so much that the outward signs of happiness would be as a flame to the moth.

"Very well." He nodded, blinking lifeless eyes. "You don't have to push yourself, to pretend. Don't do anything you can't bear, Rielle. My life isn't your responsibility."

She wanted to take him in her arms, whisper that everything would be all right, that she'd be his strength whenever he needed it. She wanted to do all that and more, but held herself in place.

If only Jon didn't still care. Didn't look at her that way. He brought all kinds of emotions rushing back in, flooding her, and if she surrendered herself to the tide right now, she would drown; with the love, passion, and wonder would come grief, resentment, anguish —and everything else she'd felt the night she'd returned to Courdeval.

No, if she gave in now, they'd never have a chance of truly rebuilding and healing the rift between them, to be friends, to be in the same room together without this burden crushing them both. Before anything else, he needed to know the truth. All of it.

But not tonight. Not until he was safe.

"Shall we?" She nodded toward the chamber, and wordlessly, he headed inside.

She followed him into the bedchamber and gave a yank on the tasseled bell pull by her bed. She just had to get through this night without letting her remaining feelings for him quiet her objections.

An awkward silence passed until Davina arrived.

"We'll have dinner now, here."

Davina bowed. "As you wish, my lady"—and she glanced at Jon —"Your Majesty." And then she was gone.

"Your chamberlain... Is she trustworthy?" Jon approached her desk, where a small vase of immortelle sat. He plucked a cluster of blooms, twirling the stem.

"Davina? She's been the chamberlain at Couronne since before my parents—" Since before Mama and Papa had died.

Jon took a step toward her but stopped. Instead, he took a sudden interest in the mundane things on her dresser, his gaze lingering on her paddle hairbrush. He was making an effort, then, to respect her wishes.

"I'll make it clear to her that I encourage the household to spread news of... us."

"Us," he said, slowly brushing the boar bristles of her hairbrush with his fingers in a lingering whisper that teased up her spine. When he brushed the last bristle, she shivered. "Right."

Warmth flowed through her, warmth that heated to fire. No, this was bad. What her body wanted would be a pale imitation of love, only the act of it, the pretense of it, and afterward, she'd only be filled with shame, and more hurt than she had now. And it would fix nothing—perhaps even deepen the rift.

Swallowing, she turned away and fidgeted. What to do? Was there anything—besides standing there and looking at his hands, his face, his eyes—

They'd eat, they'd drink, and they'd go to bed, sleep, and in the morning, it would all be over with. Her gaze landed on the bed.

Divine, *anything* but the bed.

A nightgown. That would keep her from looking at him, at least for a few minutes until dinner was served. She straightened, then strode to the armoire.

Inside, soft garments hung on white silk-wrapped hangers. One by one, she breezed through them—a long white cotton gown, one of her favorites; a flowing white silk negligee, another favorite; and a few others various lovers had gifted her over the years.

When the chambermaids entered in the morning, she couldn't be seen in a comfortable old favorite, covered from neck to toe like a crone. Her choice would have to brim with romance. Something she'd wear for the man she loved.

Her hands flowed through fine sapphire-blue silk—a low-cut nightgown embroidered with azaleas, a little white ribbon bow at the center of the décolletage, affixed with a tiny white pearl. The fine silk skirt flowed from an empire waist to the ankle, cut generously with slits past the hip. A matching sapphire-blue diaphanous robe hung over it, roomy but transparent, its closure a delicate white ribbon.

A gift, once upon a time. When she'd turned nineteen, she and

Leigh had planned to spend a week in Couronne, holed up in this room. He'd sent this nightgown, along with other gifts, but their plans had never come to fruition. Shortly after her birthday, Kieran had reported their relationship to Magehold, and that had been the end of it.

The nightgown had hung here, limp and lone, waiting for a night that would never come.

She grasped the hanger gently, lovingly. Tonight wouldn't be quite what the nightgown had awaited, but it would have its night.

Jon leaned against the dresser, twirling the sprig of immortelle, a smile on his face and a dull gleam in his eyes.

"Don't get any ideas," she blurted, cradling the nightgown against her chest.

"I'm not," he said, but his lips twitched.

She stalked up to him and jabbed an annoyed finger at his chest. "It's for appearances only," she hissed.

He pushed her finger aside with his own. "I know."

He reached for the nightgown and let the silk slip through his fingers. "You wear colors other than white now."

She eyed the nightgown—the sapphire-blue nightgown—and the dress she wore. Crimson brocade.

White. She'd worn white for years. Always. Every day. Every day since... Laurentine. When had that changed? She frowned.

He traced his gaze over her bodice, a meandering line up her ribs that made her shiver. "It suits you."

The space between them heated, electrified. His gaze darkened.

She inhaled a shaky breath. "You're too close," she whispered.

He glanced down at the space disappearing between them, then at his hand still gripping the dresser he leaned against.

It was *she* who pressed into *him*.

Too close. Much too close.

She searched his eyes, a shadowed blue-green like the waves of the Shining Sea at midnight, vast, unfathomably deep, unknowable. She pressed against the rise and fall of his chest.

Not close enough. This was bad, very bad, and yet...

She rested a palm over his heart, applying pressure to the firm muscle there before letting it glide higher toward his neck, up and around the back. He closed his eyes, exhaled, moved powerfully beneath her touch.

The doors to her bedchamber opened. Footmen and kitchen maids filed in and prepared the dinner service.

She stepped away, clutching the nightgown to her chest, clenching the fine fabric. His intense eyes remained fixed on her as he drew in deep, slow breaths.

Even now, after everything—Even now, with the fate of their relationship on the line, he was irresistible to her.

"Your Majesty, my lady," Davina announced, "dinner is served."

Rielle forced a cordial smile and nodded toward the table.

Not missing a beat, Jon mirrored the expression and gracefully pushed away from the dresser, then held out his arm to her. She took it and allowed him to escort her to the table, where he pulled out a chair for her.

Once he helped her into her seat, he pushed her chair in, then sat with fluid ease.

"Is there anything else you require, Your Majesty, my lady?" Davina asked.

"No," Jon replied, never looking away from Rielle. "That'll be all, thank you. Please give us the room."

Davina looked at her for any objection—none—and then she left, along with the rest of the staff.

A quiet settled over the chamber, and Jon leaned back in his chair, watching her with anguished eyes, fingers steepled below his chin.

She let the silence sink in, and he waited. A luxurious feast of veal loin, squab pie, fennel-seed custard, sliced cheeses, and rosewater plums filled the table, with decanters of wine varietals complementing the dishes, and a tiered tray of fruit and pastries, her favorite spiced custard tarts among them.

She looked up.

His gaze, intense and unwavering, pierced her, but he reclined in the dining chair with a dejected sigh, his head resting against the high back.

"We never really..." He took a deep breath and exhaled slowly. "We never really talked about what happened in Sonbahar."

She went rigid. What would he do if she told him about Sincuore, about Farrad, about *Sylvie*, right now? Would he leave the room? Leave Couronne? Would this entire pretense collapse? Would they fail to lure Shadow to the palace the night of Veris?

"And we don't need to." Not at this moment, anyway. There would be time enough after dealing with Shadow. A safer time. A better time.

In fact, better not to think about it at all. Better to think about other things. Like... wine. She reached for a bottle of Melletoire rosé, a pale coral hue, and poured a goblet for each of them. Rounder and fuller bodied than she had expected, it was floral on the nose, with violet notes and rose, expanding to tart sweet cherry, smoke, and a savoriness she couldn't name.

Jon poured himself a goblet of water from the carafe and swirled it. Water. How like his paladin days.

As the silence settled, he rested his elbows on the table and raked his fingers through his hair.

She'd seen him do it so many times, lost in thought, and she wanted to rub his shoulders, wrap her arms around his neck, and whisper that he could tell her anything. But those times had passed.

A line formed between his brows. "Why not?"

She quelled the fluttering in her chest. "Now isn't the right time."

"When will be the right time?" His gaze still bored into her, but she ignored him.

They ate dinner in silence, only exchanging occasional looks. She buried herself in the goblet. With time, the pain of that night would lessen; she'd live a happy life with Brennan; Jon would marry another woman; and this pain, this love, would fade, no more than a distant memory.

While he sank into his chair and sipped his water, she pushed a piece of spiced custard tart around her plate.

"And now...?" he asked lifelessly.

She breathed deep. "We go to bed."

The prospect of going to bed with Jon had once excited her, set her heart afire, long before they'd ever made love. Being near him had been intoxicating.

But the notion of lying in the same bed with him now, destroyed and hurting, made her heart turn. To be so near to him, in the very same bed, and yet worlds apart—she slumped.

Her head gently spinning with wine, she excused herself to change into the nightgown she'd picked out. Once she'd slipped into the silk, she found Jon by the bed, a pile of clothes neatly folded on a chair, down to his braies and his shirt, which he pulled over his head.

Nothing had quite prepared her for seeing his sculpted form again, and her gaze easily slipped into the familiarity of his carved lines, his sprawling tattoos, his scars, his artistry. He was beautiful.

As he settled into bed, she averted her eyes—nothing good would come of looking—and made her way there, gaze fixed on the bowl of luscious red apples on the nightstand.

He lifted the sheets and covers for her, and she raised a knee to the bed. The slit of her nightgown parted, and his gaze caught on her thigh. A small, violet mark on her inner thigh. One Farrad had made.

# CHAPTER 57

*R*ielle winced. "I didn't mean—"

"It's fine," he blurted, then looked away and dropped his head in his hand, rubbing his forehead. He sighed.

She climbed into bed and covered herself, but Jon didn't move. Divine, she hadn't even thought to check her body for any marks. She'd never meant for Jon to find out about Farrad like this. Never meant to hurt him. "I'm sorry."

He squeezed his eyes shut. "Just desserts," he said sharply. "Where is Brennan staying? He's all right with this farce?"

"Victoire, the Marcels' villa in Azalée. We thought it would confuse the plan if he stayed here." She paused. Why would it matter if Brennan was all right with their plan?

She flinched. Jon thought Brennan was her lover? "It's not—"

Jon hissed and shook his head. "Don't bother." He fell back into the pillows, staring at the bed's white canopy. "It's all right. It's as much as I deserve. And it's your private business."

She sat up and reached for his hand, big, warm, callused. He wouldn't look at her.

Some truths couldn't wait.

"Jon, after Shadow abducted me, I was imprisoned on a ship called the *Siren*," she said softly.

He looked over at her, his eyebrows drawn together, and his fingers gently closed around hers.

"It was captained by a man called Sincuore. He told me, in no uncertain terms, that I was to be sold to the highest bidder." Her heart clenched, and she was suddenly back in the captain's cabin, in a scratchy dress, the rough deck under her skin, shackled to the cannon, her mouth parched while Sincuore flaunted a bottle of wine. "He drugged me and kept me in the ship's brig. By the time my full awareness returned, I was emaciated and starving in the slave souk."

His eyes became overbright, but he didn't waver, didn't say a word.

"It was dark there, and hot. All the time. The only light appeared when the overseers would come in with slaves bearing food and water, or to take away the dead, or sometimes a woman or two. I could never get more than a handful of food every day or every other day... There were other slaves, stronger than I was, and when you're trying to survive, you lose sight of whether you're taking that survival from someone else's hands."

Pushing the bedding aside, Jon slowly rose to sitting and covered their joined hands with his palm, imparting quiet support.

"I was sold as a scribe, to one of Xir's pleasure houses. My zahibi took better care of her slaves—gave us food, water, clothing, even healing—and we somehow crossed the desert, bound in blazing-hot shackles and chains, with no shoes, no horses, no camels." She could still feel the raw blisters around her wrists and ankles.

"I'd been bought as a scribe, but once we arrived, I realized no one was going to care about that distinction but my zahibi. It was still a pleasure house. One woman, a Sileni and stronger than I was, tried to escape. She was caught by the guards, and abused to death in the barracks." Her voice broke, and she dragged an arm across her eyes.

Jon closed his arms around her, pulled her in, but she clenched fistfuls of the bedding.

"Every night in the slave quarter, they would come in and drag some of us off into the night. The house's zahib did nothing to stop it, and who could even ask such a thing when there was punishment like the Sileni woman had gotten?" She leaned against his chest. "One night..." She bit back a sob. "One night, they grabbed *me*. They were dragging *me* away—"

His hold tightened, and he rested his chin on her head. Drops wet her hair, and she pulled the fisted bedding closer.

"I had a friend there, an older girl by the name of Samara, the slave-born daughter of the zahib's grandson and heir. She held on to me, wouldn't let go, and screamed at the guards that I was her father's lover," she forced out. "It was a lie, but it saved me that night. The guards never dared touch his lovers, who were better fed, better clothed, better taken care of. Who slept in his chambers, where it was safe, not the slave quarter."

Was Samara finally free? Brennan had promised Kehani would buy Samara—she prayed it was true. She'd ask Brennan to write Kehani and ask. If not...

That night, Samara's courage, she hadn't deserved it. Not even a shred. "But if the guards discovered it was a lie, Samara would be punished. Even as the daughter of the zahib's heir, she'd get lashes at the very least. And I... I knew what would happen to me," she whispered. "But I couldn't let her suffer for my sake. I went to her father, threw myself at his mercy, and begged him not to punish her. I asked him to punish me instead. And he asked me to be his lover."

Jon's breathing stopped as he went rigid against her. "Rielle," he said, softly, hoarsely. "I should have never—"

"I knew," she blurted out before he could say anything more, "what my choices were. Refuse him, possibly face punishment, and see those guards again that night in the slave quarter. And maybe every night after that. Or agree. Be protected from the guards, have a better chance of survival while I waited for—" *For you to save me.* She swallowed. "Jon, Divine help me, but I said yes."

The tears broke free, and despite everything, she cried into his chest, curled in to him, and his hands trembled as they stroked over her back, carefully, cautiously. Tears soaked into her hair.

"I'm sorry," she whispered. And she felt him shake his head above her.

"No, I am," he rasped, his voice broken, raw. "You said 'choices.'

No, Rielle," he whispered, "to survive, you only had one choice. And it was no choice at all."

She'd known that, even then, and yet all of it had felt like a betrayal of their love, of *him*. But now she nodded faintly against his skin, and he softly caressed her hair.

*I did it to save our baby*, she wanted to say to him. *And I'd do it again if I had to, if only I had her back.* But how much more... how much more could he stand to hear?

"It was some weeks after that when he told me I'd have to serve in the pleasure house. An important guest had requested a fair-haired, fair-skinned woman, and I was the only one of age," she said. "I was distraught, but what choice did I have, if the zahib's heir didn't even have one? But when I arrived, it was Brennan. He'd found me."

Jon froze, his entire body still as stone.

"What was expected to happen... he pretended to, with me. As part of it, we kissed, disrobed, but we didn't have sex," she said carefully.

"Then he ... treated you with dignity," he said, some of that stillness fading.

"The more he helped me, the more he surprised me. After the guards left, he told me all about everyone, and gave me your letter." Her voice lilted at its mention. "Brennan wanted to break me out. But even if he succeeded, the zahib would know who'd done it. We'd be tracked back to Emaurria easily. And by then, I already had a plan. The zahib's granddaughter plotted to kill her brother, and I had access to him. She promised me false arcanir shackles in exchange for killing him. I agreed."

"Is that... how you escaped?"

"Yes. It came at great cost," she bit out, "but I'd rather we discuss that after Shadow has been dealt with."

He pulled away, just enough to raise her chin and meet her gaze. Even in the dark, his eyes had a dullness to them, something defeated, something broken. "What you suffered there," he said, searching her eyes, "none of it should have happened. I should have gone after you, and I'll never forgive myself for silencing my heart."

There was a part of her that burned, a molten anger that never wanted to forgive him for abandoning her. But as she looked at him now, defeated, broken, having suffered for his choice, it cooled a measure. She laid a hand on his cheek, the skin of her palm brushing against the coarseness of his jaw, and he closed his eyes, leaned into it, covered her hand with his.

"Even if you'd gone in search of me," she whispered, "there's no certainty you would've found me. And you might not have been able to do anything. Your kingdom would have paid the price, and coming after me might not have made a difference. So... I forgive you. And I want you to forgive yourself."

A crease etched between his eyebrows as he bowed his head, hissing in a sharp breath. He slowly drew her palm down to his chest, over his heart. "It would have mattered... here."

His heartbeat throbbed into her hand, like months of guilt, pain, and grief, like a bridge built in the past, across the Bay of Amar from Courdeval to Xir, where his wish met hers, and they saw each other clearly across the distance of time, space, and feeling.

Months of tears broke free. "Jon," she rasped.

When he looked at her, his own eyes glistening, she leaned in and kissed him.

His lips met hers, warm, soft in the quiet night, the only sounds mounting breaths and wanting kisses as she wrapped her arms around him. The sting of anguish became the fire of romance from days past, from the Red Room in Melain, and the salt of his tears and hers was the sweat of passion, of a long night of lovemaking. Memory pulsed in her blood, and his mouth opened to hers as she climbed into his lap.

Her tongue claimed his in gentle embrace, pushed for more and more and more as strong arms closed around her, as he rose to meet her desire with his own. She pressed against him, against his hardness, and he hissed a breath, resting his forehead on hers as she slowly moved against him.

"Rielle," he breathed, his voice deep, low, raw. "I think—"

"Shh," she whispered, raising his mouth back up to hers. "Don't think," she murmured against his lips between kisses. "Make me forget."

She pushed into him, urging him onto the pillows, but he resisted, despite every sign of his eager body.

His mouth broke away from hers, and breathing raggedly, he cupped her face. "We can't. Not before—"

"Why not?" Maybe this was what they needed, a night together to remind themselves of what they meant to each other, a night of passion, and maybe it would fade the wounds between them. Or at least lessen the hurt for one night. She slipped the straps of her nightgown off her shoulders, but he caught them.

"This is hard enough already," he said, squeezing his eyes shut a moment. "I would love to be with you tonight—"

Good, then that's what they *both* wanted.

"But not like this, not to forget. I can't. Not without telling you the truth. All of it."

She shifted away from him, looking him over. "What truth?"

He rubbed his forehead, then raked his fingers through his hair, once, again. Touching her shoulder, he gently urged her to sit next to him, and she did, wrapping her arms around herself.

"I betrayed you—"

"I know that," she snapped. Divine, how she wished to shut that night out of her head... and he had to bring it up again. She already knew about his lover. "Didn't you... end things with her?" Was that it?

Pressing his lips into a thin line, he nodded. "I did, but..."

But? Divine's flaming fire, was the woman with child? Could that be it?

He took her hand and met her eyes with an unwavering intensity. "You know I'm Earthbound."

She nodded.

"The Earthbinding... It required an ancient, barbaric ritual... and a coupling with a virgin."

Her lips parted, and she jerked her head back. A shudder rode her spine. "You... with a virgin..."

"Yes."

She shook her head as a hollow formed in her throat. But Bournand surged back to her, that etching in the book—*Ancient Blood Rites.*

A coupling... the king and... "Was she the same woman you... the same one as the lover I..."

"No." He didn't look away, but the intensity of his gaze dimmed.

She pulled her hand away from his and scrubbed it over her face. *Another* one?

His bare chest rose and fell, rose and fell, his paladin sigil tattoos living as he breathed, in and out, in and out. This was the same Jon who'd once sworn a vow of celibacy. The same Jon who'd once asked her to wait before making love, because it meant too much to him to rush through.

This was the same Jon who'd spoken to her of marriage and a life together.

It was a familiar darkness. When Leigh had broken her heart, he'd very publicly bedded a series of lovers after her, with no regard for her feelings. When Brennan had broken her heart, he'd done the same, all the while throwing his head back in laughter at infamously humiliating her.

But Jon... Jon was supposed to have been different. Honorable, loyal, considerate, her complement, her match. And yet... it had only been four months since they'd been together, and these acts made her shiver like that familiar darkness.

Staring at the bedding, she clenched it in fistfuls. He'd been with another woman. Two. It was...

It wasn't the same, was it?

He'd thought her dead when he'd taken a lover, had tried to relieve the hurt. He hadn't intended to hurt her. And this...

She didn't enjoy picturing him with another woman, but this had been for the Earthbinding ritual, something he'd *had* to do. A responsibility. She didn't like it, but she couldn't blame him for it any more than she could blame him for his bloodline.

It would do no good to know more, but like an ear-worm song, the curiosity was insatiable. "Who was she, the woman from the Earthbinding?"

"A servant woman," he replied with a crestfallen murmur.

A servant of *his*?

How many servants were there in Trèstellan? Did this one still work there? Had she seen this woman? Been served by her? Did she still serve Jon? "What's her name?"

He hesitated. "Manon."

She stiffened. He knew her name? "Is she pretty?"

"Rielle—"

"Is she?"

He blew out a breath. "Yes."

Of course she was. Of course. She fought back tears. "Did you enjoy it?"

"No," he blurted out, then paused. "Yes."

She shifted away from him. "Which is it?"

He closed his eyes and exhaled lengthily. "I didn't want it. Not before, not during, not after. But I did do it. I completed the ritual, so I can't deny that it... I mean, that it felt—"

She held up a hand. Listening to even a second more... She shook her head. No, if she heard even another word of that, she would explode. "Was it the only time?"

He frowned. "You think I would—"

"Was it the only time you were with her?" she hissed.

His mouth fell open, but he closed it. "Yes."

"Does she still work in the palace?"

He nodded. "I thought it would be unfair to—"

"Does she serve *you*?"

"Yes..." He lowered his gaze.

So he saw her every day? And she saw him? Did they exchange pleasantries? Did he ever think about that night of the ritual, remember the feel of her, the warmth of her skin, the press of her lips against his? Did he ever look at her and see her naked?

And the servant, this *Manon*, did she ever see him as more than her lord and king? Did she think of his hands on her body, of his kisses, his passion? Did she smile to herself as she prepared his food and made his bed?

"How did you picture it," she whispered, "if you and I reconciled?"

His pained gaze rose to hers.

"Were you going to move me into the palace, laugh and smile over breakfast with me, while your servant girl poured us tea and cleared our plates?"

He rubbed his forehead. "I didn't think—"

"Have her reassigned," she whispered. "Please. If you have any respect or consideration for me, have her serve someone else in the palace. Anyone else."

"I will."

They sat in silence a long while, so quiet she could hear the breeze rustling the oak trees outside.

More questions lingered on the tip of her tongue, but none of them would improve matters. The Earthbinding wasn't his fault, and she couldn't even be angry at him over it. As much as it hurt, it was circumstance that was upsetting, and not any intention of his. It wasn't as though he'd taken another lover just for pleasure's sake. The Earthbinding had been his duty.

"Of course I'm not thrilled with this," she said finally, her voice low. "But it wasn't your fault. I understand that."

His hand lingered over her knee before he cautiously let it rest against her skin. His touch in this moment nearly brought tears to her eyes, but she didn't hate him, didn't want him to leave her alone.

"Terra have mercy, Rielle, but there's more."

She shook her head, again and again. "No. No, there isn't. There isn't more," she said hoarsely, pulling away, "not tonight. There isn't—"

"There were two lovers. Not one."

His words lingered on the air like smoke, and she coughed. Two. *Two* lovers.

*Two.*

He'd thought her dead, turned to a lover for comfort, and what? Couldn't get enough? Had too much fun? Couldn't stop? While she was starving, suffering, while Sylvie was *dying*, this was what he'd been doing?

"I'm dying to know—" she began, through gritted teeth.

He shifted. "I'll tell you everything."

"Who ran the kingdom while you were busy tending to *two* lovers?"

Wincing, he pulled away.

"And grief must be incredibly arousing to you," she bit out. "Two,

Jon? Really? Are you certain it's not three? Half a dozen? Is there a rotation? A schedule?"

His frown deepened. "I know you're angry. You have every right to be. It was wrong, and if I could change it, I would."

She shook her head. "How could you?" It was a lot to take in. Far too much. She clutched the bedding tighter, bringing it higher, covering herself. "You thought I was dead, so you just... erased me. Like I didn't even matter."

"I thought you were dead, Rielle. *Dead.* I... Tor took over managing the kingdom while I... I drowned myself in darkness, solitude, and wine. I didn't want to see anyone, speak to anyone. The more I thought of you, the less I wanted to be here without you. When I thought you were dead, I was dead, too."

His eyes watered. "But I'd become Earthbound. Tor, Derric, Pons, the Grands... They saw the land turning. Weakening. The snows deepening, the cold biting. The Immortals emerging, destroying villages, towns... The kingdom failing with my own will to live." His face went slack. "I fell away, away from the land. Rather than giving it my strength, my willpower, *it* had been supporting *me*. One night, I drank my wine... and didn't stop."

She eyed him peripherally. "Why?"

"I needed to get out of my own head. Living death. Just for a night, or so I told myself, enough time to keep the ghosts from eating me alive." He closed his eyes and sighed. "I should have been strong, but I wasn't. It was too far, and I lost myself in it, the depth, the isolation." He shifted to sit against the headboard. "And that was the first night she came to me."

"She..."

He nodded. "Nora Marcel Vignon. I opened the door, and I let her in, Rielle." He dropped his head in his hands.

Nora? Brennan's *sister*, Nora? So she was the one Jon had been with that night?

"Terra have mercy, I was weak, I know it. I'd been empty for so long that I wanted to fill the void with something, anything, to make it stop hurting. To stop feeling the grief. And I tried."

*To stop feeling...* She took a deep breath. It was a desire she knew all too well.

"And the Grands, they wanted me to marry. The suitresses had been there for months, and King Macario had sent aid to defend against the pirate attacks on the west coast. I couldn't let Princess Alessandra leave nor her father abandon us. After losing you, I knew I couldn't marry for love, so what did it matter? Whatever the kingdom needed, I would do. We agreed to a courtship. She knew about Nora, and one day, she... and I..."

She covered her mouth. Of course. Of course they had. Why wouldn't they have?

Her eyes watered as she nodded, and she wiped at them.

The Sileni princess had expected her soon-to-be fiancé to share a bed with her. And why shouldn't she have? It stood to reason.

It all made perfect sense, and perfect sense felt like a dagger through her heart.

"That night, it was..."

He didn't need to say it. It was Alessandra she'd heard him with.

"After you returned, I told her about you. We ended it."

It was over, it made sense, and she couldn't hear another word. Something twisted, pulled, and snapped inside of her, and whatever capacity she'd had to listen and to talk, to function at all, vanished.

She lay down and turned her back to him, nestling her cheek into the pillow.

Two lovers, ten lovers, a hundred—none of it mattered tonight. Tonight was a mission. A job.

"Rielle..." His voice was soft, gentle. Apologetic.

"No more," she said brightly. "Please." She forced a smile to keep from crying. "I don't think I can stand any more truth tonight." Her silent tears soaked into the pillow anyway.

"That's everything I've done."

The quiet lengthened.

*I was abducted, abused, enslaved, had to bed my master to keep myself and our baby safe, lost her, nearly lost Brennan, nearly died to return to you... while you were bedding two lovers. Leaving me and our baby to die.*

All his sins laid bare to her, and yet she hid the gravest of them all

—losing Sylvie. A part of her wanted to tell him now, right now, and not because he deserved to know. He did.

But she wanted him to hurt like she did. She wanted to twist the knife, wanted the pain to destroy him like he'd destroyed her. Let him feel the weight of the sadness that had crushed her these past months. Let him crumble beneath its weight and meet her level under the rubble.

But she clenched her fists and her teeth, stared into the dark, and kept those words locked.

Not in the heat of anger and hurt. She had to let it fade, had to calm down, or she'd do something irreversible. Sylvie deserved better.

Everything didn't have to be revealed tonight. That wasn't why they were here.

Tonight was only a mission, only a job.

"Say something, Rielle," he said, hoarse, his voice breaking. "Please."

She curled her shoulders inward, compacted her body.

"I'm sorry I hurt you. I understand if you never forgive me, Rielle, I do. I wouldn't deserve it, or you."

She curled up in the cold sheets and let his words fade.

A mission.

A job.

# CHAPTER 58

Bright sunlight played golden behind Rielle's eyelids, and she snuggled in the cozy, soft bedding. Bed. Sunshine. Morning. With a soft yawn, she blinked her eyes open. Jon smiled faintly, a world of light silhouetting him before the radiant day.

She smiled back, wriggling closer, and eased a slow, happy breath, tracing a scrolling black sigil tattoo down his forearm with a fingertip. He watched her, a line etched between his eyebrows.

The canopied bed, the view of the oaks past the window. Couronne. Last night came rushing back in hurtful words and tears, but she pushed it all away. Lying in bed together like this, as they had so many times months ago, was too nostalgic to focus on fighting.

"How long have you been awake?" she whispered.

He looked away. "About an hour. Listening for footsteps."

Footsteps...? Of course. Her household. She nodded, licking her lips. She and Jon were supposed to be caught in a compromising position. A *scandalous* position.

*Let the pretense begin.*

She sat up, reached for the goblet of water on her nightstand, and drained it. The bowl of apples, lusciously red, waited next to it; she tried to grab one, but it tumbled from her grasp, and she just barely managed to catch it. When she turned to Jon, his brow was arched and his lips twitched. Laughing at her?

She shoved the apple against his lips.

His head jerked back, eyes wide, then he sprang and bit into it.

With a yelp, she jolted in the bed, suppressing a laugh, and bit into it herself while he took hold of her arm.

"I wasn't done," he grumbled, but his dimpled grin betrayed his play.

"Looks like you are," she joked back, then took another bite and held the apple away.

"You forget"—he pounced onto her, and she scrambled higher, laughing—"my arms are longer." He captured her hand and brought the apple to his mouth again for another bite.

"Thief."

He chewed loudly. "Witch," he said, around a mouthful of fruit.

Grinning, he chewed open mouthed, and she covered his lips with her fingers... stroked them, slowly descending, caressing his lower lip. He stilled, his gaze locked on hers.

Footsteps in the hall—

He raised his eyebrows, and she nodded; it was time to escalate the pretense.

He slid a hand under her head, his fingers buried in her hair, and lowered his apple-scented mouth to hers. His kiss was hungry, demanding, raising goosebumps on her skin, his mere touch making her shiver. A soft moan escaped as her body writhed beneath him of its own volition, arms curling around him, fingertips pressing into his firmly muscled back. Strong and familiar. Divine, he felt good. So good. Solid, warm, hers. Closer—she pulled him closer, arched her back, longed to bridge the distance between them, every distance, until she was part of him and he part of her.

The door opened, and quiet footsteps flitted about the corners. Soft voices and softer giggles. They didn't matter.

His tongue found hers, sweet and tart and wanting, taking, taking all she had, all she was and wanted to give to him. She sprawled under him, wrapped a leg around him, drew him in, close—Divine, firm and hot against her, so good, but not nearly close enough. He leaned into her. A soft whimper—hers—and his large palm found her backside, squeezed, pressed. His fingers gathered the fabric of her nightgown, feathering silk up her thigh.

A click. The door shutting.

He broke away, gazed down at her with heavy-lidded eyes, and breathed ragged, forceful breaths. His wanting gaze kept her pinned as effectively as the rest of him had.

She wanted to throw her arms around his neck and never let go. *Please.*

He squeezed his eyes shut for a moment and moved to sit next to her, pulled the sheets over his lap, and a pillow. "Gods, I'm so sorry."

She lay there, unmoving. Divine help her, liquid flame flowed through her veins, need seizing her body like an army of merciless soldiers.

A performance. It had *only* been a performance. Nothing more. He had taken two lovers while she'd been fighting for her life and Sylvie's, something she knew well, but her body had yet to remember.

"What are we doing, Rielle?" He inhaled deeply.

"Acting."

"Is that what it is?"

She looked away. "We have a lot to do before tonight. We should head to Trèstellan, so I can lay the sangremancy wards in the gardens and your quarters."

"No."

She jerked to face him. "No?"

He stared down at her, his face set, and he set the pillow aside. "There's nothing more important than mending this rift between us. Everything else can wait."

She closed her eyes. "It's not that simple."

Since that night she'd come to his quarters, he'd done nothing but try to make sincere amends. Yet that didn't mend the wound in her heart.

"Tell me how to fix this," he said quietly.

Last night, when she'd thrown herself at him like a fool, he hadn't taken her, hadn't taken advantage *of* her. He'd ended things with his lovers, had been honest with her, had promised to have the servant girl reassigned. He was already doing everything he could.

But she was still heartsore. Her heart, injured and afraid, wouldn't listen to reason.

"Forgive me," he whispered, lowering his gaze. "Please."

Her eyes watering, she reached for his hand, and he took hers. "I do, Jon. I forgive you."

He stroked her knuckles gently with his thumb. "Is it possible...? Can we... can we move past this?"

"I don't know." Wanting to and being able to seemed like two very different concepts. "I'd love to let go of everything that happened, but it's still too near, do you understand? Sometimes, just being near you, I hear it again, and it hurts."

His lips pressed tight, he nodded and looked away.

"I don't know when that'll stop hurting," she said. "Maybe... I don't know..."

"I love you," he said, his voice a smooth, deep caress. "But live your life, Rielle, and be happy. If that's with me, I'll praise Terra for the miracle, but if it isn't... That's my fault, and my fault alone."

If they took the time to fix this, it could work, couldn't it?

After Shadow, she'd tell him about Sylvie. Once everything was out in the open, they could begin mending their relationship. As long as they could resist falling into bed together prematurely, they had a chance.

She sat up, twisting her messy hair over her shoulder. "I'm going to have some tea. Join me?"

"I will. Shortly." He left the bed, dropped to the floor, and began his morning training ritual—or however much of it he could get done here. She headed for the table. And breakfast.

She poured some tea, took two sugars, and helped herself to some porridge. She eyed the empty chair at the table. The empty place setting. What was Brennan doing right now?

No doubt he was eating a meal fit for four people. She smiled and drank half her tea, then set down the cup, watching the wavering dark surface. None of this was fair to him. She'd turned down the papers to break her betrothal to him, keeping them both bound to each other.

While she attempted to fix things with Jon, Brennan didn't have a choice of bride, or freedom.

He loved her. She knew that, clear as day after he'd fought the hisaad in the desert. Even before then, that night in House Hazael. And he deserved a choice.

After this ordeal with Shadow was over, she'd offer it to him.

"SIX ARGENTS." The captain of the Sileni sloop *Tiziana* eyed Drina skeptically in the muted light of the afternoon sun.

"Four." She met his look squarely. "You're going to Bellanzole anyway. It's four more argents than you'd have otherwise."

He crossed his thick arms. "Six."

She smirked. "Five, and we set sail the moment I'm aboard."

He cocked his head, for a moment just surveying her, then spat in his palm and offered it to her. She did the same, and they shook on it.

"See you tonight." With a final nod, she adjusted her satchel, backed up, and receded into the alley.

The bitch Favrielle was back. How she'd gotten free of Sonbahar—Drina sighed, shaking her head—was a mystery. She was like vermin, impossible to get rid of, always coming back, but it didn't change anything. No, in fact... killing the king before her very eyes would be all the sweeter.

After she dealt with Favrielle's man, leaving the bitch bereft and maddened, she'd sail back to Khar'shil in style—aboard the very sloop bearing the Sileni princess home. It was his good fortune that she had no interest in slitting Alessandra Ermacora's throat.

Unsurprisingly, the captain had allowed a passenger who could be anyone; he was like most Sileni men—overconfident of himself, under-estimating of women, and thus, reckless. To her benefit.

She headed back to Peletier's, weaving through the unaware crowds. *Lyuba Vaganay* had served her well these past months, and no one had been the wiser. Even the Archmage, whose pretty little head was publicly so valued, hadn't come close.

Meandering through the Coquelicot District, she stopped at a hovel. Though small, crude, and cramped, the steps were swept clean of snow and sprinkled with salt. Sauvanne Gouin's home, and she wouldn't be at The Greasy Spoon until this evening.

Drina knocked quietly and waited, scanning the surrounding area. It was a poor district, of that there was no doubt, but the people here were good, kind, just trying to survive. Tavern wenches, apprentices, day laborers. Those who couldn't afford to live in Dandelion District, but could afford a bit more than the poverty of Chardon, for example.

Footsteps creaked on the other side of the door, and then Sauvanne's surprised face appeared. "Madame Vaganay!"

"Madame Gouin. Good day."

Sauvanne opened the door wider. "Come in, please."

With a smile, she entered. The interior was warm, with a fire in the small hearth, needlepoint decorating the walls with flowers, birds, happier things than one saw in Coquelicot. In the corner, a girl sat in the bed, her mahogany-brown hair in braids tied with ribbons. The nine-year-old Sophie. Clutching a tattered book, she smiled. "Hello."

Drina waved back.

Sauvanne directed her to a small round table, then hastily put on water for tea. She offered a tray of cookies—madeleines. "I baked them this morning myself."

"Thank you." Drina took off her gloves and helped herself to one. Its sugary sweet smell was the perfect complement to the give of its spongey, cake-like texture. "It's delicious."

Sauvanne smiled. "Sophie has been feeling better, so I wanted to do something special."

Sugar was expensive, and these cookies were indeed special for someone not swimming in coin. "Thank you for letting me share in your joy."

Sauvanne reached across the table and took her hand, her eyes watering. "It is thanks to you that we celebrate," she whispered. "Because of your generosity, my little girl is alive."

As it should be. If anyone could keep an innocent little girl breathing, there was nothing else but to do it.

With a slight nod, she hefted her satchel onto her lap while Sauvanne steeped some tea. There was no telling when, after tonight's victory, she'd return to Courdeval. Surely not in time to resupply Sophie.

She removed bag after bag from her satchel, laying out a dozen on the table.

Sauvanne stared wide eyed, reaching for one, but she'd already know it by the wrapping paper and black twine. She dropped into a chair. "Oporavak tea?"

Drina nodded. The cure for the Wasting.

"But... but—"

It was ten coronas a pound, and she'd brought twelve. It was enough to buy a new home, even in Violette District. "I will have to travel tonight, and I couldn't do that without knowing Sophie will have what she needs," she whispered.

No doubt Sophie would fully recover well before the oporavak tea ran out, but just in case, she'd brought more. Sometimes nature didn't like to adhere to norms.

Sauvanne covered her mouth, tears rolling down her cheeks. "I can never repay—"

Drina shook her head. "You don't have to. Just make sure she gets better." She sipped from her cup—a tisane—then set it down and removed a handful of argents. "And get her a few more books. They make great company."

Shaking her head, Sauvanne eyed the bounty, then looked over her shoulder toward Sophie, who carefully turned a page in the tattered book.

Drina stood, and Sauvanne stood with her.

"Why are you doing this?" Sauvanne asked with soft wonder.

"Because neither of you deserve this, and I can do something about it." She offered Sauvanne her hand, but the woman embraced her.

"Thank you," she whispered, then pulled away. "Gods bless you, Madame Vaganay."

"And you." With a final smile, she left the hovel, twelve pounds lighter, all of it from her heart. Fortune willing, the girl would recover.

There was no sense in this world if people who didn't deserve it suffered. If mothers lost their children, wives lost their husbands. In her own way, she could restore that sense.

Making her way toward Peletier's through the stalls, she grabbed a cherry-jam crêpe and nibbled it happily.

And everything—all these years of effort—would culminate in this one night. Surrounded by innumerable courtiers and guards, Favrielle and her king wouldn't even consider any threats. At least not once they retired to his quarters, where his life would end.

Her soulblade would finally quench its thirst. She patted its sheath at her back, under her cloak.

Its empty sheath.

She frowned, her pulse quickening. She checked her boot—not there either. It should be there. It was *always* there. Always on her weapons belt or in her boot, always sheathed, unless it was gorging on blood.

Before the docks, before the crowds, at Peletier's—she'd run into Max in the hall, and he'd embraced her, kissed her, made her a promise for later tonight... one she'd unfortunately miss.

Had he picked her pocket?

It might have been in the crowds—but no, she would have sensed it.

She stuffed the rest of the crêpe in her mouth and quickened her pace through the throngs to Peletier's.

There it was—the signboard. She darted to the door, threw it open, and nodded a quick greeting to Lionel at the desk before ambling up the stairs.

Perhaps—if fortune did not hate her—she'd somehow left the soulblade in her room. She'd only been gone half an hour, maybe less.

A few steps from her door, she paused. *"Mother earth, grant me your sight, / Show through your eyes, reveal all life,"* she murmured under her breath.

A large mass of anima awaited on the other side of the door, seated, no doubt at her desk. A single form.

Engage or flee?

Seated at her desk wasn't exactly an ambush. And by the shape of it, the form was a tall, fit mage.

Max.

Donning a saccharine smile, she unlocked the door and entered.

"Oh!" She raised her eyebrows and mustered an expression of pleasant surprise.

He looked over his broad shoulder, fixing a narrowed rum-gold eye on her.

"Max," she said happily, closing the door. "Moving your promise earlier by a few hours?" Hips swaying, she approached, but not within his reach. She still had a hidden blade in her right sleeve and another dagger in her left boot.

He smiled. Coldly. "Did you forget something?"

Something had changed. She leaned against the wall, trying to appear at ease. "What do you mean?"

He rose from the desk, all six feet of him, keeping his arms at his sides. Loose. Ready. "I mean the soulblade."

She raised her eyebrows again and mouthed a perfect *O*. "Soulblade? What's that?" she asked innocently, and canted her head. "Wait, do you mean my knife?" She frowned. "I found that on a body outside Courdeval on my way into town. Some poor soul who'd been robbed, it looked like, with a knife in his back."

He speared her with a glare. "You found it on a dead body? Maybe you found everything else on a dead body, too? Your satchel, your medicines, your clothes. Perhaps even your name."

"What? This is ridiculous." She backed up toward the door and turned the knob; he was on to her. It was time to run. "You know me. We'll talk after you come to your senses."

Tonight was her last chance. If Max had divined her motives, suspected her identity—if he'd shared knowledge of the soulblade, then there was no telling when word could spread. It was tonight or never.

"I think I've come to my senses. Finally." He tracked her movements with a focused gaze. "What are you planning? Who are you here for?"

An assassin. He'd put things together.

"You're scaring me, Max," she said, forcing a tremor into her voice. "I don't know what you're talking about, but I'm leaving, and when I come back, you'd better not be here, or I'll... I'll scream. I'll call the City Guard."

He exhaled a half-laugh under his breath. "You'd do more than that. I should count myself lucky to still be alive"—indeed he was—"but you're not coming back."

His eyes locked on hers, and for a moment, she dropped all pretense, let him see her true face. "Goodbye, Maxime Deloffre. You're a good lover, and a good man. Pray we never meet again."

His eyes widened, and she was through the door and in the hall, cloaked in shadowmancy. She pulled up the hood of her cloak, descended the stairs, and left Peletier's. For good.

There was no coming back. Peletier's was gone. Max was gone. Lyuba Vaganay was gone.

And as for the soulblade—well, one of her other sharp edges would have to do.

# CHAPTER 59

*B*rennan strode through the coldly gleaming palace halls toward Nora's quarters. He should have visited her long before, but Rielle had required constant guard.

Until now.

He grimaced. Word had spread to every corner of Azalée, and throughout the city, that the king had lavished the Marquise of Laurentine with gifts all day yesterday and then had arrived to spend the night at Couronne. There wasn't a tongue in Courdeval that didn't wag over the scandal, the romance, or the confusion of prizing a disgraced marquise over the region's finest suitresses.

And tonight, Rielle and the king would appear at the Veris Ball, a couple before the entire court—the entire kingdom.

A growl rumbled low in his chest. Even if it was a ruse, that ruse would find her and the king together all night, awaiting an attack by the shadowmancer. Waiting for the bitch to walk into their trap.

And since she'd gone to Couronne, there had been nothing. No messages, no pull on the bond, nothing at all. It was as if these past weeks since leaving Xir hadn't happened at all. While in the king's presence, she was completely under his influence, no matter the things he'd done.

If rumor was to be believed, Nora hadn't been his only lover. The king apparently couldn't wait a few months before tumbling other women into bed. Some paladin.

And Rielle didn't seem to care anymore. Fell under his spell completely. At this rate—

A pair of ladies greeted him, and he bit out a reply beneath a scowl and continued on his grim way.

One last sweep. He'd already checked the gardens and the great hall, and Rielle had agreed he should do one last sweep of the king's quarters before the ball tonight. Shadow would attack in the gardens, without a doubt, but at least if Rielle ended up in the king's quarters, it would be safe. He'd make certain of it after checking in on Nora.

Finally there, he knocked. And waited.

And waited.

The door creaked open, and Nora, her large hazel eyes puffy and swollen, met him with a faint smile over her grimace. "Bren... I wondered when you'd finally deign to visit your own blood."

As if she'd missed him. Snorting an amused breath, he leaned in to embrace her and kissed her cheek. "I'd ask how you've been, but"—he motioned to her unbound, hastily brushed dark tresses and her white cotton nightgown... in the middle of the afternoon—"I already have the answer."

Gaze shifting about the hall, she opened the door wider and gestured him in. "Well, come on—unless you want every mouth in the palace whispering about your pitiable sister."

He entered the disaster of a salon. Open trunks littered the floor, overflowing with gowns, jewelry, hats, boxes, toiletries, and other women's gear. Clothes lay strewn about over every available surface, including between dishes on the table, where the cold remains of breakfast lay half-eaten.

He caught their scents before the boys charged through the doorway out of the bedroom and tackled him, latching onto his legs.

"Uncle Brennan!" they shouted, and he dropped to a crouch.

Although they both had their father's coal-black curls and honey-brown eyes, six-year-old Henry's expression retained its soft earnestness, while nine-year-old Francis bore dark circles beneath his eyes, shadowed as they were, and an abyss behind his excited grin. He looked far older than his years.

"Can we have another sword fight?" Henry blurted excitedly while Francis bowed his head.

Brennan ruffled Henry's hair. "Didn't bring any practice swords this time"—he reached for his coin purse and pulled out two gold coronas—"but how'd you like to buy whatever practice weapons you want, and I'll teach you a bit next time?" He gave each boy a coin, watching their mouths fall open as their gazes shifted to their mother.

Nora heaved an exasperated sigh, closed her eyes, and gave a glamorous shake of her head.

"Please!" Henry whined, and even Francis joined in.

She narrowed her eyes at Brennan. "They're going to be spoiled because of you. You know we don't throw around that kind of money so cavalierly for toys and—"

Brennan shrugged. She certainly spent it on herself, but then it was an *investment*, meant to attract a rich lover or new husband. "Let me take a look at Vauquelin's finances for you. I have some timber connections, and coopers—"

"Timber and coopers, Bren! Really!" She threw her hands in the air, then waved him off and turned to the boys. "Fine, you can keep the coronas, but—"

Henry and Francis cheered loudly, and while Nora grimaced, he tucked a boy under each arm and spun. Their laughs and shrieks mingled, and he couldn't help but laugh either. It had been far too long since he'd seen them.

"Boys," Nora interrupted, stepping into their trajectory, "I think it's time you found Annette. Tell her we're departing in two hours, and she's to watch you until then."

Her request met with whimpers and moans, she looked to Brennan for support. He set the boys down and lowered to meet them, tapping up Henry's chin and Francis's nose with a finger. Two reluctantly dutiful sets of eyes met his.

"Listen to your mother," he said firmly, then leaned in. "She's in a mood, don't you see?"

Henry giggled, but they both nodded.

"Run along," he said, rising. "And try to go easy on your poor nanny. She's climbing up there in years and impatience."

Grinning, they hugged him, Nora, and then left her quarters.

She dropped into a clothes-covered armchair and exhaled lengthily. "The king's sending me away from court."

His back to her, he studied her things, more jars and bottles than anyone but an apothecary should own. "And? You coerced your nine-year-old son to commit treason—a capital offense. You have your head. Count your blessings."

"Blessings!" she spat. "Now I have to go back to that coastal backwater."

He shrugged. "Good. You should oversee your vineyards and make sure they produce this year."

A trunk lay open, overflowing with her nightgowns and more intimate smallclothes, a sheer black silk negligee on top that left nothing to the imagination. He grimaced and turned away.

Nora grinned broadly. "I wore that my last night with the king."

He swept an arm. "Don't tell your brother that!" *Great Wolf, if you have any mercy for your Faithful, scrub my mind clean.*

She quirked a brow. "He seemed to like it."

He shook his head. Maybe with some luck, he'd clear it.

But... for all her smugness, her bragging rang hollow. With all her things strewn about the room in various stages of packing, and her still in her nightgown, fortune wasn't exactly beaming at her. He sighed. "What a mess you've made."

She hmphed. "It wasn't a mess until you brought back your bitch of a fiancée."

"That's ironic," he grunted. "You calling someone else a bitch." Besides, she could hardly commit treason and lay the blame anywhere but at her own feet.

She made a cavalier wave of her hand. "I'm not *a* bitch. I'm *the* bitch. And she better not forget it... I owe her a reckoning."

"A reckoning? You play at court intrigues. She immolates people." He crossed his arms. "If you throw down the gauntlet and she pummels you with it, I won't step in to stop her. You need to learn a lesson."

"In what?" she snapped, turning away to pour more wine.

"Poking sleeping wolves." He turned back to the overflowing trunk. He was supposed to make a sweep of the king's quarters before tonight. Would the king win her back for good?

Brennan had saved her life, brought her back to the shores of Emaurria, only to see her into another man's arms.

*A reckoning...*

The king had taken other women to bed, Nora included. That misstep had pushed Rielle away—almost entirely. One more misstep, and she'd never want anything more to do with him ever again.

One more misstep.

Nora's black silk negligee lay on top of the heaps of clothes. The king had already dug his grave, all six feet of it. What was one more little push?

He stuffed the black silk into his overcoat. If the king somehow manipulated Rielle into bed tonight, she wouldn't fall for it so easily. She'd find this, and she'd remember he wasn't as perfect as he pretended to be. Then she'd make the right choice for herself.

"In any case, I'm probably going to visit Mother before heading back to my backwater," Nora crooned.

He turned to her and grinned. "Give her a hug and a kiss from me."

"I will." She combed her fingers through her voluminous hair. "What about you? There'll be plenty of ladies at the ball... Are you going to make your next mistake tonight?"

He laughed under his breath. "Something like that." He crossed the room, embraced her with one arm, and kissed her cheek. "Travel safe, and send me a letter when you arrive."

"I will."

With that, he left and made for the king's quarters. If the king took this ruse to bed, there'd be a reckoning—and Rielle would never trust him again.

And as for the ball, well—he grinned—he had something special in mind for her there.

～

JON WALKED the gardens of Trèstellan with Rielle on his arm, strolling in the sunlight among the other courtiers staying in the palace, while Raoul and Florian followed at a distance. After spending the night with her and waking up with her, this could have been a perfect day if not for this rift between them.

Taking a turn around the gardens on a sunny day with the woman he loved... His last days would be just so, if he were lucky, but this was pretense, and it was all it would ever be, thanks to his own idiocy.

Every so often, she squeezed his arm, and he leaned in to cover her while she poured a drop of blood from a vial—her *blood*—onto the manicured lawn.

Pouring. Her. Blood. On. The. Lawn.

Under her breath, she muttered an incantation every time. *"Ward of blood, thread of my soul, / Make this place mine, grant me control."*

"Must it be your *blood?*" he whispered in her ear, nuzzling her hair. She'd cut herself this morning, collected the blood, and healed before they'd taken the coach to the palace. All without fanfare. Was this what mages did in their Towers?

"It didn't *have* to be," she whispered back, kissing his cheek—an act —as she corked the vial once more. "Sangremancy is widely known as 'blood magic,' but it's not just blood. It's the essence of a person. That means skin, hair, fingernails." They continued along. "But blood is strongest. And somehow, I don't think marking the perimeters with my fingernails would have made this any less unusual to you."

*Unusual.* He raised his eyebrows. That was the understatement of the century. But then, he had only to think of the rituals for the dead gods to be reminded of *unusual.* "Are you sure this is going to work?"

She nodded and leaned in close. "And don't worry. We're on the third and tightest perimeter. We're almost done."

Good. If anyone were to catch them drizzling the gardens with blood and casting forbidden magic, there'd be inquisitors from both the Order and the Divinity arriving within the month. Just what a fledgling monarchy needed.

"Good morning, Your Majesty," a deep voice lulled from the left. "Marquise Laurentine."

Jon looked over his shoulder; Marquis Desmond Auvray Marcel and his wife, Elena. Duke Faolan's younger brother and Brennan's uncle. He carried himself with that quintessential Marcel arrogance that only Tor seemed to have dodged. He wore a dark-red brocade doublet and black trousers with riding boots, and it suited his six-foot long-and-lean frame.

Marquise Elena curtsied, a flourish of light-blue skirts and dark curls. "Your Majesty. Your Ladyship."

He and Rielle offered greetings in return.

"You gave us quite a scare, Favrielle," Desmond drawled with a lazy smile. "There had been rumors of your"—his gaze flickered to Jon, then back—"disappearance."

Rielle smiled, a coy twist of her mouth reminiscent of her portrait. "Everyone loves a good rumor. If only my note hadn't been lost in all the fuss after the siege. All that talk could have been avoided."

*Note.* Her story was that she'd left a note before departing for Sonbahar for her health.

"You look well," Elena offered with a warm smile and a nod. "You have some color to you."

"Thank you." A forced laugh, but Rielle's cheeks reddened as she lowered her gaze.

"Wintering in Sonbahar... Your lifestyle is beginning to look more and more like a Marcel's." Desmond speared Jon with those hazel eyes, far too reminiscent of Brennan's.

Jon's shoulders hardened. "Looks can be deceiving."

Rielle glared at him. What, angry that he'd spoken for her? He scowled back. Now was not the time, not when Faolan's brother was testing him. Had they seen the blood? The vial?

Elena chuckled. "We all have our secrets."

That was putting it mildly.

Desmond patted his wife's hand on his arm. "All the more for the unraveling."

There was still something Rielle wasn't telling him. Some wound that hid behind her sad eyes. But he had yet to tell her his own, about his heart. She hadn't made up her mind about him, and he didn't want to sway her decision. The last thing he wanted was for her to stay with him out of guilt. Better she not know, at least for now.

Elena pursed her lips at her husband and narrowed a dark eye. "Come, let's leave His Majesty and Her Ladyship to their afternoon."

Desmond straightened but arched his brow at Jon. "She asks, and I do. See you tonight, Your Majesty. Favrielle."

The two bowed, said their goodbyes, and walked on.

Rielle scowled at him. She leaned in and narrowed her storming eyes. "Did you have to be so rude?"

He scoffed. "Rude? What, because I didn't agree you belong to Brennan? What about this whole ruse?"

She uncorked the vial and spilled her blood once more, murmuring the incantation. Maddingly.

She raised her chin. "I don't belong to Brennan. And I don't belong to you either."

"I didn't say you did." He encircled her waist with an arm.

Frowning, she pressed her lips together, staring at his arm, then looking up to his face. The sunshine danced a golden sheen on her intricately arranged hair, Davina's work.

She recorked the vial. "Then what does it matter that he said—" she hissed.

He held her tighter. "It matters."

"Because?"

"Because I love you." He didn't loosen his hold as her eyes widened. "I won't pretend I don't. And I won't stand by while some man calls you Brennan's woman, unless you tell me otherwise."

Her mouth dropped. Couples walked by and whispered. *Let them whisper.* He lifted her chin, and she closed her mouth, passed her tongue over her lower lip, then pinned it with her teeth.

He wouldn't kiss her. Couldn't. Not unless they mended the rift between them, and she saw fit to give him another chance he didn't deserve.

She heaved ragged breaths in a too-tight bodice. "Let's go to your quarters."

He raised his eyebrows.

She inhaled sharply. "To... I finished the ward here."

To lay the ward in his quarters. Right. He held her gaze but let his hand fall from her waist, and took hers. He settled her hand on his arm and walked her toward Trèstellan.

They'd set the trap here, but doing so hadn't been purely practical. Pretense blurred with reality. When their cover demanded he touch her, hold her, embrace her, he did it with a loving heart, without the falsity pretense required.

And she—if he read her correctly—reciprocated? At least a little. Despite her righteous indignation, despite Brennan, despite all she'd suffered in Sonbahar—which had him in fresh agony—she still responded. To *him*.

He wouldn't cross her boundaries, but Terra have mercy, he wouldn't ignore her if she wanted him to cross them.

Inside the palace, the whispers and looks followed them and his guards until at last they were just down the hall from his quarters. He returned the greetings of passing courtiers, and then the door opened.

Brennan emerged, turned his head toward them, then swept a dramatic bow and leaned against the doorjamb between the guards, looking down the hall lazily. He had to have completed the sweep he'd promised.

"Greetings, Your Majesty." He grinned smugly. "What brings the two of you here on this fine day?" His gaze slinked to Rielle and back.

"What lovers are wont to do." Rielle raised her chin, her lips twitching. Still maintaining the pretense, even here.

"And what would that be, Marquise Laurentine?" Brennan narrowed his eyes playfully. "A game of pawns? Some light lunch? Staring at a wall? Watching dust settle?"

"Oh, your poor lovers," she remarked loftily. "How disappointed they must be." She smirked.

"*My* lovers?" he crooned. "I suppose they are disappointed eventually, when their turn is over."

She scoffed.

Terra have mercy, could they go on like this all day? Bantering? And yet... he uncurled his clenched fist. Not mere banter. Flirtation. He straightened.

"I trust all was in order?" Jon asked, before Rielle could retort.

"If she has been here, Your Majesty, it hasn't been in the last month," Brennan answered, "although it was difficult to tell, given the several—"

"My thanks." He couldn't look at Rielle; she'd stiffened next to him. Brennan no doubt aimed to injure him, but did he realize he was causing her anguish, too? "If you'll excuse us," he said firmly.

Brennan raised his eyebrows mockingly and made a show of moving aside. "Enjoy your *afternoon*, Your Majesty."

*While it lasts, he means.*

Brennan eyed Rielle, and a corner of his mouth turned up. "And I'll see *you* tonight, tripping over your own feet."

She stuck out her tongue at Brennan, who exhaled a half-laugh before Jon walked her into his quarters and shut the door.

Smiling, she let go of his arm and strolled into the antechamber, running a finger along her lip absentmindedly. Amused. Pleased.

Far too pleased.

For the past few days, the love in her eyes, her face, her voice, her movements—everything—had been plain as day, no matter that they had a lot to resolve. Just now, in the garden, they'd shared a moment, hadn't they?

Then what was this flirtation with Brennan? Mere amusement, or did she truly intend to marry him?

She turned to him and held up the vial. "Shall we?"

"Tell me what that was just now." Stiff-backed, he peered at her.

Her eyebrows drew together, a perplexed frown. "What?"

Exhaling sharply, he took her hand and led her into the study. Out of his guards' earshot. He rounded on her. "Out there. In the hall. With him."

"What? What did I do?"

He raked a hand through his hair and shook his head. Did she really not know, or was she being willfully obtuse? "The way you flirted with him."

"Flirted?" She laughed, but clipped it. "We were just talking."

"I know what flirting looks like, Rielle."

All traces of laughter fled her expression, and she narrowed her eyes. "Yes, I am certain you do. Given all the practice you've gotten in recent months."

He scrubbed a hand over his face. "You're going to equate what I have *had* to do as king with *this*? Punishing me?"

Her eyebrows shot up. "You think that was all about *you?*"

He drew in a slow breath. That wasn't it at all, and she knew it. She could have flirted with Brennan for any number of reasons, but the effect was undeniable.

"Besides, we both know you've done a lot more than flirt. And not all of it was 'what you've had to do as king.' " Her mouth twisted bitterly. "Brennan and I were just *talking*. So I'm not sure I understand... You can't tolerate me *talking* with another man, but you want me to forgive you for bedding other women? Does that make sense to you?"

*You've kissed him. You were naked in bed with him*, he wanted to say, but she'd told him the circumstances. That hadn't been her choice.

This was spinning out of control. "Whether you flirt with another man or not isn't for me to tolerate or not to tolerate." No matter how much he hated the thought. "But you told me last night that you and he are not involved. And I believed you." He moved in closer, and although she looked away, she did not recede. "You know I want to make amends. And you know how I feel. If you're in love with another man, don't ask me to stand there and watch while you pursue him." Stormy, watery eyes met his, but he continued. "If you love another man, tell me so I don't have to watch it unfold right in front of my face."

She shook her head slowly. "Maybe I do love him—he saved me, treated me kindly, nearly died for me and asked for nothing in return. But I'm not *in love* with him. You know that, Jon. Divine, you know it." Her eyes searched his.

He took her hands in his, peered down at them joined. There was a chance, this one chance, to recover what was lost, but the sun was quickly setting. "Dare I ask... Can we salvage this?"

She rested her cheek against his chest, and he wrapped her in his embrace. Terra have mercy, it felt good, natural, complete to hold her like this.

"I don't know," she whispered as he stroked her back softly. "But I... maybe we can try to start over. Slowly. Very slowly."

His breath hitched. He pulled away enough to raise her chin and see the truth of it in her face. "Then you'll let me court you? In earnest?"

They could still marry, and have two to three good years together.

Her cheeks reddened, and smiling, she lowered her gaze briefly and nodded. "Let's talk about starting over after this... after the ball and Shadow has been dealt with. So there's no confusion."

*No confusion.* For the sake of appearances, tonight they'd play the lovers at the height of passion. But that play couldn't be confused for the true state of affairs between them.

No, she was right. It would have to wait until after, and then he'd tell her what Olivia had told him about his heart, too. It wasn't what they'd dreamed of in Melain, but any time they'd have together would still be blessed for him. "Agreed."

Her smile widened, right along with his, and Terra help him, he grabbed her and spun, laughing, relishing her squeals of protest—

He set her down. "I make you a vow, Rielle. I will make you happy. Every way I can."

Blushing, she ran her fingers around the back of his neck and into his hair, urged him down, and rose on her toes to kiss his cheek. A whisper of soft lips, and then she pulled away.

"Grand plans," she whispered, tipping her head toward the bedchamber. "But first, the ward."

He laughed. Right. The sangremancy. "Yes. First, the ward."

## CHAPTER 60

The sound of clopping hooves just after dusk drew Rielle to the window, the skirts of her ultramarine silk ball gown swishing softly. Divine, tonight would be awkward. They'd agreed to start over, but tonight would be full of dancing, close contact, intimacy, pretending to be in a stable, healthy, long-term relationship. When that was very much what they both wanted, how much would be pretense, and how much sincere?

And she'd agreed to *slowly* start over, but could it truly be done, after everything that had happened?

The opulent coach-and-six had arrived, the golden carriage shining in the twilight, elaborate with painted panels and carved scrollwork, white feather plumage crowning its beauty. Immaculate white drapes hung in the windows, a striking match to the six immaculate white horses barded in gold.

She pressed her lips together tightly. It was, by far, the most luxurious coach she had ever seen. They had planned on all eyes turning to them tonight—especially Shadow's—and they would succeed. Spectacularly.

Escorted by paladin guards, Jon walked the drive to Couronne, shoulders back and chin raised, his fit frame clad in an ultramarine-dyed velvet waist-length overcoat, with long coattails, and fine white fitted trousers tucked into shining black boots. Fashionable. Handsome. Kingly.

And perfectly matched to her own attire.

She vastly preferred her trousers, shirt, and vest, and her well-worn riding boots, but this... This gown, this evening, everything, it satisfied some long-held wish from her childhood, one she hadn't remembered wanting. Born, perhaps, from a storybook read by Mama, or a doll brought home by Papa. From memories and a time when she hadn't known tragedy nor ever spent a single minute contemplating its possibility. Halcyon days.

Jon glanced up at the window, catching her eye with a corner of his mouth turned up, and then disappeared from view.

Her breath caught. *Tonight is work only. Work. Only.*

A soft knock rapped at the door.

"My lady," Davina said, "His Majesty awaits you downstairs."

After a few breaths to gather her composure, Rielle smiled tentatively at her and nodded. "I'll be right down." *Right after I put my eyes back in their sockets.*

Davina gave her a hopeful smile and gently shut the door.

This was it. Tonight, she and Jon would draw out Shadow in the gardens, or they'd made fools of themselves for nothing. And if Shadow took the bait, she wouldn't survive the night.

It would go well. It had to.

Fortified, Rielle headed for the door, but stopped at the mirror. She smoothed the skirt of her gown and brushed a fingertip over one of the many white pearl pins tucked into her hair. Davina, accompanied by a flock of maids, had taken great pains to style her to perfection, tucking fistfuls of white pearl pins into the mass of curls upon her head, painting her fingernails and toes, and coating her face in a flawless powder.

The last time she had been so meticulously styled, it had been for Farrad. With a poisoned hairpin to kill him. And she'd lost more than she could bear.

She settled an uneasy, trembling palm over her belly. *You would have been so loved, Sylvie. So loved.*

And Jon would be a wonderful father—would have *been*. She swallowed. Divine, was there really such a thing as "starting over"? After the loss, after the heartbreak, the pain? After his betrayal? Or were they just fooling themselves?

She met her own eyes in the mirror. *I love him. I want to try.*

Finding her lips matte, she reapplied some rose balm. In jeweled slippers, she left her bedchamber and headed for the stairs. She fingered the Sodalis ring on her thumb. It felt so much better there than on her necklace. More right, somehow. Over the honeysuckle-carved banister, she spied Jon chatting amiably with one of his guards.

How like him to make friends with his guards. Or perhaps, since they were paladins, he'd already known them? Although he'd once been cold to her, a stranger, on the first days of their mission, his kindness and goodness had eventually won. He'd tried, unsuccessfully, to push her away, to combat their growing love with coldness.

It had proved a losing battle. She smiled.

One of the paladin guards looked up at her, and then so did Jon. The wisp of a smile on his face gave way to wide sea-blue eyes, stillness, a mouth that fell open. His guard whispered something to him, but Jon only held out his hand and quieted him.

Eyes on her, Jon strode toward the landing, arm outstretched in invitation.

Her feet were already descending the steps before she remembered to breathe and gather her gown's skirts in one hand, taking the banister in the other. Her huge smile, implacable on her face, made her lower her chin to camouflage it.

On the landing, she released the banister and took Jon's offered arm, but couldn't meet his eyes for more than a moment.

Just that moment made her heart race, her skin pebble with gooseflesh, her knees weaken. She bowed her head. The light of the sconces sparkled in the aquamarine of her necklace, catching and reflecting the brilliance. Another of Jon's gifts.

"It's too beautiful," she whispered, risking another glance at him as she touched the necklace.

"The most beautiful jewel I've ever seen." He didn't look away from her.

Her cheeks burned. Had she burst into flames? And yet that idiotic smile still paralyzed her face. How much of this was pretense?

"Shall we?" He covered her hand with his. When she nodded, he led her to the door, escorted by his guards.

As they silently made their way down the drive, she turned to see Davina beaming in the doorway, and waved at her one last time before Jon led her to the coach and helped her into it.

Sitting opposite her, he signaled the coachman, and they departed for Trèstellan. The fading light shone on his black leather boots, and her gaze wandered along his fitted white trousers, coupled with the ultramarine velvet waist-length overcoat, its coattails elegantly tucked behind him. Fine golden embroidery adorned the velvet, its fasteners elaborate knots, and lined the closure up to his standing collar, where a white cravat peeked.

The fine tailoring of his attire showcased him to perfection, covering a large frame and chiseled muscles like a gift begging to be unwrapped. Her fingertips wriggled.

When her gaze traveled up to his face, he raised his eyebrows, a playful gleam in his eyes.

At least he had the courtesy not to call attention to her behavior.

His lips twitched. "See something you like?"

So much for courtesy. She wanted, very much, to disappear. Right now. She tried to turn away, but then he lowered his own gaze. He gave her the same treatment, looked her over with soft, placid eyes, exploring her slippered feet, the sprawling fabric of her skirt, her corseted waist, her décolletage, to at last settle upon her face.

She pulled aside the drapes to look out the coach's window... between curious glances at him. "See something you like?" she asked him back mockingly.

"Favrielle Amadour Lothaire."

She laughed. "How bold."

"The joy found in life is measured by the boldness with which it is sought."

Beneath his dauntless gaze, she shivered, masking it with a small smile. It was far too easy to melt beneath his intensity.

If their second try was to work, it would have to be slow. Careful.

She'd always wanted him, and she wanted him now. She'd loved him, and she loved him now. But she couldn't let her wanting sabotage the recovery of their relationship. If she tumbled into his bed too soon, they wouldn't be starting fresh; they'd simply be resuming where they'd left off... with all their issues ready to resurface at any moment. That couldn't happen. They had to resolve them, take the time to heal, and only then rebuild upon a steady foundation.

If only this mission weren't such a complication. She sighed.

They passed the rest of the ride in comfortable silence, watching Azalée go by the coach windows. Night had fallen by the time they arrived at Trèstellan. Their trap had been meticulously planned, and Divine willing, all would go well. Once they went to the gardens for their midnight walk, they'd trap Shadow, and this would all be over.

He escorted her to the great hall, matching her in every way; like a prized pair of birds, they paralleled each other in color and trim, differentiated only by the vestiges of gender.

Through the open doors, sapphire and golden decorations dominated every available space. Flowers in massive arrangements, ornate tapestries, and priceless art bedecked the room, an extravagant display of wealth.

A large string ensemble played a gentle tune in triple time, supporting the two virtuoso musicians the palace was currently hosting. Trestle tables piled high with food rimmed every wall, stacked with beautifully crafted hors d'oeuvres; entire roasted ducks, pheasants, and pigs; bowls of exotic fruits; cakes, pastries, and confections; and delicacies she hadn't seen nor tasted in years. She shouldn't have forgotten Trèstellan's exquisite splendor, but the lavishness before her served as an exemplary reminder.

A herald announced them. "His Majesty, King Jonathan Dominic Armel Faralle of Emaurria; Prince of Pryndon; Zahibshada of Zehar; Duke of Guillory, Verneuil, and Ornan; Count of Guigemar, Langue, Buis, Lomiere, and Sauvin; Baron of Milun, Laustic, and Bellegarde; Nawi of Ashram and Khairi; and honorary Paladin of the Order of Terra. And Her Ladyship, Lady Favrielle Amadour Lothaire, the Marquise of Laurentine, Master Mage of the Divinity of Magic, and the honorary Champion of Courdeval."

The blood drained from her face as over four hundred heads turned in her direction, a hum of whispers filling the air. Champion of Courdeval? On the gleaming ivory marble floor, a throng of luxuriously clad guests turned and bowed—courtiers, the Grands—a beaming Olivia among them, the local lords, ladies, and knights. Indeed, the crowd was overwhelming.

The attention she and Jon had courted seemed to have arrived in force. She tried to catch her breath. The mission was succeeding on one count, at least.

His hand tightened over hers on his arm, and he gave her a reassuring look and a nod. "I'm here," he mouthed.

Swallowing the lump in her throat, she nodded and raised her chin. As long as he held her, she wouldn't make a fool of herself.

Well, any *more* of a fool of herself.

He escorted her through the splitting crowd to a dais, where behind the head table a grand high-backed throne awaited, along with a smaller, simpler upholstered chair, both gilded and carved with the dragons that graced Emaurria's royal coat-of-arms. Jon helped her to her seat before taking his own. Olivia, Torrance Auvray Marcel, the Proctor, an older man she didn't recognize, and a few strangers took the remaining seats at the head table.

This was what his life had been for the past four months?

"I welcome you, one and all, to this celebration of Veris," Jon proclaimed above the din. The crowd applauded. "I encourage you all to enjoy yourselves beyond all limits tonight."

The crowd applauded again, and he motioned to the musicians, who resumed the music. A line of courtiers gathered near the throne.

Numb, she didn't move, but Jon held her hand through the masses approaching for brief greetings and niceties. After hundreds, she drooped, her head lolling to rest against his arm.

Her hand in his, he gently stroked her knuckles with his thumb. If not for him, she'd be asleep already.

"Good evening, Your Majesty," Brennan's rich, cultured voice greeted. "Lady Favrielle."

Her tired eyes quickly found him, clad in sharp black velvet from head to toe but for his white silk cravat, the fitted tailoring suiting his lean but muscular physique. She hadn't seen in him days, and seeing him again breathed some life back into her. Swallowing, she offered her hand, and he kissed it.

"It's a pleasure," Brennan intimated, maintaining eye contact as he held her hand. "You look stunning."

Jon gave her other hand a squeeze.

A servant approached with drinks, and Brennan released her as they each accepted and drank a goblet of Vercourt sparkling white. At least with Brennan there, she and Jon wouldn't need to worry about poison.

The orchestra began the overture of the dance suite.

Jon drank deeply and then turned to her. "Shall we dance?" He raised an eyebrow and inclined his head toward the dance floor.

A twirling blur of night sky, haystacks, a bonfire, and apple trees spun in her head—Jon dancing with her at Vindemia last year. She took a deep breath, a feeble attempt to slow her already racing heart, and nodded.

The orchestra played the second movement of the dance suite, the first dance—the quessanade, of moderate tempo.

The couples stood facing each other in two long rows, lords on one side and ladies on the other. Jon led her to the front, where they took their position as the leading couple, his fond eyes upon her, their sea-blue brilliance brightened by his ultramarine-dyed overcoat. Tall, confident, he cut an impressive figure down to his high-gloss boots, his misbehaving foot tapping to the beat.

Although she'd been well trained in dance, it had been years since she'd taken part in a formal ball—since... that horrible night at Tregarde. Dancing the sarabande with Brennan, only to presage the ridicule she'd faced later that night.

Jon raised his eyebrows in a silent question.

She nodded.

He took her left hand in his, her right in his. As the lively music played on, he chose a beat of the bar, extended their paired hands forward, and led her down the row with three springing steps and a hop—the quessanade courante, a livelier version than the usual. The other couples fell in line behind them.

For four bars they moved forward and posed, catching each other's eyes, a wisp of a smile, her heart fluttering as they danced from the left side of the floor to the right for the last bars and turned. Jon led her in a circle for four steps round and took her arms overhead for a quick turn, leading her his way before he turned her and chased her way.

His lips twitched.

What was so funny? He looked about to burst into laughter, and Divine damn him, he made laughter bubble in her own throat. He drew her in and led her forward.

"What are you laughing at?" she whispered.

He changed hands quickly. "I'm not laughing," he replied through pinched lips.

"Just tell me," she hissed.

He turned her, drew her in again, and led her back slowly to turn and pose. "I'm happy."

He let the smile free for one bright moment—his eyes sparkling, dazzling, lit with an inner glow—before donning his regal mask once more.

Separated, she took her position before him and swung one foot to the side, sprang onto it, and swung the other foot against it in a *pas de Bellanzole*, four times, and turned.

Happy? It could have been for the sake of the mission, but that smile cradled her heart, embraced it, and if a pretended smile could do that, then she would never know him for genuine again.

He still loved her. And despite the pain of that night, despite the hurt, despite the bleak picture of their possible future together, one smile from him, and she swayed to the breeze.

All graceful arms and intimate holds, they wove their way across the dance floor in a dizzying kaleidoscope of patterns, turning, leading, circling, posing to cheery notes until the music closed.

Breathing hard, she bent to him and he to her, bows that leaned toward one another, that beckoned, invited. He offered her his hand, and she took it.

He pulled her in. "Dance the *courante* with me, Rielle," he whispered in her ear between breaths, and she hadn't caught hers yet but nodded eagerly.

The orchestra played a movement in triple meter, playful and joyous. Jon lured her in, charmed her into steps that sped with longing, hope, expectation, and jumped into passion, soared—taking her heart along. His gaze never left hers, heartfelt, soft despite the faster tempo. His touch heated her body, warmed through the fine silk, hardy herringbone, and soft linen, and his gentle caresses and firm holds graced her body with equally delightful mystery, one she cared only to revel in and never to unravel.

Caught in his gaze, she tumbled into it as her body danced the steps, and he caught her in his strong arms, safe, secure, loving.

Eyes shadowed in smoky darkness, he held her, breathless, rippling, hungry, and Divine help her, she wanted to let his appetite run rampant. His hand slipped to the small of her back, a touch she longed for on her bare skin, and a whimper escaped her throat, barely audible.

The courante ended, just as the rest of the room and its myriad guests came back into her field of vision.

Jon helped her to her seat and kissed the crown of her head. "I have to take a few key guests to the dance floor for the gavotte, the bourrée, and the furlana. Will you join me for the volta and the gigue?"

The dance suite included the volta? It was scandalous, even for Silen where it had been choreographed.

But if anything would affirm their pretense of happiness and love, it would be the volta. Relishing his near heat, she nodded. "My pleasure."

He flashed a wicked grin, a dimple teasing his mouth. "I should be so lucky."

Then he swept away to the dance floor toward a young woman clad in Pryndonian fashion. The moderate tempo of the gavotte began, and they danced.

Rielle explored the many twirling couples, recognizing a few faces, admiring others, and when a servant offered her wine, she accepted it and drank deeply. As she returned the empty goblet, Brennan strode toward her from the dance floor.

*Damn it, damn it, damn it.* He knew the importance of tonight. He couldn't take her aside here—couldn't risk the appearance of access or intimacy. Especially not after that... *whatever that had been* outside Jon's quarters. And yet—

She straightened, scanning the ballroom for Jon.

But Brennan approached her anyway, and once at her feet, he knelt before her.

*Knelt!*

Her eyes widened. There was no way—but she blinked, and he was still there. For a long moment, he didn't say a thing, and a ripple of guests turned their attention to him, whispering behind their hands.

A Marcel did not kneel. Brennan Karandis Marcel did not kneel.

But here he was.

At last, he looked up at her gravely. "Marquise Laurentine, would you do me, unworthy cur though I am, the great honor of a dance?"

She gaped. Divine... He'd just—

Her eyes darted about the room, taking in the gasps and blanched faces. He'd humbled himself before her, in the presence of every courtier in Trèstellan Palace. *Humbled.*

If she turned him down, he'd be humiliated. Utterly. He risked social ruin with this gesture.

Ruin...

Three years ago, before a handful of nobles, he'd humiliated her. Ruined her reputation.

And now...

Now he gave her the same power.

She could make the same choice he had made, and ruin him...

Or she could let him save face. Some small measure of it.

An apology. This was his apology.

# CHAPTER 61

*R*ielle's breath caught as Brennan lowered his gaze, blinking, tensing with the effort of rising, but she held out her hand.

"It would be my pleasure, Marquis Tregarde."

A tentative smile built on his face as he took her hand and led her to the dance floor for the bourrée.

She gasped as he pulled her into position, holding her hand firmly, his skin hot against hers.

Nothing but a glimpse of Brennan's roguish grin gave her warning before he led her away, his very fast, short steps vigorous and perfect, damn him, his feet close together and on pointe as proper. He practically glided across the marble floor. Her attention divided, she struggled to keep up.

They drew in close and joined hands again. "So tell me, Marquise Laurentine," he teased, "did you honestly consider leaving me flapping in the wind?"

Her right foot followed his left, then she took a step back and then over, and a quarter step— "Doubting yourself?" she teased back.

As they breezed by back to back, Brennan leaned in close. "Indulge me," he whispered, before he swept past again in front. "Did you enjoy lengthening the delicious uncertainty of whether I should expect pain or pleasure?"

Fuming, she avoided his eyes, directing her attention to the other dancers. She wouldn't dignify his eccentricity with a response.

His husky voice swept in again. "You're doing it again. And it is exquisite."

She gaped at him, missed a step, and nearly tripped—but he caught her. He was trying to unsettle her.

*I won't allow it.*

As the music quickened, she gathered her wits and danced with all the concentration she could muster, trying to recall steps she'd learned years ago, matched with the vigor of competition; her body remembered every step, every turn, every movement. As she glared at him, his eyes burned, never once deviating from hers. She matched his intensity with a fire of her own.

If Brennan hoped for her to slip up first, she'd leave him disappointed.

Many runs, hops, twirls, and sweeps later, and neither of them had erred. The room blurred around them, entertained faces and moving bodies blended together, and the current bourrée quickly drew to its end.

The bourrée... The dance suite was slowly drawing to its end. They'd assumed Shadow wouldn't strike in front of four hundred guests —would wait until she and Jon were in the gardens—but there could be no certainty.

She leaned in. "Any sign of our friend?" she whispered.

"None," he said softly. "No scent of a shadowmancer."

If Shadow were here, Brennan would know.

The string ensemble struck up a Sileni furlana, a fast courtship dance. When Brennan assumed the proper form, her body followed suit without her prompting. She followed his lead, keeping up with his pace, searching for opportunities to unsettle him as he had her.

She made a couple strategic errors—a light brush here, a bare touch there. But he was immune; he continued to lead her in the dance, stealing glances and touches in their quick steps.

At last, the furlana faded, and he dipped her, his face dangerously close, his breath warm on her mouth. Her heart raced. She looked up into his eyes, mesmerized by how they glittered, how they drank her in. She'd just begun to lose track of how long he'd held her there when he set her on her feet, watching her.

As the tune ended, his embrace tightened, then he breathed out lengthily and cocked his head. "Here comes your true love."

Off to the side, Jon made his way toward them, his face tight but not angry. Not outwardly angry, anyway.

"Behave."

"Don't I always?" Brennan leaned in and whispered, "I'll check for our *friend* in the gardens. See you there soon?" When she nodded, he pulled away and bowed to Jon. "Your lady, Your Majesty." He gave Jon her hand.

Jon accepted it, his shoulders back despite the uneasiness of his eyes, and immediately fell into the step of the next dance, leading her into it.

"Thank you for keeping her entertained, Marquis Tregarde," he replied to Brennan, but his gaze fixed on her and did not waver, his intensity making her shiver. Being caught between the two of them for more than a moment was too much to take—thank the Divine Brennan was going out to the gardens.

The soaring notes of the volta swept in.

The last time she'd decided to perform a scandalous dance, it had been no more than a prelude to disaster. Jon's eyes flickered to the dais, but she replied with a slight shake of her head.

No, they'd come here to make vengeance irresistible to Shadow, and so they would do. They still had at least two hours to finish up here and walk the gardens before they were expected to retire to his quarters.

He inclined his head and, to the orchestra's moderate tempo, led her to the center of the dance floor. His hand to hers, he faced her, close, very close, his lindenwood scent heady in her nose, his hold constant through a series of complex hops, steps, leaps, and turns. Strong, intimate. He held her just above her right hip with his left hand and supported her through a high jump, every nuance of his touch sending frissons of pleasure throughout her body.

His touch warmed through her layers of fabric, layers of time sweeping ethereally away before her eyes, and she was in Bournand again, in bed beneath him, letting him explore her as they kissed, rising to his touch, eager to learn the sounds of his pleasure, the vigor of his passion, to know the feel of their completion. His tongue had sought hers out, earnest and curious, fine Sonbaharan cotton sheets smoothed against her skin, the lulling smoky scent of a doused candle lingered in the night air.

Jon lifted her again through her turn, his touch calling sensations longing to resurface. Every part of her awakened.

He circled her and she him, eyes following one another as the coyness of the dance splayed, flirtations that melted away distant airs.

He closed in on her again, his hand against hers, but he pulled away; again and again, they came together only to draw away, her flesh eager for the slightest contact. Never looking away, he teased and denied, teased and denied, making her heart pound, her skin tingle, her knees buckling beneath her as desire pulsed in her body. Every breath heightened her arousal, his gaze still fixed upon her, unrelenting, determined, ravenous, and she looked him over, his broad shoulders and strong arms, his sculpted chest and... and... She gasped, breathless, dizzy, her feet still moving even as her mind latched on to its deepest desire.

Controlled, he performed the dance in perfect form, his look a silent rebel, darkly sensual, kissing her wanting flesh, stroking, pleasuring.

The pulse of desire infiltrated her every movement, her every step, and she swallowed, begging for completion, for respite, two competing ends, but if she didn't achieve one or the other...

His warmth reached her skin—he was close. Much too close.

Not close enough.

He offered his arm; the music had ended. Her fingers tingled, and when she took his arm, she fought to stay standing.

"I'll recall this later," he whispered, his voice an octave deeper than usual, "fondly."

She shivered, clutching his arm tighter. "And... what will you do then?" she asked breathlessly.

With a sinful smile, he glanced down at her. "Wish you were astride me."

She bit back a soft moan. Divine, his... wish... stoked the already blazing fire inside her quivering body.

She stole a glance at him, his Shining Sea eyes, his chiseled jaw, the slash of a scar through his eyebrow. Close-cropped bronze hair that shimmered gold in the light. The scar on his neck that she'd healed so poorly, that he'd never had faded by a healer.

His good looks had always made him effortlessly seductive, but he'd shed the vestiges of a paladin's shyness and now played the game with a rake's deck.

The orchestra began another movement.

"The gigue?" he asked, his voice low. Husky.

He loved her. She loved him. He wanted her. She wanted him.

"Your quarters," she breathed.

His eyebrows rose sharply, but he corrected himself and stood a little taller. A smile eased across his face. "With pleasure."

# CHAPTER 62

utside the ballroom, Jon led Rielle through the dimly lit halls, a place for clandestine conversations and trysts, flanked at a distance by Raoul and Florian. Still two hours before the midnight walk in the gardens would be over. Still time. Plenty of time, and he led her to his quarters. Rielle.

His mind raced. He'd been bold, but she'd been bolder.

*Your quarters.*

He hissed in a breath. She glanced at him, but he only smiled at her; she snuggled against his arm, pressing her cheek to his bicep for a blissful moment.

Praise Terra, had she forgiven him? Was the rift between them mended?

Occasionally, they passed a guest or two tucked into a corner, the clicking of her shoes and the guards' armor the loudest sounds beyond the din of the distant music and chatter. He took her around the corner and to his quarters, where two paladin guards stood aside to let them in. Raoul and Florian took up posts nearby.

He walked Rielle inside, then turned back to the guards. "Do not disturb us unless the world is burning."

They saluted solemnly but exchanged the slightest of grins.

Jon ducked back into his quarters, but thought the better of it and reemerged. "Even *if* the world is burning, do not disturb us." He paused, considering the trap tonight. "No matter what, do not enter. No matter what."

One guard raised an eyebrow to the other for the briefest flash of a moment, then they both saluted. "Yes, Your Majesty."

He couldn't fathom what they thought would happen tonight—but it didn't matter. He was with the woman he loved, and the rest—the trap in the gardens, the ball, the world—could wait.

Shaking out his jittery hands, he at last closed the door, faced Rielle, and took her hand in his. Gods, she was really here, in Courdeval. In Trèstellan. In his quarters. He kissed her palm, shutting his eyes and savoring the smoothness of her skin, and a little sigh escaped her lips.

Darkness claimed the room in sensual embrace, only the ambient luminance of the night through the balcony windows penetrating its greedy claim, and the distant hearth of his bedchamber. But even in the shadows, she glittered, silvery illumination catching on her jewels, her silk, her shining golden hair. He shivered. Terra have mercy, she was the most beautiful thing he had ever seen.

A corner of her mouth turned up coyly. "Dare I ask? 'Unless the world is burning'?"

He pulled her in, against him, and took her face in his hands, raising her breathless mouth to his. "Let it burn," he whispered against her lips, her soft exhalation cool on his mouth, and he kissed her.

She melted into him, wanting hands unfastening, stealing into his overcoat, his shirt, possessing the eager flesh of his chest as he took her mouth with consuming hunger. He'd missed the taste of her, blessed water to sun-parched lips. He could drown in her. Gods, he planned to.

The overcoat unfastened, she ripped his shirt open, and he moaned, sweeping her against the wall. *Yes.*

Her back collided with the upholstery, air oomphing out of her—too rough—but before he could break away to apologize, her arms circled his neck, her fingers laced into his hair, and she urged him closer, hopped and wrapped her legs around him. She angled her hips against him, and Terra have mercy, the pleasure—he hissed—pressing against her, the hardness and the pressure hovering between ache and ecstasy. He planted a palm against the wall's corded silk, smooth and yet textured against his skin, sublime, and then the other, enshrining her between his arms. Gods, he wanted to give her everything. Everything she wanted. For the remaining years of his life and forever.

Her feet found the floor once more, and a slow hand descended from his hair down the naked expanse of his chest to his abdomen and then between them, making him shiver as she unfastened his belt. Once she released him, her touch was gentle but firm, careful and wanting, and it was all he could do not to gasp. Every part of him wanted to take her, bury himself in everything she was, in her fire, in her boldness, lose himself in her until he could no longer discern where he ended and she began—become one tonight, and forever.

Her tongue teased his, her lips playing against his, lighter, softer, until she pulled away. A shudder tore through him at the disconnect as she kissed her way down his body with a mischievous smile.

*Gods*—

A field of white eclipsed his vision. His eyes rolled back into his head, and he shut them, bowing his head. Nothing remained but sensation, unbearably pleasing sensation. And the knowledge that she craved it. Craved him.

He exhaled sharply; any more and he'd—

He reached for her, urged her up to him, and she complied, smiling demurely, only to turn and press her cheek against the wall. His maddened gaze traveled from her neck down her spine—the laces of her gown. He pulled at them, unfastening while she arched her back, the softness of her backside pushing against him.

The last of the laces yanked free, he dragged the gown off her shoulders, over her hips, and to the floor, then spun her to face him, reclaiming her mouth. One, one with her, Rielle, *his* Rielle—the need overpowered him, and he took her mouth deeply.

Not enough. Never enough.

Stepping out of her dress, she grabbed her chemise's hem and tore it to the hip, then locked her arms around his neck. When he picked her up, her legs closed around his waist, and he made for the direction of the bedchamber.

She dragged her tongue against his, slowly, firmly, rhythmically, the heat of her lower body teasing against him. His hardness became pain, pain so keen that he would either die of release or its denial. Her soft breaths shortened, urged, enticed.

The bedchamber. So far.

Too far. He made it to the study.

He spotted his desk, buried in books and documents but waist high, and he swept off every last thing to the floor in cacophony and set her upon the purple-heartwood surface.

She leaned back far enough to part her thighs and pull him close. "Please," she whispered in his ear. "I need you, Jon. Now." Her voice quivered, a fluttering plea that made him shudder.

He kissed her cheek and found her mouth once more, reaching between her thighs only to find delicate silken underclothes, delicate silken underclothes that he tore free with a yielding rip. She gasped but angled to his touch, to his reverent overture, leaned into his strokes and pressure, opened to his pleasuring, turning her face to press her cheek to his, whimpering in his ear, panting, her cries mounting and loudening until she peaked, her throaty moans descending to his furthest reaches, stroking his primal depths, calling forth a part of him wilder than the man, ancient, raw, and it answered.

"Please," came her soft voice, and he answered, poised at her entrance, her hands on his hips pulling him to her, into her. One. Her mouth dropped open and she squeezed her eyes shut, her head lolling back.

Rigid, he dared to exhale as pleasure warmed through him, and she locked her legs around his hips. Terra have mercy, he'd longed for this moment since Spiritseve, reunion with her, passion rekindled, come home. And here it was, Rielle alive and in his arms, everything getting back to the way it had been.

He took her slowly, in long, deliberate strokes, savoring the blissful feel of her, watching the blossoming revelation on her face, the tremulous breath on her lips, the flutter of her eyelashes, the rising moans.

Hers. For the rest of his life, he would be hers, and nothing and no one in this world would ever diminish his devotion again.

With a soft cry, she arched her back and her head hit the desk's gleaming surface. She blinked, writhing upon it, angling her hips against him to her liking.

But he gathered her up and lifted her. At her whimper, he said, "Bed, my love."

She nodded, clinging to him as he headed to the bedchamber. Slowly, he sat on the bed, then her knees planted around his hips and she lowered to kiss him, lightly, playfully. In a controlled descent, he reclined, his shoulders coming to rest upon the soft duvet, his mouth never leaving hers.

She reached behind her back, fidgeting, and when her corset loosened, he moved to help her. Together, they removed it, and she pulled her chemise over her head and discarded it.

Sucking in a breath, his eyes feasted upon her bare curves in the firelight—round shapely breasts, her limbs and figure no longer soft as he had remembered, but thin, slight. Yet still his love, still beautiful, still *her*.

He wanted to give her—everything. Everything she needed. Everything she wanted. Everything it would take to please her.

"Rielle," he whispered, but as she settled atop him in intimate embrace, moved, pleasured, the words evanesced in his throat. She held his gaze, a whisper of a smile upon her parted lips, huffing needy breaths as she took her enjoyment from him.

Gods, the look on her face, need and satisfaction circling one another, would be his undoing, and he watched her enjoy him, focused on the mounting pressure inside, the irresistible sensation, the promise. She closed her eyes and quickened her pace, her swift breaths becoming moans, cries, and she peaked, hitting a high note as she arched, her face tight, her hot palms catching on his thighs, bracing as she finished, tears escaping her squeezed-shut eyelids.

He sat up, catching the small of her back, and rolled her onto the bed, against the pillows. When he rose, she gasped but watched him as he shed his clothes—the open overcoat and the torn shirt, his boots and his unfastened trousers, and his braies. She pulled aside the covers, her eyes devouring him.

She licked her lips and grinned. "You look..." Her gaze descended along his body. "...irresistible."

A soft chuckle rumbled in his throat. That mesmerized look on his love's face—the best incidental perk of holding to his training rituals. Time well spent.

He descended to the bed to advance upon her; she giggled and retreated but opened to him. He pinned her among the pillows.

She raised her eyebrows and pursed her lips sensually.

When she smiled, he couldn't help but mirror the expression, resting his forehead against hers, teasing her lips to a kiss, deepening it, a pulse of need shooting straight down to his hardness. She swept eager palms over his body, clutching, pressing, but he took her mouth slowly, claiming her tongue in long, slow strokes, matching his breaths to hers until they breathed as one. With gentle fingers, he traced a meandering path over her breasts and her belly to caress the line of her hip to her inner thigh. She curled toward him, but he feathered lower and around to her hip.

Her back arched off the bed, but he anchored her, taking his time kissing his way down her neck and to her shoulder, breathing in unison, melded in rhythm. He gently closed his mouth over her shoulder, and she squirmed beneath him, her fingers threading through his hair, pulling him to her.

Inhaling and exhaling together, he took her hand, intertwined his fingers with hers, pressed it to the bed. In the silence of the fire-lit night, there was her, only her, all he needed, all he wanted, and he reveled in all that she was, longed to revere her, to exult in the oneness of making love to her. Languorous, intense.

He entered her, slowly, so slowly she gasped, drawing her eyebrows together as a shiver rode through her. Breathing together, he took her in painstaking, passionate strokes, holding her hip in his hand to patience. Her eyelashes fluttered, her lips parted, and he could watch the pleasure oscillate on her beautiful face for the rest of his life and beyond.

She embraced him, held him close, and when he slowed his breathing, she matched. Pressure throbbed in his lower body, painfully, but as her breaths grew louder, he kept pace, enjoying the smoothness of her skin, the pounding of her heart, the tightening of her embrace, sweet satisfaction he wanted to prolong, to intensify, into forever.

*I love you.*

Wild cries rending free of her, she writhed beneath him, eyes squeezed tight, body taut, her legs locked around him, and he pleasured her, pleased her, finished her as he watched the need become rapture; she dug her hands under the pillow, the pleasure in her face metamorphosing to drawn eyebrows, and she pulled her hands out from under the pillow, one of them clenching a small fistful of cloth.

Silk. Negligee.

Black as night, shimmering in the silver light.

Unmistakable. *Nora's* silk negligee.

But how—

Rielle loosened her grip, studied the small thing, a rigidity stilling her body. Her eyes widened. Her eyebrows rose. She gaped at him.

His heart stopped.

She shuddered beneath him and threw the garment to the floor, shaking her head, trying to pull away.

"Let me go," she said, panting, and he pulled away—

*"Let me go!"* she cried, her voice breaking.

He sat clear of her, beyond contact, catching his breath. Terra have mercy, how—"I have no idea how that got there."

She narrowed her eyes. "Really? Because *I* have some idea."

"I swear to you, since seeing you've returned, there's been no one else." He raked his fingers through his hair. She was his other half, forever, and she was slipping away.

She gathered the sheets around her nakedness and covered herself, then glared down at them and shuddered, curling her upper lip.

He shook his head. "The bedclothes are changed every day, Rielle."

Everything was falling apart.

She wrapped her arms around herself, folded her body together, so small, like the morning he'd barged in on her in Brennan's bedchamber. The morning she'd recoiled from him.

"Whose is it?" she asked, her voice cold, lifeless.

"Nora's."

Refusing to meet his gaze, Rielle blinked away tears, then closed her eyes.

No, he couldn't watch her cry. Not again. Never again. He moved to embrace her, but stopped short of touching her, only shifting to sit closer. "Rielle, I promise you, I haven't been with her since before the night you returned. I promise you."

She shook her head. "So, what, then? She maliciously planted it in your bed, earning your ire, to—what? Ruin any sympathy you may have had for her, any possible help or favor you might have given? Or..." She swallowed, her voice hoarse. "Or you're lying."

Heaving a sigh, he bowed his head. Terra have mercy, lying? *Lying?*

If he'd been capable of lying to her, he wouldn't have told her whose negligee it was. He would've said it was a prank, some joke he shared with Valen, who'd support whatever version of events he chose, without question. Gods above, he wouldn't have admitted to coupling with the virgin the night of the Earthbinding, or that he'd been with Nora at all. If he'd been of a mind to lie, he wouldn't have confessed to it, to any of it; she would have been none the wiser, and he'd have been a dishonorable, worthless coward. *More* of a dishonorable, worthless coward.

But he couldn't lie to her. What he wanted from her relied on truth, on trust, loyalty. What he wanted from her could never be built upon lies. "When have I ever lied to you, Rielle?"

She shrugged, burying her face in her hands. "How would I know?"

"You know me."

She drew farther away, pressed to the headboard. "I thought I did."

"You do."

She shook her head vehemently. "If he believed me dead, the Jon *I* knew would have never jumped into the arms of another woman—before my body was even *cold*." He opened his mouth to object, but she continued. "The Jon *I* knew wouldn't have sat here with his lover, his princess, and—"

"Rielle—"

Breathing raggedly, she faced him, wide eyed, reddened, livid. Hot. Every inch of her skin seemed to radiate heat, heat so scorching it blurred the air around her. "The Jon I knew would have come after us! Rescued us!"

He reached for her, but she pushed him away. *Us?*

"He wouldn't have left me to fend for myself, to fend for her on my own!" Her wild eyes pierced him. Looked through him as she trembled. "To have to debase myself to protect her! To have to kill the only person who'd protected me, to nearly bleed to death in a drugged stupor—"

Jon blinked. Shook his head.

But reality remained before him. Darkness, the bed, and Rielle unraveling, and the words she'd just spoken.

*Her.* "Her?"

Rielle's mouth hung open, but no words emerged. She closed it and covered her face, sobbing softly into her palms. She dragged her knees in toward her chest, cradled them, and buried her face in the sheets covering them. "When Shadow took me, I was... with child," she stammered into the sheets, her voice muffled. "Our child."

He stared at her, his vision blurring, questions disappearing before he could ask them. His chest tightened, knotted, then a hollow slowly formed, and deepened. And deepened. "How...?"

A child.

*Their* child.

A daughter.

He rubbed his chest, pressed hard into the flesh, but it did nothing to fill the hollow there.

Rielle's shoulders slumped. "My herbs... The eve of battle, I forgot to take them, we were together, and then the day after, I was..."

Abducted.

"Is she...?" No, it was a stupid question, and he instantly regretted it. It had only been four months, and Rielle's slight form—

She clutched her knees tighter. "I barely escaped alive... And she... I..." Her voice broke.

He took her in his arms. She fought him, pushed him, the heat of her skin bursting into a cloak of flame, and he accepted her strikes, the pain, the fight that faded into weeping. He grabbed her wrists and turned her, brought her back against him, clad her in his embrace until the violence in her blood burned out against his sigil tattoos.

She doused, cooled, leaned into him.

A family... She'd given him a family, and he hadn't even known. He hadn't even known, and he'd lost it. Lost her. Them.

"You abandoned us," she whimpered against him, her voice little more than a faint whisper. "You abandoned *me*."

His eyes watered, and he held her tighter. No matter what he told himself—that Brennan had been capable, that the realm had needed its king—it didn't change the disgusting truth. The woman he loved had been taken, and he hadn't come after her. He'd abandoned her. He'd abandoned her and their child to the cruelty of fate and to another man, a man she didn't love or count on, a man who wasn't the father of her child.

Yet a man who'd done more for her, with no promise of her love or family, than Jon had by sitting on the throne.

He swallowed past the dryness in his throat. "If I could change things, I—"

"You can't," she said, between sobs. "She's gone, I lost her, and you... I don't even know you anymore."

Pain seized his chest, clenched. Tonight... It had all seemed so possible—earning her love once more, her forgiveness.

And she'd carried this. Whenever she thought of his affairs, all her suffering and the loss of their child resurfaced. While he'd been bedding Nora and Aless, Rielle had been in agony, waiting for him, praying he'd come for her and their daughter. Abandoned.

How blind he'd been. How foolish. How callous. There was a world of hurt he'd created, unforgettable, unforgivable hurt, deeper than he'd believed, that his love and devotion might never heal. And Rielle walked the brink, one foot in this world, one foot in the other, always at risk of falling into the dark.

And he took her to it. Constantly. Every time she was reminded of what he'd chosen over her and their child.

His bones ached. In his arms, he held the only one he'd ever loved, would ever love, but she didn't want to be there. Or couldn't. Through his own inaction. And their child... their daughter... hadn't even met the world.

Because he hadn't been there.

He hadn't been there to protect her, or Rielle, to take care of them both, to love them, to support them. The man in him had submitted to the king, and it had been Rielle, and their daughter, who'd suffered for it.

"Her name," he whispered hoarsely, grimly. "Tell me her name."

"Sylvie," she whimpered against his chest, sniffling.

"Sylvie," he repeated, eyes watering. *I'm sorry.* He clenched his teeth. His failure knew no bounds, and he never would have been done letting them down. He hadn't been there for them, and he never could have been. No more than two or three years. No matter what, he had always been fated to fail them, to leave them unprotected, unsupported. To be an absent husband and father. All this time, his dream had been built on assumptions he'd too naively trusted.

He knew all that, and yet there was an ache, deep and sore, that could only ever be healed by that dream come to life. By being at Rielle's side and holding Sylvie in his arms, watching her grow up together.

If only things hadn't... He nodded solemnly. "I'm sorry I failed you both. You and Sylvie deserved so much more... so much more than me. And I will never forgive myself."

# CHAPTER 63

*ailed.* Rielle fought the tremors shaking her.

Jon wished he could change what had happened. She understood that.

But it didn't change anything. That loss would always remain, painful and real. And no matter what he said, Sylvie was gone, the person she loved above all others in this world.

She hated him for it, and hated herself even more for going to the dock in the dungeon on Spiritseve. Reckless. Naive. Overconfident. If only she'd gone with Olivia. If only she'd waited for Jon, or Brennan, or—

She blinked away tears. It hadn't been her fault Shadow had attacked her, nor Jon's, but nevertheless, she would never forgive herself. That fire would burn, everlasting, until Shadow was dead, until the one who'd hired Gilles was dead, until everyone responsible was dead, and... perhaps even then.

And Jon—he'd had to choose. He'd had to. And he'd chosen correctly for the country.

But not for her. Not for their child. He was a different man than the one she'd fallen in love with. The warmth of his chest at her back, the smoky lindenwood scent of him, the rumble of his voice—it was so much like her Jon. But this wasn't him.

"I don't know you anymore," she whispered.

"Rielle, I've never lied to you, and I never will. I know I can't undo the hurt I've caused, but my heart hasn't changed," he whispered against the crown of her head.

*Hasn't changed?* Everything about him had changed. Jonathan Ver was no more, and she didn't know His Majesty, Jonathan Dominic Armel Faralle.

"There is nothing in this world," he said softly, his voice breaking, raw, "that I would have wanted more than to welcome our child into the world. To love her, to hold her, to watch her grow up. And I will regret making the wrong choice for the rest of my life."

Teardrops hit her hair. That life he described—what would it have looked like? If Sylvie had lived, if she'd been born, delivered into her father's arms? The child of a lover, a mistress, but he would have adored her. Protected her. Raised her. Loved her.

But he would have married a princess—he would have had to. He would have had legitimate heirs. His mistress and their illegitimate daughter would have been despised by his queen, looked down upon by the court and the world, and despite it all, she would give anything to have Sylvie back, and that difficult life that would have awaited them.

But Sylvie was gone. And that future was gone.

And now, given a choice, was this pain worth starting over for? A lifetime of being second, of sharing him with his queen, of hearing them together, of finding silk negligees under his pillow? And if she and Jon ever conceived another child, she'd be bringing her into that difficult life, that fractured life, where she'd have to share her father with another family, be hated and looked down upon, be *second* to his legitimate children.

She covered her mouth. It was a sad future, a painful future.

She turned in his arms to face him, swept tears off his face.

"It wasn't your fault, Jon," she said delicately. "You couldn't have known. You made the best choice you could have made, given what you knew. I don't blame you for any of it. You should know that."

He shook his head. "I should...? What are you saying?"

She took a deep, shaky breath. "Love can't overcome everything... We never would have been able to marry... This was doomed from the start."

"No," he said, firmly, straightened. "If only you said yes, I would do everything in my power to make it happen."

"Even if it wasn't best for the kingdom?"

"Nothing would stop me, Rielle. Not in this. Nothing," he said, unwavering. "I'd spend the rest of my days—" He paused. "You are everything to me."

Divine, she wanted to believe him, so badly. She closed her eyes. Everything inside of her pleaded to believe him, except for a small, nagging voice that refused to be silent.

"Jon... you could have searched for me yourself, but you stayed here for the kingdom's sake," she said gently, and although he stiffened, she pressed on. "You performed the Earthbinding for the sake of the kingdom. You took Nora to bed to balm your grief, for the sake of the kingdom. You took a princess who could save this land, for the sake of the kingdom. You were going to marry her," she said. "Your deeds speak for you. And I can't object, because the deficiency isn't yours. It's mine. I'll never be what's best for the kingdom. Ever."

"You're what's best for *me*, Rielle," he said, his rigidity easing.

Even if that were true, was he what was best for *her*? On paper, he could never be the partner she needed. And wasn't that what mattered? A future? She didn't reply, couldn't trust her voice.

"Is there nothing I can say to convince you?" He held her hand, sweeping his thumb softly over her knuckles, his Shining Sea eyes a thousand leagues away. "Have I lost you, Rielle?"

She squeezed his hand tighter.

"Please tell me I haven't."

Things would never be the same. She loved him, but that love would ever mingle with hurt. He was irresistible to her...

But resist she would. If she let herself fall, he'd only break her heart. Jon, king of Emaurria, would have to. Marry a princess. Start a legitimate family. Choose his kingdom over his mistress.

And she'd never be able to rise again.

A sharp pain lanced her chest, forcing a pressure to her eyes. No, she wouldn't cry. Not anymore. Her tears would only invite his tenderness again, and if he tightened his arms around her now, she'd never want to leave them. She'd cry all the tears she had left for him, tell him all the words she'd left unsaid, and promise never to leave his arms again.

*I wish we could have met Sylvie.*

"I'm sorry," she whispered, and he covered her hand with his, meeting her eyes with a pained stare. His mouth twitched in an almost-smile, and he gave her a nod.

It was over.

Her chest tight, she left the bed and gathered her clothes—her chemise, her corset, her ball gown. Her tears fell heavily, but she let the darkness cloak her face and stifled her sobs. All the tears in the world couldn't change reality. "We need to go to the gardens," she said, her voice breaking. "Shadow."

Jon didn't move for a long while, then he slowly rose, pulled on his trousers, and donned a midnight-blue brocade robe that he fastened at the waist. His hands on his hips, he stared at the floor in lengthening silence.

When she'd dressed in her chemise and attempted to lace her corset, he approached her, and she swept aside the tresses that had escaped her updo. Reverent fingers tightened the laces and then those of her dress.

He would never do this again. She would never dress in his bedchamber again, never need his help to lace her corset or her gown, never leave again after spending a night in his loving arms. Tonight was goodbye.

He finished tying her laces at last, his touch lingering on them. "I've made mistakes, huge mistakes, and I'll make more," he said gravely. "But with all that I am, good and bad, I love you, and I know nothing else." He drew in a sharp breath. "So just... Promise me. Promise me you'll be happy. Promise me, and I'll be able to endure this."

She swallowed, fighting back tears of her own. *Happy.* What would happiness look like without him? Did such a thing even exist?

Glass shattered from behind. Shards flew from the massive windows.

Jon covered her and hissed. A trail of shadowed smoke sped past them into a dark corner. Shadow.

Air and fire. Flame in her right hand, Rielle gestured a wind wall with her left before herself and Jon, then reached into the sangremancy ward she'd laid around the bedchamber.

Blood darkened Jon's hair and his neck. A cut to his head?

He rolled to the bed and pulled his arcanir dagger from under it. As long as he didn't disturb the activated ward, it would work.

Shadow was trapped, and somewhere in this bedchamber.

Jon searched the dark. Rielle fixed her attention on the obfuscated corner, visualizing the sangremancy ward around the room, a crimson haze that lined the edges, forming a triple rectangle. *"Yol."*

She collapsed the first, farthest perimeter of the sangremancy curse; unless Shadow killed her or used Jon's arcanir dagger, she wouldn't be able to leave its confines. "Show yourself!"

The shadowy smoke flew for the windows. Shadow collided with the ward and fell to the floor, quickly rolling away.

Jon lunged for Shadow, his blade meeting another. They traded blow after blow.

"There's nowhere to run." Rielle set fire to all around her, everything contained in the ward's boundaries. Jon, with his sigil tattoos, would be safe. She pulled on the bond—maybe Brennan could get here in time from the gardens.

Darkness flew from Jon and darted about the confines of the sangremancy ward.

From behind a smoky, sinuous shield of shadow, laughter flowed from the corner, amused and hearty. Barely discernible, Shadow stood encased in it. "You think you've outsmarted me?"

Jon darted for her, his blade parried, but he'd grabbed Shadow's hair.

She slashed it and rolled away, a streak of black.

*"Yol."* Rielle collapsed the second perimeter of the ward. Even tighter confines. "We have."

"You think so?"

*Burn.* With a gesture, everything within the second perimeter blazed. Burning wool, silk, and wood made it difficult to breathe. Flaming bed posts collapsed. Smoke fled through the shattered windows.

Dark red drenched Jon, from the wound on his head. But he searched the blackness.

Shadow stepped out of her corner and circled from the bed in the direction of the fireplace; it didn't matter where she went. Once activated, there was no breaking the sangremancy ward without killing the caster or using arcanir.

Rielle matched her step for step. "Rat in a cage." She spelled a torrent of fire at Shadow, unending, unyielding. "And I'm stronger than you."

Her fire would win; she was no longer a shackled prisoner on a ship, and there was no room for subterfuge here, in her box.

Jon tackled Shadow. They hit the floor within the third perimeter.

"*Yol.*" Rielle collapsed the final, tightest perimeter. She, Jon, and Shadow were confined in a ten-by-ten-foot square. Until Shadow lay dead.

He forced the dagger toward Shadow's face, but she managed to turn it aside and slip out from under him, stabbing his hand into the floor with her blade. He hissed and yanked the blade free.

Rielle followed Shadow with her torrent of fire, but Shadow raised her shadowmancy shield and responded with her own force of shadow—pushing against the wind wall, costing anima, requiring ever-intensifying focus.

But against fire, it would cost her. And cost her dearly. Shadow circled, moving toward—

*Toward.*

Her fire unrelenting, Rielle glanced in the direction of the fireplace, but Shadow lunged for her instead, dispelling her force of shadow.

Her ankle burst in agony.

Shadow's hand closed around hers—

The one with the Sodalis ring. With its sage-tinted center. Its *arcanir* center.

And pushed it toward the tightest perimeter.

It broke.

Then the second perimeter broke.

*No!* Rielle formed a circle of stone on the floor and collapsed it, crumbling into the room below. Shadow clawed at the Sodalis ring.

Jon lunged for Shadow but caught only air.

Dark smoke, Shadow surged to the window.

The farthest perimeter broke.

"No!" Rielle ran to the window and caught herself on the broken edge, searching the night. Nothing.

Gone.

Shadow. And the ring.

Blood seeped from her hands onto the broken glass. After four months of torture, after losing her freedom, her child, almost her own life and Brennan's—all of that, only for Shadow to escape now? Before she could get security for Jon, and vengeance?

Shadow had to pay in blood for everything she'd caused. Because of her, Sylvie was dead, and she couldn't just *get away with it.*

Pain radiated through her jaw, teeth clenched too tight, and she tore away from the window, extinguishing all the flames in the room. Everything within the second perimeter was destroyed.

Everything was ruined. Four months of torture had been for nothing. Sylvie's death. Brennan's near-death. Her own.

Jon stood with his hands on his hips. There were no words for how utterly she'd failed him. She dropped her head in her hands.

Arms closed around her, and she allowed herself a lengthy exhalation.

"It's not safe... I failed." She breathed in. Breathed in the metallic odor of blood. She wrenched away.

The side of Jon's head was black with blood, trailing down his neck and into his robe.

"What on earth—" She reached for his head and examined the side, just behind his ear, for the wound—

No, the *piece* of his flesh missing.

"How are you still standing?" she breathed as he staggered to one of the armchairs before the fireplace. She followed him and whispered the healing incantation, closing the wound as he clenched his fists, then healed his hand. Olivia would do a better job of it later.

"Did a shard of glass hit you?" She turned the second armchair to face him, watching for any signs that he deteriorated as he leaned back into it.

He shook his head, reached for the healed wound, and stroked it. "Shadow cut me."

Rielle frowned. Shadow had cut him?

She looked at the window, the missing glass. It was massive. Both she and Jon had stood with their backs to it. Unaware, they had given Shadow plenty of time to execute precisely what she'd wanted to achieve.

Clearly Shadow hadn't needed to attack them in the gardens. She'd gotten past the guards, crossed the grounds, and had known an updraft *incantation*—a thing unheard of.

Jon had lunged to cover her, to protect her, and hadn't evaded the attack. Shadow could have killed him, but she'd cut him. Only *cut* him.

Rielle eyed the wound, missing flesh about the size of a cuivre. Hair.

She furrowed her brow.

*Flesh.*

Blood, flesh, skin, hair, fingernails... The essence of a person. *Sangremancy.* She gripped the chair's arms. Divine, there were any number of sangremancy spells Shadow could cast... She could have Jon in agony for years, decades even. She could deprive him of every one of his senses. She could kill him in the most brutal of ways, all without even laying a finger on him.

Jon was still in danger, and forever would be, as long as Shadow lived. And Shadow wouldn't pay for what she'd caused, for what she'd done, or for her looming threat. There would never be another chance like this. Ever.

It had all been for nothing.

Blinking away tears of rage, she scanned the bedchamber. The ruins of the bedchamber. Only the walls and some furnishings outside the second perimeter had survived.

Lifelessly, she studied the mantel, where Shadow had feinted, all in a ruse to use the Sodalis ring against her. And steal it.

So caught up in the end of her and Jon, she hadn't had the presence of mind to understand the detail that would have secured his life.

Above the mantel, a portrait smirked down at her, a stupid girl who thought she knew everything but would be too blind to see the truth before her very nose.

She was still that stupid nineteen-year-old chit, believing the world was hers, that she knew all there was to know. A fool. She rubbed her forehead too hard.

The door to the bedchamber flew open.

Her wind wall sprang from one hand and fire from the other.

"It's only us." Olivia rushed in, a swath of golden-yellow silk, closely followed by Brennan.

Rielle dispelled her magic.

Olivia froze just inside, agog as she surveyed the room: its scorched floor and furniture, its missing window, its gaping hole in the floor, and its drapes fluttering in the wind. Her gaze snapped to Jon. "Are you all right? Is your—"

"I'm fine," he blurted, fixing her with a steely, unwavering glare.

With a grimace, Olivia nodded. "Why aren't your guards in here?"

"I... ordered them not to enter," Jon said with a sigh.

Brennan pushed past Olivia and hurried to Rielle's side, resting a hand on hers on the chair's arm. "Are you all right?"

*All right...* She nodded. Aside from the pain of defeat, she was unhurt, but she was far from all right. Her greatest enemy had lived to fight another day.

"Thanks for coming," she said softly, covering his hand with hers.

Jon peered at their hands and looked away.

Not now. She didn't want to hurt him. She was about to pull her hand away, but...

No. Jon needed to accept it was over. Accommodating his jealousy would only encourage his feelings.

Olivia came to them and touched Rielle, probing. "Your foot!"

She crouched and pulled the skirt of Rielle's gown aside to reveal a soot-covered, bleeding, bruised foot. It was already swelling. How had that happened? In the scuffle with Shadow?

Rielle shrugged.

Jon knelt next to Olivia. "What happened?"

"Tell me you kicked her out the window," Brennan crooned next to her, smirking.

Rielle elbowed him. "I wish." She shook her head as Olivia healed her. "No... I just... I"—she frowned—"lost."

Brennan gave her a sympathetic look. Relief engulfed her leg and spread throughout her body—Olivia's magic.

"I noticed you... redecorated the place," Olivia mumbled as she finished.

"Shadow took some serious burns, but she escaped." Rielle took a deep breath. "I failed."

Wincing, Olivia rose. She took Jon's head in her hands. "Jon, did you know a patch of your hair is gone?" She urged him to the armchair, and he turned it to face Rielle's and sat.

"Balding already?" Brennan remarked. He dodged Rielle's elbow deftly.

Jon grimaced at him while Olivia tended to him, her magic glowing white.

"Fashion statement?" Brennan pursed his lips and cocked his head. "I don't think it'll catch on. Not flattering at all, I'm afraid." He knelt and picked something up off the floor. Burnt hair, by the looks of it. Shadow's?

Jon looked at Rielle, eyes haunted and intense, and it was all she could do to look away.

Olivia chuckled softly and leaned back. "Finished. No scar, and your hair will grow back."

"Fashion faux pas avoided," Brennan said.

"You're welcome to stay at court, if you so choose," Jon said to her, his voice deep, hoarse.

Her breath slowed. No matter what lay between them, she would always, always desire him. If she stayed here, even to protect him, she would find herself in this room again no matter how bleak their future was.

Distance. She needed to put distance between herself and Jon.

Swallowing, she shifted in her armchair and rose. "I... I think I need some fresh air." She glanced at Brennan. "Join me on the balcony?"

He nodded, following her as she headed for the broken doors, pushing their ruins open to head outside.

"There's already fresh air coming in through the giant hole in the wall," Olivia called behind them.

*Missing the point, Olivia.*

Outside, Rielle grabbed the balustrade and closed her eyes, breathing in the cool night air tinged with smoke.

Brennan took his place next to her on the balcony, his arm nearly touching her shoulder, his hand on the railing nearly touching hers, but just shy. "So your enemy escaped. You burned down the king's bedchamber. And now?"

She inhaled a slow, steadying breath, then narrowed her eyes, hunting the darkness. "Now I hunt Shadow until I defeat her."

"*We* hunt." He opened his other palm to reveal the burnt hair. Shadow's, no doubt.

She wouldn't turn away Brennan's help; they'd defeat her together.

"I hoped you'd say that." She covered his hand with hers. "We make for Bournand to see Feliciano, the spiritualist there, and track her down."

"No need for that. There's one at Victoire."

# CHAPTER 64

*J*on stared into the glowing embers in the fireplace. After all that had happened tonight, only one thing haunted his mind: all Rielle had told him.

The words circled in his head like ghosts, lamenting and damning, and he deserved their haunting, their judgment, their punishment. Every second. Nothing compared to what she'd suffered.

A life to protect, from dark days and unflinching inhumanity. No protector, no friend. No sword, no magic. No fists, no words. Only flesh and submission to offer. Self to sacrifice. A life for a life.

Hands and knees on hard, unforgiving floors. Blood, sweat, fears. Unfamiliar hands. A caged mind to tolerate a body made object. For pain. For pleasure. For control. For as long as it would take a lover, a father, to take action. For as long as forever, if not for Brennan Karandis Marcel.

Jon shrouded his face with a hand, blotting out the fire with darkness, the tears he didn't deserve to shed pushing against his eyes, his will; he didn't deserve to ease the grief over her suffering, and over Sylvie's death. A man who hadn't lifted a finger to fight for them didn't deserve to lessen his burden over their loss.

It was unthinkable, and it was him.

Rielle strode from the balcony with Brennan at her back.

She paused before him. "We're going after Shadow."

Jon rose. "I'll go with you."

"Brennan's coming with me." She looked over her shoulder at Brennan, who nodded.

"Rielle—"

"Brennan and I will find her together." She bowed. "We'll end her, once and for all, together."

He fought back a wince. So it had come to this. And she was leaving. Leaving the palace. Courdeval. Him. Forever.

She wanted space, distance, and he would give her what she wanted. "Terra keep you, Rielle, and your Divine."

"You, too," she said, meeting his eyes with a pained gaze, intense, unwavering, watery. She inclined her head one last time, her action mirrored by Brennan, and then she hugged Olivia. "Take care of yourself."

Olivia squeezed her tight. "Come back in one piece."

With a half-smile, Rielle nodded, met his eyes one last time, and left.

Long after the door had closed, he stood there, staring at it. After tonight, after everything, he had lost her.

She'd refused him, didn't trust him to secure their future. And why should she, when it was just as she'd said? He'd done everything expected of him as king and hadn't deviated whatsoever. He had no deeds to show her that could allay her fears, nothing he'd done to lay a foundation for a life together. Not yet, anyway.

And she'd refused his breaking of the betrothal. She would wed Brennan.

Jon dropped back into the armchair. His rigid shoulders ached.

"Did you tell her?" Olivia asked. She sat in the singed armchair next to him. "About your heart?"

"No." How could he have? When she'd clearly had enough pain, he couldn't have laid such a burden on her, guilt. It was too much.

When she'd found that scrap of silk, the pain in her face, the agony, had been overwhelming. Perhaps she believed that, with Brennan, she would never suffer it again.

With Brennan, the selfish, manipulative werewolf who'd saved her life. Perhaps his love would win over his selfish nature. Or perhaps it wouldn't.

Olivia shook her head, chewing her lip beneath a frown. Finally, she sucked in a breath. "She deserves to know. You need to tell her, or... she'll never forgive herself."

"Or maybe she's better off rid of me." He brushed a fingertip over the fresh scar on his head. "I'm bound here, but she isn't. I don't want her to be. I want her to be free, to do whatever brings her joy. And this... I..." He lowered his gaze. "I would only be another kind of shackle."

Heaving an annoyed sigh, Olivia eyed the healed wound on his head.

That wound...

Shadow carried a soulblade, had told Rielle it would kill the man she loved.

His heart pounded. "She cut me with it, and I didn't die."

"What?" Olivia's red eyebrows drew together.

"Shadow," he said, clutching the blackened armrests. "She had a soulblade when last I fought her in Bournand. Rielle said it was spelled to kill the man she loved with one cut." His voice dropped. "Shadow cut me with it, and I didn't die."

Olivia's lips parted, and she curled her fingers on her lap. A crease lined her brow before she lowered her gaze. "I—Perhaps she used a different blade."

Something tight and painful twisted in his chest. "She's been trying to kill me for months. What's likelier? That she left her most powerful weapon behind, or that the woman I love doesn't love me in return?"

Olivia looked away.

They both knew the truth. It really was over.

And here, in the palace, while Rielle was gods-knew-where with Brennan, what was he to do? Attempt to move past it, dwell on it, fight it?

There'd be no moving past losing the love of his life. That night at the Tower, he'd told her, *I am your prisoner.*

And he still was. Even now. He'd thought of her every day since he'd met her, and he'd think of her every day on. She was a part of him, whether she wanted to be or not.

And dwelling on it, as an Earthbound king... Would that be as destructive as the lies about her death had been? Perhaps he could try to ignore it, but that hadn't gone well either, as he sat in the charred consequences of that particular course tonight.

He clenched a fist. Rielle didn't want him to fight for her love, and he wouldn't. She didn't want him anymore—not as her husband, not as her lover, perhaps not even as her friend. And it was his just fate for all his egregious dark deeds.

His chest ached, and he grabbed a fistful of his brocade robe there.

"Jon," Olivia said gently, looking about the remains of the room, "should I even ask what else happened here tonight?"

He grimaced.

"A burden shared is a burden halved?" A small smile peeked from her face. "Tell me."

So he told her all of it—the disastrous circumstances the night of Rielle's return, the pain and friction between them, how she'd refused to dissolve her betrothal, the gap between them slowly closing during their ruse. And tonight. How close he'd felt to her at the ball, all the signs, their night together here, and how she'd found Nora's clothes beneath the pillow. He slumped against the armchair's button-tufted back, rubbing his forehead.

Olivia rested her head against her chair's back, too, and closed her eyes for a long moment. "She's hurt, Jon." She rolled her head to face him. "She's lost so much in her life—her entire family, Leigh, Brennan... her child. And you. And it's hurt, deeply, so badly that when Brennan broke her heart in Tregarde, she didn't want to fall in love ever again."

He pressed his lips together, thinking back to the days when he and Rielle had just left the Tower. She had stolen glances at him from time to time, flirted, but she hadn't seemed interested in love. Not until Bournand. And even then, she'd kept so much to herself; she hadn't even opened her heart to him, not fully, until Melain. "But she did."

Olivia nodded. "She did. And what do you think it would do to a person, so traumatized by loss, to lose the one they love most?"

"It would hurt."

"Yes, it would hurt, and it could break them."

Break? He frowned. But no, he'd seen it... seen the glass cracking—her wild eyes in Brennan's quarters, her haunted expression in the Grand Library.

But hadn't their bond slowly healed? In Couronne and at the ball, she'd been more like herself, stable.

Olivia exhaled shakily. "If she had to choose between the risk of loving you and breaking for it... or protecting herself by pulling away from you, don't you feel the choice would be obvious now?"

"Things were getting better." He crossed his arms.

"They were. And then she found your former lover's effects in your bed." Olivia eyed him with pursed lips.

He shook his head. "I ended things with Nora and Aless that same day I saw Rielle again. I've kept to that."

Olivia chewed her lower lip, fidgeting with her gown, then crossed her legs. "Remember the night I interrupted you in the Grand Library with Alessandra?"

He sighed. "Yes."

"Remember what I told you?"

"That I was an idiot?" he offered.

She rolled her eyes. "No, not that—but yes, you were being an idiot. But what I'm thinking of is that I was trying to keep you from making a huge mistake."

"There are many." He sighed. "You'll have to be specific."

"Sacrificing who you are for what you are."

He frowned.

"You sacrificed everything to try to be what your people needed." She stared down at her ring, the Ring of the Archmage. "You're the king. That's *what* you are. But you're Jon first. That's *who* you are. And that's who you must be before doing what you must do."

His eyes widened. "And what if I can't do what's expected of a king?"

She shrugged. "Then you can't, and you'll find another way. No one is perfect, not even a king. And if you try to be a perfect king, you'll lose yourself."

Lose himself... He already had, hadn't he? Sacrificed everything he'd loved and believed in, to do what kingship demanded. And where had it left him? He looked about the room. The burnt, destroyed room.

The ruin.

He looked up at the portrait of Rielle. He had changed. She'd told him so herself.

And he hated who he had become. What he had become.

He couldn't do this anymore, not even for two to three more years.

"I don't know if I can ever go back to who I was," he thought aloud, "but I can be who I am instead of sacrificing to try to be what a king should be."

Olivia smiled. "That's a start. You can't just be king; you have to be King Jon."

She was right, and Rielle was right. He'd become unrecognizable— the king: a man capable of doing any deed for the sake of the kingdom, the people, the land; a man with no honor; a man who had forsaken good and right for progress.

A man he could no longer be.

Perhaps the person he'd been before the crown would never make an excellent king, but it was the only king he could be, and live with himself.

And whenever the demands of rule became dishonorable and blinding, when voices required expediency, he had only but to look into his heart, where in the shadows would forever lay anguish, grief, and regret over the loss of the family he, Rielle, and Sylvie could have been—and he would be reminded of the real, human cost of surrendering to that expediency. The unbearable cost. And he'd have the strength to hold fast.

He looked back at the portrait and nodded toward it. "Do you think she'll ever forgive me?"

"I don't know. She's hurt, so she's turned to something less painful, something safe—"

He frowned.

"I don't care what some blade is supposed to mean. She does love Brennan, that's for certain, but not the way she loves *you*. I think she knows that, and that's exactly why he's safe."

Safe... Perhaps. Brennan had hurt her once, and seemed to have made amends. But tonight, the disaster in bed...

He frowned. Nora's clothes.

Nora. Brennan's sister.

He jumped from the chair and paced before the fireplace.

"What is it?" Olivia rose.

He rested his hands on the mantel and leaned against it, over the fire. How had he been so thoughtless? Brennan had come by earlier in the day to check the room. He'd had the perfect opportunity to plant whatever he'd wanted.

"How did Nora's negligee end up under the pillow?" He pounded a palm against the mantel.

"You think Brennan—"

He spun on his heel, breathing hard. "I *know* he did it."

Blanching, Olivia took a step back, and he tried to rein in his temper. "What are you going to do?"

With a shake of his head, he paced again, slowly. "I can't accuse him to Rielle—she'll think I'm just trying to undermine him," he thought aloud. "And I can't challenge him—it'll just look like I'm jealous."

"Then what's left?"

He wouldn't stoop to Brennan's level.

Brennan claimed to love Rielle. But how could he, if he resorted to manipulating her? That wasn't love. It was selfishness. And that selfishness wouldn't stop. His love would never be true, and someday, he'd make a misstep, and Rielle would see that. Someday, he'd slip up and lose her forever. And if he didn't—if against all odds, he became the man she hoped he'd become, then she'd live a good life. A happy life.

"Nothing. I will do nothing." He took a deep breath.

"Nothing? You'll just... wait?" She stared at him.

He met her stunned gaze squarely. "I'm going to return to my old life, to who I was, as much as I can." Piety, celibacy, sobriety, and—well, he could never truly live up to poverty, but he would give and give and give as much as he could.

Olivia extended an arm as if to touch him, but stopped. "Jon..." She lowered her gaze, stared at the floor. Feeling sorry for him, no doubt.

It didn't matter. This was who he was.

It wasn't just for Rielle's sake. Even if she never wanted anything more to do with him ever again, this was who he was. He was done trying to do what a king *should*. He would never bring a child into this world only to leave her behind a couple years later, fatherless. And he would never marry a woman he didn't love—for his sake, and for hers. He and the Grands would have to find some other way to settle succession.

He paced to the broken window, watching the drapes billow outside in the wind.

If he died alone and unloved, then so be it. At least he'd die being true to himself.

He lowered his gaze to the broken glass, opaque with drying blood. Rielle's.

There was a knock at the door.

"What is it?" Jon called.

Eloi entered, his blond curls angled in every direction. Frazzled. "The guards said not to disturb you, but—"

"Speak."

"There was a message, Your Majesty. From Ambassador Galvan." Eloi handed him the message.

Jon broke the seal and read.

*The dark-elves have attacked Vervewood. The alliance has been triggered...*

Olivia joined him at the window, and he passed the message to her. She gasped. "What are we going to do?"

The wind tore one of the drapes off its rod and swept it away. "We're going to war."

# CHAPTER 65

Out of the rain, Brennan strode past the footmen opening the doors to Victoire. Behind him, Rielle's footsteps clacked, still in her jeweled slippers from the ball. He eyed the footmen—if they so much as raised a brow at her ruined gown, they'd regret it—but their inscrutable masks didn't waver. Beneath the petrichor of the rain and the wet mustiness of smoke, the scent of her blood was strong—still on her hands, on her clothes.

And the king, heavy on her skin.

What had she done in that bed before she'd set fire to it? Had they found his little gift? The questions lingered, but before his mind could conjure any answers, he shook his head. He didn't want to know. For once.

Besides, there were more important matters to handle.

Preston, the elderly manservant, greeted them. Before the man's open mouth could emit words, Brennan said, "Get Her Ladyship some practical traveling attire and some tea." He shoved past Preston toward the stairs. Over his shoulder, he said to Rielle, "Wait here."

She inhaled sharply but did not object. Preston softly offered her a seat while Brennan took the stairs two at a time, his fingers tracing the hazel carving on the banister. After being exiled from court, Nora had come to Victoire to sulk before leaving for Vauquelin. For once, her mulishness was functional and not just annoying.

He made his way to her usual quarters, pulled a corona from his pocket, and worried it. He knocked on the door. Soft, short footsteps —Melanie's—and the door opened. She stood aside as he entered. "My lord! Good evening to you. My lady is—"

He held up a hand. "How are the boys?"

"Sleeping, my lord, in the adjoining quarters. Annette is watching them."

He nodded, then headed for the bedchamber. Nora's quiet breaths came from within, but not to the deep rhythm of slumber. He creaked the door open.

Clad in a deep-red ball gown, her hair elaborately arranged on her head, she lay on the bed. Her jeweled shoes caught the moonlight. Without lifting her head from the pillow, she eyed him. "What do you want?"

He leaned against the doorjamb and exhaled lazily, turning over the coin in the silvery light. "Is that any way to greet your only brother?"

She puffed, eyeing the corona. "Don't you have any other bedchamber to haunt?"

"None with a madwoman outfitted in formal attire for bed."

If looks could kill, he'd be massacred. She shot bolt upright. "And whose fault is that? If you'd left well enough alone, I'd be at the *ball* in my formal attire. Instead, you brought back a problem that ruined everything."

He laughed under his breath. "For all your cleverness, your plans are too risky."

"If only yours weren't. Then your advice would be legitimate."

He sighed. "Let's just skip the verbal tête-à-tête portion of this conversation and go straight to the point."

"Which is?"

He sauntered to the bed and leaned against one of its posts, tossing up the coin and catching it. "Do you know why you're here, Nora?"

She narrowed her eyes. "Because you couldn't leave well enough alone."

"Because Father has the funds to keep a villa in Courdeval, and *you* don't."

She snapped her face away and crossed her arms. "The point of this humbling?"

"You have no money."

Her upper lip curled as she turned back to him.

"And you don't know the first thing about how to make it. I do."

Slowly, her frown relaxed to allow her eyebrow to rise. "And...?"

"And"—he shrugged and dropped onto the bed—"I'd be willing to manage Vauquelin for you, free of charge, for a year."

She huffed a laugh. "Free. Certainly. I'm about to wake up, aren't I?"

"All you have to do is tell me where Francis's magic tutor is—"

"*Her?* Really?" Nora scrunched her face in the most unappealing way.

He winked, smirking. "You're charming, dear sister. But no, not for that. I'd like Francis to find someone for me."

She scoffed. "Did your escape-artist fiancée run off again?"

"Just say yes." The less she knew about it, the better. Any information in her hands became a weapon. And how his dear sister would put these gems to use was anyone's guess—and he couldn't have it, not until Shadow was meat between his teeth.

She arched a brow. "Who is it?"

"No questions, or you're on your own with Vauquelin." He turned the corona over and over and over.

Her eyes narrowed. "Two years."

Two years of managing the mess that was Vauquelin... in exchange for getting revenge on the bitch responsible for Rielle's captivity? "Done."

Nora's eyes glittered as a smile slid across her face. "I'll send for Master Leonne right away."

"I'll wait in Father's study." He stood and peered at her, then tossed her the coin.

She caught it and plopped back onto the bed once more. "Pleasure doing business."

If there was anything Nora loved more than money, he had yet to find it. He strode from her bedchamber and caught the gaping

Melanie's arm. "Have Marquise Laurentine escorted up to Father's study," he hissed. "Discreetly."

When he let her go, she bowed. "Yes, my lord." And disappeared.

Grinning, he entered the hall and proceeded to Father's study. The last time he'd been there, he'd confronted Father about his treason—effecting King Marcus's assassination and planning the ill-conceived coup d'état.

He raised his chin and flexed his neck; his head was still on his shoulders, so things hadn't gone as poorly as they could have. Even Jon, bleeding heart that he was, wouldn't reward treason with mercy. Traitors bought death with their schemes, for themselves and their families.

Praise the Great Wolf, he'd covered Father's tracks and saved his family. Perhaps Father could content himself with his vast holdings and wealth.

He opened the ornate oak doors and entered the study. By the moonlight coming in through the windows, he headed for the nearest candelabrum and lit its candles, then the rest of them. Father's tufted leather wing chair sat empty at the desk, and he planted himself in it. Shortly, two sets of footsteps—timid and light, and a self-assured stride that could only be Rielle's—neared from the hall.

The door opened, and she walked in, wearing a belted red brocade riding coat—one of Una's. Of all his sisters, naturally Una would be the most practical. Rielle looked about the room, her hair bound in a braid, if still soot covered in places. The scent of fresh olive-oil soap wafted, but beneath it all, blood and the king.

Brennan flinched.

"We can't stay the night." She strode to the desk and placed her fingers atop it. "We're losing valuable time."

He hadn't been able to track Shadow beyond Azalée. "Trust me, knowing where to look will help."

She grimaced and threw herself into a chair. One leg conquered the other and bounced impatiently. She crossed her arms. Ready to fight. Ready to kill.

She'd had unerring focus before, but here was a woman intent on refusing to let her mind wander.

Where might it wander to? She and the king had nearly taken one another on the dance floor. And her scent left no doubt as to what happened in the bedchamber.

She must have found his token. And the cold parting meant her affair with the king was likely at an end.

With these pieces of the puzzle, he could wait. He could be as patient as she was *impatient*. In time, she would open up of her own volition.

Two sets of footsteps neared in the hall. Light and short, and shorter. The door opened.

"Lord Francis Marcel Vignon and Master Erelyn Leonne," the footman announced.

Francis trudged in first, rubbing an eye and yawning as he stumbled over the hem of his dressing gown. He cracked a sleepy eyelid. "Uncle Brennan?"

Brennan rounded the desk to Francis and crouched before him. "I need your help. Do you think you could help us find someone?"

Erelyn Leonne entered, her dark curls an unruly mess, and curtsied. "My lord, Your Ladysh—" She gasped. "Rielle? I thought you were—"

"Erelyn." Rielle stood from her chair.

Francis's gaze shot to her, then his eyes widened and downcast them. "I'm sorry," he whispered, "I didn't mean to tell—"

"Everything is all right," Brennan said softly. "Don't worry about that now."

One step, two, three. Rielle, behind him. A hand rested on his shoulder, fingertips giving him a gentle squeeze. "We need to stop a bad person from hurting anyone else," she said delicately to Francis, "and we need you." She inclined her head. "Can we count on you?"

Francis met her eyes, his own wide and unwavering, then nodded. He looked over his shoulder at Erelyn. "I want to help. Can we, Master?"

Brennan speared Erelyn with an unrelenting glare; she met his eyes, winced, then beamed at Francis.

"Of course we can," she replied.

Brennan stood and gestured to the two chairs. He seated Rielle in one, and Francis climbed into the other. Erelyn took her place next to him, standing.

Brennan rounded the desk once more and dropped into Father's armchair. He pulled the burnt lock of hair, bound with twine, from his pocket and slid it across the desk, then nodded at Erelyn. She took it and presented it to Francis, whose eyebrows shot up.

"It's all right." Brennan smiled his encouragement.

With a nod, Francis accepted the item. Erelyn began to hum softly, an easy tune, and two pulses slowed; Rielle sank into her chair, her relaxed face and posture matching Francis's perfectly.

Erelyn's magic, a cantor's magic... the ability to manipulate the emotions of anyone not immune to magic: to relax, to desire, to hate, to panic. Hedge witches hawked such cheap tricks in every market-place of every city he'd ever visited; underneath it all, this cantor, wrapped in a fancy coat and stamped with a three-bar chevron, was no different. It was low, common magic, but it had its uses.

A faint purple glimmer dusted Francis, growing and brightening into an aura of sparkling smoke. "A small woman, clad in shadow, with hard eyes." His voice was an eerie harmony, inhuman, magical. His eyes opened, purple, intense, staring at something nonexistent with unwavering intensity. "A swaying floor. White sails and favorable winds... turned southwest."

Rielle shook her head, rubbed her eyes, and straightened in her chair. "Sailing out of the bay and to the Shining Sea. So not to the southern continent." She braced a palm on the desk and rose. "We need to find out which direction she's taking on the sea. We have not a moment to lose."

Francis blinked, and the purple aura dissipated; he breathed raggedly, and Erelyn patted his shoulder. "You did well."

"Thank you, Francis," Rielle said softly, inclining her head.

Francis beamed at her. "My pleasure, Your Ladyship. I'm glad to be of assistance." He canted his head.

Brennan half-laughed under his breath. The boy certainly had Marcel blood in him.

"Erelyn," Rielle said, "can I trouble you for a quick resonance?" When Erelyn nodded, they took to the opposite end of the study.

Brennan approached Francis and crouched next to his chair. "Well done." They shared a smile. "But I need you to promise me you won't tell your mother."

Francis flinched and lowered his gaze. "Uncle Brennan, I didn't want to lie, but—"

"I know." He rested a hand on Francis's forearm. Nora suffered from the same rare strain of seditious madness that Father did, and she couldn't be allowed to pass it on to Francis or Henry, nor risk them and the entire Marcel line on her treasonous gambles. Even Jon, who had once been a beneficent paladin, had less and less mercy to spare as king. Traitors would be punished the way they had always been. "The king has granted you mercy this once, but do not count on it again. The next time your mother asks you to do something you don't believe is right, you come to me. I'll handle it."

"You'll help me?" Francis asked, eyes bright.

"Always and no matter what. I promise." He gave Francis's forearm a gentle squeeze. The boy smiled and yawned. "Now that you've played your part in this heroic venture, I think it's time you return to dreamland."

"Yes, I think it is time we retire," Erelyn said, her face flushed. Just like Rielle's. Francis's head bobbed sleepily. "My lord, Your Ladyship?"

Brennan nodded his permission, and they left. As soon as the door shut, Rielle strode to him and raised her chin to meet his gaze firmly.

"We need to leave. Now. An hour ago." She inhaled a slow, steadying breath, then narrowed her wild eyes to slits.

He leaned against the desk. "What we need is a ship." Luckily, the most imposing frigate he'd ever seen sat in port.

"Are you thinking what I'm thinking?" A rictus grin split her face, one worthy of the Great Wolf Himself.

Brennan mirrored the expression. "Let's see how big a favor a sister's love can buy."

~

OLIVIA SET ASIDE the latest petitions from village and town magistrates across the kingdom, and looked out her study's window. The great thaw had begun, albeit still beneath a gray sky. The sun sat at its midday high behind a veil of clouds.

By now, Jon would have spent several hours on the road, with two companies of soldiers, an equal number of paladins, and the hedge witches that had been recruited into the new Order of Sages. Once an arm of the Order of Terra, at least until its intolerance of magic had become absolute, they now served the Crown—one of Jon's better ideas. Too long had magic practitioners outside the Divinity's control been ignored in Emaurria, branded "heretics" and "hedge witches" everywhere else. But there was no sense in deferring to the Divinity when it offered little in return to the Crown.

The Order of Sages would be a great advantage in the battle to come. And Jon, frayed as he was, needed every advantage now.

She curled her fingers into a fist and exhaled her annoyance. Left behind. Again. He would be fighting Immortals—the dark-elves, at that, foes they had not yet faced in battle, and so, knew little about. She should be out there with him, protecting him as best she could and ready to heal him and others if need be.

She nudged a tome beneath the petitions. Her latest project, one Jon had specifically told her to give up on, was finding a way to save his life. With Immortal beings walking the land, there had to be a way to save a human life. Jon had enough to worry about without being in constant anticipation of his heart failing him.

Whoever had hired the courier was still out there, and she'd come no closer to finding him. She pictured the sketch in her mind: a narrow face, aquiline nose, shoulder-length hair, deep-set eyes, and a birth-mark on his jaw. After staring at the sketch so many times for so long, she'd recognize him anywhere.

A large, warm palm covered hers, and she looked away from the window to Tor's comforting smile. At least he'd agreed to have his desk brought in. Jon had left management of his affairs to them both, and as much work as it was, they could get through it in one another's company.

"He'll be fine, Olivia." He patted her hand, then intertwined his fingers with hers. "Pons is with him, Valen is with him, and Raoul and

Florian, along with most of the Royal Guard. He has friends at his back."

And Cédric Fontleroy. At least he was a healer, and he'd keep Jon's condition secret.

Just not her. But she nodded anyway; he was trying to make her feel better. "I wish he trusted my prowess. I don't need sheltering."

Tor shook his head and leaned back in his chair, crossing his arms. "It's *because* he trusts you that you are here. Someone has to manage the kingdom, but not just anyone. As much as I'd like to be there, too, there is no greater duty than what we are doing here."

She sighed. Why did he have to be so sensible? "You're right. I'm just... worried about him. It's been a tough several months, and a trying several days."

He lowered his gaze and bobbed his head, the soft sunlight catching in his thick, dark hair. "He's been hit hard by the events of late, but I've known him since he was a boy. He can set aside all else and accomplish the mission before him."

Smiling her agreement, she nodded. And the mission Jon had set before *her* was assessing the results of the "interrogations" the warden had been conducting in the dungeon. He'd been torturing prisoners for information, but so far she had found nothing of use. Some Crag lieutenants in hiding, former clients, but nothing to connect anyone to the regicide.

Praise the Divine that Jon had come to his senses and ordered the torture stopped.

"How about dinner later tonight, just you and me?" Warm hazel eyes gleamed at her.

They'd gone to the Veris Ball together, but Shadow's attack had cut short what should have been a much longer, much grander night together.

She eyed him peripherally and grinned. "How about an early dinner, just you and me, minus the dinner?"

# CHAPTER 66

*B*rennan swung out of his hammock and headed through the dark for the hatchway. It had been half an hour since Rielle had awoken and left his side; she should have returned by now. He ascended the steps onto the main deck into the soft silvery light of a million stars. The *Liberté* bobbed gently, waves lapping against its hull, wind billowing its great white sails.

Sterling had the helm, standing stiff and tall as one of the masts. Or a Pryndonian. Blinking, he nodded off to the side, where Rielle leaned against the railing on the quarterdeck, staring out at the vastness of the Shining Sea. Outfitted in a turquoise coat cinched in with a white sash, she looked like one of the waves come to life.

Brennan took up a perch next to her against the railing. She looked at him, only a brief moment, before exhaling lengthily and fixing her gaze upon the waves once more. He'd expected she'd come up for some fresh air, at least after sleeping in a room full of sailors, but judging by that fine crease between her brows and the intensity of that gaze, something weighed heavily on her mind.

She gestured a spell—earthsight—then narrowed her eyes. Dispelled it a moment later.

"Are we close?" He drew in a deep breath, gazing as far as he could with his Wolf eyes. Nothing.

She deflated with a heavy sigh. "Not close enough." Her gaze dropped back to the sinuous waters.

"We'll get there." Wherever Shadow was going, she would eventually have to arrive, stop sailing, and then they would catch up with her.

"The *Liberté* is designed for speed. She's fast for her size, but compared to a small, maneuverable ship like that sloop, not fast enough." She was on her last nerve—that much was clear—but Shadow getting away again was untenable.

This was it. Whether their quarry was torn to pieces or led them to their deaths, the hunt would come to an end.

Minutes passed to the whispering of the wind and the soft splash of water; he leaned in, and she rested her head on his shoulder. He closed his eyes, savored that strange intimacy, affection that only a few months ago had seemed so foreign. But her posture was still stiff, a little too taut, too rigid. Straining to hold up more burdens than chasing vengeance.

Something had closed inside her and hardened. A grim determination, born of that night after the Veris Ball. She had arrived on the shores of Emaurria full of hope, broken and saddened, yes, but there had been a yearning gleam in those sky-blue eyes that could see happiness, no matter how far, how remote, how unlikely—hope.

That gleam was gone now. Those eyes looked straight ahead, only ahead, fixated on one goal, and only that goal. Focused eyes. Determined eyes. Cold eyes.

A hollow formed in his throat, and he swallowed, lowered his gaze to the dark waters crashing against the ship. What had it felt like? To be in the embrace of the one you love, and for your hand to close around a reminder of your love's betrayal?

And that was all it was: a reminder. No one would believe the king had been unfaithful to her since her return. Not like the few months past.

But she'd needed the reminder. That would be the life of the king's lover.

How heavy a burden had that inevitability been, of knowing that the pain of betrayal would always outweigh that uplifting rapture that was love? When she'd spoken the words, as he imagined she must have, how cold had her lips been after saying them?

The king was a changed man, no longer the one she'd fallen in love with. In time, wouldn't she have realized that, ended things anyway? It had been a mercy, saving her further pain.

Or it had been a convenience. For him. One that had cost her heartache she still paid now, and would pay for the foreseeable future.

Perhaps he could have left well enough alone, loved her from afar, waited. Perhaps he should have.

Water broke against wood, again and again, as the ship sailed on.

Her gaze didn't waver, only looked ahead, only ahead.

"Come," he said. "You'll catch cold, and I don't fancy explaining to your brother how I let that happen." When she eyed him, a corner of her mouth turned up, and he laughed softly under his breath. "Someone will let us know when we catch up to her. So let's get some sleep while we can."

She remained still a moment longer, then straightened and stretched, curving her arm over her head and then the other. "You're right. I know it. I just—"

"Need to see this done."

A nod. "So much has been taken from me... For too long. No more. I'll end this, and I'll fight to my very last breath if I have to." The starlight gleamed in those eyes like a specter on steel, cold and deadly, ethereal.

"So will I," he answered. "So will I."

IN THE DARK OF NIGHT, Leigh held up the repulsion shield, a blurry, translucent arcing wall in front of the two companies of light-elf infantry. Arrows glanced off.

One penetrated—arcanir—and he diverted the light-elf it would have hit, then renewed the shield. "Just let me use an attraction ring and—"

"No," Ambriel grunted, nocking another arrow and shooting

through the repulsion shield amid a flurry of fire. A dark-elf soldier batted it aside with a bracer. "You'd destroy the forest. We'd rather die."

"An elementalist could fix—"

"No." Ambriel winced as their forces chased the dark-elves.

"What?"

He shouted a command in Elvish. "They're retreating toward a fairy mound."

"A what?"

"A hill. Higher ground."

Divine's tits. Another arrow broke through the repulsion shield and found its target before he could divert the light-elf. Leigh hissed as he renewed the repulsion shield.

The bastards had arrived well equipped with arcanir armor, shields, and weapons, and the light-elves were being idiots about breaking a few trees.

"Once they make it out of the woods, I'll obliterate them." He searched the army for the archer shooting arcanir arrows. The origin changed every time—perhaps they'd handed out those arrows to each of them. Intelligently.

The light-elf army began to shift, attempting to push the enemy to the right, but the front lines only collided. The dark-elves continued their retreat trajectory.

Roaring, Ambriel shot arrow after arrow after arrow. The clearing shone through the trees.

*We'll have to retreat*, he wanted to say, but no doubt Ambriel already knew that. They couldn't let the dark-elves have the high ground, especially without knowing what the enemy might have left there.

But as Ambriel shouted commands, the light-elves' army only continued angling and pushing past the tree cover.

Leigh cast a repulsion wall along the tree line. If they had to retreat, only the dark-elves with arcanir would be able to pursue as he renewed the wall over and over.

Ambriel bellowed, and battle cries rose up from the light-elves. They broke from the tree cover as the dark-elves backed up onto the hill—

Pounding. Thundering. The ground vibrated.

The crest of the hill seemed to shift, a moving silhouette against the night sky. The moonlight illuminated the hundreds of cavalry units charging down the hill over the dark-elves' back lines.

As the enemy turned, Ambriel gave the signal to the archers, who loosed arrows into enemy backs.

Myriad vines wove through the dark-elves' front lines, rooting their feet to the ground, holding them in place as the charge rolled over them in a clash of hooves, arcanir, and steel.

Paladins.

Metal glinted in the silvery light. The coppery tang of blood seized the air.

The light-elves defended as the squadron of cavalry destroyed their enemies. The rumble of hooves subsided. The clash of blades died. Screams faded into gasps and silence. Small shadows slunk from the field of battle, a handful of survivors. Light-elf archers pursued.

A small contingent in tight formation broke away from the arriving force and slowly approached the tree line, stopping perhaps twenty feet away.

Moonlight reflected off blood-spattered armor. Even in the night, the imposing figure in heavy arcanir plate was unmistakably Jon. At his side were a number of people, one of whom stood in a Divinity mage coat, Ella something from the Tower—and Pons.

"Is it the Emaurrians?" Ambriel whispered.

Leigh grabbed Ambriel's shoulder and grinned. "It's the king himself."

He crossed the short distance with Ambriel and a couple of his officers as Jon dismounted and took off his helm. Leigh bowed. "Out for an evening ride, Your Majesty?"

# CHAPTER 67

*L*eigh took up a place at the table in the royal tent. With the help of the light-elves, the Emaurrian forces had set up a camp within the protections of Vervewood. They'd arrived over a thousand strong, a sizable force to face what was still a mysterious enemy.

Jon entered, his hand on his sword pommel, clad in a midnight-blue gambeson. "You've done well here."

He didn't know the half of it. Leigh grinned. "So you came with an elementalist," he said, tapping the table softly, "but not the one I expected."

Braced over the table and its map, Jon met his gaze and exhaled a lengthy breath. "Master Ella Vannier. When we requested assistance from the Divinity, they sent her to us. She fought at Brise-Lames. Talented mage."

"Yes, yes. And as for my wayward apprentice?"

That lengthy exhalation again. "She's... alive."

Leigh tore away from the table and crossed his arms, pacing the length of the tent. "Alive? She's been missing for five months, and all you tell me is 'alive'?"

"She's"—a shadow passed over Jon's face—"unharmed."

Leigh strode up to him, stood unwaveringly still until Jon moved away from the table and faced him. "What aren't you telling me?"

Jon looked away. No expression surfaced. And then he closed his eyes and shook his head. "It would be better if you heard it from her, but... she survived terrible things in Sonbahar. Horrible, unspeakable things." A rising intensity possessed his gaze, like raging waves in a storm.

The tent was deathly quiet, no breaths, even the voices outside falling to silence. "What things?" Leigh whispered, the words growling out of him.

Jon shook his head.

"What things? Speak."

He grabbed Jon by the shoulders, bored into his gaze. Terrible, horrible, unspeakable things? Rielle had unintentionally killed her entire family and razed her home to the ground. Jon knew her past. And he called what she'd suffered in Sonbahar unspeakable.

That girl, weeping and wreathed in flame, melting the snow outside her burning home, reappeared from the well of his memories. Crumpled. Broken. "You tell me what happened to her. You tell me, or—"

Jon covered the hand on his shoulder, his brows knitting together. "Shadow sold her," he said, his voice barely above a hushed whisper. "She did what she had to in order to survive."

Leigh let him go, took a step back. And another. *Sold... Done what she'd had to do.* He clenched his teeth, curled his fingers into fists.

Pirate slavers had been a fact of life during his childhood on the coast of Kamerai, and as a mage, he'd seen what slavery did to its victims. Heard what they'd had to endure.

And Rielle—his apprentice, friend, love, so much more than words could convey—she'd suffered those atrocities? "I... I should have been there."

Jon's hand shrouded his forehead. "I know," he said, his voice, low, broken. "I should've never—"

"It was just a stupid rite," Leigh said quietly. Thwarting the Divinity had been the right thing to do, but... not then. Not with the rite. Rielle had trusted Olivia's instincts, and he should have trusted hers. Should have never knowingly, intentionally stepped into her path.

Betrayed her. They could have discussed it. Figured out some other solution. Something. "I should have been there with her, every step of the way. Through the rite. Into the dungeon. Saving Olivia. All of it."

Jon lowered his hand and watched him with pained eyes.

"She was my apprentice, and that didn't end when she became an adept or a master. Guiding her, supporting her—and Olivia—should have been lifelong. And... I failed them." His fists had gone numb, so he clasped his hands behind his back.

"She'd gotten me to Monas Amar... helped me see Gilles defeated," Jon said, picking up a marker from the map and shifting it in his palm, "and I should have gone with her to see Olivia saved. But I let everything else take precedence."

"You're the king."

He set the marker back down. "I'm still Jon first."

He'd decided which side of him had won, then.

Power changed a man. Power came with duties, duties that became demands. And good men, in pursuit of good intentions, often gave in to them, sacrificed their good morals for their greater ends. Until they became something else. Someone else.

He could be himself, and do only as much good as his personal ethics would allow. And that was his choice.

Or he could become a force of greater good, unfettered, able to accomplish unimaginable good at the cost of honor, contentment, self. A man who did good even if he could no longer *be* good.

He approached Jon and surveyed the map with him. "Where is she now?"

Jon traced two fingers from the Bay of Amar out west and north to the Shining Sea. "She went with Brennan, in pursuit of Shadow."

Leigh sighed through his nose. "With *him?*" A vile, selfish, malicious man. *Monster.*

"Brennan helped her return, remained by her side for everything. And I was—"

Someone cleared her throat from the tent's entrance. "Am I interrupting?"

"Obviously," Leigh replied, looking her over. Ella Vannier. In her early twenties, hair pulled back so tight it was questionable whether blood still circulated to her freckled face. Always eager to please, to impress. Well, in the service of the Crown, she certainly had her chance now. She hadn't changed much from the Tower. "Is Cédric with you?"

Ella's frequent mission partner, a healer by the name of Cédric Fontleroy, was barely older than Ella and frequently buried in some book.

She nodded. "He was the one who cast the illusion spell to silence our arrival."

Cédric never had been content as a healer. Leigh sighed. "What do you want? The adults are talking."

She frowned and turned to Jon. "Sir Marin came to camp and said Queen Narenian and Lady Aiolian devised a plan for tomorrow, and they want to meet to discuss it."

Jon looked longingly at the map and its markers signifying cavalry, infantry, war machines—the world he knew—then turned back to Ella and nodded. "Very well. Let's find out what miracle Aiolian expects of me now."

JON LOOKED out across the battlefield, past over two thousand troops —both human and light-elf united—to the lone figure on horseback, riding back and forth, shouting. Raising his sword before the firelight rays of dawn. Rallying. Captain Perrault.

And that's where *he* should have been. At the front, Faithkeeper at the ready, prepared to charge into battle shoulder to shoulder with paladins and the Emaurrian army.

If Queen Matryona died on the field of battle, it was likely the war would be over; Leigh had said there was dissension among the dark-elf ranks. Even if the queen was highly skilled and preternaturally fast, she wasn't invincible, and so many lives could be saved with just one fight. Single combat. Only one of her Quorum—her inner circle—or another ruler could challenge her.

No matter the odds, he would have tried. For all the soldiers and paladins who'd followed him, for his people, for the light-elves, he would have tried.

But instead, here he was. Out of combat. At the back. Waiting to rally the land itself.

Aiolian stood over him in her light mail, holding a staff. Her tight gaze narrowed on him, unflinching. "It's time."

Two squads of Royal Guard surrounded him—including Raoul and Florian—as did Ella, Pons, Valen, and Cédric. None wavered in their watch.

He'd agreed to Queen Narenian and Aiolian's impossible plan, so there was no choice but to proceed. "Ella, it's your turn."

She pivoted from her post. "Yes, Your Majesty."

Her determined steps closed the distance between them, and then she stood next to him. With a gesture, her eyes became that too-vivid green Rielle's had been on the road so many times before. Earthsight. "They're inside. All is as it was last night."

Last night, she'd drawn a map of Stonehaven and its exits. A map he'd memorized down to the last detail.

He nodded to her, and she beckoned to Cédric. The lanky healer approached in his forest-green master's coat and inclined his head, shifting a dense mop of blackest-black curls. "I am ready to serve, Your Majesty."

Jon touched his own chest, his lips, and his forehead, then lowered his hand in offering, the sign of the Goddess. His Earthbound powers were nowhere near ready for this. Projecting into a tree for too long, trying to do too much, had made his head pound for hours and his nose drip with blood. And this?

*It's what we all need. It's what I'll do.*

With a fortifying breath, he lowered to the dewy grass. The circle ringing him stiffened, tightened. If an enemy did somehow manage to penetrate the thousands of troops between them and Stonehaven, they'd find no easy opposition here.

Cédric's gaze remained fixed on him, watchful for any signs of injury.

Not yet. But soon, he'd be a fountain of blood and pain, if Aiolian's training had been any indication.

Jon closed his eyes, took a deep breath, pictured Cédric, Valen, Raoul, Florian, and the circle guarding him... Hundreds of yards of open plain, carpeted with lush grass, and thousands of heads and shoulders, metal spread wide and raised high... to the growing crown of ironwood trees.

Through the small leaves, twigs, branches, and limbs, inside the bark, cambium, sapwood, and heartwood, anima flowed through the pith, brilliant and live, down, down, down... A taproot burrowed deep in the rich soil, but spread from the root crown were surface roots that anchored outward, and smaller tips and hairs that went below. He journeyed to where his roots grafted to those of another ironwood, bound together below the surface, sharing life, sharing one another, at the heart of their union, a structure of stone.

He gathered his roots closer, closer, straining against the stone, crumbling, and he flowed to further networks, bound them closer, crumbled—

One ironwood to the next, to the farthest roots that separated over structures below ground, drawing the anima closer together, restructuring—

Cold.

He curled back, a root tip twining to face the other ironwoods, but—

No, warmth.

Farther roots pulled together, breaking stone, until the ground rumbled and shifted beneath his root crown.

HIS HANDS READY BEFORE HIM, Leigh stared down the shallow ravine as the earth trembled under his feet.

"Your king is doing his part," Ambriel murmured beneath a determined frown. He held out his bow, his fingers ready at his quiver. The light-elves, as far as the eye could see, all did the same, and the humans beyond.

Leigh watched the ravine. No movement. Just mud. "Are we certain this is where they'll emerge?"

Ambriel stood frozen. "Listen," he whispered.

Tremors, and—pounding. Feet. And screams.

He sucked in a breath.

A square of mud burst open. A crowd spilled out, an indiscernible mass of moving bodies hemorrhaging like blood from a wound.

Ambriel's quick fingers nocked arrow after arrow, felling runners.

A call came from the paladin captain. A dark cloud blotted out the sun—

A cloud of arrows.

The volley fell upon the shifting crowd in the ravine, raising a cacophony of shrieks as bodies fell into the mud and piled.

"They're fleeing," Leigh shouted to Ambriel.

"They'll kill you if they get the chance!" He loosed another shot.

The dark-elves pushed out in no apparent formation, scattering in every direction. Leigh cast a repulsion shield, but... there was no need. "This is wrong," he called to Ambriel.

A bellow from within. Clear, commanding shouts. Orders.

Following the wave of dark-elves was a wall of shields. With each emerging group, it built, absorbing arrows, and spread. Each rank climbed the shields of the rank behind, rippling out of the ravine.

Ambriel shouted the attack as the paladin captain did.

The front lines pushed against the shield wall, pushed the dark-elves back into the ravine. Spears and blades shot out from between shields, but dark-elf bodies piled and piled.

The bright spark of flame lit from among the enemy ranks—and another, and another. Leigh shot force shoves through lines of soldiers, hurling them backward with trailing screams.

Tiny flames arced through the air—

He braced but was thrown off his feet. Recast the repulsion shield before Ambriel.

The soldiers, elven and human, at the front, scrambled to their feet, helping one another. Bombs. The dark-elves had bombs.

Sparks flared among the dark-elves again.

With both hands, Leigh cast repulsion shields in domes over the bombs' targets.

Some exploded on impact, raining fire and fragments onto the shield and over it. Others bounced back into the ravine and exploded.

Great battlecries rose—dark-elves scrambling over bodies, charging. Two to three squads, while at the back, bombers lit new fires.

Another repulsion shield dome. Another. Another.

"Take them down!" Ambriel barked. "The Emberaiths! Now!"

Arrows cut toward the fires, some into shields, others into flesh.

Dark-elves penetrated the front lines with shields, blades, and spears. An ear-splitting battlecry cut the air from the exit.

Queen Matryona, outfitted in battle regalia with a pair of bearded crescent axes. Protected by three squads of her Royal Guard. At the edge—

Over a face mask, a white-hot scar across a nose. Varvara.

As the Emberaiths let loose a salvo of bombs, the queen and her guard charged through the human-and-light-elf front ranks, cutting a swath of carnage and shield-bashing their way through.

Leigh cast shield after shield, gaze darting between Ambriel and Varvara. She dodged a slash at her neck, plunged a short sword between the ribs of a light-elf. As she yanked it free, she ducked low as a sword cut above her head, and whipped her shield through an Emaurrian's feet before crushing its edge onto the man's neck.

"Varvara!" he shouted, casting another shield at an arcing firebomb.

Those honey-hued eyes found his across the field.

"You can stop this!" he yelled in Old Emaurrian.

Behind her, the queen pointed an axe at him and barked out a short string of words.

With a cry, Varvara stiffened and charged for him.

## CHAPTER 68

Screams cracked every corner of Jon's blinding-white vision as he opened his eyes and blinked, his heart thudding in his chest like a hammer.

The clangor and shouting of battle rang nearby. His fingers brushed Faithkeeper's pommel. Too slow. Lethargic. "Horse," he bit out. "Bring me... my horse."

The voice sounded raspy, aged and tired, but it was his.

Hands braced his shoulders as he tried to sit up, and the world spun around him—shadows, faces—and voices blurred into one another, words braided into unintelligible chatter. And behind it all, a din of screams, calls, and metal striking against metal.

A harsh voice scolded the others, who quieted, then two hands grabbed his shoulders as a blur filled his field of vision. His head throbbed as if it were getting hammered into the ground, but he squinted his eyes until the blur came into focus and became a face.

An alabaster face, hardened with severe, angry lines, framed by tight braids white-hot like fire. Dark, night-sky eyes gleaming with ancient, burning stars. Aiolian.

He tried to speak her name, but she grabbed his face with a hand.

"Do not try to move. Do not try to stand. You have done your part, and you are fortunate to be alive." She lowered her chin, spearing him with an intense glare, then stood and faced someone. "I must join my people. He must rest. Do not let him move."

With one last glare at him, she picked up a staff off the ground and strode away.

Pressure assailed both sides of his head as if it would split in two; he reached up, but a hand held his. He turned to look, and the ground spun again.

A black mass of hair—a man. Cédric.

Warmth seeped into his palm, into his bones, and up his arm to his chest and up to his neck and head. As the ache eased, tension fled his body in ripples, and he threw his head back, colliding with—a chest.

He craned his neck—freckles, a confident nod—

"We have you, Your Majesty. You're safe," Ella declared, and glanced at Cédric.

"His entire body is under strain, and I've never seen migraines like this," Cédric said with a shake of his head. "Massive, and new ones keep forming before I can dissolve the old ones. Pressure unlike anything I've ever—"

"Horse," Jon rasped. While they sat here playing nursemaid, thousands were risking their lives on the field of battle. These two mages, and Pons, Valen, his Royal Guard, and *he*—they could be out there, saving them.

"You're in no condition for that." A warm, calm voice. Pons crouched, giving him a once-over. "I question your ability to *stand* right now, let alone mount up."

Jon frowned through the haze. "Armor."

Pons grunted a laugh, then beckoned to the Royal Guard. Two paladins came forth with his gauntlets, knuckle-dusters, and helm, the only pieces he wasn't wearing.

"Don't encourage him," a deep voice mumbled from behind him. Valen. "He could be on death's doorstep and still clamoring to fight."

"Valen," he whispered.

A massive shadow darkened over him as Valen knelt next to him in full heavy plate. "What?"

He forced a grin as he winced. "Shut... up."

Valen snorted. "On second thought, just strap him to a horse and send him out to battle."

"What... he said."

Pons sighed and rose, dusting off his black mage coat.

The warmth of healing finally began to fade. "I think that's the last of them," Cédric said, his brows drawn together. "He's as healed as I can manage, but he needs about... oh, a week's worth of rest."

Cédric let go of his hand, and a paladin armored it. Jon braced a palm on the ground and tried to rise. A canon of voices uttered objections, but he ignored them.

What strength he'd had this morning was nowhere to be found, but he labored to a knee, took several fortifying breaths, then tried to stand.

His feet planted firmly apart, he didn't dare move until the world stopped spinning, then he raised a challenging brow at Pons. Standing.

Valen moved next to him, his hand over his sword grip. "You know what a joke is, right?"

"It's a... Shut up." Knitting his brows together, Jon stared out at the churning sea of battle. He needed to be out *there*, useful, not idling here making nannies of competent fighters.

"Well," Valen announced to the rest of them with an amused lilt, "if we were worried about his wit, it's not exactly sharp, but that's normal."

He jabbed an elbow at Valen, who evaded.

But he wasn't incapable. He hadn't lost his balance. Progress.

"Horse," he said louder to his guards. "If I have to ask one more time... I'm going to order all of you to train with me... from dawn until dusk when we return to Courdeval."

A few guards shifted until one disappeared.

"You can't go out there," Valen murmured from next to him. "It's suicide."

"I can't stand around here while they fight, while they die." He would risk his two to three years for their countless lifetimes. Someone handed him his helm, and he put it on. "It's my duty."

"Surviving is your duty, my brother. Ruling is your duty."

A guard led his horse before him, and Jon put an armored foot in a stirrup, and with all of his remaining strength, mounted. On his own power. "Then I'll rule by example. No more sitting by while the world falls to ruin. For anyone."

Valen donned his own helm. "Then I'm coming with you."

A ripple of assent spread through those around him, and then everyone mounted up.

In the thick of the fighting, the Farallan dragon banner waved in the wind, blood-spattered but present. The Porte-Oriflamme was at the front, face to face with the enemy.

"Not Matryona," Pons warned from next to him. "They say she's immensely skilled, preternaturally agile—"

"I know," Jon grunted. "But someone has to try. Besides, I'll have all of you to support me."

A faint smile. "Yes, impossibility loves company, Your Majesty."

~

As Varvara leaped at him, snarling, Leigh cast a repulsion shield before himself and destabilized it.

It blasted her back, tossing her to the ground. Air heaved out of her mouth, but she rolled as a sword came down where her head had been.

"No!" he shouted to the light-elf behind her. "She's under my protection!" He wasn't about to let all the Stonehaven dark-elves die for their queen's recklessness. And Varvara was their last hope.

A blink of wide eyes before the light-elf found another target in the densely packed madness of the battlefield.

Varvara scrambled to her feet and launched herself at him once more. When he pulled up a repulsion shield, she leaped aside, then sprang from his periphery.

He moved his shield in time to stop her blade as she pinned him in the mud.

"Your people don't need to die, Varvara," he bit out, holding the shield in the face of her wild-eyed determination. "You don't want to do this!"

"Yes"—she pushed harder—"I... do!" She roared, a maddened sound.

He imbued the shield with greater focus. "Your duty ends at being ordered to die senselessly," he shot back. "Save... your... people."

She shook her head, screaming her frustration as she broke away.

Hooves thundered—a cavalry platoon charging from the side, through the dark-elves' backline. Hooves trampled through bodies as a flourish of blades rent flesh and bone.

A firebomb fell to the ground, and at the front, cloaked in red, Jon reined his horse aside as the blast exploded.

Horses screamed. Riders tumbled from their saddles. Jon hit the ground and rolled as his horse scrambled for footing in the mud. It slipped to the ground, missing him by a mere foot as it fell.

He drew his dagger to parry a strike, and angled back to where he'd lost his sword, engaging one enemy after another. One royal guard closed in, covering his flank, another nearby, while the rest of the cavalry platoon remained scattered.

Varvara darted away, but Leigh cast an attraction spell, dragging her near, and a repulsion spell, pushing her away. With both active at low intensity, she was unable to move.

"Release me!" she growled.

"Save. Your. People," he bit out, holding both spells. "If Matryona kills our king, that's it! Your people will be slaughtered!"

She cried out, a feral roar, straining with effort toward the newly arrived cavalry platoon.

A dark-elf woman, pale blue with a crown of thick, white hair, hefted two axes and cut her way toward Jon.

Matryona.

Jon yanked his dagger free of a dark-elf swordswoman's chest just as an axe came down from above.

JON ROLLED to the side as the axe barely missed him, and rolled again as another swing followed. Against her twin axes, his dagger would give him no chance at all. Useless.

Faithkeeper lay over ten yards from him. Too far. His gaze darted to the dead light-elf beside him—and a glaive.

His fingers closed around it, finding the flat of the pole that matched the position of the blade, and he sheathed his dagger.

Matryona rushed him.

He was on his feet. The point of the glaive thrust toward her chest, and she scrambled backward.

He cut downward, but she batted aside the bladed tip with an axe and jumped to her feet. Fast. Incredibly fast.

Eyes narrowed, she stood ready, and grinned. As she circled, he matched her steps, keeping more than the glaive's seven-foot pole and eighteen-inch blade between them.

She was faster than him, but the glaive's pinpoint thrusts would give her less time to react than her axes' swings would give him. And as long as he could keep the distance between them—

With a swing of an axe, she cast the glaive's blade aside and charged, but he pulled it back and thrust the point to her abdomen.

She brought up her blade to parry, and he hooked the axe with the pole, yanking her off balance.

With a snarl, she broke away, parrying the cut he directed at her side.

She caught the pole with the crook of one axe. Wound up to throw the other.

His hand released the glaive. He gestured.

The axe flew.

A repulsion shield blurred the space before him. The axe hit it and ricocheted back.

*Gods bless you, Olivia—*

Wide eyed, Matryona evaded, and he yanked back the glaive and thrust it through her shoulder.

A sharp cry.

Her arm closed around the pole where it met the blade, and she hissed, her grip so tight he could push no farther.

"Magos," she spat, and removed the blade even against his pushing.

Strong. She was immensely strong.

She forced him back, then she yanked the pole forward, and he staggered—

A roar, and a paladin with a shield and long sword moved before him, slashing toward the arm pulling the glaive. No helm—Raoul—

Matryona released it and blocked with her remaining axe, leaving her side open.

The single-combat rule—

But Jon arced the glaive around and cut.

A shallow wound as the pole met her axe. Raoul brought his sword up—

Matryona leaped back, then swung her axe across his neck.

His sword fell as his hand shot to his neck.

"No!" Jon shouted. He caught Raoul as fierce, cried foreign words rent the air.

A dark-elf woman yelling across the battlefield from next to Leigh, pointing her short sword at them.

The dark-elves and light-elves alike froze.

～

LEIGH SLOWLY DISPELLED the repulsion shield as Varvara stared down her queen. Both the light-elves and dark-elves had stopped fighting, and the paladin captain called a cease. They knew what this meant. They knew, and they would let single combat decide.

As Varvara strode toward Matryona with her sword and shield, the space around them widened. Even Jon dragged an injured paladin backward, shouting for Cédric, while Matryona yanked one of her axes from the ground. With a flourish, she shook off the mixture of blood and mud coating its edge, and faced Varvara with both in hand.

She barked something at Varvara in Elvish while Leigh edged the open circle toward Jon.

Varvara shouted back a long string of words, her face contorted in heartfelt anguish as she stared down her queen, but she took up a ready stance.

She'd done it. She'd challenged her queen to single combat.

Dark-elves filtered out of the crowd to ring the circle Matryona and

Varvara were forming. Jon and an injured paladin were on the ground near its outer edge.

"My life for Her will," the injured paladin rasped, his hand and Jon's pressed against his neck.

"Don't try to talk," Jon murmured, pulling off his own helm. "Cédric!" His sharp eyes searched the field.

"My... life... for Her... will," the paladin repeated.

A deep line between his brows, Jon winced. "With honor and valor, you have served," he replied, his voice breaking even as he said the words paladins had no doubt said for centuries.

"Her... voice... calls me."

Jon shook his head. "Answer with pride... son of Terra," he said quietly, hunched over the man.

Leigh shouldered through the dark-elves toward them. "Stand aside," he snapped at Jon, and knelt in the mud.

He pressed fingertips to the man's bloodied neck as the dark-elf circle closed before them. *Sundered flesh and shattered bone, / By Your Divine might, let it be sewn."*

Anima poured from his body into the paladin, wove into healing magic, threading through the gash across his neck.

The lines of the man's face eased and his eyes closed as he went limp.

"Will he live?" Jon fixed a pair of flinty eyes on him, unyielding, unsettling.

"He's lost a lot of blood. He'll need to rest, and then we'll see."

Jon nodded grimly and turned back to his comrade while another paladin led a horse near. Together, they hefted the unconscious man up onto it.

A roar rose up from the dark-elves, and another, and another. Those with shields beat them, and those without struck blades to armor in rhythm. Raindrops fell, sparse and light, before a downpour began, dousing the battlefield in gray and wet.

Leigh stood and angled between the heads of two dark-elves to peer into the circle they enclosed.

Bleeding from a shoulder wound, Matryona beckoned to Varvara with two fingers off an axe handle.

Her jaw clenched, Varvara advanced, shield raised and sword at the ready.

Matryona brought an axe down, and Varvara blocked with her shield, cutting down with her sword.

They clashed, each matching the other, a storm of blades and fury.

Jon came up beside him, holding his mud-coated arcanir sword. "Her own soldier?" he hissed, palming his hair back from his face.

"Captain," Leigh corrected quietly over the rain, "and she's our best chance." Whoever won this single combat would set the course of this day—and years, decades, perhaps centuries to come.

If Varvara won—peace could be at hand.

If Matryona did... the ring of rallying dark-elves would turn on them and butcher their way through. He shuddered.

Matryona beat aside Varvara's blade and hooked her shield with the beard of her axe, then head-butted Varvara. Laughed as Varvara staggered back and found her footing in the puddled ground. Snarled arrogant words.

Ripples of whispers meandered through the crowd, while the rain beat the slippery ground into submission.

Varvara, staring at her queen, heaving belabored breaths, lowered her bone-white brows. Darting from the mud, she charged. Blocked an axe cut. Parried another with her sword, then smashed the pommel into Matryona's injured shoulder. A shout.

Pure power, Varvara yanked it free. Thudded her foot into Matryona's abdomen and sent her flying backward to splash into the sludge.

In an instant, Varvara leaped onto her, kicked one axe away.

Snarling, Matryona scrambled to a knee, slashed toward Varvara's knees.

A block with the shield.

A swing of the short sword. A sharp cry.

A grinning head thudded, rolled away. Matryona's.

Varvara didn't move. As the body withered lifelessly to the ground, she didn't move. Sword still. Shield up. Tears streaming down her cheeks. A muscle working in her jaw.

Her knees plunged to the mud, and she stabbed her blade into it.

An anguished howl rent the air, loud, deafening, hoarse—a lament and a relief, rage and unbearable sorrow.

The ring of dark-elves chanted something in Elvish, beat their shields in time once, twice, three times. Then they, too, sank to their knees, set down their shields, and with bowed heads, held up their weapons in offering.

Varvara bit out a somber phrase, then raised her head, her stormy gaze alighting upon the circle of dark-elves.

Ambriel appeared at his side, his mouth a grim line of determination as rainwater streaked down his blood-spattered face. He glared at the spectacle, his expression as stony as the set of his shoulders.

"What'd she say?" Leigh asked him softly.

Ambriel eyed him peripherally. " 'Farewell, my queen.' "

# CHAPTER 69

Olivia rested her cheek on Tor's bare chest and breathed deeply, softly stroking his leg with her foot. Smiling, she followed the spirit-magic sigil tattoo on his abdomen in its winding pattern.

He was a wonderful lover. Sensitive, perceptive, generous. In his arms, the war, the courier, the horrors of Spiritseve all felt a little more distant, a little more faded. "Want to go again?"

He laughed, a low rumble in his chest. "Again? Woman, you're insatiable."

It was her turn to laugh. "Oh, no, I'm quite satiable. I just want to be satisfied again... and again and *again*—"

"Terra help me—"

"—and again, until we sleep, because it is our only choice, since being so exhausted, we can no longer move—"

"I'm fairly certain this is how I die—"

"—so we can rest up and repeat the wonderful madness when we wake." She curled closer.

"All told, it's not a bad way to go."

"Go? Nonsense. I'm a healer, remember?"

He shook his head, grinning. "Again it is."

He rolled her over, pinning her to the bed, and dipped down to kiss her, his stubble brushing against her chin. Divine, yes, this was what she'd needed—his hands, his mouth, his mind-numbing pleasure. She arched her back off the bed as he trailed kisses down her neck, her breasts, her belly—

A knock sounded from the hall.

He paused.

"Tor," she said anxiously.

Two more knocks.

He sighed lengthily. "I'll be right back," he said, dropping a kiss below her navel before rising and throwing on a robe. When she groaned, he added, "It could be important."

As much as she hated it, he was right. And if it was important, they could both be needed. She sat up and reached for her own red dressing gown, then put it on and fixed her hair. When she leaned against the large cherry-wood bedpost and looked in the mirror, she had a clear line of sight to the door.

Tor opened it, and a man stepped inside, hooded and cloaked. A man with a narrow face. Shoulder-length hair. Deep-set eyes. Aquiline nose. And a birthmark on his jaw.

Her heart stopped.

The courier.

Swallowing, she quickly looked away from the mirror, moved to the bedside table. She poured the last of the wine into her goblet.

The door snicked shut.

She casually glanced back to see Tor unrolling a message.

On his way to the bedchamber, he read it, then set it down on his bedside table.

"Was it important?" she asked, raising the goblet to her lips, trying to still the tremble in her lip, slow the racing of her heart.

His arms encircled her waist. "Not compared to this."

What was that message? Who was it from? She held up her goblet. "I think... we're out of wine."

He looked at the decanter. "So we are."

With a sigh, he tugged at the bell pull by the bed, then returned to her, brushed her hair off her shoulder, and kissed her cheek before heading for the garderobe.

She smiled, and just as he shut the door, she padded to his bedside table. Unrolled the message.

*...to Maerleth Tainn for Ignis, and we'll discuss it then.*

Faolan Auvray Marcel? That was *his* courier?

He'd been in contact with Gilles... A vastly rich, ambitious duke with royal blood.

The Swordsman? The man who'd hired Gilles to kill the Faralles?

And Tor—had Tor conspired with him?

Not possible. He would've come forward, wouldn't he? Tor loved Jon, had mentored him, raised him, known him since—

Water splashing. She moved back to her side of the bed, set her goblet down, began to change clothes.

The door opened. "Leaving so soon?"

She paused as she pulled on her chemise. "I just remembered I was supposed to write to Parliament about the coronation. No doubt the light-elves will be attending."

As she pulled on her corset, Tor helped her and then began lacing it.

"The coronation isn't for at least three weeks yet."

Stiff, she laughed and tried to loosen up. "Oh, I know, but the Master of Ceremonies made such a fuss about seating arrangements, and I just know he'll make a scene if he doesn't prepare in time."

He picked up her dress and handed it to her. "I thought you were writing to Parliament?"

She put it on and smiled. "Right. And they'll let the Master of Ceremonies know if they approve." When she finished lacing her bodice, she took his hand in hers. "I'll be right back—promise. Save some of that wine for me."

She rounded the bed and headed for the door.

"Olivia," he said, his voice lilting, almost a question. As she turned, he headed toward her, around her, faced her. He took her hands.

A look toward his bedside table. "You read my correspondence."

"Tor, I—" Her hands twisted in his grip. He didn't let go.

"Let me explain," he said.

She yanked at her hands, but he wouldn't release her. "This is—You can't—"

"Just hear me out," he said to her calmly, standing still and immovable.

She pulled and threw herself away from him to no avail—his grip was unforgiving, and without her hands, magic would be— *"Well of dreams, lush and deep—"*

He spun her in his hold, maneuvered his arm over and around her. Her back was solid against his abdomen, her hands still clutched in his, an arm over her mouth.

"It was only—"

She smashed her heel down on his toes.

His hold loosened just a touch.

A yank. A free hand. A sleep spell.

He held up his arcanir ring.

Deflected.

Retreating, she tripped and fell back onto the floor. Pulled up a calm shield.

He waved his fingers through it—dispelled—and grabbed her ankle. "Just listen—"

She held up her hand. *"Well of dreams, lush and deep—"*

"Olivia!" He dragged her toward him, grabbed her hand, as she scrambled farther.

*"—Encircle him in slumber, make him sleep."*

His hands clawed up her body, reaching higher and higher as she tried to pull away. The wide-eyed disbelief faded and faded and faded...

Until he collapsed atop her.

Her hand scrabbled for a hold on something—anything—the large cherry-wood bedpost, and she drew herself out from under him, trembling.

With shaking arms, she pulled herself to her feet, stared down at him, lying motionless on the heavy-pile rug.

Those hands—

Just a few minutes ago, those hands had been lavishing her with affection, but just now... the way they'd reached, the way they'd clawed, their strength, their potential energy—

Would he have—Had he been prepared to—

She swallowed.

A click. A creak. The door from the hallway opened.

She held up her hand, ready to cast another sleep spell.

A wide-eyed serving girl with a tray of wine froze in the doorway. "Your Ladyship..."

"Get Sir Edgar Armurier here now," Olivia said, her voice low. "No one else, girl, or Divine save you."

# CHAPTER 70

*D*rina emerged from the jungle foliage and stared up at the crumbling black tower. Khar'shil. Home.

Shifting her satchel on her hip, she jogged across the clearing, whispering, *"Wings of wind, great and soft, / Take me high, bear me aloft."* She repeated the words until her boots landed atop the tower's black stone surface, level with the massive Bell of Khar'shil.

Everything she'd read about the bell—it was true. This tower, this entire island, had once been home to the most powerful Immortals to have ever existed: the dragons. And after betraying them, ancient wild mages had bound the dragon king, Nyeris, to this bell. A tool to be summoned to do their bidding, called to arrive at Veris—when day and night were equal, a time of great power—and then banished as they pleased. Veris, less than a year away.

She rested a palm on the bell. Nyeris. Summoned with sangremancy.

Yes, come what may, her will would be done.

The metal-ring handle gleamed in the bell tower's floor. She approached it, knelt, threw open the door, and descended down the spiral stone stairs.

Bookcases lined every wall, stacked and double-stacked with every-thing of interest she'd ever collected; records from Magehold, rare books, ledgers, and journals, and the ancient tomes in Old Erudi that had been here when she'd found this place. Texts about dragons, krak-ens, mermaids, werewolves, frost giants... primordial magic and rites, some in languages she hadn't been able to decipher, containing untold knowledge and wisdom. Nearby curios contained artifacts, weapons, things she'd stolen from Magehold and anywhere her recondite skeleton key could get her.

A bed nestled in a window between two bookcases, not far from her apothecary chest and alchemy table, stocked with everything she could ever need. Pulling the satchel's strap over her head, she headed there, then placed it atop the blackwood surface.

With quick fingers, she removed the vial bearing the king's flesh and set it down. The Old Erudi tome about the bell was here some-where, and she thought back to its tattered blue cover, the creases on its spine, the scorch marks, and her feet took her across the room and up a ladder to a high shelf, where her finger traced the leathers and fabric boards until its familiar texture grazed her skin.

She pulled the book, hopped off the ladder, and ambled back to the table. A red ribbon parted the pages, and she tugged at it, opened to what she'd marked, and there it was.

A brazier, her blood, the target's blood, water, wood, a breath, and fire; three repetitions of the incantation in Old Erudi, ringing the bell after each time while thinking the command. The only way to counter-mand it would be to repeat the ritual with the bell and wish it undone. But no one would know that. Not once she destroyed this page.

Grinning, she gathered the ingredients—a skillet would have to do, and she pulled off her coat and rung it out for the water, uncorked the vial and tipped the flesh from it, cut her hand and squeezed a few drops of her own blood inside, then swiped some kindling beside her hearth and tossed it in.

That was everything.

The skillet and book in hand, she charged up the stairs, set the skillet down under the bell, then sat with it, her gaze fixed on the contents. *"Fire blazing, fire bright, / Spark to life, burn all in sight."* She blew a breath at the fire as it roared to life, then smiled.

It was time.

She looked out toward the sea, where the many sails of a frigate were a stark white against the turquoise waters. Quickly. She'd have to do this quickly.

*"Ahre, Nyeris, dragonis rexem! Meah eh vocari teh. / Verna eh aestiva ah noctur, Nyeris, te vornu, venire ah meh."* She grabbed the bell pull and yanked it—*Destroy Jonathan Dominic Armel Faralle.* It rang, deafening.

The fire wavered in the wind.

Again. *"Ahre, Nyeris, dragonis rexem!"* she shouted. *"Meah eh vocari teh. / Verna eh aestiva ah noctur, Nyeris, te vornu, venire ah meh!"* She rang the bell again—*Destroy Jonathan Dominic Armel Faralle.*

The fire flared.

Once more. *"Ahre, Nyeris, dragonis rexem!"* she screamed, her wedding brand hot on her skin. *"Meah eh vocari teh! / Verna eh aestiva ah noctur, Nyeris, te vornu, venire ah meh!"* She rang the bell the final time—*Destroy Jonathan Dominic Armel Faralle.*

The fire roared up into the bell, filling it with a great black smoke that billowed and grew, clouding the bell tower in a deepening black as the ringing reverberated through her.

Fate spun her threads in such strange ways.

Jonathan Dominic Armel Faralle would be destroyed, and Favrielle Amadour Lothaire would repay her debt in blood, know the keen pain of losing forever.

Nyeris, king of dragons—did a greater horror exist? Would he find Favrielle's love and consume him alive? Tear him limb from limb? Sunder him before her very eyes?

*A certain end. Blood for blood.*

She ripped the page in half, and again, and again, then scattered the tiny pieces to the wind.

*Marko, you will rest well avenged.*

⁓

THE CALL of land from the main deck shot Rielle from the hammock, and Brennan next to her. Securing her gear, she set her sights on the hatchway, her feet eager to tear up the deck and the stairs and to finally deliver Shadow to the Lone.

At last, her belt pouch fastened, she raced up to the main deck, where Liam manned the wheel. "The sloop sailed on," he said, "but someone rowed a boat to shore." He held out a spyglass to her, and she took it.

In the distance, an overgrowth of verdant green contrasted sharply with the turquoise waters of the Shining Sea, a gleaming ruin of a black tower spiking out of its canopy, billowing a great cloud of black smoke. And there, on the stark sandy beach, lay a boat.

She collapsed the spyglass and handed it back to Liam. "Where are we?"

"Sterling says it's Khar'shil." He pushed his hair from his face.

*Khar'shil...* There were rumors of a tower somewhere out at sea, sometimes only its jagged peak visible. Khar'shil.

Shadow's husband had been part of the attack on Laurentine, which led to her family's deaths. Shadow had been the reason for Olivia's imprisonment. For her own enslavement. For everything... everything that had happened in Sonbahar.

And if Shadow were allowed to live, perhaps ultimately, she'd be the reason for... Jon's death.

For too long, she and Shadow had been walking intertwining paths that would now end.

Footsteps thudded up the hatchway and then onto the quarter-deck. Brennan peered down at her, over six feet of leather-clad menace.

"I'll send a landing party," Liam said, his tan knuckles whitening as his fingers clenched the wheel.

"Let us take the boat," she argued.

"Absolutely not."

Brennan shook his head. "She's a highly trained shadowmancer. We don't know what we'll find. Traps, runes, magic. Just Rielle and me would be the best option. She's trained for this, and I—"

Liam held up a hand and sighed. "Save it. I'm coming with you." He shouted orders to the crew, and within moments, the boat was lowered to the waters. When Rielle glared at him, he frowned. "I'm a pyromancer, and you're used to working with a mage partner."

He was going to *logic* his way along on the mission?

"Sterling will keep an eye out for other ships and cover us."

He was right. She *was* used to working with a mage partner, and they had a better chance with Liam along.

She headed up to the quarterdeck, covered his hand with hers, and kissed his cheek. "Don't do anything stupid."

"I'll try to restrain myself." He unfastened a small sheath from his weapons belt and handed it to her. A knife.

"Liam, I—"

He closed her hand around it. "I know you don't need it. You're taking it anyway. In case she has arcanir."

With a nod, she strapped the sheath to her belt.

Brennan traversed the deck, and she followed. He climbed down the rigging and hopped into the boat, then looked up at her and opened his arms, a smile tugging at the corner of his mouth.

She looked over her shoulder at Liam, his stony gaze, the wind riffling his unruly locks of straw-blond hair. Her brother. Her *living* brother. Sonbahar had been many parts a nightmare, but in bringing Liam back to her, it still felt like a dream. One she wouldn't easily let go.

She descended the rigging down to the boat.

Brennan's hands secured her waist as she extended a leg, her foot searching for the boat's bottom. As he helped her in, Liam climbed down as if he'd done so a million times before, and hopped into the boat.

While Brennan grabbed the oars and began rowing to shore, Liam settled in next to her.

As Brennan rowed, her misbehaving eyes roved over bulging muscles and sinew in action. She could have rowed the boat herself, but Divine, it was a feast for the eyes to watch *him* do it.

He caught her gaze, cracked a smile, and she cleared her throat and looked away. "I could get us there, you know."

"You want to?" He winked. "You still can, if you feel so strongly about it." His smug grin was almost enough to make her say yes. Almost.

"Oh, I wouldn't want to delay our arrival." She pursed her lips, hoping to hide her smile.

"There's always the way back, I suppose. If you feel so strongly about it."

Smug. So very smug. She would have to retaliate later.

"I'd say 'get a room,' but we have business. Keep your heads in the game," Liam said with a sigh, although a half-laugh escaped.

They reached the shore, and Brennan and Liam dragged the boat onto the sand. Aside from the calls of birds, there was no sign of life. If Shadow was anywhere on this island, it would be at the ruined tower.

Footsteps whispered through the sand behind her, and Brennan and Liam jogged up to her side. Brennan frowned, wrinkling his nose. She inclined her head toward the jungle and started for it—

He grabbed her arm. "Wait."

"What?" The sooner they reached the ruined tower, the sooner she could deal with Shadow.

He shook his head. "Something smells... strange. The trees, the shrubs—No, maybe a—"

"Just smells like jungle," Liam said, raising an eyebrow.

"Of course something smells strange," she said. "Neither of us has ever been here before."

*"Mother earth, grant me your sight, / Show through your eyes, reveal all life,"* Liam said, using the earthsight incantation.

Brennan shrugged, but the hard look in his eyes didn't abate. There was more they couldn't say to each other with Liam along, but with any luck, he wouldn't have to Change.

Brennan's instincts were never wrong.

She cast earthsight on her eyes and looked out at the jungle, the vivacious anima in the trees and the jungle floor, small bursts of light—animals—in the sky, in the canopy, on the ground.

The life here was hidden, but not absent. Taking care to avoid the animals, she picked a path through the jungle and headed for the tower.

Liam preceded her, cleared the foliage with a cutlass, but Brennan paused and scanned their surroundings. He went taut and snarled.

"Get behind me." His voice was low, firm.

# CHAPTER 71

*R*ielle darted behind Brennan and looked in the same direction he did with her enchanted eyes. At nothing. He bent at the knees, growled.

Liam frowned, holding his cutlass ready. "Did he just... *growl?*"

"What do you see?" she whispered, ignoring Liam. Hopefully she and Brennan could explain this later.

The vibrant threads of anima remained stable, the only animals a couple of birds, monkeys, some rodents.

"You don't see them?" Brennan hissed back. "The warriors—"

"The warriors?" Liam asked.

There were no human forms in front of them—she looked around —nor anywhere around them. She dispelled her earthsight.

No less than one hundred men surrounded them. Clutching spears and bows. Faces painted and snarling. Massive jungle cats accompanied them, hungry eyed with long sharp teeth, much bigger than any normal animals. Immortals?

She gasped, conjured a flame in her hand. The men and beasts closed in—

"Rielle!" Liam shouted, grabbing her arm. "What are you doing?"

"You—you can't see them?"

"Them?"

But why... why weren't they visible with earthsight? Brennan was, and he was technically an Immortal. The kraken had been, and it most certainly was an Immortal—

A roar. Brennan's face tilted to the sky. He put out an arm and directed her backward. Above them, a massive form flew. A massive winged form. A dragon.

She shook her head. Recast the earthsight.

No anima. But for herself, Brennan, the few small animals, and the plant life, there was nothing. No men, no beasts, no dragon.

And no sounds but for her breathing and Brennan's, and the distant calls of birds.

"Brennan," she whispered. "They're not there."

He scoffed. "Rielle, I see them, I smell them, I *hear* them—they're *here.*"

Impossible. "Liam, I think there's some illusion here that we've managed to avoid with earthsight. Try dispelling yours for a second, then pull it back up."

"What?"

"Just do it."

With a grunt, he dispelled the glow and staggered backward. He quickly mumbled the incantation again. "They—they're not real?"

She sucked in a deep breath. How did Brennan smell them, hear them, when they weren't here? "Are they making noise now, Brennan?"

"You don't hear that? The roaring, the screeching, the shouting—"

"No." Magic?

No, it couldn't be magic. Magic wouldn't work on Brennan. Whatever it was, why didn't it work on her and Liam? Was it the earthsight?

What was it about this place—

She gasped. "Brennan, what was that strange smell you were talking about earlier?"

He swept around them with his hands, growling. "We have bigger things—"

He tumbled to the ground, onto his back. "Run!"

There was nothing to run from. Shaking her head, she knelt and grabbed him by the shoulders. "Brennan, believe me. There's nothing here. It's just you, Liam, and me."

His eyes darted about wildly, all around, and he remained pinned to the ground by some unseen force. He flinched, again and again, roared. "I can't—You have to run—"

With a deep breath, she grabbed him under his arms. "Help me," she said to Liam, and he braced Brennan's other side. They pulled him back to shore, and even together—Divine, Brennan was heavy.

Inch by painstaking inch, they dragged him, out of breath and staggering, and he didn't move at all but to writhe.

"Whatever is on this island, it's affected his mind and his senses," she said. The phantom enemies and attacks were as real as anything else to him, and her words couldn't cut through that reality.

"Some sort of poison?" Liam asked as they labored to the beach. "There are plants that can cause hallucinations."

Plants... They hadn't ingested anything. "Something in the air?"

"A spore," Liam suggested.

When they finally got him back to the boat, she leaned him against it. His breathing slowed, but his gaze still darted about erratically.

She stroked his face, its coarseness, and smoothed back his hair. "Brennan, I need you to wait here for me. Can you do that?"

He wouldn't—or couldn't—meet her eyes, but he didn't move. He remained in place, his back against the boat, perched in the sand.

"Perhaps in time, whatever's affected him will wear off," she said. "Could you take him back to the ship?"

Liam sighed. "Not a chance, little bee. A few minutes here, and this island has already showed us its teeth. Either I come with you, or you take him back to the *Liberté*."

Never.

Shadow had cost her far too much, and whatever it took, she'd end things here. Today.

"Fine," she snapped, using her finger to write a message in the wet sand telling him to stay.

"I doubt he'll be coming to anytime soon."

Hopefully the spore would wear off shortly... If not, perhaps they'd be paying Olivia another visit.

She turned back to the jungle, the woven tapestry of anima, then made her way to the center of the island with Liam.

She drew the knife he'd given her. The earthsight offered clarity that only a mage could achieve, but there were mysteries in this world that magic did not yet comprehend, as the kraken had so viscerally demonstrated. She was no knifehand, but even the feel of the grip in her palm gave her strength.

Among the moist foliage and tangled vines and roots of the jungle floor, they picked their way through the terrain. Unusual birds called, competing with the hooting and shrieking of small primates in the trees. The occasional predator entered her field of vision, a well-built jungle cat, not nearly as massive as the hallucinations; she gave them a wide berth, spelled a flame in her hand, and clutched the knife a little tighter in the other.

Soon, an enormous clearing, devoid of anima, lay ahead—some hundred paces.

The ruined tower. It had to be.

Liam paused, and she stopped next to him.

"I'm going to take a look without the geomancy," she whispered.

When he nodded, she interrupted her earthsight. The dark, glassy peak tore into the sky before her. She replaced the spell once more; she would not be caught unaware.

She took a step forward, and a twig snapped. Broke. There, at the top of the tower, stood one lone, bright figure of anima.

Shadow. It had to be. Waiting there, prepared, ready to fight, to kill, and a hotheaded fool would charge up that tower, through traps and any number of preparations—poisons, if Brennan's reaction was any sign—and would rush straight into Shadow's domain.

A hotheaded fool.

She hissed sharply. What was more important: that she kill Shadow immediately, or that Shadow die?

She curled a fist. "She's up there."

"I see her," he said, his voice low.

"She has something of mine. An arcanir ring. Once we get that back, I'm going to trap her in a sangremancy ward."

"Sangremancy?" he hissed. "Are you insane? If the Divinity finds out—"

"Will *you* tell them?" She didn't look away from Shadow's figure.

"No," he murmured.

"Good."

A great metallic clang. Sharp, deafening, heavy.

A bell. A massive bell.

There had to be one at the top of the tower.

"An invitation?" he asked.

Or a challenge. Regardless, she wouldn't let Shadow dictate the terms of this engagement.

"No time to waste." She pressed the blade to her palm and drew the edge across her skin as Liam winced. Blood rose to the surface. Good.

Among these enormous jungle trees, she cast the sangremancy ward while the bell rang again and again. *"Ward of blood, thread of my soul, / Make this place mine, grant me control."*

Over and over again, she repeated the incantation, creating three perimeters while Liam laid pyromancy contact runes on the ground and some of the trees. Shadow would have the Sodalis ring, no doubt, but the trap would work. *I'll make sure of it.*

The sangremancy ward laid, she sheathed her blade and healed her palm. There would be no hotheaded foolishness today. Shadow would come to them.

Still covered among the trees, she took a step forward.

"What are you doing?" Liam hissed.

"Bringing her down." She held out a hand before her, threaded her magic into the earth beneath the tower. She moved her fingers, destabilizing her earth-threaded magic. Destabilizing the earth.

A great rumble claimed the air, rippled through the ground. Leaves fluttered, branches trembled, the earth's tremors climbed up her feet, her legs. The frantic calls of birds and animals shrieked as they fled.

And the tower cracked. Great black shards and slabs fractured off its surface, plummeted to the ground. Walls broke. The entire structure crumbled into bits and pieces, a ruin pounding to the ground and shattering.

That lone figure floated effortlessly to the ground, safe. And turned her head directly here.

Rielle dispelled the earthquake, put up a wind wall before her and Liam, and waited. Shadowmancy would afford no stealth now, not when they were ready.

But another rumble shook through the ground. *Not me—*

Radiant anima streaked across her field of vision, darting past the massive trees. And the glow of shadowmancy bloomed as she turned her wind wall and deflected the spell. She shot back with fire—and her earthsight dispelled. Liam split off from her, holding up a fire shield while he threw flame arrows in Shadow's direction.

Shadow dodged, but the trees caught fire. Shadow hit Liam with a force of shadowmancy, sending him flying, then tackled her to the ground.

"No!" Rielle caught her wrist—a wrist that forced a blade right above her chest. And the Sodalis ring right there. Was Liam all right? "Liam!"

Pinning her, Shadow pushed down the blade. She laughed. "You're too late."

The tip of the blade drew nearer and nearer. With both hands, Rielle held Shadow's wrist away. With both hands.

She needed *one*.

Another rumble quaked through the earth. The earthquake had destabilized the island—the fire spread, all around, wreathing the trees in flame. Branches groaned, one directly above their heads.

A flame arrow hit the branch—Liam's.

Shadow's gaze darted upward.

*Now.* Rielle gestured a fire spell, flame bursting around her hand—and Shadow's wrist.

Shadow hissed, her sleeve afire, and Rielle deflected the blade into the ground next to her and yanked off the Sodalis ring. She pounded the pommel deep through Shadow's hand, tremors of pain snaking up her arm.

A crack came from above, and she rolled Shadow over—they both did. Right into the sangremancy ward.

~

RIELLE ROLLED BACK OUT and activated the first perimeter. A fire shield appeared before her as Liam darted to her side.

Shadow followed—and met with an invisible wall. She was trapped inside the ward, with the burning tree and flaming branches falling from above.

And no arcanir to escape with.

"You all right?" Liam breathed.

Rielle lay on her back, breathing heavily amid the smoke, ash, and flame of the burning jungle. "Fine. You?"

He narrowed his eyes at Shadow. "She knocked the wind out of me."

Rielle propped herself up, fixing her gaze on the cause of so much pain, and put the Sodalis ring on her thumb. Shadow pounded against the invisible wall, face contorted.

"Only one other way out"—killing the caster—"and I'm on this side of the ward." Rielle scrambled to her feet as another tremor shook the earth, trying to maintain her balance as she recast her earthsight. There wasn't much time left before the entire island would be destroyed.

Shadow hit the wall again and again, but Rielle closed the second perimeter, pushing her back. The burning branch hung directly above Shadow and faltered.

"You killed Marko. I will have my justice." Shadow stood, chin raised, staring her down.

Rielle shook her head. "Justice would be him paying for that crime. And he has. And now so will you."

Her eyes narrowed, Shadow looked her over. "Your precious king is still alive."

"Our child isn't!" As soon as the hissed words left her lips, she regretted them.

As Shadow's eyebrows rose, laughter bubbled from her mouth, laughter that rose and rose and rose.

"What are you laughing at?" Rielle spat, flinching as Liam rested a hand on her back.

Shadow shook her head with a bemused smile. "And you want vengeance for that, do you? I didn't intend to kill your child any more than you intended to kill my husband. And yet, here you are, looking to repay blood with blood in the endless dance."

*No.*

No, it wasn't the same. Wasn't at all the same.

"Don't let her get into your head," Liam said.

Sucking in breath after breath, Rielle tried to scramble to her feet but tumbled backward, and he caught her. "It's not—You can't—"

"Oh, but it is. And you dare judge me? Judge Marko? *You* killed your own family. *You* should pay for the crime. He wasn't there to kill anyone."

Liam stiffened behind her. "What?"

Rielle stood on shaky legs. Divine, no, not like this—

He shook his head. "The invaders were pirates—"

Shadow scrutinized him. "You look like her. Family? If so, you should get away while you can."

"Liam," Rielle breathed, "I can explain—"

"Liam Amadour Lothaire?" Shadow asked, with a tilt of her head. "The brother. Alive? Ha!" She laughed to herself. "You didn't think it strange that 'pirates' attacked and didn't kill anyone? Not even as a show of force?"

Shadow pressed her palms against the sangremancy ward's invisible wall and turned to Rielle. "Just how stupid are you, Favrielle? After all these years, you never thought it strange that your older brother had his éveil a year before the attack, but his twin, your sister, still hadn't? And that an éveil occurs during moments of great stress?"

"Dominique," Liam whispered.

Rielle clutched her chest. Took a step back. And another. The jungle burned around her, the circle of fire reaching to the sky.

The pirates weren't pirates? The attack had something to do with Dominique's éveil?

And Great Divine, Liam now knew the truth.

"Sometimes an éveil needs to be provoked." Flames filled the sangremancy ward, devoured the ground toward Shadow. "Your brother was to be the next marquis of Laurentine," she said, nodding in his direction. "And her mother was a quaternary elementalist. The world sorely needed her progeny."

The world? "What are you talking about? Who needed—"

"Marko had come to awaken your sister. She would have had her éveil and served the world, served the Most High. But you—you just couldn't wait to kill, could you? Hovering on the edge of battle fury, about to fall into fureur with the slightest provocation. You are corruption festering on the pure flesh of magic, a curse to be eradicated—"

"Shut your mouth," Liam snarled. "Enough of these lies."

"Liam," she said, her voice breaking. "They're not... they're not lies."

His head snapped in her direction, his sky-blue eyes a glittering tempest.

"It is... as she says," she whispered, her chin quivering. "I had my éveil during the attack... and the fire... killed everyone."

Shadow's laughter rumbled from the ward, permeating the air.

His eyes widened, maddened, as he stood still but for the ragged breaths heaving his broad chest. "And you think," he bit out to Rielle, "that this is *your* fault?"

He took a step toward her, and she flinched. If he wanted to yell at her, punish her, she deserved it.

"You believe this madness? What this woman has to tell herself in order to accept the death of her husband?" The wildness in his eyes deepened. "What wife would want to believe her husband a murdering pirate bastard? Better to paint him a hero, some benevolent force feigning attacks for the greater good!"

"But I—"

"You were a keg of black powder they unexpectedly lit while trying to burn our family," he gritted out. "You're no more to blame than a bolt of lightning or an earthquake." He turned to Shadow. "This is over."

"It has only just begun." Flames slithered up Shadow's boots and trousers. "*O Divine,*" she murmured, "*blessed be Your reign, / Share Your might, numb my pain.*" The skin of her hands reddened and crisped. "For all the innocent lies you've taken, you will suffer. I have made certain of it."

"Innocent lives she's taken? You madwoman!" Liam rounded on her, stomping up to the ward.

Made certain if it? "What have you done?" she asked Shadow.

Flames embraced Shadow, burning her like an effigy, and as she blinked, her eyelashes caught fire. "You will suffer as I have suffered. Blood for blood," she croaked. The branch above her plummeted. Consumed by fire, Shadow collapsed to the ground.

The brilliance of Shadow's anima faded... and faded... and faded until she became nothing, nothing but ash returning to the earth.

"Good riddance." Liam spat.

With a gesture, Rielle cleared the flames around her, then knelt, turned the ground to sand, and pulled free the knife. She tucked it into her boot and looked up at Liam towering next to her. "I'm so..."

He shook his head and held out his hand to her. When she took it, he pulled her up into an embrace. "You should've told me," he whispered, stroking her hair. "You've carried this too long."

He didn't blame her? He forgave her?

"If not for me—" She cried into his shoulder.

"No," he whispered. "If not for *them*. We didn't ask to be attacked. *You* didn't ask to be attacked. Something happened that you couldn't control."

A charred bough cracked and fell next to them. He pulled back and took her hand. "Let's go. It isn't safe."

Not safe... *Blood for blood.*

"Whose blood?" she whispered. When he frowned, she added, "Shadow said 'blood for blood.' Whom could she hurt here?" Great Divine. "Brennan."

"Come on!" She raced through the burning jungle, dousing the flames as she passed through.

If Marko had been the one Shadow had loved and lost, and she had targeted Jon before, whose blood had she sought to claim here? Brennan's? She couldn't have done anything to Jon from here, could she? Or had she cast a sangremancy spell of some kind already?

*Please be all right. Please be all right. Please be all right—*

The white sands of the shore came into view. But not the boat.

She searched the shoreline with her earthsight.

"There!" Liam pointed.

At last, a bright figure shone in the distance. She dispelled the earthsight.

Brennan. Still leaning against the boat. She hurried to him, to his pallor, his sweat, his panicked murmuring.

"Brennan." Her knees dropped to the sand, and her hands roved over him, tapped his face. "Are you all right? Speak to me."

His murmuring continued, and she brought her ear to his lips. "*... not going to die like this, let me up, let me up, let me up... Run, Rielle... Don't look back... will kill you all... all of you... tear me to pieces... let me up, let me up...*"

Swallowing, she pulled away and cupped his face in her hands.

"He needs healing. Badly," Liam said.

Healing Brennan could never get, as a werewolf.

And still... "*Sundered flesh and shattered bone, / By Your divine might, let it be sewn.*"

Nothing happened.

"Arcanir poisoning?" Liam suggested.

Healing magic didn't work on him; it never had. Nothing had happened, but she'd needed to try.

"Let's get him into the boat." She slung Brennan's arm around her shoulder, and Liam took the other. They tried to rise with him, to help him into the boat, but the best they could do was to topple him into it.

Even at that, he didn't flinch, didn't wince, nor react at all.

*Oh, Brennan... What's happened to you?*

They arranged him carefully, comfortably, pushed the boat bit by painstaking bit out into the water, and then Liam began rowing them back to the *Liberté*.

But Shadow's words rang in her head. *And you dare to judge me?*

# CHAPTER 72

Olivia strode through the malodorous darkness of the dungeon, keeping her head high despite wanting to jump out of her own skin.

After Spiritseve, if she'd never returned here, it would have been too soon. But here she was. Again.

"You really think he would have killed you?" Edgar asked quietly from next to her.

His evergreen eyes were soft, his mouth set just slightly in a contemplative line. Cautious. Caring.

She offered him a thin smile. "I... I don't know."

The look in Tor's eyes when he'd grabbed her... It had been this wide-eyed disbelief, like he couldn't believe she'd accused him, or couldn't believe she'd read his correspondence... or couldn't believe what he was about to do. As for which it was... would she ever know? Did he?

"What do you think His Majesty will do when he returns?"

Divine, she couldn't even imagine. Jon had lost his parents, his whole family, a child, Rielle, and now... one of the few people he'd considered closer than blood had betrayed him.

She shook her head. "I don't know that either."

Edgar sighed. "What *do* we know? Other than we've just thrown the Lord Constable into a dungeon cell?"

It was risky. For Edgar, with his new position in the Royal Guard, it was risky. But she'd take responsibility. She'd already written and signed affidavits. If Jon needed anything else, she'd do it all, and keep Edgar's name out of it. He didn't need to make an enemy of the Marcels, or their many allies—nor of Jon, for that matter, if all this went sideways.

But all this... There was something to it. There had to be. "He'd said... 'Just hear me out.' Why would he say that? What would there be to hear? If there was nothing damning, why wouldn't he just let me leave?"

The moment Tor had suspected she'd read the correspondence, he'd tried to prevent her leaving.

But she'd read the message. Again and again. And so had Edgar. It was little more than an invitation to Maerleth Tainn for Ignis.

Except for the "it" Faolan suggested Tor discuss with him there.

Whatever "it" was, perhaps it had been enough for Tor to stop her, to fight her, perhaps even to...

"Maybe he thought you'd get the wrong idea about something," Edgar suggested carefully.

"What wrong idea would be worth hurting me?" She rubbed her hands, which she'd resisted healing of their bruising. Evidence.

"Something important."

"Something seditious." She stopped in the hall, rested her palm against the moldy wall.

Sedition.

Faolan employed the courier. That courier had delivered coded messages between him and Gilles. Those coded messages had likely contained instructions for the regicide.

And for James's murder.

She grabbed at her chest, a fistful of gray velvet.

If Tor had hidden Faolan's crimes, he was responsible for more than just lying to Jon. Much, much more.

Edgar's touch on her shoulder was feather light. "Are you all right?"

She shook her head. "No, I'm not. But this isn't about me."

Straightening her back, she gathered her composure and walked on. "But I appreciate your care."

He huffed.

"No, truly," she said, pausing to touch his arm.

His gaze settled on her, skeptical beneath knitted eyebrows.

"I couldn't do this without you, Edgar. And I'm glad we met. I'm glad we've gotten to know each other. I'm grateful for all your help, and your friendship."

His smile had grown with every word until he looked away. "It's my privilege, Your Ladyship."

She gave his arm a squeeze. "We're friends. It's Olivia, if you please."

He grunted and grinned at her. "Oh, *now* it's 'Olivia'?"

Pursing her lips to hold back a smile, she resumed her steps to Tor's cell.

A few feet away, Edgar took up a post at the wall, with a clear line of sight. He nodded to her, and she proceeded.

Behind the iron bars, Tor sat cross-legged on the floor, his palms up and open in prayer. Someone had brought him a change of clothes—Edgar, perhaps—proper boots, pants, and a crisp white shirt. His robe sat neatly folded atop a cot in the corner.

He blinked, and those once-sunlit hazel eyes found hers, dull like the grave, somber, old beyond his years.

"Olivia." He rose, and she took a step back. Wincing, he froze, lowered his arms to his side. "Olivia, I'm sorry. I never meant to—"

"To what?" she bit out, schooling her face. He wouldn't see her waver. Not if she could help it. "What, exactly, were you going to do?"

His gaze fell to the floor for a moment. "Would you believe me if I told you I don't know?"

She'd never forget it—the wide-eyed look on his face as he'd attacked her. Eyes that didn't understand what his hands did.

She nodded to him. But none of that mattered. "Somehow, the idea that you didn't know is just as frightening, if not more so. You can't tell me... You can't tell me, with certainty, that you wouldn't have killed me."

He drew his eyebrows together, opened his mouth, closed it. "I... I wish I could tell you that. But I don't know."

She swallowed and nodded. Once. Twice. "Tell me the reason, Tor. Let's not pretend there was none."

His gaze lifted to hers, and he blinked. "I won't lie to you. We're past innocent explanations now, aren't we?"

"Far past." If any innocent explanations had even existed.

He took slow, cautious steps to the bars and grasped them, lightly, thoughtfully. "I've spent all my life looking out for my family, as well as I could, and much of my life looking out for Jon. When I learned they might be at odds, I wasn't going to choose a side. I decided I would make peace."

The Marcels and Jon at odds. "And how would you do that?"

He exhaled a soft breath. "I would dissuade my brother from his ambitions."

*We'll discuss it then*, the letter had said. "When did you know Faolan was responsible for the regicide?"

A contemplative frown. "About two months ago, I was certain. But my suspicions are older. Much older. In my family, the aspirations to the Crown, the notion that it was rightfully ours, never quite faded. Everyone knows that, right? It's no secret among the Houses. I wanted no part in it, content to join the Order. And no one was reckless enough to act on it, of course." A slight smile, soon fading. "But then... Faolan had lingered close to the capital during the siege. Appeared quickly. Taken King Marcus's bastard daughter as a mistress. Many of Faolan's allies in Parliament stalled Jon's legitimization. And my niece so desperately courted Jon's favor. Perhaps she didn't realize he would never be as ruthless with his justice as my brother would, if he got wind of treason."

A shiver rode down her spine. "So your brother... was responsible for hiring Gilles, the Heartseekers, for the regicide, the siege?"

Tor frowned grimly, but nodded. "Yes."

"And you knew? You knew and didn't tell us?" Her voice broke. "Did you think Jon would see your entire family executed? Why didn't you tell us?"

He shook his head. "Can't you see, Olivia? It's far beyond him now.

Hundreds of paladins and priests died. He has the Order of Terra to account to. And this is an atrocity that has shaken the world. He can't be lenient. Any leniency will be seen as weakness, and weakness will be seen as opportunity."

"So you believe Jon—our Jon—would execute your entire family?" It was unthinkable. Even to such considerable pressures, he wouldn't submit. Not when it would mean loss of innocent life.

"Even if Jon wanted to be merciful, the Paladin Grand Cordon would not. The Grands would not. The world stage would not allow it. His hands would be tied. Faolan would be executed, no question. His wife, my sister-in-law? Would anyone believe Caterine would have been unaware? And Nora, who was ingratiating herself to the king? And what about Brennan, who stood to gain everything if Faolan succeeded? A man who'd no doubt swear vengeance if his father, mother, and sister were executed? Do you believe they'd spare him? With the Order, the Grands, and the region watching, Jon would have no real choice."

She opened her mouth, but no words came out. Faolan Auvray Marcel had ordered the deaths of an entire *family*. All of the Faralles, down to the last child. If the Marcels anticipated response in kind, they clearly didn't know the man whose family they'd killed. Whose father they'd killed. James. *Her* James.

Faolan Auvray Marcel had swept away James's life as if it had been meaningless. Allowed Gilles to use him for information, to torture him, with no honor, no respect, no humanity.

And out of fear of retaliation for that atrocity, Tor had kept it all secret. Tried to dissuade—

"You said 'dissuade,' " she whispered. "That means he *still* aspires to the throne."

Tor's face went slack, and his grasp of the bars loosened. "I've convinced him not to act on it, to wait until after we meet during Ignis. I was hoping to put his ambitions to rest."

Jon was still in danger.

And if any word left the capital that Tor was imprisoned, that anything at all had changed, it would alert Faolan to their knowledge. "How did he plan to take over now, after the siege?"

A deep breath. "He believes in redundancies. He's bought allies in many corners. The only reason he didn't succeed before was because he wasn't aware of Jon's existence until—"

"Until..." She swallowed. "Until Gilles tortured that information from James."

Tor bowed his head. Nodded. "Olivia, I'm—"

She held up a hand.

There could be no apology that would ever assuage the grief and the rage over what Gilles had done to James. Over what *Faolan* had done to James. No words Tor could ever say.

Her fists clenched, she struggled to draw in deep breaths, to release them slowly. Not to scream. Not to cry. Not to reduce the bars to rust and cast spell after spell until the pain abated. Which it never would.

No. They had answers now. That was something. More than they'd had before.

Faolan had left them in a web, paralyzed, unable to act for fear of alerting him, and yet unable to ignore the rot of betrayal that had corrupted the very heart of the High Council. Of Jon's inner circle.

But as long as Faolan remained unaware of their knowledge, they'd be at an advantage. One she would push, with Jon's blessing, after she told him all of this.

She turned back the way she'd come.

"Olivia," Tor called, his voice raw, broken, "I know it would be pointless to ask you not to tell Jon. To let me handle this—"

The audacity... She shook her head.

"But when you do tell him, make sure he knows all I've wanted is to protect him, and to protect my family. To make sure both survive."

She pinned her lower lip bitterly and glared at him. "You're a liar."

When he only blinked, she continued, "All you've done is drag this out, give Faolan the time to put every last piece into position. You think a man who spent millions of coronas to overthrow a dynasty was going to change his mind after a *talk with his little brother*? He was never going to be dissuaded. He was never even open to it. All he did was manage a liability. Manage *you*."

He recoiled from the bars, shuddered.

"To him, Jon's assassination was always an eventuality. And you

—*you*. 'A blade may not be wielded by two men.' You know this. You know it, and yet you expected to serve both your king and your diametrically opposed family? No, you're no fool. You knew it could never end peacefully. But you told yourself it could, lied to yourself, all so you could stall the inevitable."

From between two bars, he gaped at her, his hazel eyes wide, unsettled, his breaths escaping in gasps. At his sides, his fingers trembled.

She walked back the way she'd come, and when he called her name, again and again, she didn't stop.

Edgar hadn't moved from his post, although his gaze darted toward the cell, then back to her, unsettled in that same way, haunted.

Tor's calls for her didn't stop.

"We're done here," she said to Edgar, and continued down the corridor. With a bewildered nod, he moved alongside her.

She'd find a way to bring Faolan Auvray Marcel to justice, and save Jon's life—no matter who plotted his death.

～

AS CHEERS ROSE UP among the light-elves and the Emaurrians, Jon winced, rubbing his temples. He'd slept through most of the night and the entire day, and yet that headache from the battlefield had stubbornly lingered.

A palm clapped his back, and he staggered over the table, spilling his water onto the ironwood surface.

"What are you so sullen about?" Valen asked with a chuckle as he downed his cup of mead. "The war is over, the dark-elves surrendered, a peace has been negotiated. What could there possibly be to brood over?"

Jon scowled at him. "Well, my guts flying out of my chest and onto this table, for one."

Valen snorted and broke into laughter.

Their alliance with Vervewood had now been blooded, and was strong. Stonehaven had surrendered and accepted terms—the new queen to serve as a governor with an Emaurrian observer, the dark-elves free to live among his people if they so chose, an exchange of knowledge, trade relations...

Emaurria was stronger than it had been on his first day. But there would always be the next battle. The next Immortals. The new crisis. "There's just no end to this in sight. Today, we have peace. Tomorrow, there will be some new Immortal creature wreaking havoc on our people."

Valen set his cup down and sighed. "Hope for the best, but prepare for the worst, my brother. You can't tunnel into seeing only conflict after conflict."

He shook his head. "But the loss of life—"

"Every life counts. That means not just lives lost, but lives saved. How many lives were saved yesterday with that surrender? On all sides?"

Terra's teachings. "You're right."

"Of course I am." A laugh as Florian, next to him, poured him another round. Raoul was still recovering, but seemed better since last night.

"But His Majesty isn't wrong either," Leigh said from across the table. He sat with Ambriel, cozy, intimate, but a grim line creased between his brows. "The dark-elves surrendered, and they may yet prove themselves to be peaceful. But can we expect that of other Immortals? Wyverns, frost giants... werewolves?" He pierced Jon with dark eyes. "What if we come across entire races wanting to annihilate us?"

"We have help in Vervewood and now Stonehaven. If there are problems, we'll all face them together." Valen drank deeply of his mead, and Florian nodded next to him.

"And how big of a problem can we manage?" Leigh challenged. Ambriel took his hand, but Leigh shrugged him off. "We should be making peace where we can, but this is also a new world to us. Our ancestors knew it, and their answer to uncooperative enemies was the Sundering."

Ambriel straightened and glared at him. "Dreshan, they sealed entire peoples, *our* people," he bit out in Old Emaurrian. "You can't possibly—"

"And that was wrong," Leigh said softly, turning to him. "They never should have done that to the light-elves. Or any life not hellbent on destruction. But wyverns? Frost giants? Whose only goals seem to be destruction and death, who are incapable of forging a peace? Was it wrong to seal them?"

A silence settled over their portion of the table, while cheers and laughter still rang around them from the celebrating light-elves and humans.

"Even if we all agreed as an alliance, even if we chose only to seal the beasts among the Immortals, the Sundering happened millennia ago," Jon argued in a low voice. "We don't know how it was done."

A sly smile claimed Leigh's face. "And if we did?"

Jon raised his eyebrows. Based on the rituals he knew of so far—"I have no doubt an immense sacrifice would be required."

"And if it could stop armies before they could kill a single Emaurrian, what wouldn't you sacrifice for peace?"

Peace often came at the cost of lives. But this—sealing off entire species and races *before* they could wage war—was that "peace"? That was what they were discussing. It didn't sit right. "If you have any knowledge of it, send it to me, or to Olivia. We'll consider all options, but only if our allies agree."

"Dreshan," Ambriel began, "our peoples just survived a war. Let us celebrate that, at least, before you wage another war of your own."

Leigh shot him a lopsided smile, then sighed and raised his goblet. "To peace."

Jon raised his, as did everyone else around. "Hear, hear."

As he drank his water, he looked out over the crowd. Light-elves and humans, celebrating together, allies, united. Perhaps someday soon, the dark-elves would be among them. The face of Emaurria was changing, growing stronger, finding strength in the chaos of the Rift.

Since Spiritseve, life had changed for everyone here—and everyone in Emaurria and beyond—and he aimed to make that change for the better, if he could, with whatever time he had left, *without* sacrificing who he was.

He set down the goblet, smiled as Cédric poured him some more water, and then some wine for Ella.

What was Rielle doing now? Had she found Shadow? Was she well, happy?

When she'd left, she'd taken a piece of his heart with her, but even so, it was fuller now than it ever had been. And maybe she didn't love him anymore, but he loved her, and always would.

*Stay safe, live well, be happy. I will see you again, in this life or the next.* Whether as friends or more, he'd always be there for her. Whatever she needed of him.

And until then, he'd... What had Valen said? *Prepare for the worst.*

Yes, it was time for that. While danger lurked in every shadow, Emaurria couldn't afford to house power that didn't earn its keep.

It was time to bring the Tower of Magic into the fold.

IN THE DARK, Leigh gazed at Ambriel's hand on his chest, stroked it lightly. Next to him, Ambriel slept soundly.

The celebration had gone on long into the night—and in this bedroom, well past midnight—but now, just a couple hours before dawn, all of Vervewood was quiet. The night air blew in, fluttering gossamer curtains and carrying in the sweet smell of spring blooms and dewy leaves. Lying here with his lover in his arms, Vervewood and Stonehaven at peace, and the land so lively, it seemed enough to content just about anyone.

Just about.

But he had fought a wyvern. Been tortured by a werewolf. Knew the accounts of the Emaurrian army fighting the mangeurs. It would only get worse. From what he'd read about the dragons, it was only a matter of time until they mobilized and reconquered the world.

And what loss of life would accompany that? How many humans— and who knew who else—would have to die for that conquest?

Not if he had anything to say about it.

Jon, former paladin that he was, couldn't be trusted to do what must be done. Too honorable. Too soft-hearted. He'd rule by his personal code, and that would eventually invite every monster to eat Emaurria, and mankind, alive.

Narenian had said the last living mage to perform the Sundering had gone to an island—Venetha Tramus, a realm of the sky-elves—and never returned. That any who went there never returned.

He'd never heard of it until her mention, but he had to try. Someone had to. Maybe there would be answers there about the Sundering, dragon mages, anything that could help.

"I'm going there," he whispered. "To Venetha Tramus."

A slow, lengthy exhalation. "I know that, dreshan. I knew it since your fit at dinner."

Leigh stiffened, covering Ambriel's large hand with his. "You're not asleep?"

"No," he replied without opening his eyes. "And I'm coming with you."

"Coming with me?" It was a journey with no direction, no map, and even less hope of success. "Why on earth would you even want to?"

A low, rumbling laugh that faded. "Because you're going to kiss me, dreshan. Right now. You're going to kiss me so well, and so long, and so deep, that it's going to be worth it."

"Oh?" Leigh took that hand, pinned Ambriel among the soft cotton sheets, and leaned in, curtaining him with his long platinum hair, lips almost touching his. Oh, he could most definitely make it worth his lover's while. "Yes, Captain," he whispered, and kissed him.

# CHAPTER 73

*R*ielle turned the page in her elementalist tome, glimpsing
Brennan asleep in bed. Liam had sailed into the port of
Stroppiata to resupply, and they'd been staying at The Lady and the
Lynx for days. She'd sent word of Shadow's defeat to Jon; he could rest
easier.

At least *he* could.

If Shadow was to be believed, the pirate attack on Laurentine had
never been a pirate attack at all, but some maneuver designed to
provoke Dominique's éveil. A maneuver gone terribly wrong.

If Shadow was to be believed, her husband had been working for
the Most High, the Grand Divinus, somehow. Officially or unofficially?
Were these truths or lies?

*I'll find out. One way or another.*

And Shadow had called her a hypocrite. A pawn in the "endless
dance." *And you dare to judge me?* she'd remarked.

And hadn't been wrong.

Shadow had been driven by unbridled rage, set aside all else in her
quest for vengeance, to take a life for a life.

*And I...*

She had overcome fureur, become herself again, allowed herself to feel fear, love, grief, and rage—and had nearly become a shadow of herself, too, in her own quest for vengeance. It had begun as protection for Jon, yes, but after Sylvie...

After Sylvie, it had become something else. Anything else to fill an emptiness that would never be filled.

*Blood for blood.*

No, she couldn't judge Shadow.

And she wouldn't become her, either.

*Blood for blood* meant no peace until all blood had been spilled. A world steeped in it. A destroyed world. A dead world.

She shook her head. No. She wouldn't have any part in it. No more vengeance. Her shadow self would end her reign here, diminish, and become part of the only self that would move forward.

And forward was... *For all the innocent lies you've taken, you will suffer,* Shadow had said. *I have made certain of it.*

How had Shadow "made certain" Jon would suffer? A spell of some kind? She'd written to Olivia and Jon about the threats Shadow had made, but there was nothing specific to them at all.

And what about Brennan? Had Shadow "made certain" he would suffer, too?

Brennan tossed in bed. Was this how? His sickness?

He'd spiked a fever and been delirious for days, hallucinating, speaking nonsense like a madman. He'd barely eaten, slept fitfully, and required constant watch lest he leave bed and do Divine-knew-what.

He wasn't invincible. The thought would have once given her hope, but now it only made her shiver.

*Please be all right.*

She moved her chair closer and took his hand. Sun-kissed and hot to the touch. A large, broad palm. Strong yet elegant fingers. Long, muscled arms that had held her tight. Broad, powerful shoulders. Dark, dense stubble on an imperious chin and chiseled jaw. Long, black lashes almost too feminine for someone like him. Thick hair she wanted to comb her fingers through.

He'd never been sick a day in his life, and now, here he was, lying in a bed, vulnerable, helpless. The notion of leaving his side made her cringe, and she did so only when Liam himself relieved her.

She squeezed Brennan's hand. "You have to wake up sometime."

When a knock came from the hallway, she opened the door and accepted a tray of food. Brennan had eaten precious little; getting him to eat or drink had been a game of luck during his moments of delirious consciousness.

But his fever had broken. Maybe he'd wake soon.

She set the tray down on his nightstand and sank back into her chair.

Blinking sluggishly, he stared at the ceiling.

She shot up. "Brennan."

His eyes shifted toward her, clear hazel eyes. "W-where...?" He coughed, and she quickly held a cup of water to his lips.

As he drank, she answered. "We're in Stroppiata. You got really sick on Khar'shil... Some kind of spore, perhaps, that affected your mind and caused you to hallucinate. You've been ill for a few days."

His thick, dark brows drew together. "Shadow?"

"Dead. It's over." She took the cup, helped him sit up, and joined him in bed with the tray of food.

He eased back against the pillows, eyeing her with a peripheral once-over. "And you?"

She gestured to herself. "Whole. Liam's fine, too."

He nodded. "Good." For a moment, he frowned, staring into space. "Jon's safe," he said carefully.

"And so am I. And so are you." She held a spoonful of hot oatmeal to his lips, but he took the spoon and bowl from her and dug in himself.

Then he was already feeling better. She grinned. "You had me worried."

"I don't get sick," he said between bites. He grabbed an apple and bit into it.

"But you did." She buttered a roll and handed it to him.

His eyes gleamed. "Feeling better." He popped the entire roll into his mouth, stuffing his cheeks like a chipmunk.

She laughed. "And hungry."

"Always hungry," he said around a mouthful of food.

She refilled the cup and gave it to him, and he gulped it down instantly.

"So what now?"

She'd been asking herself that, too. After writing about Shadow's cryptic remarks to Olivia and Jon, there remained the question of how to investigate these new allegations herself. "I need to write a report and send it to the Grand Divinus. In the meantime, I thought we'd go to Laurentine. Or if you prefer, Tregarde or Maerleth Tainn. It doesn't really matter where. I'd like you to write to Kehani, too, and find out whether she's gotten Samara."

"Of course. I'll find out." But he raised an eyebrow and set down a half-eaten cheese-and-pinenut fritter. "Not Courdeval?"

An ache formed between her shoulder blades. No, not Courdeval.

She'd said all she'd needed to say in correspondence, and it was best that she and Jon kept some distance between each other.

And it was time to tell Brennan about the papers she'd refused from Jon.

~

BRENNAN EYED the crease between her brows. Great Wolf, what he wouldn't give for just a glimpse into her head.

But she sat there, silent, her pink lips pursed, looking him over with those summer eyes, a slight smile tugging at the corners of her mouth, a glimmer in that gaze. It was even bluer matched to the turquoise overcoat she'd worn on their voyage, which she wore now, left unbuttoned at the top, a tease of her smooth chest visible above her lily-white shirt.

She wore her golden curls plaited from one side of her head, around the back, to pile over her other shoulder in a thick, practical braid secured with a ribbon. What he wouldn't do to pull that ribbon, shake that mane of hers free, run his fingers through it—

Her eyes softened, and she squeezed his hand. "Brennan?"

"Hm?"

She rested her shoulder against his arm. "The night I left Claudine's for the palace, when I met with Jon—"

He winced. He didn't want to hear this, how she'd fallen for Jon again, made some promise, or how he'd stolen her heart, how she needed to return, despite Veris, despite everything, and—

"—he granted my petition to dissolve our betrothal. He had the document ready that night."

Of course he had. Brennan grimaced.

Was there a man alive who wouldn't remove impediments to marrying his beloved, if he could? A king was no different, other than possessing all the power he needed to do so.

Why was she telling him this here and now? Letting him down gently? Prefacing her exit?

"I refused," she whispered.

Naturally, she'd—

*Refused?*

He jerked his head back, his heart racing. "You what?"

"I refused the papers."

A ripple tingled through his body, and he did everything he could to not jump out of his skin.

She'd refused the dissolution.

She'd *refused* it.

For years, she'd worked tirelessly to dissolve their betrothal contract, but when the reward had been in her grasp, she'd turned it away?

Why?

His gaze darted to her but dared not linger. She didn't want to dissolve the betrothal. That meant... That meant—

He tried to slow his breathing. "Have you... changed your mind?"

As the moment drew on, his thundering heart threatened to explode lest she answer.

"Yes." With a widening smile, she tightened her hold on his hand.

Rielle wanted to marry him.

He stilled, held his breath, then finally had to breathe. It all rushed in with one inhalation.

"If you have the patience to wait for me until I'm... myself again—"

"I do," he blurted. "Of course I do."

"As long as you can wait however long it takes until I'm ready to consider having children... which may be never—"

"I can," he said, sitting up. He'd get to be with her. Forever. They could worry about the rest later.

She winced. "You say that, but... if you want a different bride, one who isn't... If you want someone else, I'll take the document. I don't want you to feel locked into—"

He put an arm around her shoulders, and she eyed him with a tentative smile before leaning against him. Great Wolf, he'd never wanted to kiss her as much as he did right now.

"I don't feel locked," he said, playing with her fingers, intertwining them with his. "If you really want to do this, then so do I."

She smiled up at him, her cheeks reddening, and nodded.

He gave her hand a squeeze. "Then... tell me how this goes, Rielle, because I find myself in uncharted territory."

Chuckling, she rolled her eyes.

He grinned. "Shall I court you?"

She shoved him, but he resisted, biting his lip to keep a straight face.

"Send you flowers?"

She laughed into his chest.

"Take you dancing, even?" he asked, but she only laughed harder. "Moonlit walks in castle gardens?"

She yanked at his arm, and he held her closer. She looked up at him with a smirk.

"Well?" he asked, trying to suppress a grin.

Her lips twitched, her sky-blue eyes sparkling. "You forgot chocolates."

He finally cracked—and laughed. "I'm just trying to decide how best to impress you."

She shook her head and looked away for a moment, then turned back to him. "You don't need to. You already have."

He raised their joined hands and kissed hers. "When?"

"Countless times. On this chase after Shadow, in Courdeval at the ball, Sonbahar—"

"Not that." He grinned. "The wedding. How else can I count down the days?"

She raised her eyebrows. "It's short notice, but... why not this autumn?"

In five months?

"Done." He looked her over. His fiancée. His soon-to-be bride. *Wife*. His chest warmed.

Great Wolf, he was going to marry her. Finally.

The woman he loved, his curse broken—and all would be as had been intended.

## END OF BOOK TWO

Thanks for reading *By Dark Deeds*! If you enjoyed the adventure, please consider leaving a review. The review rating determines which series I prioritize, so if you want more books in this series soon, review this one!

Ready for the next installment in the Blade and Rose series?
The next book in the series is called *Court of Shadows*, available now!

# AUTHOR'S NOTE

Thank you for reading *By Dark Deeds*, the second book in the Blade and Rose series. Rielle's journey continues in *Court of Shadows*, the third book in the Blade and Rose series, available now! If you haven't yet read "Winter Wren," the prequel short story to the Blade and Rose series featuring Rielle's first meeting with a certain paladin, be sure to sign up for my newsletter at www.mirandahonfleur.com. You'll also receive updates about my new releases, cover reveals, giveaways, and more.

If you enjoyed this book and would like to see more, please consider leaving a review—it really helps me as a new author to know whether people like my work and want to read more of it. Writing a review is probably the most important way readers can show support for their favorite authors, especially independent authors like me, who don't have the help of a big publisher.

As always, there are people in my life without whom this book wouldn't have been possible. I'd like to thank my husband, Tony, who gave me the courage and the nudge to pursue my dream. And my mom for dreaming big, far bigger than I'd have the courage to dream on my own.

I'd also like to thank my friends at Enclave—Katherine Bennet,

Emily Gorman, and Ryan Muree—you're all amazing, and I couldn't have done this without you. See you all at Disney (I'll bring the suitcase full of chocolate). Thanks also go to Sue Seabury, Imogen Keeper, Elkin Kennard, M. Lavena Murray, Susan Stuckey, and Deborah Osborne, whose enthusiasm and thoughtful and constructive help encouraged me to complete this book.

And you, my readers. I couldn't do this without you! Your thoughts, art, and excitement have meant the world to me. I love hearing from you, so please feel free to drop me a line on: www.mirandahonfleur.com, Facebook, Twitter, and miri@mirandahonfleur.com. Thank you for reading!

Sincerely,
    Miri

# ABOUT THE AUTHOR

Miranda Honfleur is a born-and-raised Chicagoan living in Indianapolis. She grew up on fantasy and science fiction novels, spending nearly as much time in Valdemar, Pern, Tortall, Narnia, and Middle Earth as in reality.

In another life, her J.D. and M.B.A. were meant to serve a career in law, but now she gets to live her dream job: writing speculative fiction starring fierce heroines and daring heroes who make difficult choices along their adventures and intrigues, all with a generous (over)dose of romance.

When she's not snarking, writing, or reading her Kindle, she hangs out and watches Netflix with her English-teacher husband and plays board games with her friends.

*Reach her at:*
www.mirandahonfleur.com
miri@mirandahonfleur.com

facebook.com/MirandaHonfleur

twitter.com/MirandaHonfleur

instagram.com/mirandahonfleur

amazon.com/author/mirandahonfleur

bookbub.com/authors/miranda-honfleur

goodreads.com/MirandaHonfleur

pinterest.com/mirandahonfleur